THE MAHONEYS
OF WEST SEATTLE
STEPHEN BURKE

A sequel to
The Chieftains of South Boston

The Mahoneys of West Seattle
Published by Stephen Burke
Copyright 2021 by Stephen Burke
www.MahoneysofWestSeattle.com
www.WriterBurke.com

Cover art by Joel Ertsgaard

Copy Editors
Nicole Curry
Randy Hilfman

Special Thanks to
Finbar Benson
Joe Benson
Jim D'Isidoro
Cheryl Elkins
Joel Ertsgaard
Amado Floresca
Tiffany M.

To Artie Sullivan
Professor Without Portfolio, Disruptor of Formal Curricula.
Thank you for teaching me how to forgo the Life Expected
in favor of a Life Creative.

Book I

In the Direction of Home

Chapter 1

The Heist

Friday, September 10, 1999

"Let's not do a bank, Matt. I think it's a bad idea."

Anne Boushay waited for her husband to reply, but the battery on her cellphone went dead. She was standing outside HighLife Records at a busy West Seattle intersection commonly known as the Junction. The sidewalk was crowded with people getting off work and heading to happy hour at one of the many local watering holes.

Anne tucked her dead phone into a pocket of her jeans and tried to look inconspicuous. She stood six feet tall and wore embroidered Western boots that were badly in need of a new set of heels. Her light brown hair was tied in a French braid that curled into the hood of her red sweatshirt.

A pickup truck with three ladders strapped to its roof rack eased to a stop near Anne, and her husband stepped out of the passenger door. He worked as a foreman on a roofing crew, and he was dusty from ripping old shingles off a large brick Tudor home in the nearby neighborhood of Gatewood.

Anne held up a hand when he reached her. "I have a bad feeling about this, Matt. Let's not do a bank. It's a lot of risk with little return. We have other options."

Matthew Mahoney had a soul patch on his chin that covered a scar he earned playing hockey in South Boston, where he grew up. Although the short black hair on his head was turning prematurely gray, the soul patch was dark and had a tinge of red. He gave it a tug and asked, "What happened to your confidence? I can remember a time when you weren't afraid of anything."

A woman carrying a bunch of flowers walked past them on the sidewalk. As a familiar sweet fragrance reached Anne, she turned in the direction of the flowers. They had round blooms with bright coral petals. Anne smiled and said, "Wow, can you believe that? Peonies. In

September." She turned back to her husband and realized that he would never catch the reference to the twelfth anniversary flower.

"It's been 12 years, Matt. Can you believe it?"

He smiled back. "I still do."

Anne's expression became more serious. "Alright. We'll do the bank."

"Good, I hope you finished your research," Matthew said.

Anne extended her hand. "I need to add something to the list. Did you bring it?"

Matthew pulled a pen and small notebook out of his pocket and handed it over. After jotting something down, Anne said, "OK, here we go." And they walked into HighLife.

The store was a mecca for music lovers wanting to buy or trade CDs and vinyl, get concert tickets, or just kill time by flipping through obscure recordings by their favorite artists. Colorful posters and album covers were plastered on every wall up to the 20-foot ceiling. Staring down from some of them were the faces of music legends, including Aretha Franklin, Jimi Hendrix and Johnny Cash.

Matthew and Anne headed for the rockabilly section, where a set of windows looked across Alaska Street to a branch of Seafirst Bank. The wooden CD bins rose to cover half of the windows, but Anne and Matthew were tall enough to get a clear view over them.

"How many security cameras did you count?" Anne asked.

"Enough," Matthew said. "I checked them out on my lunch break today. They've got two in the parking lot, two at the front door, one at the back door, three in the lobby and two behind the teller windows. They'll get a look at us from every possible angle, so our disguises better work really, really well."

"Where's the escape route?" Anne asked.

"We come back to this side of the street, then go up the alley behind HighLife," Matthew said, pointing to the back of the store. "We cross Oregon Street and continue up the alley. There's a parking garage behind Pagliacci's."

"Is it a closed garage, like, with a door that only opens when you have an ID?"

"No, it's open, but it has plenty of cover from the alley. No cameras inside or out. The lighting is bad, which we want. We'll go to the back and change out of our disguises. We'll be carrying a green bag with the cash and a yellow bag that's holding two black backpacks. In one of the backpacks, we put the disguises and the two bags. In the other one, we put the cash.

"When we leave, we'll no longer be two people carrying a green bag and a yellow bag. That's what they'll be looking for. We'll be wearing black backpacks. We continue north up the alley. At Genesee, we turn left and walk to Glenn Way, where our car is parked. None of the houses along that route have security cameras. I checked. We'll drive home, staying as far away from the Junction as possible. Then we'll burn the bags and disguises in the backyard fire pit."

Matthew stopped talking as someone walked down their aisle and reached for a Sleepy LaBeef CD. He turned to see who else might be nearby. The clerk at the front register was looking his way, but Matthew dismissed it. In a lower voice he continued, "It's just after 4:00 on a Friday afternoon right now. Look how light the customer traffic is inside the bank. We could be in and out of there in three minutes, five tops."

"But look at how many people are outside right now," Anne said. "They're all potential witnesses."

"If you want, we can do the credit union instead. It's a block away from all this traffic."

"Our credit union?" Anne asked.

"They have money too, you know," Matthew said.

"I'm not going to rob our own bank. If I want money from our credit union, I'll write a check or use my ATM card."

Matthew smiled. "It doesn't work that way, Anne. When you rob a bank, they don't take the money out of your account."

"I know how it works, Matt. What I'm saying is that the idea of robbing a credit union that you've trusted with your own money is ridiculous. It would be beyond embarrassing to get caught doing something like that."

Matthew reached out a hand. "I just remembered something for the list." As Anne pulled the notebook out of her sweatshirt pocket, she noticed a woman in the next aisle looking directly at her. She turned back toward the window and spoke more softly. "OK, so it's this Seafirst branch. Are you done?"

9

Matthew jotted something in the notebook, then said, "That's my end of it. How about the dye packs?"

Anne took a deep breath. "So there are two kinds we have to worry about. One uses a timer. It's set to go off a certain number of minutes after it's activated, which happens when the teller removes the stack of cash from the drawer. Typically, the dye pack is set to explode 30 minutes after activation. Whether it's 30 minutes or even 20 minutes, we should have plenty of time to leave the bank, reach the garage before they go off, and get rid of them there.

"The second kind of dye pack is RF controlled. It's set off by radio frequencies that are emitted at the bank exits. For those, we have a Faraday cage." Anne used her hands to outline an imaginary box. "I'm using an extra-large briefcase that's lined with conductive material—aluminum foil. It totally covers the inside of the case when it's closed. The foil creates a seal that will block electromagnetic fields. We'll put the cash in the briefcase, and the briefcase inside the green bag before we leave the bank."

"OK," Matthew said, "but are you sure aluminum foil will work? That seems a little..."

"Excuse me, who's the engineer here?" Anne then gave Matthew a longer explanation of exactly what constituted a Faraday cage and also a technical explanation of how it blocked electromagnetic fields.

"Alright, I think I get it," Matthew said. "So we put all the money in the briefcase. Then we sort through all the stacks in the parking garage, identify the ones that contain dye packs and leave them behind."

"Latex gloves," Anne added. "We each have a pair."

"Right. We'll handle the dye packs with latex gloves. In fact, we'll be wearing the gloves when we enter the bank. Our jackets have long cuffs, so people won't notice."

"Both kinds of dye packs will be easy for us to detect. You can tell just by feeling the stacks of money. If you can flex the stack, it's clean. If it's stiff, it has a dye pack." Something out of the corner of Anne's eye caught her attention, and she glanced toward the front door. A police officer was talking to one of the register clerks, a 20-something man wearing a Mother Love Bone T-shirt and fuzzy green wristbands.

"Hey, Matt," Anne said. "Look who's here."

He turned around casually and saw the officer. "Don't worry. It has nothing to do with us."

They began flipping mindlessly through the CDs in front of them. After a minute, Matthew turned around and saw two more police officers walk into the store. They spoke briefly with the first one, who stayed at the front door while the other two approached Matthew and Anne from different ends of their aisle.

To block any escape, Matthew thought. He noticed that both of the officers had their right hand resting on the handle of their service pistol. Not a good sign.

Anne saw them as well, and said, "This is your idea. I'm not saying anything to them."

Matthew grabbed the nearest CD and pretended to examine it. He heard the approaching steps, then on his right a man asking in a friendly voice, "Excuse me, I'm Officer Park. What brings you folks to HighLife today?"

The police were so much nicer in Seattle than they were in Boston, Matthew thought. He turned and smiled. The officer was a good ten years younger than him. "Oh, hi. We're looking to add to our rockabilly collection." Matthew held up the CD to the officer, actually looking at it himself for the first time. Marshall Crenshaw. Matthew had a strong dislike of Marshall Crenshaw, and he had never understood quite why. Almost everyone he knew loved, or at least liked, his music. Even the pickiest critics praised the guy, but Matthew had disliked him from the first song he'd heard.

"He played Buddy Holly in that *La Bamba* movie, you know," Matthew said, hoping to strike up a rapport with Officer Park. Anything to ease the conversation toward an innocent explanation for what was going on.

"He asked what you're doing here," the other officer said. She wasn't smiling, and Matthew sensed that whatever patience she had when she showed up on the scene was pretty much gone. Her name tag read "Officer Morsom." Pointing at Matthew's hand, she continued, "Can I see that notebook?"

Matthew put the CD back, then handed over the notebook. Officer Morsom scanned it quickly, then began reading a list: "Bans, check for

11

bruises, really check…avos, three ripe, three not…" Officer Morsom read the next several items silently, with her lips moving. Then she looked up. "TP. Who is TP?"

"That stands for toilet paper," Matthew said, trying not to smile.

She closed the notebook, then held it up. "What is this?"

"It's a list of groceries," Matthew said.

"Also known as a grocery list," Anne added.

Matthew turned to his wife and said softly, "I thought you weren't going to say anything."

Anne looked at her watch and said to both officers. "As you can see, we have to go shopping. We also have to pick up our daughter at soccer practice in about 15 minutes."

"Do you really have a daughter at soccer practice?" Officer Park asked.

"Every Friday, I leave work early so I can get her at school and take her to practice. When it's over, I pick her up," Anne said.

Officer Morsom didn't seem to care about shopping or soccer practice. She said, "Let's see some IDs. One at a time. You first," she said, nodding to Matthew. He pulled out his wallet and handed over his driver's license.

"Now yours," she said, looking at Anne.

Once the officer had both of their licenses, she took a few steps back and reached for her radio. Matthew saw two more officers enter the store. He knew there was no easy way to talk their way out of this, but he also knew that if he didn't explain everything as quickly and directly as possible, he and his wife might be spending the next several hours in a police station—or worse—a jail.

He turned to Officer Park. "Someone overheard us talking about a bank. I'm sure that's why you're here."

"What about a bank?" Officer Park asked.

"Someone overheard us talking about robbing a bank. Planning a robbery."

"Are you planning to rob a bank?" Officer Park asked.

Matthew could hear Officer Morsom on her radio, reading his driver's license number and his address. From the information on his license, she also described him as Matthew Mahoney, a White male, 40 years old, six feet three inches tall, blue eyes. The officer did the same with Matthew's wife—Anne Boushay Mahoney, White female, 38 years old, six feet tall with blue-green eyes.

The half dozen shoppers and the two register clerks were trying very hard to follow the unfolding drama while pretending not to do so. Anne scanned the store quickly and prayed, really prayed, that none of the people there recognized her or Matthew.

"Look, this is just a game we play," Anne said, which was the truth. "We imagine what it would be like to do something exciting…challenging. Then we think about all the steps we would have to take to actually do it. But we never do. We just pretend. Then we score ourselves on how well we planned it, OK? That's all we do. Pretend to steal the Porsche 959 that Bill Gates owns, or break into a museum or…"

"Or rob a bank?" Officer Park asked.

Anne responded quickly. "A bank was his idea."

Matthew shot his wife a look. She shot one back.

They could hear the report coming back on their licenses. No criminal records. For Matthew, one speeding ticket; for Anne, two speeding tickets, one in a school zone.

Matthew sensed that Officer Park was not completely convinced.

"It's our twelfth wedding anniversary…" Matthew began.

His wife interrupted him. "You don't have to tell them every little thing about this."

Matthew turned and spoke to her as calmly as he could. "I think that's the idea right now." Turning back to Officer Park, he continued, "We do this kind of thing every now and then, usually around our anniversary. It's the bank across the street we were going to…imagine robbing." Matthew continued the story with some of the details they'd researched.

"We decide on disguises. Then we pick a day and a time. The plan was to scout the place today, then come back next Friday afternoon at this same time. We'd stand out on the sidewalk, watch the bank to see how long it takes for the last person in line to reach a teller, add two minutes for the teller to hand over the cash…the imaginary teller to hand over the imaginary cash…and see if any police or security guards happen to walk into the bank during that time. After that, we'd walk up the alley behind this store and see if we encountered anything or anyone who might be a problem for our plan...our imaginary plan. We'd look for possible weaknesses in it, then decide if it would have been successful or not."

Officer Park seemed to be studying Matthew's words. "Am I hearing a little East Coast in your accent?"

"Yes, I'm from South Boston. Originally." Matthew immediately regretted not simply saying "Boston."

"Really. South Boston. And your last name is Mahoney. I don't imagine you're related to..."

Matthew shook his head and interrupted, "You'd be amazed how many Mahoneys there are in South Boston. It's such a common name. When I was a kid, there were two other Mahoneys on my hockey team one year."

"OK, well, let me give you some advice. It's really not a wise idea to talk in public about robbing a bank," Officer Park said.

Anne looked around the store with growing impatience. "Right. We get it."

Officer Morsom approached Matthew and Anne and returned their licenses. To her partner, she said, "No records." Then in a louder voice, she added, "Except they both have lead feet, including one speeding ticket in a school zone."

That was just a parting shot, Matthew calculated. Officer Park looked like he had been convinced by the explanation. All they needed to bring the scene to a graceful close was an apology that was heartfelt, or at least one that sounded heartfelt.

"Thanks," Anne said without a smile, and with more than a hint of contempt in her voice. She stared at Officer Morsom. Over the years, Anne had developed a slight squint that could sometimes unnerve people or make them feel as if they were being scrutinized for some reason. She squinted outdoors because she hated to wear sunglasses. They made her feel claustrophobic. Squinting also became the thing she did when she was very focused on a particular person or thought. Or when something annoyed her.

Officer Park might have been willing to let them leave at that point, but Officer Morsom didn't appreciate Anne's stare. She took a half step toward Anne and asked, "Did you grow up around here?"

"No," Anne answered.

"Where do your parents live?"

Anne hesitated, then said, "My father lived in Alaska, but he's dead. My mother lives in Ipswich, Massachusetts."

Officer Morsom stared at Anne for a long moment before asking, "What if I called your mother right now and told her what you've been doing today? What if I told her that you were being questioned by the Seattle police for plotting a bank robbery?"

Matthew looked at Anne, expecting her to answer. Instead, he saw something remarkable. His wife's face displayed a complex series of emotions. First came confusion. That was followed quickly by shock, then extreme embarrassment, resentment and contempt. After a brief return to embarrassment, it seemed to settle firmly on anger.

That was Matthew's cue. "I think my wife and I realize now that we made a big mistake. It is just a game, but you're right. Playing this kind of game in public is a bad idea. We're really sorry about that. And we promise to never do this sort of thing ever again." Turning to his wife, he added, "Right?"

Anne had parked their car nearby, and as they left HighLife Records and walked slowly down Alaska Street, Matthew was sure that all five cops were back on the corner watching them, some confused, some amused, and at least one regretting the fact that they didn't take the couple downtown to scare them a little.

Anne sensed it as well and pulled the hood of her sweatshirt over her head. They rounded the corner and walked up to their Subaru. Anne unlocked Matthew's old steel-frame hardtail mountain bike from the back rack. He'd be riding to QFC for the groceries while Anne picked up their daughter, Nora. "Your backpack should hold everything. It's in the front seat."

As Matthew stood over the bike and put on the pack, he said, "We'll try again next week. Something different."

"I told you a bank was a bad idea. You should listen to me."

As she said it, Matthew began to smile broadly.

"What?" Anne asked.

"Your expression. When the cop said she was gonna call your mother. That was the best anniversary present you've ever given me."

Anne brushed some dust from his jacket and leaned in for a kiss. "Enjoy it because it's the only one you're getting this year."

15

They lived in the Arbor Heights section of West Seattle. It was a sleepy neighborhood of modest homes, many of them built between the '30s and '50s when Boeing dominated the Seattle economy, and the middle class wanted the suburban dream of a cute little house with a backyard. In the '90s, it became the place where many Seattle couples headed when they were ready to start a family and wanted to escape the cramped, noisy life of the city. The Mahoneys rented a small Craftsman home near the top of the Heights.

It was different in many ways from the gritty Old Colony housing project where Matthew had grown up in South Boston, but it was similar in the sense that everyone looked after each other, and each other's kids. For Anne, the neighborhood made her feel welcome, the way she was welcomed in Anchorage when she moved there at the age of 12 after her parents divorced.

It was typical of almost any neighborhood by being in a slow state of flux, with families occasionally moving in and moving out, but Matthew and Anne seemed to arrive during a sort of high-water mark of conviviality. There were block parties during the summer, and sometimes a simple stage would be set up with a few amps and microphones so teenagers could blast out a set of grunge favorites or a dad band could revive the hits of the '70s. Birthdays, graduations and anniversaries had a way of turning into get-togethers that were open to everyone within a couple of blocks.

From late spring to early fall, a handful of the gatherings were held in the Mahoneys' backyard because of the giant outdoor movie screen that Matthew and Anne had built against the side of their garage. Anne had salvaged a swath of white industrial fabric left over from an irrigation project at work, and they stretched it across a wood frame that was 14 feet wide and 8 feet high. Their neighbor Kurt had an expertise in all things audiovisual, and he modified a projector and sound system that did a convincing job of mimicking a big-screen movie experience.

At 7:30 on Friday evening, when the sting of their encounter with law enforcement began to fade and a string of party lights cast a cheery glow in the fading light of dusk, Matthew and Anne were joined by some neighbors and several friends to celebrate their twelfth wedding anniversary. A table on the large backyard deck held three salads of the green-leafy and black-bean variety, chips and salsa, potato salad, hummus, cheeses, cookies, cakes and brownies, with room made for new plates as more neighbors joined the party. Beside the table was a quarter keg of Hale's Pale Ale chilling in a plastic barrel filled with ice.

The sound of music mixed with the voices of children playing tetherball and running around. There were no fences between the six backyards on their side of the block, so there was an ebb and flow of kids and a rise and fall in noise.

Matthew stood at the grill tending a couple of steaks, and the last round of burgers and sausages, along with veggie versions of both. At his side was his ten-year-old son, Dylan, with tongs in hand, attentive to the task of toasting the rolls.

By 8:00, the sky was just about dark enough to play the first movie, so Kurt turned on his projection equipment and tested it. Another neighbor plugged in the professional popcorn machine she had inherited from her uncle's theater in Tacoma. Inside a brightly lit glass cabinet decorated with old-fashioned graphics was a big kettle, the lid of which began to rise and jump as popped corn spilled forth to be salted, buttered, scooped up, and poured into red-and-white-striped paper bags.

"The kids' movie starts in three minutes!" Kurt called out.

The seating in front of the big screen steadily grew with a random assortment of chairs hauled over from neighboring yards. When the screen grew bright and the opening music to *A Bug's Life* began playing, the backyard filled with the sound of children cheering and clapping. A few stragglers came running barefoot across the soft, cool grass with popcorn bouncing out of their bags. Matthew and Anne's seven-year-old daughter, Nora, and two of her friends were given permission to watch from the branches of the tall maple tree in the backyard, but halfway through the movie that permission was revoked when the girls chose to amuse themselves by tossing popcorn onto the movie watchers below.

Just before 10:00, the children's movie ended, and the younger kids headed home. It was a thinned-out crowd that remained for the second show. Matthew had really wanted it to be *The Matrix,* which had just been released on video, but to nobody's surprise Blockbuster didn't have any copies available when he called. So they settled on *The Empire Strikes Back*, which they owned. It was one of those movies that everyone had seen at least once and almost everyone enjoyed seeing a second, third or fourth time. Those who didn't were happy to hang out on the deck or inside the house, where a card game had broken out.

When the end of the second movie drew near, only the die-hard viewers remained. The air had grown cool enough for Matthew to bring out jackets for Anne and himself. Nora was doing her best to stay awake. Her head was resting on her mother's lap and she had a sleeping bag wrapped around her. Dylan had gone inside, brushed his teeth and climbed into bed, where he was reading about a machine that could create anything starting with the letter "N" in a story by Stanislaw Lem.

A lot of the cleanup had been done, so when the movie was over, Kurt packed up his equipment and carried it home. The popcorn maker was stowed inside the garage, and Matthew and Anne said goodbye to the last neighbor to leave. That happened to be Janice.

As Janice put on her jacket, she asked, "So it's 12 years. That's not exactly a milestone like a 10th or 25th, but did you do anything special to celebrate?"

Matthew and Anne glanced at each other, then Matthew said, "It was a real low-key thing this year. We just went to HighLife. Trying to fill out our rockabilly collection."

"Oh, nice," Janice said. "Did you find anything good?"

Anne said, "A couple of police…a couple of CDs by The Police."

Matthew smiled and nodded. "Yup, pretty low-key."

Janice gave them both a hug. At the front door, she hesitated and turned around. "I wouldn't expect to find The Police in the rockabilly section."

"We were surprised too," Anne said. She smiled, then looked at Matthew, and he smiled.

Janice looked back and forth between them, then slowly began to smile as well. "Alright, whatever that means I'm not going to ask you about it. Happy anniversary, and I'll see you both next week at Ryan's birthday party. Anne, be sure to bring some of your homemade hummus. People can't get enough of it."

When Janice had disappeared down the sidewalk, Anne closed the door and let out a laugh. "I almost…"

"You're not a good liar. You better watch what you say about your homemade hummus. Someday they're gonna find out you buy it from a shop in Montlake."

It was almost 1:00 when they finally went to bed. Matthew was asleep within two minutes, but Anne lay awake in the dark with her eyes open. Their bedroom was on the first floor of the house, and the kids' small rooms were on the second floor.

There were often nights when Anne would be awake like this, thinking about one thing or another while Matthew was sound asleep. She would hear things in the night: the wind chimes on their back porch sounding out a breeze, a ferry horn bellowing across a foggy Puget Sound, a jet coming in for a landing at Boeing Field, or the occasional fireworks, which were technically illegal but which could be heard on any holiday and whenever a Seattle sports team won a big game.

There were some nights when she thought she could hear the sound of her children breathing in their rooms above, and she would see them in their typical sleeping poses: Dylan on his back or side with an arm covering his eyes, Nora on her stomach with her pillow tossed onto the floor.

What was keeping her awake on this night was something that two people mentioned at the party that night. They had both asked Anne about Alaska and whether it was still in the future for the Mahoney family. Of course it was still in the future, Anne had said. Yes, definitely. It was still the plan, just delayed. That is, it was further delayed, since the deadline for moving to Alaska had changed a number of times. As each new year found the Mahoneys still living in West Seattle, the story they told about their future had to be revised once more. And Anne had begun the latest revision in her answer that night.

"It's happening in the next year," Anne had said. "In the next 12 months." That meant September 2000, she thought. It was a totally arbitrary date that she hadn't discussed with Matthew. It just came to her in the moment because she sensed it was time to set a firm deadline for a goal that had been slipping away from them for years. Something had to stop the slide. She didn't want to look the same people in the eye the following September and admit that, yet again, the plan had not come to pass.

She rolled onto her side and gave Matthew a nudge. His slow, steady breathing continued. Not only did he have an easier time falling asleep, he also had an easier time staying asleep. She tried again with a firm punch to his shoulder. He groaned and slowly drew in a deep breath.

"Matt, wake up. We need to talk about The Plan."

Chapter 2

The Mahoney Plan

(And How Life Mocked It)

Like all their close friends, Matthew and Anne had a plan. Almost everyone they knew had a plan. And they all had a practiced, ten-second version that could be delivered like an elevator pitch at parties or while waiting in line for a double tall skinny at Starbucks.

My wife's a tax attorney. I'm still at the bank, but I'm taking some night classes to learn computer programming so I can get a job at Microsoft. When our third kid finishes college, we're selling the house and moving back to Utah.

My partner has a house in Wallingford. My cat and I just moved in. The house needs a lot of work, so we'll probably spend the next ten years fixing it up. We'll still be going to Mexico twice a year. We love Mexico.

We need to get out of debt before we can buy a house. My sister and I are planning to open a daycare in West Seattle. There are so many young families there now. My husband drives for Metro. It's a reliable paycheck with good benefits.

I remarried last year and got back into the restaurant business. Cooking is my thing. I have two kids from my previous marriage, and that's enough for both of us. Our plan is to open a small bistro in Madison Park or Madrona. And build a cabin in the mountains. Someplace off the grid.

Right after they were married in 1987 and living in a small two-bedroom apartment in the Ballard neighborhood of Seattle, Anne would describe The Mahoney Plan this way: *I'm starting a career in environmental engineering. Matthew is bartending while he goes back to college to finish his degree, so he can work in the computer field. We're planning to have two kids. Before they're in grade school, we'll move up to Alaska and live in our cabin outside of Anchorage. Our future's in Alaska.*

It was the same cabin where Anne had moved at the age of 12 after her parents divorced. As a teenager, it was difficult adjusting to life in Anchorage, even though her community made her feel welcome. That's why she wanted to move back before her kids were in grade school, so that the transition wouldn't be as disruptive to them.

Anne had been an only child. Her father, Dylan, who died in a climbing accident before Anne's marriage, had left her the large cabin. It was unoccupied the first year after her father's death, and Anne intended to keep it that way until she, Matthew and the kids moved in.

That's how The Mahoney Plan officially began all bright and shiny in December 1987. Matthew signed up for a full load of classes at Seattle Central Community College and continued his bartending shifts at Donovan's Steak and Oyster House in downtown Seattle. Anne was working as an environmental engineer at a company based in Kirkland, Washington. It paid well, and it gave them healthcare benefits.

On September 26, 1988, The Mahoney Plan started to go off the rails when Anne got called into an unscheduled meeting at work. She and her 14 coworkers were told that the company was filing for bankruptcy and everyone was, as of that moment, laid off. There would be no severance pay and no extension of benefits beyond the end of the month, which was three and a half days away. Because the company employed less than 20 people, Anne and her coworkers were not eligible to continue their health insurance under COBRA.

A week later she discovered she was pregnant, which was part of The Plan but way ahead of schedule. The health insurance that had covered her and Matthew, and that would have covered the birth of their now unborn child, had expired. Even if she got a new job, her pregnancy would be considered a preexisting condition by her new employer's insurer and wouldn't be covered.

That meant they had to pay out of pocket for all the expenses involving the pregnancy and the birth. Anne's mother, Joan Boushay, learned of the situation and offered to pitch in, even to cover the entire cost. She could certainly afford it, but Anne had always been steadfast about not seeking or taking financial help from her mother. Publicly she said it was because of the self-sufficiency she had inherited from both of her parents. Privately she also wanted to maintain a ground of separation—the unnamable and sometimes uncomfortable distance that Anne stubbornly insisted on maintaining between herself and her mother. Taking such a large gift or—even worse—a large loan, would be an unacceptable intrusion upon that sacred ground.

It went back to the time of her parents' divorce, when Anne chose to live with her dad rather than stay with her mom at the Boushay family farmhouse in Ipswich, Massachusetts. That created a rift, and a wound that was still healing. Anne dealt with it by relating to her mother as an equal, and being an equal in Anne's eyes meant being financially independent. She thanked her mom for offering to help but politely refused, softening the blow by saying that if she and Matthew couldn't make it work financially by themselves, she'd reconsider.

Their savings were depleted soon after the bills started arriving. There were days when the mailbox in the lobby of their apartment building was difficult to open because it was so tightly packed with statements from doctors, X-ray labs, blood-testing facilities and various departments at Swedish Medical Center. Fortunately, they qualified for some financial assistance, information that was not shared with Joan Boushay. The remaining expenses, which were considerable, went onto credit cards.

A month into the fall semester at Seattle Central Community College, Matthew dropped out, sold his textbooks for pennies on the dollar and got a full-time job working in the claims department of an insurance company in downtown Seattle. His salary and the money from his bartending shifts covered their living expenses. Matthew absolutely hated insurance work, but the job came with health benefits, which they needed.

In December, they gave up their small apartment in Ballard and moved to the Arbor Heights section of West Seattle, where they got more space for the same rent in a small house.

It was an abrupt transition. A few months before, Anne had a great job and Matthew was a few semesters away from qualifying for a professional job in a rapidly growing field. They had been newlyweds living in the busy city with cafés, restaurants, pubs and music venues within blocks of where they lived. Most nights and weekends were theirs to spend however they pleased. Now their lives were structured around the coming birth of a child, and living in a quiet neighborhood of families that went to bed early.

When friends would ask how The Mahoney Plan was going, the response was: *It's a little off schedule but still on track.*

In the months before the birth, Anne worked part-time as a cook at Roy's, a neighborhood restaurant near their new home. Matthew had told her about the opening. He had started bartending there a couple of nights a week because it was more convenient than the restaurant downtown. With Anne working in the kitchen and Matthew at the bar, they joked that it would be like the old days when they worked together at Donovan's, the place where they first met.

It was a lot like the old days. Roy's had an open kitchen, so customers could see the cooks swirling sliced vegetables around a sizzling sauté pan, or slapping a fresh salmon fillet onto the cherrywood grill. As Matthew was pouring an ale or shaking a vodka gimlet, he could hear through the clattering of pans and bar chatter the clear sound of Anne's voice calling out: two fish and chips, one with no tartar; a New York steak medium well, no potato and extra vegetables; a grilled chicken burger, no cheese, no tomato, with a side of house slaw.

Their son, Dylan, was born in May 1989. In the fall, Anne returned to full-time work for an environmental engineering company that provided health benefits. Matthew added to his evening and weekend shifts at Roy's, but quit his daytime insurance job to be a stay-at-home dad.

Keeping up with their hefty credit card payments was a monthly challenge, and looming in their financial background was the cabin in Alaska. They would live there eventually, but in the meantime, it was a drain. The place had to be heated during the cold season to prevent the pipes from bursting. They made occasional visits in winter, so draining the system wasn't practical. And there was the accumulation of large and small things that needed attention, like new windows, worn-out gutters that had to be replaced and a garage that needed fixing after a tree fell on it during a windstorm. All the cabin expenses went onto their credit cards, including the property taxes, which ran over two thousand dollars a year. Whatever Matthew and Anne managed to pay toward their debt each month was more or less replaced by new charges, so that the overall balance never varied much.

Matthew moved delicately around the subject, but eventually convinced Anne that they should rent the place to cover expenses until they moved north. The solution Anne agreed to was to have Blue Star Management, the best regarded property management company in Anchorage, oversee maintenance and screen potential tenants. Matthew realized what being "best regarded" meant when he saw what the company charged, but he kept his mouth shut. The compromise was one they could both live with.

After Nora's birth in the winter of 1992, the goal became to move to Alaska sometime in the next few years. That version of The Mahoney Plan hit snags in 1994 when Anne got laid off again, and in 1995 when their West Seattle landlord told them that the house they were renting was being sold. They had less than two months to find a new place and move.

That setback by itself wasn't a concern. They could find a new rental house in Arbor Heights, and they quickly did. It's what happened before the move that sent The Plan off the tracks again. On the day they announced to their kids that they'd be moving to their new home, Dylan freaked out. The initial tantrum lasted 48 hours, with breaks for the bathroom, sleep and, on the second day, food. He was extremely upset with the idea of change. "Home" was the rented one-story rambler where they lived. "His room" was the last room on the south end of the house, arranged the way it was right now and not any other way.

Dylan's strong reaction surprised Matthew and Anne. Neither one had seen it coming. Yes, he had a thing about routines—for example, eating the same breakfast at the same time every morning, always being driven to their local Safeway along the same route, lining up his Transformer toys before bed every night in the same order, with Optimus Prime always, always in the center—but he'd never been so difficult about the occasional exception to routine either.

The behavior issue lasted beyond the move to their new rental. When Dylan started first grade that fall, the problem spread from home to school. Matthew had begun roofing that year, and more than once he got a call from the school while standing on the top of a house with a nail gun in his hand. He'd leave the jobsite, drive to the school and either have a long, calming talk with Dylan or take him home and end his workday prematurely.

The problem at school wasn't rooted in Dylan's academic skills. That's what Anne and Matthew were told at their first parent-teacher meeting.

Dylan was considered intelligent by his teacher. But when things didn't go the way he wanted them to, either in the classroom or on the playground, he got frustrated and acted out. He also had trouble focusing in class and was easily distracted by simple things, like the sight of a plane flying by outside.

Matthew remembered how things had gone for him growing up in South Boston, and Dylan's behavior didn't really strike him as being particularly abnormal. It was a phase. He'd grow out of it, like he'd grow out of other phases yet to come. For Anne, the teacher's report was more disheartening.

It was clear to her that relocating the family to Alaska anytime soon was out of the question. Moving Dylan four blocks to another house had been traumatic. Moving him more than a thousand miles to a different environment and without the few friends he had was too much to put him through. At least right now. Time would tell when The Plan could get back on track.

Over the next couple of years, people would ask from time to time how The Mahoney Plan was going. In the beginning, Anne would insist that everything was still going as planned and that additional small setbacks were being managed. Matthew learned to be evasive with his responses and usually smiled and said something like, "Let me get back to you on that, OK?"

The question was asked less and less frequently until it was no longer asked at all. Their friends and families were good enough not to torture them with what was now obvious. The Mahoney Plan had failed. They had become what they were most afraid of becoming: people adrift in the world without a plan, moving through life from one year to the next, simply reacting to the circumstances that life threw their way.

As Anne lay awake that night, she counted the years when they had lived without a plan while pretending they still had one. There didn't really seem to be anything in their way now, though, because Dylan's situation had improved enough in the last year that, in Anne's opinion, he seemed ready for a move to Alaska, as long as the move occurred in an orderly fashion. If all the details were explained to Dylan ahead of time, it would give him the space he needed to adjust to the change.

It was time, Anne decided, to resurrect The Plan.

Matthew wasn't happy to be woken up in the middle of the night, and he was eager to get to the end of the discussion so he could get back to sleep. But he listened to what Anne had to say, then added his own thoughts, like maybe scheduling the move at the end of the school year or that summer, which is when their current lease also happened to expire. After covering a few more points, they came to an agreement. The Mahoney Plan was officially back on track, and they vowed to move the family to Alaska in the year 2000, ideally by the end of July.

The first step was for Anne to research job openings in her field, specifically in the Anchorage area. They would have to be full-time staff positions that included health benefits for the family. She had been tempted in the past to take a temporary contract job because there were lots of them available and they were easy to get, but contract work was generally short-term and didn't come with benefits. Regardless of what kind of work Matthew got and when he got it, they agreed that one of them had to land a stable staff job in Alaska before they would move. And with Anne's experience and education, she was in a much better position to be the one.

Chapter 3
The A Crew

Monday, October 18, 1999

The alarm clock was set for 5:15, but Matthew woke at 5:10 to the distant sound of a ferry's foghorn. Anne was deep asleep beside him. With just the light from the clock, he put on his running gear, grabbed a small headlamp, set the timer on the coffeemaker in the kitchen and headed into the morning fog.

Matthew Mahoney was a creature of habit, and the habit he was most religious about was his morning workout. Come rain or shine, he started by running a loop through his Arbor Heights neighborhood, heading south on his street until it reached Marine View Drive, then returning north. As the name suggested, the road was filled with homes spread out on a high bluff, with five-star views of Puget Sound, Vashon Island and the Olympic Mountains beyond.

In early summer, the sun would have just risen and he'd see salmon fishers clustered around Three Tree Point and ferries traveling back and forth across the Sound. This time of year, it was still dark, and sunrise was over two hours away. There were no views, just the slapping of his soles on the wet pavement, a spot of light jumping on the road ahead, and a trail of vapor from his breath rising into the damp air.

His route brought him north, passing a few blocks from where he started, then the road dropped steeply. It was 350 feet of descent that he'd have to earn back in about ten minutes. At the bottom of the hill was a bakery and Roy's, where Matthew bartended part-time.

Light shining from the restaurant lit up the wet sidewalk out front. Matthew rapped a knuckle on a window as he passed. The opening cook Jeremiah had his shoulders hunched over a rolling pin, and he sent up a cloud of flour as he answered with a wave.

Two more turns in the road and Matthew passed the Fauntleroy ferry terminal. The first boat from Vashon Island was pulling up with early-bird commuters. Cars sat idling on the pier, as their drivers waited to board the 5:50 departure to Southworth.

The last stretch of his run took Matthew along the paved beach trail in Lincoln Park. As he approached the first picnic shelter, he offered a greeting to a pair of runners, a middle-aged man and woman he assumed were a couple, passing him in the other direction. Their morning routines were as regular as his, so that they almost always encountered each other along this stretch.

Where the trail curved out to a point, a few harbor seals on the beach waddled casually across the smooth stones that clattered together with each wave, and again when the water receded. At the point, Matthew turned around and headed back. Waiting for him on a windowsill outside Roy's was a paper bag. He grabbed it without losing a step. The scones inside were fresh from the oven, and he cupped his hands around the bag to warm his fingers. The final push up the steep hill took around 600 steps.

When he wasn't feeling well or hadn't slept soundly, the hill could be pure agony. When he was feeling OK, as he was this morning, he climbed it quickly and even picked up his pace toward the end. Each step was incrementally more taxing, so by the time Matthew reached the top of the hill his legs were spent, his lungs were burning, and a steady cloud of vapor rose from his jacket.

The easy two-block walk home gave him a chance to cool down and eat one of the blackberry scones. There were three more for Anne and the kids. He dropped the bag on the kitchen counter, drank a glass of cold water and changed his wet shirt for a dry one. With a hot mug of coffee, he headed out to the garage to finish his workout: 20 minutes of lifting weights, stretching, then hitting a speed bag while listening to the news on a radio.

After Anne left on her commute to Kirkland, carpooling with two coworkers, Matthew dropped the kids off at their different schools, then headed for work as foreman of a roofing crew, wherever that happened to be for him that day.

Every other Monday morning, he started his workday by driving to the top of Capitol Hill for a management meeting with the brothers who ran Rieger Roofing. He hated crawling in rush-hour traffic over the West

Seattle Bridge but he liked Coastal Cuisine, a neighborhood restaurant that was a lot like Roy's but slightly more upscale.

Sal Camacho was waiting for him at the horseshoe-shaped bar that wrapped around the open kitchen. He was just ordering a coffee, and changed the order to two coffees when he saw Matthew walk through the front door.

He was Matthew's assistant foreman and a good friend of more than three years. Sal was one of the few people, other than his wife, who Matthew trusted with the great secret of his life—the identity of his older brother Francis.

Sal was originally from Yakima, Washington, to the east over the Cascade Mountains. He and his brother, Luis, had moved to Seattle in the early '90s. Like Matthew, he had done stints in landscaping and restaurant work before settling on roofing. He was more than strong enough for the physical demands of the job, and he was smart enough to know how to get a crew to put out its best work. When he caught anybody slacking, a few sharp words in his deep, gravelly voice snapped them back into focus.

"Happy Monday," Matthew said. He took a stool next to Sal as their coffees arrived. In his opinion, Coastal Cuisine served the strongest, richest coffee in the city. It bordered on abusive for people with weak stomachs, but it agreed with Matthew as long as he drank no more than two and a half cups.

"Wiley called. He's gonna be a few minutes late," Sal said. "He mentioned a bonus job today for whoever wants it."

Matthew blew across the top of his mug before taking a sip. He thought about the last time their boss offered them a bonus if his A Crew worked on a Saturday to shingle a building at a local winery. As they were finishing the job, the sound of their nail guns overlapped the first ten minutes or so of an outdoor jazz concert on the winery property. As a result, the bonus vanished.

"If I remember correctly…"

"I know," Sal said. "Beware the bonus from the Wiley one."

"Hey, so how was the Showbox last night?" Matthew asked, referring to the concert venue on First Ave where Sal and his girlfriend, Malia, talked about seeing Maceo Parker and the Seattle band Maktub.

"We got there too late, and they were sold out. Malia blamed me, but the reason we were late is because we got into a fight, which was about me hanging out with my brother and his friends the night before. So when we found out the show was sold out, we got into another fight. Then we went to the Crocodile. They had a couple of '80s bands that were barely worth seeing. Did you guys catch any shows?"

"No. I bartended yesterday. On Saturday, we drove to Snoqualmie Pass and did a little hiking. Then we stopped for dinner in North Bend. Nora ended up getting sick and was sick all day yesterday. This morning she seemed OK. I'm hoping I don't get a call from her school. But we are gonna see Joe Strummer at the Moore in two weeks."

"Anne likes Joe Strummer?" Sal asked.

"Not really. But, as usual, we're trading. She'll go to Joe Strummer if I go to Luna at the Crocodile the week after."

"By the way, Diego's already here," Sal said.

"He's out back?" Matthew asked, referring to the meeting space off the rear dining room.

Sal nodded. "Let's see if he left us anything to eat."

Matthew told the bartender to put their coffees on the Riegers' bill, then they walked to the small meeting room. At the far end of a long table sat a man reading the *Seattle Post-Intelligencer,* known as the *PI.* He was slightly shorter than Matthew and had a thicker build. He was the other foreman for Rieger Roofing and, like Matthew, he oversaw two work crews. His name was Diego Espinoza. Matthew heard that Diego had quite the temper, although Matthew had never witnessed it himself. Matthew also heard that he was originally from Medellin, Colombia and had emigrated to Washington State as an adult.

Diego didn't get along with Matthew or Sal, so they generally ignored each other at these biweekly morning meetings and other work situations that put them in the same room or on the same jobsite.

On all but the hottest days, Diego wore a sweatshirt and jacket. This morning was no exception. When he saw Matthew and Sal step into the room, he put down his newspaper, cupped his hands and blew into them. It was as if he were standing outside on a cold winter day, but the meeting room was comfortably warm, at least for Matthew and Sal, who weren't wearing jackets.

They took seats across from each other in the middle of the table and stared at the plateful of muffins and scones sitting very close to Diego, so close that when Diego held up his newspaper again, the treats disappeared from their view.

They were fresh-baked at Coastal Cuisine that morning and paid for by Wiley Rieger, the owner of Rieger Roofing, who'd be arriving any minute. But Diego was in the habit of showing up to these meetings first, ordering the baked goods and keeping the plate out of everyone else's reach. Matthew had gotten a brief glimpse of the muffins. They looked delicious and he was still a little hungry, but he wasn't about to ask Diego to push the plate his way.

Sal saw this and swept a dismissive hand at the other end of the table.

There were also two carafes of hot coffee on the table. Matthew pushed one in Sal's direction. As Matthew was topping off his own mug with the other carafe, their boss walked into the room. He was wearing an expensive athletic suit and the aviator sunglasses he wore everywhere. Wiley had just come from his gym, the Washington Athletic Club in downtown Seattle. With a nice restaurant and pub, finely appointed conference rooms and upscale lodging, it was more of a resort, in Matthew's opinion. The gyms he had belonged to were filled with the smell of sweat and the sound of clanging weights, and usually overcrowded.

Matthew had been to the Washington Athletic Club a couple of times as a guest, once for a workout and once for drinks, and he really liked it, although it was far from his home in West Seattle. More importantly, there was no way in hell he could afford it. But if he ever did show up there while Wiley was working out, Matthew knew he'd find his boss spending all his time in the weight room, building up show muscles and never breaking a sweat.

The first time he shook Wiley's hand, Matthew was shocked at how soft it was. From what Matthew understood, his boss hadn't driven a single nail through a shingle in his entire life. It seemed the toughest thing his hands did every week was sign some checks. There was only one occasion when Wiley visited a jobsite and stayed for more than five minutes. Even then, he stayed on the ground the whole time, and when he left his fair skin was painfully sunburned.

Diego lowered his paper when he heard Wiley walk in. Then he poured two cups of coffee, one for Wiley and one for his brother, Willard, who was running a little late. Wiley sat at the head of the table, then focused on his appointment book for a moment. "OK," he said, looking up. "We'll keep this meeting short because there's a rush job that one of you guys needs to finish by 5:30 today. It's right here on the Hill. The Reynolds Estate next to Volunteer Park. Willard's getting supplies lined up for it now. They'll be on-site soon."

Wiley stopped suddenly and looked down the table at the plate of baked goods. "Let's see, Diego...I'll take a poppy seed muffin and..." He paused to peek over his sunglasses. "Aaaand...a cranberry scone."

Diego carefully placed them on a paper napkin and delivered them to Wiley. "We can save the other poppy seed for your brother. And also the cinnamon scone," Diego said, placing them onto a napkin that he pushed toward the empty spot where Willard liked to sit. With his hands on the plate and his eyebrows raised, Diego looked at Sal.

"Cranberry scone," Sal said. Diego placed it on a napkin and handed it to Sal.

Matthew saw only one decent muffin left on the plate. A blueberry one. He called down the table for it.

"That one's mine," Diego said.

A half-eaten blueberry muffin sat next to Diego's coffee mug, so Matthew said, "I don't mean the blueberry muffin you're eating. I mean the blueberry muffin that's still on the plate."

"That's mine too," Diego said. "We each get two items from the plate. That's my second."

Diego then picked up one of the remaining muffins. Without placing it on a napkin, he pushed it in Matthew's direction. It was not just a bran muffin; it was a bran muffin with raisins, so Matthew had two reasons to hate it. He turned to Sal with a knowing look.

Over time, Matthew had learned not to let people get to him. It was a lesson that took several years to sink in. Ten or so years earlier, he didn't let any slight, whether real or perceived, pass without response. It usually ended with words, but occasionally ended in a fistfight. The last time it happened, he sent a guy named Colton to Harborview Medical Center unconscious. It happened after Colton, a total stranger, accused Matthew of cutting in line for tickets to a Soundgarden show.

Luckily, Colton woke up, but it could have gone the other way and resulted in criminal charges and a civil suit. All at a time when Anne was about to give birth to their first child. After that wakeup call, Matthew got used to ignoring the occasional slight, whether it was intended or not. It kept the blood pressure down and made life in general a whole lot easier, particularly when he was bartending. It took him a while, but he eventually got to the point where people couldn't push his buttons.

The one exception now was Diego, who had succeeded in getting under Matthew's skin when they first met two years before. It led to an ongoing grudge match, where each would take any opportunity to slight the other. It was always about minor stuff, but it held the potential to escalate into acts of greater consequence, Matthew knew.

While he picked at his bran muffin, Wiley began reviewing a list of expenses that Matthew and Diego had charged to Rieger Roofing in the previous two weeks—shingles, felt paper, nails, caulking, flashing, propane for the heaters used on torch down roofs, gas for the work trucks—anything and everything that showed up on the debit side of the ledger.

The review helped Wiley assign expenses to each roofing job and thereby determine how profitable each was. The tedious task was also Wiley's way of making his two foremen more "expense conscious." He was questioning Diego's purchase of a new nail gun when Willard Rieger showed up and took a seat at the table.

Willard was shorter than his older brother and had a wiry build. His thick, drooping moustache and stoic attitude made Matthew think that Willard, like so many Seattle motorcycle cops, had seen way too many cowboy movies growing up.

"Sorry I'm late," Willard said.

"I saved you a poppy seed muffin and a cinnamon scone," Diego said.

"Thanks, Diego."

"Hey, Willard," Diego began. "I'm still having trouble with the heater in my truck. It was blowing only cold air all the way over here this morning. I was freezing."

Matthew had heard the complaint before about the heater in Diego's truck. It seemed to come up every few meetings. Whereas Matthew drove his own truck to work and got reimbursed for mileage, Diego drove a company truck, which meant two things. First, it was a piece of shit. Second, the Riegers managed all the maintenance, so any repairs were done as cheaply as possible or not at all.

"Didn't you bring it back to Jay's shop?" Willard asked, referring to a garage on Queen Anne.

"It was OK for three weeks. Now it's blowing cold air again."

"Alright, we'll talk about it later, Diego. I have to take care of this business first. OK," he said, addressing Matthew and Diego. "I just finished unloading a truck at the Reynolds Estate. Which one of you guys is doing the job? Did my brother mention the bonus?"

"We were just getting to that," Wiley said. Then he explained in detail what the job would entail, including the square footage of the roof and the number and size of the dormers, and the fact that the current shingles didn't have to be removed but could be shingled over. That information was important for the foremen in calculating how many man-hours would be needed to complete the work.

"I'll pay a $350 cash bonus if the job is done at the end of day today and clean," Wiley said. He looked at Diego. "Can you pull your A Crew off that job on Delridge and get them all up here in the next hour?"

Diego leaned back in his chair and picked a piece of blueberry from between two teeth. "Well, it might take a little longer. And you know my assistant is out hurt. So that's just me and the four others. Would the owner of this Reynolds place be OK if we finish by noon tomorrow?"

"Absolutely not, Diego," Wiley said. "This guy is having a dinner party tonight. It's a fundraiser, and he wants his place looking perfect. All lit up and clean, like something out of *Better Homes & Gardens*. He said the roof looks dreadful, although it doesn't look that bad to me. Anyway, it has to be done by 5:30 today."

Rieger Roofing had to be charging a premium price on this job, Matthew knew. He was watching Diego carefully to see if he was going to commit to the deadline, but it was looking like he wasn't. That worried Matthew. His worst fear was that Wiley would ask Matthew and his A

Crew to work side by side with Diego's crew on the Reynolds Estate. That would be bad. They had tried it a year before and it was a disaster.

Wiley had called it "poor team dynamics" and warned both Diego and Matthew that they better learn how to work together if the situation called for it, or work someplace else. All the same, Wiley hadn't asked them to bring their teams onto the same job since. With such a tight deadline, however, he just might.

For that reason, and because he saw this as a chance to show up Diego, and because there was bonus money involved, Matthew said, "My crew can get it done by 5:30."

Both Wiley and Sal turned to Matthew with a look of surprise. Wiley said, "You've got a torch down in Rainier Valley due today, plus that big house in the U District. The Hendersons, am I right?"

"My B Crew is doing the torch down. I trained them all on it last month. They've done two on their own with me inspecting. I talked to the Hendersons on Friday. They said they'd be fine if we wrap up their place by Wednesday or Thursday."

That wasn't technically accurate, Matthew knew. In fact, it was an outright lie. He hadn't spoken to the Hendersons at all about delaying the completion of their roof. But he felt confident he could make a deal.

"Alright then," Wiley said as he stood up. "We're done. Make it happen, Matt."

Before the brothers walked out together, Willard said to Matthew, "Meet me at my truck. I'm parked on Harrison. I've got something for you."

Matthew looked down the table at Diego. "I think I can guess what Willard has for me in his truck: $350 cash. That'll buy a lot of blueberry muffins, don't you think?"

Diego pretended not to hear Matthew. He folded up his paper, tucked it under his arm and walked out.

When he was out of sight, Sal and Matthew had a good laugh. Sal said, "You didn't really talk to the Hendersons on Friday, did you?"

"Of course not."

"What's your plan?"

"I remember the owner complaining about birds getting into both chimneys on the house. I've got two chimney caps sitting in my garage left over from a job last year. They're not exactly new, but they're in very good condition. We'll install them free to compensate for the delay. Hopefully that works."

"It better," Sal said. "And by the way, our A Crew is short today. The Mole has the day off because he was out celebrating his birthday last night."

"Oh shit, that's right," Matthew said. He began tugging lightly on his soul patch. He needed to do some quick thinking. "OK, here's what we'll do. You call the guys up at the Hendersons. Tell the Professor and the Major to pack up and come to the Reynolds Estate."

"Have Major start on the dormers. I don't trust Professor to make them look good. And tell Buck to stay at the Hendersons and keep working, so they hear the sounds of progress on their roof. I'll pick him up when I go there and explain my deal to the Hendersons in person. After you get Major and Buck set up at the estate, head to Rainier Valley and make sure the B Crew isn't fucking up the torch down. Before I pick up Buck, I'll stop by the parking garage and wake Mole."

"He's not gonna like it, Matt. He probably got to bed about two hours ago. The Mole doesn't party much, but when he does, he goes all out."

"I'll make it worth his while."

Matthew found Willard sitting in his truck around the corner. When Willard motioned him inside, Matthew noticed a brown paper bag on the seat between them, which immediately put Matthew on guard.

"I hope that's not what I think it is, Willard," Matthew said.

"It's part of the bonus for the Reynolds Estate. Just swing by the lumberyard before noon today."

"I told your brother I wouldn't be making any more trips to Granite Lumber for him. And I really meant it. Telling me now that it's part of the Reynolds bonus is bullshit."

"Well, it's not something I wanted to bring up inside the restaurant. But it is part of the deal."

Matthew had not once opened any of the bags he delivered to Granite Lumber. Nor had he sniffed them to guess their contents. He knew they had to be either cocaine or heroin. If it had been the '80s, it probably would have been coke, but heroin was everywhere now, especially Seattle. Matthew couldn't recall a week that passed when he didn't hear about someone dying from an overdose. Mexican black tar heroin was cheap and could be found easily in lots of places around town.

According to Willard, the bags Matthew dropped at Granite Lumber were for a contractor who steered work in the direction of Rieger Roofing. If the drops were made, everybody worked. If the drops stopped, there might be layoffs. Matthew had made four previous drops for the Riegers. He was told that everybody did it—Wiley, Willard and Diego. It was a burden of being in management, a burden that had to be shared equally. Matthew suspected two things. It was almost certainly not being shared equally because the Rieger brothers would never expose themselves to that kind of risk. Second, it was a maneuver that could only be carried out for so long before somebody got caught.

Even if the Riegers didn't draw attention from the Seattle cops, who knew what kind of federal or state law enforcement might be keeping a close watch on every move made by the mysterious contractor? Any kind of trap set for the guy would scoop up everybody involved, including Matthew if he was unlucky enough to be doing the drop that day. He had seen it happen plenty of times before, from the projects in South Boston to "The Ave" in Seattle's University District.

Matthew weighed his choices quickly. He could walk away from the whole bonus, which he didn't want to do. There was the cash, and there was the chance to show everybody that his crew could deliver. Finally, there was not wanting to have Diego find out that the bonus had been botched.

So instead of walking away, Matthew decided to double down. "The bonus is going up to $500, Willard."

"I can make it $400, but $500 is too high."

Matthew asked Willard to hand him the bag. It looked larger than other drops Matthew had made. When he got it in his hands, Matthew felt the weight. He raised and lowered it a few times to get a better sense. "This is at least twice as much as any drop I've done for you and your brother. It's 500 or it's nothing." He extended the bag to Willard, who clearly did not want to take it back.

"Alright."

"500?"

"Sure, that's good." Willard said it with so little conviction that Matthew thought, If there's a cheaper son of a bitch in this world than me, his last name is Rieger.

"I want to hear you say it, Willard. $500 cash bonus paid at the end of today."

"Fine. The bonus is $500 cash paid end-of-day today. If you finish the job right."

Before stepping out of the truck, Matthew said, "You tell your brother that I won't be doing any more drops. I have a family. If your brother tries this again, the price will be more than he can afford. Please tell him that exactly."

Willard was technically his boss, and Matthew had just put him in his place, so he wasn't surprised when Willard tried to reassert a little authority by calling out, "Just make sure you get that roof finished and everything cleaned up by 5:30, or your bonus will be nothing."

*   *   *   *   *

Beneath the Emerald City shopping complex in downtown Seattle was a parking garage that Matthew referred to as the Seven Levels of Hell. It was a labyrinth of dark, narrow passageways that smelled of car exhaust and an acrid odor akin to burning rubber. Matthew hated it more because he struggled around the tight turns in his crew cab, long-bed Ford F-350 pickup truck.

Before arriving at the garage, he had dropped off his ladders at the Reynolds Estate. If he was carrying them, he couldn't enter the garage at all. Without them, he had no more than two inches of clearance between his roof racks and the countless cross pipes suspended from the ceiling. As a betting man, he gave even odds of one day smashing into a pipe and unleashing a jet of high-pressure steam or some foul chemical.

Round and round he went on the spiral ramp, all the way down to level seven, the lowest level of parking hell. In the far corner, surrounded by empty spaces sat an old Chinook camper, essentially a small pickup truck with a cabin mounted on the back. The white fiberglass was now a splotchy gray, and its faded horizontal stripes in pumpkin orange and avocado green showed classic '80s flair.

For the last year and a half, the camper had been the home of Travis Platt, nicknamed the Mole for where he chose to live currently and for his aversion to bright light. He was the only person Matthew knew in Seattle who enjoyed the region's gloomy, wet winters and disliked its bright, sunny summers. Matthew didn't care how much Mole complained though. He was a skilled roofer, who could be relied on to show up on time and do a decent day's work.

In an attempt to save up money, Mole had made a deal with OK Parking, the company that managed the underground facility. In exchange for sweeping the garage three times a week with their vacuum truck, he was allowed 24-hour parking privileges, as long as he kept his camper in the wasteland of level seven.

Mole was able to save lots of money because he didn't pay rent anywhere. He slept in his camper, a detail that OK Parking managers knew about but never officially acknowledged because it was against company policy. Mole's only fixed living expenses were a small box at the post office and an $18 monthly fee to shower at a bare-bones gym nearby.

The frugality was all in an effort to save up $20,000 as quickly as possible. When he reached that milestone, Mole explained that he would quit his job and travel at a leisurely pace around the country, stretching his dollars and avoiding the yoke of labor for as long as possible. Nobody knew how close the Mole was to reaching his $20,000 goal, but the rest of the A Crew loved to speculate.

Matthew knocked on the camper's back door and listened. He heard nothing, so he knocked a little harder. From inside came a rustling and a grunt. Matthew knocked again.

"What? Who is it?" Mole moaned like someone who still had one foot firmly planted in the land of sleep.

"It's the sound of opportunity knocking, Travis. I have a deal for you that involves a bonus."

The door opened with a squeak. Travis stood hunched over in the middle of the camper. He had curly brown hair, a thick brown beard and a fluffy brown sleeping bag wrapped around him. Even though level seven was poorly lit, the slight increase in light within the camper set off a flurry of blinking by Mole. He waved his pale, pink hands around in front of him, flapping them open and closed as if he were searching in the dark for something. Finally, he found his round, blue-tinted glasses on a nearby shelf. He put them on and let out a sigh. "Matt, what the fuck? I have today off."

"I know, Travis. And I know how shitty it is to have somebody wake you up on your day off. But you know that I wouldn't be here if I didn't have a really important reason. Right?"

"Is that how you talk to your kids when you make them do something they don't want to do?"

"Pretty much word for word."

"What is this opportunity you speak of?"

Matthew walked over to his truck and returned with a quad shot latte and a fresh cinnamon roll he picked up on his way to the parking garage. The combo was Mole's idea of a perfect breakfast, Matthew knew. He handed them to Mole, who held the latte beneath his nose and inhaled deeply.

Matthew explained the rush job at the Reynolds Estate—how it had to be finished by the end of the day, and how he needed Mole's help in getting it done on time. "There's a bonus involved. For ruining your morning, you'll get $90 on top of a full day's wage. The other three guys will get $60. How does that sound?"

Mole perked up at the mention of a bonus. Besides knowing his favorite breakfast, Matthew knew that Mole liked the idea of tax-free income even more.

"Are we talking cash money?"

*   *   *   *   *

Their first stop was in the University District, where Matthew told the Hendersons that he'd need to pull his crew off their roof for one day. When he proposed offering them two free chimney caps as a way to compensate them for the inconvenience, they happily agreed to the deal.

Buck climbed into the back seat of the truck, where Mole had been trying to maybe catch a few more minutes of sleep. Since he and Buck, a loudmouthed hothead from Philly, spent half their time antagonizing each other, the dozing promptly ended, and the two began bickering about the quality of air in underground parking facilities and the inevitability of death by smoke inhalation versus actually burning alive in the case of an underground fire. Since it was a topic Buck had broached more than once before, the discussion soon grew tedious for Mole. After asking Matthew if it would be OK, Mole climbed into the front seat.

Buck continued to voice his comments loudly from the back. He was barely five foot six, so Matthew could only see the top of his head, but he could hear Buck's booming voice. It annoyed Mole, but not Matthew as much. He thought he understood Buck. They were both from the East Coast, where people were more likely to express their emotions rather than describe them. Buck was still going through a phase of cultural adjustment and didn't quite realize that he didn't need to play the role of a small dog with a big bark anymore. People were more laid-back in the Pacific Northwest. You just had to roll that way.

Plus, the last thing you wanted to do in Seattle was draw attention to yourself as being from some big East Coast city like New York, Philadelphia or Boston. When Matthew had arrived in Seattle back in December 1978, it was in the middle of Boston's desegregation crisis. Some of the people he met wanted to remind him of the racism in his hometown.

Matthew didn't need them to tell him anything. When he was coming of age in South Boston, he discovered racism in his neighborhood, on his street, and finally within himself. He learned that he couldn't change the place where he grew up or some of the people he grew up with. But he could learn to deal with the assumptions he made and the reactions he had. And that, he knew, would have to continue for the rest of his life.

Lately in Seattle, Matthew had also been hearing the term Masshole, referring to an asshole from Massachusetts. He had talked about it with Buck as a means of warning him, but Buck brushed it off, saying he wasn't from Massachusetts. It didn't matter, Matthew told him. The point was not to be that guy from the East Coast who thought that acting like an asshole was somehow supposed to impress people out West.

It was a lesson that had yet to sink in, and Matthew was only gonna have so much patience as he waited for Buck to come around. If he wasn't a real hard worker who showed up every day on time, and someone who could be trusted to finish a job on his own, Matthew would have dropped him from his crew a long time ago.

Just as Buck's commentary on the quality of air in underground parking garages was running out of steam, they arrived at Granite Lumber on Elliott Ave. Matthew told them he'd be back in a few minutes and pulled the paper bag from beneath his seat.

"I'm guessing I shouldn't ask you what that is," Mole said.

"You're a good guesser," Matthew answered.

Buck, who was still in the back seat, couldn't see what they were talking about, nor did he care. He was more interested in teasing Mole. "Tell me something, Mole. Do you have to wear those blue glasses everywhere you go?"

"Tell me something, Buck. Do you have to wear that dimwitted expression everywhere you go?"

"Alright, kids, now I want you both to behave while I'm gone," Matthew said.

Mole pulled a CD player and a pair of headphones from his jacket. "Excuse me while I quickly disappear into the sanctuary of Radiohead."

As he had done on his previous drops at the lumberyard, Matthew stopped by the main office, where the guys behind the counter knew him. He explained that he was going into the yard to take a look at some cedar siding. There was nothing unusual about it. Matthew visited Granite often enough to pick up lumber for Rieger Roofing or one of the many side jobs he did in the off-season.

Once in the yard, he made his way to the farthest shed, and meandered among stacks of cedar siding and tongue-in-groove boards. He spent about five minutes checking out the siding—he actually needed to pick up some soon for a project he was doing for a neighbor. There were two employees working in the yard, and when Matthew was sure they weren't watching, he walked to the far end of the shed and placed the paper bag into the dark recess behind the last stack of cedar.

On his way back to the truck, Matthew wiped the front and back of his hands on his shirt. It was more of a ritual, his way of promising himself he'd never do another drop for the Riegers again.

It was almost 10:30 when they arrived at the Reynolds Estate on Capitol Hill, a large home on 14th Ave, nicknamed "Millionaires Row" because of all the mansions built there at the turn of the century. It was an impressive Bavarian-style place with two porches and plenty of steep dormers. Matthew counted four in front. There were probably that many out back, he figured. What caused him concern right away were the two turrets on either end of the house.

Ladders and staging had all been set up on the front side, where Major was finishing his second dormer and Professor was starting on the main roof. The air was filled with the sound of their nail guns firing to separate beats, and the steady hum of a generator powering the compressor. Matthew spotted two small rose bushes bordering the main entrance. They were just waiting to be damaged by a tool or a few shingles sliding off the roof. He grabbed a couple of large trash barrels from the back of the truck and placed them upside down over the bushes.

"Where do we start?" Mole asked.

"Let's tackle the front first," Matthew said. "We've only got enough staging for one side of this beast. Besides, if we run into a problem today, I want to at least have the front looking finished."

Travis and Buck strapped on their tool belts and headed for the roof. Matthew followed them up the ladder so he could check in with Major. First, he climbed to the peak to catch a quick view, something he loved to do on most houses he worked on. It was amazing. To the east, he saw down the back side of Capitol Hill to Lake Washington and the Cascade Mountains beyond. To the west was an unobstructed view of downtown Seattle, Lake Union and the snow-capped peaks of the Olympic Mountains about 60 miles away.

"Nice view, huh?" Major called out.

Matthew carefully crossed to the dormer that Major had just finished. "Now this is fucking real estate. How's it going up here?"

"Not bad," Major said. "I'm ready for the next dormer. There's another four out back."

"I saw. Can you do the turrets too?"

"By 5:30? I wouldn't bet on it. I shingled turrets once before, and they're a bitch."

"That's alright. I'll have Sal do them. You focus on the dormers. You need anything up here?"

"Maybe a new nail gun that doesn't keep blowing air in my face. Otherwise, I'm fine right now. Hey, doesn't this place make you want to yodel?"

Matthew's mobile phone began playing a ringtone from the song "Insane in the Brain" by Cypress Hill. It was one of Sal's favorites.

"How's it going down there?" Matthew asked. Then he listened as Sal explained one problem after another with the torch down roof. The B Crew had rushed that morning. Instead of laying out the rolls of roofing material so they could relax, they had installed them right away. That created wrinkles.

There were also several of bubbles in the material from improper heating and sealing. Bottom line, Sal had to pull up two hours' worth of work and start over. If done again properly, it was a simple job that could still be finished by 4:00 or 4:30.

Assuming his B Crew could handle the torch down job without supervision was Matthew's first mistake of the day. Hopefully it would be his last. Having Sal stay with the B Crew to manage their work meant one less set of hands to finish the Reynolds Estate on time. But he couldn't risk having the B Crew miss their deadline. If they did, he could kiss the bonus goodbye.

"You better stay there, Sal, and make sure it's done right. I'll see you back up here when you wrap things up," Matthew said. He closed his phone and turned to Major. "Looks like the turrets are all mine."

*   *   *   *   *

At 2:00, they took a 15-minute break to eat a quick lunch. Professor and Major both had a smoke. The Professor, whose real name was Quinlan Price, earned the nickname because he had been an actual college professor before having a kind of nervous breakdown related to his work in quantum mechanics. Matthew suspected the breakdown had more to do with the Professor's wife running away with some guy who worked in a chicken slaughterhouse in Seattle's International District. In either case, the Professor, who had never smoked a cigarette before the age of 38, was now a heavy smoker and would often have a lit cigarette dangling from his mouth as he fired off his nail gun on a roof. Each shot secretly meant for the chicken slaughterer, Matthew sometimes mused.

When they finished the front roof, they moved on to the back. Shingling the turrets was painstaking work. Matthew had to set up staging and wear a harness that was anchored to the peak. They were six-sided turrets, so he had to shingle six separate surfaces and install six rows of capping where they joined.

At 4:00, the turrets were done, and Major was on the last dormer. Matthew kept the other guys fed with shingles and coils for their nail guns by climbing up and down the ladders over and over again. The particular kind of shingles they were using on the estate weighed 65 pounds per bundle, so it was a real workout.

The other guys hated lugging shingles to the roof and always chose to use the power lift. When it was working, the lift let you load a few bundles, or other supplies, onto a platform. When you turned a switch, a small gas engine pulled the platform up to the roof along tracks attached to a ladder. Then someone on the roof unloaded the platform. No lugging the bundles step by step up a ladder.

The problem with the power lift was that it broke down a lot. Matthew was never too quick to fix it. He actually enjoyed carrying the bundles manually. It was as good a workout as any gym could provide, and it was free. Over the last few years, it had helped him get into the best shape of his life. When he wanted to test himself, or show off, he'd carry two bundles, or even three slung over a shoulder.

A few minutes before 5:00, the nail guns went silent. While the others worked on removing the staging, Matthew walked around the house and picked up every stray piece of shingle that had fallen off the roof. The trash containers he had placed over the fragile rose bushes had done their job. More than one falling shingle had been deflected.

Sal showed up while Matthew was cleaning all the tools and storing them in the back of his truck. From the front yard, Sal scanned the new roof.

"Turned out nice," Sal said.

Matthew walked over to a stack of ladders that stood near the truck. "It wasn't all that bad really. No complications," he said.

Sal went to the other end of the stack, and one by one they carried the ladders over to the truck and placed them onto the roof racks. After tying them down, Matthew ran short chains through rungs on both ends, then secured them with padlocks. "Did everything get straightened out with the torch down?" Matthew asked.

Sal nodded. "The customer is satisfied. Gladisfaction all around," he said with a laugh. "Gladisfaction" was the stage name of a stripper who Buck had been obsessed with for a couple of months, and Sal loved using the name in different contexts.

How is the new guy doing?" Matthew asked, referring to someone the Riegers had recently added to the B Crew.

"He seems to be learning OK." Sal paused for a moment. "Except he keeps talking to me in Spanish. I had to tell him again today that not every Latino speaks Spanish. I know maybe a hundred or so words. I can't tell if he has a memory problem or if he's messing with me."

"He's messing with you. When I worked with him last week, he kept calling me 'McMahoney.'"

A white pickup truck with the company name spelled out in dark crimson letters on the front door approached the driveway.

"Looks like we got ourselves a Rieger on the scene," Sal said.

After Willard parked, he did a walk around the house to inspect the work.

"It looks good, Matt. Nice job," Willard said. He reached into his pocket and pulled out a wrinkled envelope.

"It went pretty smoothly," Matthew said. "We just cranked away on it. Sal helped out with the torch down. That one's finished too."

Willard extended the envelope to Matthew, who felt its thickness between his thumb and fingers.

"500?" Matthew asked.

Willard gave him a vaguely confused look that slowly changed to one of awareness.

"Oh right. Sorry. My brother gave me the envelope before you and I talked this morning." Willard pulled a wad of bills out of his back pocket and peeled off seven 20s and a 10. "Here's the rest. Thanks again, you guys."

When Willard left, Matthew said to Sal, "I forgot to mention this…after breakfast this morning, Willard asked me to do another drop."

Sal gave him a harsh look. "I thought you were done with that shit."

"I know, but he wrapped it up with the bonus. This was the last time though. For real."

When all the staging had been loaded into the back of Sal's truck, Matthew called the guys together. "Nicely done, A Crew. Here's a little bonus for your efforts. This is on top of your regular pay, of course." Matthew began counting out money and handing it to each of them. "Buck gets $60, Major gets $60, Professor gets $60, Travis gets $90 because we dragged his tired ass out of bed on a day off, Sal gets $115…thanks for fixing the fuckup on the torch down today…and I keep $115."

"Was it worth it, Mole?" Sal asked.

"It's tax-free cash. What more needs to be said?"

"There you have it," Matthew said. "I'm a river to my people."

*   *   *   *   *

On his drive home, Matthew dropped off the Mole at the entrance to the garage rather than inside since he had ladders strapped to the roof, then he picked up two pizzas. Anne had called in the order, and they were just coming out of the oven when Matthew arrived at Pagliacci's. When he got to the house, he headed straight for the dining room, where he slid the pizzas onto hot plates Anne had set up, then reached on top of the hutch for a Mickey Mouse ceramic jar the kids had gotten at Disneyland.

He lifted Mickey's head and dropped a small roll of cash inside.

"What's that?" Anne asked.

"A little bonus I made today," Matthew said proudly. "$115 cash."

When Matthew went to the bathroom to wash up, Anne called the kids to the table and retrieved the large salad she had made—spinach and mixed greens with tomatoes, red onions, mushrooms, sliced peppers and steamed broccoli, all drizzled with a spicy vinaigrette. That was for her, Matthew and Nora. In front of Dylan's chair, she placed a small bowl of iceberg lettuce smeared with ketchup and topped with crushed potato chips.

Once Anne had registered what Matthew said, she replied, "Sorry to rain on your bonus, but I got a call from Blue Star this morning. They said the washing machine at the cabin died yesterday. I gave them the OK to send somebody out with another one."

"So…another one. You mean a new one?"

"Of course. It's a really good one. And it's high capacity, which we'll need when we move up there. They installed it today."

"What's the damage? $300…$400…"

"$740. That's with installation. And the extended warranty. We have to have the extended warranty."

Matthew looked up at Mickey Mouse. What had seemed so impressive just a moment before was now overshadowed by yet another cabin expense. There had also been the drug drop at Granite Lumber. Later on, after the kids went to bed, he'd have to tell Anne about it. She wouldn't be happy, Matthew knew. He had told her a month ago that he would never do another one.

Still, it had been a decent day, he thought. Better than most.

Chapter 4
Roy's

Sunday, November 21, 1999

When Anne was growing up in Ipswich, Massachusetts, she and her mother had a Sunday morning ritual. Not a minute later than 8:35, they would leave the Boushay family farm, which bordered the salt marshes of Essex Bay. In their robin's-egg blue 1968 International Harvester Travelall, they would drive five miles along Plum Point Road, named after the Boushay plum orchards planted by Anne's grandparents in 1920, to the First Presbyterian Church on Route 133.

After the 9:00 service, they would have breakfast at the Choate Bridge Bistro, a longstanding eatery perched on the banks of the Ipswich River, near the center of town. Anne would order French toast ("I'm half French, you know," she would sometimes mention nonchalantly to their food server). It would come dusted with powdered sugar, pats of melting butter, real maple syrup and a side of fresh fruit—berries when they were in season. Their Sunday morning routine endured until Anne moved to Alaska at the age of 12.

Matthew had a similar but simpler Sunday morning ritual with his mother, Nora. After attending the 8:30 mass at Saint Augustine Church in South Boston, they would walk several blocks to a bakery on West Broadway and pick up a dozen donuts, two of which would not survive the trip back to their Old Colony housing project. His mother had grown up in Roscommon, Ireland, and was a devout Catholic. Not the preachy, holier-than-thou kind, but a salt-of-the earth variety. As his mother would sometimes remind Matthew, "You're not Kennedy Irish. You're Mahoney Irish."

As adults, neither Anne nor Matthew attended any kind of church service outside of weddings, funerals and baptisms. It became a point of discussion when the kids were very young. They briefly considered raising them as Catholic and also talked about sending them to Sunday school.

In the end, they decided on neither. On Sundays, the Mahoney family skipped the service and went straight to breakfast, and the place they chose for Sunday breakfast was Roy's. Its official name had been the Fauntleroy Junction, which combined the nearby Fauntleroy ferry terminal and an old trolley line junction that had been located in front of the restaurant. After it opened in 1976, locals shortened the name to Fauntleroy's. When the neon sign above the entrance began failing in the late '80s, and only the last syllable in "Fauntleroy" remained illuminated, people began referring to it as "Roy's."

The place included a restaurant and bar, and was not far from the Mahoney home. If the weather was clear on their leisurely walk down the hill, they could see ferryboats sailing back and forth from the Fauntleroy terminal to Vashon Island, and farther up the Sound between downtown Seattle and Bainbridge Island and Bremerton.

On that Sunday, however, a brisk wind was blowing off the Sound and light rain was falling, mostly sideways, so everyone wore rain jackets. They moved at a pace brisk enough to get them to breakfast a few minutes earlier than their usual 8:30 arrival.

Punctuating their walk down the hill was the sound of a soccer ball bouncing off the sidewalk, off the short stone walls along some home fronts and occasionally off parked cars that lined the road. The ball was scuffed and faded from being used on the street as much as on a soccer field.

"Please don't kick the ball into cars," Anne said.

At almost eight years old, Nora was into a number of sports, from snowboarding to climbing, but soccer was her obsession of the moment. Regardless of activity, she didn't like being coached by her parents. "I'm not hitting the cars, Mom," Nora said. "I'm hitting the tires. That's where I'm aiming."

Anne was about to explain to Nora that car tires were part of the car when ten-year-old Dylan, who had been totally focused on his Game Boy, walked straight into a sign. It was a "For Sale" sign that hadn't been there the previous Sunday. His forehead struck the thick wooden arm extending from the center of the signpost. As he fell flat on his back, his Game Boy went skittering along the gravel at the side of the road.

51

"Oh, hell! What the hell?" He cried out, not knowing exactly what had happened to him.

The rest of the family stopped and turned to stare, equally confused as to why he was suddenly sprawled on the ground. Matthew saw a big red spot on Dylan's forehead and a small trickle of blood forming at the center, then noticed the signpost. "D-Man, you walked right into a sign." Matthew pulled a paper napkin from his jacket pocket and handed it to his son.

With the napkin pressed to his forehead, Dylan stood up and stumbled forward to pick up his Game Boy. When he found it still functioned, he called out, "Oh, thank God it still works! Thank God!"

They arrived at Roy's just in time to beat a breakfast rush that seemed to be growing by the week. The neighborhood had become a popular place for people wanting to escape an increasingly crowded Seattle, and as people moved in, they discovered Roy's, arguably the best restaurant and watering hole in the southern half of West Seattle. The old brick building had large windows overlooking a front deck that was almost always full when the weather was warm. Next to the front door, a six-foot wooden pig in a waiter's uniform greeted customers.

"Leave your ball with Wilbur," Matthew said, using the name that the pig had been given by the restaurant staff. Nora tucked the wet soccer ball into the crook of Wilbur's arm, where someone had also looped a leash for a golden retriever that was resting at Wilbur's feet. An awning shielded Wilbur and the dog from the rain. Inside the restaurant, the sound of the breakfast crowd mixed with a clattering of pots and pans from the open kitchen.

Jennifer was working as hostess, and she led them to a free booth. Matthew was surprised to see her working a hostess shift because she normally bartended. "Are you still working with me later?" he asked.

"Yes, but I'm also picking up all the shifts I can this weekend—in the bar and dining room—because my boyfriend and I will be away for a race in Arizona next weekend." Jennifer turned to Anne and added, "It's a triathlon."

"Good for you," Anne said. "I'm lucky if I get to the gym twice a week these days."

Matthew had worked with Jennifer for almost two years. They usually worked together on Sunday nights, and occasionally a Friday or Saturday night. Jennifer also bartended solo two or three nights during the week. She was ten years younger than Matthew, but he considered her as good or better a bartender than he was. She had a great memory for drinks, for tracking multiple drink orders and for maintaining a sense of calm on nights when the bar and restaurant became a zoo. And she had no trouble shutting down someone who made the mistake of harassing her.

Bartending was one of the jobs she held down while going to school at the University of Washington to get her master's degree in physical therapy and rehabilitation medicine. Somehow, she also found time to do triathlons and volunteer at Seattle Children's Hospital. She had a way with kids, and it showed in how Nora and Dylan had both taken a liking to her the first time they met her.

Jennifer handed out menus, then said to Nora and Dylan, "I bet you guys don't even need these. You probably have the breakfast menu memorized by now."

Dylan patted the menu in front of him. "For the regular items, yes. Not for the rotating menu from around the world. But I'm still about 85 percent accurate in predicting what everyone in my family will get. Maybe more like 90."

When their food server, Gregory arrived, Dylan said that he would order for everyone. He began saying what he wanted first, but his mother reminded him that the polite thing was to start with other people and finish with himself.

Dylan collected the menus and handed them to Gregory. "OK, so my mom is getting the spinach and goat cheese omelette with a side of fruit. And cranberry juice and a coffee with cream. Right?"

Anne winked and gave him a thumbs-up.

"And my dad is getting the huevos rancheros with extra sauce, a side of fried potatoes and black coffee." Matthew nodded, and Dylan continued, "And my sister is getting…" In a moment of uncertainty, he stared at Nora.

On the word "sister," Matthew noticed Gregory looking back and forth quickly between Dylan and Nora. He had just started that week, so he hadn't seen them before, and he was making the same assumption other people would often make—that the two weren't siblings. Dylan had his father's fair Irish skin, and his hair was reddish brown, while Nora's long hair was jet black. She also had a rich olive complexion that came from the

French side of Anne's family. It wasn't evident in Anne, whose father had been Welsh, nor in her mother, but it was the same complexion that Anne's grandmother had.

Finally, Dylan said, "My sister will have the apple cinnamon French toast."

"No," Nora said.

"You never go two weeks in a row without getting it," Dylan said. "You didn't get it last week, so you have to get it this week."

"No, I don't," Nora replied. Turning to Gregory, she said, "Instead..." She raised a finger and repeated the word for emphasis. "Instead, I will get the apple cinnamon French toast. With fruit and cranberry juice."

"Which is exactly what I said," Dylan muttered. "OK, so I'm getting the grand slam with three pancakes, three slices of bacon, or more if you happen to give me one or two extra, which you guys do sometimes, and a large orange juice."

A while later, after everyone had finished most of their meals, Anne brought up some family business. Looking at the kids, she said, "So you both know that we've talked about moving to Alaska before..." She noticed the anxiety in Dylan immediately at the mention of Alaska, so she looked right at him. "That means eventually, Dylan. Sometime in the future. Not now."

Nora rolled her eyes. "You and Dad keep talking about this, but we never get to move. When are we really gonna finally move? I want to move to Alaska."

"No!" Dylan said.

"Squids," Matthew said, using the nickname he had given Nora when she was very young, "Let your mom finish."

"I'm starting to apply for jobs," Anne said, "but it'll be a long process, so we're not moving anytime soon."

"So not next month?" Dylan asked.

"No," Matthew said. "Not for a number of months..."

"So...like two or three?" Dylan asked.

Matthew continued, "Not for at least six months. Not until you and your sister finish this school year. Not until next summer."

Anne added, "So Dylan, we're not moving for a while. And when the time comes to move to Alaska, we'll all be ready. We'll all be prepared to make the change, right?"

She saw some of the anxiety drain from Dylan's face, but not all of it. He slowly returned to his breakfast and took a bite from his last piece of bacon.

Nora sighed and pressed her forehead into her palm. "I'll be dead before we ever move to Alaska."

*   *   *   *   *

When Matthew returned for his bartending shift at 4:00, Roy's seemed like a different restaurant, but he had learned over the years that visiting the place as a customer was different than experiencing it from behind the bar. As a customer, he could be more or less oblivious to what was going on, outside of his food and drinks being delivered as ordered and in a reasonable amount of time.

However, when he was on shift, he had to see and hear everything, and manage the flow of alcohol to all 12 barstools and every table—there were 9 in the bar area, 22 over the half-wall in the main dining room, and 14 more in the rear dining room.

At Donovan's, by comparison, the restaurant side had twice as many tables, and the bar area was as big as a ballroom. On weekend nights, there would be six bartenders on duty. The din of the crowd would still be ringing in Matthew's ears at 2:00 in the morning when he was counting his till in the break room upstairs.

Roy's was a saner place to work, even when it got busy. And it was the kind of place that Matthew wouldn't mind owning himself someday, or at least a smaller version of it.

The actual wooden bar at Roy's was as good as any he had seen in his life. It was 30 feet of hand-carved oak that came from an old brothel in Walla Walla. Along with the bar came an ornately carved backbar that held rows of bottled liquor and an eight-spigot beer tap with a rotating selection of local microbrews.

Every three months, Roy's featured the cuisine of a different global region alongside its regular menu of American comfort food like buttermilk fried chicken with mashed potatoes, baked macaroni and cheese, and smoked barbecue pork. With the food of Chile came Chilean artwork hanging on the exposed brick walls, along with colorful papier-mâché animals suspended from the ceiling rafters.

In October, Matthew had to make himself familiar with the Chilean menu. He also had to learn how to make a few drinks that were either native to Chile or inspired by the same. It was extra work, especially when he forgot how to make one of the new drinks, but it made things interesting, and he liked the special food items better than the standard American fare.

He had just finished mixing up a Bodacious Borgoña when a regular named Eric walked into the bar. He did carpentry work on restaurant renovations and liked to place sports bets with Matthew, who had nicknamed him Eric the Red when he learned about his reputation at other bars.

Eric lived almost ten miles away in Des Moines, and for a long time Matthew wondered why Eric didn't go to a bar closer to home. There were certainly plenty in Des Moines. It wasn't like he was in Roy's every night, maybe once or twice a week. But Eric also talked about hanging out regularly at another West Seattle bar, so for one reason or another, he was avoiding bars in his own neighborhood.

Then Matthew found out that Eric had been banned from every one of them, not all at once but one at a time over the course of about two years. Word was that when Eric was between renovation contracts, he'd camp out in a bar all day and evening. Near the end of the night, if he was in a particularly bad mood, he'd pick a fight. In the last place he got banned, The Salty Scupper, Eric challenged the whole bar to a rumble. Nobody took him up on the offer, so Eric broke furniture and smashed a pinball machine before running out the back door when he heard police sirens. That's when Matthew gave him the nickname.

At first Matthew had trouble believing the story because Eric seemed so mellow, at least when he was at Roy's. Then Matthew remembered a couple of guys at his old bar who could flip from happy drunk to belligerent in a split second. As long as nobody pushed Eric the Red's buttons, Matthew figured, he wouldn't create a problem at Roy's. There was only one regular customer capable of doing that. It was the Balloon Man.

When Matthew spotted the Balloon Man walking through the front door shortly after 5:30, he waved him over toward the opposite end of the bar, where Matthew mixed him a tequila sunrise.

The Balloon Man's real name was Daniel Hastings, but everyone called him by his nickname. He earned it two decades earlier when he began twisting thin balloons into the shapes of various animals at Pike Place Market in downtown Seattle. Before showing up at the Market around ten in the morning, the bald, heavyset Balloon Man would paint his face with clown makeup. It was something that caught the eye of every kid. They'd drag their parents over to watch his magic—turning balloons into flowers, dogs, birds, alligators, bumblebees, hearts, swords and the like. More often than not, the parents ended up buying one of the balloon creations, so the Balloon Man was able to make a modest living with his craft.

Everyone seemed to love The Balloon Man. Eric was the only exception that Matthew was aware of. He hated him.

It had been that way since an evening four months earlier when The Balloon Man showed up at Roy's wearing a balloon cowboy hat, along with a balloon pistol in a balloon holster. Being in an especially playful mood after downing his third tequila sunrise, The Balloon Man walked over to Eric and poked him in the side of his head with the balloon pistol. Eric jumped off his stool and swatted The Balloon Man out of the bar with a plastic-sheathed menu.

Eric thought that was the end of it, but The Balloon Man took a seat in the dining room and waited for his moment. Twenty minutes later, he snuck up behind Eric and popped a balloon right behind his ear. It sent Eric into a frenzy, and he chased The Balloon Man out of Roy's and several blocks down Fauntleroy Way. Eric had to give up the chase when he got winded. The Balloon Man may have been overweight, but his lungs were in excellent shape from blowing up balloons all day, so he escaped the wrath of Eric the Red that evening.

It was two weeks before The Balloon Man dared to show up again at the bar. When he did, Matthew took him aside and informed him that balloon pranks of any kind would no longer be tolerated at Roy's.

Violating the rule would result in The Balloon Man being banned from the establishment for six months. A second violation would earn him a lifetime ban.

The Balloon Man and Eric settled into a fragile truce, although Matthew kept a close watch on the two when they were at the bar together. On this evening, Eric wasn't even aware of The Balloon Man's presence, which is how Matthew preferred it.

"I can't believe you got me to bet against the Seahawks, Matt," Eric said as he laid a $20 bill on the bar. "I'm never gonna do that again. Not even for ten points."

Matthew picked up the $20 and tucked it in his back pocket. Vegas had favored the Seattle Seahawks by about a point, but Matthew believed they would win it big, so he took the Seahawks and gave Eric ten and a half points. The offer was too tempting for Eric to pass up.

Matthew had watched the last quarter of the game on the bar TV, and Seattle won it by fourteen. He had made the same bet with two other guys, so he had $40 more coming. After pouring a beer for Eric, Matthew asked, "Do you want to win it back tomorrow? The Broncos are playing the Raiders in the Monday night game."

"Sure, I want the Raiders though," Eric said.

Matthew nodded.

"Give me three and half points," Eric said.

Matthew shook his head. "Vegas has the Raiders by one and a half. I'll be generous and give you half a point. That's a good deal."

Eric tilted his head to the side and gave Matthew a withering look. "How about giving me two and half?"

The drink ticket machine on the backbar began printing out orders for dining room tables. Matthew shook his head. "Half a point, Eric. I'm here all night if you change your mind."

By 6:00, the restaurant was starting to get busy. The drink tickets were printing at a faster pace, and Jennifer, who had just started her shift, was tearing them apart, lining them up on the backbar and calling out the drinks to Matthew. "Two martinis, one extra dry, one house red, one Macallan 12 neat, water back..."

The TV at the far end of the bar had been playing the Cardinals and Eagles game, but the local station cut in for a quick look at traffic, weather and top national stories. Matthew had just finished mixing a margarita when something caught his attention on the TV. He heard a name mentioned by the newscaster, and it made him take in a quick breath. Then he heard Eric saying something, but Matthew ignored him. Instead, he walked to the other end of the bar to see if anybody needed a refill. As he did, he let his breath out slowly and told himself not to react, not to look like he was paying attention to the story. But he was very much paying attention to it and waiting for it to end. When it did, he returned to Eric's end of the bar.

"Hey, Matt," Eric called. "You missed it. There was a story on the news about a guy named Mahoney from South Boston. You're from South Boston, right? Are you related to the guy?"

Matthew gave Eric a confused look. "What are you talking about?"

"On TV a minute ago. I was trying to get your attention. A guy named Francis Mahoney from South Boston, who was head of the Irish mob there. He's on the FBI's Ten Most Wanted List. You must have heard of him."

Matthew smiled and nodded. "Oh, that guy. Of course I've heard of him. People are always asking me if we're related. We're not. Not that I know of." Matthew turned to pour a couple of Mirror Pond ales and continued, "The name 'Mahoney' is like Smith in Boston. There must be about a million Mahoneys in the Northeast. But you never know...maybe there's something my parents never told me." Eric let out a laugh as Matthew carried the beers to the end of the bar.

He was hoping that would be it, that Eric would drop the subject. But when he got back, Eric kept at it. "The guy went into hiding 12 years ago, they said, but the FBI has never come close to catching him. Nobody knows where he is, but every now and then somebody somewhere thinks they see him. Like the retired guy in Fort Lauderdale. He said he saw him at a health club down there. There's a two-million-dollar reward for being the one who spots him. I'd drop a dime if I saw Francis Mahoney. I could easily retire with that kind of money."

Eric went on about how he'd spend the reward money, and Matthew just kept wishing that he would shut the fuck up. On TV, the second half of the Cardinals and Eagles game started, and Eric finally turned his mind back to football.

*   *   *   *   *

By 9:45, the kitchen had served its last bowl of Chilean *porotos con riendas,* and the crowd at Roy's was down to a handful of regulars in the bar and a dozen tables finishing their meals in the dining room. The bar would stay open for another hour or so with Jennifer on duty, but Matthew's shift was over. He stood at the bar terminal, closing out his checks and running his sales report, then went to the back room to drop the report, along with cash and credit card receipts, in the office safe. He stashed his clip-on tie and black apron in his small locker in the break room. Before heading out, he grabbed a sparkling water behind the bar and wished Jennifer luck in her triathlon the next weekend.

It was a peaceful walk home. Matthew took the same steep hill where he finished his morning runs. Light rain was falling, and the air was chilly, but it was a refreshing contrast from the bar, as was the relative quiet of the night. He could hear raindrops tapping on the hood of his jacket, the distant sound of car tires splashing along pavement two streets away, and from one of the houses nearby a TV was blaring the opening credits of the TV show *ER*.

The slow walk home alone was his way of decompressing from work. In the old days at Donovan's, he'd do it by going out for drinks with the other bartenders. That didn't work so well anymore for a number of reasons, including having kids and needing to wake up for a workout at 5:15 the next morning. He'd cut back a lot on his drinking since he became a father. He'd also finally said goodbye to the occasional cigarette.

Halfway up the hill, Matthew's quiet walk was disturbed by the crowing of a rooster a block away. The sound startled him, even though the same thing happened about once every other month, seldom enough that he'd forget about the rooster's existence. Eventually his mind went back to his conversation with Eric.

The truth was that Matthew did know Francis Mahoney. He knew him very well. Francis was his older brother. One of his older brothers. There was also Jimmy, who still lived in South Boston and was a career politician in his 13th year as president of the Massachusetts State Senate. But Jimmy wasn't the one that made Matthew's life complicated. He wasn't the one who gave Matthew the occasional nightmare and made him avoid hanging out with anybody from any part of New England, let alone Massachusetts, because those people couldn't help but know about Francis Mahoney.

It was like learning about Plymouth Rock or Paul Revere when you were in grade school. Everybody knew about Francis Mahoney before they were old enough to have their first legal drink. And when any of those New Englanders met Matthew at some backyard barbecue in Seattle and found out two things—that he was from South Boston and that his name was Mahoney—none of them could resist trying to dig for a connection to Francis Mahoney.

As careful as Matthew was to avoid those situations, he couldn't escape them altogether. Sometimes it would happen twice in the same month; other times, he could go three months without being asked if he was related to Francis. The question usually came from out of the blue, which was the worst part of it all—being blindsided.

But Matthew had mastered a response. It came automatically and was delivered naturally. It followed the script he had used with Eric. Acknowledge it with a smile—of course he knew about Francis Mahoney, no they weren't related, introduce a made-up statistic about the number of Mahoneys, throw in a joke. Then let the subject fade and die. If it didn't, Matthew would physically separate himself from the discussion—walk to the end of the bar, go to the bathroom, take out the trash, remember an important phone call he needed to make.

Only three people in Matthew's Seattle life knew that Francis was his brother—Anne, Sal and Jennifer—and he trusted all of them completely. With acquaintances, Matthew didn't mind lying, but he did feel bad when he lied to someone he knew better. And he didn't like that Anne had to occasionally lie about it herself. Someday, he knew, he would have to tell the kids, and they too would have to lie. Or maybe not. The decision would be theirs once they were old enough to know. However Dylan and Nora chose to deal with it, their connection, their relation to Francis Mahoney would be a burden. Or, at the very least, a nuisance.

Anne had gotten home ten minutes before Matthew and had relieved the babysitter. Once a month, she got together with girlfriends from her engineering world for some kind of activity: bowling, playing cards, watching a movie, kayaking or biking when the weather was good. This evening they had gone to trivia night at the Blue Moon Saloon, a dive bar in Morgan Junction.

When Matthew stepped through the front door, he heard Anne in the kitchen opening and closing drawers. "How was trivia night?" he asked.

"Pretty good. We made it to the semifinals when we knew what element Hg represents on the periodic table. It's mercury, if you're wondering."

"I never would have gotten that," Matthew said.

"That's why I told you. So what real-life person was the movie *Raging Bull* about?" Anne asked, as she finished checking the last drawer, at which point she turned her attention to the cabinets.

"Jake LaMotta," Matthew said.

"That's the question we lost on," Anne said, then turned to Matthew. "Where are the bulbs you said you were going to get for our weird lamp. I was just about to read, but the bulb is still burned out."

Their neighbor Jeremy had given them an unusual lamp as a housewarming gift years before. It was a handmade porcelain design in the shape of a tree trunk with two holes. An owl was peering out of one, and an alien head was sticking out of the other. Matthew and Anne weren't crazy about the lamp, but the kids loved it, and every time their friends stopped by the house, they commented on how fantastic it looked on the old oak end table. Beyond its appearance, the lamp had the disadvantage of requiring bulbs that were only available at a specialty lighting store in Fremont. They were also expensive and burned out frequently.

"Quit searching," Matthew said.

"Where are they?"

"I forgot to get them yesterday when I had to deal with the truck fuses. I'll pick them up when I'm in Seattle tomorrow."

"I guess I can read in the dining room," Anne said.

"Or…" Matthew said. He walked over to the kitchen light switch and turned it off.

"What are you doing?" Anne asked as Matthew walked into the dining room, pulled two large candles out of the hutch and pressed them into candleholders. When they were lit, he turned off the remaining lights and handed one of the candles to Anne. The incandescent brightness was replaced by two warm, glowing flames that moved slowly into the living room and stopped at the couch.

"I think this will work," Anne said. "If not, I'll get a headlamp from the closet. I just like our couch. I need 20 minutes on this couch at the end of the day."

Anne lowered her candle onto the end table and tried placing it in different positions to see where the light would be best cast for reading her latest issue of *Alpine Trekker*.

Matthew put his candle down on the coffee table, then bent over to take off his shoes.

"So how was your shift?" Anne asked.

"Not bad. At least until someone started asking me about Francis. There was a story on TV."

A creaking sound came from the stairway. When they looked over, they saw Nora staring at them with big eyes through the banister rails. "Ooh, candles. Spoooooooky," she said.

This was becoming almost a nightly ploy where Nora would be put to bed at 9:30, only to appear sometime later when she would attempt to negotiate her way out of bedtime.

"You need to go back upstairs right now," Anne said.

"Read me a story."

"I read you two stories, Nora," Anne said.

"I want Dad to make up a story."

When Matthew stood, Nora scampered up the stairs and called back, "Bring your candle!"

Matthew climbed the stairs to the kids' bedrooms on the second floor. It was actually a converted attic, so that all three rooms—Nora's on the left, Dylan's on the right and a storage room at the back—had sloped ceilings that required adults to stoop over. Both Matthew and Anne had banged their heads regularly on the ceilings before learning to drop into a constant hunch whenever standing in either of the kids' rooms.

Light shone from beneath Dylan's door, so Matthew cracked it open and looked inside. Dylan was lying on his bed reading a book about three boys conquering a far-off galaxy.

"Ten minutes, buddy. Then lights out."

"I know. I just want to finish this chapter," Dylan said.

In Nora's room, Matthew found a safe place for the candle, then took a seat at the end of her bed. He tugged at his soul patch as he considered what should be the next episode in the adventures of Nora, child explorer. After settling on what he thought could be an interesting opening, he began to tell his story.

Nora interrupted him. "Wait, Dad. I want to tell the story tonight. I already have one made up."

Matthew had been making up stories ever since his daughter was old enough to listen attentively, but she had never once said that she wanted to make up a story herself. He wasn't sure if he was more sad or more excited about this development. "OK, I'm ready when you are."

Nora began her story and wasn't three sentences in before Matthew asked, "What's this girl's name?"

"Oh, right. It's Runa. That's her name."

"So, it's kind of like the name Nora."

"Yeah. But it's not. It's Runa."

Matthew nodded and leaned back against the wall. "OK."

"There was a girl named Runa, and she loved to go snowboarding and she was a really good snowboarder. Whenever she would race her friends, she would usually win. And whenever they had a contest to see who could go highest off a jump, Runa would go higher than anybody else. Her friends still liked her because she helped them learn more snowboarding tricks.

"One day Runa decided to go to the biggest mountain in the world, which is up in Canada…"

Matthew interrupted. "Are you sure the highest mountain in the world is in Canada? It might be somewhere else."

"It's the biggest mountain where you can snowboard, and it's way up in Canada. So Runa walks into the lodge and asks them where the big jump is. She goes over to the big jump and looks down and says, 'This is a pretty big jump, but I can do an even bigger one,' so she goes back to the lodge and asks them if there's a bigger jump on the mountain.

"They tell her there's one more, but nobody is able to go off that jump because it's so high and everyone is afraid to try it. They tell her it's up at the very top of the mountain, so she rides a chairlift there."

The story continued with a successful execution of a jump by Runa, followed by a celebration back home with her friends. Matthew enjoyed it, and when Nora got to the end, he found himself in a far sleepier state than she was. He groaned as he pulled himself onto his feet. With a kiss on Nora's forehead, he wished her sweet dreams and picked up the candle.

"Good night, Squids," he said.

"There's gonna be another story about Runa," Nora said. "I just have to think about what's gonna happen."

As Matthew was closing Nora's door, she added, "There might be a scary animal in it too. Like a bear or a tiger or a dragon."

Chapter 5
Sound and Vision

Sunday, November 28, 1999

When the last Sunday of the month rolled around, Matthew and Anne enacted a ritual by clearing the dining room table, then spreading out all of their bills, credit card statements, bank statements and the notebook that tallied progress on their debt. They had been carrying large balances on four different credit cards, but they had managed to pay off one balance in October, which was good because its 0 percent interest rate was scheduled to go up to 16.9 percent in November. They had grown skilled over the years at using balance transfer checks to shift debt from one card to another whenever a low promotional interest rate was due to return to a much higher rate. It was critical to have one credit card paid off and available to receive a transfer.

They called it their musical chairs of finance. They had gotten good at the game, but they didn't like having to play it. In seven years, they'd had a few close calls but always landed in a safe place at the end of every billing cycle. Over that time, they'd managed to cut their credit card debt almost in half. Still, there were occasional setbacks when unexpected expenses caused the balance on one or more cards to shoot back up. The latest was Dylan's need for braces, something that their health insurance only half covered. When they complained about it to Anne's mother, her response was, "I could see that one coming years ago. He's got the Irish teeth."

The comment didn't surprise Matthew. Anything about the kids that could be considered a weakness, shortcoming or flaw, Joan Boushay attributed to their Mahoney genes. Whenever they showed any kind of talent or developed an impressive skill, it obviously came from the Boushay side.

With all the paperwork laid out on the table, Matthew settled in a seat across from Anne. She had brewed a pot of Mountain Moon herbal tea. According to Anne's friend, it was the best tea for soothing nerves and

66

putting a person in a calm, relaxed mood. She handed Matthew a large mug.

They started with utilities (the water bill was higher than it should be…was anybody lingering in the shower longer than necessary?), then moved on to rent (the landlord gave them a $50 discount if they maintained the landscaping…no, Matthew told her, he didn't need to mow the lawn again until spring) and their three credit cards, on which they paid a total of $700 a month. When all the checks were written and balances tallied, they moved to the remaining miscellaneous items.

Anne brought the teapot from the kitchen and refilled Matthew's mug.

"Whoa, that's enough," he said.

"Ingrid told me about this tea. It's pretty good, isn't it?"

"Sure, but I think three mugs is plenty," Matthew said.

Along with the teapot, Anne also brought a letter to the table. It was from Blue Star Property Management in Anchorage. "So there's still one more thing we need to talk about," she said, holding up the envelope.

"I saw that in the mailbox Friday. What is it?" Matthew extended his hand for the envelope, but lowered it when it was clear that Anne wasn't going to hand it over just yet.

"There's something at the cabin we're going to have to deal with before spring."

"Like what…more firewood? Is the garage door broken again?"

"It looks like we'll need to do some work on the roof."

"What kind of work?"

Anne stared at the envelope and spoke deliberately. "Well, the thing is…we've done a lot of small fixes over the last couple of years. Apparently, some of them…the leaks…"

"Anne, please, just tell me what it is."

She looked straight at Matthew. "We need a new roof."

Matthew was stunned into silence.

Anne continued, "Some of the old leaks have opened up again, and there are new leaks. And a lot of the nails that hold the sheeting down are popping up, which means…"

"I know what that means," Matthew interrupted.

"It definitely needs to be replaced. Blue Star works with the best roofing company in Anchorage, and they say it's actually better that they do it now while it's cold and below freezing. Once it warms up in spring, the leaks will open up more. That's what they're telling me, and they're really honest about these things."

"They better be honest with what we pay them. The cabin's got a metal roof. I've never installed a metal roof, but I know they aren't cheap. It's probably gonna cost us like $10,000."

"Um…$14,000," Anne said.

Matthew tilted his head back and looked up at the ceiling. "Holy shit," he muttered.

"Somebody better not be swearing!" Nora called from the living room couch.

Matthew continued, "That's $14,000 on a place that brings in $1,200 a month after Blue Star takes their cut. Plus, we've got property taxes coming up in a few months. That's over two grand."

"We get $1,250 a month after Blue Star takes their commission," Anne said. "And, by the way, if we were living there as residents right now, the annual Permanent Fund Dividend that I, you and the kids would get could cover property taxes, so don't forget to include that if you're going to bring up property taxes."

"Right, whatever. So how do we want to do this?" Matthew asked.

"We've only got the one credit card free," Anne said as she sifted through a stack of convenience checks from different banks. When she found the ones she was looking for, she read the details. "It's zero percent interest until…December next year. The transfer fee is two percent, which isn't bad. Our limit is $12,000."

"We need to come up with $2,000. Which is most of our savings," Matthew said.

"I'll stop by the Kirkland branch of our credit union at lunch tomorrow and take care of everything."

Matthew watched as she wrote the check to their credit union account, then tore it from the page of transfer checks. He considered saying something about what would happen if they hit another big financial pothole anytime soon. In short, they'd be fucked. Then he thought that saying anything wouldn't really do any good. It would just state the obvious, ominous truth. But he decided to say it anyway. He began slowly, "You know, if anything else…"

"I know, Matt. OK? I know."

*   *   *   *   *

Wednesday, December 1, 1999

Matthew had one last task before his Wednesday workday was done. His B Crew had finished installing flashing around a chimney, and he needed to make sure they didn't screw it up. It was on a 5,500-square-foot chalet-style home that sat on two acres of wooded property just below Marine View Drive in West Seattle. The place overlooked the water and was worth millions, and if the flashing wasn't installed properly, it could cause expensive water damage in the next rain.

His A Crew was supposed to do the work, but a windstorm the night before sent trees falling everywhere, some onto roofs, and they were busy on two separate emergency repair jobs. If they had done the flashing, Matthew wouldn't need to check it.

On the drive to the house, Matthew was surfing the dial on his FM radio and stopped when he heard a song that brought him back to his teenage years. It was "Sound and Vision" by David Bowie. He had never figured out what the song was about, but he had loved it from the first time he heard it on a cheap transistor radio. How lucky he was to be a teenager when Bowie showed up on the music scene. His sound colored so much of Matthew's life in those early, crazy years.

As the song ended, Matthew was pulling into the long driveway, dark with the shade cast by tall Douglas firs on either side. The sun was dipping below the Olympic Mountains to the west, so there wasn't much daylight left. Matthew parked his truck in front of the three-car garage and grabbed a water bottle from the back seat. He'd use it if he needed to check whether the flashing would cause rain to pool anywhere.

The owners were out of town, but Matthew rang the front doorbell just in case. People didn't like hearing unexpected footsteps on their roof. Nobody answered so he got to work, pulling a ladder off his roof rack. He had brought the longest ladder the company owned. It was a 40-foot fiberglass model that weighed over a hundred pounds and was a real bitch for one person to set up. He preferred to set a ladder on grass or dirt, where

69

he could plant the safety feet into the ground for peace of mind, but the only place around the home that was close to level was the paved parking area, so he settled for that.

The house was three stories tall with lots of large windows facing Puget Sound. On his way up, Matthew passed a large one and got a glimpse inside. He figured the house couldn't be more than ten years old, but the exposed woodwork inside looked like it could have come out of a century-old mansion. It had an open floor plan, with lights casting a warm glow up to the vaulted ceiling.

Thirty-three feet above the ground Matthew reached the gutter, where he stepped onto the roof and climbed up to the massive brick chimney at the peak. Six feet high, it stood almost as tall as Matthew and contained six separate flues. He took a moment to admire the view from the top. A container ship from Asia was making its way south on Puget Sound to the port of Tacoma, casting ripples in the glassy water. The sun had just finished setting behind the Olympic Mountains, and the sky was streaked in pale orange and purple, with the mountains silhouetted in charcoal gray. Directly across the sound were The Brothers, two adjacent peaks frosted white with the first snow of the season.

With daylight fading, Matthew got down on all fours and began crawling slowly around the base of the chimney, checking where the top of the lead flashing was sealed between layers of brick with fresh grout. On the bottom, it overlapped the shingles to direct rain down the roof. All it took was one small error to channel water beneath the shingles. Crouched down, Matthew pressed on the flashing and ran a finger along the fresh grout. Then he checked where the various pieces of flashing overlapped in a cascading line that followed the slope of the roof.

When he completed his check and was satisfied that the work was done properly, he stood up again. As he did so, he reached a hand onto the top of the chimney to steady himself. Rather than brick, his hand felt the edge of a shallow metal pan that was just hidden from view. At the light pressure from his hand, the pan tipped toward him and spilled its contents.

It all happened in less than two seconds. Matthew's first instinct was to look up at the pan. As it tipped, he felt his fingers become wet. When he realized what that meant, he instinctively turned his face away. But not before some of the liquid splashed into his eyes, which immediately began to burn.

One of his feet slipped on the shingles. He began to lose his balance, so he dropped down on all fours and grabbed onto the peak of the roof to stabilize himself. From the burning sensation and the smell, Matthew knew it was a solvent of some kind, probably left behind by his crew or someone else doing work on the roof recently. The metal pan, which had slid down the shingles and off the roof, clanged onto the pavement a moment later. Then all was silent.

Matthew wiped a sleeve across his face to brush away the solvent. When he tried to open his eyes, the burning pain intensified so much that he immediately shut them again. He remembered the bottle of water he had taken from the truck and reached behind him. It was still in his back pocket. He'd seen this kind of accident before, and he knew he needed to wash his eyes right away.

He pulled the bottle out of his pocket, unscrewed the plastic cap, tilted his head back, opened his eyes and poured. Through the pain he felt the cool liquid flushing his eyes. As it ran down his face, some dripped into his mouth and he could taste the solvent.

He sat up and coughed. A quick shake of the water bottle told him he had a little left. He lay back and poured the last of it into his eyes. He wiped his face with a dry patch of his shirt, and gave himself a minute to catch his breath and calm down. When he tried opening his eyes again, the burning began immediately and just as intensely as before, as if the water hadn't helped at all.

But it did. He knew it must have. Now what, Matthew thought. He needed to get off the roof. If the owners were home, he'd try to get their attention. He thought of the neighbors, but the wooded property was big enough that there were no houses close by. And he had no idea where the nearest house was.

For a moment, he thought he might have his cellphone with him. He patted all his pockets. Nothing. The phone, he remembered, was down in the truck. So he knew he had to get from where he was to the ladder. Once there, the climb down was easy, even with eyes closed. So was walking to his truck and finding his phone.

First, he had to get a line on his ladder. It should be directly below him. If he made his way down feet first on his stomach, and he kept a straight line, he'd hit the ladder. But he didn't want to hit it so hard that he knocked it off the gutter.

Maybe he could see where the ladder was. When he opened his eyes, the pain intensified. His vision was blurry, but he was able to spot the top of the red fiberglass beams against the gutter. He'd need to move about eight feet along the peak.

With his eyes closed, the pain faded. He began crawling along the peak slowly, measuring the distance with his open hands, which he knew were eight inches long. At the count of 12, he turned and began backing down the roof feet first. The pitch wasn't so steep that he was likely to slide, but with his eyes closed, he found his sense of balance wasn't as certain. After what seemed about a minute, he thought he must be getting close to the gutter. He began tapping down with the toe of his boots to make sure he didn't go too far.

A few feet later, Matthew heard a metallic ping and felt his boot slip into the space of the gutter. He took a deep breath. OK, first task done. He lay down flat and extended his legs over the roof a little, then slowly swung a leg to his left to feel for the ladder. He found only air.

Then it had to be to his right. He swung his right leg out slowly but didn't hit anything. Maybe he hadn't moved down the roof in a straight line. Still, the ladder had to be there, either to his right or his left. He guessed right and slid himself in that direction before swinging his foot out again. It hit the ladder.

Now the last part. He lined himself up with the ladder and got back up on all fours. You've done this a million times, he told himself, and moved one leg over the top of the ladder while keeping his weight on his hands and one knee. He landed his foot on a rung and brought his other foot over the top. With both feet planted, he walked his hands down the roof until he could move them onto the top rung and stand himself up.

It was the slowest, scariest ladder descent he had ever attempted, but he felt better with each passing rung. It ended when he extended his foot and it finally touched solid pavement. He knew it would hurt to open his eyes again, but he did it to get a blurry view of his truck a short distance away. When he reached it, he opened the back door and found another water bottle to rinse his eyes again. In the front seat, he found his phone and called Anne, getting two wrong numbers from misdialing before reaching her. She had just picked up Nora and was almost home.

"You don't want an ambulance?"

"We're not gonna pay $500 for a cab ride to Highline," he said, referring to the Burien hospital where several of the staff in the ER knew him, either from bringing injured coworkers there or going there himself for treatment a few times. He'd had friends get there by ambulance, and they all got nailed with big bills despite having insurance. If you're not bleeding to death or completely mangled, they told him, skip the ambulance. And if that was the shape you were in, someone else would be making that decision for you anyway.

"Just don't run any lights on your way here," Matthew told Anne. He gave the address, then added, "See you in five minutes."

As he sat in the front seat of his truck with the door open, he could feel it getting dark. Cool air was rising up from the Sound.

Just as he felt his breathing become regular again, his phone rang. It was Sal.

"We're done over here. It took us a little longer because we ran out of sealer. How'd it go at the big house?"

"I'm still here. Somebody left a pan of thinner or acetone or something on the chimney and I knocked it into my eyes. Burned like a motherfucker. I just got off the roof. My eyes should be fine. I rinsed them out with water…"

"Oh, shit. I'll come over right now…"

"Don't rush. Anne's gonna be here in two minutes to take me to Highline, but bring someone with you who can take down the ladder and drive my truck to the house. I'll leave the keys on the front seat. Then give the owner a call. Their name is Dwyer. Keith or Kyle…"

"I've got their number," Sal said.

"OK. Tell them everything's all set. Their beautiful house has a beautiful chimney and flashing that won't leak. Also, when you're here…there's a metal pan that fell in the driveway somewhere. Grab that."

Even with his eyes closed, Matthew could see the approaching light of Anne's Subaru.

From the back seat, Nora was asking if they were still going to have takeout Thai food for dinner. That was followed by more questions. "What did you do to your eyes? Can you open them? Are you gonna go blind? Last year at school we had two pet salamanders that were blind. They're born that way. They find things by smelling them and they can smell with their tongues. No, wait, they can smell through their skin. Snakes smell with their tongues."

Dylan was also sitting in the back seat, but he was silent for the entire ten-minute ride. As they were getting close, Matthew turned to face him with his eyes closed. "Hey, Dylanator, I'm gonna be fine. You don't have to worry."

It seemed that Dylan wasn't going to respond, but then he said, "We have Star Night on Friday." Star Night was when he and his dad went to Lincoln Park to look at the night sky with a borrowed telescope, weather permitting.

The scene at the Highline Hospital emergency room was a familiar one to Matthew, except for the fact that he couldn't see anything. He could only hear what was going on, and held onto Anne's arm as she guided him through the waiting room to the front desk.

"Matt, is that you? What happened?" The voice of the attendant was familiar. Matthew recognized it as Melissa's.

"I spilled some kind of solvent in my eyes, Melissa. Paint thinner maybe. So are you working the evening shift now?"

"I'm covering for Chelsea while she's on vacation. Has your insurance changed at all, Matt?"

He was covered under Anne's insurance, so he turned in her direction. "It hasn't changed," Anne said.

"It's pretty slow tonight, so I can take you back right now," Melissa said. "Then I'll keep an eye on your kids."

Melissa took Dylan and Nora into the waiting room, where *The Simpsons* was playing on an overhead TV. With Melissa leading the way, Anne guided Matthew through a set of swinging doors and into an examination room. When the doctor showed up, she asked what happened, then applied anesthetic drops for the pain. The next set of drops dilated the pupils.

"That'll reduce the small activity in your eyes, which should help with the pain. I know you rinsed out your eyes, but I'm going to irrigate them again." That was followed by antibiotic drops. She finished by placing adhesive patches over both eyes. All in all, it was Matthew's shortest ER visit ever.

"Is there any damage to the corneas?" Anne asked. "What's the prognosis?"

"There's irritation, but I don't see any damage. It should resolve itself in a couple of days. Keep the eyes patched for 48 hours. If there's an increase in irritation or if you see any reddening or inflammation when you remove the patches, see an eye doctor right away. In fact, you should set up an appointment with an eye doctor regardless to make sure everything is OK a week or two from now."

The doctor gave Anne replacement patches and prescriptions for anesthetic and antibiotic drops, along with instructions for changing the patches twice a day.

*   *   *   *   *

On Thursday morning, Matthew woke automatically at 5:00, then rolled over, hoping he could fall back to sleep. He woke again at 6:15, so he shuffled out to the kitchen to make coffee. Usually he prepped the coffeemaker the night before but that hadn't happened. He began fishing around the cabinets and drawers for everything he needed. A paper filter, the bag of coffee from the cabinet, a soup spoon to measure it, using his fingers to make sure each scoop was rounded, grabbing the pot and filling it from the sink, once again using his finger to feel when it was full and to guide the process of pouring the water into the coffeemaker reservoir. Feeling the heat with his hands and hearing the fresh coffee splash into the pot told him that he had indeed hit the correct switch on the front of the machine.

While it continued to brew, Matthew took care of something else. He needed to pee. The night before he had simply gone in the shower. Now he stood in front of the toilet, seat up, and took aim. Rather than hearing his pee splash into water, he heard it hitting the floor. He quickly adjusted his aim, but adjusted too far and hit the floor on the other side of the toilet. By the time he found the bullseye, he was almost finished. The next couple of minutes were spent mopping the floor with toilet paper.

Things went a little better back in the kitchen. He poured a cup of coffee, and it tasted perfect. That gave him a small sense of accomplishment. Next came a bagel, which he successfully sliced, toasted and smeared with cream cheese, although it took him at least twice as long as usual to complete the process. With that done, he carried his bagel and coffee cautiously into the dining room and settled down to enjoy his breakfast. Between bites, he listened to the sounds of his family waking up.

Anne's alarm went off, which turned on the bedside radio. A minute later, drawers were opened and closed, and the closet door slid open. Eventually Anne walked into the kitchen.

"You made coffee. Well done. Can I bring you anything?"

"No thanks. I'll be here all day. Plenty of time to eat my way through the kitchen."

Anne poured herself a cup before preparing bowls of fresh fruit and cereal for herself and the kids. Matthew listened to a buzzing sound coming from the kids' rooms. It was Dylan's alarm, which drove Nora crazy. A pair of feet hit the floor upstairs. Dylan...no, they were moving too fast. It was Nora, who came tearing down the stairs.

"Good morning!" she called as she ran through the living room in her pajamas.

"Morning, Squids."

Because their only bathroom was on the first floor, the morning began with both kids going straight to the bathroom. They hated having to make their way downstairs in the middle of the night. It was easier to hold it until morning if they could.

Matthew was taking a bite out of the second half of his bagel when he heard Nora scream from the bathroom. "Gross! Who peed all over the bathroom? Was it you, Dad? It's all over the place in here!"

Anne made her way to the bathroom. "Stop it, Nora!" she said.

"Look, Mom..."

"Stop it right now! It's not a big deal, OK? It's not everywhere. Don't exaggerate. Give me a minute to clean it up."

"But I have to pee now!"

"One minute, Nora. You can wait one minute. Now step out of the bathroom and count to 60."

"Sorry, girls," Matthew said.

Nora interrupted her count to respond. "It's really gross. Why do we have to clean up Dad's pee?"

"He can't see right now. Remember?"

"Well, then he needs to pee sitting down like we do."

Anne was able to finish the job in a little over a minute, much to Nora's relief.

"I thought I wiped it all up but apparently not," Matthew said. He heard Dylan descending the stairs and knocking on the bathroom door.

The door opened and Nora said, "Dad peed all over the floor."

"Nora, enough!" Anne said.

Dylan surprised Matthew by how quietly he made his way to the table and took a seat next to him. He was so engrossed in his latest favorite book, *Voyage to Star System Zero*, that he wasn't paying any attention to what was going on with the rest of his family.

"You owe me one, Mahoney," Anne said to Matthew.

Dylan suddenly looked up. "Mom, did you just say 'Obi-Wan Kenobi'?"

Anne put a bowl of Kashi and a bowl of fresh-cut fruit in front of Dylan. "No, I didn't say 'Obi-Wan Kenobi.'"

"You just said it a second time," Dylan said.

"I didn't say it a second time because I never said it a first time. Not a first time in the way that you mean 'first time,' which is actually when I said something completely different."

Mother and son stared at each other for a few seconds. Then Dylan lowered his eyes to his breakfast and said, "I don't understand you…in so many ways."

"That's pretty deep," Matthew said.

"Are we still gonna do Star Night?" Dylan asked.

The question caught Matthew by surprise. He had forgotten about it with everything that had happened to him, even though Dylan had mentioned it on the way to the hospital. "Sure. The doctor said my eyes should be OK. Let's hope the clouds stay away until Saturday."

"I checked the forecast," Dylan said. "It's supposed to be clear."

Anne circled back to the bathroom conversation. "Nora exaggerated, of course. But she's right, Matt. You're gonna have to sit down when you pee."

"That's right," Nora said as she joined them at the table.

After breakfast, Matthew settled on the couch in the living room, where Anne removed his patches, washed his eyes with a wet cloth, applied the various drops and put on new adhesive patches.

The drops cleared up the itchiness Matthew had been feeling since waking up. The brief moment of sight was a relief because the patches made him claustrophobic. Although he could see, his vision was blurry, just as the doctor had said. When he took the patches off for good on Friday, he'd find out if there was any lasting effect.

Anne brought him his phone so he could check in with Sal. He had called his boss the night before to let him know about the accident and that he'd be out of work for the next couple of days. Wiley Rieger wasn't happy. The company was behind on its list of houses to roof before winter weather caused work to slow way down until spring, and the forecast called for a week of steady rain moving in at the end of the weekend.

Unlike the roofers he managed, Matthew got a week of sick pay. His boss hated it when people actually used the benefit. For the next couple of days, Matthew wouldn't lose any money, but if he had any complications with his eyes that kept him out more than five days, he would.

Before Matthew could punch in Sal's number, his ringtone began playing. Everything had been taken care of at the Dwyers' house. While he was picking up Matthew's truck and ladder, Sal had called the owner, who told him that a painter had been up on the roof to finish some trim work around the dormers.

"Why would he leave a pan of solvent on top of the chimney?" Matthew asked.

"No idea, but at least we can be pretty sure it wasn't one of our guys."

"I'll call you later," Matthew said and hung up.

There was a bit of a frenzy getting the kids ready for school. Matthew usually dropped them off on his way to work, but Anne let her team know she'd be a little late because she'd be taking care of that task herself.

"Just relax and enjoy the downtime," Anne said. "Call if you need anything."

Matthew heard car keys jingle, felt Anne's kiss on his cheek, and listened as they all climbed into the Subaru and headed down the street. Sitting there all alone in a quiet, empty house, Matthew's first thought was whether Anne had locked the front door. He hadn't heard the deadbolt. It's not something he would really care about if his eyes weren't covered, but he felt a little vulnerable. He carefully rose from the couch and maneuvered his way around the coffee table by sliding his shins along its edges.

The way across the living room should be clear, he thought, and it was. At six steps, he stopped and reached out, expecting to be able to touch the door. Nothing. It took him one more step. The door wasn't locked, so he turned the deadbolt and tested it to make sure.

Seven steps back to the coffee table, where he felt around for his empty mug. His first order of business was a refill. He moved cautiously toward the kitchen, but when he was halfway through the dining room, his knee smacked into a heavy oak dining chair. The chair had not been put back at the table where it belonged.

He made contact just below his kneecap, and the pain was sharp enough that he dropped his ceramic mug, which smashed into many pieces on the hardwood floor.

The rest of the morning passed slowly. There was nothing on cable TV that interested him. Sound with no picture proved to be an empty experience, no matter what channel he tried. For a while, he listened to news on the radio, then found a show on earthquake danger in the Seattle area that seemed promising, but it ended five minutes after he tuned in. That was followed by a show on politics.

Matthew didn't care much for politics, no matter the party or position. It's not that he didn't vote. He did. But he avoided political debates and arguments, and didn't get himself worked up by listening to radio or cable TV shows that spewed nonstop hate chatter.

He had become immune to all that, or maybe just jaded, by his experience growing up. His father, nicknamed "Salty" for his caustic wit and combative personality, ran for mayor of Boston three times. As a kid, Matthew would become a reluctant volunteer to hold an election sign at a busy intersection to catch the attention of rush-hour commuters. They would sometimes beep at him in support, and sometimes spit at him. He would stand there for hours in sweltering heat or steady rain until his shift was over, and not a minute before then, or he risked punishment.

Later, his father went on to start a talk radio show that pushed every anger button that people in Boston had. And people in Boston had a wealth of buttons they were happy to have pushed by tuning in at 1:00 every weekday afternoon. Anger, Matthew learned, was a drug just as powerful and addictive as any other. And like other drugs, anger needed two things to thrive: pushers and addicts. Salty Mahoney was the consummate pusher, and his talk show ran for eight straight years, ending only when the man died.

Matthew's older brother Jimmy felt differently. He followed their father into the world of politics, but where Salty Mahoney failed, Jimmy Mahoney succeeded. He rose through the ranks to eventually become President of the State Senate, the second most powerful position in Massachusetts politics, and he still held that post after almost 13 years.

Matthew didn't care much for Jimmy. He didn't hate him. It's just that they had never been close, and Jimmy seemed to operate by different sensibilities. Unlike Matthew, Jimmy had been well-educated, graduating from Boston College Law School, and came off as very intellectual when he wanted to. Jimmy was also 12 years older than Matthew, so he was already in college when Matthew was in first grade. More important than the years that separated them was the lack of warmth and closeness of brothers, and when Matthew was growing up, the distance seemed to be intentional on Jimmy's part.

Francis, on the other hand, was ten years older than Matthew and very much a part of his early world. Matthew turned to Francis, not his father, to learn how to live on the streets of South Boston. Francis provided the education that no university offered: how to defend yourself and your friends, how to read people, how to sense their intentions and motives and, if need be, how to make people fear you. Fear, and how to wield it, was something that his brother Jimmy understood as well. The difference was that while Jimmy restricted himself to political uses that fell generally within the law, Francis' use of fear—his mastery of it—was unrestrained by ethics, morality or legal concerns.

Matthew wasn't really aware of his brother's deeds in Boston's underworld until Francis went into hiding in 1987. In the years that followed, Matthew would read the stories at newsstands in Pike Place Market, which carried newspapers from all over the world, including the *Boston Globe*. From them, Matthew learned things about the brother who raised him—that he had murdered or ordered the murder of several people.

Matthew read as many of the details as he could bear, which were few. There was the man whose arms and feet were bound with electrical cords, then lowered over the side of a rowboat in the middle of the night to drown in the depths of Squantum Channel. A woman who was going to testify against Francis was choked to death with a rope wrapped around her neck and fed into a garbage disposal. Another woman was strangled in front of her 15-year-old daughter because she threatened to end a relationship with Francis' friend. Then the daughter was strangled to keep her from talking.

As horrible as those murders were, one was even worse. The victim's name was Bradley Michael Driscoll. He and Matthew had grown up together in the Old Colony housing project and were close friends from the age of five. By the time Bradley turned 12 and made his start in the world of drug dealing, he became known as Buzzy because he was high so much of the time. Although he was good at dealing, Buzzy wasn't good at fighting. On the streets of South Boston, that was a problem. But Buzzy had his friend Matthew, and Matthew became his protector and occasionally his collection agent.

They were best friends, and Buzzy was the best man at Matthew's wedding in 1987. The reception took place at the Boushay seaside home in Ipswich, and before the sun had set on the big striped tents in the backyard, Francis and Salty got into a knock-down, drag-out fight that shocked guests from both sides of the aisle. The next morning, Salty Mahoney was found dead, and the police were looking for Francis, who was already on the run from the threat of federal indictments.

It was a week that turned the Mahoney world upside down. When it was over, Matthew knew two things for sure, and believed a third just as certainly. Buzzy's father was not named Driscoll. His father was Salty Mahoney, the same as Matthew. The best friends were half-brothers, a secret kept from Matthew until the week after his wedding. The news was even more disturbing because their father's rejection of Buzzy led him to commit the murder himself, then frame Francis for it.

Buzzy confessed to it all when he was caught and questioned by the police. He even provided them with evidence. Then Buzzy disappeared. He had been locked up at police headquarters on Berkeley Street in Boston, which is not a place people generally escaped from. Nobody could say what happened, but when Matthew heard the news of Buzzy's disappearance, he got a very strong feeling. He didn't have any proof, but he believed as deeply as he had believed anything in his life that Francis had managed Buzzy's disappearance and had killed him. The fact that Buzzy's body had never been found didn't change Matthew's mind in the least. Matthew had come to realize in the years since his wedding that he'd been a sucker in the loyalty game with Francis.

It was true that Buzzy had framed Francis for the murder. As Francis saw it, there would be no other option in dealing with such a betrayal. And yet in the whole complicated situation, who could say what was an act of betrayal, and what was an act of loyalty or an act of justice? They were questions that Matthew struggled to answer, but one thing seemed clear: in the grand family bargain, Buzzy was the one who had been royally screwed. And taking the life of your brother, or half-brother, was something that could never be justified. At least not to Matthew, and he'd had 12 years to consider and reconsider. He missed his best friend, and he was still angry about it all.

*   *   *   *   *

The last of the morning was an exercise in home layout dynamics: studying the location of every object on the first floor of the house and its position relative to every other object as exactly as possible. That is, every object that Matthew could potentially walk into. It was also a way to kill time and keep his mind occupied with something other than disturbing memories.

Step by step, he counted his way from the bookcase near the front door to the cutting board and knife block at the far end of the kitchen. He made note of edges and corners that posed the most danger, like the angle irons sticking out of the fireplace (two and a half steps from the end of the couch, a little over seven steps away from the far side of the room) and the heavy cooking pans hanging where Matthew might smack his head into them.

He confirmed all of his measurements by walking them out twice. A few adjustments were necessary, but he soon had all the dimensions of the first floor's walking space memorized. With that, he declared the project a success and set about making lunch. Two slices of bread, provolone (he felt all the plastic bags in the fridge's deli compartment until he detected a round shape), ham (a rectangular shape; it actually smelled like ham, whereas what he suspected was sliced turkey had almost no smell) and mustard (a small, plastic, squeezable container on the top rack inside the fridge door).

He also grabbed a bottle of pale ale from the lower shelf. If there was ever a time for drinking during the day, this was it. Matthew settled on the living room couch to eat his lunch and turned the TV on again, only to turn it off almost immediately.

This was the middle of the day when most people in the neighborhood were at work, with their kids in school or at daycare. It was fairly quiet, which made it easy to discern individual sounds: the subtle purring of the fridge, the barely audible rumble of a jet…was it taking off or landing? He knew from hearing the weather on the radio that the wind was blowing from the southwest, so the jet would be coming into Sea-Tac from the north and landing into the wind. Several blocks away, someone started up what sounded like a leaf blower.

Matthew's thoughts drifted to his eyes and what would happen if he had permanent damage, even to one of them. There might be no more running on dark mornings or riding a bike. He probably wouldn't be able to roof. Maybe he could still bartend, depending on how bad his vision was. If he couldn't earn a living, how could they ever pay off their credit cards, all of which were practically maxed out?

He decided not to dwell on the possibility of losing one or both eyes. There was nothing to be gained in such speculation. Remember what the doctor said, he told himself. Give it a couple of days and everything should be fine.

The forced air furnace clicked on, and a minute later the fan started up with a whoosh. The sudden warmth and the effect of the beer made

Matthew drowsy, so he threw his feet up on the couch and rested his head on a pillow. He hadn't slept well the night before, and he felt himself slipping off slowly, his thoughts drifting beyond the confines of the house in random dreamlike directions. Every so often, his consciousness surfaced briefly before sinking back. This happened several times before he was startled awake by the sound of a voice. Matthew sat up and turned his head from side to side, listening in different directions.

"I'm here," was what Matthew heard. Or what he thought he heard. He had been dreaming about Buzzy, or maybe not, but he automatically connected the voice to his old friend. This sort of thing had happened a few times before, where Matthew would project the end of a dream into a waking moment. Sometimes it was a voice that seemed to be real in the conscious world. One time it was a wasp that his mind had re-created in remarkably accurate detail, crawling across the striped bed sheets and disappearing over the side of the mattress.

Matthew thought about removing his patches to make certain there was nobody in the house. He didn't like the idea of not knowing. The furnace fan had been blowing but it shut off, leaving the house silent. Matthew listened carefully for a moment, more carefully than he had ever listened in his life. No, there was nobody there. Almost certainly. He decided to believe that this was another dream projection.

On the mantel above the fireplace were three photos from the wedding reception at the Boushay home in Ipswich. The center photo was one of Matthew and Buzzy wearing tuxes and standing in a garden full of flowers in bloom. Matthew was a little drunk and had a cocky expression, while Buzzy's eyes searched for the yellow jackets that had singled him out for persecution on that warm September afternoon.

On the many occasions when a fire blazed in the fireplace, Matthew had been tempted to toss that photo into the flames, frame and all. The image of his friend alive at the wedding, then gone forever a week later, had the power to ruin an otherwise good day. And it happened all the time. He'd be coming through the front door while finishing a phone call or herding the kids in front of him and carrying a few bags of groceries. Then, inadvertently, his eyes would glimpse the photo.

There had been a lot of speculation at the time that Buzzy was hiding from enemies in the drug world. He had begun pushing heroin for Francis,

Matthew learned. When time passed and Buzzy never surfaced, people believed that he must have been killed by a rival in the business, by someone he shorted in a deal or maybe by one of the many cops he had pissed off over the years.

Other than burning the photo, the only tactic Matthew had was to hide it somewhere, then reposition the remaining two photos. His son, however, thwarted him every time. The photo with Buzzy had never mattered to Dylan until he learned that he had been given his middle name Bradley because of Matthew's bond with his best friend. The mysterious Buzzy, whose story had a frustratingly murky ending, suddenly became important to Dylan, and if he couldn't get a more accurate account of what happened to his namesake, he could at least keep his image front and center in the pictorial history of his family.

On top of that was Dylan's sense of continuity. For him, everything in life had a proper place, and collections of things had their proper order. The clothes hanging in his closet had to be grouped by color. Nora once tormented him by taking a shirt from the blue group and placing it in the middle of the red group, then planting a plaid in the middle of solids.

Everyone in the family had learned to accommodate Dylan's eccentricities. The color grouping of his clothes was one. The arrangement of wedding photos on the fireplace mantel was another. Dylan had originally selected the three himself from the album of wedding photos and had positioned the one of Matthew and Buzzy dead center.

Approaching the situation diplomatically, Matthew suggested that a photo of the whole Mahoney family might be better in the center since it included so many of Dylan's East Coast relatives, some of whom he had yet to meet. Or maybe the picture of Anne and her mom in the Boushay plum orchard on the day of the wedding, just as the sun began piercing the morning fog. The more Matthew tried to change his son's mind, the more Dylan insisted on keeping his arrangement.

Matthew walked over to the mantel, felt around for the photos and located the center one. He carried it to the dining room hutch and shoved it to the back of the bottom drawer, where other framed wedding photos were stored. Fishing around, he found one the same size and placed it in the spot between the other two. The tactic would almost certainly fail, but it was new, so worth trying.

85

With that done, Matthew found other ways to distract himself and kill time. He sorted through a pile of CDs and sampled each until he found a few of his favorites to play. He did sit-ups, pushups, stretches and every kind of exercise possible in his situation. That was followed by a shower. He thought that shaving might not be a good idea in his situation, but he did it anyway without suffering any cuts. After dressing, he phoned Sal to talk about the jobs they had lined up for the following week. Then he called to order sealant for a torch down roof after calculating in his head the square footage, the number of seams to seal and the amount of sealant required.

Around 4:00 he sensed the sky outside beginning to lose its light. He finished the afternoon with more music and a return to the couch as the light outside vanished completely. The next thing Matthew noticed was a sudden return of brightness and the sound of his family pushing through the front door, all of them talking at once and driving the cloud of solitude out of the house.

Small feet approached him, and he smelled a chocolate peppermint breeze. Nora had just eaten a piece of candy and was blowing gently on his face. Matthew smiled and heard her giggle.

"I'm an angel sent by the spirit that can see everything, the future and the past," she whispered, "and I have a message from the spirit: tomorrow you will see." With that, she took a few steps back toward the door.

"Thank you for delivering the message. May I ask the spirit a question?"

Nora responded in her normal voice. "The angel's gone. She had to go. Dad, can my friends from soccer come over for indoor movie night on Saturday? Mom said I have to ask you. I already promised Juliette. She's my best friend on the team."

Indoor movie night was a smaller version of outdoor movie night, meaning that not as many kids and adults could attend because of space limitations. It took place once a month and was hosted by different families. In December it was at the Mahoney's house. The event included all the silliness and spilling of soda that occurred in the outdoor version, but with more cleanup on Sunday.

"Your mom and I will discuss it. But it can't be the whole team. I can tell you that right now. Also, Dylan may want to invite some friends over too. You have to consider that," Matthew said.

"I already asked him," Nora said. "He told me he's not inviting anybody."

Anne sat down beside Matthew "You spent the whole day on the couch, didn't you," she joked.

"Worse than that," Matthew said, "I spent it in my head."

"Mom, Dad said you guys have to discuss whether I can invite my friends from the soccer team over for movie night. Can you discuss it right now?"

"No, later," Anne said. "You've already invited two neighborhood friends and two school friends."

"Some soccer friends don't live in the neighborhood, and they don't go to my school."

"We'll let you know in the morning," Anne said.

The sweet, spicy smell of Thai food reached Matthew's nose. "Something smells good."

"We picked it up at the Buddha Bar," Anne said. "Let me change your patches first."

They moved to the bedroom for the procedure, and Matthew lay down on the bed. When Anne peeled the patches off, the air felt cool to Matthew's now-exposed eyes. He blinked several times. The bedroom ceiling looked a little blurry, but better with every blink. With a few drops in each eye and fresh patches, Matthew was back in the dark.

"How were your eyes today?"

Matthew was about to answer when he was interrupted by Dylan shouting from the living room. "Who moved the picture? Again! It's not even here anymore."

"Where did you put it?" Anne asked.

"In the bottom drawer of the hutch," Matthew said. "The photo was annoying me."

"You can't even see it. How can it bother you?" Anne said.

Matthew stood up. "Let's have supper. I'm starving."

Once the photo situation was resolved, everyone sat down at the dining room table. Dylan scooped portions of rice, garlic shrimp and curried vegetables into a bowl for his dad. Matthew used a big spoon and held the bowl close to his mouth to keep from spilling, or spilling much. After dinner, Nora retrieved some Magic Markers and asked if she could draw on her dad's eye patches.

"Squids, what are you gonna draw?" he asked.

She giggled. "I'm not telling. You have to guess."

There was more giggling than drawing. Matthew had no idea what she was creating.

"It looks very interesting," she declared when finished. Anne and Dylan were loading the dishwasher and putting away leftovers. Nora called them back to the table to judge her work.

Dylan laughed. "Dad's an alien."

"I think he's an insect," Anne decided.

"No, he's a lizard!" Nora insisted. "See the green and the yellow?"

"Alright, homework time," Anne called out. She sat down at the dining room table with Nora while Dylan went to study in his room upstairs. Matthew brought a radio into the bedroom, where he lay down and listened to the Seattle Sonics game against the Golden State Warriors. It was still early in the season, but Seattle was off to a strong start.

Homework was followed by an hour of TV, then getting the kids ready for bed. At 10:00, Anne came into the bedroom. She undressed, turned off the light and got into bed.

"The Sonics won," Matthew said, then turned off the radio.

"Wonderful."

"Listening to sports helps me stay sane. I should have found some games to listen to today."

Anne moved close to Matthew and stretched an arm over him. "I could stay home tomorrow." She waited for Matthew to respond but he didn't, so she continued, "There's nothing pressing at work. If anything, I've got less to do than usual. It's like they know I'm looking for work in Anchorage. What do you think? We can drive each other crazy all day here."

Matthew smiled. "OK, that would be nice. Thanks."

Anne propped herself up on an elbow. "Another thing—what videos do we want to rent for movie night? And Nora's friends from the team. I say she can bring two. That'll mean six friends in all, and that's more than enough."

"Agreed," Matthew said. "What were you thinking for the movies?"

"I wasn't. I was hoping you would be thinking about them today."

"OK, so for the adult movie, *The Matrix*."

"That might work," Anne said. She knew better than Matthew that the taste of their neighbors had to be the top consideration when choosing movies. In general, they didn't like movies that were too serious. They liked satire, irony, noir, indie tales with an antihero and anything in the *Star Wars* series. Anne grabbed a notepad and pen and started a list that included *The Matrix, The Truman Show, Smoke Signals, Chinatown, A River Runs Through It, Cookie's Fortune* and *Office Space.*

"I'll make a few calls tomorrow to see what people think," Anne said. "What about a movie for the kids?"

That list was shorter. It would be either *Muppets From Space* or *Who Framed Roger Rabbit.*

"Done," Anne said, putting down the notepad and pen on her nightstand. Then she leaned over and brushed a finger across Matthew's chin. "You know, you're usually asleep by the time I get to bed. It's kind of nice having you here awake."

Matthew leaned over to kiss her. His lips ended up on her nose instead of her mouth. Anne laughed. "A little lower."

She was rolling on top of Matthew when he whispered something.

"What?" she asked.

He pointed to the ceiling. "Squids is sitting on the stairs right above us."

Their daughter had a bad habit of eavesdropping on them when she thought her parents would be discussing something about her, like whether she could invite her friends from the soccer team to movie night.

"Are you sure?" Anne whispered.

Matthew nodded.

She put on her robe and moved quietly to the foot of the stairway, where she hit the light switch.

Matthew heard Nora squeal, then Anne marching her up the stairs. A brief interrogation was followed by protestations of innocence, all of which were discredited or dismissed. It ended without tears but with a stern warning. The whole interaction lasted two minutes, then Anne was back in bed.

"We really need to break her of that habit."

"That might have done the trick. You sounded pretty convincing."

"How did you know she was on the steps? I didn't hear her."

"When you can't see with your eyes, you have to use your other senses," Matthew said.

"That's very zen, Matt," Anne said. Then she whispered as softly as she could, "Can you hear this?"

Matthew nodded.

"OK," Anne whispered. "I want you on top."

*   *   *   *   *

With Anne home, Friday was a lot easier on Matthew than the day before, although when Anne went into cleaning mode, he couldn't settle down anywhere without her eventually saying, "Can you move, please? I need to clean there."

Later in the afternoon, Anne left to bring Nora to soccer practice, then pick up Dylan at South Seattle Community College, where he was enrolled in an after-school program in astronomy. On their way back, they stopped at Blockbuster to rent the DVDs for movie night a day before the Saturday rush emptied the store shelves. By 5:30, they were all home and sitting around the dining room table, waiting for teriyaki take-out food to be delivered and waiting for Matthew to take off his eye patches.

"Hurry up," Nora said. "I want to see if you can see."

Matthew tried taking the patches off himself, but the adhesive proved too much. "It's like glue," he said.

Anne ended up removing the patches, pulling them slowly off Matthew's face. "These really are stickier than the others," she said.

With both patches gone, the skin around his eyes felt cool. He blinked a few times and his vision went blurry, then clear, then blurry. Anne handed him a warm, wet napkin and he moved it gently around his eyes and over his lashes. With each blink, the blurriness diminished, and the clarity increased. He stopped blinking and looked around the table. Everyone was staring back at him. It seemed to be something of a solemn family moment.

"Can you see OK?" Dylan asked.

"Give us the word," Anne said.

Matthew turned around and looked out the front window. Mrs. Whitcomb's white Honda was parked in her driveway. It was dark outside, but a streetlight illuminated the back bumper. Matthew could see the license plate clearly, and the number and letters were in sharp focus. He could read them all. Relief, that was what he felt. Relief at dodging a bullet. He turned back to his family.

"It's good to see you again."

*   *   *   *   *

After dinner, Matthew and Dylan drove down to Lincoln Park with a telescope Dylan had checked out from his after-school program. It's something the two of them had been doing together once a month since the previous summer. That's when Dylan's interest in astronomy began, although he had always liked science fiction and was obsessed with the *Star Wars* series. The one exception was the most recent movie, which both father and son deemed profoundly disappointing. Even six months after seeing *The Phantom Menace*, Dylan cringed at the mention of the character Jar Jar Binks, who he considered the most awful character ever created. Dylan took it so personally that if asked what the worst thing was that he had ever experienced in his ten-and-a-half-year life, he would simply answer, "Jar Jar Binks."

When Dylan was younger, Matthew expected he'd spend time teaching his son how to hit a baseball, throw a football and shoot a puck. But after a short Little League stint, Dylan expressed absolutely no interest in organized sports. Matthew occasionally nudged him toward easier ones, but to no avail.

Dylan's preference for hobbies like astronomy was an adjustment for Matthew. He was the parent and used to being the one teaching, but with astronomy he was the one learning from his son.

They parked in the lower lot at Lincoln Park and walked down a steep road to the path that skirted the beach for almost a mile. The air was chilly, which according to Dylan made the sky clearer for viewing the stars. A few hundred yards down the beach, they found a spot where large pieces of driftwood provided a comfortable place to sit.

Nearby at the Fauntleroy terminal, a ferry bound for Vashon Island fired up its engines and moved slowly away from the dock. Matthew settled on a log and watched as Dylan set up the telescope in a methodical series of steps, something he liked to do on his own. Matthew opened up the notebook he had brought from the house. It held star charts inside.

"What are we looking at tonight?"

Dylan turned to face his father. "I circled the five constellations I'm supposed to map. They're in the Ursa Major family."

Matthew was wearing a headlamp, and he turned it on to see what had been marked.

Dylan turned away quickly. "Dad, don't! I told you not to turn on the light when I'm looking in your direction. My eyes will have to adjust all over again now."

Matthew apologized and swiveled around on the log, so his back was to his son. After waiting a minute, Dylan lowered his head to the viewer and asked what the first constellation was.

Matthew did his best to pronounce the name. "Canes Venatici. It looks like it's due west."

Over the next hour, Dylan mapped out all the stars that made up each of the five constellations. He needed to refer to the star charts several times, using a small red light so his eyes wouldn't be affected, but some of it he knew from memory. He didn't speak much to his dad during the process, but as he was working on his last constellation, Leo Minor, he said something unexpected.

"I don't have a best friend," Dylan said, staring straight at his father.

Matthew considered the statement, which caught him off-guard. It was Dylan's typical way of broaching a subject, but the jarring effect was something Matthew hadn't gotten used to. "What about Samuel? You guys do a lot of things together, and Samuel's into astronomy too. Right?"

"I asked him if he wanted to be best friends, but he said he's already best friends with Joshua Diaz."

Matthew considered mentioning that a person could have more than one best friend, but it didn't sound like Samuel was open to that notion. He went down a mental list of all Dylan's friends he was aware of. Dylan eliminated each of them in turn, citing one reason or another, until Matthew ran out of names.

"Nora is younger than me, and she already has a lot of best friends," Dylan said. "I know more girls who want to be best friends with her too. I even know a boy who wants to be best friends with her."

Matthew looked at his son, but didn't respond right away. He knew Dylan, and he knew that he didn't want a hug. He wanted to understand why one thing that was seemingly easy for lots of other kids, including his younger sister, was proving unattainable for him.

Matthew launched into a discussion about friends of his over the years, how his different friendships had begun, how some had ended. The talk moved into areas he had discussed with Dylan before, like the idea of popularity and how it changed for people over time, especially among kids.

Dylan was growing impatient and interrupted. "I found an article in the school library that says it takes 200 hours to become best friends with someone, but I did a calculation and I spent around 325 hours with Samuel before he mentioned that he was best friends with Joshua, so that can't be right. Do you know if that's right? About 200 hours? Is it a lot more?"

"It does take time, Dylan, but I'm afraid you can't put a number on it. It's more about other things. Like who you can trust the most. Someone you tell things to that maybe you can't tell anybody else. It's about who you can depend on. A best friend will always have your back, and you'll always have their back. And another thing: best friends forgive each other."

Matthew saw Dylan starting to look away, at the bluff behind them, at the ferry dock, where cars were unloading. "So, D-Man, here's the thing. Not everybody has a best friend, and that's OK. I don't think I have a best friend right now…"

"What about Sal?"

"Sure, maybe Sal is, but maybe he's not. He's got a lot of other friends he's known for a long time, and we don't hang out all the time together outside of work. And that's OK. Look, a best friend is more important when you're younger, and I know that. So here's what you might try doing differently if you really want a best friend. Next time when you're with a buddy, ask them what they've been up to instead of telling them what you've been up to. Ask them what they like instead of telling them what you like. Ask a lot of questions and really listen to what they have to say."

Dylan said nothing as he stared out into the distant dark of the water. They heard small fish jumping just offshore as they were being chased by larger fish.

Finally, Dylan turned back to the telescope to map the final stars of Leo Minor. Five minutes later, they packed everything up and headed toward the parking lot.

"You and Buzzy were best friends," Dylan said as they walked.

Matthew had intentionally avoided using Buzzy as an example in their discussion, but now Dylan was forcing his hand. "Sure, Buzzy and I were best friends going way back. We went through a lot of craziness together. He was a pain in the butt sometimes…"

"Why don't you try to find him? You said he moved away somewhere, but you never said where he moved to. Does he still live in the United States?"

Matthew found himself slowing down as they walked. With the discussion about Buzzy, he saw one gigantic fork in the road directly in front of him. The same thoughts and questions he'd had about what to tell Dylan and when to tell him all went rushing through his mind, and there was no way to sort through them all in the moment at hand. He'd become good at deceiving his son about Buzzy, but he was also growing very tired of it. In the moment, Matthew made a quick decision.

"Here's the thing about Buzzy," he began. "He disappeared after your mom and I got married. It happened a week after the wedding. Nobody knew where he went or what happened to him. Nobody could find him. I've never seen him or heard from him since then…"

Dylan stopped walking. "You told me that he moved."

Matthew stopped as well, and turned to face his son. "I know, Dylan. I didn't tell you everything about Buzzy before because you were too young to hear it. Buzzy was involved in drugs, selling drugs, and some people think…" Matthew paused, knowing that what he said next would amount to a lie, that he was only sharing part of the truth. Maybe it was the part that Dylan could handle, or maybe it was the part that Matthew could bear to tell his son right now. "Some people think that Buzzy did something that upset someone in the drug world. And that's why he disappeared."

"Someone killed him? Someone murdered him?"

"Yes. Probably."

"Who do you think did it?"

"I don't know, Dylan. Nobody does. Not for sure."

Matthew waited for more questions. That was Dylan's nature when faced with new, unfamiliar situations, but further questions didn't come. Instead, he picked up his equipment and the two began walking again.

"That's why you keep moving the picture," Dylan said. "It reminds you. If you want, you can replace it with another one."

"It can stay where it is, now that you know what happened. I think that will make it alright."

"Does Mom know about this?"

"Mom knows everything."

"I thought maybe I could meet Buzzy someday. Your first best friend."

"First and best of them all," Matthew said. Then he added, "Dylan, it's important that you don't tell your sister about this, OK? I'll explain it to Nora when she's older and can understand."

"Don't worry, I'm good with secrets," Dylan said.

*   *   *   *   *

When they got home, Matthew waited until Dylan and Nora had gone to bed and were asleep. Then he took Anne onto the back deck and told her what he had revealed about Buzzy.

"I don't know, Matt." She spoke in a quiet voice that still seemed too loud in the calm, cold air. "I think it's too soon."

"He seemed to take it well. I think it's alright."

"How much did you tell him?"

"That Buzzy disappeared after the wedding, that he was involved in the drug world, that he was probably killed by someone with a drug connection. I left it at that. And I told him to keep it all from Nora."

Across the yard came the sound of a neighbor's back door opening and a dog being let out on a long leash. They could see the dark Yorkshire terrier by the faint reflection of light in its eyes—two dots of dim illumination gliding over the grass. They stood perfectly still on the deck, but it seemed that the terrier sensed their presence. It moved cautiously toward the point where the leash grew tight, and remained motionless there for a moment. Then it lifted a hind leg, peed onto a nearby shrub and returned to the house.

"You didn't tell him anything about Francis, I hope."

Matthew shook his head. "I dread the day."

Chapter 6
Goat Creek Lodge

Wednesday, December 22, 1999

"If you really want to argue the point, fine," Mole said. "We'll start with mythological architecture. *Star Wars* has it; *Star Trek* doesn't. Also, the special effects in *Star Wars* humble and embarrass the special effects in *Star Trek*. Next, *Star Wars* has the Force and *Star Trek* has…nothing. And please, don't tell me that Khan is more impressive than Darth Vader. The Dark Lord is the ultimate badass."

Buck was sitting across from Mole and grew furious in his defense of *Star Trek*. He looked straight into Mole's blue spectacles and said, "You're forgetting the Borg, you're forgetting that Kirk and Picard are both better lead actors than Luke Skywalker, you're forgetting supporting actors. Spock kicks Han Solo's ass…"

Mole countered, "I'm not forgetting Captain Kirk's painfully stilted dialogue. Even in a crisis, when a cheesily costumed alien threatens the Enterprise's destruction, Kirk can barely utter a coherent sentence. I think that's something you really struggle to process, Buck, because whereas my cerebral cortex contains the requisite four cognitive lobes, your brain cavity seems to be wholly occupied by a reptilian stem that gloms onto the simple and the banal. Hence your embrace of white bread, heavy metal, tube socks and *Star Trek*."

The rest of the A Crew was mostly ignoring the argument between Mole and Buck. It was just more of the same background static they had gotten used to from the two. Everyone was sitting around a table in the rear dining room at Roy's, which put the boisterous A Crew mostly out of earshot from other diners in the front of the restaurant that evening. This was the annual bash that Matthew threw for his A Crew in late December, when roofing work slowed down for winter.

They were on their second round of drinks and working their way through a few appetizer plates that the kitchen prepared specially for them when a round of tequila arrived at the table.

"Enough with the *Star Trek* shit," Sal said. "I want you guys to tell me what you think about this tequila. I tried it last weekend at the Matador."

Matthew was sitting beside the Major, who was sharing his idea for a new set of miniature war depictions by drawing rough sketches on a paper napkin. Like Buck and Mole, Major was a White guy in his late 20s. What earned him his nickname was his hobby. He had grown up in Hawaii, and his father had been a general in the U.S. Army. As a kid, Major became obsessed with creating miniature representations of classic battle scenes.

He had no interest in joining the military himself. Instead, he talked of moving to Montana someday and owning property. How he would earn a living and pay for the property was over Major's horizon for now. All he knew was that his future lay somewhere "over there" in Montana. His girlfriend, who sold handcrafted wax candles at Pike Place Market, was in on the Montana plan as long as it involved apple orchards, so she could press cider. The two were saving together, and Matthew thought they might actually make it to the Big Sky state if they kept saving for a few more years.

Major sniffed his tequila, then took a sip. "This will be the most complex project I've ever done, skipper. It covers the Battle of Waterloo. I'll create maybe seven or eight separate scenes...the first with French Marshal Ney trying to break Wellington's center. He was out of infantry reserves and tried the attack with cavalry charges alone."

Matthew listened as he enjoyed his tequila. He knew his window of attention to Major's battle descriptions would slam shut in about a minute. Luckily, the Professor was sitting on the other side of Major, and he was paying much closer attention to the Battle of Waterloo. The Professor usually wore contact lenses, but this evening he was wearing tortoise-rim glasses. That and a worn cardigan sweater made the Professor actually look professorial for perhaps the first time ever to Matthew.

Major continued, "So Wellington's infantry soldiers see this and go into square formations with about 500 soldiers in each square. It's the perfect defense against a purely cavalry attack because horses won't charge into a wall of bayonets. At the same time, soldiers inside the square can fire on the cavalry. Marshal Ney tries 10 or 15 charges before he finally has to give up. That's just the first scene."

Mole had been savoring his drink and took one final sip before declaring it a fine tequila that didn't have that initial funk you got with cheap ones. He then sniffed the empty shot glass. "The aroma's not bad. The taste has a sort of sweet, caramelized agave flavor and a creamy vanilla finish that stretches nicely."

Sal smiled. "Mole, once again, you're a fucking genius about the weirdest shit. I love it."

Buck didn't miss an opportunity to undermine the compliment. "The real reason you like it, Mole, is because it's free. That's your number one reason for liking anything."

"What did you think, Buck?" Sal asked.

"I don't know shit about tequila," Buck said. "But it went down OK."

Matthew nodded and gave a thumbs-up. "We started carrying this a last month. It's top on everyone's list. And it's not crazy expensive."

The Professor was the last to weigh in. "I really don't drink tequila anymore because I had a bad experience with it about ten years ago…"

"From where I sit," Buck said, "your glass looks empty."

"I was getting to that…so I haven't had it in ten years, but I liked this. It didn't bite back." The Professor raised his first two fingers to Major, the only other regular smoker at the table, and they both left to have a cigarette beneath the awning out front.

Buck stared at Mole. "When was the last time you spent any money?" Buck asked. "I bet you haven't spent any today. Or yesterday either. All you do is save."

Mole responded, "You can't calculate the value of everything in life with a cash register, Buck."

"You sound like an American Express commercial," Buck said. "Aren't you the guy who's counting every penny on his way to $20,000? Why don't you tell us how close you are to reaching the grand goal?"

As always, Mole was coy about the subject. His focus was on the remaining appetizers, specifically the two Dungeness crab cakes. "I'm as close to my goal as I need to be."

A server stopped by the table to deliver another round of drinks and take dinner orders. As she began clearing appetizer plates, Mole scooped up the crab cakes before they were taken away. From a jacket pocket he pulled a small plastic bag, into which he placed the salvaged snacks. He zipped the bag shut, then discreetly returned it to his jacket.

Buck noticed the move. "Are those crab cakes gonna be your free breakfast tomorrow, Mole?"

"The cornbread and jam packets that were left uneaten earlier will be my free breakfast," Mole said as he patted his other pocket. "The crab cakes will be tomorrow's free lunch."

"You know, when you hit your goal and quit working, you're gonna have to start spending that money to survive."

When the entrees arrived, most of the conversation at the table focused on what Mole's life would look like when he did reach his goal. He had explained it all before, more than once, but he indulged the crew again. It was like hearing a story from someone who had just won the lottery, or was about to. At one time or another, they all had the fantasy of heading out on a road trip that had no fixed itinerary and no end in sight.

"I intend first to travel down the Northern California coast. The area is reasonably warm, and it also has a comforting morning fog. I'll stay in campgrounds, ones that are free. I have books for that. From there, I'll continue traveling around the country, mainly west of the Mississippi, with no particular destination other than to reimmerse myself in a certain sense of subculture, spending time in communities that embrace a spirit of life that doesn't cut so much against the grain of nature."

"Hippie chicks and hash brownies!" Buck laughed.

The Professor asked, "How long do you think you can you make your money last?"

"Well, I intend to supplement my reserves by selling handmade items at craft fairs. Not the ubiquitous bars of sandalwood soap or abrasive hemp clothing, but items that are both unusual and useful in everyday life. At the last fair I attended in Paonia, Colorado, I did reasonably well selling fountain pens made from the bones of birds of prey. The hollow of bird bones is fairly spacious, giving them greater ink capacity. Creating a reliable seal between bone and roller tip is the greatest challenge, but I've perfected a method that guarantees no unwanted discharge."

"Bird bones?" Sal asked with a look that fell somewhere between confusion and disgust.

"I have a process to ensure a clean and sterile product at the end," Mole said. "It begins with searching for bird carcasses on my long hikes in the mountains. Occasionally I'll spot a hawk or eagle nest and search beneath it, but mostly I use the bones of burrowing owls. I also use their talons and skulls for necklaces and earrings."

"That's disgusting, Mole," Buck said. "You shouldn't be touching dead birds. What the hell's wrong with you?"

"That's interesting," the Professor said. "I don't think I've ever seen you wearing a necklace or ring like that though."

Mole turned his head slowly in the Professor's direction. "I dislike embellishments of any kind. But that's for me personally. I really enjoy crafting jewelry from the remains of those beautiful creatures. I would have no objection if somebody did likewise with my remains when I die, as long as they made something tasteful."

Buck shook his head in disbelief. "You are one sick motherfucker."

Sal felt it was time to distract Buck from his critique of Mole because he knew it would only get worse. "Buck, don't be so critical of Mole starting his own business. I hear you're doing the same thing."

Buck gave Sal a surprised look. "I'm not discussing that publicly yet. It's still in the research stage."

The enigmatic denial only made everyone more curious. Especially Mole. "What sort of business do you consider yourself capable of running? You're underskilled in every capacity I can think of. If you tried for a job at a waste recycling plant, your application would be thrown directly into a composter."

A smile began to spread across Sal's face. "Oh no, Mole. It's not a messy business he's starting. In fact, it's a very classy business, isn't it?"

"Look," Buck said as he sensed the possibility of evading the discussion rapidly diminishing. "Let me just say that the whole world is moving online right now. Every business that has existed in the real world for centuries will exist more and more in the virtual space of the Internet."

"So you're opening an online blacksmithing shop?" Mole asked, which caused everyone to laugh.

It was the Professor who finally cracked the code of Buck's description. "If I'm right, it might be even older than blacksmithing. Are you creating a website for porn?"

Sal let out a deep belly laugh. "But not just any kind of porn, Professor. Buck's website will feature only the most tasteful porn there is. Classy porn. Right, Buck?"

Buck nodded. "The online porn business right now is like a bad amateur hour. It's trashy or it's homemade or it has insufficient quantity of images. I'm building a website that will feature only classy porn and plenty of it. I'll sell monthly access subscriptions..." Buck paused to point in Mole's direction. "Once I acquire sufficient inventory, I'll be making way more than $20,000. I'm telling you, a year from now, I'll be hanging up the roofing hammer forever."

Now that the cat was out of the bag, everyone at the table was firing questions at Buck. What did he consider classy? Would he hire models and set up photo shoots? Where would he get the money for that?

Buck explained that he would acquire the images for his site by scouring the World Wide Web and copying all of the images he could find that met his standards of classy. Buck said it involved swanky settings, silk lingerie, soft lighting, expensive-looking jewelry and plush accessories.

"So you're stealing the images from other websites," Mole said.

"Only the ones that meet my strict standards. Once I have enough, I'll purchase a web domain and hire a technology consultant. Then I'll sit back and watch the cash roll in."

As the evening wore on, different names were suggested for Buck's website. The most popular ones involved replacing the word "fuck" with the word "Buck," like the Buck Palace, Cluster Buck, What the Buck and Just Bucking Around.

As Matthew was finishing his second shot of tequila, it suddenly occurred to him that he hadn't handed out the bonuses he gave his A Crew every Christmas. He reached into his jacket and pulled out five envelopes. The one marked for Sal held $250. The others each held a $100 bill. Matthew would also be paying the restaurant and bar bills for the evening. This was the first year when he'd succeeded in squeezing $75 out of Rieger Roofing to spend on his A Crew as a holiday treat, which only covered a small part of the dinner tab.

"Hey, I almost forgot," Matthew said as he stood and handed out the envelopes. "It's nothing much, but I want you to know that I appreciate all your hard work…that is, on those rare occasions when you actually care enough to work hard…"

Matthew waited for, and received, the expected reply of colorful protest. "No, really, you all do work hard, and you work well together, which is just as important. I promise to do my best to keep you earning money this winter until the Rieger work goes back to full-time again in spring."

"The feeling's mutual, Matt," Buck said. "By the way, everybody, if you listen really hard you can hear the Rieger brothers wishing us a Merry Christmas too. Don't be confused, though, if it sounds like they're saying "'Fuck you, A Crew!'"

Matthew announced that his neighbor, Kurt, the evening's designated driver, would be arriving in about ten minutes with his van to give everybody a ride home. Drinks were polished off and final bathroom pit stops were made. But the evening was not quite over.

Mole had opened his envelope and pulled out the crisp $100 bill. It was what he had received the previous year, so it's what he expected to receive again. Now that he had peered over the top of his blue-tinted spectacles and confirmed the amount, he could deliver his news.

Mole rose from his chair just as the Professor stood to leave. He steadied himself, then spoke. "If I could have your attention for a moment, I have an announcement to make. With the receipt of this $100 bonus…thank you very much, Matt…I have, as of this moment, reached my stated goal of $20,000. To be exact, my confirmed total is now $20,017. Having said that, I must now give my immediate notice to you, Matt. I know I technically have been employed by the Rieger brothers, but I like to consider myself your employee. So I want to say that I've enjoyed very much working for the Mahoney enterprise and with all of you…" Mole glanced momentarily in Buck's direction. "For the most part anyway. I leave for points south first thing in the morning, or maybe late morning. I promise to send postcards. They may arrive by hand if I can find someone traveling to Seattle. In that way, I can avoid the cost of postage. And, really, who wouldn't prefer a hand-delivered greeting?"

The whole crew was stunned by the news, and nobody seemed to know what to say. They had just been speaking about Mole's trip in the abstract, something that wouldn't become a reality for months to come. But now it was suddenly happening, and the news brought a mix of emotions.

Buck was the first to speak. "What the fuck, Mole?" He paused before continuing in a soft voice that revealed more hurt than surprise. "You can't say you're leaving, then leave just like that."

The Professor stood frozen with one sleeve of his coat on. Sal just stared at Mole from his seat. For the first time that evening, Major fully shifted his attention away from talk about his Waterloo battle scenes. As hard as Mole was trying to keep a casual attitude, he too showed how uneasy he felt and how hard it was to deliver his message.

Matthew was surprised and a little annoyed that Mole would spring his surprise like this. But it was still a free country and he wasn't quitting the A Crew in the middle of the busy summer roofing season.

Wanting to end the awkward moment, Matthew smiled and said, "Well, congratulations. I had no idea you were so close to reaching your target. Nicely done. We're gonna really miss you, man. You're a good guy and a solid worker." Matthew reached for his glass of beer, which wasn't quite empty. He raised it and said, "Here's wishing Mole…" Matthew paused after saying the nickname, which had been bestowed by the A Crew. Now that Mole was leaving, Matthew had the odd thought that maybe he should now be addressed by his name in the outside world. "Here's wishing Travis a safe journey and good times on the road."

There were a couple of faint "good lucks," but nothing like the hearty endorsement Matthew was hoping for. He looked around the table and said, "C'mon guys, he's quitting his job for an adventure we'd all like to be going on. That's a move that takes some balls, and I respect that. The least we can do is wish him well."

Sal said, "You totally surprised me here. I think we're all shocked, but we wish you the best. Really."

"This is an amazing moment, Mole," the Professor said as he finally finished putting on his jacket. "You gotta keep in touch and tell us how it goes."

Major gave a few claps and smiled. "Who's gonna be there to take the last of my french fries before I'm done eating them?" It was a running joke between the two.

Mole's shoulders relaxed as the awkwardness of the moment ebbed. He gave a half smile. "Well, thank you all. I appreciate it. And I will keep in touch." He went around the table and shook hands. Mole was very uncomfortable with the idea of hugging, a fact that everybody was aware of.

"If you ever need a job, Travis, let me know. You'll always have a spot on my A Crew," Matthew said. When Mole turned to leave, Matthew added, "Kurt will be here soon. He can drop you at your garage downtown."

"That won't be necessary," Mole said. "I anticipated the bonus this evening and knew it would likely put me over the top, so I vacated my berth on level seven of the garage this afternoon. I'm currently parked on a side street two blocks away, where I'll be spending the night. Matthew, could you send my final check to my downtown post office box?"

"Will do, Travis."

With that, Mole quietly walked out of Roy's and out of the A Crew's world.

"Well that was an ambush if I ever saw one," Sal said. "I'm gonna need another drink. Who else wants one?"

"Sure, why not?" the Professor said. He took off his coat and sat back down. Everyone else seemed like they wanted to stick around for a bit, so Sal called for a fresh round for everyone minus Mole. He took a look at Buck, who had been unable to speak since his first comment. Buck looked completely dazed, so Sal slapped him on the back. "C'mon, breathe, MotherBucker."

When the drinks arrived, Sal said to Buck, "Take a drink, big guy."

Buck stared at the glass and shook his head. "Why didn't he tell us he was so close? He just sprang it on us like that."

"It's not the end of the world, BuckleHead. We'll get a replacement for the Mole. I mean, you hardly liked the guy. You were always arguing with him. Now you're acting like your girlfriend just dumped you."

"Lovers' quarrel," Major joked.

That remark seemed to snap Buck out of his stupor. "Fuck you and your toy soldiers," he said.

Sal let out a long, raspy laugh. "Yeah, that's more like it!"

105

A few minutes later, Kurt arrived. "Matt, I'll see you sometime tomorrow afternoon," Sal said. "We should be at the lodge by around 4:30."

"That's perfect. Here…" Matthew walked to the bar and grabbed a pen and a blank credit card slip, on which he wrote the security code for the front door at Goat Creek Lodge. "In case we're running late."

Sal started to leave, then turned back to Matthew. "Fucking Mole," he said, shaking his head.

"I know. At least it's not summer. It's actually better to have a smaller crew for winter, but we'll need to replace him in spring."

Sal laughed, "There's no replacing the Mole. He's one strange creature."

Dennis, the manager, was tending bar at Roy's that night. He walked to the front door and flipped a sign telling the world that the restaurant was officially closed. Matthew joined him at the bar to pay the bill along with a tip. He paid with a fat roll of cash he had taken from the Mickey Mouse jar back home.

"Alright, I'm out of here. Enjoy your Christmas, Dennis. I'll see you on the other side of 1999."

"Don't forget Y2K, Matt. The world might be ending in about ten days."

*   *   *   *   *

When Matthew woke the next morning, the first thing on his mind was brussels sprouts. Christmas was only two days away, and every Christmas since marrying Anne, the bitter vegetable had made an appearance on the Mahoney dinner table. Matthew loved all kinds of food, and he could stomach almost anything in a pinch, including leftovers just short of rancid. There were only two items of food that repulsed him: liver and brussels sprouts.

The vegetable arrived every Christmas in the checked baggage of Anne's mother. On her small farm in Ipswich, Joan Boushay grew her own brussels sprouts. Since retiring from her role as professor in the math department at Salem State College, she had plenty of free time to devote to agrarian pursuits.

A greenhouse protected her sprouts from a killing frost, and fertile, well-drained soil with a pH of 6.8 ensured optimal growth. There were Christmases when Matthew hoped Joan's sprouts would fall prey to insects or the kind of blight that wiped out the potato crop in Ireland, but his mother-in-law was too competent a farmer to allow anything like that to happen. The sprouts of Christmas were unstoppable, and they cast a bitter shadow over what had been Matthew's favorite holiday.

"Just tell her you don't want any," Anne would say. But that was missing the bigger point, as Matthew saw it. While Anne's father had wholly approved of him the day the two met for the first time in Alaska so many years ago, Joan Boushay had always been ambivalent at best. Matthew knew for a fact that she discouraged Anne from marrying him because of who he was and where he was from.

To Joan, the pastoral milieu of Ipswich did not match well with the housing projects of South Boston. Then there was the wedding reception in 1987, when the Irish-American Mahoney family lived up to more than one negative stereotype. And finally, there was Matthew's brother Francis. To her closest friends, Joan had to confess that her daughter's brother-in-law currently sat near the top of the FBI's Ten Most Wanted list. To the rest of her world of acquaintances, it was a dark secret waiting to leap into the light of day at any random moment and deeply embarrass her, should one of them connect the Boushay-Mahoney dots.

Matthew felt that telling Joan he simply didn't want any of her brussels sprouts was in no way the same as passing on a second scoop of mashed potatoes or a slice of pie. More than once, she described them as "the most virtuous vegetable nature ever blessed us with." Rejecting them would be tantamount to rejecting Joan and the values that the Boushay family was built upon. No fucking way was he going there.

His only hope was that Joan's airline would lose her baggage. He considered the possibility as Anne began to stir beside him. They both had the day off, and Matthew was a little hungover from his night at Roy's, so it was one of the rare mornings when they both slept late and lingered in bed for a while.

"Did you guys have a good time last night?" he asked.

Anne yawned and rolled onto her side. "It was very nice. Mom took us out for Indian food. Then we went to Southcenter and saw that movie

Stuart Little. It's a story about this little mouse that a family adopts. Stuart's a mouse but a person too, if you know what I mean. Nora absolutely adored it. I'm thinking you might not want to set any more mousetraps in the house. Not even in the garage."

"I haven't set any in the house for at least six months. I swear. And I think I have just one in the garage. Maybe two. Three at the most."

"Well, you better get rid of them or put them where she'll never see them. Mice are now people to her."

"Alright," Matthew said. Then, as casually as he could, he asked, "So did everything go OK with your mom's flight?"

"Did everything go OK? What do you mean?" Anne replied with a straight face.

"You know, the flight, the landing, the baggage..."

Anne laughed. "Yes, Matt, everything went OK, and I'm sorry to tell you that her brussels sprouts arrived safely."

Matthew closed his eyes and groaned.

*   *   *   *   *

Everybody was a little slow getting out of bed and getting dressed that morning. It wasn't until 10:00 when they met Joan for breakfast at Roy's. As she did every year when visiting, Joan stayed nearby at the Giffordshire House, a cozy bed-and-breakfast on the West Seattle waterfront.

In the year after Anne and Matthew were married, they invited Joan to stay in their small Ballard apartment, and it was a disaster right across the board. After that, local bed-and-breakfasts saved them all from family civil war. Fortunately, the Giffordshire House was only five blocks from Roy's.

Although Joan always arrived alone when visiting Matthew and Anne, she was, in fact, in a relationship. The man's name was Brian Livingston, and he worked as an optometrist in an office in downtown Ipswich. Although they had been together for the last 20 years, they each maintained their own residence. To Anne, the relationship seemed to be more of a close friendship.

Since her divorce some 30-odd years before, Joan never expressed any interest in remarrying. Whenever the Mahoneys visited Ipswich, whether it was the whole family or just the kids on their annual two-week summer visit, Brian would make an occasional appearance but would mostly remain on the periphery. And when Joan visited Seattle, she would always bring along Brian's best wishes for everyone, but never Brian himself. To Anne and Matthew, Brian had been charming company, but they always had taken him in small doses. Anne suspected her mother knew that an extended period of time in Brian's company might not be quite as pleasant.

Breakfast was followed by a walk along the beach at Lincoln Park. A chilly breeze was blowing off the water, and the rocks exposed by low tide glistened in the misty rain. It was standard winter weather in Seattle, and the Mahoneys neither liked nor disliked the conditions. They just wore their rain jackets and carried on.

On the other hand, Joan was enjoying the walk. Compared to the much harsher winter climate along her Ipswich shore, which could include temperatures well below freezing and strong winds off the ocean, this was a pleasant break.

Dylan explained to his grandmother that it was on this beach where he and his dad fished for salmon every summer. "We go up by the point because that's where the salmon come close to shore, chasing the bait fish. We've caught some kings and sockeyes, but last summer we caught a bunch of pinks. Every two years, a whole lot of them come back, and they're super-easy to catch with Buzz Bombs. They're these heavy lures that come in different colors."

They watched an eagle gliding high in a circle over the water. Anne had heard about the barred owls spotted recently in the park, but they were nowhere in sight at the moment. When they reached the point, they stopped to watch some harbor seals barking on the beach.

"Dad, do you murder mice?" Nora suddenly asked.

The statement was so jarring that Matthew could only stare at his daughter. "What?" he finally asked.

"Mom said you have mousetraps in the garage. That's how people murder them, you know. With traps. Or they use poison."

Then Matthew remembered the conversation about *Stuart Little*.

"No, there are no more mousetraps in the garage. I got rid of them all," he said, with as much conviction as he could muster.

"That's a good thing because when you kill a mouse in a trap, you're committing murder. You're taking an innocent life, and that's illegal. Plus, it's very inhumane to the mouse."

*   *   *   *   *

It wasn't until 2:00 when they finally had everything packed for the drive to Goat Creek Lodge just outside Mount Rainier National Park. Anne rode with Joan and Nora in the Subaru. Matthew and Dylan left earlier in the pickup truck, which gave them room for all the firewood they'd need for four nights of fires in the big lodge fireplace and outdoor fire pit. Then there were the snowshoes, poles, snow sleds and, most importantly, gifts.

Matthew had always gone through the trouble of hiding the gifts in the lodge because Nora still believed in Santa Claus. But at Thanksgiving dinner, Nora announced that she no longer officially believed. She also added that she hoped her loss of faith would not negatively affect either the quantity or quality of gifts she received at Christmas.

Dylan used the one-and-a-half-hour drive as an opportunity to tell his father all about black holes. He'd learned about them recently in science class. Ever since watching his first *Star Wars* movie, anything related to space, including stargazing, became an immediate obsession.

Talk of "event horizons," where the force of gravity is so strong that even light could not escape, lasted the whole drive to Tacoma, where they left the freeway and turned onto Route 7. Strip malls gradually gave way to open fields, dense groves of towering conifers and steep drop-offs with views of the Nisqually River. The trees were shrouded in a chilly mist that turned to wet flakes of snow as they approached the town of Elbe.

Matthew rolled down the window to take in the smell of firewood burning in a distant cabin and the scent of damp, musty earth. It was more subtle than the rich aroma of the woods in summer with its symphony of wildflowers, fir needles, sweet ferns and nearby farm soil warming in the sun.

Passing through Elbe meant they were only 15 minutes from the lodge. Dylan enjoyed seeing the old railroad cars parked on tracks by the side of the road. They were dining cars and cabooses that had been turned into a motel, a restaurant, a gift shop and a lounge called the Side Track Room, which had a sign out front saying, "Sorry, honey—I got sidetracked."

A mile before the Nisqually entrance to Mount Rainier was Goat Creek Inn, a roadside restaurant with rooms and suites on the second floor. The old inn hadn't changed all that much since it was built in 1914. During the summer, the small counter and dining room overflowed with tourists, hikers, climbers, bicyclists and the occasional pack of Harley riders, but in winter months it was mostly locals who stopped by for a meal or maybe a slice of blackberry pie that was made fresh on the premises.

Right before reaching the inn, Matthew turned onto a narrow dirt road with cedar trees forming green walls on both sides. The road eventually opened onto a large grassy field with three cabins and the big red lodge, arranged in a circle around the field. Everything was covered in three inches of new snow. Seeing no car tracks told them they were first to arrive.

The lodge was built in 1914, the same year as the inn, and constructed of Douglas firs. Inside, the exposed logs were stained an amber color that had aged over the generations to deep tobacco brown. On the west end of the great room, windows stretched up 15 feet to let in the fading afternoon light. A wood-slab dining table that seated 18 had a surface scarred with an assortment of gouges, scrapes, discolorations and burn marks accumulated over the decades.

On the other side of the room, couches and easy chairs were arranged around a massive fireplace made of smooth stones pulled from the nearby Nisqually River. Its hearth was six feet wide, and on both sides it still held the swing-arm cranes that let a cook swivel cast-iron kettles in or out of the hearth's heat as needed.

The first task was to unload the truck. From the back, they grabbed luggage and bags of wrapped gifts, and hauled them through the great room and down a long hallway that led to four bedrooms. Around a corner and through a door, the hallway ended at a master suite that gave Joan a sense of privacy and quiet when the holiday spirit in the great room grew too loud or went on too late for her liking.

Snow continued to fall as they retrieved the firewood and kindling from the truck, organizing it in two big stacks, one next to the stone fireplace, the other at the fire pit in the center of the snowy field. Next came all the snow gear and the cases of beer, which they stored in the lodge's unheated sun porch. A case of wine went to the kitchen, along with some of the food for the stay. More of it showed up in the Subaru just as Dylan was putting a match to crumpled newspaper in the fireplace.

By 4:30, the sky was dark and the snow was falling more heavily. Cars began arriving with people who were staying in the other cabins: Anne's friend Renee Lambert, who had worked at the same engineering firms as Anne for years, along with her husband, Doug, and three kids—Nathan, Emily and Diana. Next came Nicholas and Zoey Schuler, with their two kids, Randy and Maeve. The Schulers now lived in Redmond, but for years had lived in Arbor Heights, where they became friends with the Mahoneys. Matthew had once repaired the chimney on the roof of their home, telling the younger neighborhood kids that it had to be made wider to accommodate Santa Claus.

The last to arrive were the Engebretsens, an older couple whom Matthew and Anne had befriended back in the '80s when living in Ballard, a neighborhood with a proud Norwegian heritage. Andy Engebretsen was the son, and the grandson, of a locksmith, but he chose a career in city government and had two years to go before retiring. He and his wife, Trine, had both been married previously, with neither having children.

The same four families had gathered at Goat Creek over the Christmas holiday almost every year since 1994. The one exception was 1997, when the second-generation Engebretsens traveled overseas to celebrate the holidays with their Norwegian kin.

Sal had joined the Goat Creek circle the previous two years, and this Christmas he'd be bringing his girlfriend, Malia. At 5:30, they were nowhere to be seen and the snow was falling heavier still. Cellphone reception at the lodge was notoriously bad, and the great room was the absolute black hole of tower signals, so Matthew stepped outside to call Sal, who said they had been delayed in leaving. He had tried to call Matthew but kept getting voicemail.

Seattle traffic was a mess with the snow. That was one reason why Sal and Malia hadn't left town. The other reason—the bigger one—was that they'd gotten into a fight. Sal would be arriving the next day when the snow eased up. He promised to be at the lodge in plenty of time for Christmas Eve dinner. But he said he'd probably be arriving alone.

The lodge served as the epicenter of social activity for everyone in the Christmas crew, and by 6:00 it was in its usual state of pre-dinner bustle with kids chasing each other around or playing board games. Joan, Renee and Doug were trimming a tree along with the Engebretsens, who had carried it from Ballard on the roof of their old AMC Pacer. Over it all played *Christmas in Norway with the St. Olaf Choir* on the lodge's stereo system, which dated back to the '70s.

With that, Matthew hurried back inside and rejoined Anne in the kitchen. Cooking duties over the holiday were split among the families, and Thursday evening belonged to the Mahoneys. They had already put out appetizers and uncorked a couple of bottles of wine.

Dinner included a fillet of grilled king salmon that Matthew had caught the previous summer, boiled new potatoes tossed in melted herb butter, grilled vegetables and two different kinds of salad. At 6:30, all the dishes arrived without incident at the big dining room table, where 16 hands raised a glass and gave thanks.

*   *   *   *   *

"I don't think Nathan Lambert likes me," Dylan said to his dad early the next morning before anyone else had gotten out of bed. They were in the kitchen, and Dylan was sitting in the breakfast nook staring at his toast. The nook had windows that looked out on a winter scene, where snow continued to fall.

Matthew had heard Dylan, but he was busy crawling around the kitchen floor in search of mousetraps the owner might have set, which was typically the case. In past years, it hadn't been a big issue, either in the lodge or back at home. But Nora's current attitude toward mice made it critical to avoid any scenes. He had already pulled three traps from behind the fridge and stove. That seemed to do it.

He got to his feet, brushed off his hands and knees, poured himself a cup of black coffee and joined Dylan in the nook. "When we were all out at the fire pit last night, I heard you talking to Nathan about black holes."

"Yeah, we were talking about black holes, about wormholes, neutron stars...a lot of different things."

"Well, you say that 'we were talking,' but I don't remember Nathan really saying anything, D-Man. I only remember hearing you talking. Now I know it's Christmas, and you're excited. You've just learned a whole lot about black holes, and you can't wait to tell people all about them. Even when you're excited, though, you have to remember what we've talked about."

Dylan looked down at his toast and let out a long sigh, not in a dramatic way but so quietly that he himself seemed unaware he was doing it. "Sharing a conversation," he said finally.

"It's been a whole year since you've seen Nathan, right? So he's got a lot of news he wants to share with you too. He started playing football last fall. I'm sure he wants to tell you what that's been like."

"But I don't play football."

"Right, and Nathan probably isn't fascinated by black hole theory and event horizons the way you are. And that's OK. But you can't expect him to care about black holes if you don't try to care about his first year of football. I never played organized football either, but I had friends who did, and I would talk to them about it all the time. Try it today. Nathan will be snowshoeing with us."

"OK, I will," Dylan said after a bit of hesitation.

Just then, his sister came charging into the kitchen, waving her hands wildly over her head and shouting, "It's still snowing! This is so amazing! I can't wait to go up to the mountain today! It's gonna be super-awesome!"

Nora looked up at the ceiling and spun around a couple of times before stopping in front of the nook and grabbing the tabletop to steady herself. She looked at her dad, then at Dylan. Both seemed to lack excitement about the day of snowy adventure that lay ahead.

Half out of breath, she asked, "So what are you guys talking about?"

Matthew was about to repeat his breakfast options, but before he could, Nora reached in front of her brother and grabbed a piece of his toast.

"Can I have a bite?" Without waiting for an answer, she said, "Thanks," then took a bite. "If it's about Nathan, don't worry. He's not mad at you. I talked to him when Dad and Mr. Engebretsen were putting out the fire. He doesn't want to hear anymore about black holes, though."

"Do you guys feel like pancakes or eggs for breakfast?" Matthew asked.

Nora said, "I want pancakes, Dylan. Do you want pancakes? Just say 'yes.' Right now."

When he said "yes," Nora ran with her piece of toast back into the great room, saying, "This is the snowiest Christmas we've ever had ever. It's blowing my mind!"

*   *   *   *   *

After breakfast, they loaded the snowshoe gear into the back of the Subaru and headed into the national park. Behind them were the Lamberts in their 4Runner. The Engebretsens would be staying at the cabin and relaxing in their outdoor hot tub, and the Schulers were going cross-country skiing on a nearby trail.

Once inside the park, the road wound through a forest of enormous old-growth trees coated with snow. It created a somewhat spooky, somewhat fairy-tale atmosphere. Occasionally they got a peek at the Nisqually River, its frigid glacial runoff roiling milky white as it rushed downstream. The road continued climbing on its way to Paradise Inn at 5,400 feet, and as it did, the wall of snow on either side rose higher and higher.

Nora was sitting in the back seat. She had cracked the window beside her just wide enough to stick her hand outside. It was something she had been doing for the last year or so, the way a dog loves to stick its nose out a car window and catch different scents. She claimed it was to cool her hot hands, but Anne suspected it was her way of catching a rush from the fast-moving air. At first, the open window was only a small annoyance to the other passengers, but when the elevation of the road reached 3,000 feet, the air outside and inside the Subaru grew noticeably colder.

"Do you mind closing the window?" Dylan asked.

"My hands are hot. I have to cool them down," Nora said. She had been switching hands more frequently as the elevation increased.

Joan was sitting in the back seat between the kids. "I think I'm quite ready for you to close that window as well, Nora," she said.

Nora moaned in protest but complied. "If I don't have the window open, I might get carsick and throw up."

"Nora, stop," Anne called from the front seat. "You haven't gotten carsick in years."

Just before reaching 4,000 feet, they crossed a bridge at the headwaters of the Nisqually River. Off to the left was the foot of the glacier that fed the river. Ten thousand feet above was the peak of the mountain itself, visible on clear days but now shrouded in clouds and mist.

Anne was explaining to her mother how it took about a hundred years for the ice at the top of the glacier to make its way slowly to the bottom. Over the decades, there had been climbers who had fallen to their death on the glacier, and their bodies couldn't be recovered. They would, in time, emerge at the bottom, along with a number of Air Force planes that had crashed into the glacier in the '40s and '50s.

Joan was listening, but instead of looking up at the glacier, she was looking down at the tremendous 250-foot drop to the icy river below. Then her eyes traced the course of water up to the dirty glacier, to the place where it climbed into the clouds. "My goodness, this view could give you vertigo. I've got butterflies in my stomach."

Dylan had his head in his hands with his eyes shut. Crossing this bridge always made him dizzy to the point of panic, and Joan's comments made the scene come alive.

A mile later they approached Paradise, the end of the road.

Just before the parking lot, Anne pulled off at the Jackson Visitor Center, where Joan would spend the day. As an academic with an interest in all things natural, she never tired of exploring the center's nature exhibits and sitting in on a busy schedule of lectures and movies about the flora, fauna and geological history of the mountain.

The only thing Joan found odd was the round, flying-saucer shape of the building itself. When she first saw the visitor center, it looked like someone had cut the top off the Space Needle and stuck it on the mountain.

"Do you know that they can use up to 500 gallons of diesel fuel a day for a heating system to melt all the snow on the flat roof? It's a ridiculous modernist insult to the natural landscape," she said.

"I think you've mentioned that before, Mom," Anne said.

Joan gestured for Nora to open the door and let her out. "But still, what they have inside is wonderful. I could spend a week in there and never get bored. Alright, I'll see you all around 3:00. Be safe."

They backtracked two miles down the mountain road to the parking lot at Narada Falls, where the Lamberts were waiting for them. Everybody put on their snowshoes and tromped a few hundred yards down a wide, flat trail, covered in three feet of snow, until they reached Reflection Lake. There, they took the Pinnacle Peak trail, which climbed up through a dense forest, where there was a hushed quiet. It was chilly at first, but climbing up the trail quickly warmed everyone. The snow had stopped an hour earlier, and now the cloud ceiling was lifting and the sky lightening.

At certain places, it was hard to tell which way the trail went because they were leaving first tracks on the new snow. Anne had hiked up to Pinnacle Saddle a number of times, and had even climbed the crumbling volcanic rock to the peak, so fortunately she knew the route without a visible trail. She reminded everyone that being first in the woods that day meant they could more easily spot fresh tracks of animals.

Marching ahead of the others were Anne, Renee, Diana, Nora and Emily Lambert, who was the same age as Nora. They came upon a boggy spot created by a spring. Around the edges, much of the snow had melted and there were animal prints in the mud leading from one side to the other.

"Mom, what's this?" Nora asked, pointing down.

"That's deer," Anne said. "See the shape of the two cloves and how they come close at the top but don't touch?"

Nora pointed to a set of tracks that looked different. "How about these?"

"That might be a fox," Anne said.

Emily and Diana followed another group of tracks that led into the deeper snow, where she called out "Deer poop!"

Nora rushed over to see, and the girls got into a discussion about how many deer there had been and where they might be headed.

"C'mon," Renee called. "You don't want the boys to pass us, do you?"

The boys weren't too far behind, but they were in no hurry. Rather than looking for real animals in the snowy landscape, Dylan was describing the imaginary. "I could totally see a herd of Tauntauns running through here," he said to Nathan.

"What's that?" Nathan asked.

"From the *Star Wars* movies. They're reptile-like creatures that look like a small T-Rex with the head of a ram. Tauntauns are warm-blooded and covered in white fur because their planet, Hoth, is icy cold like these woods, but with no trees. The Rebel Alliance rides them when they're out on patrol. Plus, they use them to carry supplies. I don't think they would be a threat to us if we saw two or three Tauntauns right around those trees up ahead. But one thing I know for sure, I would not—definitely not—want to meet even one Wampa up here. They're about 15 feet tall with big claws and razor-sharp teeth and they live on Hoth too. They hide in snowdrifts and completely surprise you. Then they take you back to their cave and rip you apart in, like, two or three seconds. You wouldn't even have a chance."

Matthew and Doug Lambert were several steps ahead of the boys. Doug worked as a manager at Kozmo.com, a new startup company that made a name for itself in the online retail world by guaranteeing free one-hour delivery of everything from food to videos. Matthew had seen plenty of the delivery cyclists with their orange messenger bags flying around Seattle.

Buck found their delivery riders annoying. Despite Matthew's warning about accumulating bad karma points, he would contact Kozmo.com and place an order for one chocolate muffin, one razor blade or one small bag of potato chips. When the delivery rider arrived sweaty and out of breath at Buck's apartment on the top of Queen Anne Hill, Buck would pay with pennies and never tip.

"Our business is growing like crazy," Doug said. "Don't repeat this to anyone, but in the coming weeks we'll be announcing major partnerships with a couple of Seattle's largest companies. One of them sells a lot of coffee, by the way. Analysts are predicting that we'll be a dominant player in the retail industry for decades to come. I'll be happy if they're even half right."

As Matthew listened to Doug with one ear, he caught some of what the boys were saying with the other. He turned around and waited until he caught Dylan's attention. When he did, he gestured with his arm as if he were throwing a football.

After a few seconds of confusion, Dylan's eyes opened wide. "Oh yeah," he said. "Hey Nathan?"

"What?"

"How did you like playing football this year?"

Nathan had been walking two steps ahead of Dylan and not really paying attention to the talk of *Star Wars* creatures, but he stopped and waited for Dylan to catch up.

They traveled for another half hour up the trail, emerging from the trees occasionally to cross small meadows. As the sky continued to clear, the jagged peaks of the Tatoosh Range came into view and the trail made an abrupt shift. It had been rising gradually over fairly level ground, but directly ahead it crossed a snowfield that angled down too steeply to cross without ice axes. Anne announced that this would make a good spot to rest and have lunch.

They ate quickly because a chilly breeze had kicked up. Nathan, who hadn't followed his mom's advice to wear two layers, was complaining about the cold.

As they got ready to leave, Anne asked, "Does anybody else hear that?"

With a few conversations going on at once, it was hard to hear anything but voices.

"I think I do," Doug said.

"What?" Nathan asked.

Anne pointed south across the snowfield to the nearest peaks, where they could hear a faint rumbling. It diminished, then increased again. A slab of snow had broken loose and was crashing down a steep chute, gathering up loose rocks and more snow as it rushed downhill. It eventually collided with a field of boulders and exploded in a cloud of snow.

"I see it!" Emily said.

"Is that an avalanche?" Nathan asked.

"That's right," his dad said.

One of Nora's boots had become untied on their hike in, and she was busy retying it while the others watched the avalanche. "Where is it?" Nora finally asked.

Emily pointed, "Right there. On the side of that mountain. But it's over now."

"When will there be another avalanche, Mom? I want to see one."

"We have to get going right now, Nora. We might see another one tomorrow."

"No, I want to see one here. We have to wait."

"Honey, we can't wait for another avalanche here today," Anne said. "We happened to get lucky."

Nora insisted. "If we wait, we'll see another one."

Everyone else had started the return hike, but Nora refused to leave. Anne gave her one last chance. "We're not staying here any longer. If you don't get moving down that trail, I'll pick you up and carry you. Either way, we're leaving in ten seconds."

"No. We just need to wait five more minutes."

"Nine, eight..."

Nora remained defiant until the end of the countdown. As soon as Anne moved in her direction, she took off running. Anne was more skilled in moving quickly in snowshoes, so it was a short chase. A minute later, she was walking down the trail with Nora slung over her shoulder.

Soon Nora said, "OK, you can put me down now."

"Will you behave?"

"Yes, I will."

They moved more quickly with Nora walking on her own, and they had almost caught up with the rest of the group when Anne felt a tug on the back of her jacket and turned around. Nora was holding a finger to her mouth with one hand and pointing down a slope of trees to a clearing at the base with the other. A fox was staring down at the snow and twisting its head in one direction, then the other. It took a few steps forward and shoved its snout into the powder. Then it took a few more steps and poked the snow again.

Its fur was black with silver highlights, and the tip of its tail was white.

"A fox," Nora whispered with excitement. "What's it doing?"

"It's hunting something." Anne almost whispered "mouse," which was most likely the case. "The fox can hear things moving under the snow."

"The snow makes its face look like a raccoon," Nora whispered.

They watched it repeat the same behavior a few times before going into a crouch, then springing three feet in the air and diving nose first into the snow. The fox plunged so deep that only its hind legs and tail were visible.

Usually Anne would want the fox to catch its mouse, but she was crossing her fingers for this hunt to be unsuccessful. There was no telling how Nora would react if she saw Stuart Little chewed to death. Fortunately, the fox emerged with nothing but a face full of snow. The next pounce was equally unsuccessful. After a third, the fox stood up, looked around, then trotted out of sight.

When they caught up with the others, Nora told them all about the fox. She repeated the story to Joan when they picked her up at the visitor center just after 3:00.

"It was a silver fox," Nora said.

"I was looking at the very same creature in an exhibit today, but of course it was stuffed. And it's actually a red fox."

"No, it was silver and black," Nora insisted.

"Yes, I'm sure it was, but the kind of fox you saw was a silver-phase red fox. When a red fox has babies, they can be born with different colored fur, including red, or brown, or silver and black like the one you saw. But they're all part of the red fox family." Joan went on to explain more about the *Vulpes vulpes,* including its range and natural enemies, from wolves to bald eagles.

"I bet we'll see more of them when we move to Alaska," Nora said.

"I wouldn't hold your breath on that one, dear," Joan said. "With every Christmas visit, it seems less and less likely that you'll ever be moving north."

"Oh, we're definitely moving there," Nora said, then turned to her mother. "Mom, tell Nana B about the job you're gonna get." Turning back to her grandmother, Nora added, "When this summer comes, we're outta here."

Dylan had been focusing intently on his Game Boy but had become distracted by the conversation. At Nora's comment, he let out a faint groan.

"You didn't tell me you had a job," Joan said.

"I'm applying for jobs. Two, actually," Anne said. "I was waiting to see if I got at least a phone interview before telling you. The job situation is a little complicated. First, I want a staff role with health benefits for the family, not a contract job. But you know that. Also, some of the jobs require me to be a resident, which I'm not these days. And with some of the openings, I'm supposed to have a state license that needs to be renewed every two years."

"What are the two jobs you've applied for?"

"Well, one is working with the DoD, Department of Defense, but that's a long shot because most of my experience is in water resource engineering. Long story. Anyway, the other job is with an oil company." Anne waited for the reaction she was sure would come.

Joan didn't waste a moment. "I really don't think you need to repeat your father's mistake of supporting the fossil fuel industry, dear. You wouldn't be doing the planet or the next generation any favors, no matter how well the job might pay."

"Mom gets paid pretty good," Nora said.

Joan peered over her granddaughter's head and out the window at the snowy peaks in the distance. "It really makes you think about the word 'environmental' in the term 'environmental engineering.' If we really want to, we can live without petrochemicals and we can wean ourselves off fossil fuels. But we can't live without clean air, clean water and a globe that maintains a relatively stable temperature. By the way, did I tell you I'm getting a Prius? They'll be available next year, and I've already placed my order. I'm sure you've heard about them. They're a big step in the right direction."

Anne had heard it all before, with the exception of the Prius comment. And she'd explained to her mother more than once that the work she did as an environmental engineer was in support of the environment, not in opposition to it.

She also knew that her mother's comment was as much about the opinion she had of Anne's father. He had divorced Joan and moved to Alaska, where he worked on the famous oil pipeline. After the divorce, Anne had made her mother's life very difficult, so difficult that a year later, Joan agreed to allow Anne to move to Alaska and live with her father full-time.

It was a mother-daughter wound that would likely never fully heal, Anne knew. Consciously or not, her mother had taken any fair opportunity over the years to cast anything related to her father in a less than favorable light. Had Dylan Sr. been a surgeon who saved scores of lives over his career, Joan's first comment on the medical profession would no doubt have been about the number of malpractice suits filed against surgeons for leaving behind sponges and surgical instruments in their patients after cutting them open.

Not that her father did anything close to what a surgeon did. He worked as an engineer on the Trans-Alaska Pipeline that ran 800 miles from Prudhoe Bay to the port of Valdez. His primary work was to help design a support system that kept the above-ground sections of the pipeline from rupturing in the event of an earthquake. He did preliminary design work in the field, then support work back in the Anchorage office. He did it for the engineering challenge, for the pay, which was very good, and as a way to distract himself from the biggest failure of his life, which was his marriage.

For his design work, Anne was proud of him. She had never worked for an oil company herself, and would prefer a different industry, but in Alaska the lion's share of engineering work was in oil and gas.

There were times when she would bristle at these kinds of comments from her mother, but more often now she let the urge pass. "I'll tell you when I hear back for certain on anything, Mom. But like Nora said, we're definitely making the move."

Nora smiled at her grandmother. "See, I told you."

*   *   *   *   *

When they got back to the lodge, it was dusk. The sky had cleared, and the air was cold and crisp. Sal had arrived. He had joined Mrs. Engebretsen in setting up the dining room table with everything needed to make Christmas cookies. They were also organizing the ingredients to construct several gingerbread houses.

"Will your girlfriend be coming to the lodge in her own vehicle?" Mrs. Engebretsen asked across the table.

Sal pulled another handful of gingerbread squares out of a box and stacked them on a plate. He shook his head, then said, "No, we had a last-minute change in plans. She won't be coming to the lodge."

A look of concern came over Mrs. Engebretsen. "I hope Malia is not ill."

"The thing is…" Sal began but paused, because even though he knew that he and Malia would not be together again, he had not actually delivered that news to any person face-to-face, and he found himself

123

struggling to get it out. "Yesterday, we kind of had a fight and now we're not…it looks like now we're not really…"

Sal didn't have to finish his thought. Mrs. Engebretsen did it for him. "Oh no, Sal. You and your girlfriend have broken up? I'm so sorry. Do you think it's a temporary thing?"

Sal shook his head again, this time slowly, as if to put a fine point on the finality of the breakup. "This time it's for good. I have to admit it took me by surprise."

"Yes," Mrs. Engebretsen said with a few solemn nods. "They happen so often at Christmas, Sal. It's the end of the year approaching fast, and people tend to assess the state of their relationships at this time. Also, we have a big crowd of people here, and Malia has never really met most of us, so there may be some anxiety about that."

"She gets really nervous about meeting new people and staying in new places. It's always been that way."

"Well, there you go, Sal. And this year, there's so much more anxiety floating around because of Y2K."

After helping Mrs. Engebretsen, Sal went into the kitchen to assist Mr. Engebretsen in making Norwegian glogg, a mulled wine served at Christmastime. They stood at the stove, heating up two pots that were spiced with cinnamon, ginger, clove, cardamom, flaked almonds, raisins and orange peel. The pot for adults included red wine and a little cognac, while the kids' was made with fruit juice. The simmering glogg filled the lodge with the wonderful aroma of holiday spices.

As they stirred the pots, Sal and Mr. Engebretsen discussed what, if any, of the predicted Y2K disasters might take place a week later when the date on computers changed from the year 1999 to 2000. It was a giant digital cliff that the world was about to step off, and speculation was leading to wild, catastrophic scenarios. Some thought planes would drop from the sky at midnight because the computers that controlled their engines would stop functioning. Others believed that the banking system would seize up. People wouldn't be able to withdraw any of their money, and companies wouldn't be able to process any online transactions.

"I think it's a bunch of crap," Sal said. "I think everything's gonna be fine."

"Then you don't understand what's at the heart of the problem," Mr. Engebretsen said. "You see, data storage in the first computers was very limited and costly, so the engineers shortened the year on dates to two digits. Right now it's 1999, but computers only see the year as 99. Instead of the year changing to 2000, computers will think it's the year 1900. That's a recipe for complete chaos."

Mr. Engebretsen had a brownish red beard trimmed short and a thick moustache that curled back toward his ears. He twirled one end of it as he continued, "Just make sure, Sal, that you're not out driving on New Year's Eve because at midnight all the traffic lights are going to malfunction. They're all controlled by a central computer, you know. I work for the city, so I'm aware of these things. When you see the traffic light ahead of you turn green, you won't know for sure that the other fella is getting a red light. He might be seeing a green light as well. We've trusted the traffic light system for generations, but that all ends on New Year's Eve. This could result in numerous accidents. Other systems will also experience disastrous breakdowns."

In the event of a food shortage, Sal admitted that he would be unprepared. Back at his apartment, his backup supply amounted to a few canned goods. The Engebretsens, on the other hand, had a cellar stocked with jars of canned vegetables and tins of mackerel, herring and anchovies. Their basement refrigerator also contained many jars of lutefisk packed in oil. If the power grid went down, Mr. Engebretsen stressed, the perishable lutefisk would need to be eaten very quickly.

As Mr. Engebretsen was calculating the shelf life of unrefrigerated lutefisk, Matthew walked into the kitchen and said, "That smells amazing. I think you've outdone yourself with the glogg this year."

Turning to Sal, Matthew continued, "So what's the word? Did you come alone?"

Sal nodded. "We're done. The last fight was a rehearsal. This one is the real thing."

"Oh, man, I'm sorry," Matthew said. "The holidays make it worse. There are so many breakups at this time of year."

Mr. Engebretsen poured out glasses of glogg, and the three men had a discussion that began with Sal's breakup but quickly moved along to the dissolution of Mr. Engebretsen's first marriage and the tragic ending to Matthew's first real romance.

In the end, Matthew brought it back to Sal. "What about that woman who works at the café on Capitol Hill. The one on 15th. You should stop by and see her."

"We've chatted a two or three times, but I'm pretty sure she's got a boyfriend."

"Find out if she's happy with him," Matthew said.

"My head's not anywhere near where it needs to be for that. I just want to survive the holidays. Maybe in a month or so."

"Ha!" Mr. Engebretsen said. "You assume there's going to be a January. Y2K might just make everything disappear, including the calendar."

By 4:30, the lodge glowed with a crackling fire. Mr. Engebretsen took the pots of spiced glogg off the stove and ladled the warm, ruby liquid into mugs, serving the children first. They were sitting around the big table, where Mrs. Engebretsen distributed cookie cutters in various shapes: trees, stars, snowflakes, bells, holly, candy canes, angels, stockings and snowmen. The children pressed the cutters into the dough, then placed the floppy shapes onto baking sheets. When one was filled, Mrs. Engebretsen brought it to the kitchen for baking. As the last of the dough was being cut into shapes, the first batch of baked cookies arrived at the table to be decorated.

Next, she led the kids in the making of gingerbread houses. Mrs. Engebretsen was a tall woman, a good four inches taller than her husband, and she raised the pitch of her voice when giving the children instructions, so all paid close attention. Big plates of gingerbread in different shapes—squares, rectangles and triangles—sat in the middle of the table, along with icing to hold the pieces together, powdered sugar, candy canes, M&Ms and other sweet adornments.

Five of the seven kids had experience from previous years but for the two youngest kids, Diana Lambert and Randy Schuler, this was their first attempt. For inspiration, Mrs. Engebretsen gave each a few pictures of simple gingerbread houses. Dylan had made one every Christmas at Goat Creek Lodge. This year, he informed Mrs. Engebretsen, he wanted to build a gingerbread Naboo Starfighter. She was initially flummoxed by the notion until Dylan drew a rough sketch of the *Star Wars* spacecraft. With a serrated knife, she carved pieces of gingerbread into the special shapes required. She also made him an extra-thick batch of icing that behaved more like aviation adhesive than regular frosting.

Four gingerbread houses were finished, one was abandoned, and one ended up looking like a lean-to. The Naboo Starfighter was declared a limited success. When Dylan brought it back home, he would need a razor knife to round out the many odd angles.

The Schuler family prepared the Christmas Eve dinner. They cooked a turkey in their cabin's oven, and at 6:00 they carefully walked the turkey across to the lodge. Other adults carried the side dishes, while kids lit the way with flashlights.

Dinner stretched slowly into a dessert of Christmas cookies and more glogg. At 7:30, Matthew and Sal put on jackets and boots and headed out to the fire pit, where they brushed snow off the stack of madrona wood, started a good-sized fire, then arranged several Adirondack chairs around the upwind side of the pit.

The lodge didn't have a dishwasher, so the kitchen was busy with people washing, drying and putting everything away. When that was done, they all headed out to the pit, where the kids were making snow figures—a snowman, a giant lizard and a shark. Dylan and Nathan were finishing up a four-foot-tall Death Star. To the uneducated eye, it was nothing more than a giant snowball.

The discussion around the fire moved from the growth of dot-com businesses to the more personal. Zoey Schuler talked about the rough fall the family had experienced. In October, their Jack Russell terrier was hit by a car and had to be put to sleep. The kids had named the dog Freckles, and Zoey explained how it was not the first time Freckles had gotten loose and dashed across their busy street, oblivious to the traffic. In that sense, it wasn't the smartest dog in the world, but the whole family mourned the loss nonetheless.

On top of that, Zoey's mother had been diagnosed in November with breast cancer. The news arrived just as they were beginning to get over Freckles' death, and it cast a pall over the Thanksgiving holiday. The cancer had been caught early enough that the prognosis was fair to good. Still, the family was looking at a challenging winter and spring.

Renee shared the story of her sister, who had been diagnosed with breast cancer in 1996 and, so far, hadn't had a recurrence. Her treatment included chemotherapy and partial mastectomy. Zoey explained all the options her mother was considering, and various opinions were offered. They were actually more like thoughts and sympathies than opinions, because nobody wanted to suggest that they were disagreeing with the course of action Zoey's mother was taking.

The adults settled into a somber silence, and the wind shifted just enough to cause Matthew and Anne, who were seated at one end of the semicircle, to pick up their chairs and move them to the opposite end. The mood lightened with the return of Mrs. Engebretsen. She had gone to fetch her guitar. As she began tuning it, an errant shot from a snowball fight among the kids almost knocked Doug Lambert's mug of glogg out of his hand.

With a raised voice, Mrs. Engebretsen called the children over to the fire pit. When they settled onto empty seats, the lap of a parent or on the snow, she announced, "I want to share a traditional Norwegian folk tune that's sung around the holidays. It's called *Musevisa,* or *The Mouse Song.* I'll tell you the story in English, then sing it in Norwegian." As Mrs. Engebretsen strummed the guitar, she told the children about a mouse family on Christmas Eve. Father Mouse warns his children about a dangerous device called a mousetrap. If the little ones avoid the trap, they will celebrate a happy Christmas.

"That's what my dad does," Nora called out. "He murders mice!"

Her comment drew plenty of laughter and a sympathetic look or two in Matthew's direction. Anne asked Nora to please not interrupt Mrs. Engebretsen, and for the record, her father had sworn off mousetraps.

"That better be true," Nora said. Turning to Mrs. Engebretsen, she added, "I'm sorry I interrupted."

Mrs. Engebretsen continued with the story and told how the mice swept the house clean with their tails while dancing a polka. Then they made a Christmas tree out of an old boot by decorating it with nails and cobwebs. They danced around the boot and listened to Grandma Mouse sing a fairy tale. The story ended with a final warning:

Old Granny's getting tired, soon comes the early dawn.

As morning is approaching, she cannot help but yawn.
Christmas is a lot of fun for each and every mouse.
Be careful of the mousetraps in this trap-infested house!

Mrs. Engebretsen then sang the tune in Norwegian, which was followed by more familiar Christmas songs. After the fire was stoked a couple more times, the younger kids were sent off to get ready for bed. The older ones were allowed to stay up with the adults, at least until the flames subsided to embers. Eventually, it became too chilly around the pit, and everyone said good night and Merry Christmas, then headed off to sleep.

*   *   *   *   *

The first one to wake up on Christmas morning was Nora. Like everyone else, she was tired from the previous day and wanted nothing more than to stay under the warm covers. With her belief in Santa Claus a thing of the past, there was no need to rush to the tree and discover what he had brought. Her parents had told her they would be opening their gifts together after everyone had breakfast.

But Nora did have another reason to climb out of bed early: thirst. At 7:00, just as the dawn sky began to cast a faint glow, she got out of bed, put on her slippers and shuffled down the chilly hallway to get a glass of water in the kitchen. The kitchen was still too dark for her to see what she was doing, so she turned on an overhead light.

There on the floor, barely three steps in front of her, she saw a dead mouse facedown with its little forelegs stretched out in front of it. Across its lower back, the metal bar of a trap held the tiny body in a death grip. During the night, the mouse had been caught in the undiscovered trap but not quite killed. With its upper body free, it had dragged itself from behind the trash can and across the kitchen floor as far as it could before expiring.

Nora instantly jumped back and screamed. It took her less than a second to decide where the blame lay. She dashed out of the kitchen, through the great room, and into the mudroom, where she pulled on her boots and grabbed her jacket. Out the front door of the lodge she raced, down the front walkway, past the fire pit and across the snowy field until she reached its center. The chilly morning was as still and peaceful as

129

anybody could hope for on Christmas Day, but all that peace was pierced as Nora shrieked, "My father murdered the Christmas Mouse!" She broadcast the accusation over and over again, like a lighthouse sending its pulse of brightness at regular intervals.

A light came on in one of the surrounding cabins, then in the one next to it. In the lodge, everyone was rousted from sleep by the noise. Matthew stumbled out of bed and slammed his big toe into a dresser.

"Son of a bitch!" he yelled.

Anne immediately recognized what was happening and what needed to be done. As she pulled on her pants, she said, "She's yelling about a mouse...oh God, there she goes again...didn't you get all the traps in the kitchen?"

"Yes, I did! Jesus, I hope I haven't broken my fucking toe."

Anne dashed down the hall, past Sal, who asked if anything was wrong, past her mother, who asked, "What in the Lord's name has possessed your daughter on Christmas morning?" and past Dylan, who had conducted a quick investigation in the kitchen and confirmed, "Dad missed a trap."

Anne burst out the front door of the lodge and interrupted Nora mid-shriek. When Nora saw her mother bounding across the field with clouds of snow kicking up behind her, she ran in the other direction. Her feet sank deep into the loose powder while her mother began rapidly closing the distance between them.

The chase ended before Nora could reach the far side of the field. She kicked in vain as her mother picked her up and slung her over a shoulder the same way she had done the day before. "Stop it right now, Nora! Not one more word."

Mrs. Engebretsen appeared on the porch of her cabin in a bathrobe and called, "Anne, it sounds like I may have given poor Nora nightmares by singing *Musevisa* last night. Tell her that no mice are injured in the story. Nobody gets murdered."

When Nora walked into the great room, she was greeted by a jury that was very much awake, although none of them wanted to be. They were still in their sleepwear and drowsy, looking like apartment residents who had been forced to flee their homes in the middle of the night because of a fire.

Anne looked at Nora and said, "Now I want you to apologize for waking everyone up and scaring them half to death."

Nora, however, was anything but contrite. She pointed a finger toward the kitchen. "Look for yourself! Somebody in this room murdered the Christmas Mouse, and I think we all know who that is."

Matthew sat on a couch, rubbing his foot. He looked up and said, "Squids, I didn't set that trap. It was the owner of the lodge." She began to rebut his statement, but Matthew interrupted her. "We'll talk about it later. Right now, you need to do what your mother told you to do and apologize to everybody."

Joan added her own testimony. "For heaven's sake, child, you can't go running into the first light of day screaming like a banshee because a mouse gets caught in a trap. It's how the mouse herd gets thinned and how their gene pool gets stronger. Someday, traps won't work because mice will evolve beyond them. That's the day we'll be in real trouble. And by the way, there is no such thing as a Christmas Mouse. I've never heard that term in my entire life."

"Well," Nora began, "it's Christmas, and it's a mouse. Or it was."

Sal yawned as he ran a hand over the stubble of hair on his head. "You know, I really want to go back to sleep, but I know that ain't gonna happen. So let's all move on to breakfast. It's my turn to cook. What does everybody want?"

"Pancakes!" Nora said.

Sal turned to Nora with a mean expression on his face. It wasn't real mean, but as mean as he could look without really meaning it. "Oh no, there will be no pancakes or anything for you until we hear an apology, and I don't think we've heard one yet."

"Alright," Nora said. "I'm sorry that I woke you all up this morning."

Anne prompted, "And that you won't do it again."

"I promise I won't ever do it again. Unless somebody decides to murder…"

"Hey, hey, don't get all political," Sal said. "Just keep it simple."

"OK, I won't do it again. Can we have pancakes now, please?"

Dylan had built a fire and had turned on the coffeemaker, so everybody grabbed a cup and found a place to warm up around the fireplace.

While Sal got breakfast going, Nora successfully pleaded a case to her parents that she be allowed to give the mouse a decent burial. She went to get Emily, who had also been smitten by the movie *Stuart Little*, and the two of them conducted a ceremony down by the creek behind the lodge, where the wet, sandy soil was not frozen solid. Matthew found a shovel in the shed out back and dug a small grave. The mouse had been removed from the trap and placed on a bed of moss inside a matchbox. A few words were said about the fleeting nature of life, the capricious hand of fate, and how everyone needs to learn to respect all creatures, great and small.

As Matthew placed the matchbox into the damp grave and began covering it with sand, tears were shed. "Goodbye, Stuart...I'm sorry you got murdered," Nora said with a solemn wave.

Breakfast managed to wake everybody up and elevate their mood. Sal grilled up some pancakes and bacon. He had planned to have his girlfriend help him cook breakfast, their assigned meal. In Malia's absence, Renee agreed to step in and whip up a dish she had been experimenting with: eggs bhurji, or Indian scrambled eggs. All the special ingredients she needed were in the food supplies she had brought.

The spicy dish brought tears to some eyes. Joan felt compelled to issue a general reminder that she was a native of New England, where hot spices were used very sparingly, if at all. Nora had her stack of pancakes, but instead of covering them with syrup, she rolled them up with eggs bhurji stuffed inside.

The plan for the day was to go sledding up at Paradise, but first the kids had to open their gifts. Anne and Matthew followed the "one big or many small" gifting model, where Dylan and Nora would receive one large gift or many smaller ones if their wish list didn't center on something like a bike. Both kids were used to adjusting their expectations accordingly.

This was a "one big" Christmas for both. Dylan was the first to tear off the wrapping paper. Even though he helped carry the gifts into the lodge the day before and had made a prediction of what his gift was based on the size and weight of the box, he still was amazed when he saw the name of the telescope across the front of the package. It was a Star Surfer 2, the same one his friend Samuel owned. For a long moment he simply stared at the box with wide eyes, then said almost in a whisper, "Perfect."

Nora's gift was even larger than Dylan's and had to be dragged from behind the tree before Nora could get to it. Standing on end, it was half a foot taller than her, and she needed guidance on how exactly to open it. After it was tipped on its side, she tore off the paper, opened the box and pulled out a snowboard. Nora was beside herself with joy. It was called the "Yeti Betty" and had white snow creatures against a purple and red background that made Matthew's eyes hurt. The snowboard came with boots and step-in bindings, which were new that year.

Anne had used Nora's measurements from the snowboarding classes she took at Snoqualmie Pass for the boots. The board was a little on the long side, but the instructor told Anne that Nora had a natural talent for the sport and would be able to manage a longer board. Plus, she wouldn't outgrow it so fast.

Nora held the board above her head and jumped up and down. "This is so rad! I'm gonna bomb on it like nobody's business!"

Nora was whirling with her eyes closed and moving dangerously close to the 12-foot Christmas tree, so Anne brought the celebrating to an end.

"I can ride this today, right, Mom? Up at Paradise? First, I have to show Emily. I have to show her right now. Can I go over to Emily's cabin, Mom?" Nora didn't wait for an answer. "I'll be right back," she said, and went running out the front door holding the board up high. She fell halfway across the snowy field, got up laughing and covered with snow, then continued her charge to the Lamberts' cabin.

"That girl certainly knows how to express her excitement," Joan said.

The adults then opened their gifts. For Anne, they included a bathrobe and a graphing calculator to replace the one she accidentally dropped in a creek while working outside. Among Matthew's were a pair of new work boots and a set of tickets to see the Seattle Thunderbirds hockey team play the Portland Winterhawks.

*   *   *   *   *

The sky was clear on Christmas Day, so when they arrived at the Paradise parking lot, the mountain was out in all its glory. At 5,400 feet, Paradise was near the top of the treeline, and some of the fir trees scattered about were buried so deep in the snow that only their tips showed. Further

133

up the mountain, Rainier rose in jagged rock formations, between which were ancient glaciers with the look of pale-blue waterfalls frozen in motion. Against a deep-blue sky, the 14,410-foot summit was crowned with steam-like clouds.

At 10:30, there was a handful of people in the designated snow-play area, trudging up with their plastic sleds and saucers before flying down. The Engebretsens had brought thermoses with coffee and hot chocolate, along with some of the Christmas cookies baked the day before. They set up a break area at the bottom of the sled runs, so kids and adults could rest and have a snack.

Emily and Nora climbed with their snowboards to the top of the run, then hiked another 300 yards onto a vast open snowfield, where snowboarders and skiers were carving through six inches of fresh powder. Anne joined them for the first hour to make sure that the girls understood the boundaries and knew where not to go, namely toward the western edge of the field, where it dropped steeply down to the Nisqually Glacier.

Matthew, Dylan and Sal had brought snowshoes and began a leisurely trek up the mountain. Unlike summer, when the hiking trails were clearly marked, the snowshoeing routes above Paradise were determined mostly by where previous snowshoers had trod. They went in one direction for a while, then in another, without any danger of being lost because the terrain was all open. After a good two hours of stomping through the snow, they began their descent to the bottom of the sled runs.

"So, Dylanator, have you seen any sign of Wampas up here today?" Sal asked.

"No," Dylan said. "I've been looking around for places they might attack from, but I think there are too many people up here now. They would probably wait until sunset and look for somebody who got lost or maybe someone whose car won't start. But I know for sure where they'd have their caves. Right over there," Dylan said, pointing west across the valley to where the Nisqually Glacier connected with the Wilson Glacier, which rose steeply on the opposite side.

Just as Sal looked in that direction, a low rumble came from high on the mountain, where the sun had melted ice and snow above the 10,000-foot level. They all turned and saw a huge avalanche of rock and ice crashing down from the top of the Nisqually Glacier. It gathered speed and sent a cloud of dirt billowing in front of the main flow.

Matthew felt Dylan back into him and stay there. "Are we OK here?"

He put his hands on Dylan's shoulders. "We're fine. It'll stay down there in the valley."

The dirt cloud grew so large that it concealed the flow itself, and the sound intensified and continued for a full minute before fading away. The cloud dissipated as it rose and drifted east. Below they could see a field of stones and dirty snow covering the glacier.

They continued down to the snow-play area and found their group. Nora and Emily had just taken their last run and were reclining on a snowbank, soaking up the sun. After two hours of repeatedly hiking up the slope and snowboarding down, they were exhausted. Everyone was talking about the avalanche. Sal asked Anne, "Where's your mom and the Engebretsens?"

"They left about an hour ago. My mom is cooking dinner tonight, so she needed to get back early and finish prepping."

Sal smiled at Matthew. "Did you hear that, Mattissimo? Dinner is being prepped."

Matthew was confused, then it hit him. "Oh, yes. I forgot."

Sal had witnessed the brussels sprouts drama over the previous two Christmases, and he thoroughly enjoyed it. After a good laugh, he said, "C'mon, Mahoney. Take it like a man."

*   *   *   *   *

The final dinner at the lodge was served at 5:30, with the great room glowing in the light and the warmth of a big fire. Matthew sat at one end of the table enjoying a beer, but feeling resigned. Joan and Anne delivered one dish after another from the kitchen. Matthew watched them arrive, starting with a platter of odd-looking chicken pieces. They were white mounds the size of Cornish game hens. Next came a bowl of Spanish rice, followed by a sweet potato casserole, stuffing, and a bowl of cinnamon apple cranberry sauce.

He waited for the brussels sprouts to arrive. Instead, he watched Anne take her seat, then Joan, who led the table in saying grace. The sprouts appeared to be a no-show. Could that be possible, Matthew wondered. He wanted to silently celebrate, but something told him it was too soon.

As the dishes made their way around, he took scoops of everything. Anne was sitting beside him and used a pair of tongs to place a piece of chicken on his plate.

"Joan, this all looks terrific," Renee said. "But where are your wonderful brussels sprouts? We look forward to them every year."

"What?" Nora said, looking down the table at her grandmother. "No brussels sprouts, Nana B?" in a voice that revealed her disappointment.

Joan smiled. "I think you're all going to like this." She sliced her mound of chicken in half, then held up the plate for all to see. It was a thin layer of white meat wrapped around a bright green interior. "It's chicken stuffed with brussels sprouts and gruyere cheese. They're all wrapped together. *Ç'est tout d'un morceau.* It's all of a piece!" She said with delight.

"Oh, that's very clever, Joan," Renee said.

"Yay, brussels sprouts!" Nora shouted.

Matthew sliced into his chicken and the familiar acrid smell hit him. When he glanced toward the other end of the table, Sal was looking back at him with a smirk. Matthew scratched his nose with a middle finger, took a generous gulp of beer and got on with the unpleasant task.

*　　*　　*　　*　　*

When twilight faded, the evening sky grew dark enough for stars to shine bright. Being so far from city lights made it much better for stargazing, which is what Dylan wanted to do with his new telescope. All bundled up, he and Matthew headed across the field to the dark fire pit and set the Star Surfer 2 on its mount. Dylan had read through the operator's manual, but he knew most of it already from using Samuel's scope.

"I wish I knew where to look for the space shuttle," Dylan said. "It's up there now. They're repairing the gyroscopes on the Hubble Telescope. The shuttle might not even be over our hemisphere right now though."

The brisk night air was refreshing to Matthew after dinner. He watched Dylan adjust the telescope, quietly bringing the stars into view. The two of them took turns peering through the scope and identifying constellations, from Orion and Andromeda to Taurus and Gemini. After a while, Anne and Nora came out to get a glance at the heavens. Dylan told them how to spot the different stars and planets, then gave Nora explicit instructions on which of the knobs and dials she was not allowed to touch.

With an eye to the scope, Nora said, "I see Jupiter...no, wait, it's Saturn...no, wait, it is Jupiter. I'm 90 percent sure."

As clouds drifted into view and obscured some stars, Dylan said, "Mom, I can't remember what the night sky is like in Anchorage."

"Oh, it's absolutely beautiful. On a clear night in winter, when you get one, it's even darker than this. My dad and I would turn out all the cabin lights and set up a telescope on the second-floor deck. He would borrow one from a friend. In Alaska, you can see the Big Dipper and Little Dipper rotating around Polaris, the North Star. They make a full circle every day. Then there are the meteor showers."

When Dylan turned to face her, she reached out and brushed a hand across his hair. "And from fall to early spring, you can see the northern lights. You're gonna love that. We'll make hot cocoa, wrap ourselves in blankets and watch the colors rippling. It's like a magic show. There's green, red, blue, pink, purple..."

"How do they get the colors?" Dylan asked.

"Well, if I remember correctly," Anne said, "it's from charged particles meeting the atmosphere. When they react with nitrogen, it's one color. If it's oxygen, that's another. And it depends on whether it happens high in the atmosphere or lower down."

"It's pretty cool, D-Man," Matthew said. "I saw it on my first winter trip to Anchorage. Your grandfather had speakers on the deck. We sat back and listened to classical music as we watched the show."

From the front door of the lodge, Renee called out to them. "Hey, Mahoneys, it's time for the lanterns."

Matthew disconnected the telescope from its mount and handed it to Dylan, who cradled it in his arms and carried it safely to its case. Then they all joined Joan, Sal, the Engebretsens and the other families behind the lodge. Small lights illuminated the path down to the banks of Goat Creek. During the snowmelt in spring, it would become a bubbly, gurgling rush of water, but in winter it flowed at a slow, serene pace. Its surface shimmered from the battery-powered lamps set up by Renee and Doug.

137

On the last night at the lodge every Christmas, it was a tradition to light candles and send them floating downstream. Joan had seen it done on a trip to Thailand after she retired from academia. During the Yi Peng Lantern Festival in Chiang Mai, she watched people release hundreds and hundreds of glowing lanterns into the night sky as a way of symbolically letting their problems and worries float away. The lanterns were made of thin rice paper and held small candles to heat the air inside and lift them into the darkness.

The sight of so many bright lanterns rising gracefully, and the meaning behind the ritual, impressed her so much that she introduced it to the Goat Creek Christmas circle in 1996. She altered the ritual in two ways, though. First, she replaced sky lanterns with floating lantern rafts made of rice paper and other biodegradable materials. Second, as the glowing lanterns floated slowly down Goat Creek, they would not only carry away problems and worries of the previous year, but also each person's greatest wish for the coming year. The only restriction on the wish was that it couldn't be for oneself.

When Joan first proposed the idea, it surprised Anne. Such a selfless sentiment didn't exactly fit her mom's personality. Then again, people did change, or at least grow, and if this was the direction her mother's life was beginning to take, Anne wasn't about to question it. And for the last three years, the ritual was one that gave everyone something to feel good about.

The evening air was chilly and damp along the creek, so Joan wasted no time in passing out her handmade lanterns. When that was done, she asked that everyone take a moment to consider what wish they wanted to make. "Remember, it has to be a special wish for somebody else. We can't make the wish for ourselves."

"I have a question, Nana B," Nora said. She was tapping the toe of her boot against the soft, wet sand along the bank. "Can I wish for somebody else to get a million dollars, then give me half of it?"

That drew a few chuckles. "No, you cannot, Nora," Joan said. "That's selfishness in a very thin disguise. This is about focusing on someone else and how they can be helped in the struggles they have with life, about wanting them to succeed or survive, to grow or learn, to endure or blossom. When you focus on improving life for someone else, you might be surprised at how that wish can lead to action that changes both of your lives for the better."

Anne lit one of the long matches used to light the fireplace and lit the candle inside Nora's rice-paper lantern. She moved from one person to the next until all the lanterns were bright. The flames illuminated the translucent paper and made it glow golden amber. Nora stared into her flickering light as she bent down. She waited for the others to do the same before placing her lantern raft on the water and giving it a gentle nudge toward the center of the stream. The 17 lanterns bobbed on the dark surface and were drawn slowly into the current. As they moved downstream and followed the winding course of the creek, their glimmer remained visible through the bare branches of the alder trees along the bank until, one by one, they rounded a bend and disappeared into the night.

Chapter 7
The Crux of Winter

Sunday, February 13, 2000

Ever since 1996, Nora and Dylan had flown east to Ipswich for two weeks to stay with Nana B in the Boushay farmhouse where Anne had grown up. However, the trips never occurred in winter when the New England weather could be harsh and the seashore inhospitable.

Instead, the trips always took place during the summer, when the beaches were open and life was in bloom. From the Boushay farmhouse, it was a very short drive to a nearby beach. It was officially named Crane Beach, but all the locals and people as far away as Boston always referred to it as Cranes Beach. There Joan would take the kids to spend the day splashing in the surf and running through the dunes. She'd pack a lunch that included fresh fruit and greens grown in her own gardens and orchards. On some evenings, they would dine in the screened gazebo on the vast back lawn, where Joan and the children could watch birds hunting for dinner on the flats of the Essex River.

On other evenings, however, Joan and the kids would pile into her Saab at dinnertime and go in quest of the world's best fried clams. Nora and Dylan had grown to love them, and enjoyed traveling to different local restaurants to see whose fried clams were worthy of being crowned that summer's blue-ribbon champion. Past winners included Woodman's of Essex and The Clam Box of Ipswich.

It was a special thing for Anne to know that her kids were growing up with the same sense of place that she had in her early years in Ipswich, and she was grateful that her mother packed as much fun and learning as she could into those two weeks each summer. Having been a teacher helped in making both happen easily.

The ritual meant a lot to Joan as well. She looked forward to it so much that she gladly flew round-trip to Seattle twice each summer so that the children would fly alongside her in each direction rather than be left in the hands of airline employees during their flights.

The talk of a move to Alaska during the approaching summer put the ritual at risk for the new year, since it was unclear exactly when the move would take place and if the kids would be available for a trip back East. Joan let it be known after Christmas that she was willing to have Nora and Dylan visit Ipswich in February.

At first, the plan was to have them visit for one week during the February school vacation. It was the third week of the month. Then Joan suggested the trip be extended to two weeks. When Anne hesitated to take the kids out of school for that extra time, Joan reminded her that she had been taken out of school on two occasions to travel with her parents. Anne finally relented.

"Just explain to the school that it's for family reasons, as well as the children's education," Joan said. "Ask their teachers to assign them a week's worth of homework, and I'll see to it that they complete every exercise."

On February 10, Joan flew to Seattle and checked in again at the Giffordshire House, where she was now on a first-name basis with some of the staff. Over the next few days, she made the rounds of her favorite Seattle museums and saw a pre-Broadway debut of *Martin Guerre* at the 5th Avenue Theatre.

That Sunday afternoon, Anne and Matthew drove Joan and the kids to Sea-Tac for a nonstop flight to Logan in Boston. On the way, Anne gave her mom an update on the job hunt. As expected, she didn't get the job at DoD. The phone interview lasted less than fifteen minutes. Things went better with the ConocoPhillips position. She had two phone interviews, and they wanted to fly her to Anchorage for a final third interview. Before that could happen, the subject of availability came up. They asked if Anne could start work no later than February 15. She explained that she wouldn't be available until the summer when her kids finished school. She might be able to start sometime in May and leave Matthew to care for the kids for a month or so, but the middle of February definitely wouldn't work.

"So that was that," Anne said. "Everything was fine except the timing. I guess I should have thought of that."

"When companies hire, they usually want you to start yesterday," Joan said. "Plus, where would you stay if you moved up there on short notice? Your house is rented right now, isn't it?"

"That's another thing we have to deal with. The tenants gave their notice last month, so the place will be empty on March 1," Anne said.

"Can't you just rent it to someone else until you all go up there?"

"It's not easy to rent a place that size for just four or five months." Anne was going to add that the place being empty meant that she and Matthew would have that much less money in a budget that was already tight. But she knew that would only prompt her mother to offer to help them out financially.

Nora had been bored by the conversation, and was more interested in talking about her coming two weeks on the East Coast. She explained how it would be different from summer trips when beaches were the main venue. "We'll be spending a lot of time with witches, Mom. Salem has a ton of witch stuff. We'll be going to the witch museum, the witch dungeon, the witch house, the witch history museum and...ah...the witch village."

"And the pirate museum," Dylan added.

"Yes, the pirate museum too," Nora confirmed.

"As long as you both finish all your homework assignments on time," Anne said.

"For sure," Nora replied.

"Definitely," Dylan said.

After Joan and the kids boarded their flight, Matthew and Anne headed into Seattle for a museum visit of their own. It was an exhibit of *Titanic* artifacts that was traveling to different cities around the country.

It had caught Anne's attention when she was watching a story on TV about how a submersible vessel had discovered the *Titanic*'s wreckage and retrieved various items. Some of them were quite fascinating, like glass vials of perfume that were still sealed, a set of silver serving dishes, a matching Edwardian cobalt and gold dinner plate and teacup, and an assortment of jewelry worn by some of the wealthier passengers.

Many of the items were made of gold: a man's pocket watch, a set of stickpins, and a brooch in the shape of a bow with a diamond centerpiece. There were gold rings with clusters of diamonds, one that had diamonds surrounding a large sapphire, diamond cuff links set in onyx and gold, a

142

gold link bracelet with scripted silver letters spelling out the name "Amy," and a silver necklace and pendant with an array of sparkling jewels.

The collection gave Anne an idea, and when she shared it with Matthew, he agreed. They would visit the exhibit twice to determine exactly what it would take to successfully complete a heist. Like all their other adventure games, it was meant purely for fun.

They parked in Belltown around 4:30 and walked toward the Seattle Center. Matthew brought a small backpack so they could pick up a few things at a favorite wine and cheese shop. It was on the way and closed at 5:00. The plan was to spend a couple of hours walking around the exhibit, looking for cameras, motion detectors, emergency exits, alarms and the like. But when they got in line at the ticket booth just before 5:00, an attendant closed the front doors and announced that the last tickets were now being sold and the exhibit itself would close in one hour at 6:00.

"Excuse me," Matthew said as the attendant was returning to the booth. "I thought you closed at 7:00 tonight, not 6:00."

The attendant was a guy who looked to be around 30, and Matthew sensed that he either hated his job or had grown bored with it. On the pocket of his starched white dress shirt was a silver name tag that read "Mel." He didn't seem to have much patience for Matthew's question and answered with more than a hint of sarcasm after pointing to something above the booth.

"We made a sign with the hours printed really big up there, so people wouldn't get confused. See, Saturdays we close at 7:00, Sundays at 6:00."

Mel then went into the booth, where another attendant was selling tickets. She and Mel proceeded to get into an argument about closing duties. They were short-handed and had a long list of tasks to complete by 7:00 when all the night alarms switched on and they needed to be out of the building. It was helpful information for Matthew and Anne to learn.

After they paid cash for their tickets, which were designed to look like White Star Line boarding passes for the RMS *Titanic*'s fateful maiden voyage, they found a quiet spot to chat for a moment.

"I'm not seeing any cameras in the lobby," Anne said.

"Me neither," Matthew said. He gestured toward the entrance. "The front doors have contact alarms. That's all."

The last people to buy tickets were a couple with a boy about Dylan's age. Matthew and Anne followed them into the first exhibit room, which detailed the vessel's construction in a Belfast shipyard. The room had a 15-foot ceiling and contained several salvaged artifacts, as well as some re-creations. At one end of the room, an enormous propeller was positioned at an angle against the wall. As large as it was, a printed description stated that the center propeller, called the mid-propeller, on the *Titanic* was actually a little more than 16 feet tall, while the two wing propellers were 23 feet tall and weighed 38 tons each.

Matthew became so engrossed while reading all the details about the ship—how it was made, what each deck contained, and how it was divided into 16 watertight compartments—that after many minutes passed, Anne had to remind him why they were there. "Focus, Matt. Finish looking around, then let's move on. I saw one camera as we entered this room, and there's another in the archway as we leave."

The exhibit flowed through rooms full of other artifacts, including sections of the ship's hull and interior; assortments of cutlery, china and cookware; and clothing and personal items. Placards detailed the living conditions of the passengers in the various classes: first, second and third, as well as steerage. One hallway between rooms was a re-creation of a corridor through a first-class deck, with a doorway opening into a suite of elegantly appointed living quarters. Another room showed typical third-class accommodations—a small space with two bunk beds. As spartan as third-class lodgings were, they included electricity and running water, more typical of second-class quarters on other ships.

Anne herself had a little difficulty staying focused on their task. She made a mental note of the one emergency exit they had passed so far, and estimated that the door opened onto another interior part of the building rather than the exterior. The cameras in each room were counted, as well as alarms and motion detectors, which were located near the most sensitive areas.

As far as security guards, they had only noticed one. He moved slowly through the rooms, pausing occasionally when an overly curious visitor leaned too far into a display, causing an alarm to sound. Anne counted three times that he had looped through the exhibit while they were there.

When Matthew and Anne entered the second-to-last room, Anne's eyes were drawn immediately to the jewelry. It sat in sealed cases that were expertly lit, so that the gold and silver shimmered brightly, and all the precious stones sent sharp, piercing reflections off their many facets. The brilliance of the display drew Anne closer. As she peered through the protective glass, it was easy to imagine seeing the jewelry shining in all its splendor across the table from her at dinner on the doomed vessel. She also imagined the eight-piece band—the one that played on deck until the bitter, cold end as some of the passengers boarded lifeboats—playing during dinner service in the first-class dining room.

"Focus, Boushay," Matthew said. His comment brought Anne back to the moment.

He drew Anne's attention to an exit door nearby. Then they began to scan the room for security features. As they did, an announcement over the speaker system told them that the exhibit was closing in five minutes and could everyone please proceed directly to the lobby exit.

There were seven other people nearby, and one by one they moved into the final exhibit room. The last to leave the room were Matthew and Anne. She said softly, "That exit door near the jewelry cases should lead directly to a parking lot or the street. That's good."

The final room was a re-creation of the *Titanic*'s forward grand staircase with rich wood panels and ornately carved details. The staircase had gilded balustrades made of polished oak and wrought-iron railings. They rose to a large landing, where the staircase split right and left to continue up to the next deck of the ship. The whole scene captured the luxury and grandeur of the actual *Titanic*.

One by one, the other visitors took their final photos and headed down the hallway to the lobby. Matthew began to walk in that direction himself when Anne grabbed his arm and pointed to a poorly lit space at the rear of the staircase, where, on the real *Titanic,* stairs would have descended down to another deck.

Matthew didn't understand. "What?"

"I think there's another exit back there. I want to check."

Matthew heard a woman's voice in the lobby thanking people for visiting. Whoever was speaking wasn't in view, nor was the remaining guard, who presumably was still working.

"Nobody knows we're still here," Anne whispered. "C'mon. We'll just be a second."

The long velvet rope stretching in front of the staircase held a sign reading "No Visitors Beyond This Point." They stepped over the rope and looked around for security devices. Anne pointed to a box shooting a thin red beam of laser light a foot above the floor. They carefully stepped over it and continued to the back of the staircase.

Small lights that Anne thought might mark an emergency exit turned out to be part of an electrical panel. Just as they were about to return to the front of the room and leave the exhibit, they heard footsteps and someone speaking over a two-way radio. It was the security guard. He had come from the first room of the exhibit and was confirming that each successive room was clear of visitors.

As the guard approached the room with the grand staircase, Matthew and Anne looked at each other, wondering what to do. If they stepped out from behind the staircase now, the guard would see them standing where they weren't supposed to be. That could be a problem. If they stayed where they were, they might get locked in the exhibit overnight.

Back in his days as a teenager in South Boston, Matthew had always had the same reaction when he was somewhere he wasn't supposed to be and confronted with someone wearing a badge and uniform. Either run or hide, but never surrender. If he'd had the time to think about it in this situation, he would have chosen to surrender, but his instincts from decades before kicked in. He quickly crouched down in the shadows. Then he pulled on Anne's sweatshirt, and she followed suit.

They listened as the guard walked further into the room. When he reached the front of the staircase, he stopped. For several seconds there was no sound other than the ticking of a clock and a door closing out in the lobby. Matthew and Anne looked at each other, waiting to hear whether the guard had detected them somehow.

From the radio came Mel's voice, echoing in the vaulted staircase. The guard responded, "Staircase is clear." Then the guard resumed his slow walk toward the lobby.

"Matt, what are we doing?" Anne whispered when the guard was out of earshot.

"Shhh. He might come back."

"Why didn't we just say we didn't see the sign or something?"

Matthew had been staring in the direction of the lobby and listening intently. He turned toward Anne and gave her a look. "Why did we come back here in the first place? Whose idea was it to see if there was another exit?"

"It looked like there might be one, OK? That's what this visit is for. To gather information."

"Well, we've definitely confirmed that there is no door back here."

"We should walk out there right now and say we got lost," Anne whispered.

"I think it's a little late for that. We could be in serious trouble, especially if that guard has a gun and gets all freaked out. Did he have a gun? Did you see one?"

"I don't know. Maybe. I can't remember. Still, we should…"

Matthew interrupted, "They said they had to be out before seven when the night alarm comes on. I don't know what happens when the alarm comes on, but I think we want to leave before then, too. But we'll have to wait until they all leave. Then we make our move."

"How are we supposed to get out of this place?"

Matthew took a deep breath, then remembered their conversation in the previous room. "You said there's an exit back there that goes to the exterior. We'll leave that way. And we'll leave before seven."

They listened in silence for a few minutes. They could hear Mel's voice and the voice of the other attendant, but the sounds were muffled. From being inside the ticket booth, Matthew assumed. He pulled his phone out of his pocket and checked the time. It was 6:12.

Suddenly the lights in their room went out. Not all of them, but enough to give the space a somewhat spooky feel.

Anne whispered that she was going to stand up because her knees were starting to ache from being crouched down. Matthew did the same and noticed that half the lights in the previous room had been turned off as well.

Anne pointed to the top of the staircase. "Let's wait up there," she whispered. "We'll have a better view."

They walked to the front of the stairway and slowly climbed 12 steps to a landing. On the wall above, an antique-looking clock with Roman

147

numerals ticked off each second. Anne gestured to the right and they climbed nine more steps to the top. After sitting down, they had a good view of the room below while remaining hidden themselves in the shadows.

"This is the second time things have gotten really weird," Anne whispered. "I was hoping we had used up our bad luck at HighLife last year."

Matthew took off his backpack and zipped it open. At the wine and cheese shop, they had picked up some Camembert, two kinds of goat cheese, a strong Stilton and a Wensleydale. They had also bought three bottles of their favorite wines, including a pinot noir with a screw top. Matthew pulled it from the backpack. "We could be here more than a half hour. I think I could use a drink while we wait."

He opened it, and they passed the bottle back and forth. As their eyes grew used to the dim light, they were able to see more details of the grand staircase. At the very bottom, a shiny gold cherub stood atop a railing that ran up the middle of the steps. In its left hand, the cherub held a light in the shape of a torch, which had gone out when the main lights were turned off.

Anne stared at the figure. "That's a really big cherub," she said.

"Is it?" Matthew asked idly.

"Yes, for a cherub that's pretty big."

"You've seen a lot of cherubs, have you?"

"I've seen my share," Anne said.

"I'm sure there are bigger cherubs somewhere," Matthew said.

Anne turned and gave him an incredulous look. "Really? Well, that's easily the biggest cherub I've ever seen, and I'm pretty sure that I've seen more cherubs than you have."

"Maybe you have seen more cherubs than me, but not necessarily. I've seen a lot of cherubs myself."

"OK, tell me the last time you saw a cherub," Anne said.

Matthew handed the bottle to Anne, then folded his hands in thought. Seconds passed.

"See, you can't remember," Anne said.

"OK, when was the last time you saw a cherub then?"

Anne raised the bottle slowly and took a swig. "You mean, before this cherub here...the one that we're looking at down the stairs..."

"You're stalling," Matthew said. "You can't remember the last time you saw a cherub either."

Anne was silent for a moment. It seemed she wouldn't remember, but suddenly she said, a little too loudly, "the Junction."

"Shhh."

"The Junction," Anne whispered. "The bakery...the French bakery. In the front window last week, I saw a chocolate cake with two cherubs holding up a big red heart. It was a display of different cakes. They all had a Valentine's Day theme." She turned to Matthew and handed him the bottle. "You remember Valentine's Day, Matt, right?"

"Sure."

"So, when is it?" Anne asked.

"It's soon. Let's see..."

"It's tomorrow, Matt. Monday, the 14th. Valentine's Day is less than six hours from now."

"I know it is."

"And you planned ahead and got me something, didn't you?"

Matthew paused. "I did, actually. I have a gift that's all wrapped up and hidden away."

Anne shook her head and laughed softly. "You lie, Mahoney. You shouldn't lie about things like that."

Matthew turned to her. "So tell me that you got me a really amazing gift that's wrapped and waiting for me to open tomorrow."

"Shhh. You're louder than me," Anne whispered. "I'm just teasing, you know. Mostly."

They both leaned back and listened for a minute to the clock above the landing ticking away the time. Anne swept a hand slowly across the dark floor. When she found Matthew's hand, she squeezed it. "I didn't buy you a gift for this year yet. I had trouble deciding. Or even coming up with a good idea. Last year I got you running shoes."

"Which was fine," Matthew said.

Anne turned to look at him. "No, it wasn't fine. There's nothing romantic about running shoes. What's the point of giving someone running shoes for Valentine's Day when you could do it on their birthday, or when they could just buy them for themselves? Which you would have done within a couple of weeks. The whole point is just...lost. I hate to say it, but

149

I was going to drive to Home Depot tomorrow morning and get you a gift card. That would have been the absolute rock bottom of Valentine's Day gifts."

"I was planning to get you something for you at the art museum gift shop downtown…" Matthew began.

"That's what you did the last two years. You went in there and asked one of the women in the gift shop what to get me."

"Yes, I did. What's wrong with that?"

"Nothing, Matt. The earrings are nice. I mean that. I like both sets of them. Especially the little bears. But the thing is…and don't take this wrong…someone I don't know is deciding what jewelry I wear. That shouldn't bother me really. I know that. And as I said, I do like the earrings. There's nothing wrong with them. My point is that the holiday itself is really corrupt. It's all about getting people to spend more money. I never used to think this, but now I think it's the least romantic day of the year. The whole day, the whole 24 hours, should just be carved out of the calendar. February is already a screwed-up month as it is."

Anne turned back toward the cherub to consider what she had just said. "So here's what I'm thinking, and I'm deciding this right now…no more Valentine's Day gifts for either one of us, OK? From now on, let's do something special for Valentine's Day instead. Something we'll remember for the rest of our lives."

Matthew had been anxiously trying to follow whatever course of thought his wife's mind was taking, and he felt a sense of relief to hear it end at a place that would probably make their lives simpler and not more complicated. "Sounds good to me. When do you want to do something?"

"Tonight."

"OK," Matthew said. "Where do you want to do it? Downtown? We're practically there already."

"On the *Titanic,*" Anne said.

Matthew was confused for a moment. "What do you mean, 'on the *Titanic'*?" A moment later, he understood. "Oh, you mean 'on the *Titanic.*'. Like right here, right now."

"What's wrong, Matt? Are you afraid?"

"No. I mean, I'm not afraid afraid." Matthew paused as he struggled with an image. "But I guess I am afraid of literally getting caught with my pants down if somebody walked in."

"I can remember a time when you weren't afraid of anything," Anne said.

Matthew looked around for the screw top and when he found it, he capped the bottle. "Alright, but if the cops show up, you're doing all the talking this time."

They undressed slowly, careful not to make much noise. The only thing close to a loud sound was when the metal buckle of Matthew's belt dropped down one of the steps. After that, they paused only once so that Matthew could slide his pants between the cold floor and his bare skin.

When the clock above the grand staircase showed the time as 6:48, Anne was pulling on her boots. She turned to Matthew and smiled. "That was nice." She leaned in and gave him a kiss. "It was really nice. I think it was worth having us get stuck in here."

Matthew opened his phone to check the time. "I'm definitely not gonna forget this Valentine's Day."

"Now that I think of it, Matt, there is one gift you can get me this year. I guess it's more of a favor. Since you've got free time this week, could you take my boots to that cobbler on Admiral Way and get them resoled? I've been putting it off for the longest time. Maybe that's what's messing with our luck. My boots. It might be their cry for help."

Matthew noticed that Anne's braid had come loose. He felt around on the floor until he found her elastic hairband. Anne asked what he was doing.

He showed her the band. "Turn around," he said. "Let me fix your hair." One of Matthew's unsung skills was knowing how to do a French braid. In their current situation, he went with a quick version. As he braided, they listened to the two attendants, who were still chatting away in the lobby, trading opinions about a new bistro that had opened across from Key Arena.

"I'm thinking about a cherub lamp," Anne said. "One with a cherub holding a torch underneath the lampshade. Or maybe it doesn't need a shade. That way, you can always see the torch, which would be kind of cool. As long as it's not too bright. I'll discuss it with Jeremy."

151

When Matthew finished the braid, he wrapped the band around the end. Then he checked the time again. It was 6:51. Just as he was starting to grow nervous, there came different noises from the lobby—cabinets opening and closing, the jingling of keys, comments about having a good night—that made it seem like the attendants were preparing to leave the building. Next came beeping noises, followed by a loud boom as a heavy metal door slammed shut, and finally, the sound of locks being turned.

The lobby went silent. Matthew nodded to Anne. They both stood up and held hands. The ticking of the clock seemed louder as they walked down the stairway and took one giant step over the thin red laser beam. They paused for a moment when they entered the room with the jewelry and looked one last time at their imaginary treasures, some of which sparkled alluringly even in the dim light.

At the exit door, Matthew checked his phone one last time. 6:55. Anne looked at the wiring around the door and at the push bar that emergency exits typically had. She put her ear to the space where the door met the frame and felt a faint breeze. She could also hear the sound of voices, many voices.

"I don't know where this leads," she whispered, "but I think it's street level, and I think it's outside."

"When we get out there, if it's outside, we need to walk away," Matthew said. "Just keep walking no matter what anybody says to us. Not too fast."

Anne pulled her sweatshirt sleeve over her right hand so she wouldn't leave fingerprints on the metal bar. "Attention, all passengers," she said. "Prepare to abandon ship." Then she pushed the door open. An alarm began ringing immediately. It was loud, shockingly loud. She reached for Matthew's hand, and they stepped into the cool evening air. They were on the landing of a fire escape. They could see streetlights through a row of trees that stood between their landing and the nearby street. A staircase to the right led up. Anne pulled Matthew to the left, and they descended a half flight to a cement walkway.

The walkway led between two trees and onto the sidewalk, which was full of people moving in one direction, from left to right, up Second Ave. To their left was the intersection with Denny Way, where they saw a cop standing in the middle of the street. While directing heavy traffic, the cop was looking around to pinpoint the source of the alarm, but the sound was bouncing off different building surfaces and the cop was trying not to be hit by passing vehicles.

"There's a hockey game tonight," Matthew said. "That's where everyone is going. The Thunderbirds are playing at Key Arena."

They had parked on Broad Street, which was on the other side of Denny Way, but Matthew and Anne both knew they'd stand out by walking against the flow of people; plus they'd be doing it right in front of the cop. So instead, they stepped into the stream of Thunderbirds' fans and flowed with them toward Key Arena. They would gladly take the long way back to their car if it meant getting away from the scene cleanly.

Behind them, the door alarm still rang loudly, but nobody on the crowded sidewalk was paying attention. It was just one more bit of background sound in a big, noisy city.

*   *   *   *   *

In the winter of 2000, a fever was sweeping across Seattle. The city was caught up in the dot-com boom. Everyone was either working for or investing in a dot-com startup, or knew someone who was. During nearly every shift Matthew bartended at Roy's that winter, he overheard people talking about the latest, greatest idea for a new online business. More than simple conversation, it was a buzz that revealed the sense of excitement people feel when they hear about a deal they think will make them a shit-ton of money.

As someone who had placed plenty of bets over the years, Matthew could see the look in a person's eyes, he could hear it in their voice, and he could sense it in the way they slapped a credit card down on the bar when it came time to pick up a big tab. Everyone wanted in on whatever kind of deal they could get, whether that meant investing money or slaving away for 80 hours a week in a startup job that promised a pot of gold in stock options once the company went public.

Matthew couldn't count all the different business ideas he had overheard at the bar, but he remembered one night someone saying they'd secured $4 million of venture capital to start an online store to sell only blue jeans at www.justjeans.com. Two nights later, he overheard someone

153

else who had pitched an idea for a dot-com delivery business to sell fresh vegetables at www.justgreens.com.

The fever wasn't affecting Matthew personally. He was staying on the sidelines and trying to keep his household budget in the black. Winter was the lean season for him and his A Crew, and the year 2000 was turning out to be the leanest winter ever. In January, they got a total of five paid days with Rieger Roofing; in February, it was four. Fortunately, Matthew didn't have to worry about spreading the work between two crews. His B Crew was hired by the Riegers every spring and dismissed in the fall. Matthew and Sal had also found side jobs that helped make up somewhat for the lack of roofing income.

Work for the A Crew stretched a little further with the absence of the Mole and the Professor, who had taken an offer from a former academic colleague to work for a semester at the University of Hawaii. The colleague was trying to get him an adjunct professor position in the physics department, but a background check by school officials pulled up police reports from Seattle that dated back to the Professor's marital troubles. The best he could do was a position as university groundskeeper. But, as Matthew reminded him, no matter what he was doing, he was doing it in Hawaii, and that beat scrounging for roofing work in chilly, rainy Seattle.

Matthew didn't know whether Diego was getting as few jobs for his A Crew. In previous winters, the work had been split evenly between Matthew's crew and Diego's, but he suspected that might not be the case this time. Matthew's hunch came from a meeting with Willard Rieger in the first week of January.

They met at the Starbucks in Green Lake and spent two hours going over accounting for the previous year, as Rieger Roofing prepared for tax season. During the talk about material costs, equipment rental fees and mileage reimbursement, Willard asked in a casual way whether Matthew still felt the same way about making drug drops at the lumberyard. When Matthew said he hadn't changed his mind about it, Willard simply nodded.

Matthew had a strong suspicion that he and his A Crew were being punished for his refusal to do any more drug drops. The lion's share of work must be going to Diego's crew, he reasoned, which would mean that Diego was now handling the drops. Whether that was true or not, the matter was out of Matthew's hands.

In the previous year, Sal found someone who needed several acres cleared of trees. They borrowed chainsaws to cut the trees and rented a wood splitter to turn it all into firewood. The scheme let them pull in money from two sources: the landowner who paid them for getting rid of the trees and the people who bought the firewood.

They couldn't line up the same kind of side gig in 2000, so they found a new one that didn't require a lot of investment or training: home insulation, specifically blow-in insulation for houses that had been built without any at all. There were plenty of them in the Seattle area. Rather than insulating attics, they focused on walls. It was a little more complicated than doing attics, so most homeowners preferred to hire someone else to do it.

They did a little research and found that the only major equipment they'd need to buy was a primitive-looking metal hopper that broke up the blocks of cellulose insulation into tiny fibers. A blower fan sent the fibers through a long hose, out a nozzle and into a wall. Most of the work involved removing select clapboards around the outside of a house and drilling holes to access the wall space between studs. Depending on how the house was framed, it could require hundreds of holes. After insulation had been blown in, each hole had to be plugged and caulked watertight before the clapboards were put back on.

The price for a new metal hopper shocked Matthew because they seemed to be such simple machines. The bigger ones cost almost $10,000. The cheapest they could find was $2,000, which was more than they wanted to pay. But at a used-equipment clearing house in South Seattle, they found a small hopper for $400. It was selling cheap because it had a blown motor. When they called around for a replacement, they discovered that the model was no longer manufactured and nobody stocked replacement motors. They turned to Sal's brother, who did electrical work. He was able to rebuild it with $60 worth of parts.

The crew practiced on the uninsulated walls of Sal's small apartment building in Fremont. They made a few mistakes but only charged his landlord $1,000, plus material, for the job. They put ads on Craigslist, and Matthew spread the word to customers at Roy's.

At the end of January, they picked up their first insulation job, a 1,700-square-foot house in West Seattle. Matthew estimated it would take a day and half for the four of them to finish it. It turned out to take two days but brought in $2,000. After deducting $300 for supplies, Buck and Major each pocketed $350, Sal and Matthew each $500.

The total was well below the $3,000 or $4,000 that an established business would charge, but Matthew and Sal didn't have the experience. Nor did they have a business license and the contractor insurance that established businesses like Rieger Roofing had. The Riegers might bribe their way into roofing jobs with drugs, but they had contractor insurance to protect the homeowner in case of a problem and workers' compensation insurance to cover roofers who were injured on the job.

Matthew and Sal had neither. Their crew knew it, and if a homeowner asked about it, Sal and Matthew would be honest. But it wasn't something they advertised when they bid on insulation work. The fact that they only accepted payment in cash tipped off some people. On the plus side, Sal and Matthew had built a good reputation from all the roofing work they had done in the Seattle area over the years. Many customers were willing to offer a recommendation when asked.

In early February, they got their second and third insulation jobs, which the crew was happy about. They waited almost until the end of the month before landing their fourth. During that dry spell, they only got one paid day of roofing work. It was becoming a sore spot for Matthew, and he intended to confirm his suspicion that he was being punished when he met with the Riegers on the 28th.

*　　*　　*　　*　　*

Monday, February 28, 2000

It was a chilly morning with light rain coming and going. Matthew and Sal arrived at Coastal Cuisine on Capitol Hill at almost the same time. They grabbed coffee at the bar, then found Willard and Diego sitting at a booth instead of in the meeting room where they normally met.

Once again, Diego was dressed in layers despite the restaurant being reasonably warm. He and Willard were eating muffins, but Matthew saw no plate with extras for him and Sal, not even a bran muffin with raisins.

"Is your brother coming?" Matthew asked.

"No, that's something I have to tell you guys about," Willard said as Matthew and Sal slid into the booth. The vinyl-covered bench seat was shaped like a horseshoe. Matthew slid in first, so he ended up sitting right next to Diego. "Wiley's gonna be pretty busy the next few months with a project we're investing in, so I'll be managing the roofing work myself," Willard said.

Matthew and Sal glanced at each other. This was an interesting development. Matthew wanted to know more. When he asked, Willard seemed eager to share.

"It's a dot-com startup for people to buy gourmet foods over the Internet. Nobody is doing it right now, so there's huge potential. Last week we signed the papers. My brother and I now own 51 percent of the business, which means we make all the final decisions, but the day-to-day operations are managed by the couple who founded it. The company office is up by Golden Gardens," Willard said, referring to the beachfront park in Ballard.

"That's interesting," Matthew said. "Seems like everybody is investing in a startup these days."

"Gourmet Menu dot-com," Diego said.

"What's that?" Sal asked.

"That's the name of the company," Willard said. "Beside the office is a refrigerated warehouse where we store all the inventory. People from all over the country can go to the website and shop from a gourmet store bigger than any that's ever existed. They don't have to get in their car and drive, and they don't have to pay for parking. They get on their home computer and place an order. We receive the order and have it packed within an hour. Then we ship it overnight. People can place an order at noon today and have it in their kitchen by noon tomorrow. Everything from prime steaks that are flash-frozen, to salmon, live crabs, cheeses, coffee, truffles..."

"Caviar," Diego said.

"Right, caviar," Willard repeated. "Like I said, we're the first to market this idea. The sales we're projecting are off the chart. The Internet is so...amazing." Willard gazed off in space, as if he were looking through a portal to a whole new universe that no human had yet set foot in. A virgin market.

"It's like magic," Diego said.

"Yes," Willard said, coming back to planet earth. "It's also a ton of effort to get the business up and running. Wiley's been working with the team seven days a week, fifteen hours a day. That's why you won't be seeing him around for a while."

Matthew was mildly impressed. If they were the first to market the idea, it could be really successful. But it sounded like the same pie-in-the-sky talk he had been hearing from people at Roy's. Everyone was going to be super-rich with their dot-com startup, and their pot of gold was just around the corner.

"OK, enough about that for now," Willard said. He opened a notebook and pulled out two sheets of paper, handing one to Matthew and one to Diego. "There's not much work right now as far as roofing goes. Once May comes around, you're all gonna have more work than you can handle." Looking at Diego and Matthew, he added, "Make sure you have full crews starting in May. We don't want to miss out on any work because either one of you is short a man."

"Before I forget, Willard," Diego said, "The heater is broken in my truck again. I'm gonna bring it to the shop this afternoon."

"Are you serious? I thought they fixed it last time," Willard said.

"I thought so too. But they definitely did not. Maybe there's air in the antifreeze system. I don't know."

Matthew looked at his job list. For the next two weeks, he had one patch job, one chimney cap to install, and a new roof on a small ranch house. That was barely two days'-worth of work for a four-man crew. He looked over at Diego's list and counted seven roofing jobs. Four of them involving tearing off the old roof as well as installing a new one, which could mean an additional half day of work, and an additional half day of pay, for each job. Matthew considered whether he should be direct about addressing the imbalance or be more diplomatic. He decided on direct.

"Hey, Willard, I'm seeing our two lists here, and it looks like my crew is coming up short. Very short. What's up with that?"

Willard shot him a look that was so earnest, Matthew wanted to roll his eyes. "Matt, you know the work is scarce in winter. We just have to take what little there is, then it's up to you to fill in your workweek with what you guys can find on your own. That's what you did last winter. You know how it goes. We split the work as evenly as we can between you and Diego. Everyone is gonna have plenty of work starting in May."

Matthew laid his worksheet on the table. "I've got maybe two days of work for my crew. On Diego's sheet I'm seeing seven new roofs, four of them with a rip. That doesn't seem like a fair split."

Diego began to speak, but Willard talked over him. "Your crew works out of Seattle and West Seattle, Matt, and the jobs you're talking about are all jobs down in Burien, which is Diego's territory. That's why he gets those jobs."

"I understand that, Willard, but would it be too much to ask for my crew to get maybe one or two of them? Everyone here has to pay the rent until May, you know. That's all I'm saying."

Matthew could tell that Willard was on the fence about the matter, and might just agree to his request, but Diego jumped in. He swept an arm across the table in the direction of Sal and Matthew, and his elbow pushed into Matthew's chest. A half-full coffee cup ended up in Sal's lap, and he jumped up in his seat. "You guys have an insulation business!" Diego began. "You're making plenty of money these days. My crew has nothing else except a few hours flipping burgers or bagging groceries. They need these jobs more than your people. That's what's fair. And these jobs are all in my territory. You're not stealing my work, Mahoney."

Diego's voice was louder and angrier than Matthew had ever heard it. So this was the temper, he thought. Half the people in the restaurant turned toward the booth to see what the outburst was all about. When Diego finished, his face was right up in Matthew's, and the two stared at each other. Finally, Matthew spoke. "Take your arm off me, or I'll make you suffer."

Willard slapped a hand on the table. "Knock it off!" He grabbed Diego's jacket and tried pulling him away from Matthew. "Diego, get your arm off him. We don't need a goddamn scene in this restaurant. The owner was the best man at my brother's wedding."

The last comment made Matthew want to laugh. He felt Diego slowly withdraw his elbow, then watched him ease back in his seat.

Willard's face was red as he spoke. "If you guys start trouble like this again…either one of you…you're fired. Matt, the jobs on the sheet aren't changing."

159

"I was only asking," Matthew said. "Politely."

"Don't question my assignments again. They are what they are. End of story."

Diego picked up the last piece of blueberry muffin from his plate. He raised the morsel to eye level, then turned to Matthew. "The muffins were delicious today."

*   *   *   *   *

The only other thing Matthew and Sal had on their calendar that Monday was an estimate for an insulation job in Redmond.

"Thank God it's a leap year," Sal said as they drove across the 520 bridge. "That gives us one more day to land some work before the month is over. Diego's crew is not gonna have any trouble making rent. I can't believe how fast he went off at the idea of sharing some of the work. He acts like he's got a right to it all."

Matthew took a sip of lukewarm coffee from a stainless steel travel mug that had been so battered over the years that little remained of its black and gold Bruins logo. "It has to be about making drops at the lumberyard. I don't know if Diego was doing any before, but I guarantee you he's doing them all now. And Willard probably told him that I'm refusing to do them anymore. That's why he was so defensive. He feels like he's already paid up front for the work."

"It's only a matter of time before somebody gets busted on those drops," Sal said.

"I'm curious how much the Reigers actually get for the drugs. It's not like we're all buried in work right now. Maybe the drops have nothing to do with roofing jobs at all. I wouldn't shed a tear if Diego got busted in the act. He rubs me the wrong way, and every time I see him it's worse."

Sal was half listening as he studied a worn paper map of the Eastside. "OK, you want to take 405 north to 70th." Sal turned to Matthew and said, "I forgot to ask—what band did you guys end up seeing on Friday?"

"Yo La Tengo," Matthew said. "They played at the King Cat."

"What'd you think?"

Matthew nodded slowly. "They were good; I liked them. I was already 80 percent there. But it was Anne's pick, so I have to be careful not to get too enthusiastic." He turned to Sal. "I have to hold back a little. Otherwise, she'll think she gets to pick the next band too. Then I lose a turn."

They had no trouble finding the McEvers' home, a ranch house on just under an acre of wooded property. Two golden retrievers barked from the porch, then ran out to greet them in the driveway.

"A ranch. *Bueno,*" Sal said. One-story houses were easier to work on because it meant less time on ladders and less distance for things, and people, to fall.

Matthew grabbed his notebook and they went to meet the owner, a guy in his late 30s who had moved into the home recently with his wife and three kids. They introduced themselves, then took a slow walk around the house as Matthew explained the work they'd do. He opened his notebook and showed photos of the insulation steps. A light mist began to fall and drops hit the plastic lamination covering the photos. It all went smoothly, including the $2,500 price Matthew gave.

"That's definitely less expensive than a quote that I got yesterday," Christopher McEvers said.

"We've gotten pretty efficient with the whole process," Matthew said. "We use quality insulation and source it at a good price. My crew has a lot of experience with the work. There's Sal and me, plus two other workers. We could probably have everything finished in two days. Two and a half at the most."

They discussed when the work could start. Sal suggested Wednesday, when the light rain was supposed to let up. Christopher agreed to that, and everything seemed to be settled until Christopher asked the question that made Sal and Matthew squirm.

"So, you guys are licensed and insured and all that stuff?" Christopher asked in a way that was apologetic for even suggesting that they might not be.

"Well, as a startup," Matthew began, surprised that he was actually using the word "startup" in relation to their insulation work, "we haven't gone through all of those steps yet, so I have to honestly say no. However, and this is important, we've done excellent work in the West Seattle area, and those homeowners would be more than happy to speak with you about how pleased they are with the results. Some could tell you how much money they're saving every month now because their houses are insulated. I can give you a list of names and phone numbers if you like."

Christopher flashed a weak smile that was mixed with confusion at first, then with embarrassment as he asked, "So you guys aren't insured or bonded then?"

"No, not yet," Matthew said, and left it at that because he knew they were already screwed. He watched the firmness return to Christopher's expression.

"Oh yeah, well…I'm sorry. We really can't have people working on the house if they're not insured. It's a liability thing. I'm sure you understand."

"Not a problem. We understand," Sal said.

"I'm really sorry you guys came all the way out here…" Christopher went on for a couple of minutes with a long, drawn-out guilt-ridden apology before Matthew and Sal were finally able to free themselves and leave.

"Well, this whole day is becoming a real clusterfuck, and it's not even half over," Sal said.

Matthew suddenly got an idea. "Hey, what time is it?"

Sal checked his watch. "Quarter to 11."

"You know what we need? Some good barbecue. Let's go meet 'The Boss.'" Matthew said. He was referring to Ruby's Barbecue, where the owner, Earl, walked around with a battered pot of home-brewed hot sauce known as "The Boss." On the back bumper of Matthew's truck, he proudly displayed a sticker that read, "Have You Met The Boss?"

Sal rolled his eyes. "Oh brother, I don't know if I can handle it today."

Matthew knew that Sal wasn't referring to the hot sauce, which was painfully fiery, at least for Matthew. Instead, he was afraid of the treatment the owner's daughter, RJ, gave him when he didn't order properly. The place was owned by a Black family that had moved from the Deep South in the '80s. Earl smoked the meats out back, while mother and daughter worked inside. Ruby Sr. was a small, quiet woman who managed the back of the kitchen. Ruby Jr., or RJ for short, had a presence that was both commanding and intimidating.

If customers didn't place their order in a way that was clear and certain, RJ would sometimes send them to the back of the line. To the

162

many white-collar workers from nearby high tech companies, the show was quite entertaining unless, of course, it involved them. Sal lived in terror of screwing up his order with RJ, and it had happened more than once.

The last time they came to Ruby's, RJ seemed to recognize Sal in line. Before he could give his order, RJ said, "Don't you dare fumble your order to me and change your mind halfway through." Which, of course, is what Sal ended up doing.

"Back of the line, Fumble Man!" she commanded, adding another ten minutes before Sal could eat.

Lunch at Ruby's Barbecue officially began at 11:00, although it could run five minutes to either side of the hour, depending on when the smoked meats were ready, and when the cornbread had been pulled from the oven and cut into squares.

Sal and Matthew were first in line and waited between the seating area and the ordering area. The walls there were lined with framed stories about Ruby's opening and with articles from publications such as *Chile Pepper Magazine*. An old, faded map of the world held a few hundred push pins placed by customers marking their hometown.

From the kitchen came the smell of burning hickory and barbecue sauce. There were two versions of it: spicy and sweet. Stainless steel pans clanged, and oven doors were pulled open and slammed shut as food made its way to the serving line. Matthew stood behind Sal, and the two remained a respectful step away from the threshold, where they had only a partial view of the kitchen and prep activity.

Every now and then, someone would get curious and poke their head through the doorway to see how lunch was taking shape. It was always a first-time customer who tried the move. When RJ would spot the violation, she would berate them. "Did you hear me open my kitchen for lunch? Don't come in here until you're told to step forward!"

One car after another pulled into the parking lot, and the line of people behind Sal and Matthew grew longer. RJ carried long stainless steel warming trays over to the steam table. They were heaped with smoked ribs, shredded pork, hot links and chicken. Further down the serving line were sides of baked beans, potato salad, coleslaw and cornbread.

"So what are you gonna order?" Matthew asked.

"I don't want their small ribs," Sal said in a low voice. "If she brings out big ribs, I'll get those. Otherwise, I'll get the shredded pork sandwich."

"Hot sauce or sweet?"

"Hot, of course."

"Lunch plate or dinner plate?"

Sal hesitated. "Ah…"

"Salamander, you better know when you step up there."

"Why do I keep forgetting…what's the difference again?"

"Lunch plate comes with one side dish, dinner two. And the large rib dinner gives you more ribs than the large rib lunch."

"I'll get the lunch. I'm not that hungry yet."

"What's your side?"

"I'll probably get the beans…no, actually I'll get the potato salad."

Matthew shook his head. "Don't do that when you step up, man. Know exactly what you want. She preys on people who hesitate…"

Sal elbowed Matthew. "I know what you're doing, Mahoney. You're trying to get me all freaked out, so I make a mistake when I order."

From the kitchen came the sound of metal serving tongs tapping on the counter. "Alright, let's go!" RJ called.

Sal crossed the threshold and stepped up to the counter. The steam table that kept all the food warm was protected by a glass window in front and a stainless steel counter on top. As Sal was looking through the window to see what was available, RJ dropped the last tray of smoked meat into its place over the hot water. It sent a cloud of vapor onto the glass, obscuring Sal's view.

"OK, what do you want?" RJ asked.

Sal shifted his view to the left, then to the right as he tried to see through the fogged window. "Well, I'm trying to see if you have the ribs I want…" Giving up on the window, he bent forward over the counter to look directly down.

"Hey," RJ said. "Don't you lean over my counter!"

The rebuke stunned Sal. "I'm sorry. I'm trying to see if you have the large ribs. If you…I mean, if you don't, I'll take a pork…the shredded pork…"

"Step out of line, Confused Man." RJ pointed her tongs to the wall behind Sal. "Go on, take a step back."

She turned to the line of waiting customers relishing the show. "Next!"

"Excuse me," Matthew said as he stepped forward and gave Sal a gentle nudge toward the wall. "Shredded pork dinner with sweet sauce. A side of baked beans and a side of coleslaw."

RJ laid a bun open on a plate, buried one half with shredded pork, drizzled it with sweet barbecue sauce, put the plate on the counter for Matthew, then walked toward the side dishes, which were already portioned into styrofoam bowls.

After Matthew paid, RJ called out to Sal, "Step forward, Confused Man. You get one more chance before I send you to the back of the line."

"She's so fucking sadistic," Sal said after Matthew had returned from the soda machine with two cans of Coke.

"If I didn't love this barbecue so much, I'd never come here," Sal said. "She knows we're addicted, and she tortures us."

"Not all of us," Matthew said. "She's a blues singer too. Did you know that?"

"RJ?"

"Anne and I heard her sing at Bumbershoot last year. She has a beautiful singing voice. It's different from the voice she uses with you."

Earl was making his way through the casual dining area with his pot of hot sauce. When he reached their table, he asked, "Who's ready for 'The Boss'?"

"Serve it up generous here," Sal said. He leaned to one side so Earl could reach in and drop a half spoonful onto Sal's open sandwich. Matthew held out his plate. "Half as much for me, Earl. Thanks."

Earl placed a smaller amount on Matthew's plate, then nudged Sal. "He can't handle it like you and me."

"He's a lightweight, Earl, but I'm trying to teach him the ways."

Earl laughed and patted Sal on the back. "Alright, we'll see you boys later. You be good now." Earl waved and moved on to the next table.

They took a few bites of their lunch before Sal said, "We've got two problems right now. We're getting practically no roofing work, and that probably won't improve until May. Second, we're missing out on some insulation jobs because we're not bonded and insured."

"You're forgetting about Y2K," Matthew said.

"Don't remind me again. I'm still pissed about that. All the build-up about all the shit that was gonna go wrong, and nothing happened. Like a fireworks show that just fizzles. But let the record show that I predicted it would do exactly that."

"You should talk to Mr. Engebretsen. I bet he knows what went wrong about everything not going wrong."

"Trust me. I am gonna talk to him. I want answers."

Matthew had mixed his drop of sauce into his beans and eaten a few bites. He had to pause to blow his nose and wipe sweat from beneath his eyes. "Back to the Riegers. Their gourmet startup business surprised me. Maybe they're waiting to see if it takes off. If it does, maybe they'll get out of roofing altogether."

Sal and Matthew glanced at a table to their left, where a group who had just sat down was being greeted by Earl. They were all clean-cut young guys, and they all wore khakis with an open-collar dress shirt: the classic tech-worker look. They told Earl they were first-time customers. By tradition, all new diners at Ruby's had to try at least a toothpick taster of The Boss. On later visits, they could pass.

Three of them reacted to Earl's outstretched spoon with trepidation as he placed a tiny bright drop of The Boss on their plate. The fourth, however, had a big grin on his face. He insisted Earl put two big spoonfuls of it on his open sandwich. Earl seemed insulted by the request and mentioned something about respect, but the guy insisted on the large double dose.

Sal scratched his head and chuckled, "Matt, check this out. He made Earl give him two big scoops. This should be interesting."

Sal pulled a piece of bread off his sandwich and used it to mop up sauce on his plate. "Enough with the Rieger machine. I want to talk about a plan I have. Actually, it's a plan my brother and I have. We've been talking about it since you told me you were definitely moving to Alaska. We want to run our own roofing show starting this summer. Luis' electrical work is pretty steady. He's got a sweet contract on the Seattle waterfront right now. I'll tell you, that guy is making more money than I've ever made, but he's ready to branch out. And he's familiar enough with the roofing business.

"We're gonna do it legit. Get the business license, insurance, everything. We've got enough saved up to buy all the equipment we need: ladders, nail guns, compressor, generator…the works."

The news didn't really take Matthew by surprise. He and Sal had talked about going into business together themselves. "You guys should definitely do it. If I wasn't moving, I'd be all in."

"My brother probably won't spend any of his time on the roof. He'll mostly take care of the books. I hate doing that shit. And he'll also build a website for us and set up a bunch of online ads. He's taking a class on Internet advertising. Like Buck said, the future's on the Internet. Even Willard said it today. By the way, part of the plan is to steal your A Crew when you leave for Alaska."

"Steal away," Matthew said. "They'll be happier working with you guys."

They both turned their attention again to the guy at the next table who had taken the large double dose of The Boss. His friends had been cheering him on as he took one bite after another of his sandwich.

"This'll be a life lesson," Sal said as the guy's chewing slowed down. "I bet he won't take another full bite."

The smile slowly faded from the young man's face as he lowered his sandwich. His face had been red and now grew redder.

"Watch this," Sal said. "He's gonna push his plate away."

As the man nudged his plate toward the center of the table, Matthew said, "Now he's gonna drink the rest of his Coke."

"Then he'll go to the machine and get another one," Sal said.

They watched the young man pat the sweat from his forehead with a napkin as his friends continued eating their meals. He smiled occasionally at the good-natured ribbing they were giving him, but the expression of brazen audacity had been replaced by a subdued, slightly ashen look.

When the guy returned to the table with his second Coke, Earl walked by and said, "I hope you learned your lesson. Nobody disrespects The Boss."

"There will be one less arrogant prick working in the tech industry this afternoon," Sal said. Turning his attention back to the previous discussion, he asked, "So how is Anne's job hunt going?"

"Nothing so far," Matthew said. "Actually, she did get an offer, but they wanted her to start two weeks ago, which is about four months too soon."

"At least she's got a steady job right now that gives you guys benefits," Sal said.

"It's not all rosy. Her company got bought by an engineering business in California. They're shaking things up and moving people from one position to another. Anne got a new director in January, and she's not crazy about him. It's the second time she's had her company go through a change like this. It didn't end well the first time. She's definitely ready to move. That reminds me. Anne was gonna let me know if she heard back on another job possibility."

Matthew pulled his phone from his pocket and opened it, but the screen was blank. He shook his head. "It doesn't hold a charge the way it used to."

"What do you expect?" Sal asked. "Your phone is ancient. Don't be such a cheap bastard. Buy a new one."

Matthew finished off his Coke, then tossed the can toward the opposite wall. It sailed in a high arc, banked against the cinder-block wall, and clanged into a metal barrel. He stood up and put on his jacket.

On their way out, Sal stopped at the table where the young man was now resting his head atop folded arms. Sal leaned over and tilted his head sideways, so they were looking directly at each other. "It's gonna get a whole lot worse before it gets any better," Sal said, then walked away laughing.

*   *   *   *   *

After lunch, Matthew had time to kill, so he brought the truck in for an oil change. The shop had a sale on tires, and the prices were so good that Matthew considered buying a set. Once all the extra costs were thrown in and Matthew saw the total, however, he got sticker shock and told the guy behind the counter, "My wife would kill me if I didn't talk to her about this first."

With nothing else to do, he headed home. It was a little after 2:00 when he got there, and a light rain returned once again. As he walked through the front door, he was reliving the moment that morning when Willard said the restaurant owner had been the best man at his brother's wedding. What an odd thing to say in that situation, Matthew was thinking, when his eyes fell upon the fireplace mantel.

He stepped up to the photo of Buzzy and stared at his old friend. Matthew remembered the yellow jackets in the garden that day and how they were only interested in attacking Buzzy, for some reason. They swirled around his shaggy mop of reddish-brown hair. The photographer had captured the look of suppressed fear on Buzzy's face—half of his attention turned to the camera, the other half to defending himself from an indiscernible threat.

Matthew leaned forward and tried to spot a yellow jacket in the image. He had tried before but had never succeeded. Maybe they were camouflaged by the tall hedge in the background or moving too fast for the camera to capture. It wasn't the yellow jackets that had haunted Matthew for 12 years though. It was the look of fear on Buzzy's face. He had seen it again a week later on that awful day in the Copley Square subway station, where Matthew wrongly condemned his good friend. That would be the last time he ever saw him.

As he stared at the photo—staring through it, really—Matthew smelled a burning cigarette. He turned and looked to the other end of the house. Through a kitchen window, he saw a figure moving on his back porch. First he thought it was a burglar. Then he heard laughter and recognized it as Anne's.

He headed for the back porch, where Anne and Renee, along with two guys they worked with—Leonard and Craig—were all sitting around a table with an ashtray and two bottles of wine, one empty and one half-empty. Craig was the smoker and, counting from the ashtray, he had gone through four cigarettes. Matthew had surprised them when he suddenly opened the sliding glass door, and for a moment the only sound was the light rain tapping on the porch roof overhead.

He laughed at the scene. "Are you guys playing hooky or something?"

"We all got laid off today," Renee said, raising the glass in her hand.

Anne turned to him. "I called you and left a message."

Matthew pulled his phone out, then remembered. "The battery went dead on me again today." After the news sank in, he said, "Well, that truly sucks. I'm sorry, guys." He sat down beside Anne and reached for her hand.

"They let six of us go this morning," Renee said. "We're having a little pity party."

"I'm still in shock," Leonard said. For him and Craig, it had been their first job out of college. They were both hired the last week of June 1998. "It's like, we had jobs and careers and lives this morning, and now suddenly we're not sure about any of it anymore." He lit another Marlboro. "I wanted to puke when the HR rep told me. We were in the conference room that got painted two days ago, and it's still majorly off-gassing. My manager didn't even know it was happening today."

"I kind of wonder if that was really the case," Craig said.

Leonard insisted it was. "No, really, I called him after I left, and he said he didn't even know until it was done. They didn't want him to be involved. They told him he couldn't call me to check on me. He couldn't reach out to me in any way and could only talk if I contacted him first."

"He might just be saying that to keep us from...," Craig began.

"Killing him?" Renee said, finishing his sentence for him. They all laughed except Matthew.

"Excuse the gallows humor, Matt," Renee said. "We have to find a way to deal with it right now."

"Because tomorrow morning's gonna suck," Craig added.

"The director is from the California office," Anne told Matthew.

"They called in an outsider for the hit," Matthew said.

"Yes," Renee said. "So how is your day going, Matt?"

"Pretty shitty but still better than yours. So did they give you a reason?"

"We're all in the water resource management group. Or we were. The company has moved away from that kind of work in California. They focus on soil science, and that's what our office is going to do starting tomorrow, I guess."

For the next hour, Matthew listened to more of the drama, from how everybody got the news to the humiliating task of having to clean out their desk with coworkers looking on awkwardly. They had all seen layoffs as a possibility after their company was bought out, but nobody was really prepared for it to happen so soon.

When Leonard and Craig announced they were going to head home or, more precisely, to the Hop Haven, which was a brewpub in their Ravenna neighborhood, Anne invited Renee, Doug and their three kids over for dinner. It might help everyone if both families could adjust to the new reality together. And, they reasoned, it could help if the kids all got the news at the same time.

Renee had already phoned Doug about the layoffs, but she called again to discuss dinner at the Mahoneys'. As she waited for Doug to pick up, she asked, "Matt, how do you guys feel about chicken? I've always found grilled chicken to be comforting in times of high stress. You know, like chicken soup for colds?"

Matthew smiled. "Sure, we can grill out back. We've got plenty of veggies here, plus cheeses and the sweet potato fries that your kids like. We also have plenty of beer, but we might be out of wine."

Renee told Doug that before or after picking up the kids, he should buy some chicken breasts, avocados, and a bottle...no, a few bottles...of Columbia Crest merlot. If he couldn't find Columbia Crest, any red wine would do as long as it wasn't from California. And a chocolate truffle cake.

Matthew picked up Dylan at his school, then Nora at the soccer field where her team was finishing practice. They got home right after Doug had arrived. Before the chicken went on the grill, they gathered the kids together in the living room and told them about their moms both losing their jobs that morning. The kids were quiet initially. Nora had the first question.

"Are we still gonna move to Alaska?"

"Yes," Anne said. "It's the same as before."

"Can you still get a job in Alaska after you got fired today?" Nora asked.

"We didn't get fired, honey. We got laid off. And yes, they'll still hire me. People get laid off in all kinds of companies. It's a business decision that we just have to live with." Anne listened to herself and didn't know where the last part of her statement came from. It was shock talk, she decided.

Through the course of dinner, the consensus among the kids was that they'd enjoy having their moms around more often. Among the parents, the consensus was that the family budgets were about to take a big hit.

171

*   *   *   *   *

The cold reality didn't really set in until the following morning when the palliative effects of the wine and chocolate truffle cake had worn off. After his morning run and an intense session with the speed bag, Matthew woke the kids and got them ready for school. He told Anne to sleep as late as she wanted. Hadley Epps, a neighbor, would be shuttling the kids to school. Hadley had no children herself, but regularly drove three other kids on the street to the same schools where Nora and Dylan went. She worked part-time at a flower shop in Admiral Junction, so she had the time to shuttle them most days. She also did it as a way of giving back to neighbors, who were always helping out her and her husband. When Matthew called Hadley, she said there was plenty of room in her minivan for Dylan and Nora.

In the darkened bedroom, Anne was lying on her stomach and drifting in and out of sleep. The wine from the night before was causing a mild headache that she hoped wouldn't get any worse. Outside, rain tapped on the bedroom window, and the wind chime on the back deck tinkled in a faint breeze.

When Hadley pulled up in her minivan, Anne heard the sound of the sliding door open, then the voice of her daughter announcing in a most piercing way, "My mom doesn't work anymore. She got fired!"

Anne groaned and pulled a pillow over her head. She listened to the minivan driving away and realized the chance of getting any more sleep was now slim to none, so she pulled on some socks and a pair of sweats.

"I'm making oatmeal," Matthew called from the kitchen.

"OK," Anne said. She grabbed a recent *Pottery Barn* catalog and sat down at the dining room table. After flipping through a few pages, she thought—why am I looking at stuff I can't afford to buy anymore? She closed the catalog and pushed it toward the center of the table. After staring at it for several seconds, she grabbed it and picked up where she left off.

Matthew brought two bowls of oatmeal to the table, along with mugs. Anne gazed at her coffee, which looked infinitely dark and probably too strong for her stomach at the moment, so she started with the bowl of oatmeal. A spoonful of brown sugar was slowly melting across the beige surface. She stared at it and thought the oatmeal without the brown sugar looked something like the popcorn ceiling in their bedroom.

"What are you seeing in there, Boushay?" Matthew asked from the other side of the table, where he was already halfway through his bowl.

"I'm still half asleep. And I'm not hungry at all."

She reached for her coffee and tried taking a small sip, but was distracted by the sight of Matthew shoveling big spoonfuls of oatmeal into his mouth.

"I don't know how you can eat so energetically," Anne said. "Aren't you feeling hungover at all?"

"Well, I went for a long run. But mostly it's because I went to bed at 10:00 when Doug took the kids home. That's about when you and Renee cracked open a fresh bottle."

"Yes, I remember. I really wish we hadn't done that. It was around midnight when I called her a cab. But it really was an exceptional day."

The furnace kicked on and stirred a light breeze, which gave Anne a chill. It reminded her that the gas bill was sitting unpaid on the fireplace mantel. "Renee and I only got two weeks of severance pay," she said. "Plus, I have a few days of vacation left that they'll include in my last check. I don't know how much I'll get paid in unemployment benefits, but it'll be a lot less than I was making and it won't kick in for weeks. I don't know why they make people wait. I'm unemployed now."

Anne began taking small bites of the oatmeal. It was still warm and went down easier than she thought it would.

"We'll need to take a look at our finances," Matthew said. "The big picture."

Anne sighed. "It's not going to be pretty. I'm unemployed and you're not getting any work. By the way, there's $40 on the mantel from Eric. He stopped by the house before you got home. Did Eric lose a bet?"

"He lost two," Matthew said.

Anne thought about the transaction and wondered what would have happened if Matthew had lost $40 instead of winning it. And what would happen if he lost a series of bets like that. Where would the money come from to pay the winners? "If you had lost both bets and had to pay up, you wouldn't involve our checking account, would you?"

"I told you before. I never touch family money," Matthew said.

"But if you lose a big bet, who's going to pay?"

"Mickey."

Anne was confused, then remembered.

Matthew walked over to the hutch and reached for the Mickey Mouse cookie jar that sat on top. "I never bet more than Mickey can cover."

He put the jar on the table in front of Anne. When she looked inside, she saw a small pile of bills, mostly 20s. "How much is in there?"

"$430. $470 with Eric's payment."

"That's impressive," Anne said. She pushed the cookie jar across the table. "Just don't get carried away with it."

After Anne showered and dressed, they returned to the dining room table and took stock of their finances. They had already mailed their rent check for March, leaving a little over $1,000 in their checking account. Coming due were payments on their three credit cards, all with high balances. The largest balance was on the card used to fund the new roof in Alaska. They had been paying more than twice the minimum due on all the cards, but Matthew suggested they drop to the minimum for each.

"That'll be about $550 total, due in the next couple of weeks." He wrote it down on a fresh page in their home budget notebook.

"We owe another payment on Dylan's braces," Anne said. "The statement came yesterday. It's $350. Our insurance company has already paid their half of the bill. We'll owe the final $550 when he actually gets the braces."

As she mentioned insurance, Anne suddenly remembered that when she lost her job, she also lost the share of insurance coverage paid by her now former employer. It made her queasy to think about carrying the full cost. "Matt, one other thing. We'll have to pay for our own health insurance through COBRA starting in April. Technically they only had to pay through the end of February, which is today, but they extended it a month."

"Any idea what it'll cost?"

"I can't be sure until we see the paperwork, but it could be $1,000 a month. Maybe more."

"Jesus," Matthew said. "I'm really hoping that the roofing work will start coming back in a few weeks."

"In the meantime, can you get more bar shifts?" Anne asked.

"I keep asking Dennis about that, but all they can promise is two shifts a week until late May or June. I'm thinking about calling Donovan's and seeing if they need any help."

Donovan's had a massive bar that turned into a mob scene on weekends and anytime there was a sporting event at the Kingdome. There were a lot of big-money shifts, but the work was brutal. On many nights when Matthew had worked there, he had to jump over the bar to break up a fight or throw somebody out. There were times when he enjoyed that aspect of it, but that was when he was in his 20s, not a 40-year-old with two kids.

"I don't want you going back there, Matt. Stick to Roy's."

He took the empty bowls to the kitchen and began washing them out. Anne sat alone at the dining room table with a headache and a cup of coffee that was growing cold. She could see what kind of trouble they were now in, and how quickly things could fall apart. They would survive March with her severance, but sometime in April, maybe early April, they would go off a cliff.

Anne knew she could call her mother for help, and she would get it. She had said no to that option before, and didn't want to reach for it now, but there was no other choice, was there? Anne imagined how that conversation would go, and she felt herself recoiling from the thought. She stared down into her cup, into coffee that was dark as oil.

Then it came to her. Another option. She called into the kitchen. "Matt?" When he joined her at the table, she said, "I'm gonna call Andre this afternoon." Andre was a long-time friend of her father, dating back to the construction of the Alaska pipeline in the early '70s. They had even opened a bar together, the Big Wall Bar & Grill in Girdwood. Andre had almost retired from the oil industry but still did occasional consulting work for Bluff Rock Oil Group, which was commonly referred to as BG. After Anne let him know that she wanted a staff job in the industry, he had started keeping his eye open for an opportunity that might fit her.

In previous years, Andre would entice her to take a contract job in Alaska, especially one on the North Slope, which required working seven days a week on the cold tundra but also paid very well. In the past, Anne and Matthew had decided that the contract option was too drastic for their situation. But now their situation itself had become drastic.

Anne explained her idea to Matthew, who wasn't on board at first. After they went over all their expenses again, Anne said, "We're going to get buried, and it's going to happen soon. You know that. I can call Andre, and I'm sure he can find me a contract on the Slope."

"How long would a contract be?"

"I'll have to find out. It could be two months. It could be six."

Matthew said nothing for a moment as he considered the option. He really had nothing better to offer. As he imagined exactly how things would play out with Anne away in Alaska for months, and with him and the kids back in Seattle, his thoughts turned to Dylan and how this new option would affect him.

Chapter 8
Saint Boushoney Day

Friday, March 17, 2000

It was a made-up holiday named after a made-up saint. Saint Boushoney Day had no fixed date on the calendar, but usually took place once a year when the Boushay-Mahoney family felt themselves fraying at the emotional edges. Anne and Matthew would take the day off from work, and the kids would have notes written to excuse them from school in order to "participate in a ritual essential to the cultural and spiritual health of their family." Anne had learned that if she made it sound vaguely religious, school administrators wouldn't question it.

What happened on Saint Boushoney Day changed from year to year and depended on what the family agreed to the night before. However, one part had remained constant for the last three years. At Nora's insistence, the day had to begin at Pike Place Market. So, early Friday, which also happened to be St. Patrick's Day, they parked beneath the Alaskan Way Viaduct and walked through a light drizzle to Pike Place, where Sal joined them for his first Saint Boushoney Day celebration.

Dylan was just happy to be out of school, but Nora was beside herself with excitement as she climbed atop the big bronze pig sculpture that stood at the entrance to the covered part of the Market. At 9:30, it was already busy with shoppers and tourists streaming in both directions, sipping their morning coffee and watching the show put on by the fishmongers at Pike Place Fish Market. When a whole fish was purchased, it was plucked from its bed of shaved ice and tossed in a high arc to the other end of the counter, where it was caught, weighed and wrapped in a matter of seconds.

The seafood stand faced the bronze pig. When one of the fishmongers recognized Nora, he whistled to her and waved. Even though her sneakers were wet from the rain, Nora quickly gained stable footing on the pig's surface. It had become smooth over the years from one tourist after another sliding onto its back for a photo op. The piercing sound of Nora's voice

177

caused more than a few heads to turn. "Hey everybody, do you know what day this is?"

From the far side of the Market, someone said in a hesitant voice, "St. Patrick's Day."

Nora did a little dance on the pig's back and waved her arms in the air. "It's Saint Boushoney Day!"

A couple of the fishmongers cheered. Some of the shoppers and tourists weren't quite sure what to make of the strange-sounding holiday, but nevertheless responded by clapping. Sal, who stood ready to catch Nora on one side of the pig, was laughing and shaking his head at Matthew, who stood on the other side. He shrugged at Sal. "Don't ask me. It's just what she does."

Anne, who was equally ambivalent about Nora's theatrics, stood a few steps away. Beside her and with his back to the scene was Dylan, who grew more embarrassed by the spectacle with each passing year.

"See you next Saint Boushoney Day!" Nora cried. She jumped off the pig and grabbed the arm of Sal's jacket. "C'mon, let's go to the next spot!"

"Where are we going now?" he asked.

Nora led Sal down the nearby stairway to Post Alley, a narrow cobblestone walkway beneath the main floor of the Market. One side of the alley was filled with posters for plays, operas, music events, and gallery openings, along with cryptic propaganda statements. Opposite that was the Gum Wall, where the brick edifice was covered with maybe millions of globs of chewed gum that had been pressed onto it over the years. The actual bricks had long been obscured, and in some places the accumulated gum was inches thick. The grotesque gallery spanned an area 15 feet high and 50 feet long.

Sal had seen the Gum Wall before. He thought it was cool from a distance but disgusting once he got within a few feet.

"If you want to be in the Saint Boushoney club, you have to lick the Gum Wall," Nora said.

Anne had gone off to find a bathroom, but Matthew and Dylan watched from the foot of the stairway. Dylan held a hand over his mouth in a gesture of revulsion. He turned to his dad and spoke through his fingers. "She's gonna do it again. You should stop her."

Nora pulled a reluctant Sal closer to the wall. "You don't have to actually lick the wall. You just have to come very close. Like this." Nora put her hands behind her back and leaned forward. She giggled lightly as her outstretched tongue came within an inch of the gummy surface. Then she took a step away from the wall. "See, you just do it like that."

Sal wasn't sure if he wanted any part of the ritual and turned to Matthew for reassurance, but Matthew was pretending to read an old poster announcing the 1998 performance of *The Nutcracker.* Dylan was shaking his head in a very unambiguous way, but Sal didn't notice the warning. Instead, he took a step forward and leaned cautiously toward the wall. "Like this?" he asked.

"Yes, except you have to hold your hands behind your back and stick your tongue way out," Nora instructed.

Sal did as he was told and leaned in.

"Closer," Nora said. "Just a little bit more."

As Sal came within an inch of the wall, Nora slid behind him, put her hands on his lower back and gave him a shove. Sal's tongue came into momentary contact with an assorted pre-chewed patch of spearmint, strawberry and cinnamon gums.

Dylan watched in horror. It was the same trauma Nora had inflicted on him at the very same wall a year earlier. He called out in sympathetic pain, "Oh my God!"

Nora giggled as Sal regained his footing, then spit several times onto the cobblestone. "You little shit. I could tell you were up to something."

"Cheer up, Sal," Nora said, patting him on the back. "Now you're a member of the Saint Boushoney club! Not many people can say that."

*　　*　　*　　*　　*

With the formalities over, the day moved on to activities that everybody could enjoy. There would be a trip to the waterfront aquarium, then a walk to the Pacific Science Center, where they'd see two short IMAX movies—*Alaska: Spirit of the Wild* and *Into the Deep,* the first 3D IMAX movie to be shown in Seattle. Between the movies, they'd have lunch at Zeeks, their favorite place for pizza in the city.

If the rain let up later, as forecast, they'd drive 30 miles out I-90 and spend the afternoon hiking up to Rattlesnake Ledge. They'd finish the day with dinner at the North Bend Bar & Grill, a favorite of Matthew and Sal because their bar poured all the microbrews from nearby Snoqualmie Falls Brewery. Dylan also liked studying the black-and-white photo over the fireplace. It showed an old Western scene with a dozen men drinking inside a turn-of-the-century bar, three of them on horseback.

Before all that, the very first stop of the day was at a donut stand near the bronze pig in the Market. Through a glass screen they watched small rings of dough riding a conveyer belt into a bath of hot oil, where they crackled and sizzled, were flipped over to have their other side cooked, then emerged at the end ready for a sprinkling of cinnamon or powdered sugar. Matthew bought a dozen and a half of the mini donuts. Dylan carried the warm, oil-stained bags and led everyone to his favorite café.

It was only two levels down from the donut stand but you had to choose one of many possible stairways, then follow a very specific course through the labyrinthian corridors within the belly of the Market. Only Dylan could remember the correct route to take past the many small shops selling comic books, miniature cars, antique books, imported tobacco, used records, embroidered clothing, exotic jewelry and so much more. Anyone else attempting to navigate the route invariably led the family far astray.

At the café, they settled into a window booth with a sweeping view of Puget Sound, where they could watch the green-and-white ferries sailing back and forth across the choppy water. In the distance, the peaks of the snow-capped Olympic Mountains were shrouded by low-hanging clouds.

Matthew told Sal he'd pay for his mocha. When it arrived with the other drinks, Matthew said, "The cacao bean and the coffee bean have enzymes that work together to kill germs and scour the bad taste from your mouth."

"You better be right about that, Mahoney. You let it all go down without warning me. This fact shall not be forgotten," Sal said. When Nora smiled, he pointed to the side of his head and added, "You better watch your back, little girl. Sal Camacho has a very long memory."

Their server had been kind enough to break the house rule about bringing outside food into the café. Dylan emptied the bag of donuts onto a plate and said, "Nora did it to me last year, Sal."

Anne didn't realize that Nora had intended to repeat the prank and told her that she was very disappointed in her behavior. "I think you owe Sal more than a mocha for not stopping it," she said to Matthew.

"You don't see all the pranks he pulls," Matthew said. "Believe me, he's still better than even at this point."

The donuts were gone in a matter of minutes. As Nora pressed her last piece into the remaining sugar on the plate, Anne said she had something to tell the kids.

"You know that the plan for us was to move to Alaska this summer when you kids got out of school. Well, things have changed since then."

Nora was busy licking sugar from her fingers and wasn't paying full attention. Dylan hated any kind of uncertainty about the family's future, and he sensed immediately from his mother's tone that something big was up. He waited anxiously for her to continue. Matthew knew what was coming and had shared the news with Sal the day before.

Anne continued, "You know that I lost my job a couple of weeks ago, and your dad's roofing business is a little unpredictable right now..."

Dylan interrupted, "Are we moving?"

"No, Dylan." Anne tried to pick up where she left off, but Dylan interrupted her again. She had made sure to sit beside him in the booth for this very reason. Anne put her arm around him and said he needed to listen right now. He could ask questions when she finished.

"Last week I spoke with people up in Anchorage who are looking for someone who does the kind of work that I do..."

"You got a job!" Nora said.

"It's not the same as a permanent position. They need somebody to work in Alaska for a few months, then probably...probably...it will turn into a permanent situation. They want to see how I do on the job first."

Dylan squirmed nervously. "You said we weren't moving."

"We are not moving, Dylan," she said firmly. When that sank in, she added, "I will be moving, or going up there for a while so that we have money to pay the bills and have everything we need. Three months can pass very quickly. And in three months, we'll all be together again."

Nora finally realized what was going on and was quick to voice her disappointment. "Why can't we go with you?"

"No!" Dylan yelled across the table at his sister. More than disappointed, he was upset. Turning to his mom, he said, "Why do you have to go up to Alaska? Why can't you do the work down here?"

Nora didn't let up. "You said we'd all be going! This isn't fair. I want to go to Alaska. You said we would all go!"

Matthew was sitting on the opposite side of the booth from Anne. They looked at each other with the same thought: why did we think it was such a good idea to tell them in a public setting?

They expected Nora to be let down by the news, but they didn't anticipate Dylan's reaction. As long as he didn't have to move, they assumed he'd be OK with the arrangement. But now they realized it was just as upsetting for him to hear that his mom would be living away from the rest of the family, even for a short time.

"We already have a plan," Dylan said. "Going to Alaska by yourself is not the plan. You can't make up a new plan. You can't just change things like that."

Nora chimed in with her own definition of "the plan," which caused Dylan to protest even more. The conversation was drawing attention from other customers in the café. The situation threatened to go into full meltdown, so Matthew and Anne signaled to each other for a tactical withdrawal.

Anne grabbed Dylan's arm. "C'mon, we're going," she said, and slid out of the booth. Matthew left money on the table for the bill and tip. When they reached the exit, he, Sal and Nora went up the nearest stairway, while Anne and Dylan went in the opposite direction. They would all meet at Seattle Center for the first IMAX movie in an hour and a half when, hopefully, things would have settled down.

Light rain was still falling as Anne and Dylan walked beneath the viaduct and headed toward the waterfront. She tried to hold his hand as they crossed Western Ave, but Dylan was having none of it. They headed straight to the Seattle Aquarium, which was built on a pier extending over the water. It was where they were all supposed to be going as a group, but Anne still thought it would be a good place for her to spend time alone with her son. When they stepped inside the lobby, it was so quiet that she wasn't sure if the aquarium was open or not.

Behind the ticket counter she spotted a young woman, who was wearing a dark blue cap embroidered with the slogan: *I Work With a Porpoise.*

Anne smiled at her and said, "I like your hat."

The woman smiled back and said, "Thanks. We don't actually have any porpoises in the aquarium these days, but sometimes you can spot one in the harbor. There's still lots to see here though. We're pretty quiet right now. You guys will almost have the place to yourselves for a while."

After paying for admission, they wandered over to the tide pool exhibit, which held sea stars in a rainbow of colors from yellow and pink to orange and magenta. There were also purple sea urchins, bright-green anemones and spiny red sea cucumbers.

"Dylan, do you remember the sea stars and urchins we saw at the coast last summer?" Anne asked.

The surface of the pool rippled from a stream of water flowing off a rock ledge. Dylan stared down and didn't answer at first. Finally, he said, "It's not the plan that you told me would be happening. I'm not agreeing to anything else."

Anne walked over to him and put her hand on his shoulder. "C'mon, let's go see some fish." At the other end of the exhibit, they entered a dim hallway that had a cave-like feel. An eerie blue-green light spilled from a series of thick windows along the left wall, offering views into an enormous fish tank.

"You probably didn't know this," Anne said, "but your dad and I had our very first date here at the aquarium. That was all the way back in..." She had to think for a moment. "...1985."

Against the right wall Anne spotted a couple of couches, which seemed out of place. As she considered sitting down, the woman from the front desk came walking their way. Before Anne could ask, the woman said, "Feel free to relax. We used them for a private function last night, and they won't be picked up until this afternoon."

Anne sat down in the middle of a couch, which was surprisingly comfortable. It made her think about their couch at home and how uncomfortable it was by comparison. She sat back and watched the bright tropical fish moving slowly in and out of view: orange-and-white striped clown fish, yellow cowfish, mottled red leaf scorpion fish, orange spotted filefish, elegant Moorish idol fish with bands of black, yellow and white.

She had a flashback to when she was 11 years old and seeing the colorful tulips that would bloom outside the Boushay farmhouse in Ipswich. Suddenly the larger memory of a particular day came back to her, and it flooded her with a surge of emotion.

As the emotion subsided, she was left looking at Dylan, who was standing in front of one of the windows with his back to her. She called to him, and he walked over to the couch. For a moment he hesitated, looking to his mom's right, then her left, before realizing she had picked the middle so he couldn't sit too far away from her. He sat to her left and settled back against the cushions.

"I know how you're feeling right now," Anne said.

Dylan stared at the window onto the fish world, then turned to his mom. "I hate it when you say that. If you knew how I was feeling, you wouldn't be going to Alaska."

Anne's mind wandered to a time when she was six years old and sitting at the kitchen table with her grandmother, the original Nana B, who was making French macarons. As Nana B measured her ingredients from memory, she looked across the table and gave Anne one of her weekly lesson in French.

"Écoute: Il pleut. D'accord? Répète."

Anne repeated the phrase as her grandmother stirred the ingredients together in a large, heavy bowl.

"Il pleut, il pleut," Nana B repeated.

Anne had to keep practicing the phrase until Nana B was satisfied with her granddaughter's pronunciation. It was a memory Anne had never recalled so vividly.

She turned to Dylan and said, "I'm going to tell you a story, and I want you to pay attention."

The memory Anne shared with Dylan involved a day when she was 11 years old, the same age as Dylan. She was playing with friends in the family plum orchard. It was a blustery day in late March, when winter was just beginning to loosen its grip.

As Anne was climbing to the upper branches of a plum tree, she heard her father's voice calling to her. She climbed down and ran to meet him at the other end of the orchard. He said he had something important to explain back at the house. His Welsh accent flowed in its relaxed, musical way, but when her father put his arm over her shoulder, she felt his hand trembling.

They went to the study, which faced onto the sprawling back lawn that sloped down at the far end to meet a salt marsh. Outside the windows were planter boxes where her mother's early-season tulips had just bloomed in yellow, white, salmon and dark purple. As the strong breeze blew in from the ocean, it rattled the windows in their frames and made the tulips jostle each other.

Her parents were getting divorced. That was the first thing her father told her. They had not been getting along well, which had been obvious to Anne for more than a year, and it was now time for them to move on to separate lives. When Anne heard the word "move," she felt as if she were losing her balance. With one hand she reached for her father's arm, and with the other a desk in the study. She thought she heard rain falling outside, and in that moment she remembered the phrase that her grandmother had taught her. As Anne watched the tulips swaying outside the window, she whispered to herself—*Il pleut. Il pleut.*

Her father explained what would happen next. He would be moving out, and Anne would be staying in Ipswich with her mother. There would be visits at certain times every year and regular phone calls. When Anne asked where he was going to live, he said he was moving to Alaska.

She had always been closer to her father, and the thought of him moving so far away and leaving her behind pushed her off an emotional cliff. She screamed "No!" in such a loud voice that her mother, who had been standing just outside the door to the study and eavesdropping on the conversation, gasped audibly.

She wouldn't stay behind with her mother, she insisted. She wouldn't live in Ipswich while he moved to Alaska, where she had never been and knew little about. She was going with him when he moved out. She was going to live in Alaska too.

None of that was possible, he told her. Everything had been settled in a legal way. Plus, the job he would hold through the end of the summer wouldn't allow it. He'd be working as an engineer at the remote Prudhoe Bay Oil Field in preparation for the Alaska pipeline project. It would be seven days a week, working long hours and sharing a housing trailer with several other men. That was no place for an 11-year-old girl.

In the end, when her many pleas were exhausted, all Anne had left was one question: When would she see him again?

There was no way to know exactly, he told her. Maybe at the end of summer or early fall, when the work up north finished and he had time to find a permanent home in the Anchorage area.

In the study that afternoon, she hugged her father for a very long time, and over his shoulder she watched the tulips fighting back against a breeze that just wouldn't quit. Through her eyes, it looked like it was raining outside, but it wasn't.

"I didn't see my dad again for a year," Anne said to Dylan. "I felt so hurt that he would leave me behind like that with less than a day's warning. I was hurt, and I was angry for months. And my mom didn't handle the divorce very well, so it was even more difficult living in that big house with just her.

"A friend and I talked about running away to the Florida Keys. My friend wasn't serious about the idea, but I was. We saw a magazine article about the Keys, and it showed beautiful pictures of people scuba diving around coral reefs. They were swimming with brightly colored fish, like the ones in the tank here. It looked so amazing. That next spring, my mom let me move up to Alaska to live with my dad for good.

"So that brings us to my temporary job in Alaska. You know that I'll miss you when I'm gone, Dylan. And I'll be thinking of you all the time. I promise to call you and your sister as often as I can, and we won't be apart that long." Anne was about to say more but decided to leave it at that because Dylan's face was pressed into her jacket, and he was weeping quietly. She held him close as she stroked his back. *"Il pleut,"* she whispered. *"Il pleut."*

*   *   *   *   *

Sunday, March 26, 2000

It was a quiet Sunday morning in West Seattle, but the Mahoney household was in a minor state of frenzy. Matthew stood on the back deck

186

calling to Nora, who had decided to climb high up the backyard maple tree to see if any robins had laid eggs in their different nests. Matthew told her they were leaving for the airport in five minutes and she needed to come down right now, but she insisted on inspecting one more nest.

Inside, Anne was trying to double-check the mental list of everything she'd need for her time away, while Dylan was asking her to confirm all the activities marked on his handmade calendar. In the time since Saint Boushoney Day, he had come to terms with his mom's departure by making the calendar. It marked her location each day for the next three months and the activities she'd be doing, at least generally, as far as Anne could determine.

"So you take a plane to Deadhorse on the 27th...no, wait, the 28th, right? You get there in the afternoon. You said you get there in the afternoon, didn't you? Will it be early or middle or late afternoon? And will it be dark already when you get there?"

Anne put a hand on Dylan's shoulder as she stared down at a suitcase packed with clothing, toiletries, and a couple of engineering books. "Give me ten seconds, honey." She knew there was something she was missing that she needed to pick up that morning, but she couldn't remember what it was.

"Squids, leave the birds alone and get your butt down here right now!" Matthew called from the deck. "If I don't see you climbing down in the next minute, I'm coming up there after you."

When Dylan began to speak, Anne placed a hand over his mouth. Then it came to her. "Floss!" she said. She went to the bathroom and rummaged around in Matthew's toiletry kit until she found a full roll of dental floss. As she tried to leave the bathroom, Dylan blocked the doorway.

"What time is sunrise in Deadhorse on the 29th, which is your first whole day on the North Slope?"

"8:17 a.m." Anne blurted it out quickly and pushed her way around him. In a louder voice, she called in the direction of the porch, "Matt, we have to get going now! I hate being rushed at the airport."

He appeared at the back door along with Nora, who was annoyed at being called down from the tree. "I was five feet from the last nest, Dad! Why couldn't you let me just finish?"

"It's too early in spring. They're not laying eggs yet," her father said.

Anne held up the floss. "I'm stealing this from your kit."

Dylan waved his calendar in front of his mother's face. "I think you made up that sunrise time. I think it's earlier."

On the 20-minute drive to Sea-Tac Airport, Nora annoyed Dylan by rolling down her back window on the freeway and holding her hand in the breeze. It created a swirl of air in the back seat. Dylan had recently started putting gel in his short hair to make it stand up straight. The breeze was messing with the look, but he knew better than to argue with his sister directly.

"Mom and Dad, Nora is doing the window thing again. She needs to close it."

Without turning around, Anne called back, "Honey, please close the window."

"I'm warm from climbing the tree, so I'm cooling down through my hand. Otherwise I'll overheat."

"Close it now, Nora," Anne said.

The drama stretched out for a few minutes, with Nora closing the window in increments. Even after they arrived at the airport and were walking toward the Alaska Airlines terminal, Dylan and Nora both found ways to annoy each other or their parents. Only after Anne had checked her bags and they all went to the platform where a tram would take her to a satellite terminal did they focus on the fact that their mom was really leaving.

Anne crouched down in front of Nora to say goodbye. "OK, sweetie, I'll see you in three months. You be good to your brother while I'm gone and help your dad, alright?"

As her mom hugged her tightly, Nora answered, "Alright."

Anne was about to turn to Dylan when she spotted a small dab of blackberry jelly on the side of Nora's face. She reached in for a kiss, and licked the jelly away, which made Nora giggle.

"OK, that's gross, Mom," Dylan said.

Anne gave Nora a kiss, then turned to Dylan and kissed him as well. "I know you'll be OK, Dylan, and I know you'll be good to your sister. There's always a chance my schedule up there might change slightly, but remember that I am coming home in about three months."

"June 18. Your flight gets back here at 1:20 in the afternoon. I'll be checking your activities every day."

Anne looked into her son's face, which seemed so peaceful compared to how he had been nine days earlier. His blue eyes suddenly reminded her of the time when she was 11 years old and looking into the face of her father as he was about to board a plane for Alaska. She tried to push the memory aside.

They heard the droning sound of a tram pulling into the underground station. Anne felt a flood of emotion and had to hug Dylan again quickly. "I love you so much," she whispered.

"Mom, your train's here!" Nora yelled over the sound of doors opening.

She stood up and kissed Matthew. "Take care of yourself, Matt. And take care of our babies."

"I will. Call when you get to the cabin. And tell Maddie I said 'hi,'" Matthew said, referring to Anne's neighbor in Anchorage.

Anne grabbed the handle of her wheeled carry-on bag and rolled it onto the train with her. Matthew and the kids stopped at the threshold.

"What are you guys gonna do today?" Anne asked as she waited for the doors to close.

"We're gonna watch the Kingdome blow up," Dylan said.

An announcement on the tram speakers said to stand back, as the doors were about to close.

"One last thing, Matt," Anne said. "Promise me you won't use the Subaru for any work that you and Sal do."

As the doors began to close, Matthew smiled and held up his right hand as if swearing an oath.

Anne blew a last kiss through the window. Then the tram slid forward and disappeared into the tunnel with a whoosh.

*   *   *   *   *

On the drive to downtown Seattle, they stopped at a bakery to pick up fresh muffins before making their way to Capitol Hill. They found a place to park on the street, then walked to the top of a parking garage, which gave them an excellent view of downtown and the ill-fated Kingdome.

Beyond it was the new baseball stadium, Safeco Field, which had opened the previous July. The garage was becoming crowded with other people who had the same idea. There was a casual, festive mood to the scene, with people announcing the countdown as it reached 20 minutes to the scheduled time of destruction, then 15.

Matthew stared at the gray cement dome. He had always thought it was an ugly building. He never cared much for seeing a baseball game played indoors on artificial grass either. But he was feeling unexpected nostalgia for the old place. He and Anne had seen U2 play there in December 1997 during their PopMart Tour.

"Look at all the boats in the bay! It's crazy," Dylan said. He checked his watch. "Three minutes to go."

Nora stared up at the sky. They were directly beneath the flight path for Sea-Tac Airport. About every minute a jet roared above. "Can you tell which plane Mom is on, Dad?"

"It's hard to tell exactly because they're so high up. But it's close to the time she's taking off, so it has to be one of the planes going by soon."

The implosion was scheduled for 8:30, and as the time drew closer, anticipation built in the crowd. Then it happened. The detonation began with a series of loud cracking sounds echoing across the clear, quiet morning. The sounds corresponded with puffs of concrete dust rising from the ribs that ran from the top of the Kingdome roof and down the supporting columns. It was a rapid series of explosions that alternated from one side of the building to the other.

After the first set of blasts ended, the Kingdome remained standing for a brief moment. It was a strange magical pause lasting no more than a second or two, when the structure seemed to be defying the carefully calculated attack upon its integrity. Then slowly, the center began to collapse like a balloon losing air. The sides crumbled and fell inward. 125,000 tons of concrete came crashing down in a matter of a few seconds.

As it began hitting the ground, a cloud of dust billowed into the air and obscured the site. The cloud dust expanded up and outward, rolling over downtown buildings, cars and people observing the event close-up. It coated everything and everyone in a white concrete dust.

A cheer rose from the garage crowd as if they had all just witnessed the finale of a fireworks show on the Fourth of July. As amazing as the implosion was, Matthew considered it strange to cheer for the destruction. After all, there were tens of millions of dollars in construction debt on the Kingdome that had yet to be paid off.

Dylan was beside himself with awe. "That was incredible, Dad! Really incredible. I'm not kidding when I say that it was honestly better than the collapse of the Death Star!"

Matthew turned to see Nora's reaction. Instead, he saw the back of her head. She was facing in the opposite direction with her eyes to the sky, waving both hands slowly at a plane heading north in the hazy morning.

Chapter 9

Spring Breakup

As soon as her flight began its descent over Prince William Sound, Anne had that strange mix of feelings she got every time she returned to her home up north. She had a window seat on the right side of the plane, and when the cloud cover broke over the town of Cordova, she caught a glimpse of the College Fjord and the snow-covered mountains that began close to shore and continued inland as far as the eye could see. It was the Chugach Range, and Anne knew parts of it very well. Five minutes later, the plane touched down at Anchorage International Airport.

"Welcome home, baby!" Maddie said as she gave Anne a great big hug at the Alaska Airlines baggage claim. At 62 years old, the one-time California girl turned oil pipeline worker was old enough to be Anne's mother. It was a role she began to play when Anne first arrived in Anchorage, all tall and skinny in 1972.

Maddie Beardon was one of the rare female pipefitters who worked on the construction of the oil pipeline running south from Prudhoe Bay, which is where she befriended Anne's father. It was Maddie's husband, Charley, who helped Dylan Sr. select a cabin to buy in their neighborhood just south of Anchorage. Maddie and Charley lived next door, and a short path through a grove of Sitka spruce connected the two properties. Anne traveled along that path countless times through her teenage years to spend time with Maddie, who gave her guidance on everything from dating boys to hunting willow ptarmigan.

Maddie's wavy hair had been chestnut brown back then, but it had grayed over the years and she had recently cut it short. Anne complimented her on the new look, although Maddie said it felt a little strange feeling a breeze on the back of her neck for the first time since she couldn't remember when.

Soon Anne's bags showed up on the carousel, and they wheeled them out to Maddie's Bronco. They were met by the barking of two German shorthaired pointers inside. Whenever Anne visited, she liked to borrow Luna and Biscuit from Maddie and take them on long hikes.

"The girls are happy to see you," Maddie said.

"I wonder if they even remember me. It's been over a year," Anne said as she took off her jacket on a surprisingly warm afternoon. She climbed into the passenger seat and was immediately overwhelmed by the four-year-old, brown-speckled pointers licking her on both sides of her face. She laughed as she struggled to hold them back. "OK girls, alright, I missed you too!"

"And you thought they didn't remember you," Maddie said.

Anne petted them roughly on their necks. "Who wants to go for a hike today?"

The question set off a series of barks from the dogs and laughter from both women. When she was picking which breed to get, Maddie chose pointers because their need for regular exercise would keep her active as well. Three or four times a week, she took them on long hikes in the local foothills.

"Alright, that's enough. Settle down," Maddie commanded.

As they drove south, Anne didn't notice much snow on the ground, just small dirty mounds here and there where shade had slowed its melting. The grass was brown, the trees were bare, and the roads and sidewalks were all thick with dust from courses of sand laid down over winter. Anne opened her window and rested her arm on the door. The breeze felt good. It was just warm enough not to feel chilly.

"Breakup came early this year," Maddie said. "You'll be needing your mud boots soon at the cabin." "The Breakup" was an Alaska term for the time in spring when the ice in the rivers and lakes broke apart, and when the snow melted away. Warm temperatures also thawed the frozen ground and made walking off dry pavement a messy, muddy business.

"Some bears are waking up early too. I've heard stories from a few people down at the Big Wall who've had surprise encounters already," Maddie said, referring to the bar in the town of Girdwood, 20 miles away. "Take protection with you on the trail."

"I should stop by the bar to see Andre," Anne said. He and Dylan Sr. had opened the Big Wall Bar & Grill together in 1978, and it served as a popular watering hole for lots of people, particularly the community of climbers in the area. Andre and Dylan Sr. were both avid rock and ice climbers, and wanted to create a gathering spot for the like-minded to share route reports and inspiration. Running the bar was more a labor of love for them in the beginning, but over the years it built a core of regular customers. In recent years, however, the crowd of regulars had been diminishing.

"I believe Andre's out of town right now. You may have to wait until your break in May to see him."

"I need to thank him for helping me get this contract," Anne said. "He said that if they like the work I do, there's a really good chance they'll give me a staff job in the Anchorage office. Which is exactly what I want."

Maddie asked how Matthew and the kids were doing, so Anne gave an update of everything since her last visit. She also described the sense of panic she felt when she got laid off and Matthew's work had been cut back.

"Matt and I had agreed that I would never work on the Slope because I'd be away from the kids too much."

"Working up there usually means two or three weeks at a stretch," Maddie said, "followed by the same amount of time back home. I know people who have raised a family that way, but it's not ideal having one parent absent half the time."

"I know. I've heard stories about working up there. From you, my dad and others. But I don't really have any choice at the moment."

"There are 15 men for every woman on the Slope, and that's always been a big problem. If you do as much work as the men, you shouldn't have any trouble. You can't take any guff, but you also need to have a sense of humor about things. Above all else, beware of Texans. When I was up there, they were hands down the best pipefitters on the job…that is, once they figured out what permafrost was…but most Texans I met were chauvinistic assholes, and that's putting it in polite terms." Anne remembered her dad expressing a similar sentiment.

"How are things for you at the mountain?" Anne asked. Maddie worked as a supervisor at the Snowbird Café, one of the local ski resort's restaurants. She and Charley had earned enough over the years so that Maddie didn't need to work, but she'd told Anne that since his death, working helped to give her life some structure. It also kept her in better touch with the local community.

"We haven't had much snow this winter, so it's been a tough year. Less than half the lifts are operating now," Maddie said. "We had a lot of guests through last month, but the crowd has thinned since then. We'll probably close for the season in a week or two at the most."

They had been driving due south on Route 1, also called Seward Highway, but when the road reached the water, it turned southeast. Anne stared out at Turnagain Arm, a 40-mile-long branch of Cook Inlet. It was a wide body of water, almost five miles at its widest, with snow-covered mountains on the far shore.

The road and an adjacent railroad line hugged the water's edge from Rabbit Creek to the town of Portage, which was almost entirely destroyed by the Good Friday earthquake in 1964. The 9.2-magnitude quake caused the ground to sink six feet, putting most of the town below sea level and causing the waters of Turnagain Arm to come rushing in.

Anne remembered driving down to Portage with her dad during her first week in Alaska. She was shocked by the sight of so many abandoned buildings. On the drive back north along the highway, her dad gave her a stern warning as he pointed out to the mudbanks of Turnagain Arm. "Here's one of our rules, girl. We never walk onto those mudflats, OK? It can be tempting to go exploring out there, but that stuff is like quicksand. Your boots will sink down deep and the suction will hold you like cement. You see how it's low tide right now, and the water is way out there? When the tide comes in, it doesn't move in slowly. It moves in very fast. The water rises 35 feet from low to high tide, which is one of the biggest tide shifts in the world. It comes rushing in so fast that if you're stuck in the mud, there's likely nothing anybody can do for you except pray."

The warning proved accurate when Anne was living at the cabin. Several times a year, people got stuck in the fine, silty mud and had to be rescued by the Girdwood Fire Department, sometimes with the help of a dive team that used rods to blow air into the mud around a victim's feet. Every now and then, someone died. Anne remembered hearing the gruesome story about a last-minute rescue attempt by a helicopter crew that tried to pull a man out of the mud as the water was closing over his head. The rope they had tied around his waist ended up pulling his body apart.

From bears to earthquakes to deadly mud, Anne learned that life in Alaska involved a fair share of nature's dangers. Then again, it also had more than its fair share of nature's beauty and wonder. She and her father experienced plenty of it. There was no other place she'd rather be. As her father once told her, "We're not here to see Alaska, girl. We're here to live it. That's what makes it special. Let the rest of the world view it from the deck of a cruise ship. They'll never know the Alaska they're missing."

Twenty minutes south of the airport, they left the highway and turned onto Lower Potter Creek Road. It wound its way through neighborhoods in the foothills of the Chugach Mountains and climbed steadily. After a couple of miles, it became Upper Potter Creek Road and changed from pavement to gravel. They were 1,200 feet above sea level, where almost a foot of snow still covered the ground. Alder, cottonwood and Sitka spruce trees lined the way. Homes were spaced much farther apart on the upper road, and most couldn't be seen from the road itself. Every hundred yards or so, they'd pass a driveway that disappeared into the trees.

After a mile, the gravel road leveled and continued to where the treeline met the open tundra, followed by foothills that led to a ring of high mountains beginning with McHugh Peak, two and a half miles away. A quarter mile before the end of the road, Luna and Biscuit began barking. Maddie turned up the long driveway to Anne's cabin, and after a few twists and turns, the home came into view. It was a beautiful structure built in the '50s by a Scandinavian couple, with a stone foundation supporting massive white spruce and Sitka spruce logs up to 18 inches in diameter.

The cabin was two stories high, and the west end had a first-floor deck over down-sloping ground. On the second floor were three bedrooms, including the master suite, which had its own south-facing deck. Both decks had sweeping views out to Turnagain Arm, Cook Inlet and the mountains beyond when the weather was clear enough.

Off to one side of the cabin was a large garage that Anne's father had expanded to provide space for their "tools and toys," as he liked to call them, including a Land Cruiser FJ60, a Ford F-250 pickup, a trailer, a snow machine, a chainsaw, a log splitter, skis, snowshoes, gardening equipment, a cement mixer, a large assortment of tools, climbing gear and more.

They came to a stop in the driveway and stepped into air that was cold, crisp and still. Light flurries were falling.

"They did a good job," Maddie said, looking up at the red standing seam metal roof.

Anne opened the back of the Bronco and grabbed her bags. "I hope it lasts a long time. It cost us a pretty penny. I thought Matt was going to pass out when I told him the price."

"You should get 50 years out of it, or close to that anyway. To put it differently, you'll never need another roof in your lifetime."

They walked the bags to the front porch, then Maddie went back to the Bronco to retrieve a container of dog food and bowls. Luna and Biscuit were busy chasing each other back and forth on the path to Maddie's house.

"I better get going," Maddie said. "I have to do payroll work before my dinner shift begins at four. Call me if anything comes up. Otherwise, it's breakfast at my place tomorrow at seven, right?"

"I'll be there," Anne said.

"By the way, I went through your place this morning." Maddie said, "It looked like the cleaning crew did an excellent job."

"I appreciate it. And thanks again for the ride."

"You bet. And don't forget to change your watch. You're an hour behind Seattle time now," Maddie said and waved goodbye.

Making sure the cabin was cleaned up thoroughly after tenants left was important to Anne. In fact, it had become an obsession over the years to have it remain, or at least appear to remain, as it was when her father was still alive.

Anne stood for a moment before the front door, which had originally hung on the home of a wealthy fur trader in Three Saints Bay, a Russian settlement on Kodiak Island. The dense cedar door had ornate iron hinges that branched out like the horns of a caribou, and a heavy iron knocker in the shape of a standing bear.

When her father installed the door, he had burned his last name— BARRY—across the top. Anne reached up and traced a finger across each letter. After Anne had lived there for a few months, her father added a hyphen beside his name, and beneath it the name BOUSHAY.

When she arrived in Alaska in 1972, Anne's legal name was Anne Rhoslyn Barry, but her father politely insisted that she legally change her last name to Boushay. He knew how terrible it was for his ex-wife back in

Massachusetts to lose primary custody of her only child, and how important the family name had been to the two generations of Boushays he had known.

Anne unlocked the door and carried her bags inside, where she was met with the familiar smell of leather from the three couches in the great room. In front of the couches lay a large 19th century Tibetan rug with a colorful image of a tiger. Her father had served as an engineer in the British Merchant Marine, and on his travels around the world, he searched for cultural treasures he could bring home. Some of them he shared with friends, some he sold for a nice profit, and others he kept for himself.

The rug reached within three feet of a broad stone fireplace. Anne flipped a light switch, and a dozen Japanese wall lanterns bathed the room and the high vaulted ceiling in soft light. As she had done every time she returned alone to the cabin after her father's death, Anne placed her left hand on the wall and slowly walked clockwise around the room, feeling the bumps in each log, the places where one log was scribed precisely into the next, the gritty mortar between fireplace stones. With every step, she remembered the moments that mattered most to her while living in this home.

There was the day she climbed Ptarmigan Peak, the most difficult among the ring of peaks in the surrounding mountains; the time she had her first encounter with a grizzly bear while salmon fishing along the Nushagak River; she and three friends surviving a two-week backpacking trip through the Brooks Range; her first boyfriend at the age of fifteen and breaking up with him six months later; all the boyfriends and breakups that followed; braces, toothaches, and a broken arm; a snowstorm that trapped her in the backcountry for two days; a Fourth of July celebration when her Swiss mountain dog, Cunedda, knocked over a lantern on the back deck and set an American flag on fire; countless birthday parties; bagging her first deer; going to senior prom with Jared; finally understanding the concept of quantum spin; and mimicking her father's Welsh accent, much to his delight.

Then there was the time when Anne brought Matthew to meet her father. She had never seen him so happy with any guy she had brought home. She didn't quite understand why he liked Matthew so much since he had never fully approved of any of her previous boyfriends.

During the following week when the three went camping and salmon fishing together, a strong bond developed between her father and Matthew. As Dylan Sr. explained it to Anne, Matthew had been forced to leave the place where he had grown up and struggle to make a new place for himself in the world. And when it came to what mattered most in life, Matthew lived without fear.

At the end of that trip, Anne confessed to her father a reluctance to commit to a serious relationship with Matthew because he didn't share all the same interests as her, such as climbing. Her father replied that it was their differences that would make their relationship stronger. He assured her that Matthew had qualities she had not yet begun to appreciate. Dylan Sr. knew people and knew which ones were worth making part of your life. In his opinion, Matthew was a very good fit for Anne, despite what surface perceptions might suggest.

Those were the times that came rushing back to Anne. Through all those moments, her father was there to teach her so many important lessons. He was beside her to celebrate the successes, to soothe the pain when life proved unkind, and to share the most mundane of moments, each of which Anne now cherished as a polished gem.

When she completed her walk around the room, Anne reached up to a row of pegs and grabbed her Western straw hat. She wore one most of the time in Alaska, as long as it wasn't too cold—rain or shine, hiking or fishing. There were a couple more just like it kicking around the cabin. She had a bad habit of misplacing them or leaving them behind at a restaurant or a friend's house, so she always picked up an extra when she caught them on sale.

There was still plenty of daylight outside, and the sun wouldn't set until about 8:30 this far north. Anne thought about running to a grocery store to pick up a few things before it got too late, but when she checked the fridge, she saw that Maddie had stocked it with everything Anne would need for the next couple of days. At the front door, she called to Luna and Biscuit, who came charging into the cabin.

Anne picked up the container of dog food and the stainless steel bowls, then led the dogs into the spacious kitchen. She filled both water dishes because she knew the creeks they'd pass on their hike would still be covered in snow and ice. As the dogs drank, Anne carried her bags to the other end of the great room, where a stairway led to the family bedrooms. On that end of the first floor were her father's library, an office and a guest room with bath.

Once upstairs, Anne plopped her bags down on the king-size bed in the master suite. She changed into comfortable hiking clothes, then went to the end of the walk-in closet. A six-foot-tall safe held some important papers but mainly served as a place to securely store firearms and ammunition. She dialed the combination, then swung the steel doors open.

Firearms played no part in her life in Seattle, but when she was in Alaska, she considered them a necessity in the backcountry. She also carried pepper spray and always reached for that as a first means of dissuading a bear, which had worked for her once. Her father, however, disagreed. He believed that a charging bear was not a threat to be addressed with what he called "half measures."

Inside the safe were a Remington pump-action shotgun for upland bird hunting, a .30-06 rifle, a .45-70 Marlin 1895 lever-action rifle, two handguns and two cans of pepper spray.

Anne grabbed the Ruger .357 magnum and loaded the cylinder with hard-cast bullets. She hated the kick of any magnum. That was especially true with the other one in the safe, which was her father's .44. She fired it once at the range and received such a god-awful kick that she swore she'd never fire it again. There tended to be a lot of arguments about whether a .357 was enough to stop a grizzly. Anne would always answer that a .44 she couldn't control might only let her get in one shot. With a threatening bear, the goal was to land as many hits in the shortest time, and she could manage that far better with the .357.

From a hallway closet, she got a chest pack to hold the pepper spray and the Ruger, and a small backpack that she loaded with a few essentials, then led Luna and Biscuit outside. The flurries had stopped, and the sun began to burn through the low cloud ceiling. Before she forgot, Anne took out her cellphone and called Matthew. She got his voicemail, so she left a message saying she had arrived OK, was heading for a hike with Maddie's dogs and would call him again later that night.

They walked to the end of Upper Potter Creek Road, then headed in the direction of McHugh Peak. The trail was covered by snow, but Anne had practically memorized it over the years. They'd hike up a couple of miles, then loop back. Enough of a workout to satisfy the dogs and enough for Anne to work up a good appetite for dinner in downtown Anchorage.

*   *   *   *   *

The 1985 Land Cruiser started easily once Anne reconnected the battery. Every few weeks when she was away, Maddie would come over and run both vehicles for a while to keep oil circulated around the engines and the batteries charged. Her father had bought the Land Cruiser new and had only driven it 17,000 miles in the year and a half before his death, so despite being 15 years old, it was in excellent condition.

On the way downtown to meet her old boyfriend Jared at Humpy's Alehouse, Anne ran into a little rush hour traffic. She remembered how, growing up, she'd consider a two-minute delay a huge traffic jam. Back then, Anchorage seemed like a full-size city to her. With every visit north from Seattle though, it seemed more and more like a small town.

Wow, Anne thought, when she realized that in August it would be 20 years since she had lived in Alaska full-time. It didn't seem nearly that long. Some of the oldest memories remained the most vivid for her. She remembered driving downtown in late spring of her senior year with Jared in his dark green and white 1972 lifted Chevy K20 pickup. With a warm evening breeze blowing through the open windows of the truck, they'd blast music into the night.

On the floor between them was a box full of carabiners and cassette tapes, and the tape Jared liked reaching for most that spring was *Damn the Torpedoes* by Tom Petty and the Heartbreakers. On a Friday or Saturday night, he'd play it all the way through, then a second time, and a third. They had been dating less than ten months, but by that point their lives had melted together in so many ways that Anne never considered that their relationship could end.

They had met at Service High School, where they were both freshmen in 1976, but they didn't really become friends until the end of their sophomore year. That year and the next, they each had their share of high school romances but never with each other. It was the beginning of their senior year when it finally happened, and it grew into a relationship that was far more intense than either of them had experienced before.

She and Jared both had a reputation at school for their athletic ability: Anne at track for the 400-meter hurdles, hurdle relay and the 800 meters, Jared as a running back on the football team. Away from school, they were known for being especially adventurous at rock and ice climbing on difficult routes.

At school and around town, people got used to seeing Anne in Jared's truck. During the week, they'd ride back and forth from school and maybe head to a lake or creek in the Chugach for some afternoon fishing. On weekends, they'd drive up to the mountains to climb, hike and camp. In winter, they'd snowshoe, backcountry ski and occasionally snow camp. During school vacations, they'd disappear for a week at a time in the wilderness. Over that year, they were seldom apart.

Like Jared, Anne intended to go to college in Alaska, either at Alaska Pacific University or one of the state schools in Anchorage, Fairbanks or Juneau. She wanted to study environmental science and maybe follow her father by pursuing a degree in environmental engineering. In the fall of her senior year, she applied to three Alaska schools. At her father's urging, she also applied to the University of Washington in Seattle and California Polytechnic in San Luis Obispo.

She was wait-listed at Cal Poly and accepted at the other four colleges. Although Anne was leaning toward Alaska Pacific, her father made a strong effort to persuade Anne to go to UW. As he saw it, the UW had a much better engineering program, both at the undergraduate and graduate levels. Secondly, as someone who had been born in Swansea, Wales, sailed several times around the world as a young man, then lived in New England and Alaska, he wanted his daughter to spend time living away from home, even if it was only as far away as Seattle.

She fought him on it because she believed her father had a third—unspoken—reason. Namely, her boyfriend. He'd never openly disapproved of Jared. At the same time, her father never indicated that he approved of him, at least as far as Anne could tell. Jared was welcome at the cabin anytime—for dinners, holidays, whenever. Her father was always nice to him, and the two would have long conversations about climbing, football, world travel and other topics.

But Anne could tell that her father never really warmed up to him. He was strangely neutral about Jared the whole time he and Anne were a couple. Anne would ask her father why, and he would always avoid answering directly. "He's a good football player, a solid climber, and he's learning how to tie his own flies. What's not to like about that?" he would say. Or "The important thing is that you two get along well, Anne. If you're happy being with him right now, I have no objection to that. Truly."

Jared had high hopes of receiving a football scholarship, and had applied to UW when Anne told him she had applied there because of pressure from her dad. He didn't get in, but he wasn't too disappointed about it. Jared really had no interest in moving out of Alaska for any reason. He'd attend UAA, the University of Alaska in Anchorage. He could afford a trip to Seattle once a semester, he promised Anne, and he'd see her back home during school breaks.

Anne made an agreement with her father that she would attend UW for at least two years. After that, if she wasn't happy, she could finish her degree any place she wanted, including Alaska. She and Jared both expected that when the two years were up, she'd be back home and they'd be together again.

In August 1980, she moved into a dorm on the UW campus in Seattle. Her father flew down to see her a few times that first year. And Jared made a trip at the end of October for a three-day weekend. He didn't care much for Seattle and resisted commenting on some of the friends Anne had made at school. They saw each other when she returned home for Thanksgiving and Christmas, and again over spring break. By that time, Anne was feeling more comfortable with life in Seattle. She was doing well academically, and she helped to start an intramural soccer team with the other women in her dorm.

When she returned to Anchorage for the summer, Jared told her that he wouldn't be going back to college in the fall. Instead, he and his friend Toby would be taking jobs up on the North Slope. He'd be earning good money right away, instead of slogging it out for three more years at UAA. With the boom in oil production brought on by the building of the pipeline, a lot of guys Anne had gone to high school with had already headed north. It was hard to pass up the lucrative pay being offered even to laborers, which is how Jared and Toby would start.

That summer, she and Jared spent a few weeks together fishing, camping and climbing, then he was on a plane to Deadhorse. He'd see her in Seattle that October, he promised. But when October rolled around, he called Anne at her dorm and said his work schedule had been changed and he wouldn't be able to make it to Seattle after all. As Anne listened, she heard a difference in his voice, a change she couldn't identify except that he sounded like he had lost a piece of himself somehow. Or maybe it was nothing more than a weak phone connection.

On her first night home over Thanksgiving break her sophomore year, she and Jared went to a party at a waterfront home in the Bayshore neighborhood. Jared introduced her to a lot of new friends he had made on the Slope. Outside of him and Toby, Anne didn't know many of the 30-odd people in the place, and almost all of them were high on something. There were two stereo systems competing with each other, and Anne seemed to be the only one who noticed how annoying the resulting effect was.

In a number of rooms, including one of the upstairs bathrooms, people were doing drugs, and not just the pot and speed that were commonplace in high school. The sound of people snorting cocaine didn't stop until Anne left the party.

This was something she had seen when she was 14 years old and her father was dating a woman who ended up becoming seriously involved with coke, then heroin. Her father called it the "slope sickness," brought on by too many people making too much money too fast. And now Anne was seeing it again.

The third time somebody at the party offered her a line of coke from a mirror that held a pile of powder as big as a plum, she told Jared she wanted to leave. They argued until he finally agreed to drive her home. Over the course of that long weekend, she found out how deeply he had fallen into the trap. When she asked if they could go backcountry skiing that Sunday, he said he had misplaced his skis and that he wasn't really feeling that well anyway, so maybe they should postpone a trip into the mountains until her semester break.

When she returned home for Christmas, he told her that he wouldn't be able to pick her up at the airport because he didn't own a truck anymore. He needed to sell it but would be getting a new one...a brand-new one, in fact...when spring rolled around. In the meantime, could she borrow one of her dad's vehicles and meet him at the apartment he was sharing with Toby in Mountain View?

Anne knew that the Mountain View neighborhood wasn't the best place to live in Anchorage. When she showed up at the apartment, she was even more shocked at how disheveled Jared looked and what a mess the apartment was.

He had a drug problem. That was obvious. But he refused to admit it to Anne, and he wouldn't admit that he sold his truck, his backcountry skis and so many other valuable possessions for bags of cocaine. After a half hour of pleading with him to at least admit what was going on, she left. When she got back to the cabin, she went straight to her father, explained everything and asked what she could do about it.

"Nothing," was his first answer. Her father had seen Jared around town a couple of times that last month and knew right away that he had a problem and what that problem was. Jared was not the first one to catch slope sickness and he wouldn't be the last, her father explained. And based on Anne's visit to Jared's apartment, there was nothing she was going to be able to do in her short break from school to help him. Her father said he would be able to do something himself, however, along with the help of some friends. It would take time to get Jared into rehab, and his treatment would take several weeks. Until that was complete, Anne shouldn't be in touch with him at all. If the phone rang at the cabin over the next few days, her father would answer it.

It was the worst Christmas of her life, and it couldn't pass quickly enough. Anne went back to school early, and for two nights she practically had the whole dorm floor to herself. Her father called that first day to let her know that he had gotten Jared into the Tikishla Recovery Clinic. He would be there for eight weeks, which was a long time for treatment programs, but her father assured her it was the best program in town. He told Anne not to set her expectations too high for Jared once he gets out, especially any hope for continuing their relationship.

That was the hardest news of all for Anne to hear. She had already been going there in her own mind, and she had discussed her situation with her roommate and a couple of close friends at school. But to hear it from her father somehow made it more real.

When she did hear from Jared, it was on a rainy Saturday in March. Anne was about to head over to the football practice field for a game of intramural soccer when Jared called. He sounded better and he was calm, much calmer than Anne. But from his voice she could still hear it—the sense that he was missing a piece of himself, and now Anne realized that no matter what Jared did, he might never get that part of himself back.

He was moving to Florida for construction work, he told her. Toby had gone through a rehab program as well, and the two of them would start rebuilding their lives outside of the environment they had been used to in Alaska. Someday they'd return, but not for a while. Before Jared could ask her a question she might have trouble answering, Anne told him the six words she had been practicing for days: I can't be with you anymore.

It was the most difficult thing she had ever had to say, and she was surprised at how well Jared took it. He had been expecting to hear something like that anyway, he said. She was perfectly justified in feeling that way, and he would respect her decision. Would she mind if he sent her an occasional postcard or letter, he asked. She told him that would be OK. Jared said he needed to get going because somebody else was waiting to use the payphone, and besides, he was running out of quarters.

The field quickly became muddy during the soccer game that day, and the rain didn't let up at all. Anne's team won, but her mind was so far away from the game she was surprised she could even run straight.

The end of her time with Jared and the life she was building at school in Seattle gave her all the reasons she needed to continue studying at UW when the promised two years were up. After their breakup, there were postcards and occasional letters between herself and Jared, but it wasn't until the death of her father in the fall of 1986 when Anne saw him for the first time in six years.

From there, they rebuilt a friendship, and on her visits back to Anchorage she would meet up with Jared for dinner, coffee, a hike, or some fishing if it happened to be the right season. He had bought a small place on the north end of town, and every few years they'd go in together on a big load of birch and spruce rounds, then spend a weekend using her father's splitter to turn them into firewood for his house and her cabin.

As sad as their breakup had been, Anne was grateful that she and Jared had been able to stay in touch over the years, especially with the loss of her father. It kept her connected to those early years in Alaska that were so important in shaping the life she was living now.

*　　*　　*　　*　　*

Humpy's Great Alaskan Alehouse was one of Anne's favorite places to meet downtown. It had good beer, decent food and live music some nights. On a random visit there, she was likely to run into one or two people from her Alaska past. It was a little after six when Anne walked through the back door. She quickly scanned the wraparound bar in the center of the pub, then the tables, but she didn't see Jared. The place had a fair crowd for a Sunday night and it was somewhat noisy, with lots of conversations going on and Nirvana playing on the jukebox.

Jared surprised her by coming up from behind and tipping the back of her hat up. It was an old trick.

Anne spun around and smiled. "Hey, I should have known you'd do that!" She gave him a big hug. He was wearing a faded plaid shirt, and Anne couldn't smell any cigarette smoke on it. "You quit smoking again," she said.

"Yes, again. Three and a half months this time," he said.

"Nice. And the beard is back, I see."

Jared stood slightly taller than Anne and had kept himself in decent shape over the years, mainly due to the demands of the welding and fabrication work he did with Toby. He had gone back and forth with facial hair since high school, but once again had grown out his thick black beard. It had been a few years since Anne had seen him with one. She gave it a gentle tug. "It's looking good on you. Although I think I spot a few gray hairs in there," she teased.

"You can't pick on me until you've had at least one beer. C'mon, let's grab a table up front," Jared said, reaching out for Anne's hand, then leading her through the crowd to one of the open high tables at the front of the bar. He caught the eye of a server, held up his beer glass and signaled for two more of the same.

"Besides," he said once they sat down, "I'm not the only one. I bet I could find a few gray hairs under that hat."

Anne laughed. "Those gray hairs are from my kids. They don't count."

Jared smiled warmly at Anne and she smiled back. "Speaking of the kids, how are those little creatures doing?"

207

"Oh, they're doing great. It's only been…" Anne turned and stared out the front window of the pub and tried to count the hours of a day that had passed in something of a blur. Just then, the server showed up with two pale ales and set them down, along with two dinner menus.

Anne continued, "It's been 11 hours since I left Seattle, but I miss them already. It was all I could do to keep from tearing up as we said goodbye at the airport. Yes, Dylan and Nora are growing up well. Most days, one of them does something that really pisses me off. Then they do something that blows my mind at least a little bit. Nora started doing this thing with animal crackers last week, and I don't know where it came from. She'll eat a camel, then say the spirit of the camel is inside her."

"Sounds like quite the imagination," Jared said.

The server stopped by again and took their orders. Anne picked the fried halibut and Jared ordered a reindeer burger. Then she gave Jared a 15-minute update on everything she, Matthew and the kids had been up to since Jared's last visit to Seattle. Their dinners arrived just as Anne was finishing her report.

"The plan was for all of us to move into the cabin together this coming summer once I landed a job with benefits and once the kids were out of school. Matthew's been really good just rolling with it and seeing what kind of work he can get once he's up here. But, like I told you, we got hit hard financially. To pay the bills, I had to take this contract work. Tuesday morning I'm heading for the Slope. I really hoped to avoid working up north. No offense to your time there."

"Not at all. I wouldn't go back there for all the money in the world. You'll be alright though. It's just a temporary gig. What exactly will you be doing?"

"Contracting for BG. My dad's buddy Andre set me up with it. I'll be doing different things, like soil sampling. It's ironic because the company that laid me off didn't think I had enough experience in that area. I'll be outside a lot of the time, which'll be nice."

"Which'll be cold," Jared said.

"Which I've never had a problem with, unlike some other people I know," Anne said with a smile. When they went snow camping, Jared would always be the one to complain about his sleeping bag getting cold even though his was better insulated than Anne's.

She continued with the details of her job, which would start with a stretch of almost seven weeks. After that, she'd come back to Anchorage for a four-day break, then return for another four-week stretch.

The company would pay for any flights back and forth from the Slope to a contractor's POH, or point of hire. In Anne's case, that was technically Anchorage. She would be responsible for getting back and forth between Anchorage and Seattle, except the one round-trip flight agreed upon as part of her contract. So the final trip back home at the end was covered. She and Matthew had agreed that on Anne's four-day break, she should relax in Anchorage, rather than fly all the way to Seattle and spend precious money.

"Seven weeks is a long stretch up there, and a four-day break is crazy short," Jared said. "Everybody I know does two weeks on, two weeks off, or three weeks on, three weeks off."

"I know, but I need to be making as much money as I can. This is a one-time thing, and I'll just handle it. I have to. My break starts on May 15, and the fishing season begins down here on May 16. I'd like to catch some kings and ship them down to Matt and the kids."

"May 16 is a little early for kings around here. We'd have to go down to Seward or Homer and take a boat out. Seward if you only have one day. Even down there, it might be on the early side."

"When they find out I'm fishing for them, they'll be right on time. As you know, the salmon and I have always been like this," Anne said, smiling and holding up two crossed fingers. Jared was more experienced than her when it came to fishing of any kind, but Anne always seemed to have better luck catching big kings. Her record was a little over 37 pounds.

"So how's it going with setting up the charter fishing business? Have you and Toby gotten financing for a boat yet?"

"Well…," Jared began as he picked up a french fry and dragged it through a small puddle of ketchup. "It seems Toby and I have very different ideas on what kind of boat we should get. He thinks we should get a flat-front Munson, but I think we should be getting a Glacier Craft with a deep-V front so we can take people fishing offshore, and not just in the rivers and around the inlet."

"You guys need to work together," Anne said. "The season's only two months away. I think Toby is more the expert on boats, and you know

209

more about the actual fishing. So I think you should let him pick the boat, and you can focus on the rest, like working on the financing, the licenses, Coast Guard inspection, gear and all that."

Jared ate his ketchup-soaked fry, then began tapping his finger on the table for emphasis. "The boat you pick determines the kind of fishing you can do, so it's not as simple as you're making it sound."

Anne had known Toby almost as long as she'd known Jared. They could both be stubborn, but when they decided to work together—like opening the Arctic Machine and Welding Shop in 1994—they could really accomplish a lot. She wanted to say more, but she didn't want to get too deep into how he and Toby did business. "Well, when you guys settle on a boat, I think you'll be most of the way done," she said.

By 7:30 the dinner crowd had thinned. Many of the people arriving at Humpy's now were there to see a band that had been setting up on a stage near Anne and Jared.

Anne immediately recognized their first song. "Hey, they're playing 'Sweet Jane.' It's on the Cowboy Junkies CD I bought a couple of days ago. I listened to it twice on the flight this morning."

"Their version's too slow for me," Jared said. "I like the original by Lou Reed."

Anne told him that Matthew had the same reaction, but that she couldn't stand Lou Reed's voice. The only musician whose voice bothered her more was Elvis Costello. Matthew loved Elvis Costello but learned to never play him if Anne was in the house. One Saturday morning, when she was eight months pregnant with Nora, he accidentally put an Elvis Costello CD on the carousel, then went to do some work in the backyard.

Maybe it was the pregnancy, she told Jared, but she found the sound of Elvis Costello's voice so grating, especially since Matthew agreed never to play him in her presence, that she took the CD to the front porch and flung it into the street. Before Matthew could retrieve it, a passing car shattered the disc into shards. Anne laughed at the memory. "I promised to buy him a new one, and I did, but Matthew was so…so pissed at me!"

Between songs, Anne asked Jared about the woman he had been dating the last time Anne had visited. Her name was Marie, and they were still together, although not seeing each other as often. She had moved to the Mat-Su, he said, which was the Matanuska-Susitna Valley north of

Anchorage. Marie was working as a nurse at the regional medical center and wanted Jared to move up there with her, but he wasn't willing to commute 40 miles every morning and evening. She was doing a six-month assignment at the center and would be back at her regular Anchorage hospital by the end of summer.

They ordered another round, but Anne only sipped her beer over the next half hour. When the band finished their first set, she told Jared that it was time for her to get going. She'd see him on her return to Anchorage in mid-May. They fought over the bill, but Jared insisted on paying.

It was noticeably cooler out in the parking lot. The late March sun had already set behind Mount Susitna across the inlet, but the light of dusk still lingered. Anne enjoyed the drive back to the cabin and was feeling good about how Jared was doing. It was important to her that he live as good of a life as possible. He and Maddie were two of the main lights still burning in her Alaska life. Although she would never say it to either one, Anne felt personally responsible for making sure they both kept burning bright.

When she got home, Anne took the dogs outside. It was dark, so she turned on the outdoor lights and kept the dogs on a leash. Once they had both peed, she brought them inside and got a fire going. After settling on the couch with the dogs, she gave Matthew a call. First she spoke with Dylan and Nora before they went off to bed. Nora explained that they had just finished watching the video *Scooby-Doo on Zombie Island,* and asked her mom, as she had done regularly over the last few years, if they could please get a dog, and it didn't have to be a dog that talked. They would be getting a dog, Anne promised—in fact, two of them—but not until the family moved up to Alaska. Anne dodged any further commitments until Nora handed the phone back to her dad.

Luna and Biscuit were both resting their heads on Anne's lap. "The kids would love these pointers. I took them on a hike this afternoon, and we'll do a short one tomorrow morning. Then I have to give them back to Maddie. We should think about getting pointers."

They talked for another 15 minutes and made plans to speak again once Anne arrived on the Slope and found out the phone number in her dorm. From all she had heard, the oil companies were good about making sure workers were able to stay in contact with home, particularly those with families.

After saying goodbye, Anne found she was so tired that she might have fallen asleep right there on the couch, so she led the dogs upstairs. Maddie had made up the bed in the master suite that morning. As Anne climbed in, the dogs settled down on top of the red Hudson's Bay wool point blanket. Barely more than a minute later, Anne was sound asleep.

*   *   *   *   *

At quarter to six the next morning, she woke refreshed, dressed in running gear, and took the dogs on a quick trail run. After breakfast with Maddie, she headed downtown and picked up her ticket for the flight the next morning and her fishing license for when she would return in May. The bulk of her day was taken up by health and safety training classes for her NSTC—North Slope Training Cooperative—card, which was required for work on the Slope. Some information she knew from her previous experience, but most of it was specific to northern Alaska and was new to Anne.

Back home that night, she rummaged through the walk-in closet for all the cold-weather gear she'd need for working outdoors on the Slope. That included a couple of good hats, a pair of warm gloves and mittens, and a down parka with hood and fur fringe. She was also bringing her best pair of Sorels, although she was told the company would provide cold-weather boots and some other gear on-site.

There was a light rain falling the next morning when Maddie gave Anne a ride to the airport. They said goodbye, and Anne promised to call when she settled in over the next day or two. Anne checked her bags, then made her way to the gate and onto the tarmac, where she climbed the ramp stairs into the Boeing 737. The plane was not even a third full, so she picked a window seat near the front. There were three seats in her row, and just as she was buckling her seat belt, a man stopped nearby in the aisle.

He looked to be in his 40s and was dressed in a blue business suit and dress shirt. As he laid a briefcase on the middle seat next to Anne, she noticed he was wearing a Rolex watch and a wedding ring. After stowing his parka in the overhead, he sat down and offered Anne a friendly smile. He was an attractive man and neatly groomed, and his overall appearance made him seem a little overdressed and out of place with the rest of the crowd on the plane.

"Good morning. I'm Bert," he said and extended a hand.

Anne shook it. "I'm Anne."

"I'd ask you where you're going, but I think we all have the same destination today, isn't that right?"

Anne smiled at the comment. "This is my first time going to the North Slope."

They made small talk about their respective families back home as the last dozen passengers boarded, then the plane taxied to a runway and took off. Once it leveled out, a refreshment cart came around with drinks and snacks.

"I'll have a mimosa, please," Bert said to the flight attendant.

The woman showed a confused expression before breaking into a smile. Anne overheard the remark and was surprised as well. No alcohol was served on any flights going north, only the ones returning from Deadhorse, and Deadhorse itself was a completely dry town.

Finally, the flight attendant said, "Ah, I think you mean orange juice, don't you?"

Bert smiled and nodded graciously. "Yes, of course. Forgive me. I'll enjoy that mimosa on the way back, but right now I'll be perfectly content with a glass of your best orange juice."

Anne had brought a bottle of water with her, so she passed on the refreshment cart.

"You say this is your first trip to the Slope," Bert said. "If you like, I can give you a tour once you get settled. I'm the director of new drilling operations up there for Burtonwood Oil Company. That makes it easy to remember my name, by the way. Bert from Burtonwood. I work out of the Houston office. I've spent a whole lot of time on the Slope, so I can give you a personal tour around the little town of ours. Then, if you like, we can grab some dinner. It's a good idea to have a friend or two up north. You know, to pass the idle hours. Maybe we could catch a movie every now and then. I bet you like a good romantic adventure."

The comment caught Anne off-guard, and she wasn't sure if it was just her imagination or if the conversation had just taken a strange turn. It was the sort of moment when some people might let the comment pass, while others might bring the conversation to a polite close by reaching for a CD player and headphones. But that wasn't Anne's style.

"I'm married. I told you that."

Bert showed a very convincing look of surprise and raised his hands in a gesture of innocence. "Of course you are, Anne. And yes, you did tell me that. And as I mentioned earlier, I'm married as well. My wife is back in Houston right now. I typically spend two weeks with her and two weeks away from her."

Bert paused at that point to let his words sink in. A couple of minutes later, he picked up where he left off. "This is your first trip to the North Slope, so I was just trying to give you the lay of the land, an insight into the North Slope subculture. While you're there, it's important to remember how people interact and how our lives up north can differ from our lives back home."

Bert smiled as he continued, "There's a saying that I believe captures the essence of that difference quite concisely: there are no husbands and wives on the Slope. There are just men and women."

Anne was now completely through with the whole matter. What she had to say next, and the volume with which she said it, caused heads to turn in half the plane. "Find yourself another seat. Now!"

The command wiped the smile off Bert's face, but he didn't move. "There's no need to overreact, Anne. If you've taken my comment the wrong way, I apologize. Let's get our conversation back on track and enjoy the rest of the flight."

Anne stared at him without saying a word. None were required. She had an intense way of looking at people that could be unnerving. It usually wasn't intentional, but in this case it was. After several seconds, Bert was sufficiently rattled to pick up his briefcase, retrieve his parka from the overhead and retreat to the rear of the plane.

Anne put her head back against the seat, took a deep breath and let it out slowly. She was barely 20 minutes into the hour and a half flight, and she was already having second thoughts about this contract job. Maddie had warned her. Even her father had made certain comments that she could remember. If every guy she had to deal with was going to be that big of an asshole, the weeks were going to pass painfully slow. But there was no turning around now. Not in any sense.

The flight attendant stopped by and asked Anne again if she'd like anything to eat or drink. Anne asked for an apple juice.

"Apple juice coming right up." Continuing in a more confidential tone, she added, "If he gives you any more trouble, just let me know. We can divert to Fairbanks, and he'll be taken off in handcuffs. It happens every blue moon on this shuttle."

Anne did her best to shift her thoughts beyond the present moment. The rest of the flight was uneventful, and she spent much of the time staring down at the pristine, white landscape. The sky had cleared, and the sun reflected brightly off the snow. Anne had never traveled this far north outside of summer months, and she found the stark landscape to be quite soothing.

Further north, soft hills grew into the sharp peaks of the Brooks Range, where she had spent time backpacking with friends. On the other side—the north slope of the range—there were more small hills and eventually just flat, white-frosted tundra that stretched to the horizon. It gave Anne the impression that sometimes what made something beautiful was not the presence of elements but their absence.

Chapter 10
Pingos & Permafrost

When Anne stepped out of the plane at Deadhorse Airport, the North Slope welcomed her with a temperature of -10°F and winds at 20 mph. Blowing snow whipped around her boots on the long walk across the tarmac to the green bus that would take her and everyone else on the flight to their respective company camps. As people began boarding the bus, which was a small step up in luxury from a typical school bus, the driver announced that anyone who might need to go to the bathroom anytime soon should head over to the nearby terminal and return within five minutes.

Anne walked to the back half of the bus and lifted her bags onto the overhead rack before settling into a seat. Through the window, she watched as Bert walked to a waiting pickup truck and climbed inside. Good riddance, she thought.

A man wearing a New York Yankees baseball cap and a patch over his left eye took a seat across the aisle from Anne. The driver gave one more bathroom warning. When nobody took him up on the offer, he put the bus in gear and headed for the main road. Outside of the airport, Anne could only see a few low buildings. The town of Deadhorse was nothing more than an outpost surrounded by flat tundra covered in snow. The vastness of the landscape made the human encampment feel small and insignificant.

Out the right side of the bus was an elevated silver pipeline running parallel to the road. Anne noticed that the sky was mostly clear, but snow was blowing over the tundra and the roadway ahead for as far as she could see. She thought she saw a small animal run across the road maybe a hundred yards in front of the bus, but it was hard to tell.

"What's your camp?" the man with the eye patch asked.

Anne turned and saw that he was speaking to her. She didn't answer right away. The encounter on the plane made her cautious. He smiled and pointed to the eye patch. "My five-year-old girl back in Portland got a little too enthusiastic with her plastic sword. It should be fine by tomorrow. This is more of a precaution. I'm Terrence. I'm headed to ConocoPhillips. I do accounting up here," he said.

Anne smiled. "I'm Anne. Environmental engineering with BG." Then she added, "This is my first time on the Slope."

"Welcome to the ice paradise." Terrence pointed out the window at some buildings they were passing. "You'll notice some of them are built on stilts. Piers. It's one way to keep heated buildings from thawing the permafrost beneath them and sinking. Sometimes they use foundations with passive cooling systems. Or deep gravel pads. This is all tundra, and the permafrost is up to 2,000 feet deep in places. But if you're an environmental engineer, you know more about that than me."

"I know some, but I'm still learning. I'll be doing soil sampling, so I've been reading up on permafrost," Anne said. Looking out the front window of the bus, she added, "It's a nice day, but there's a lot of snow blowing around."

Terrence nodded. "That's how it is until the thaw. It doesn't really snow much up here. Very low precipitation throughout the year. But the snow that does fall just keeps getting pushed around by the wind all winter long. That stuff blowing across the road right now might have fallen last October."

Anne saw another animal run slowly across the road in front of them. It was closer this time, and it looked like a fox.

"You'll see a lot of foxes up here," Terrence confirmed. "Along with other critters. The foxes aren't afraid of vehicles at all."

As they rounded a bend in the road, a large structure came into view ahead of the bus. It was a giant oil drilling rig on the move to another drill site. The structure took up both sides of the road and didn't appear to be moving at all. Anne guessed it was about five stories tall.

"This rig might delay us," the bus driver announced through his intercom. A couple of groans came from the 20-odd passengers.

"They crawl along the road to another drill site at one or two miles an hour," Terrence said.

They caught up with the massive rig and followed behind it for a few minutes before the driver called out, "We're lucky. There's a turnout ahead."

"They have turnouts along the road every so often for this situation," Terrence said. "Traffic on both sides will be able to pass around."

Right after they overtook the rig, Anne saw a sprawling network of modular prefabricated structures coming up on the right. They looked like a bunch of extra-long shoe boxes on stilts, some of them two or three stories high. Other structures were sitting on the ground. "This camp has a lot of BG people. It might be your group," he said.

A minute later, the driver announced as much. When the bus stopped, Anne got up and grabbed her bags. "Thanks for the info, Terrence. I hope the eye heals OK."

"You bet. And good luck to you," he said.

Anne followed the instructions in her welcome kit and checked in at the administrative office. Behind the front desk was an older man pouring a packet of coffee into a coffeemaker. He turned when Anne stepped in, and when he saw her bags, he said, "Ah, you're checking in, I see. You must be Anne. I saw you on this week's list. The only woman."

"Yes, I'm Anne. I'm supposed to report to Seth Berkowitz."

At the sound of Seth's name, the man chuckled. "Nobody calls him Seth anymore. He's 'the Dude.' You know, like in *The Big Lebowski.*"

When Anne stepped into her supervisor's office, she understood why he had the nickname. Seth Berkowitz, a native Nebraskan, was not the spitting image of the famous movie character, but he did bear a very close resemblance. That included the long, wavy hair, the scraggly goatee, even the chunky cardigan sweater. Underneath it, he wore a colorful polyester Hawaiian-print shirt.

Seth had his feet up on his desk and was flipping through a Tommy Bahama catalog, but when he saw Anne, his eyes grew bright and he stood up. "Well, well, it looks like she has arrived. Indeed she has. And you must be the very same Anne Boushay Mahoney I had the distinct pleasure of speaking to over the phone not two weeks ago." Anne put her bags down, and they shook hands. "Please, have a seat," Seth said, and motioned her to a rattan lounge chair on the other side of his desk.

"All kidding aside, Anne, I'm glad you've arrived OK, and I'm super happy to have you on my team of engineers." Seth asked if he could get Anne anything, including coffee, which he said with an encouraging nod would be on the fresh side, but she said she was good. He shared a little bit about himself, then went on to explain first that he had a laid-back style of supervising, and that Anne should feel free to mostly "self manage," as he called it. Next he briefly went over the details of her assignments, her designated partners for field work, and the general expectations of the soil sampling she'd be doing.

Then Seth looked on the floor behind him, searching for something. "Ah, here it is," he said, and handed Anne a green hard hat. "This is for when you might happen to find yourself in an area where a hard hat is required. When that happens, you may notice that while your hard hat is green, the hard hats worn by some other people are not green. The color would be the dead giveaway indicator that you are in your first year of work on the North Slope. A newbie, or greenhorn, if you will. I have every confidence, Anne Boushay Mahoney, that you will graduate from your first year on the Slope with flying colors and shall leave behind the rookie helmet as soon as the clock allows. Until then, though, please wear it when one is required.

"OK, with the helmet discussion behind us, let's commence with the grand tour, where I shall point out the many places to find all the free, tasty food your stomach can handle; followed by our very fine gym; our decently sized movie theater; the building where you shall check out and check back all the equipment required for your fieldwork; the office where you may receive and replenish your supply of gear, such as gloves, boots, jackets, goggles, etc.; and finally, your living quarters."

Anne left her bags and helmet in Seth's office for the tour. It began with a stop in the large dining hall. It offered a wide variety of restaurant-quality food, including fresh fruits and vegetables, steak, seafood, including lobster tails on special occasions. There were four different menus each day—breakfast, lunch, dinner and a midnight meal—because work on the Slope went on round the clock.

There were also a couple of "spike rooms" open 24 hours a day. They had snacks, fruit, soda, juice, coffee, frozen pizzas that could be heated up, nachos, soups, sandwiches, ice cream and more.

Seth swept a hand in the direction of all the shelves and coolers. "This is like fantasyland for someone with the munchies. A 7-Eleven that never closes and where everything is free and constantly replenished. But it serves a more important purpose. You'll be working outside a lot of the time in subzero temperatures, so you're going to be burning calories at a much faster rate than usual. If you find yourself hungry a lot of the time, that's normal. Let me repeat that another way. Don't be concerned if you want to eat a lot more food than you're used to eating. Like my Italian grandmother would say if I had an Italian grandmother—*mangia, mangia, mangia!* Always stuff a few of these snacks in your jacket before you head outside for any length of time. Also, drink lots of water. This is a dry climate. Finally, if you brought skin moisturizer, use it generously. If you don't have any, pick some up today at the employee store."

Anne nodded. "I've got plenty."

"OK, good," Seth said. "I know I'm repeating a lot of what you heard in your training classes. It doesn't do any harm, and it might just do some good."

Next stop was the large gym, which included a cardio area, weight machines and even a small swimming pool. A bathing suit was not among the items Anne brought with her from Seattle, but Seth told her she could buy one at the employee store. "In my opinion, the BG gym is far better than any other you'll see up here, even without the pool."

After the gym, they walked to the movie theater, which could seat more than 50 people. It had a full schedule of classic movies and recent releases that played round the clock. It even had a concession stand with a big popcorn machine.

"I heard *High Fidelity* will be playing here soon," Seth said. "I'm looking forward to that one."

They looped back to Seth's office to pick up Anne's bags and hard hat before heading to the women's dorm on the second floor of a nearby building. The room was on the smaller side, and everything in it was on the smaller side: a twin bed, dresser, closet, TV with free cable hookup, desk and phone. Anne plopped her bags down on the bed.

"Here's another BG perk," Seth said. "You've got your own bedroom. At some other camps, you'd be in a room with another woman or sharing a room with a woman working the opposite 12-hour shift from yours." Seth pointed at the small TV sitting on the desk across from the foot of the bed. "It has all the news and entertainment you could want. And the bathroom..." Seth said, opening the only other door in the room, "...is right here. It's a Jack and Jill setup, so you'll be sharing it with the woman who has a bedroom on the other side of that door. Her name is Sarah Ketchins. She's on my team, and you'll be working alongside her sometimes in the field, but not right away. She's got a break coming up, so it'll be after that.

"Which reminds me, Anne. I know you requested an assignment where you'll be on for about seven weeks straight before taking a break. A very short break at that. If you discover that you've bitten off more than you can chew mentally, emotionally, whatever, you need to let me know right away."

Seth turned to the hallway door and pointed. "Now for the end of the tour. We're almost done. I'll show you the laundry room downstairs. Which reminds me, there's a housekeeping person who'll tidy up your bedroom and bathroom regularly, but you'll want to make their life bearable by picking up after yourself as much as possible."

They stepped into the hallway and began walking to the stairway when Seth suddenly stopped and put a hand to his forehead. "We need to talk about phones. Did you bring a cellphone with you?"

"No, I was told that there was free phone service in the dorms. And my cellphone company told me I'd have to pay out-of-network charges if I made any calls up here."

"OK, you did the right thing. I've seen people really freak out when they looked at cellphone bills after making calls from Deadhorse. I'm expecting that will change at some point, but yes, for now it's best to use the free phone service provided here.

"At the moment, however, there's a problem. The phone in your room, all the phones on this floor of the dorm, aren't working for some reason. They may be fixed tomorrow. They may be fixed in a year. I honestly don't know. You'd think with so many engineers around, they could figure out what the problem was. In the meantime, there's one phone that does work in the lounge at that end of the floor." Seth pointed behind them. "To make sure everyone gets a chance to call home and keep in touch with their loved ones, there's a clipboard with a schedule. If you could kindly write your name on the list ahead of time, and thereby reserve your half hour...the reservations are broken into 30-minute segments...then the world of the women's dormitory shall continue to spin peacefully on its axis. If something urgent comes up, you can always ask around to trade phone times."

Before Seth left Anne to settle into her room, he told her he was available to provide company at dinner if she liked, and she only needed to call his extension or stop by the office. He'd be there until six.

When she was alone in her room, she opened her bags and began storing her clothes in the dresser and small closet. At the bottom of one bag, beneath her cotton sweats, she found a dark blue T-shirt that didn't look familiar. When she pulled it out of the bag and held it in front of her, she recognized it as one of Matthew's workout shirts, which he must have left on the bed when Anne was packing. She held the shirt to her nose and smelled deodorant and sweat. It was a familiar, intimate scent she'd be able to detect with her eyes closed. The bottom drawer had some room left, so she folded the shirt and stashed it there.

After unpacking her bags and becoming familiar with everything in her bedroom and shared bath, where the first flush of the toilet was loud enough to startle her, she walked to the lounge at the end of the hall to see the phone reservation list. It was a clipboard holding a stack of pages, one for each day, with a line for every half hour. The sheets for the next few days had names filled in for the slots from early to late evening, prime time for calls home after work and dinner for people on a day shift.

Anne filled in her name for a few slots in the coming week. It was only 4:00 and nobody had reserved the next half hour, so she settled onto the couch next to the phone stand and called Matthew. They talked for the full 30 minutes before the woman who had reserved the next time slot walked into the lounge and Anne had to say goodbye.

More women showed up in the dorm as their work shifts ended, and Anne was able to meet some of her neighbors, including Sarah Ketchins. She was almost ten years younger than Anne and was suntanned, which made her stand out in her current environment. They sat down in Anne's room to talk. Sarah had a touch of a Southern accent, which Anne had always found pleasant.

She told Sarah all about herself and her family back in Seattle, and pointed to two photos pinned to the corkboard beside her bed. They were recent ones of Nora and Dylan.

"Oh, look at those two cuties," Sarah said. "I bet you miss them already. But don't worry. Time passes quickly up here. I keep track of my time by watching my tan. Just when it starts to fade, it's time for my three weeks back in Miami."

"You fly back to Miami every three weeks?"

"I'm on a three-week rotation, so it's every three weeks."

"Isn't that expensive?"

"Nope!" Sarah said, and smiled in a carefree way that reminded Anne of her friends in high school. "You can't tell anybody about this, OK? But my POH isn't Fairbanks or Anchorage, like everybody else's. It's a long story, but at least through the end of this year, Miami is technically my POH. So they pay to send me back and forth. Pretty sweet deal, huh?"

"I bet," Anne said. "If you ever get sick of the cold tundra, you have Florida beaches just days away. You know, I've been wanting to go to Florida my whole life, and I still haven't been there. It's been like a dream for me to go diving in the Keys."

"The Keys are amazing," Sarah said. "A little overbuilt in places, but as beautiful above water and below as all the pictures you've ever seen. Miami has a different vibe, but it's still all about the sun and the surf. I wouldn't live anyplace else. My partner, Jasmine, and I have a two-bedroom place that's not far from the beach. You all are welcome to stay with us anytime. We're sorta, kinda near Calle Ocho, but you probably have no idea where that is. One of the small art galleries in our neighborhood finally...finally agreed to commission one of my pieces. It's sitting in a back corner of the gallery right now, waiting for someone to fall in love with it."

Sarah then walked through the bathroom to her bedroom and brought back a folder with glossy photos of the many works of art she had created, including three tables. Two of them were coffee tables, one three-cornered, the other rectangular. The third table was small and tall with thin, elegant legs and a skirt of rooster feathers that were shiny black.

All were painted in black lacquer, but what really made them remarkable was that each had a box built into the top of the table. The boxes were covered with glass tops that looked down into scenes depicting underwater tropical landscapes. There were jagged pieces of coral, along with wispy strands of seagrass and many-armed sea anemones swaying in an imaginary current. Each scene was bathed in a different tropical color cast by a tube of neon hidden from view.

"These are amazing," Anne said, and she truly was amazed. "How did you create everything down inside each...box?"

"That's what they are. Shallow boxes. Inside them are clay sculptures, and each one has a different kind of scene and a different color that represents...well, a mood, I'll say. I decided not to paint the clay, but have the light and shading do everything I wanted each piece to express. The frames are made of ash. Designing them and painting them were the hardest parts really."

Sarah laughed and raised her fists in mock anger. "These things actually drove me fucking insane for weeks on end. I almost destroyed the first one with a hammer. Hiding the neon tubes and the power boxes was very frustrating work too. But they all pretty much ended up the way I imagined them being."

"So is one of these in the gallery?" Anne asked.

"Yes, the tall one. Because it takes up less floor space. They absolutely would not take the coffee tables. But if tall girl sells soon, then the gallery will take the others. I'm sure of that." Sarah stared down at her photos, and a smile slowly broke out on her face. "I've worked on all kinds of projects, but I think these tables are the craziest thing I've done." She looked at Anne and asked, "Can you remember the craziest thing you've ever done?"

Anne drew a blank on the question at first, and it frustrated her. Sarah was so young and had already created such amazing art. Anne couldn't think of anything she had ever done that was so crazy and original. Then something came to mind, and she just blurted it out. "I had sex on the *Titanic.*"

Sarah's eyes grew big, and she laughed. "You did what?"

Anne smiled, then explained.

Sarah enjoyed the story. "That is crazy," she said. "Truly crazy. And you're both survivors."

There was a knock on Anne's open hallway door. Two more of her neighbors announced they were heading to the dining hall. After Sarah returned her folder to her room, she and Anne joined the others and headed off for dinner.

Later on, Anne had a chance to see more photos of Sarah's art, including bright, colorful work in different mediums. It all captured Sarah's interpretation of light, sky, earth and sea in Florida. Anne finished up her evening by reading some of the material she had brought with her on thermokarsting. It was a subject that would put most people to sleep, but it kept Anne engaged for almost two hours. At that point, her eyes grew heavy, so she turned off her reading lamp and slid beneath the covers. The last thing she saw in her mind's eye were the faces of Nora and Dylan as she kissed them goodbye at the airport.

* * * * *

Anne's alarm went off at 5:30 the next morning. Twenty-five minutes later, she was ordering breakfast. Through the windows in the dining hall, she could see that it was still dark outside. She vaguely remembered Dylan asking what time sunrise was on her first full day on the Slope. Well, this was it and she still didn't know.

As she was scooping up her last bite of scrambled eggs, her field partner showed up in the dining hall and headed straight to Anne's table. David Herbst, a 26-year-old engineer from Minnesota, had curly blond hair and a wide smile.

"You're Anne. I'm David Herbst," he said, then took off his jacket and sat down at her table. "Take your time, please. We have no rush to get out there today."

"I'm all done actually." Anne looked around the dining hall. There were about 25 people there, but David had walked straight up to her. "So how did you know it was me?"

David smiled and looked around. "Well, I think I'm familiar with most everybody here. Plus," he said, and tapped a finger on the green helmet sitting between them on the table, "this helped."

Anne smiled. "Of course."

After stopping by the spike room to grab a few things for lunch, they stepped into the morning air and felt the sting of a -19°F temperature. Their company pickup truck was waiting for them in the lot, which was well lit so workers could see if bears or other critters were close by. A fuel truck was just finishing its rounds.

"Up here," David said, "the gas stations come to you."

Anne looked around at all the diesel exhaust plumes, then noticed that none of the seven trucks in the lot were occupied. David said, "They keep the engines running all winter long unless they're in the shop for repairs. Otherwise, they'd be hell to try and start in this cold."

They had 60 miles to drive that morning before beginning work, and they used the time to get acquainted, which was turning into something of a practiced drill for Anne. As young as David was, he told Anne that he had worked on the Slope for almost four years, so he was considered fairly experienced among the environmental engineers working for BG. He pointed to the noticeable scars across his nose, which Anne had indeed noticed, and said they came from a dog attack when he was a small child.

"I didn't hold a grudge," he told Anne. "My girlfriend and I have two Chesapeake Bay retrievers, and I miss them as much as I miss her. Well, almost as much. But they're family, you know."

David told her that most people who worked on the North Slope were up there for one reason: to make money. They worked jobs that kept them busy twelve hours a day, seven days a week for one to three weeks, usually two, followed by the same back home before repeating the cycle. Their time on the Slope could be summed up in three words: work, eat, sleep.

"Not me," Anne said, "at least not yet. I'm fascinated by this place, as barren as it is. I've been wanting to experience it for a long time. My father worked up here almost 30 years ago, in 1972 when the pipeline started. He always told me stories about it, but now I'm experiencing the place firsthand."

"It is a unique place," David said. "Speaking of unique, our boss is quite the original, or actually a very good copy of an original. Wait until our next team meeting. He always ends it by saying 'the Seth abides.'" The comment made them both laugh.

They had been driving for almost an hour, and the light of dawn was casting streaks of gray across the snow, which took on tones of blue as the light increased, then finally orange when the sun broke above the horizon. The light revealed a large mound of snow in the distance on the right, and it sent a long shadow pointing west.

Anne squinted into the light and felt the warmth of the sun on her face. "Oh my God, this is beautiful."

"Hearing you say that reminds me that you're absolutely right. I can forget it sometimes."

In the light of day, Anne had a better view of the snow mound. It was bigger than she first thought.

"They're called pingos," David said. "They're mounds of soil-covered ice that can reach over 200 feet high. Think of them as giant frost heaves. Pingos are one of the favorite denning spots for animals up here. Everything from grizzly bears and polar bears, to Arctic ground squirrels, foxes and wolves. Hunters like them, too, because they can climb up to the top and spot game way off in the distance."

As they got closer to their worksite, David explained that they'd be surveying the surface stability across a mile-wide map grid and replacing some equipment. The survey work was fairly simple and would normally be done by technicians rather than engineers, but Anne's supervisor wanted to give her a practical knowledge of all the projects their engineering team did on the Slope. At some point, she'd likely be called on to design a similar survey project herself.

The site was an old oilfield where pipelines and power cables had once been buried in the tundra. When the trenches were initially dug, the moss had been ripped up and the permafrost exposed to sunlight. The trenches had since been backfilled and either seeded with native grass or covered with sod, but the area had to be surveyed regularly because erosion or other natural occurrences could cause the situation to repeat itself, even years after the new ground appeared to have stabilized.

The technical term was thermokarsting, and it was exactly what Anne had been reading up on the night before. It happened whenever the top layer, or active layer, was torn up. The active layer insulated the permafrost and kept its temperature from rising above the freezing point. The active layer could be soil, sand, moss, or a mix of those, and its temperature would typically rise above the freezing point for some part of the year. In the case of this site, it was moss.

The moss layer was only ten inches thick generally, but it kept the temperature of the permafrost steady at around 31 degrees and insulated it against the summer sun. In turn, the solid permafrost kept precipitation from percolating down into the soil, making moisture available to the moss and thereby keeping it alive. With only a few inches of rainfall a year, the tundra would quickly become a frozen desert without a stable permafrost, Anne learned. She found the dynamics of the relationship fascinating.

When the relationship was disturbed by having the moss torn up, the permafrost began to melt. The melting formed pools that expanded and created pits and depressions across an otherwise smooth terrain. As these pools, or thermokarsts, grew they melted more of the permafrost below them, which released water and organic matter that, in some cases, had been trapped and frozen for millennia.

Thermokarsting was a process that could occur naturally in different environments around the world. But on the North Slope it was also oil drilling, and all the associated human activity, that produced the phenomenon. In the last 30 years, a lot had been learned about how to avoid disturbing the permafrost. Still, every time a new worksite or drill site was created in the tundra and every time one was decommissioned, environmental mitigation was required. For Anne, it provided a good-paying engineering contract and a foot in a new world.

When it was time to leave the warmth of the truck, Anne zipped up her down parka, tightened her Sorel boots and put on a hat. She also pulled on a pair of gloves that weren't too thick, and over them big mittens, which she'd remove to take measurements. When they stepped outside, the air was still. Anne looked around and noticed floating ice crystals. As they moved, the crystals glittered and sparkled in the bright sunlight. This was something she had seen before. Sometimes called "diamond dust," it was a magical effect that also gave the sun a thin halo.

The temperature had warmed all the way up to -14°F according to a thermometer on the outside of the truck. It was cold, but Anne had spent time outdoors in colder weather. One time when she went snow camping with Jared, they encountered temperatures around -25°F. But that had been a long time ago, and right now -14°F was more than cold enough for her.

They stuffed some instruments into backpacks, grabbed a tripod from the back of the pickup, and wandered a hundred yards onto the tundra in the direction of a red-and-white striped surveying pole.

"When they built the pipeline back in the '70s," David explained, "they didn't understand what they were working with. You don't get a lot of permafrost in Texas, you know. So the Texans laying the pipe just did what they did when they laid pipe in the Middle East or wherever. They dug trenches, laid the pipe and buried it. The trouble is that the oil they were pumping was hot, around 150 or 160 degrees. That quickly melted the permafrost. Then the pipes sank down in the mud.

"That's why they ended up putting pipeline above ground on VSMs—vertical support members—wherever there's permafrost. Seth said that your dad worked on those."

"He was one of the original designers," Anne said.

"Very cool," Seth said. "So the VSMs keep the insulating moss intact. It's the same principle with the buildings in our camp. Most of them are built on stilts. Even with the roads up here, they have to use a lot of gravel to insulate the permafrost. It takes five feet of gravel to insulate as well as ten inches of moss."

He then told Anne about a company doing exploration in the Arctic ten years before the pipeline was built. They had an airstrip for planes to bring in camp supplies. Because the pilots sometimes had difficulty seeing the strip from the air, they used a bulldozer to carve giant initials of the company at the foot of the runway. That exposed permafrost, which continued melting every year. Ten years later the initials were still there, but they were 35 feet deep.

"The oil companies made a mess of things in the beginning," David continued. "Luckily they didn't do as much harm to the wildlife. You'll see the big animals when the weather warms up in late May, but there's a really cute critter I'm pretty sure you'll get to see today."

When they stopped to take their first reading, David motioned for Anne to turn around. They were being followed by an Arctic fox. It had fluffy white fur and blended in well with the snow-covered landscape. The fox kept its distance, but when Anne and David walked to a new spot, the fox advanced along with them. This continued several times until they put on their backpacks yet again and moved.

When Anne looked back, the fox remained sitting in the same place. "Why did it stop following us?"

David pointed in the opposite direction. Anne saw two new foxes trotting toward them from far away. "We just crossed into the territory of a different group. They know exactly where their boundaries are and won't trespass. Not unless they're looking for a fight. By the way, don't let any of them get too close to you. A good number of the foxes up here have rabies."

By 1:00 they had completed almost half of their measurements and headed back to the truck for lunch. After Anne hoisted the aluminum tripod onto her shoulder, she turned to look at the sun's position in the sky and said, "It seems like it's still morning."

"It's not quite April, and the days are already long up here," David said. "The sun won't set until almost 9:00 tonight. By the way, I need to mention something about that tripod. Our team has six of them right now, and that's the only one that works properly. We won't get new ones until May or June. That one's number five. Hence the number five spray-painted on it. The others have legs that get stuck, clamps that won't hold, or some other problem that will have you cursing whenever you have to use them.

"So here's the deal: we can check out equipment like tripods for up to three days. That gives us two more days with number five before we have to return it. But we have to keep it overnight in one of our rooms, or else someone else on our team will find a way to steal it. Everybody knows number five is the best, and it becomes a game of who can get it next. One time, Dominic took it with him to the dining hall after work. When he went to use the bathroom, I switched it with number three. He didn't notice until the next day when he went to use it."

Anne smiled. "I'm sure he was happy about that."

"We all had a good laugh. Like I said, it's our little game, and it helps to keep things light on the team."

They settled into the warmth of the truck, and after David did a radio check-in, they spread out their lunches. They had each picked a chicken salad sandwich along with a number of snacks. As Anne was peeling the plastic wrap from her sandwich, she watched David open his own and squeeze packet after packet of mustard onto the chicken salad. After he had emptied a sixth packet, she watched him reach into his lunch bag and pull out several more.

"Um, David...don't you think that's enough mustard for one sandwich?"

He seemed surprised by her comment, then stared for a few seconds at the pile of bright yellow mustard.

"You're building a pingo," Anne said.

David finally nodded and returned the unopened packets to the bag. "You know, I'm already seeing the value you bring to our team."

*   *   *   *   *

Life on the Slope soon fell into a pattern that was neither too comfortable nor too uncomfortable for Anne. Most days, she and David would leave camp at 7:00 or 8:00 in the morning and return between 5:00 and 7:00 in the evening, with maybe an hour or two for reports or the processing of soil samples. Their days in the field could be cold and tedious, but there was enough variation in the routine to keep things interesting.

Most of their work involved drilling for soil samples at various depths. They'd sometimes be joined by a technician or two, depending on how many sample cores needed to be retrieved and how deep they needed to drill for them. The drills they used varied from a simple hand auger to a large drilling unit mounted on the back of a pickup truck. One drilling machine was so big they had to tow it on a trailer. It moved like a tank on special treads designed not to destroy the moss layer. Anne had no idea how to operate it at first, but after watching David and the technicians use it a few times, she learned to work it herself.

Once they had the soil samples, they'd typically do testing on them in a small lab back at camp. Sometimes they packed the frozen core samples in a cooler with dry ice and shipped them to a BG lab in Fairbanks for more extensive analysis.

Bad weather was sometimes a factor. When a storm kept them in camp, they'd spend their day in the lab or writing up findings. Anne had her first taste of a really fierce storm about a week after she arrived.

She and David were scheduled to visit a site fewer than 20 miles away, but during the middle of the night the temperature dropped to -27°F and the wind began gusting up to 60 mph. There wasn't any snow falling, but the strong winds whipped up what was on the ground and created whiteout conditions that made it impossible to see more than 20 yards.

"They're calling it Phase Three conditions," David told Anne as they watched the storm through the window of the dining hall where they were eating breakfast. He explained that Phase Zero was normal road conditions,

231

which was most days in spring and summer. Phase One meant that only necessary travel was allowed, and you had to get approval from a supervisor. In Phase Two conditions, only essential travel was permitted, and vehicles had to travel in convoys and be in constant radio contact.

"When it gets to Phase Three, all roads are closed and nobody can travel unless it's an emergency or critical to operations, and then it's in convoys again. I pity anybody who gets stuck out there in that stuff. In the middle of winter, it can drop to 60 below."

By that evening, the storm had ended, and the next several days in the field passed quickly. Anne's thoughts were usually focused on the work she was doing or the landscape around her. It was at the end of the day, as they drove back to camp, when her thoughts would shift to Matthew and the kids. She missed them, and she missed the many small moments, like sitting down with Nora to help her figure out a problem with her homework. Or braiding her hair, which Nora had mentioned the last time they spoke on the phone. "Dad can do a braid, but sometimes he does it too tight," she said. "A mom braid just feels better."

Dylan sounded like he was taking her absence in stride. Anne heard a lot of "Dad and I" when she spoke with him. "Dad and I just got back a while ago from Lincoln Park, where we were using the telescope…yesterday Dad and I patched the movie screen, and we'll be putting it up in the backyard before you get home…" They both had worries about Dylan slipping back into a negative space, but according to Matthew, he was doing well in and out of school.

The only major challenge she saw was coming that Saturday morning, when Dylan would have his braces put on. Matthew never had braces as a kid, but Anne did. She told Matthew to definitely be prepared for a reaction. "There's some pain involved, but I'm guessing that won't be a big problem. It's having the metal braces in his mouth, having his mouth feel so different…you know how he feels about change, Matt."

Chapter 11
Bubble Trouble

Saturday, April 15, 2000

Business was on the slow side when Matthew started his shift on Saturday afternoon. It was the calm after the storm, or the latest storm, for dot-com startups. Matthew had worked the night before, when the buzz at the bar had been all about the tech-heavy Nasdaq Composite Index dropping 9 percent in one day, ending a week in which it fell a whopping 25 percent. That was on the heels of the Federal Reserve raising interest rates and a court finding that tech giant Microsoft was guilty of antitrust violations. All bad news for the tech sector.

Smart money was returning to the lower-yielding, but safer, traditional stocks. Startups that had been burning through money on their way to becoming the next big thing on the Internet were now running out of cash. The dot-com bubble was starting to burst big-time, and everyone who owned a startup company or startup stock was freaking out about it. One guy at the bar on Friday night was Edward Smith. He told Matthew that, according to his calculations, he had lost more than $1 million in less than a month. He had to repeat it to Matthew twice because the bar was so loud and Edward, in his state of shock, could only muster a strong whisper.

On Saturday afternoon, Matthew saw Edward, and other regular customers who had invested heavily in startups, return to the bar. They all showed up wearing their bravest faces, but they all moved liked survivors from the *Titanic,* wrapped in gloom, with the glitter and giddiness all gone. As each arrived, they took a seat at the large community table at the end of the lounge, where a growing number of them were sharing their misery. With every passing hour, the table began to look more and more like a leaking lifeboat.

From what Matthew had heard, this was just the beginning. As capital continued to dry up, more Internet wonders would come crashing to the ground. And to think just a few months earlier, 14 of those companies paid an average of $2.2 million for a 30-second advertising spot during the Super Bowl.

All Matthew could do was offer an encouraging word here and there, but mostly he just kept their glasses full. He only had so much sympathy for people who brought an amateur gambler's mindset to the business world. Plus, he was having his own bubble troubles, specifically the bubble of debt that he knew was going to burst around the end of April.

Anne's contract pay was supposed to head off that problem. The first paycheck should have shown up in their checking account on April 5. Anne called to say that there had been a problem with the paperwork she filled out for direct deposit. She had to fill it out all over again and resubmit it. Her supervisor promised her that her regular pay, and all of her back pay, would show up in their account on April 19, but it made Matthew worry.

He had already used what little available credit there was on all but one of their credit cards to pay for gas, food and everything else. That morning, he had almost emptied the Mickey Mouse jar so he could make a final payment on Dylan's braces, which were being put on at the orthodontist's office that day. Working a double shift, he had a three-hour break with a few tasks to accomplish before returning to work at 4:00. He had the kitchen prepare him a Cuban sandwich, then grabbed a sparkling water and headed out to his truck. The first stop was the soccer field, where he picked up Nora. They had to swing by a Safeway to buy a small box of animal crackers, Nora's ongoing snack obsession, before picking up Dylan at Samuel's house.

They all arrived at the orthodontist's office for the big event of the day. Dylan was approaching the moment the way a prisoner approaches his execution. Matthew did his best to lighten the mood by talking about the upcoming fishing season. It was the kind of subject that always got Dylan jabbering away about what kind of lures might work best on the salmon, but this time it only elicited a blank stare.

The silence continued in the doctor's waiting room. When Dylan's name was called by the orthodontist assistant, he let out a long sigh before walking slowly toward the back room and the chair that awaited him. Matthew had brought his phone charger, and he moved to a seat next to a plug. He intended to use the next hour to catch up with a number of people.

Nora spent five minutes studying the outside of her animal crackers box, where a polar bear, tiger, lion and buffalo were pictured behind bars. She was soon bored and felt like talking, so she walked up to the receptionist's desk.

"Do you want to know why I have to eat animal crackers every day?" Nora asked.

The young receptionist flashed her a pleasant smile, but she was busy typing information into her computer. Just then her phone also rang, so she gently waved to Nora as a way of letting her know that this was not a good time to chat.

There were ten chairs in the waiting room, and Nora made her way to the one at the far end, where a doorway led into a long hallway. Dr. Anderson's office occupied half of the first floor in a very large Victorian house, with living quarters occupying the rest of the downstairs and all of the upper floor.

The door to the hallway was partially open, and Nora could hear music coming from a distant room. Her father was busy on the phone and the other two people in the waiting room were focused on their magazines, so none of them saw Nora disappear down the hall. She walked slowly in the direction of the music, which was coming from a room just ahead, where a boom box was playing the classic British tune "Rule, Britannia."

When Nora reached the doorway, she was awed by what she saw inside. The room was decorated with a large red rug and crushed red velvet fabric adorning the walls. At the opposite side of the room stood a tall, gilded throne. Sitting on it was an older woman in full regal splendor. She sat straight as a rod, and wore a sparkling tiara, a luxurious white mantle and a royal blue sash draped across her chest. Her right hand rested atop a golden scepter.

Nora needed a moment to take it all in. When she finally did, she whispered "Wow."

She stared at the queen while the queen stared back. Finally, the queen raised her scepter, held it up momentarily, then lowered it once again. "Enter, child," she said in a voice brimming with authority.

Nora advanced into the room and stopped several steps away from the throne. There was another moment of silence before she asked, "Are you a queen?"

"I am Queen Victoria, but you may call me 'your royal highness' or 'your majesty.' Do you know how to curtsy, child?"

Nora shook her head. "What's that?"

"No matter. What is that box you carry?"

Nora raised her right arm and looked at the box of animal crackers she was holding by its string. "These are animal crackers, your majesty. They give me special powers." Nora opened the box and pulled out a cracker. "This is a bear. See?" She bit off its head, chewed it and swallowed. "Now I have the brain of a bear inside me." She pulled another cracker from the box. "This is a rhino…no, wait, it's a hippopotamus, I think." After eating its head, she said, "Now I have the brain of a bear and the brain of a hippopotamus inside me. And that's beside my own brain, so I have three all together." Next came a tiger. "Now I have the brain of a bear, the brain of a hippopotamus, the brain of a tiger and my own brain inside me. That's just the first step. Next I eat their bodies, and that gives me the spirit of the animals. But it only lasts until midnight. That's why I have to eat animal crackers every day."

Victoria's eyes grew big, and she smiled. "Ah, you are a sorceress! How impressive. And what land do you come from, sorceress? What is your clan?"

"You mean my family?" Nora asked.

"Yes, in what land do they dwell?"

"Well," Nora began uncertainly, "my dad's family is from Ireland, and my mom's family is from Wales and France."

Victoria smiled again. "You have relations on the continent! How fortuitous. I've been looking to form a new alliance with the French crown. You, with your French blood and your powers of sorcery, could be the key that unlocks it all. Together, we can bring about a new empire. Once this is accomplished, if you like, I could make you dauphin. Or, rather, dauphine. Now let me teach you a proper curtsy."

By the time Nora returned to the waiting room, her father was asking the receptionist if she had noticed where his daughter had gone.

"There she is," the receptionist said, pointing to the doorway.

"I was talking with Queen Victoria," Nora said with noticeable excitement. "She lives in this house, and she's a real queen."

The receptionist turned to Matthew and smiled. In a lowered voice, she said, "Victoria is Dr. Anderson's mother. She used to work in the theater, and playing a queen was her favorite role. She really misses it, I guess." The receptionist paused to consider how to word her next statement. "There's some mental decline, I think, but her spirit is…definitely super strong."

Matthew made Nora sit next to him for the remainder of the wait, during which time she told her father a number of things about her new acquaintance. "Queen Victoria said I have magic powers, but I think she's really the one with magic powers. You know what she told me? She said if I wanted, she could turn me into a dolphin."

It wasn't long before Dylan finally reappeared. Matthew went to the receptionist and counted out $550, while Nora told her brother all about her encounter with royalty. Dylan's arms were crossed, and he was staring down at the checkerboard carpet with a look somewhere between detachment and annoyance.

When Matthew finished with the receptionist, he said, "Let's have a look at your braces, D-Man."

Dylan turned toward his father, shook his head, and with his mouth closed tight returned to staring at the carpet.

"Alright," Matthew said. "You can show me later. Let's go."

Jennifer was waiting for them at the house. She'd be babysitting the kids until Matthew's shift ended at 10:00 that evening. When she said hello to Dylan and asked how it went at the orthodontist, he shook his head, then marched into the house and up to his room.

Jennifer looked at Matthew and said, "That's how it can go the first day. I remember it well. Braces are no fun."

"He's being very quiet," Matthew said. "That might mean nothing, but it might possibly…"

Nora interrupted to inform Jennifer that "Dylan always gets real quiet before a meltdown."

"Let's not assume the worst, OK, Squids," Matthew said. Then to Jennifer, he added, "I'll have my cellphone on me tonight. Call if he gets worse. I'm gonna walk to work, but I can be home in five minutes if something comes up."

Matthew gave Jennifer most of his remaining cash to buy dinner and rent a couple of movies. He also told Nora she needed to go to bed when Jennifer said it was time. No arguments, no games. Turning to Jennifer, he said, "If you need an easy dinner, they both like pizza."

Nora disagreed. "Dylan can't eat pizza anymore because of his braces. I heard the cheese gets stuck in them."

"Actually the hard crust is a bigger problem," Jennifer added.

"We can get Thai food," Nora said. "Noodles are OK with braces. Jennifer, I know the place to order from and what's good there, so you can leave that to me. First, we should pick up movies at Blockbuster."

A half hour into Matthew's shift, and before the dinner crowd had arrived, a tall, thin woman wearing faded jeans and a sweatshirt walked up to the bar and asked for Matthew Mahoney. She looked young enough that he would card her if she tried to order a drink. Her long hair was pulled back in a ponytail, and she wore black plastic-frame glasses.

"That's me," Matthew said. "What can I do for you?"

She extended a hand, and Matthew shook it. "I'm Lyka Ancheta," she said. "Sal Camacho's brother is friends with one of my brothers. He told me you were looking to hire someone as a roofer."

"Indeed I am. Do you know someone looking for roofing work?"

Lyka gave Matthew a skeptical smile. "Umm, yes. Me. That's why I'm here."

Matthew was taken aback and replied apologetically. "Of course…wow, sorry about that. I've never had a woman apply for a roofing job with me. I'm sure there are lots of women who roof though." He thought of all the roofers he had ever known, but in that moment he couldn't actually remember any who were women.

He got over his embarrassment and continued, "I'm looking for someone to start the first week of May. Can you do that?"

"Yes, I can."

"OK, that's good. And let's back up a little. Have you ever done any roofing?"

"Sort of. A brother and I were visiting the Philippines last year, and we helped an uncle on that side of our family install new gutters on his house. And I shingled a shed in his back yard. It was a pretty small shed, but I used a nail gun on it. Sal's brother said you use nail guns."

"We do. Here's how this'll work." Matthew turned around and reached into a drawer in the backbar. He pulled out a generic job application used at Roy's and handed it to Lyka. "First, you need to fill this out. If you're hired, I'll pass it along to my boss. You want to make sure all your information is complete and up to date. The part that I'm going to pay most attention to is this…" Matthew took a pen from his shirt pocket and circled the section titled "References."

"I need two recent references. If they give you a good report when I call them, you can show up on the job and we'll see how it works out."

"Great," Lyka said. "Can I fill it out here?"

The bar wasn't too crowded yet, so Matthew said, "Sure. Have a seat."

After Lyka sat down, she pulled the sleeves of her sweatshirt up to her elbows and scanned the application. Matthew handed her a pen. As she accepted it, he noticed how thin her arms were and wondered if she'd be up to the physical demands of the job. Then he noticed a tattoo on the underside of her right forearm. The tattoo was hard to miss. It stretched from her elbow to her wrist and spelled out in very ornate script the word "FORGIVE." Matthew didn't want to be caught staring at it, so he immediately looked up and continued, "If you like, I can call your references when you finish filling out both sides. If that goes well, I can tell you where to show up for work."

Fifteen minutes later, Matthew had spoken to all of Lyka's references and gotten solid recommendations. "We start work on Monday, May 1. I'll give you a call once we have the address for the house we'll be working on," he told her. "Keep in mind: it can be a dirty job, so dress accordingly."

*   *   *   *   *

Word had gotten around about the new menu at Roy's, so Saturday dinner was busier than usual. After three months celebrating the cuisine of Greece, the new focus was on the island of Cuba. Matthew was pleased with the change because he found the Greek cuisine, at least as presented by Roy's, to be a little on the bland side. Not that he would ever say anything to the kitchen crew. He didn't have to—they admitted privately to the rest of the staff that their Greek presentation was decidedly underwhelming. But they had to follow the recipes as handed down by the head office, where Roy's and two other restaurants were managed.

The Cuba menu brought a welcome boost of flavor, like the omelette stuffed with Caribbean spiced yams, chayote squash, poblano peppers and queso fresco. Along with a more vibrant menu, the brick walls of the restaurant were covered in new paintings and photographs depicting Cuban culture in bold, unapologetic colors.

Dennis had to open the back dining room at 5:30, rather than 6:00 or 6:30, to accommodate all the customers showing up to try a taste of Cuba. Along with the dining rooms, the bar was also busy. Matthew's work didn't start to slow down until a little before 9:00.

It gave him a chance to chat with Eric the Red, who had been parked on a barstool for the last hour and a half. Eric was questioning Matthew about his finances, specifically how Matthew could make any money when he had to pay for a babysitter.

"I'm definitely in the black tonight," Matthew said.

"OK, tonight for sure. But I've seen you here on slow nights. Everything you make must go to paying Jennifer. So what's the point of working those shifts? Tell your boss you'll only work weekends when it's busy."

Matthew smiled. "I can't cherry-pick the good shifts. That's not how it works. Dennis has to spread the lucrative ones around, so everyone has a chance to make money. Maybe I break even some nights when she babysits, or even lose a little money, but I keep my job. On the other end of the equation, Dennis isn't scheduling us to work the same nights, and Jennifer is willing to babysit whenever I need her. Do you know how hard it is to line up a reliable babysitter who your kids really like? The arrangement makes my life a lot easier, so I don't care if I'm losing a little money. Besides, the whole situation is temporary. Anne comes home in June."

Roger, the other bartender on duty that night, told Matthew they had a blown beer keg. It was the second one in the last hour. Thanks to the Cuban drinks on the new menu, they had also pulled their last rum from the storeroom. All that remained were the three open bottles sitting on the shelves of the backbar. Matthew guessed it would be enough to see them to closing.

Just as he was mixing what seemed like his thousandth mojito of the evening, Matthew heard something that caught his attention. It was a guy speaking in a Boston accent. As Matthew poured the cocktail into a glass and garnished it with lime and mint, he continued listening. There was something strangely familiar about the voice, and it wasn't just the accent.

Matthew looked down the bar and spotted a middle-aged man sitting next to Eric the Red. They were talking about the baseball game between the Mariners and the Blue Jays earlier in the day. Highlights were playing on the bar TV. The man was wearing a dark sweatshirt, and his neatly trimmed beard was mostly white. The moment before Matthew consciously recognized who it was, he felt his scalp tingle. Then it struck him. The beard threw Matthew off since he had never seen his brother with any facial hair.

There was Francis Mahoney, chatting away with Eric. For a moment, Matthew wondered if he might be hallucinating. Then a waiter walked up to the bar and asked if the drinks were ready for table 24. After placing the mojito with the rest of the drink order, Matthew turned back toward his brother in disbelief. Yes, it was Francis. It absolutely was him. What in God's name was he doing at Roy's? The man was wanted by the FBI. Even Eric the Red talked about how he'd love to turn in Francis Mahoney and collect the reward money. And now Eric was sitting one foot away from the infamous fugitive without realizing it.

Francis nodded as Eric praised the performance of Alex Rodriguez in the game. Then he looked over at Matthew and showed an easy smile. "I'll have a Chianti. Something very dry."

Matthew turned to the backbar and stared at a row of bottles in front of him. Why is my brother here, he wondered? To see me. That was the only thing that made sense. But why? The ticket machine began spitting out more drink orders, so Matthew located the driest Chianti that Roy's had. He uncorked the bottle and poured out a glass. The bar had a mirror behind the rows of liquor. Matthew used it to watch his brother talking to Eric and gesturing at the TV to emphasize a point. This could end badly, Matthew thought. The last thing he wanted was to have someone in the bar identify Francis and make a scene.

As Matthew delivered the Chianti, Eric excused himself to go outside and answer a phone call.

Francis picked up the glass and scrutinized it for cleanliness before tasting the wine. "Not bad, little brother. Not bad at all." Then Francis smiled again. "You're nervous, aren't you? You think this guy Eric is gonna figure out who I am. Or maybe someone else. Listen, nobody is gonna recognize me, OK? Relax."

Matthew registered his brother's words, but he was still in shock. The two hadn't seen each other in more than 12 years. Matthew noticed the toll time had taken. There were new wrinkles on his brother's face. His reddish-brown hair had receded further and turned a light rust color. But the eyes, Matthew could see, were the same steely gray eyes that more than once had put the fear of God into Matthew when he was younger.

Suddenly he thought of Buzzy and wondered if Francis' eyes were the last ones he had looked into before dying. Matthew felt something that might have been anger and he wanted to let Francis know about it, but that emotion was mixed up with so many others that Matthew simply asked, "What brings you here?"

"An important favor. I have not asked you for any favors since we were last together at your wedding. Nor will I ever ask you for one again."

As confusing as the moment was, Matthew was certain of one thing. He wanted to see his brother leave Roy's and never interrupt his life again, so he got straight to the point. "What's the favor?"

Francis took another sip of his Chianti, then carefully placed the glass down on its cocktail napkin. "I'll visit you again in a while. I needed to know if you were receptive." With that, Francis stood up and began to leave. On his way out, Francis walked right past Eric, who was in front of the restaurant finishing his phone call. Even with the noise of the bar, Matthew could hear Eric yelling into his phone, "OK, well fuck you too!"

When Eric returned to his seat, he unloaded his frustration onto Matthew. "That cocksucker won't let me back in his bar! He said it was a six-month ban, and six months are up, but now he's telling me he never said it was six months. 'No,' he said, 'I told you it was at least six months, not just six months.' The fucking bar is right at the end of my street. I can leave there and walk home in two minutes. No DWIs, no accidents." Eric paused for a moment, and continued in a softer voice. "That motherfucker's gonna pay. I'm telling you, he's gonna pay."

Eric hadn't been looking at Matthew during his rant. When he finally did, he saw a blank stare on Matthew's face. "What the fuck's wrong with you? You look like you've seen a ghost."

Before Matthew could reply, he felt his cellphone ringing. He held a finger up to Eric, suggesting he'd return soon. Then he told Roger he was taking two minutes out back. As he stepped into the cool evening air, he opened his phone.

"I wanted to give you a report," Jennifer said.

"OK, thanks," Matthew said, anxious to hear what kind of update she was going to deliver.

"He didn't eat any dinner. He's sitting on the couch with his arms crossed. He hasn't really been talking much. Hardly at all."

The information told Matthew everything he needed to hear. It was not good, but it helped to pull him out of his stunned state. "Roger should be OK alone. I'll be up there soon."

Matthew let Eric know that he had to leave because of a family situation. After printing his sales report and dropping his receipts in the safe, he hung his black tie in his locker and headed up the hill. Halfway there, he began to jog. If he got home in time to avert a disaster, it would be worth breaking a sweat.

He was too late though. Nora was waiting for him at the open front door. Pointing up the stairs to the second floor, she yelled, "Major meltdown!"

Matthew could hear Dylan screaming, but he wasn't prepared for what he saw when he walked into his son's room. There was blood on the hardwood floor and on the oval beige rug. Dylan was sitting on the edge of his bed with his hands over his mouth. His face, his hands and his shirt were covered in blood. When Matthew caught his son's eyes, he could see that he was terrified.

Jennifer was kneeling on the floor beside Dylan and dabbing at his face with a bloody washcloth. When she saw Matthew, she said, "He just did it, Matt. He was trying to take the braces off with this." She handed Matthew a bloody steak knife. A cook at Roy's had sharpened the whole set for Matthew only a week earlier.

"Jesus," Matthew whispered as he knelt down in front of Dylan and took hold of his hands gently. "I need to see in your mouth, Dylan. Open it for me, OK?"

A tear ran down Dylan's cheek as he slowly moved his hands. When he opened his mouth, he said in a strained voice, "I want them out, Dad. I want them out." As Dylan spoke, blood trickled down his chin and small flecks of it hit Matthew's face.

Jennifer handed Matthew the washcloth and said she would get a fresh one. "Make it a bigger one, a clean one from the closet. And wet one end of it, please."

As he pressed the cloth to Dylan's face, he could see that his son had sliced open his lip pretty good. When Matthew looked inside his mouth, it was hard to tell clearly if there were more cuts. Then he saw a pulse of blood emerge from Dylan's upper gum.

Mouth wounds usually bled a lot, Matthew knew. With the initial shock wearing off somewhat, he took a deep breath. He had never seen his son injured this badly, and it wasn't easy to shake off. Another trickle of blood moved over Dylan's chin, but it was thinner than the first. Dylan flinched when Matthew tried to open his mouth a little wider.

"Don't!" Dylan moaned and moved his hands over his mouth.

"It's OK if you swallow some blood, Dylan. There's no harm," Matthew said.

Jennifer returned with the towel and Matthew used the wet end to wipe Dylan's hands and face. He wanted to see if there were more wounds besides his lip and gum. He didn't see any.

"I'm not sure about the inside of his mouth," Matthew said to Jennifer, "but his lip is gonna need stitches at Highline."

"No," Dylan moaned.

"Sorry, D-Man. There's no other option here."

"I can go with you guys, Matt," Jennifer said. "Or I can stay with Nora until you get back. I don't work until tomorrow afternoon, so it's alright."

Dylan was the only one in the room who noticed that Nora was now standing in the doorway. "I'm going to the hospital with you," she said.

Matthew turned around. "It's not necessary, sweetie. Jennifer will stay here with you."

Instead of agreeing, Nora appealed the case to her brother. "Dylan, do you want me to go with you?" Dylan stared at his sister, but gave no sign of an answer. Then she added, "You need a friend to be with you."

Dylan looked at his father, then looked back at Nora before nodding slowly.

"Hold this to your mouth," Matthew said as he folded the towel and handed it to Dylan. To Jennifer he said, "You don't have to…"

"I said it's alright. I'll go with you," Jennifer said.

The emergency room at Highline Hospital was more crowded than the last time Matthew visited. It's what he expected with it being a Saturday night. Chelsea was one of the people working the front desk, and she recognized him when he walked in.

"I heard about your eyes, Matthew. They're all better, I hope." Then she saw Dylan, and her expression changed. "Uh-oh, what do we have here? Is he your boy?"

"Yes," Matthew said. "He'll probably need stitches on his lip, and he's got cuts inside his mouth. Same insurance. Nothing's changed."

Chelsea asked a number of questions, including Dylan's full name, birthday and medical history, before printing out an ID band and wrapping it around his wrist. "Don't worry, honey," she said. "We've got doctors who are gonna take good care of you. You'll be cleaned up and feeling better before you know it."

It took a little longer than Chelsea suggested before Dylan was seen by a doctor. As they all waited in the examination room, Nora began reaching into the clear plastic bins along the back wall to see what kind of medical supplies they held. When Matthew noticed what she was doing, he said, "Please don't touch any of that, Squids."

In an attempt to occupy Nora, Jennifer asked, "How did you get the nickname 'Squids'?"

Nora shrugged. "It's what my dad calls me."

"He gives some of the people at Roy's nicknames too," Jennifer said. Turning to Matthew, she asked, "What's your deal with nicknames?"

Matthew explained that where he came from, everybody earned at least one nickname growing up, if not more. Young children were often given one by their parents or older siblings. As they grew older, it was their friends who labeled them with a nickname that could live with them for the rest of their lives. The one bestowed by friends typically were more harsh. And in the end, most nicknames proved more durable and indelible than any tattoo.

One of Matthew's nicknames was Goldfinger. He earned it when, as a teen, he and Buzzy went to the Massachusetts State House one night and attempted to remove some of the gold leaf from the building's dome. Whenever he visited South Boston now, all he had to do was walk down Broadway or stop at one of the town's many bars to hear someone call out "Goldfinger."

Nora's nickname came about during a visit to the Seattle Aquarium. They had a family membership when she was very young, and Matthew liked to take her there during the week when it was less crowded. She loved everything in the aquarium, but she especially enjoyed seeing the octopuses. When she was two years old and saw them for the first time through the large windows, she traced their movements on the glass with her finger.

Her father, not being well informed on the subject of marine biology and not really caring that he wasn't, called them squids. The term stuck with Nora. From then on, all octopuses were called squids. So were eels, salamanders, earthworms and anything else that resembled an octopus in any way. Nora loved calling it out loudly as she pointed at the various creatures in the aquarium, in the backyard or in the living room when they were watching a wildlife show on TV.

Matthew even found that it helped distract Nora when she was crying about something or throwing a tantrum. He would call out "Squids" and point to the back door. Nora would pull herself out of whatever emotional tailspin she was in and follow her father to the backyard, where they would hunt beneath bushes and under rocks in search of earthworms.

Anne wasn't a fan of nicknames in general, and she didn't like that Nora was being misinformed on the names of sea creatures. During the next family visit to the aquarium, Anne brought Nora to a window that looked into one of the large tanks. When she spotted an octopus, she pointed to it and said, "Octopus. See? Octopus."

"Squids," Nora replied.

Anne shook her head. "That's an octopus. Can you say 'octopus'?"

"No! Squids! Squids!"

Nora soon moved on to other obsessions and eventually stopped using the term. But the nickname stuck and became a name that she instinctively responded to, as much as she did to her real first name. Only when she was four years old did she begin asking about its origin, and by then she had come to embrace it as her own.

The story about Nora's nickname succeeded in distracting everyone for ten minutes. When the doctor finally arrived, he examined Dylan, cleaned his wounds, rinsed his mouth with two different solutions and announced that the boy would indeed require stitches on his lip but not inside his mouth. The worst part of it all for Dylan was not the needle being shot into his lip to numb it. Instead, it was the second needle that was required because the doctor disappeared for a half hour and the anesthetic from the first one had worn off.

Dylan was far from the ideal patient. He kept insisting that he didn't need stitches, and Jennifer and Matthew had to hold him still as the doctor's curved suture needle came into view.

"It could be worse, Dylan," Nora said from her seat next to the examination table. "At soccer practice I heard about a man who went into the hospital for, like, a broken toe or something and they cut off his whole leg by accident. That's what I call bad hospital luck."

"Not now, Nora, please," Matthew said as he struggled to hold Dylan still until the final stitch was knotted tight and its stray ends clipped.

Everyone was exhausted when they finally left the emergency room just after 1:00 in the morning. Jennifer tried to refuse the extra $50 that Matthew wanted to give her as combat pay, but he insisted. His one request was that she not cash the check for a couple of weeks.

Later that night, as he lay awake in bed, Matthew was finally able to put aside his son's crisis and consider what had happened earlier that evening. It was so bizarre to have Francis just show up. It had completely surprised Matthew. Looking back at the moment now, Matthew wished he had responded better.

He hadn't confronted Francis about Buzzy. It would have been impossible to do it at the bar, but Matthew could have taken a break so they could have a private conversation outside. He could have demanded that Francis explain what he did to his best friend. Matthew also could have told his brother that he wouldn't do him any favors until Francis answered for Buzzy's disappearance. But Matthew didn't do any of those things, and now he was feeling guilty about it. Francis had managed to control the whole conversation, the way he had always done with Matthew in the past.

The reward money came to mind. He could drop a dime on Francis and collect two million dollars. That would certainly solve his money problems, but Matthew immediately dismissed the idea because it was wrong in a number of ways. Where Matthew was from, you never turned family or friends over to the law. You dealt with the person inside your own community. If the news ever came out that he had handed Francis over to the FBI and collected the reward, the reaction in South Boston would be that Matthew Mahoney would turn in his own mother if he could make a buck off the transaction. He didn't want to cheapen his grievance with his older brother by making it about money. That would be the easy way out. Instead, Matthew would deny Francis what he wanted most.

Fuck him, and fuck any favors he wants from me, Matthew decided. I'm not doing a goddamn thing to help him. He caught me off guard today, but that's not gonna happen again.

*   *   *   *   *

At Sunday breakfast later that morning, three groggy Mahoneys slid into a back booth at Roy's a good hour after the time they normally arrived. The hostess tried to seat them at a window table, but all agreed that the bright sun was a little too jarring for them in their current state. Their back booth had a comfortable dimness. Jennifer showed up unannounced and joined them soon after they sat down. They were all happy to see her, especially Dylan and Nora.

"You're like family now, Jennifer. My dad will probably give you some kind of a nickname. What are you getting to eat?"

"I'm not too hungry," Jennifer said. "Plus, I'm training in an hour, so I don't want to put too much food in my stomach." Jennifer looked more tired than any of the Mahoneys. "For now, I think I'll just get a coffee, and maybe a fruit plate."

"That's what my mom gets with her omelette here," Nora said. "I don't know if she can get good fruit plates at the North Pole."

248

"North Slope," Dylan mumbled, but then immediately regretted moving his lips to speak.

While Nora and Matthew ordered their usual breakfast meals, Dylan's was anything but usual. Matthew walked over to the open kitchen and explained to the staff that his son wouldn't be able to deal with solid foods for a couple of days, and would it be possible for the kitchen staff to make him something that he could handle? They were fairly busy, but took the time to prepare a breakfast suitable for his condition. Several menu items were mixed in a blender and poured into coffee mugs. Some items required the addition of water or milk to achieve a viscosity that would allow them to be drawn through a sturdy straw.

Dylan let Nora preview each one and offer an opinion. Jennifer sampled a few as well. The potato, cheese and eggs with gravy combo had to be watered down so much that it was on the bland side. The goat cheese and herb egg scramble got a thumbs-up for taste and ease of sipping. The breakfast burrito was also to Nora's and Jennifer's liking, although not so much for Dylan because of the effect of the spices on his wounds. The buttermilk pancakes and syrup, on the other hand, were exceptionally good. As were the blended eggs and bacon, light on the bacon because of the sting from the saltiness. The surprise favorite turned out to be a blackberry scone mixed with vanilla bean ice cream and a little milk. It was the last mug to be tasted, and Dylan finished every drop.

When Matthew's third cup of coffee finally succeeded in rousing him from his sleepiness, he began mentally preparing the email he would have to send to Anne when they returned to the house. He had a phone number where he could reach her on the North Slope in the case of an emergency, but it seemed the emergency phase of Dylan's situation was now over. He'd have to begin the email by saying something like "everything is fine now, but Dylan had a little accident last night..." But that wouldn't cut it. It wasn't "little," and it was not completely an "accident," considering that Dylan himself attempted the orthodontic mayhem with a steak knife.

Which reminded Matthew that he needed to call Dylan's orthodontist to set up an appointment for Monday. The emergency room doctor hadn't seen any damage when he looked at the braces, but to be sure he urged Matthew to have them examined by Dylan's orthodontist. That would be another $50 to come up with.

"Jennifer," Nora said, "you should come back tonight and watch TV with us. We're gonna see *Futurama, The Simpsons, Malcolm in the Middle...*"

Dylan interrupted his sister by banging on the table. When she looked at him, he shook his head, then used his fingers to indicate numbers. Somehow Nora understood what he meant and corrected herself. "Right, *King of the Hill* comes after *Futurama*. Anyway, then it's *The X-Files*, although my dad won't let me watch that, even though I did watch it twice before and it didn't scare me because nothing really scares me. It's true."

"Jennifer has to work here tonight," Matthew said.

Jennifer smiled at Nora and said, "I'll be babysitting Tuesday night. We'll watch TV then. After we go over your homework."

Before leaving, Matthew stopped by the kitchen to thank everyone for taking such good care of Dylan and making breakfast enjoyable despite the circumstances. Dylan conveyed the same to the staff by clasping his hands over his head and nodding.

"You guys should put all of the blended stuff on the menu," Nora suggested. "It could start a whole new blended breakfast thing."

It was an hour later when Matthew finally sat down to write the email. He wondered if he should mention the appearance of Francis, but immediately dismissed the notion. Dylan's situation came first, and Matthew didn't want to complicate that. More importantly, he couldn't put what he wanted to say in an email. Never put anything incriminating in writing, Matthew knew, and that included emails.

He didn't know exactly which statute it violated, but there had to be at least one and probably more involved when you communicated with someone on the FBI's Most Wanted list. The phrase "aiding a fugitive" came to mind. It was one thing for him to be guilty, but to tell Anne about it would implicate her as well. And an email detailing Francis' visit could do just that.

Maybe he could do it in a phone call at some point, but he'd have to figure out how to communicate it to her in some sort of code. In the email, he focused just on Dylan. Two hours after he sent it, and as he was folding a load of laundry in the dining room, the home phone rang. It was Anne. She had just read the email.

She told him that she knew something like this would happen, that it was almost guaranteed. Since Matthew hadn't had braces, she said, he didn't realize how irritating they can be until you get used to them. She reminded him that Dylan's reaction would always be on the extreme side. Finally, she asked how many stitches he'd gotten.

Matthew could hear the note of alarm in Anne's voice, and he wanted to tell her it was fine now. The crisis had been managed and was over. But he knew that for her it was all fresh, only minutes old. "I think it was four stitches. Maybe five. It's on his lower lip."

Anne stressed to Matthew that Dylan had to take care of the wound as it was healing. Otherwise, there could be a bad scar. Matthew also had to make sure that Dylan kept the stitches covered until it was time to take them off. Dylan would want to pick at them, she said, and maybe try to remove them himself. Then Anne asked Matthew to put Dylan on the phone.

He called Dylan down from his room and handed him the phone. Matthew went back to folding the laundry and watched his son get comfortable on the couch and listen to his mother. A good 20 minutes passed with Dylan saying very little. Mostly he said "OK." Occasionally he would nod, and a few times he raised a hand to touch the bandage covering his stitches. When he was finished, he called out to his father, who had moved on to washing dishes.

Matthew went to the phone and said, "You had a good talk with him then?"

Anne said she did, although Dylan probably wouldn't remember half of what she told him. It was difficult not being there, Anne said, and that dealing with it over the phone was not good enough. She went silent for a few seconds before saying that she trusted Matthew, and that she was thankful for how he had handled the situation. She asked him to thank Jennifer for her.

"I will," Matthew said. "She was a big help through the whole thing. And the kids have really taken a liking to her as a babysitter, so it'll take a load off me when my work really picks up next month."

They talked for another few minutes before Anne had to surrender the phone to a woman who had reserved the next half hour. She had traded places on the list to make the call, so unless she could make another trade, she told Matthew that it might be a few days before she called again. He promised he would email every day with updates on Dylan's recovery, and he promised to make Dylan email her as well. That should be enough, they both agreed, then said goodbye.

Later in the afternoon, as Matthew was finishing chores and wondering what to make for dinner in light of Dylan's condition, there was a knock on the door. It was Jeremy from down the street. He and his partner, Benjamin, had stopped at Roy's for lunch and had heard about Dylan's "accident." Jeremy said that they were having a couple of friends over for dinner, and they'd love to have Matthew and the kids join them.

"That sounds great," Matthew said. "But there's one problem. Dylan can't really chew anything right now."

"We heard. That's why we're inviting you. You'll know what I mean when you come over. Is six OK?"

Dylan and Nora were more than happy with the dinner invitation. They were always excited to see what kind of interesting new lamps Jeremy was building. They would occasionally knock on his front door unannounced to see if a new one had been added to the collection of lamps around the house. They weren't disappointed when they arrived Sunday evening. Jeremy showed them his two latest inventions, which would both be sold at a specialty shop in Fremont once they had been put through their testing phase.

The first lamp was called "Asteroid." Beneath its bulb and shade was a base that was round and slightly smaller than a basketball. The glazed material was a mixture of dark, dull colors and had a heavily cratered surface, but through various fissures came a pulsing orange glow meant to simulate a molten core. Dylan considered mentioning that asteroids usually didn't have molten cores. In his current condition, though, he had difficulty speaking. He also thought the glowing core effect looked really impressive.

The second lamp was titled "Railroad Crossing." Beneath its shade, it featured all the important elements of its name: two long arms with stripes of paint that alternated between bright red and reflective gray. The foot-long arms stood vertically on either side of the base and, as Jeremy explained, they lowered just like real crossing gates at the top of every hour. The base itself was an old-fashioned railroad lantern that had been used on the Great Northern Railway. Jeremy had purchased it at an antique shop in La Conner, Washington. The four-sided lamp had large glass lenses, two red and two green.

Jeremy reached behind the base and advanced the lamp's clock to the next hour. Just then, a small speaker on the top of the lamp emitted a loud clanging sound and the bright lights on the lantern began flashing in an alternating pattern. After a few seconds, the gates lowered and stayed that way until the clanging and flashing ceased.

"That's so cool!" Nora said.

"It is cool the first few times you hear it, honey," Benjamin said. "Then it gets a tad piercing." Turning to Jeremy, he added, "Don't get me wrong. I really like this concept. I do. But Billy manages that shop in Fremont, and believe me, if he can't sell this lamp on the first day, he's gonna take it down the street and toss it in the Ship Canal. Good concept. A little too loud."

Jeremy took the criticism in stride. "I'll make some adjustments tomorrow. This is why testing is important," he said to Matthew, who was still seeing spots from the flashing lights.

"What can we get you all to drink?" Benjamin asked.

"I'll take a beer," Matthew said.

"Very good. And for you kids, do you still like the usual?"

They both nodded. The usual was Sprite or 7 Up with a dash of grapefruit juice and a wedge of lime in a tall glass. As Jeremy began making the drinks in the kitchen, Benjamin walked the Mahoneys onto the back deck, where he offered Dylan a list of possible menu items suitable for his situation. Benjamin worked as a chef at Usonia, a fine dining restaurant perched on a bluff in Queen Anne overlooking Lake Union. As Benjamin explained, during his time working as a chef in the Los Angeles area, he also had a number of private clients. On one occasion, he needed to prepare meals for someone with a broken jaw, and another time for someone undergoing treatment for oral cancer. In both cases, he had to create dishes that were both delicious and sippable through a milkshake straw. From the different options Benjamin presented, Dylan selected a couple for his dinner.

"How long will he need liquid food?" Benjamin asked Matthew.

"Just another day or two. Mouth wounds heal quickly. In the meantime, I'll be making good use of our blender. You've given me some great ideas."

When the other guests arrived, there was more clanging and flashing in the living room as Jeremy demonstrated how "Railroad Crossing" celebrated the arrival of every new hour. Then they joined the Mahoneys on the back deck. They were the Andreassens, a couple from Vancouver, Canada, who surprised Matthew by asking him more detailed questions about roofing than anyone had ever done before. They were genuinely curious about the craft and how it had changed through the decades and centuries. When they were done asking questions, Matthew found himself wanting to do more research on the subject himself.

As the evening air cooled, everyone moved inside for dinner, where Mrs. Andreassen captivated the table with a story about her grandfather, who had emigrated from Sweden in 1893 with the plan of making a new home in America. He settled in Seattle and met the woman who would become his wife. A few years later, when news of gold being discovered in the Klondike region of the Yukon territory reached the Pacific Northwest, they made the bold decision to head north. They were among the few to return home from the Klondike with a relatively modest, yet still impressive, sum of money, while so many other prospectors returned with little more than their lives.

Dylan was taking the first sip of his dessert when Nora mentioned, "My mom used to go camping in the snow in Alaska. She's up there now at the North Pole."

"North Slope, Squids," Matthew said.

"Oh, right. I mean the North Slope."

At the end of dessert, Matthew thanked Jeremy and especially Benjamin for going through the trouble of making a dinner suitable for Dylan. When it was time, Benjamin asked for a favor. If Matthew had time in the coming weeks, could he take a look at their roof? There seemed to be a leak up there, specifically around the chimney, and they would be grateful if Matthew could locate it. They'd pay him for the work, of course. Matthew said that as long as it was a straightforward job, he wouldn't charge them a penny.

Chapter 12

The Bundle Test

Wednesday, May 3, 2000

The weather on the North Slope had improved toward the end of April. Temperatures were averaging 15 degrees during the day and zero at night. With the arrival of May, the amount of sunlight was also increasing. The sun rose around 4 a.m. and set well after 11 p.m. Anne noticed the presence of more small animals, and she was told the grizzlies would start coming out of hibernation within a couple of weeks. The males, that is, for the most part. Female grizzlies that were nursing cubs wouldn't show themselves until sometime later. The same was true for pregnant polar bears, although males typically stayed active all winter.

Another change that Anne noticed was a drop in her weight. Part of it was due to her visits to the BG gym four or five times a week. But mostly, she believed, it was due to spending long hours in the cold during an active workday. She had followed Seth's advice about taking extra snacks with her when she was working outside, and she was glad she did. There wasn't a day that went by when she wasn't reaching for a bag of thick pretzels or a pack of Fig Newtons. Aside from pregnancy, she couldn't remember having such an appetite since her days playing soccer in college.

And she didn't skimp on meals in the dining hall either. Breakfast was always some version of eggs, toast, muffin and occasionally potatoes. She always skipped breakfast meats, like sausage and bacon, but when the menu included fish cakes, she got two or three. She indulged herself the same way at dinner, which was usually centered around some form of chicken, fish or steak, and occasionally lasagna, burritos, casseroles or savory pies. The only item she avoided was meatloaf. A bad experience in high school gave her a mistrust of meat in any restructured form. It was years before she ate hamburgers again, and she still avoided hot dogs.

Anne noticed her weight loss around the four- or five-week mark. First it was in the fit of her jeans. She usually went without a belt, but now she was making a point of wearing one all the time.

She also noticed it in her rings. She wore two. One was a wide gold wedding band with images of leaping salmon engraved around the outside. It was made to match the original gold band that had belonged to her father. After his death, she wore his on a chain around her neck until her wedding day when she slipped it onto Matthew's finger. Unfortunately, Matthew managed to lose the heirloom in the week after they were married. They had a replica made when they returned to Seattle, and Anne decided that as long as they were remaking her father's ring, she should have her own version of it. So they got a matching pair.

On her right hand, she wore a wide silver band that her father had given her as a high school graduation gift. The ring showed a profile of Eagle Peak in the Chugach Mountains. Rising beside the peak was a gold inset of a moon. Eagle was the first of the big peaks that father and daughter had successfully summitted together.

After a month on the North Slope, both rings had come close to slipping off Anne's fingers in the shower, not once but several times. Rather than risk losing them, she stashed them away safely.

To confirm her weight loss, she made a point of doing something she hadn't done since leaving Seattle: stepping on a scale. The BG gym had one. Before leaving for Alaska, she was in the same weight range she had been in since giving birth to Nora, and her weight had never varied more than a few pounds up or down. The scale at the BG gym showed that she had lost 12 pounds. If it wasn't for everyone telling her that her situation was normal for someone working on the Slope, she'd swear she had a tapeworm, or worse.

Anne was telling Sarah about it at dinner one evening, and Sarah said she experienced the same thing, to a lesser degree. "I'm here for three weeks at a stretch," she said. "And it's right around two, or two and a half weeks, when I begin to feel like maybe I've lost a couple of pounds. But then I go home and put it back on. You've been here for five weeks now, so it's really kicking in. Just be careful to cut back on how much you eat when you get home. Otherwise, you might put on more than what you've lost here."

After dinner, Sarah said she had to do some homework. The gallery in Miami had sold her first table, and they had emailed her the details of the deal. She had to approve the sale and inquire about having the gallery commission one of her larger pieces. Anne had no other plans, so she went to the theater alone to see a movie called *Deep Blue Sea*. It was a sci-fi horror flick in which a team of scientists drained fluid from the brains of mako sharks to produce a cure for Alzheimer's disease. It was definitely far-fetched but interesting enough to keep her watching. Around 45 minutes into the movie, someone walked into her row and sat down in the seat next to her. The theater was almost half full, so it didn't strike Anne as odd until she heard a familiar voice say, "Well, what are the chances?"

She turned to her left. It was the guy from the plane: Bert from Burtonwood. He leaned toward her and said, "I said we'd enjoy watching movies together and, lo and behold, here we are in our intimate little theater." He paused, then added, "I know we got off on the wrong foot, Anne, but I would really like the opportunity to get things back on track. You're an impressive woman." Bert smiled and continued, "And, I have to say, you have the most extraordinary eyes, and the most extraordinary spirit."

Anne had almost forgotten about the incident on the plane, and Bert's sudden reappearance caught her by surprise. When she finally took in what he had said, she was repulsed. She stood up to leave, then realized she'd have to walk past him to reach the aisle.

Two people were sitting directly in front of her, but there was nobody in the row behind. She grabbed her jacket and stepped over her own seat. "Creep," she muttered before walking toward the aisle.

It was after 9:00 when Anne returned to her room. In the bathroom, she couldn't see any light coming from beneath the door to Sarah's room. She didn't want to wake Sarah if she was asleep, so she got into bed and flipped through a three-week-old copy of *People* magazine until she grew tired enough to sleep.

The next morning, she met Sarah for breakfast in the dining hall and told her what had happened.

"The fact that he used your name would bother me for sure," Sarah said. "I don't think I know who he is though. Gloria might know." Sarah called to a woman who had just gone through the serving line and waved her over to the table.

Gloria worked at BG's medical clinic, and when she heard Anne's story, she nodded. "Bert from Burtonwood. I don't know him personally, thank goodness, but I know about him. He's a director here, and I've heard about a few women he's harassed. Then there are the ones you don't hear about. If I were you, I'd do everything I could to avoid him."

"I've been up here five weeks," Anne said, "and I haven't seen him once the whole time, except that first day on the plane. Then he just shows up in the movie theater and sits next to me?"

On Gloria's plate was a mushroom omelette and three sausage links. She held a link in her right hand and pointed it over her left shoulder. "They placed some Burtonwood buildings next to your camp. They move buildings all the time up here, you know. They just jack 'em up and move 'em."

"That's probably it," Sarah said. "He must live in one of those buildings they moved."

"But why did they let him in the theater?" Anne asked. "It's BG's building, not Burtonwood's."

"Bert's a director, honey," Gloria said. "They're big honchos up here. I'm sure he can go into any company's buildings without much of a problem."

After eating the first sausage link, Gloria picked up another. When she pointed it in Anne's direction, a drop of grease flew in the air and landed on Anne's sleeve. "Oh, sorry..." Gloria said. She grabbed a napkin with her other hand and dabbed at the spot, but the grease had already soaked into the gray cotton fabric.

"Don't worry," Anne said. "It's an old shirt. Thanks for telling me what you know about him. I guess I'll avoid going to the theater alone from now on."

*   *   *   *   *

(earlier that week)
Monday, May 1, 2000

The beginning of the month was when the A Crew went back to roofing full-time. On that Monday, Matthew met Sal before work at a café in Westwood Village. He reminded him that Lyka would be joining them for her first day on the job.

Sal was pleased. "Thanks for reminding me. I think you might owe somebody a referral bonus."

Matthew said he was a little concerned about whether Lyka would make it through the two-week trial period every new member of the A Crew had to undergo. The tests included mastering the use of the tools, installing shingles in a straight course, and applying flashing correctly. The test that people were most likely to fail was showing up at the jobsite every day for two weeks straight and showing up on time. With Lyka, Matthew's biggest concern was the bundle test.

It was nothing official, just a random test Matthew's first roofing employer made him take when he started. It involved carrying ten bundles of shingles up a ladder and dropping them at the peak of a two-story roof within 20 minutes. The weight of a bundle varied depending on the type of shingle, but a typical one could weigh around 60 pounds and was held together by a thick paper wrap. You'd sling a bundle over your shoulder, hold it in place with one hand while using your other hand to grasp the rungs of the ladder as you climbed.

When he became foreman at Rieger Roofing, Matthew made the bundle test a requirement for every new hire. Everybody he had ever roofed with could do it. In fact, he couldn't remember any hire of his ever struggling with the test. But he had the feeling Lyka might. It was one thing learning to control a heavy nail gun over the course of a long day, but for a person with a light frame to carry 600 pounds up a two-story ladder in 20 minutes was another. He had made it a requirement for years though, so he couldn't simply say it no longer mattered, or that it didn't apply to specific hires, unless he wanted to hear a lot of backlash about favoritism and double standards.

There was something else worrying Matthew, but it had nothing to do with roofing. It had been two weeks since Francis had shown up at Roy's, and Matthew hadn't told a single soul about his brother's appearance and his request for a favor.

At one point during a phone call with Anne, he tried to let her know by talking about a visit from a person back home whom he hadn't seen in a while. He was speaking with the kids sitting right near him, so he couldn't exactly mention his brother's name. The vague reference left Anne confused enough that Matthew had to change the subject.

He had hesitated to tell Sal for the same reason he worried about telling Anne. If Sal knew that Matthew had seen his brother and was supposed to see him again, it would cast a legal shadow over Sal. That resolve had lasted for two weeks, but now it was crumbling. Matthew needed to unload it all on someone he could trust. Sal was a good choice because he was among the few people who already knew about Matthew's brother.

After Matthew finished sharing all the details of Francis' visit, Sal asked, "So when is he coming back?"

"He didn't say. And he didn't mention where he'd show up, except it won't be at the bar."

"What kind of favors would you do for him?"

"I've already decided. I'm not doing him any favors. Whatever he asks for, I'm saying 'no.'"

They downed the last of their coffee, then headed for the parking lot. Before getting into his truck, Sal called over to Matthew, "Just be careful how you say 'no.'"

*   *   *   *   *

When Lyka showed up at the job on Thistle Street in West Seattle, Buck and Major were pulling ladders from Sal's truck and extending them at the front of the house. Matthew introduced Lyka to the crew and said she'd be going through the same two-week test period that everyone else had gone through.

They'd start with showing her how to rip off an old layer of shingles, which they'd be doing that morning before putting down new shingles in the afternoon. As Matthew was walking to the back of Sal's truck, he heard Buck say quietly to Major, "You've got to be shitting me."

It was what Matthew had expected from Buck. Hopefully none of the others would be so quick to judge. "Hey, Buck," Matthew said. "Why don't you train Lyka this morning. You can show her how we rip a roof."

It was always a dirty job when an old layer or two of shingles was being removed. They would start at the peak, shove pitchforks underneath the old shingles and pry them free. It created a filthy mess. Shingle fragments, old felt paper, nails, and a lot of dust and dirt would go sliding down the roof. Tarps were used to protect shrubs, flower beds and anything of value below from the rain of debris. Then hundreds, or thousands, of remaining nails had to be pulled out with a hammer to make a smooth surface for the new underlay. Matthew kept a close eye on Lyka that morning, first to see if she was moving safely while on the roof and ladder, and also to see how well she managed a pitchfork.

When the old roof was lying in scraps on the ground, it was Lyka's job to shovel it all into the back of a dump truck, either directly from the ground or by shoveling the pieces into a wheelbarrow that she carted over to the truck. It was a good workout, even for someone who was used to doing it every day. Matthew had her on the task for a couple of hours, then sent her back to the roof, where Major showed her how to apply underlayment and nail a course of shingles properly.

They started work at 8:00 and finished a little after 4:30. With a half-hour lunch and a couple of short breaks, it was a full day. After Matthew did a walk-around to make sure the cleanup had been done correctly, and after the ladders and other gear were returned to Sal's and Matthew's trucks, everybody either headed home or rolled down to Roy's to grab a beer at the end of "Ferry Hour." Matthew would skip Ferry Hour because he had to pick up the kids from their after-school programs, but before leaving he spoke to Lyka to ask how things went. She said it went OK.

Matthew could tell she had mixed feelings, but wanted to sound positive. Her shoulders were rolled forward, so he knew she was worn out. Like the others, she had been covered in dust from ripping the old roof. Sweat had run tracks down the side of her face and neck. Her glasses were covered in the same fine-grain dust. Earlier in the day, Matthew stopped her as she was about to wipe her glasses and told her to wash them off first. Otherwise, the fine dust would scratch the lenses.

261

"You had a good first day," he told her. "If you stay with this job, you'll probably never have a day harder than this one. Everything was new to you, including the guys who you were working with. When you start feeling sore tonight, you'll think back on what you had to do today, and it'll seem more awful than it really was. At least that's the way it was for me and most of the roofers I know."

He gave Lyka a slip of paper with the address for the house they'd work on the next day. "If you can show up at the job tomorrow morning at eight, you're at least halfway there. You'll still be sore. In fact, you'll be sore until Thursday or Friday or maybe even next week. But every day you'll be less sore, and every day you'll be a little stronger, and in a matter of weeks you're likely to master this work. OK, that's my pep talk. Drink plenty of water tonight, sleep well and I'll see you in the morning."

As it turned out, Matthew didn't see Lyka the next day. After dropping the kids off at school, he had to go to a different jobsite to train the new B Crew that the Riegers had hired. Training a new B Crew was a task that neither he nor Sal enjoyed. They flipped a coin the evening before, and since Matthew lost, he got stuck with it.

Roofers on the B Crew were paid barely more than minimum wage, so the jobs they worked on were more profitable for Rieger Roofing, as long as the B Crew didn't fuck up, which they did far more often than the A Crew. They weren't as reliable, they had trouble following instructions, and some had attitude problems, at least in Matthew's opinion. They were also more likely to not show up for work without telling anyone. But Matthew and Sal were responsible for training the B Crew properly when they were hired at the start of the season.

*   *   *   *   *

It wasn't until the following week when Matthew rejoined his A Crew. He was surprised at how quickly Lyka had earned everyone's respect. That included Buck, whose opinion of a person was either very negative or very positive. Never in between. He had been skeptical of Lyka's ability at the outset, but now was supportive of her joining the crew. Major and the Professor felt the same way.

On Thursday afternoon, Matthew and Sal took a drive to Home Depot for some caulking, and Sal asked straight out, "So is she in?"

"I think she'd be great on the crew," Matthew said. "Has she passed everything?"

"Sure, pretty much."

"The bundle test?" Matthew asked.

"When we fix the motor on the hoist, that'll be carrying all the bundles for us again, so I don't know how much it really matters."

On the drive back to the jobsite, Matthew stopped at an ATM so he could pay back a loan from Sal. Anne's checks had finally started showing up in their checking account, so their finances were now back in order. Then he and Sal talked some more about the bundle test.

"I wish I had never introduced the stupid thing," Matthew said. "But every roofer on the crew had to pass it. If she can't, everyone will take note. It's something that could work against her at some point. And against me for letting it slip."

"I understand," Sal said, "but I saw her lift a whole bundle…or try to lift it, I should say. She got three rungs up the ladder and had to step back down."

"Maybe there's a way. We still have tomorrow before the two weeks are up, so let's think about it overnight."

"By the way," Sal said. "What does that tattoo on her arm mean? It says 'FORGIVE.'"

Matthew shook his head. "I don't know. I've been curious, but I don't want to ask. It seems kind of personal, you know?"

"Personal? It's right there in big letters for the world to see." Sal held up his right forearm and pretended to write on it. "I came this close to asking her yesterday because I keep wondering."

"So why didn't you ask her then?"

Sal thought about it. "I don't know. I figured maybe…"

"It's too personal?" Matthew said, finishing Sal's sentence.

"Yeah, maybe. My best guess is that it's a family thing. Maybe something about her dad, you know."

"I was thinking it was more about religion in general," Matthew said. "The whole idea of forgiveness and how important it is. I mean, we both know the Catholic side of that."

"It's possible," Sal said, "but I really think it's specific to a person in her life. That's just how I read it."

When Lyka showed up at the jobsite on Friday morning, Matthew pulled her aside. She had proven herself over the last two weeks, he told her, and she had earned a spot on his A Crew. There was one test she hadn't passed, but that didn't really matter because in the end it was Matthew, and Matthew alone, who made the hiring decision, and the bundle test wasn't a deal-breaker as far as he was concerned.

On the other hand, he told her that if she could somehow pass the test before he announced to the rest of the crew that she would be hired, that would put her on equal footing with them because they had all passed it. She agreed it would be better for her, but she also recalled her attempts at carrying a bundle of shingles up a ladder.

It was a cool, cloudy morning, and Lyka wore a black sweatshirt with a green logo of the band L7. The logo was peeling and Lyka picked anxiously at it while she spoke. "If the bundles were smaller I could, but 60 pounds is just…I don't know if I can even make it to the top of the ladder with one."

"Would you like to pass the test?" Matthew asked.

"Yes, of course I would!" Lyka said with more than a touch of irritation.

There were two ladders leaning against the house, and they were standing at the foot of one. The two-story house was going to get a new layer of shingles nailed over the existing one. As soon as Buck and Major set up the staging, the crew would start nailing. "Wait here a minute," Matthew said.

He and Sal made a few trips back and forth from the pallet of shingles in the driveway. When they had a stack of ten bundles piled up beside the ladder, Matthew said to Sal and Lyka, "I have to deliver some supplies to the B Crew. I'll be gone for about an hour and a half. Sal, you and Lyka work it out when you want to time her on the test."

Turning to Lyka, who was staring at the stack of shingles, Matthew said, "There's only one way to pass. You have to bring ten bundles worth of shingles to the peak in 20 minutes. The shingles we're using today are 29 to a bundle. That means you have to carry 290 shingles to the peak." She was still staring at the pile and not looking too enthusiastic about her chances, so Matthew said, "Lyka, you can do this, but you're going to have to solve it with your head first. Think about what I said."

Turning to Sal, he said, "Call me if you need me. I'll be back before lunch." Then he headed for his truck. The house they were roofing was on Palm Ave near the northern tip of West Seattle, overlooking Alki Beach and Elliott Bay. As Matthew drove up Massachusetts Street, he wondered whether he had just made it even easier for Lyka to fail. What a stupid little test it was, he thought, and once again cursed himself for making it matter at all in hiring a new roofer. But if Lyka could pull it off, he knew it would matter to her. And probably everyone else.

After driving a few blocks farther, Matthew found a place where he could park and get a decent view down the hill to the house. He could see three guys on the roof, and Sal and Lyka standing near the ladder. After about five minutes, he saw Sal and Lyka bending over and tearing the paper wrapping from the ten bundles.

When he returned a couple of hours later, everybody was on the roof. Major and the Professor were shingling the back side, and Buck and Lyka were working their way up the front. Sal was handling the flashing. When he saw Matthew pull up, he called out to the rest of the crew. They all put down their nail guns and made their way to the ground.

Lyka's mood had completely changed. She was grinning, and so was everybody else. Thank heavens, Matthew thought. He didn't want to say it, but he felt more relieved than anyone else.

"She did it, skipper!" Sal yelled. There was a smattering of claps and yells from the others.

"She got all the shingles up there in under 20 minutes, Matt," Buck affirmed. "Sal timed it."

"Nineteen minutes and twenty-three seconds," Sal said.

"All the way up to the peak," Buck said, pointing to the roof. "Two hundred ninety shingles in all." He patted Lyka on the back. Matthew noticed that the side of her neck had been rubbed raw from the shingles she had carried over her right shoulder. Normally, the smooth paper wrapping would have prevented that.

"How do you feel?" Matthew asked.

Lyka smiled and pushed the bridge of her glasses up her nose. "Good. Tired," she said with a laugh.

"So that's it Matt, right?" Buck asked. "She's in. No more tests."

Matthew nodded. "For better or worse, she's officially on the A Crew now."

They finished work early, then everybody headed to Roy's to celebrate. Everybody except Lyka, who had to pick up her niece from daycare and babysit her. However, she'd be joining the rest of the crew at Matthew's house for a barbecue the next evening. That, Matthew said, would be the official celebration and much better than a couple of hasty beers at a crowded Ferry Hour.

The A Crew, minus Lyka, sat at a big round table in the bar and shared a few appetizers: gambas al ajillo, which were spice-rubbed shrimp; tamales stuffed with spiced ground beef, with a serrano pepper sauce; and Penn Cove mussels sautéed in ginger-infused coconut milk. Along with the cold microbrews, the scene was a little more enjoyable than Matthew had led Lyka to believe, but he didn't want to make her feel bad about missing it.

"I think she's gonna be even better than Mole," Buck said as he waved his empty pint glass to signal the waitress for another round for everyone except Matthew, who had to pick up the kids soon. Matthew also had a small insulation job to do with Sal the next morning, so he wanted to limit his drinking.

"Don't get me wrong," Buck said. "Mole was a good roofer."

"So has anybody heard from him recently? Wasn't he somewhere in Arizona?" Major asked.

"Bisbee, or just outside of Bisbee," the Professor said. "It's in Arizona. Mole was paying two dollars a night to stay at some hippie camp there. That was in the last postcard I got, which was a couple of weeks ago."

"We'll never see him again," Buck said. "He'll make his bankroll last for 20 years. Plus, he'll add to it by selling his freakish fountain pens."

"Speaking of freakish," Sal said. "How is the building of your porn business coming along, Buck? Have you stolen enough classy pictures to open your online shop soon?"

Major tried to stifle a laugh but couldn't. Buck tossed the tail of a spice-rubbed shrimp in his direction.

"As a matter of fact," Buck said, "I happen to be more than halfway to my goal of gathering 20,000 of the world's best photos. The day of my financial independence is approaching fast."

"So, when exactly?" the Professor asked.

Buck closed his eyes and shook his head slowly. "You will find out when you find out," he said.

"You're being a mystery man," Major said. "Just like Mole."

Sal laughed. "But he's classier than Mole. Right, Buck Naked?"

The appetizer plates were cleared, and Matthew pulled some cash from his pocket and paid the tab. Before the gathering broke up, one more topic came up for discussion: Lyka's tattoo. As it turned out, everybody at the table had a different opinion about what it meant. As Matthew listened, he realized that everyone, including himself, had come up with an interpretation that reflected their own background and experiences, and he said as much.

"It's called projection," the Professor said.

Buck found one more shrimp tail hiding behind a salt shaker. "Here, let me project this," Buck said, and tossed it in the Professor's direction.

*   *   *   *   *

Saturday, May 13, 2000

Nora, and especially Dylan, enjoyed sleeping late on weekends, but Matthew woke them at 7:00 on Saturday morning. Once they were dressed, he walked them down to Jeremy's house. He and Benjamin had agreed to take care of the kids while Matthew went off to do an insulation job with Sal. In fact, they had been bugging Matthew for the chance to pitch in with the childcare during Anne's absence.

Benjamin was already in the kitchen preparing a breakfast of pancakes and bacon, and he allowed Matthew to steal one of the slices cooling on a plate.

"We signed them up with us for a stewardship project down at Lincoln Park," Jeremy told Matthew. "It's only for a couple of hours. Clearing brush, picking up trash, that sort of thing. Then we'll head downtown for lunch and a movie."

Benjamin said, "We're thinking of going to the Omnidome to see *The Eruption of Mount St. Helens.*" Benjamin paused to offer the plate of bacon to the kids, who were soon, like their father, nibbling on a piece. "Unless you've already seen that movie."

"They have," Matthew said. "Twice, but they'll be happy to see it a third time."

"I love watching that mountain blow up!" Nora said. "It's awesome. During the movie, Dylan will sound like he's about to get motion sickness, but don't worry. He won't."

Matthew said goodbye and headed back to the house, where Sal had just pulled up. The insulation job that they were doing in Tukwila was supposed to be simple, and it did indeed turn out to be. As they were prying off clapboards and drilling holes in the house, Sal shared a piece of news with Matthew.

"You know that woman who works at that café on Capitol Hill?"

"The one who works at the Adagio?" Matthew asked, referring to the café on 15th Ave.

"I finally got the courage to ask her out."

"It's only been about five months. What's her name?"

"Inessa. She grew up in Tacoma. Her dad is Russian, and her mom is Polish, and she can speak both languages. As it turns out, my timing is good. Inessa has been in a relationship for the last year, but they broke up last month. We're going out the weekend after next."

"Are you gonna take her to a show?"

Sal shook his head. "We didn't really decide exactly where we're gonna go, but I don't know if a show is a good idea for a first date. She plays the violin, and she's in a group that rehearses and plays in a real orchestra. I get the feeling she's good, so I don't want to get off on the wrong musical foot with her. Maybe we'll go to dinner, then catch a movie."

By 2:00, all the holes in the house were plugged, the clapboards were secured, the gear was loaded in the truck, and the owner of the house had handed over a cash payment.

As they were driving back through Burien, Matthew spotted something in the parking lot of a local bar. A smile broke out on his face as he turned suddenly into the lot, a move that caught Sal by surprise.

"We've got plenty of beer back at your house, Matt," Sal said.

Matthew pulled up next to a vehicle familiar to both of them. It was Diego's work truck, and it was parked at the far end of the lot. The window on the driver's side door was open a few inches.

Still smiling, Matthew said, "We're not here for a drink. We're here to help our friend Diego. We're gonna make sure he's never cold inside his truck again."

Matthew then pointed his thumb toward the back of his own truck, which held the insulation hopper and hose, a generator, and three packages of insulation left over from that day's work. Sal immediately figured out what Matthew had in mind and began smiling too. He tilted his head back and let out a big laugh. "Oh, we should do it. We should definitely do it."

They formulated a quick plan. Sal helped Matthew prepare the hopper and hook it up to the generator. Two packages of insulation were opened. Each package was a two-foot by three-foot block of compressed cellulose. Once broken up by the hopper, the insulation expanded to fill a much greater space. They agreed that two would be more than enough.

Sal went up to the front door of the bar. He would stay outside and make sure Diego didn't suddenly want to return to his truck. If he did, Sal would keep him occupied for as long as was needed.

Matthew's first task was to jam the nozzle of the hose into the opening in Diego's truck window. Then he fired up the generator, turned on the hopper and began feeding it insulation. Halfway through the second block, he could see the inside of the truck rapidly filling with a white, fluffy material that looked very much like cotton candy. In the next 30 seconds, Diego's truck was completely filled. Like beer foam overflowing the top of a glass, fluffy insulation began spilling out the opening in the driver's window.

Matthew turned the hopper and generator off, then jumped from the back of his truck to retrieve the hose and secure it. The sound of the generator powering down was Sal's cue to return. The whole operation had taken barely five minutes. As they resumed their drive back to Matthew's house, their only problem was trying to figure out a way to stop laughing.

*   *   *   *   *

Throughout that morning, there had been light rain on and off, mostly off. It didn't affect the insulation work Matthew and Sal were doing, but it made Matthew wonder whether he should postpone the barbecue scheduled for that evening. But the forecast called for clearing, and by four that afternoon, the sun began to poke through the clouds.

Everybody in the A Crew showed up, except the Professor, who was attending a lecture on the future uses of laser technology. Matthew made the mistake of mentioning it to Dylan, who asked if they could cancel the barbecue and join the Professor at the lecture instead.

Matthew also invited a number of neighbors, including Jeremy and Benjamin. Everyone showed up with some kind of side dish or dessert, and something to throw on the grill if they didn't like the burgers and dogs Matthew would be cooking. The first thing they all asked about was how Anne was doing in Alaska. Matthew filled them in on what life on the Slope was like, from the weather to the work to the fact that Anne somehow got to see the new movie *High Fidelity* in BG's little theater even before it was showing in local Seattle venues.

Lyka brought her niece, Analyn, who was three and a half. The backyard grass was still too wet to sit down on, but the deck was big enough to hold plenty of folding tables and chairs, which were brought out of the garage and dusted off.

Matthew had spent 20 minutes getting the hickory and oak lump charcoal going. Now the grill was crowded with hamburgers, hot dogs, and veggie burgers, as well as asparagus and garlic scapes, which were both in season locally. Dylan was on duty next to his father, tending to the burger and hot dog buns to ensure that both sides received a proper and equal amount of toasting.

It was Nora's first time meeting Lyka, and she took to her right away. After dinner, Matthew watched Lyka as she worked Nora's hair first into waterfall braids, which Matthew had never seen, then into a pair of Dutch braids. As Lyka braided, Nora told her all about her mom going up to Alaska. "She has her own room up at the North Pole…"

Matthew heard it and corrected her. "North Slope."

Nora protested this time. "You know what, Dad? I looked it up on a map, and it really is almost practically the North Pole."

"Whatever," Matthew said.

Nora continued, "One day when she first got up there it was way below zero and there was a blizzard going on. That was totally crazy. She told me all about it on the phone. Anyway, I'll get to see all of Alaska when we move up to Anchorage soon. We're gonna live in my grandpa's cabin, which is my mom and dad's now, and I already know where my room is and where Dylan's room is. It's right by the mountains and my mom sees bears walking around all the time. Pretty much every day. She caught a salmon one time that was bigger than I am right now. When the salmon show up in the rivers next spring, my mom's gonna show me how to fish for them. And we're gonna be getting dogs. Not just one dog, but two big dogs."

When Lyka asked how long Anne had been up in Alaska, Nora looked around for Dylan. She spotted him at the grill, then called out, "Hey, Dylan, how many days now?"

Without having to ask what his sister meant, Dylan answered, "Today is day 49."

Nora turned to Lyka. "Our mom's been in Alaska for 49 days now," she repeated.

"And when is she getting home, Dylan?" Nora asked.

Dylan thought for a moment, then turned around to reply, "On day 85 she flies to Seattle. That's June 18th."

Matthew listened to the numbers as he flipped a burger, and it gave him a heavy feeling. Anne's return home was still more than a month away.

Nora continued talking about Alaska until Matthew suggested she give Lyka a chance to talk. Nora obliged and listened as Lyka told her about her family, including her niece, who was growing tired of carrot sticks and calling for a hamburger. At one point, Matthew overheard Nora asking Lyka about her tattoo. "I know what it says, but why did you get it?" Nora asked.

As casually as he could, Matthew turned his head halfway around so he could hear the answer better. As he did, he noticed Sal, Major and Buck doing the same thing at their table. Instead of hearing the answer, they saw Lyka bend down and speak softly to Nora. A few seconds later, Nora whispered something in Lyka's ear. Then Lyka whispered to Nora again.

When Lyka finished, Nora's eyes grew big. "I get it. That's so cool."

All the guys looked at each other to see who might have caught some of the answer, even a word or two. None of them had. Matthew shrugged and turned back to the grill.

When the cooking was finished and all the burgers and dogs had been paired with a perfectly toasted bun, Matthew filled a plate and sat down at a table with his neighbor Ron, who worked at a tech startup company in Seattle. He began talking to Matthew about the dot-com bubble, how it had recently begun to burst and which companies were likely to survive it.

"Everybody's been borrowing a lot, and everybody's been acting like growth is more important than turning a profit. Then Alan Greenspan decided to get aggressive with interest rate hikes. That was one of the sparks, but the groundwork was laid by a crazy growth mentality," Ron explained. "My company will survive. In fact, we're in a good position to pick up market share because we didn't overextend ourselves."

Ron wore a fleece jacket to stay warm in the cool evening air, but like Matthew he was also wearing shorts, a wardrobe choice for all but the coldest months. He got up to use the bathroom and returned with another beer for himself and Matthew. "By the way, Matt, I wanted to ask you about something. A buddy at work was talking about having to get his house reshingled, so I mentioned your name to him. He's from Massachusetts, and when I said you were from South Boston, he asked if you were related to that guy Francis Mahoney. You know, the one the FBI is looking for."

It was the same question that Matthew had fielded many times, and he automatically shifted into denial mode. But this time, the question made him more nervous than ever because of his recent encounter with Francis. "I've heard about him, but no, thank God, I'm not related to that guy. You'd be surprised how many people are named Mahoney in Boston. It's like the name Smith." Matthew said, delivering his practiced response.

But Ron continued, "Because the guy said that Francis Mahoney has two brothers, and the younger one is named Matthew."

It was the first time anybody had brought up that detail, and Matthew had to think fast. "You know, I have heard about that. It seems strange. But it's really the same thing that goes for the name Mahoney. Matthew is a common name for Irish Americans, and South Boston is full of them. I think there were two or three other Matthew Mahoneys in the grade school that I went to. Maybe more. It could get confusing sometimes. Matthew is the name of a saint too, and Catholics love naming their kids after saints."

Ron had listened carefully, and Matthew couldn't tell if his explanation had been convincing. Matthew glanced to his left and saw Dylan standing by the back door and looking his way. There was a good chance Dylan had heard part of the conversation, maybe the whole thing. Matthew felt a desperate need to change the subject without seeming to do so. Usually he would crack a joke at this point to dismiss the topic. That didn't feel right in this instance, so he tried a different tack.

"It's sort of like that phenomenon with birthdays," he said, turning back to Ron. "You know that if you have 23 people in a room, there's a 50 percent chance that two of them will have the exact same birthday. That seems unlikely, right? And that's despite the fact that there are 365 days in a year. Or 366 in a leap year."

"I don't think I've ever heard about that," Ron said.

"And if you have 70 people in a room," Matthew continued, "what do you think the chances are that two people will have the same birthday? Take a guess."

Ron thought for a moment, then said, "70...80 percent?"

Matthew turned to Dylan and repeated the question. Dylan walked over to the table and said, "Approximately 99.9 percent."

"That's crazy," Ron said. "Are you sure?"

"It's called the birthday paradox," Dylan said. "We studied it in school this year."

Matthew thanked his lucky stars that he had helped Dylan with that particular homework assignment. He stood up and gestured for Dylan to take his seat. "Tell him how it works, D-Man." Turning to Ron, Matthew added, "I'm gonna go clean up the grill before it cools down. It'll be a real pain if I leave it 'til tomorrow."

There were no more difficult questions from Ron that evening, and the rest of the barbecue went smoothly. The crowd thinned around 9:00, and by 10:00 Matthew was in the kitchen putting away the plates, silverware and grilling utensils that people had washed and dried for him.

Nora pestered her father to let her tell a story before she went to sleep, so Matthew listened in on a tale about Runa and her friends rafting down the Snake River. There were lots of rapids they had to navigate, as well as two waterfalls that they managed to survive thanks to Runa's extraordinary rafting skills. At night, they camped on shore and had a big bonfire. Matthew had to correct Nora twice when she insisted on calling it a "bomb fire."

During the rest of the adventure, Runa's crew successfully evaded grizzly bears on land and giant serpents in the river. Matthew urged the story forward to a happy ending that featured a party with soda, chocolates and three different kinds of cake.

Dylan was reading in bed when Matthew stopped at his doorway to say goodnight and remind him not to stay up too late. It was a rule that Matthew had been lax about enforcing since Dylan got his braces, and he knew his son would probably end up reading until midnight.

After locking the front and back doors, Matthew climbed into bed and turned out the light. In the darkness, he thought about what had been said on the back deck as he listened to the sound of light rain hitting the thick green leaves of a rhododendron bush outside the half-open window. He was lying on the far side of the bed, with an arm stretched across the half where Anne usually slept. It would make sense for him to sleep on her side because it was closer to the bedroom door and didn't require him to circle the bed every time he got in or out. But after sleeping for so many years on the right side—his side—of the bed, it would feel strange to suddenly sleep on her side.

She had been gone over seven weeks, and, according to Dylan's count, it would be another 36 days before her return. He missed her in many ways, but on that particular night he missed simply having her beside him in the darkness. She alone knew how to reassure him when thoughts of his brother plagued him enough to ruin a good night's sleep. She alone could help him deal with the part of his family that was forever threatening to leap out of the shadows and screw up the life he had worked so hard to build.

Chapter 13
Tripod Number Five

(the previous day)
Friday, May 12, 2000

As the time approached for Anne's short break in Anchorage, her days on the Slope seemed to go by faster. She was looking forward to the time off. She'd fly out on the morning of the 15th and return on the 18th. After another four more weeks of work, she'd finish her contract and head back to Seattle, which she was looking forward to even more.

On Friday, she spent the day conducting surface measurements with David, using a laser mounted on a survey tripod. It was tripod number five, and Anne guarded it closely when they returned to camp. She kept it at the dining hall table when she ate; she took it with her when she needed to use the bathroom; she carried it to the lab, where she worked for the next couple of hours to complete her report; and a little after 9:00, she leaned it against the wall in her suite, then proceeded to take a long, hot shower.

After toweling herself dry and putting on her robe, she opened the door to her room and stepped inside. It took her a fraction of a second to realize there was someone sitting on the far end of her bed. It was Bert from Burtonwood. Anne took a step back and gasped.

"Hello, Anne," he said in a soft voice. "I'm sure you don't mind an impromptu visit."

Once she got over her shock, Anne was furious. "Get the hell out of here!"

Instead of leaving, Bert stood up and said, "We're past the stage of being coy, don't you think?" He began stepping slowly toward her.

Anne felt a wave of panic. She tried to think of what to do. Yell...Sarah wasn't in her room, and the door to the hallway was closed, so she might not be heard. She was going to have to deal with him alone. She thought of hitting him with something, and her mind leapt to tripod number five. It was leaning against the wall right next to her.

The heavy-duty metal device was three-and-a-half-feet long with the legs retracted, and it weighed over 15 pounds. Anne quickly grabbed it with both hands. Like a baseball batter reaching for a high fastball, she swung hard.

Bert drew a hand up to deflect the blow, but it wasn't enough. The thick baseplate for the laser mount struck his hand and continued onto the side of his head. The blunt force sent him spinning backwards until he slammed face first into the door. He groaned and began searching for the doorknob with his uninjured hand. When he found it, he pulled the door open and took one wobbly step into the hallway.

In that moment, coordination failed him. Like a giant tree falling, his descent was almost silent, but as soon as he crashed onto the hallway floor, he let out a thunderous howl. Doors were soon opening because of the commotion. Bert rolled across the hallway, holding both hands to his head and screamed, "You crazy bitch!" When he bumped into the wall on the far side, he began rolling back to the near side. Blood flowed steadily from his wounds, and as he rolled around, he left bloody prints on the hallway carpet wherever his hands made contact.

Anne watched in horror. She still held the tripod and wasn't sure if she'd need to use it again. Women from neighboring rooms slowly moved toward the strange scene. There were voices coming from the stairs leading down to the first floor. Then she heard the footsteps of someone climbing to her floor.

She suddenly felt a chill as cold air from outside was blown up the stairway through the open front door. After she leaned the tripod against the hallway wall and turned toward her room, she realized that Bert might be able to grab the tripod and attack her with it. So she brought it with her into the bedroom. Her hands were shaking, and she had trouble closing the door behind her and locking it. How could this happen, she wondered. How did this happen?

The door to her bathroom opened quickly, and Anne turned toward it with a renewed sense of panic, as if Bert might suddenly be attacking from a new direction. But it was Sarah, who had just returned to the dorm. When Anne recognized her, she unclenched her fists and exhaled.

"What the hell!" Sarah began. "Are you OK?"

Anne pointed toward her door to the hallway. "He was in my room when I got out of the shower. That guy, Bert..." She paused to take a deep breath before slowly explaining everything to Sarah.

A few minutes later, they heard a knock. Somebody announced himself loudly as camp security. Sarah went with Anne to the door. When Anne unlocked and opened it, she saw Bert back on his feet and holding a bloody towel to his head. He wasn't looking in her direction and Anne didn't want to see him, so she took a step back. There were two security officers, and one of them asked if they could come inside.

They entered her room and closed the door. Anne looked at the officer who seemed in charge and thought he couldn't be older than 25. He also looked to be more shaken up by the incident than her. "Are you OK?" he asked.

"I'm OK," Anne said, and felt a dryness in her throat.

"You're not hurt at all?" he repeated.

"Not physically. No." Then Anne noticed that the other officer was writing her responses down in a notebook.

"Can I ask you what happened?"

Anne took a deep breath and pointed to the bathroom. "I just got out of the shower and when I stepped into my room, he was sitting on my bed."

"He said he tried to leave when he saw you."

"No, he stood up and came toward me..."

"He's saying that he made a mistake and didn't realize it was your room."

"He looked at me and called me by my name: Anne. He damn well knows who I am, and he knows this is my room." Anne took a quick breath before continuing. She felt herself getting more pissed off at the security officer for what his questions were suggesting. "He's harassed me a couple of times already."

"OK. I'm just trying to get a clear picture of what happened."

Anne went on to describe in greater detail her interaction with Bert on the flight, in the theater and that evening.

The officer went to her hallway door to see how easily it opened and closed, and to see if it remained closed after being shut. Then he tried turning the lock, which was a sliding deadbolt. "So your door was not locked when all this happened, right?"

"No…" Anne began.

"Then it was unlocked while you were taking a shower. Is that right?" the officer asked.

Anne got the troubling sense that the officer was implying something, and she didn't like it. "This is a women's dorm. No, I don't keep my door locked one hundred percent of the time. And neither do the other women staying here. We visit each other's rooms all the time, and I can't remember a door ever being locked unless it's at night and we're sleeping."

The officer was somewhat taken aback by Anne's reply. He raised a hand and said, "I'm just gathering the facts. That's all."

"Well, the fact is that I do lock my door, OK? But not until I'm ready to go to sleep."

The officer nodded. "OK, fine. We're done with the lock. Now the tripod. Can you show me what you did with it?"

Anne picked up the device and explained how she had swung it. When she was done, the officer asked her to hand it to him. He underestimated its weight and almost dropped it. "Wow," he said. "Alright. We'll need to hold this as evidence for the time being."

"Oh, great. David's gonna kill me."

"That's number five, isn't it?" Sarah asked.

Anne nodded.

"Don't worry," Sarah said.

A medic had shown up, and there was a fresh round of howling in the hallway as Bert's wounds were examined.

The officer continued, "We're bringing him to the clinic so he can get treated, then we'll be taking his full statement. If we happen to have more questions for you, we'll contact you and ask you to stop by our office." With that, the officer taking notes closed his book, and the two left.

Anne sat down on the edge of her bed. "I can't believe this happened," she said, shaking her head. "What did I do to make him come after me?"

"Nothing. He just does it," Sarah said as she put a hand on Anne's shoulder. "You're not the first one, Anne, but something tells me you'll be the last."

Sarah walked to the hallway door, then looked out at all the blood stains on the carpet. "Head wounds tend to bleed a lot, you know. If he was able to leave here on his own two feet, he'll be fine." Sarah walked around the hall so she could see the stains from different angles. "I'm seeing an interesting pattern here. It's like some weird experimental roller art project."

Three other women living on the second floor stopped by Anne's room to hear directly from her and offer support. She spoke to them briefly, making it clear that she was tired and wanted to go to sleep. Sarah went back to her room, but told Anne to wake her up if she needed anything before morning.

When everyone left, Anne closed her hallway door and locked it. She wondered whether she'd be able to sleep at all and wasn't even ready to try. What she really wanted to do was call Matthew. She would have to walk to the lounge at the far end of the hallway. She hoped that the other women on her floor, the ones she hadn't talked to, would be sympathetic to her once they heard the whole story. But she just didn't want to invite a big discussion at the moment, and if she walked into the hallway, that's what might happen.

Maybe she could wait a while for everyone to go to sleep, then head to the phone lounge. She considered what she'd say to Matthew. She knew it would make her feel good to unload the whole event into his ear. But she also knew how he'd react. First, he'd get really pissed off. Then he'd want to fly north and get involved in the whole situation. She didn't want that. She didn't need him to fix anything for her. She just wanted to talk to him about it. Talking would make her feel better, she knew, and so would hearing that he was on her side in this, that he was backing her up whatever the fallout might be. And he would be, of course.

Anne unlocked her door and opened it just enough to poke her head out. In the phone lounge, she saw someone's shadow moving and heard them talking on the phone. She closed the door and locked it again.

The small clock on her bedside table told her that it was almost midnight. It was an hour later back in Seattle. If she waited until the phone was free to call Matthew, she'd definitely wake him. He wouldn't be able to fall back to sleep when the call ended. Instead, he'd stay worked up about things until the sun came up.

Anne had time reserved in the phone lounge on Sunday. She'd wait until then. To distract herself, she reached for the copy of *People* magazine she had been half-reading that week. After flipping slowly through the pages, seeing images of glamorous celebrities on the red carpet or on the set of a blockbuster movie, she tossed the magazine on the floor and turned out the light.

She lay in the darkness with her eyes open and tried to calm herself down. If only she could be with Matthew. Even to hear his voice for a few moments would bring her enough peace to get to sleep. But she was alone now, and she would have to get through it alone, at least for the next day or so.

Suddenly she remembered something and got out of bed. In the back of the bottom drawer of her dresser, she found Matthew's workout shirt, which she had accidentally packed in her bag weeks before. The shirt still carried his scent. She brought it back to bed with her and placed it next to her face on the pillow. With one hand on the shirt, she closed her eyes.

*　　　*　　　*　　　*　　　*

Anne's first stop the next morning was her supervisor's office. Seth was waiting for her.

"I think you should apologize," he told her as he rocked back in his creaky chair.

Anne's eyes grew big. "You're kidding me," she said.

"I'm not kidding you, Anne. Really. Bert Galland's story is that he had a long day and was very tired, and he went into the building that he thought was his dorm. They just moved his building, you know, so he was a little confused. Bert lives on the second floor of his dorm, just like you, and he walked into your bedroom thinking it was his own. You surprised him and hit him on the head before he had a chance to explain his mistake."

Anne tensed up with anger. "Listen, Seth. He looked at me and called me by my name. He said, 'Hi, Anne. I hope you don't mind a visit.' Then he stood up and came toward me. He knowingly broke into my bedroom, for Chrissake! I can't believe you're siding with him."

"OK, alright, Anne. Let's not get too worked up," Seth said as he raised his arms, then lowered them slowly. "I'm not saying he's telling the whole truth. But the thing is, Bert ended up in our emergency care clinic in the middle of the night, needing several stitches on his head and a cast for his hand."

"His hand?"

"Apparently he broke a number of bones in his left hand. Or you broke them, to be more accurate."

"Do you think I'm lying about what happened?"

"I'm not calling you a liar. Not at all. What I'm saying is this: Bert Galland is a big deal up here. He's the director of new drilling operations for Burtonwood. Everybody is going to hear about this thing...this incident, let's call it. And he's going to need an outcome that doesn't make him, or Burtonwood, look bad."

Seth had his hands folded on his desk. He rolled his right palm up and continued, "On the other hand, you've been contracting up here for almost two months now...and you've been doing a great job, by the way...and I know you're hoping to parlay this experience into a staff job with BG back in Anchorage."

Anne shook her head and gave Seth a look that questioned why he was bringing her job hopes into the discussion.

"Am I right about that?" Seth asked.

"Yes, you are right about that, Seth."

"OK, so let's not drive into a big pothole that you can just as easily drive around. If you're willing to apologize...and what I'm saying here is completely confidential and off the record...then Bert won't take any action against you as a result of the incident. He won't take legal steps or say anything disparaging about you. He'll simply describe it as an unfortunate misunderstanding where neither person is at fault."

Seth's office had one window. It was to Anne's right. She turned to look onto the parking lot outside. Two men were having a conversation in the chilly morning. She saw great puffs of vapor coming from both of their mouths, but it was hard to tell who was actually saying something and who was simply breathing.

Anne felt a sinking feeling and realized she should have seen events taking this kind of strange turn. They were going to hold her staff job hostage unless she went along with a story that made Bert look innocent.

She turned to face her supervisor. "This is wrong."

Seth's chair creaked again as he leaned back. "I'm just saying how it is, Anne. There's only so much influence I can have on the outcome here. But you can walk away a winner if you apologize. And I'm sure you'll never be running into Bert again. Not after this kind of public…incident. You'll be leaving for Anchorage the morning after tomorrow, right? Before you catch a ride to Deadhorse Airport, just stop by his office." Seth pointed out the window. "His office is in the reddish building behind those two guys. It's the first one you see when you go through the front door. He said he'll be there all Monday morning. You simply have to pop your head through the doorway and say those two little words: 'I'm sorry.'"

There were, in fact, two words Anne really wanted to say to Bert Galland. But they were very different from the ones Seth was suggesting.

*   *   *   *   *

David worked in the lab until Anne had finished her business with Seth. He didn't like the fact that Anne had temporarily lost possession of tripod number five, but when he heard all the details on their drive to a drill site, he had a more positive reaction.

"You clocked him on the head with a survey tripod? Holy cow! You go, girl!"

Anne smiled. "I wish Seth could see things your way."

"What do you expect? He's a middle management weasel. Please shoot me if you ever see me in a job like his." Then David smiled as he added, "Or knock some sense into me with a tripod."

They were driving south on the Dalton Highway. Rather than being snow covered, the highway now had a mix of snow and sand over its gravel surface. The daily temperature had been slowly rising, and that afternoon it was supposed to hit the mid-30s. Anne could see spots out on the tundra where the snow was beginning to melt.

"You can't apologize to the dude. You know that, right?" David said.

"I don't want to, but Seth is suggesting I might lose my chance at a staff job if I don't."

"No job is worth that."

"I know what you're saying. The thing is that I have two kids, and I'm trying to move the family up to Anchorage. I've been trying for years now…" Anne felt a surge of resentment and had to pause for a moment. "God, I hate being so close to making it finally happen just to have some jerk screw it all up. It's that feeling of having something you deserve, and you've earned, taken away from you just as you're about to grasp it. You know what I mean?"

David had been paying more attention to the conversation than the road in front of him and didn't see the pothole he was about to hit. The left tire went right into it. The truck bounced and everything inside rattled. "Sorry about that," he said.

"Maybe that was the pothole that Seth warned me about," Anne said.

David laughed. "What does Matt think you should do?"

"I haven't told him yet. I wanted to last night, believe me. But someone was using the phone when I checked. Plus, I know how he'd react if I woke him up and told him what happened. There's nothing he can do about it where he is. Except lose sleep. I'll be calling him tomorrow. I've got time reserved on the phone."

"I don't know," David said, unconvinced. "If something like that happened to my girlfriend or my wife, I think I'd want to know about it right away. Not two days later."

"I hope nothing like this ever happens to your girlfriend, David. Or your future wife. But if it does, and if you trust her...and that's the important thing, David, trusting her with the decision...then you'll appreciate being able to sleep well at night until the time is right for her to let you know all about it."

*   *   *   *   *

The next day was Sunday, and Anne only worked until 1:00. She spent the rest of the day getting everything ready for her flight to Anchorage the next morning. She didn't even notice the time until it was 5:08. Her reserved phone slot was 5:00 to 5:30. She walked down the hallway to the lounge, settled into the end of the green fabric sofa next to the phone stand and dialed her home number.

The first thing she heard when someone answered was giggling. Anne wondered if she had dialed correctly.

"Hello?" she asked.

There was silence for a moment, then Nora and Dylan launched into a kind of rap:

Although you're far away
And skies above are gray
We hope you're still OK
Please don't overstay
Or they'll be heck to pay
Oh, and by the way
We have something to say
Happy Mother's Day!

When they finished, Nora burst out giggling. The song had taken Anne completely by surprise and she was overwhelmed.

When Matthew came on the line, he said, "Well, if that doesn't bring you tears of joy, I don't know what will."

Anne wiped away a tear as she laughed awkwardly. "How dare you ambush me emotionally."

"I hope you liked it."

"I loved it, Matt. It was beautiful. In fact, it was just what I needed."

"You know it's Mother's Day, right?"

At the mention of Mother's Day, Nora and Dylan began repeating their rap in the background.

Anne laughed. "This is going to sound awful, but I completely forgot. I mean, I knew it was coming…that it was this Sunday…but I haven't been thinking about it at all this weekend. I've had something else on my mind that I'll tell you about later."

"Didn't you get the Mother's Day package? The kids put one together, but we might have sent it too late."

"The mail's been delayed a couple of days up here, but I'm sure the package will be waiting for me when I get back from my break."

Matthew put the kids on the phone, Nora first. Her highlights included scoring a goal in two soccer games. She also said that the robins' nests in the maple tree out back had two confirmed blue eggs. The second nest was on a branch that Matthew forbade Nora from climbing onto because it was too close to a power line, so she had no egg report regarding that nest. Also, she mentioned that she had come up with another story about Runa and her friends. In this story, they all went surfing in Hawaii rather than snowboarding on a mountain. But, of course, they surfed waves that were bigger than any waves ever recorded in Hawaii.

Nora then went into some detail about the new takeout dinners they had been ordering. The Buddha Bar, the Mahoney family's favorite Thai restaurant in West Seattle, had closed suddenly. They were now ordering Thai dinners from the Laughing Monk in Morgan Junction. Nora liked them a little better but said their pad krapow gai, or Thai basil chicken, didn't have the same spice as the Buddha Bar, whose sauce had the ideal blend of sweetness and fire.

When Dylan got on, he reported that he and his dad had brought the telescope down to Lincoln Park last week and witnessed the general alignment of the sun and the inner six planets of the solar system. They had also seen a lunar occultation. That was when the moon or a different solar system body passed directly in front of another celestial body and thus obscured it from a viewer on Earth. Dylan clarified that it was only a partial occultation, which technically probably made it more of a transit than an occultation, although he seemed a little shaky on the distinction. He shared some of the conflicting information he had read on the subject.

He finished by telling his mom that his braces had been tightened that Friday, and his mouth hurt again, just as his mom had told him it would happen each time. But he had followed her advice and bought two calendars, one for 2000 and one for 2001, and he had marked down all the orthodontic appointments for the next six months and the one for December 18, 2001, when Dylan was tentatively scheduled to have his braces removed. They didn't represent actual appointments because Dylan didn't yet have an orthodontist in Anchorage, but they showed him a progression from a life with braces to a life without them. Anne took the opportunity to stress the tentative nature of the date when the braces would be removed, and that the day could shift earlier or later. If so, it would most likely be later but not by much.

Matthew came back on the line and gave Anne a quick rundown on things back home. As expected, the roofing work had picked up. Between that, his bartending shifts and making sure the kids got to and from school—and everywhere else they needed to go—on time, his days were full. But Jennifer was doing a great job babysitting and shuttling the kids across town regularly, so he wasn't overwhelmed.

He made another attempt to tell Anne about Francis in an indirect way, but it proved to be just as confusing as his other attempts, so he abandoned it, then asked, "So what was it that you wanted to tell me about? What's happening up there?"

"Well, it started on the flight up here in March..." Anne began but stopped when Virginia, a woman living on the floor, walked into the phone lounge. Anne looked at the clock above the doorway and saw that she had gone a few minutes past her half hour. She stood up and waved Virginia toward the phone.

"You know what, Matt, my half hour is up. Someone else has the phone reserved. Anyway, it's not a big deal. I can tell you all about it when I call from Anchorage, OK?"

As Anne lay in bed that night, she thought about the next morning. She'd be getting on a plane and flying south and couldn't wait for that. But it was something else that kept her awake. Whether or not to apologize.

It would be plain wrong, and it went against everything she believed in. At the same time, she hated to think that she'd lose her chance to get a BG staff job in Anchorage. In a little more than a month, the whole family could pack up, leave Seattle, move into the cabin and begin their new lives. It was the dream that Anne had been chasing for years. All of that could be lost if she didn't apologize.

Even worse, not apologizing might also make it harder, or even impossible, to secure any job with BG or any other oil company in the future. If word got around among those who mattered, maybe she would even be barred from working for other industries in the Anchorage area. It wasn't that big of a city, and people did talk. What a terrible decision to have to make. Two simple words; three syllables.

She didn't sleep well at all, and when her alarm went off at 6:30, the only thing that got her moving was the thought that she'd soon be standing knee-deep in the Talkeetna River, casting a fly across the chilly waters flowing down from Talkeetna Glacier. She was so looking forward to that.

David showed up at 8:00 and helped her carry her bags down to his work truck. The morning was cloudy, cold and windy. Anne hoped the wind wouldn't cause her flight to be delayed or cancelled.

"This is nothing," David told her on the short drive to the airport. "You'll be in a 737, and I've seen them take off in winds twice this strong."

"I'm so sleepy I think I'll nod off on the plane no matter how bumpy the ride is."

David carried one of her bags out to the tarmac. They handed them to a worker who threw them onto the luggage belt that carried them up to the cargo hold. Anne gave David a hug and thanked him for the ride. As she began climbing the steps at the front of the plane, David called out to her.

"I'm sorry, but I really have to know," he said.

She turned around, but with the wind blowing so hard, it was difficult for Anne to understand what he said. "What's that?"

David cupped his hands to his mouth and yelled, "Sorry for asking, but did you apologize?"

Anne showed him a tired smile, then yelled back, "Hell no!"

Chapter 14
Fish On!

Monday, May 15, 2000

Maddie was there to pick up Anne at the airport, and they spent the afternoon hiking the Penguin Peak Trail with the dogs. It was a cool day in the 50s and drizzling, but to Anne it felt like a welcome heat wave. She had gotten some sleep on the flight down, and although her neck was a little stiff, the fresh air brought her fully back to life.

The trail took them through heavy brush as it climbed steeply on the lower portion. Anne had hiked it plenty of times and would occasionally trail run it. Seven weeks working outside on the Slope with regular workouts at the company gym made it easy for her to keep up with Maddie and the dogs, who were charging up the trail.

They emerged from the brush eventually, and the trail opened onto an expansive meadow. They continued farther onto a ridge, where they sat down to enjoy the view and have lunch. The trail gained another thousand feet on its way to Penguin Peak, but the ridge would be as far as they'd go.

Maddie took a look around to make sure there were no wild animals in sight before she let the dogs off their leashes. They obeyed her as well as any dogs would in normal circumstances, but if a bear or moose showed up, they might give chase. Biscuit and Luna had seen bears on the trail before, and Maddie had trained them not to bark wildly, but they were always on a leash where Maddie could hold them close. When most dogs encountered a bear, they would charge and attack until it landed a good swipe or bite, at which point the terrified dog would quickly retreat and lead the bear straight back to its human.

Anne pulled a couple of plastic bags from her pack and handed one to Maddie. They placed them on the wet moss, then sat down. Three thousand feet below were the beautiful blue waters of Turnagain Arm. The mountains beyond were now showing new green vegetation. Maddie had packed sandwiches for her and Anne. For the dogs, she had brought dry food and water, which she put into plastic bowls.

Anne took a deep breath and let it out slowly. "That felt good. I haven't done any uphill hiking since leaving for the Slope." As Anne leaned forward, the small pack where she carried her handgun pressed into her chest. She was too lazy to take it off, so she leaned back and spread her hands into the soft moss.

Maddie talked for a while about her job. Although the ski season was officially over, she was still busy at the lodge, with skiers and snowboarders being replaced by the first wave of tourists. Things would pick up even more in June, when the weather got "a little friendlier to outsiders," as she described it.

"You'll have to take Matt and the kids on this trail when they move up here. They'll love the view. Even when the weather isn't great, which it usually isn't, the view is wonderful."

The mention of Matt and the kids moving up made Anne think of her situation and her growing doubt that she'd be offered the staff job she wanted so badly. She had already given Maddie a partial rundown of how the first seven weeks on the Slope had gone. Now she told her about the incident in her room.

Maddie's first reaction was to just shake her head. "It's been almost 20 years since I worked up there, but no matter how much they tell me things have changed for the better, there are some ways that it hasn't changed at all. I'm glad you knocked that guy on the head though. I just wish I had been there to see it."

Maddie had made grilled chicken sandwiches with fresh pesto from the basil plants she put out on her deck when it was warm enough. They were good-sized sandwiches, but Anne had finished hers before Maddie had eaten even half of her own. When Maddie noticed, she held the other half out to Anne and said, "Take the rest of mine if you like. I had a big breakfast."

"You don't have to, Maddie," Anne said.

Maddie smiled. "C'mon now, I saw you staring at it just like you used to when you and your dad would come over for a summer barbecue. You'd gobble down a big hamburger, then stare politely at the platter where there were more. You'd never get out of you chair for seconds no matter how hungry you were. I'd have to pick up the platter and walk it over to you."

Anne laughed out loud and put a hand to her face. "Oh my God, I remember that. I'd do it every time we came over for dinner. I didn't want to be greedy, I guess."

"But that's why I grilled extra burgers. So here," Maddie said, extending the sandwich half again. This time Anne took it.

"I wouldn't worry about whether you get a job out of it or not, Anne. There's plenty of work up here for someone with your skills."

They were quiet for a while and simply enjoyed the scenery. Then Anne picked up one of the plastic bowls and played tug of war with Luna. Biscuit didn't appreciate being left out, so Anne grabbed the other bowl and let her tug at that.

Maddie laughed. "They're gonna miss you when you're gone."

"Likewise, for me," Anne said. She stood up and shook the water from the bottom of her plastic bag. Maddie did the same and handed hers to Anne, who stuffed them both into her pack before strapping it on her back.

"Do you plan on stopping by the Big Wall to see Andre?" Maddie asked as she stowed the dog bowls and put Biscuit and Luna back on their leashes.

"Definitely. I'll swing by tomorrow or Wednesday. It's been too long, really."

The clouds began to break up during the hike back to the trailhead, and they made better time than on the way up. As they approached the valley and entered the thick brush, Maddie was telling Anne how much she disliked this part of the trail because of how easy it could be to stumble onto a bear and how often it happened in Bird Valley. She suddenly paused mid-sentence and stretched out an arm to signal Anne to stop.

In front of them at a fair distance, they heard the sound of branches cracking, then a couple of low guttural grunts. In her time in Alaska, Anne had had several encounters with both black and brown bears, although usually she was able to see the animal. The biggest danger was getting between a sow and her cubs, but so far it only sounded like one bear.

The dogs smelled it, and they began growling. Maddie took a few steps forward, and as she did, she shortened up on the leashes. "Shush, girls." Then turning to Anne, she spoke softly, "I can't see anything, but I'm sure it's a bear. I told you I hate this brush. If it sounds like it's moving toward us, we'll need to make some noise."

Maddie reached up to the shoulder strap of her pack, where she kept her bear spray. Anne's handgun pack had a Velcro closure. There was a ripping sound as she opened it and pulled out the heavy Ruger.

"The wind blows every which way in this valley," Maddie whispered, "but it was coming in our direction when the dogs smelled it. I don't think the bear knows we're here. It sounds like it's moving away from us, doesn't it?"

The sound of breaking brush, along with the occasional grunt, continued but with the passing minutes, it seemed more certain that the bear was heading northeast up the valley, which was away from their trail.

"This is why I really don't like to hike along Bird Creek by myself anymore," Maddie said. "Too brushy. A couple of people got mauled in this valley over the last year."

They waited silently until they could no longer hear anything from the bear. Biscuit and Luna had loosened their pull on their leashes and were noticeably more relaxed.

Maddie returned her bear spray to its holder, and Anne did the same with her Ruger. They started slowly down the last stretch of the trail, making enough noise to alert the bear if it was still anywhere close.

"I'm thinking of making green chili with pork for dinner," Maddie said. "How does that sound?"

*   *   *   *   *

Jared showed up early the next morning in his black Dodge Ram pickup. It was three years old, fully paid for and splattered in mud up to the door handles. Along with his fishing gear, he brought a thermos full of strong coffee, a few ham sandwiches and a bag of fresh muffins from a bakery in his neighborhood. Anne put her gear in the back and climbed inside with a thermos of her own, which she put on the floor of the back seat.

"We've got some of Maddie's chili for lunch. She made a big batch of it last night. There's plenty for all three of us," Anne said, meaning herself,

Jared and Jared's friend in Seward, who would be taking them out on his boat.

Jared was still a little sleepy, but word of the green chili woke him up. "Awesome! With pork?"

"Green chili with pork," Anne said as she closed her door.

"Yes! Maddie makes the best green chili I've ever had. We've got to bring her back a fillet. If your king salmon show up, that is."

"I was just talking on the phone with them," Anne joked. "They're on their way."

It was a rainy two-hour drive south on the Seward Highway, and Anne used the time to talk about her first seven weeks on the Slope. Jared was familiar with life up there, so Anne didn't need to explain much. Then she told him about what happened over the last few days.

"You're fucking kidding me," Jared said with obvious anger. "Actually, I'm sure you're not kidding me. I saw it happen more than once in my time up there. It's sad, but some things don't change."

Anne described her predicament and her decision not to apologize.

"You made the right call. Apologizing just keeps them in the clear and keeps them repeating the same bullshit. Don't worry about the job. Give it some time." Jared was silent for a minute, then turned to Anne. "Actually, you know what you should do? Talk to Andre. Tell him what happened. That guy's been in the business a long time, and he knows a lot of people."

It was still raining on and off when they arrived at the marina in Seward and boarded *The Redemption.* The 32-foot aluminum Glacier Craft was owned by Jared's friend Walter, who had started a charter fishing business the summer before. It was early in the season, and Walter was only booking trips every other day, so he kept the 16th free and gave his crew the day off.

"See, this is what I'm talking about," Jared said to Anne, pointing at the bow of the boat and sweeping his hand toward the stern. "A deep-V-front Glacier Craft that you can take well outside of the bay. This is the boat Toby and I need."

Anne introduced herself to Walter, a short heavyset man in his late 30s who had moved to Alaska when he was 22 years old. His plan was to only stay seven years, long enough for his drug possession warrant in Oklahoma to expire. But he got hooked on the fishing business and seven years turned into seventeen as he worked his way up from mate on different charter crews in Homer and Seward to captain of his own boat with a crew of three.

Jared met Walter when he and Toby took a trip on a fishing boat that Walter used to crew. On subsequent fishing trips that summer, Jared and Toby told Walter they were planning on starting their own charter business and asked him all kinds of questions, from what kind of boat to get to what the licensing procedures were. In the meantime, Walter had gone ahead and started his own business, while Jared and Toby were still in the talking stage.

They left the dock at 8:30 just as the rain began to let up, and cruised at a good speed out to where Resurrection Bay met the Gulf of Alaska. The boat rose up and down on long, rolling swells and the air was chilly, but everyone was dressed appropriately in wool, fleece, fishing overalls and rain jackets. Walter slowed the boat down, and Jared set up a line of rods on multiple downriggers. He and Anne had been getting everything ready on the ride out, so now they simply had to bait the hooks with herring.

Walter stepped out of the cabin and called back to Jared, "Set the downriggers to 80 feet for now. I'm seeing a decent bait ball around there." *The Redemption* was equipped with new sonar equipment that was essential for any charter captain who wanted to return to dock with happy clients.

They spent the first couple of hours fishing for king salmon, trolling back and forth in different spots until they started getting some hits. By 10:30, they had six good-sized kings draining in the hold. Then Walter fired up the engines and headed east to some places where the deep water came up against shallow slopes. Bait fish tended to gather there. The halibut knew it and would rise to feed on them.

In the first hour, they caught a few "chickens"—small halibut not worth keeping. Then they hooked two big ones, 27 pounds and just under 45 pounds. The rods were set up in holders until there was a hit, when either Jared or Anne would grab that rod while the other would reel in the two remaining lines so the fish wouldn't tangle in them. Then they'd get ready to assist in bringing the fish on board. Both the kings and the halibut put up a good fight, but it was Anne who reeled in the larger halibut. It took longer than she thought and wore her out.

Around 1:00, when the rain had finally stopped, they stepped into the cabin to warm up and have a quick lunch of green chili, corn muffins and ham sandwiches. Halfway through the meal, Walter called out "fish on!" when the third big halibut struck. Just as Jared grabbed the rod, a fourth struck on a line that Anne was reeling in, so Walter throttled down and came to the back of the boat to assist.

They stayed on that slope for an additional hour, then moved on to a different one, but the tide had shifted and their luck ran out. By 3:00, they called it good and hauled in all the gear.

Anne and Jared cleaned and filleted the fish on the way back to the marina, where Anne brought two kings and one halibut to a local processor that Walter used. The fillets were cut into smaller pieces, flash frozen, vacuum sealed and packed in a shipping box that would arrive in West Seattle the next afternoon. Anne called Matthew and left a message that the fish were on their way and when to expect them at the house. He had let her know that he would be hard to reach until the next night because he was booked solid with roofing work and closing shifts at Roy's.

When they set out that morning, Walter had told them that the fishing trip was on him—payment for the fabrication work that Jared had done on Walter's boat in March—but they still gave him some cash to cover at least half the fuel. After cleaning up, they headed into town for beer and nachos at the Klondike, a neighborhood pub that brewed its own amber and pale ales, and pilsner. An hour later, Jared and Anne were driving north on the Seward Highway.

It was a good day of fishing, and it left Anne happy and exhausted. Jared dropped her off at the cabin around 8:00 with a salmon fillet. Anne delivered it to Maddie along with the cleaned chili thermos. After she took a hot shower, Anne dressed for bed and closed the curtains to block the mid-May sun that wouldn't be setting until 10:45. A minute after her head hit the pillow, she fell fast asleep.

*   *   *   *   *

As satisfying as the fishing in Seward had been, it was the following day that Anne had been really looking forward to. She woke at 3:30 in the morning, had a quick breakfast, made a pot of coffee for her thermos, packed a lunch and gathered up her fly-fishing gear.

The sky was just beginning to lighten when she passed through downtown Anchorage, heading north on the Parks Highway in the direction of Fairbanks. It took a little over two hours to reach the small town of Talkeetna, and in that time the sun rose above the horizon. Being farther north, the temperature in Talkeetna was 35°F, colder than at the cabin. Before reaching the center of town, Anne turned onto a side road that led her eventually to a bend in the Talkeetna River, where she parked the Land Cruiser under trees that were shrouded in morning mist. A short trail took her to a sandy patch of riverbank.

Some of the bank on both sides was still covered in snow and ice, and in places the ice extended for several feet over the water as well. Bare branches of nearby trees glistened where they dipped close to the fast-flowing current. The sound of rushing water was all Anne could hear, and when she sat down on the sand to pull waders over her fleece pants, she felt a cold wave of air from the river washing over her.

The thick fleece pants would keep her legs comfortable, although not quite warm, in the frigid water for a while. She also wore a down vest under her jacket. With every hour, the temperature would inch up until it reached about 50°F at midday, so it was just the first hour or two when she'd feel the chill.

With rod in hand, Anne stepped into the river and slowly walked to where the sand ended and slick, smooth river rocks began. She stopped several yards from shore, where the water almost reached her waist and the current applied a steady pressure against her legs.

One hundred yards upstream, tall trees shaded much of the river, and snow-covered ice extended over half of the water. As Anne was tying an old White Zonker Streamer to her tippet, she heard a crunching sound followed by a loud crack that could have been a rifle shot. The noise came from a large piece of ice breaking off the main sheet. The sound faded in a slow echo that was replaced once again by the sound of rushing water.

There was barely a breeze at 6:00, and Anne's first cast sent her line unfurling gracefully upstream. As the fly drifted downstream, she stripped the line so the fly would dart forward, then paused for a moment before repeating. On her third cast, she saw a fish rising on the deep side of the zonker, so she shifted her aim away from the shore.

On the next cast, Anne saw water swirling as a fish charged downstream and attacked, then the quick flash of a rainbow trout as the fight began. She felt the rush of the moment, of being connected so closely to a beautiful, strong creature. Catching salmon and halibut the day before was enjoyable in its own way, but to Anne, stepping into a river and being able to see the fish react was a much more intimate experience and far more satisfying. It's what she had been looking forward to for so long and what she missed so much.

She drew the rainbow closer and closer, until she had to raise her rod to bring the fish right to her. With one hand, she reached for the small net draped over her back, then slid it beneath the rainbow. It was a good 15 inches long. Its speckled green skin was especially dark, and the stripes along its side were a deep violet-red. She kept the fish underwater as she gripped it firmly, worked the hook from its mouth, then pointed it upstream before letting it go. The fish swam away just as pieces of ice from the breakup came floating by. Anne usually didn't keep rainbows. Besides, the Talkeetna was all catch-and-release this early in the season.

She fished the same spot for another 20 minutes before moving upstream a little ways and changing flies to a Purple Leech. As she was tying it on, she heard snapping and crunching noises coming from the opposite bank. A large cow moose emerged from the brush and began munching leaves off willow and cottonwood trees, which had recently sprouted new growth.

Anne waited to see if a calf or two might appear as well, but it was only the solitary moose. She seemed to notice Anne but didn't pay her much attention. It was a mature cow, Anne could tell, maybe seven or eight years old. She was old enough to have had a number of litters in her life. Maybe she hadn't bred the previous fall, Anne thought, or maybe she had given birth, then lost her litter to a bear or wolf pack, or to a bitterly cold night.

The Purple Leech didn't catch the attention of any rainbows, but Anne kept casting and watching the moose. Her thoughts began to drift, first to Nora and Dylan, then to her father. The Talkeetna was where he taught her how to fly-fish when she was 13, and the two returned every season to challenge the rainbows together.

As Anne's mind wandered, something strange happened. In a very sharp sense, she could feel the distance between herself standing in the Talkeetna River, and her children and Matthew back in Seattle. The moment felt stranger still because Anne could imagine her scene on the river from above, as if she were detached from her body. There she was, standing thigh deep in frigid water, and there was the cow moose ripping bright green leaves from a willow tree. There was the sound of ice groaning, then cracking as another section broke free and began drifting downstream.

She had been so busy since leaving her family—working seven days a week on the Slope for 12 or more hours a day—that she hadn't really had the chance to feel how separated she was from them. This was her first real moment being alone with the time to reflect on it all.

For the whole stretch she had been away, Anne had been thinking that they were all still connected because they spoke regularly on the phone. She had heard all three of them tell stories about how their days and weeks had been going.

Now she saw it, and felt it, differently. For the last several weeks, despite the phone calls and packages, they had been drifting apart, farther and farther. She could see it from above: she and her family being so far apart that all they had now were the memories of times when they had been connected. Soon they would be little more than strangers. Standing in the frigid waters of the Talkeetna, this new perspective hit her in a painful way. It was like a voice inside her saying you shouldn't be here.

She had discussed this break with Matthew months ago, and they both agreed that it made no sense for Anne to spend a lot of money to fly down to Seattle for less than three days when the company would pay for her flight home just a month later. And it made even less sense for Matthew and the kids to spend a lot of money to fly up to Anchorage for three days when they were financially strained.

Matthew had told her to use the break in Anchorage as a chance to rest and recharge. Here she was doing exactly that, but now it seemed that it was the absolutely wrong thing to do. She could have flown home for her break. Her previously delayed paychecks had all been deposited, so they had the money now. They could have made it work.

It would have given her two or three nights sleeping in the same bed with Matthew. Sex aside, just sleeping together and waking up together would reconnect them. She could sit down for breakfast with Dylan and talk to him about his braces and about the stars. She could lie on the couch with Nora and tickle her as they watched some silly TV show that Anne would almost completely ignore. She would hold them both close and whisper how deeply she missed them.

Anne reeled in the Purple Leech for the last time. Usually it was breaking clouds and bright sunlight that would instantly alter fishing conditions on a river. This time it was her mood. It had dropped so quickly that it scared her. She pulled a nail clipper from her tackle vest and snipped the fly free of the tippet, then hooked it onto a vest pad. Sloshing her way toward shore, Anne's legs moved slowly. When she sat down in the sand to pull off her waders, her shoulders felt stiff and sore.

It was exhaustion she was feeling. She understood that. If it had only been in a physical sense, that would be easy, even welcome. But it was emotional as well, and included the trauma inflicted by Bert. That magnified the effect in both senses. She laced up her trail shoes, gathered her gear from the bank and made her way up the trail to the Land Cruiser.

The sky darkened on the two-hour drive south to Anchorage. Rain began to fall, sporadically at first, then steadily. It was a cold rain, the kind that could get inside you and take hours to shake off. To fight off sleepiness, Anne pulled over twice to refill her mug with coffee. It was just before 9:30 when she stepped through the front door of the cabin. She had just enough energy to pull off her shoes and start a fire before curling up on a living room couch under a heavy patchwork quilt that Maddie had made for her long ago.

*   *   *   *   *

When Anne opened her eyes again, the fire had died down. She was barely awake and just lay there on the couch, staring at the glowing embers. Occasionally they sparked and popped. She was on the verge of sliding back into sleep, so she slowly pushed herself up and looked at the grandfather clock in the far corner of the great room. It was almost 3:00 in the afternoon. She heard a faint tapping high above. The rain was drumming steadily against the new metal roof.

It was one of those odd instances when a very long nap interrupted a day so thoroughly that it was like starting the day all over again, or beginning a new one in the same stretch of daylight. As groggy as she was, Anne didn't want to sleep anymore. She pushed the quilt aside, stood up and stretched. Now, what would she do with the rest of her day, she wondered. It occurred to her that Andre was back in town and would likely be at the Big Wall, so Anne went upstairs and washed her face. She changed into jeans and a plaid shirt, and pulled on a pair of Western boots.

Outside it was still raining and chilly, but the brisk air woke Anne up. She stood under the roof covering the front porch and spent a few minutes just watching the rain fall before zipping up her jacket and walking to the Land Cruiser. The rain let up on the ride to Girdwood and the sun began poking through the clouds.

Girdwood was a small town that had once been populated by gold miners working their claims on the creeks that fed into Turnagain Arm. Now its claim to fame was the Girdwood ski resort, which turned the place into a destination for skiers and snowboarders from all over the world. In summer months, the town drew a modest stream of tourists.

The community was made up of 20-odd streets spread on either side of Glacier Creek, with a small airstrip, a grocery store, a handful of restaurants, a health clinic, a couple of bars and coffee shops, a library, three bed-and-breakfasts, two guide establishments for backcountry adventure, a ski and snowboard shop, a post office and a chapel.

Sitting on the western edge of it all was the Big Wall Bar & Grill, within view of California Creek. It was a two-story lodge built in the '30s that was converted and expanded in the '40s to house a sawmill. In 1960, it was sold and remodeled as a Bavarian-themed inn that provided lodging to skiers at the recently opened resort. By 1977, it had fallen into disrepair and stood empty until Anne's father and Andre bought the place in 1978.

They spent the better part of a year making it presentable and applying for the licenses required to serve food and liquor. Anne and Jared volunteered many weekends hauling away truckloads of debris to the dump, cleaning and painting the place, and sanding and sealing the old wooden floors. Once it opened, the Big Wall Bar & Grill became a popular watering hole for the local climbing community.

With its stucco and exposed beam façade, and planter boxes outside the second-floor windows, the building still had a Bavarian look, but with an Alaskan twist. Hanging directly above the front door was a massive moose rack. Higher up were three sets of caribou antlers and old snowshoes nailed on either side of two small windows to the loft.

By the mid '90s, the Big Wall's popularity began to fade as many of the climbers that Andre and Dylan knew grew older and began to hang up their harnesses. The last time Anne had visited was in 1998, when there were barely more than a dozen people there on a Friday night.

So when Anne showed up that afternoon, she was surprised to see the gravel parking lot almost full. After working seven days a week on the Slope for so long, she had fallen out of the weekday/weekend rhythm, so it took her a moment to realize that it was only Wednesday. That made the crowded parking lot even more of a mystery, but the mystery was solved when Anne pulled open the creaky front door and stepped inside. The bar had a good crowd, around 40 people, and most of them were under 30.

The customers might be younger, but Anne sensed right away that they were still climbers. That was confirmed when she overheard a few snippets of conversation mentioning routes familiar to her. The conversations weren't necessarily loud, but many of them had the kind of energy that came from people who were exchanging firsthand tales of adventure. The din was almost enough to drown out a song by the band Everlast, which was playing on a jukebox that looked a lot newer than the one Anne remembered from her last visit.

As she made her way to the bar at the back, she passed by a wall full of framed photographs that showed climbers on various summits. The photos dated back to the day the bar opened in 1979, but the wall was also crowded with many newer pictures, some simply tacked up with pins pushed into the old barn-wood wall.

All eight stools at the bar were taken, but two people were standing to leave so Anne grabbed one of theirs. It was a strange feeling being back in a public place that brought so many personal memories to the surface for Anne, but it was also a good feeling. The bartender eventually stopped by to see what Anne wanted to drink. She looked to be in her early 20s and had elaborate tattoos running down both arms, as well as piercings on her nose, eyebrows and ears.

Anne ordered an amber from an Anchorage brewery. The bartender nodded and looked at Anne as if studying her. Then she tilted her head slightly and said, "I hope you don't mind me asking, but do I know you at all? I'm getting the feeling that we know each other from somewhere."

Anne shook her head once and said, "I don't think so. Not that I can remember anyway."

The bartender turned around, and as she was pulling the pint she looked up at a large, framed photo sitting high on the wall behind the bar. It was a faded image of three people taken in 1976 on the summit of Bird Peak. On the left was Andre, on the right was Anne's father, and in between them with her arms around both stood 15-year-old Anne, nearly as tall as the two men and wearing a pair of mountaineering pants that were almost two inches too short for her.

The bartender had a big smile as she placed the beer on a cardboard coaster in front of Anne. She turned to point up at the photograph and said, "That's you, isn't it? In that photo."

Anne nodded and smiled, "Yup, that's me. A long time ago."

"I knew it!" the bartender said with a sense of satisfaction. "So you're Anne, the daughter of the original owner…not Andre…but the one on the right."

Anne nodded again.

"I've been looking up at that photo since I started working here five months ago, and I wondered if I'd ever meet that girl."

"Well, here I am," Anne said with a smile. "It's 20-something years later, but I remember it like it was yesterday. That was my first time up Bird Peak. I'm smiling in the photo but believe me, I wasn't smiling inside. It was a long, hard haul to get there."

"That's what I've heard," the bartender said. "I've done some of the other peaks around here, but not Bird yet. By the way, I'm Eileen."

"Good to meet you, Eileen," Anne said. She was about to ask if and when Andre might be showing up, when she heard his voice coming from the kitchen area. Even after living in Alaska for 25 years, he still spoke English with a thick French accent. At the moment, it was being used to criticize a cook who obviously wasn't paying enough attention to the pommes frites to notice that the oil in the fryer was well past the point of being fresh enough to produce fries that were worthy of sitting on a plate next to the freshest grass-fed beef burgers in the greater Anchorage area, if not all of Alaska.

"Yes, yes," Anne heard the cook saying. "You're absolutely right…I will…OK…exactly."

Then Andre emerged from the kitchen carrying a sheaf of papers and wearing a look that said he was not even close to being done with his inspection. He stood straight as a rod and had the same thin comb-over across his well-tanned scalp.

When Andre turned and saw Anne sitting at the bar, his expression changed entirely. He raised his eyebrows and his brown eyes lit up with surprise. "Ah…*ma gougère…salut!*" Andre used the nickname he had given Anne when she arrived in Alaska and had shown an appreciation for the small cheese-filled pastries that he would bake.

They embraced across the bar. "So good to see you. What brings you into town? Oh wait, this is your break from work on the Slope, isn't it? Your insane tiny break after seven weeks up north." Andre scanned the restaurant, then pointed to an empty table. "*Allons y*, OK? Bring your beer."

They sat down at a table with a view of California Creek, which eventually fed into the much larger Glacier Creek. It was flowing high and fast with the last of local snowmelt. Andre put his stack of papers on the table between them, then cursed and put them on the floor instead. "I'm telling you," he muttered. "This business can be worse than a bad marriage sometimes, and I've had two of them, so I know." He sat back in his chair, took a deep breath as he watched the creek flowing, then let out an easy laugh.

"I'm such a complainer," Andre said. "Everything is OK, really. I just put on a show for the people working here. They're very good people, believe me, but they're all young, so their minds are always on other things, you know?"

"It's definitely a younger crowd," Anne said. "How did you manage to fill the place again? This is like when you opened it with my dad."

Andre shrugged and threw up his hands. "I swear to God, I have no idea. They just started showing up. A lot of them are into climbing or mountaineering or hiking. In the winter, it's the skiers and the snowboarders, mostly snowboarders for some reason. I ask people how they like the menu. I change it to what they like. Within certain limits, you know. I won't do chili cheese hotdogs and other disgusting things like that. It's good food, fresh food, everything made just right, as long as I keep my eyes sharp on the kitchen."

Andre glanced out the window and noticed something on the loading dock at the side of the restaurant. He caught the attention of a food server and asked her if she could please take a moment to go to the back door and bring in the case of apples left there before the very observant raccoon family living along the creek made a feast of them.

Turning to Anne, he said, "Maybe you can tell, but I'm a little tired."

"You need a vacation, Andre. You need to visit Europe for two or three weeks, and relax. Have some fun. You'll come back refreshed. You never take vacations, and that's what wears you out."

The comment hit Andre with a sort of directness that pulled him back into the moment. "You're right. I need a vacation."

"Promise me you'll schedule one."

"OK. I will," Andre said with a solemn nod. "Someday, many years from now, I suppose I'll sell this place." He paused to point a finger across the table at Anne. "When I do, you'll get a check for half the amount."

Anne held up a hand to counter Andre's finger and shook her head dramatically. "Not again, OK? You need to stop saying that. You owe me nothing." It was an old argument between the two. When Anne's father died, Andre offered to pay her a settlement for her father's half of the business. The two men were very close friends, close enough to make all the big decisions with a handshake, a nod or an "OK." Plus, they were both too lazy to ever draw up the proper documents identifying them as equal owners. Nobody planned on dying in a climbing accident. Everything was in Andre's name.

He had been threatening to write Anne a check almost every time they got together, and each time Anne told him no. If he wrote her a check, she would burn it. If he gave her a bag of cash, she would bring it to his office at the Big Wall and leave it on his desk.

"OK," Andre continued. "Enough from me. Truly. How is everything with you?"

"Le bien," Anne began. She would slip into French sometimes with Andre, when it came easy. It was her way of trying to maintain at least a faint grasp on her family's native language. She started by telling him about Matthew and the kids before getting to her seven weeks on the Slope. It was a fascinating place, and she was glad to finally see where Andre and her father had played a small part in the history of the famous pipeline. She gave him all the details about the conditions, the work, even the food, which she assured Andre was better than she expected.

"But you're not sure if you like working up there," Andre said, when it seemed Anne had finished her update.

"Pas du tout. Je l'aime," Anne said. "The work is great." She paused for a moment, then added, *"Il y avait un problème la semaine dernière."*

Andre folded his arms and sat back in his chair. *"Que s'est-il passé?"*

Anne explained everything that happened with Bert, from the plane trip north to the meeting with Seth, where he told her to apologize.

"You didn't apologize, did you?"

Anne shook her head.

Andre nodded. *"Bon. Alors.* First, I'm glad you hit him."

Anne then added the detail about the broken bones in Bert's hand.

"Quel dommage! The asshole deserved it. He deserved far worse, OK?"

"My boss told me that if I didn't apologize, I might not get a staff job with BG. And it made me wonder if it would affect my chances with other…"

Anne didn't get a chance to finish her thought because Andre interrupted. "Absurd!" He shook his head dramatically, "No, no, no." He then leaned forward and swept an arm slowly across the tablecloth as if clearing a collection of scattered crumbs. "When you go back to the Slope, you just do your work and don't worry about losing your staff job, OK? You're not losing anything."

"D'accord," Anne said.

"You fly back tomorrow, right?"

"Tomorrow morning," she said.

"So, are you free for dinner tonight or do you have plans?"

"No plans, but I am hungry."

"Good. I need a few minutes to place an order over the phone. Then we'll have dinner together right here. Copper River king salmon and a special Beaujolais that's the absolute perfect pairing. I'll grill some fresh asparagus and the little potatoes you like."

*   *   *   *   *

When Anne got back to the cabin, she did a load of laundry and began putting things away. Maddie would drop her off at the airport, then come back to the cabin to empty the fridge of anything perishable and generally tidy up the place, but Anne wanted to take care of as much as she could herself.

When the laundry was done, she brewed a big mug of fennel tea. Along with the tea, she carried the basket of clean clothes onto the second-floor deck, where she began folding them. At dinner, she only drank half a glass of Andre's Beaujolais. It was wonderful wine, but after spending seven weeks on the Slope without alcohol, her tolerance was low. One beer and a little wine had been plenty.

Anne wore a down vest over a fleece jacket on the deck because by 10:45, the air had cooled into the 30s. Across Turnagain Arm, the low cloud ceiling was breaking up. Darkness had already settled onto the lower slopes, but the setting sun sent a final burst of light between the mountain peaks. In an open field 200 yards away, Anne spotted two deer moving quietly toward a stand of white spruce on the other side.

Just as she was starting to feel at home, it was time to leave again, she thought. But it wouldn't be long before that would change in her favor, and in the whole family's favor. She didn't know whether Andre would be able to help her with her problem, but she would trust him and not worry about the matter. In the morning, she'd return to the Slope and simply carry on. The work would keep her plenty occupied.

After bringing in the folded pile of clothes and packing them, Anne called Matthew. He had just stepped through the front door after his closing shift at Roy's, and yes, he had received the message about the fish as well. It was all sitting safely in the chest freezer out in the garage.

Anne told him that she had dinner with Andre, then finally told Matthew about what happened up on the Slope with Bert. His reaction was

305

what she expected, at least as far as the encounter with Bert was concerned, but not what she expected in another sense.

He didn't like the fact that he was being told the news after Anne had shared it with Maddie, with Jared and with Andre. Anne said that she had tried to tell him on Mother's Day but had run out of time on the dorm phone. She also reminded him that he had been busy with roofing work during the day and bartending shifts every night, and that he had warned her he'd be unavailable unless there was an emergency. Didn't this amount to an emergency, he asked?

No, Anne said. It was an emergency when it happened, yes, but she had handled it and now it was in the past. Matthew was silent for a moment before finally coming around.

His reaction caught her by surprise at first, but it made sense. For her, it was old news, but for Matthew it had just happened. It reminded her of Dylan's trip to the hospital. She heard about it the next day after Matthew had managed everything, and she had to experience a delayed version of the event, first with the email, then with the phone call.

She remembered back to the night of her own situation, seeing Bert in her room, feeling a sense of panic, even how her hands were shaking when it was all over. That's where Matthew was, living in the moment of the event itself.

He told her again that he got it, and he understood why she hadn't told him sooner. He trusted her. He trusted Andre too, and he'd let them handle it. That was what she had hoped he'd say, and finally hearing it put her at peace. A few more weeks on the Slope. That was all she had to endure. A few more weeks, and this disconnection from her family would end.

Chapter 15

Dreams Lost and Stolen

Monday, May 29, 2000

Memorial Day brought beautiful weather to Seattle, and by late afternoon the bar at Roy's began to fill up with regulars, one being Eric the Red. Matthew was working the early shift, and was surprised to see him suddenly show up after an absence of several weeks. Eric explained by holding up a court document.

It detailed an event six weeks earlier when Eric had emerged from a convenience store carrying a small bag of groceries. On his walk home, he was stopped by a police car. The officer behind the wheel accused him of having broken into a bar the previous night after it had closed and flooding the place by turning on the kitchen faucets and plugging the sink drains with rags.

Eric responded by placing his grocery bag on the hood of the police car, removing a carton of eggs and pitching them, one after another, at the vehicle. He might have gotten away with only a trip to the station and a night in jail, but with the last egg Eric managed to hit the police officer on the side of his face as he was emerging from his car. A possible night in jail turned into six weeks.

"Well," Matthew said after listening to the tale, "a couple of puns come to mind, but I'll spare you."

"I appreciate that," Eric said as he folded the document into his shirt pocket. "And by the way, they don't have enough to charge me with that flooding bullshit. OK, give me two of those Scotch ales, please. One now and one in three minutes. Then check with me again in 15."

Normally Jennifer would be working alongside Roger on a Monday holiday, but Roger was on vacation and Jennifer had broken a bone in her foot during a trail-running race in early May. Instead of bartending, she was now babysitting Nora and Dylan, while Matthew and Dennis were covering the shifts behind the bar.

By 7:30 the dinner crowd had peaked and was ebbing, so Dennis told Matthew that he could finish up and head home. After closing all his tabs, Matthew made his deposit in the safe and hung up his tie and apron in the locker room. He got home a little after 8:00. When he walked through the front door, he could hear the TV playing *That '70s Show,* something neither Dylan nor Nora was allowed to watch. There was a scrambling for the remote, and Nora quickly changed the channel to *7th Heaven,* a show she was allowed to watch.

"Squids," Matthew asked, "did you tell Jennifer that I said it was OK if you watched *That '70s Show?* Because I didn't say it was OK."

Nora was sitting on the couch next to Jennifer, whose broken foot was in a cast that rested on a pillow at one end of the coffee table. Dylan was sprawled across the love seat with his face in a science-fiction novel.

"She told Jennifer you said it was OK," Dylan said.

"Tattletale!" Nora said. "I wanted to see what it was like when you were growing up, Dad. You know, in South Boston. In the '70s."

"You won't learn much about it from watching that show. That's for sure," Matthew said.

Jennifer looked at Nora. "You told me your dad allowed you to watch it." She poked Nora in the side and began tickling her, which caused Nora to erupt with giggles.

"Matt, if you're hungry," Jennifer said, "there's some Indian food left over from dinner. Dylan put together a plate for you."

Without looking up from his book, Dylan said, "It's in the fridge. If you're wondering why there's no chicken pakora, it's because Nora decided to eat the ones that were supposed to be for you."

"That's a lie! I only had four!" Nora protested. "You screwed up because you didn't tell me that you only asked for one order of pakora. You were supposed to order two. That's what we always order. But you only ordered one, and I didn't find out until after I ate my usual amount!"

Dylan let out a long sigh and turned a page.

"Sigh me a river," Nora said. It was something Anne had taken to saying in response to Dylan's long sighs, which had been growing increasingly audible.

"OK, that's enough pakora drama," Matthew said. "I'll eat what's there. But first, I want to hear a homework report from both of you, and Jennifer will tell me if it's not accurate. Squids?"

Nora quickly went through her homework assignments, ending with the apparent failure of a science project because the worm she was studying either escaped from the flowerpot where she had placed it, or it was refusing to emerge from the dirt so Nora could make her observations. Dylan ticked off a list of four tasks, all completed.

"And did you both thank Jennifer for helping you complete everything?"

"Yes," Nora said.

"Of course," Dylan said.

Matthew turned to Jennifer. "I think we're good here if you need to head out."

"No!" Nora said, grabbing Jennifer's arm as she leaned forward to get up. "You have to stay until the end of the show. That's 9:00. You really have to stay."

"You're welcome to," Matthew said to Jennifer.

Nora pulled harder on Jennifer's arm and repeated her plea, so Jennifer relented and sat back on the couch. "Just until 9:00, Nora. Then I have to go."

"I'm having a beer," Matthew said. "Can I get you a drink...beer, wine? There's a bottle of red open."

"Sure, I'll take a glass."

Matthew returned a few minutes later with a glass of wine, a beer and a plate of microwaved Indian food. He made Dylan scooch over on the love seat and settled in for the remainder of *7th Heaven*. During commercial breaks, he chatted with Jennifer about her schedule for the next couple of weeks.

Her broken foot meant she couldn't work any bar shifts until late June, but it also meant she was available to babysit the evenings that Matthew worked at Roy's. Because it was her left foot that was broken, it also meant she could still drive her automatic SUV, and pick up and drop off the kids from school, soccer practice and other after-school activities. On the few days when Jennifer had other commitments, Hadley Epps had been available as backup shuttle driver.

Matthew considered himself lucky to have Jennifer watch over the kids, even with her broken foot. Ever since Dylan's episode with the steak knife, Dylan had developed an attachment to her despite sometimes pretending otherwise. Nora didn't hide her affection for Jennifer at all, and had recently asked her if she would consider changing her last name to Mahoney because she was practically officially family now.

*　　*　　*　　*　　*

Friday, June 2, 2000

The weather for roofing had been ideal all week, at least as far as Matthew saw it, with temperatures in the low to high 60s, steady cloud cover most of the day, no rain and an easy breeze. At 3:00 on Friday afternoon, the A Crew was close to finishing its third big roof of the week. It was an old Victorian at the northern end of West Seattle.

Willard was due to show up with the paychecks soon, and the crew's plan was to cash them at the bank on the way to Roy's for Ferry Hour.

That morning, Lyka had asked Matthew if she could shingle the one turret at the front of the house. She had never shingled a curved surface before, and Matthew wasn't sure if she was ready to deal with all the complications a turret involved. On top of that, he told her, it would mean working on staging and wearing a harness. For Matthew, it meant having to check on her work every 15 minutes. If the turret wasn't being done right, someone else would have to take over so the whole Victorian could still be finished by 4:30 at the latest.

The turret took Lyka almost six hours to complete, during which time she threatened to give up twice. After some initial mistakes that required a course, or row, of new shingles to be torn off and thrown away, she progressed steadily with only a few minor adjustments needed.

At 4:00, the only one left on the roof was Buck, who was nailing down the final pieces of cap, and caulking the flashing around the chimney. Everyone else was on the ground cleaning up and putting away gear.

"Payday!" Buck called out after he spotted Willard's truck coming down Admiral Way. When Willard arrived, he climbed out of his truck and walked toward Matthew, looking as earnest as ever. What seemed to be missing, Matthew noticed, were the crew's paychecks. At least Willard wasn't carrying them. That was clear.

Matthew wasn't the only one who noticed. Major, Professor and Lyka had all gathered to receive their checks and all were watching Willard silently. Even Buck on the roof had stopped nailing and was resting against the chimney.

Willard ignored the staring eyes and looked at Matthew. "I want to talk to you back at the truck," he said, and the two walked down the street. Once inside the truck, Matthew asked, "What's up?"

"The thing is, we had a little problem with the checks today. I don't have them. Not right now. Tell your crew that I'll be back next Tuesday with them, OK?"

"What kind of problem did you have?"

"This is a one-time thing. It's not a big deal."

"Did the B Crew get paid?"

"Next Tuesday, Matt. Tell your crew."

With that, Matthew realized that the conversation was over. He walked back and told the ones who were on the ground what was going on. As he did, he noticed Willard ring the front door of the Victorian. When the owner showed his face, Matthew overheard Willard ask for a check to cover the 60 percent that was due on the completion of a roofing job. The owner retrieved his checkbook, but insisted on a walk around the house to inspect the new roof and ensure the grounds had been cleaned properly. Then the check was signed and handed to Willard, who thanked the owner but didn't look at the crew or say anything to them as he left.

*   *   *   *   *

Sal had been supervising the B Crew on Friday, so when he showed up at Roy's he didn't quite understand why everyone in the A Crew was in such a bad mood. After Sal heard about the paychecks, he looked at Matthew. "You don't have my paycheck with you?"

They were sitting at a large table in the rear dining room, and Matthew responded by shaking his head and gesturing for Sal to sit down. Buck poured a glass of beer from one of their two pitchers and slid it to Sal. "He stiffed us all," Buck said. "We have to wait until Tuesday for our checks."

"It's a good thing I already had rent money for June," the Major said. "Sometimes I'm waiting for that first check of the month to put me over the top. I'd be screwed in this case because Tuesday is the sixth, and my landlord only lets me slide until the fifth of the month."

"Willard told me there was a problem with the checks," Matthew said. "But he wouldn't tell me exactly what it was."

Sal pulled the fresh beer toward him and turned the glass slowly on the plastic tablecloth. "Well, Willard didn't have any trouble getting paychecks for the B Crew. He showed up with them this afternoon and handed them out. Everybody got paid. And I assumed Willard left my check with you, like he always does," Sal said to Matthew.

"The B Crew got paid and we didn't? That's fucking bullshit!" Buck yelled. "They're the fucking B Crew. There's a reason they're second in the fucking alphabet!"

Matthew gestured for Buck to sit down.

"Easy, brother," Sal said.

After everyone went silent for a moment, the Professor looked at Matthew and asked, "What do you think the problem is?"

Matthew shrugged, then turned to Sal. "After he told me 'no checks,' he knocked on the front door and asked for the last 60 percent. Right in front of us all."

"Maybe they're losing money at roofing and they only had enough today to pay one crew," Lyka said.

Matthew shook his head. "No, they're bringing in good money this spring. We busted out three jobs this week without any rework needed. It's been that way for at least a month straight. The B Crew is earning the Riegers steady money too."

"What is it then?" Sal asked, and as soon he did, he knew the answer. "Wait, I bet it's Wiley's side business."

Matthew nodded. "That's what I was thinking."

Sal continued, "He's losing money with Gourmet Menu dot-com."

Matthew nodded again. "And whatever investment money he had coming in is drying up because dot-com investment money is drying up all over the place. Every week at the bar, I hear about one or two more startups going belly up."

"They're using our paychecks to keep their startup afloat?" the Professor asked.

"I swear to God, I will fucking…" Buck said.

"Don't go there, Buckaroo," Sal warned.

Matthew realized that it probably wasn't a smart idea to be spinning a conspiracy that would get people worked up, even if it was just Buck who was getting worked up and even if the conspiracy was most likely true. He raised his hands and said, "Look everybody, I don't know what's going on exactly or why we didn't get our checks today. Willard said we'd get them Tuesday, so let's just be patient until then." He paused to stare at Buck and said, "And let's keep our powder dry, OK?"

The Major chuckled at the gunpowder reference.

Matthew continued, "If anybody needs a payday loan, I can front you some cash until you get your checks."

Lyka said she could use $50, and the Major asked for $100. Matthew pulled out his wallet and counted out the bills. A bell rang at the bar, signaling the end of Ferry Hour, when the after-work party generally broke up. The Professor did an even pour-out of the two pitchers, and Lyka passed around the plate holding the last beef empanada, which Buck took.

Matthew told everybody the address of the house they'd be roofing on Monday. "The weather sounds like it'll stay good for us. No rain, no big heat. That makes for happy roofing, y'all."

One by one, the crew finished their beers and left until it was just Matthew and Sal at the table.

Suddenly something occurred to Matthew. "Hey, I forgot to ask you about your date with Inessa. Did you guys go out last weekend?"

"We did. It's been such a crazy week, I forgot to tell you about it. So, on Saturday night, we had dinner at Serafina up on Eastlake."

"Fancy," Matthew said.

"Expensive," Sal said. "I was actually kind of nervous when I saw the menu because it had things I've never even heard of. And, like, some of it was in Italian. Inessa spent a year abroad in Italy…"

"She speaks Italian too?"

Sal nodded. "The sound of it is beautiful. I just closed my menu, and Inessa ordered everything. It was great. Then we went to the Guild 45th and saw *High Fidelity. Gladiator* was playing there too, but I didn't want to push my luck."

"It went OK then?"

"I have a good feeling about it. I really do. I'm gonna take it slow though. I don't want to screw this up." Sal picked up his glass and downed the last of his pale ale. "As far as our work situation goes, I've got to be honest. I'm done with the Riegers. I really am."

Matthew rested his head on his hands and closed his eyes for a moment. "I was done with them, like, a year ago."

"No," Sal said, "I mean done. My brother and I have everything ready."

Matthew opened his eyes and turned to Sal. "Really, you guys are ready?"

Sal nodded. "We've got all the equipment we need for a small crew. Are you ready to jump ship and start working for the Camacho brothers?"

"Absolutely," Matthew said. "Do you have any jobs lined up?"

"We've got two customers ready. I'm working on a third," Sal said.

"OK, so that's maybe a week's worth of work."

"Hey, at least it's a start," Sal said. "What's your fucking plan?"

Matthew realized his mistake and sat up. "Sorry about that. You're right. It is a start. That's how businesses get going, I guess. I've never really gotten one off the ground myself, aside from the insulation thing you and I do together sometimes. And that's still not off the ground."

"By the way, this is when I'll also be stealing the rest of the A Crew."

"I think every one of them will be OK with the switch." Then Matthew considered how to drum up some business. "I have an idea. We'd only have a few days or so to make it work because once the Riegers found out what we're doing, they'll put a stop to it. Or maybe not. Anyway, we know all the houses we've worked on this spring. And the ones we worked on last year. We have the names and addresses in our notebooks. Let's pay a visit to all the owners. We tell them that the crew that installed their roof is now working for a new company and is available to roof the house of any of their friends or family."

"Offer them a discount," Sal said.

"Maybe. Maybe not. If they liked the job we did, they'll probably refer us without a discount. And a certain percentage of houses out there need a

314

new roof right now. I'm gonna say five percent, easy. If we knock on a hundred doors, we could get about five solid referrals. And while we're there, we ask them to send us a recommendation, in writing. Better yet, we ask them to do it right there on the spot. One sentence, like...I'm completely happy with the new roof...they're the best roofing crew in Seattle...or the whole Seattle area. They're trustworthy...reliable...honest. You know, shit like that."

"And what if they didn't like the job we did."

"'Have a nice day' and we go to the next one on the list."

"I like it," Sal said.

"Roofing is all about lining up the jobs," Matthew said. "The actual roofing work is nothing."

Sal laughed. "Listen to you. Suddenly the fucking business expert."

*   *   *   *   *

The Mahoney Plan for Friday night was to grill one of the pieces of halibut that Anne had shipped south from Seward. Matthew had taken it out of the freezer the night before and prepped some side dishes. Earlier in the day, Jennifer had picked the kids up from school and brought them to Lincoln Park to go swimming in the public pool. Or at least Nora, who was taking a break from her usual Friday afternoon soccer practice.

Matthew knew that Dylan would probably opt to chat with the people fishing for salmon at the point to find out which lures were proving the most productive on that tide. It was still early in the season. Fishing for king salmon in Puget Sound wouldn't begin for real until around mid-July, although Matthew had heard at the bar that a few sockeyes were starting to show up.

The sun was out all afternoon, which made for a nice time at the pool and the beach. Nora loved the sun, but Dylan, like his father, had fair skin. He returned from Lincoln Park with a somewhat reddish face despite reapplying sunscreen twice during the afternoon. He reported one sockeye salmon being caught, although he didn't witness it himself. He did, however, see one guy catch a shaker, a juvenile salmon that was too small to keep.

As he helped his father prep the grill for dinner, Dylan gave a rundown of the lures he saw being used. "A lot of spoons, just like last year. All different colors. Green and white Octopus Squid. Buzz Bombs, mostly pink. I heard that some guys on a boat had luck with a Cookies n' Cream spoon. Nobody on the beach was really catching anything. I think it's still too early, but we should get out licenses so we're ready when it's time."

Jennifer had been dropped at the Mahoney house that morning by her boyfriend, Alex, and she had used the Subaru to shuttle the kids to and from Lincoln Park. Alex was supposed to return and join them for dinner, but Jennifer made her way to the back deck on her crutches to say that he wouldn't be able to make it after all. He worked as a sales rep for a software company in Bellevue, and one of his larger clients from San Francisco was in Seattle on other business. They asked Alex at the last minute for a consult on a proposal they'd be making Monday to their team back in San Francisco. Alex and his regional manager both had to drop everything and schedule a dinner meeting with the client.

"He said he'll still be able to pick me up around 9:00 or so," Jennifer said. "He's gonna call me when they're finished."

"It sounds like an important meeting," Matthew said.

Jennifer raised her eyebrows and nodded. "Yeah, I think so," she said, without doing a very good job of hiding her disappointment.

The sliding screen door opened with a bang. Nora, fresh from the shower, sprang onto the deck and announced loudly, "I can't wait for this fish! I've been thinking about it all day." To Jennifer, she added, "My mom caught it herself when she was fishing on a boat in Alaska. She said it weighed, like, a hundred pounds."

It was a perfect evening for dinner outside. They ate at a leisurely pace while discussing the latest weather reports from Anne and the recent changes to Matthew's roofing situation. Jennifer talked about her recuperation schedule and said that she expected to be back in top running condition for a late-summer, high-elevation trail race in the North Cascades. The course would start at Rainy Pass and end at the Cutthroat Pass trailhead.

After dinner, the plan was to watch a movie inside, but the evening was so nice that Nora challenged Dylan to a game of tetherball in the backyard. After a quick game, Matthew suggested they play ladder ball instead in two-person teams. As far as physical intensity, the game was similar to horseshoes, so it would allow Jennifer to join in the fun.

The game was briefly interrupted at 9:00 when Alex called to say that his dinner was running a little late, but that he should be able to break free soon. By 9:30, the light in the sky had faded so much that it became difficult to see and aim at the ladders. Matthew declared the game over, which irritated Nora. She was teamed up with her dad, and they were very close to tying the score after a long comeback. It was time to get ready for bed soon anyway, Matthew told her, and they still needed to clear the dinner table and wash some dishes.

As they were putting everything away in the kitchen, Alex called again to apologize and say that he had become involved in a technical discussion at the end of dinner. He and his regional manager really needed to walk their client through a set of very important and complicated steps. He promised, absolutely promised, that he'd be able to pick Jennifer up no later than 11:00.

Once the kids were in bed, Matthew and Jennifer sat down on the back deck with the bottle of wine they had opened at dinner. It was cool enough that Matthew was wearing a sweatshirt and Jennifer was wearing one of Anne's hoodies.

They talked about the possibility that the Mahoney family might be moving north sometime soon and all the changes that would involve. Then the conversation shifted abruptly to Alex's absence at dinner.

"It's happening more often," Jennifer said. "I know that things can come up, but his work is really starting to interfere with our relationship. Like, too much. Last weekend we were supposed to meet a group of friends in Belltown for brunch. On Sunday morning, he gets a call from his boss and tells me has to skip brunch. I was so pissed off. These are my three closest friends from when I went to UDub," Jennifer said, referring to the University of Washington. "We get together for brunch or dinner every year around graduation time. They're all married now. I show up alone and make some excuse. I actually made up a lie because I was too embarrassed to say that Alex couldn't show up, that pleasing his boss on what was supposed to be a day off was more important."

Jennifer paused to sit up and stretch her back by twisting in one direction, then the other. "It happened a couple of other times too, in the past month or so. He knows it annoys me."

"It might be the economy, you know," Matthew said. "A lot of people at the bar tell me they're afraid of losing their jobs right now. Maybe he doesn't want to admit he's worried about that."

"He's not respecting my time, Matt. He's dropping the ball."

Matthew smiled, then let out a quick laugh. "Sorry," he said. "It really does sound like Alex is dropping the ball. It's just that Anne would use that same expression on me for years. 'You're dropping the ball, Mahoney,' she would say if I called to tell her I couldn't pick up one of the kids as planned, or because I had forgotten the avocados or the bananas on a trip to the grocery store. And she was right. I was dropping the ball."

"I don't see you guys having any problems like that," Jennifer said.

"Well, eventually things improved. I stopped dropping the ball so much, and Anne learned to cut me some slack when things were beyond my control. Making a grocery list every week helps. It still happens though occasionally. And believe me, she still lets me know when it does."

From the opposite yard came a loud noise as the neighbor with the Yorkshire terrier let the dog go outside to pee. Matthew and Jennifer watched the dog move cautiously and sniff the grass as it made its way toward an osoberry shrub.

"As long as you don't think it's something else," Matthew continued. "And from what you've told me before, he's good about traveling with you to your triathlons, especially the ones that are out of state."

"He's doesn't compete himself though. He hardly ever goes to the gym or joins me for a run. For me, the physical challenge is everything. But it's more than that. It's a way of life. I'm getting my master's in physical therapy and rehabilitation medicine, so it'll also be my career. I've been thinking that maybe Alex and I are just too different."

Matthew let the thought hang in the air for a moment before responding. "You could be talking about Anne and me, you know. I work out every day. She goes to the gym up on the Slope, but when she was down here, she might have gone once a week, if that."

"But you guys are different," Jennifer said. "You're as close to an ideal couple as any couple I know."

That drew another laugh from Matthew. "You didn't see us 15 years ago. Even six or seven years ago. The road is fairly smooth most of the time now, but it was plenty bumpy for a number of years. When we were first together, we were even more different than you and Alex. Believe me. I grew up in a rough part of Boston. She grew up in a comfortable suburb, then moved to Alaska, which was like another planet to me. She grew up hunting and fishing and camping. I never did any of that. I knew my way around a subway system; she knew her way around the Chugach Mountains. Then there's my family. Anne's mom still hasn't figured out how to deal with it. But at some point, we knew we wanted to be together for good."

"What made you know that?"

Matthew considered the question. Finally, he said, "We haven't really talked about it a lot. But my theory is that…or maybe I should just say that we had a couple of common experiences. When we were young, we both lost the parent that we were closer to. And we both fell very hard for someone in high school, and had that relationship fail in a big way. That didn't exactly make us soulmates, but it was a way we had of looking inside each other and seeing something familiar and painful. Or something like that. It was a small connection really, but I think it made the difference in those years before we were married."

"So who did you fall for in high school, if you don't mind me asking?"

"I don't mind telling you. But it might be a long story."

Jennifer smiled. "Alex won't be here for a half hour."

"Alright. By the way, part of it involves my brother. You know, that one," Matthew said, referring to his brother Francis. Like Sal, Jennifer knew that Matthew was related to the notorious fugitive.

"It starts about a week after my mother was buried. I was 15 years old."

Matthew explained how the moment was a turning point in his life, not just because he had lost his mother, but also because he was forced to leave South Boston forever. It was the summer of 1974, and school desegregation was about to tear the city of Boston apart. His mother had been the parent who Matthew had been closer to, so with her gone and with things not going well between him and his father, Matthew didn't object to being shipped off to live with relatives in Quincy, which was just south of Boston.

The move put him beyond the reach of Boston's desegregation court rulings. His father refused to send Matthew to a private high school, which would have kept him from being assigned to a Boston public school. The only other way many parents had of keeping their kids out of the coming turmoil was to send them to stay with relatives beyond the boundaries of Boston, and that was the choice his father made.

He moved in with his cousins, Richard and Bobby, who were more than ten years older than Matthew. Richard worked as a fisherman, and he and Bobby had recently opened a store in Quincy called Mahoney Seafood. During Matthew's first week of his freshman year at North Quincy High School, he would take the train every afternoon into South Boston to hang out with his old friends. It was the start of desegregation, and he got into so much trouble in one week that the police came to his new home in Quincy and threatened to arrest him if he showed his face again in South Boston anytime soon. After that, Matthew's ties with his old home were limited to occasional visits.

He got along well with his cousins and settled in at his new school, but he woke up every morning and went to sleep every night feeling like he was living in exile.

Two things kept him going during those years. Hockey was the first. He made the junior varsity team his freshman year and moved up to varsity as a sophomore. He played defense and scored more goals than someone in that position usually did. He was big for his age, he was strong and fast, and he knew how to dominate at both ends of the ice. He also got into a lot of fights, which ultimately got him kicked off the team toward the end of his junior year.

The second thing that kept him going was Lauren DeLuca. She lived four houses away on Billings Street, close enough to North Quincy High that they both walked to school every day, but not together.

He would see her walking a block ahead of him sometimes. She was a tall girl, and she seemed even taller because she stood so straight. But there was something else about Lauren that made her stand out and catch Matthew's eye. When he would see her at school, she always moved in an easy, comfortable way, and in the freshman math and English classes they shared, Lauren displayed a quiet certainty about herself, even in situations when most people would feel their confidence waver. Yet she didn't seem to be pretentious at all, or to be loud and bragging like some of the girls Matthew knew from South Boston.

It was Lauren who approached him first one day while he was studying in the cafeteria during his free period. He was sitting by himself at a table, and suddenly there she was, standing across from him and asking if he would be interested in buying a ticket to the freshman dance. She was looking at him with the hint of a smile when she added that it might be a chance for him to meet the girl of his dreams.

It was the first time they had ever looked directly at each other, and in the bright lights of the cafeteria, he saw that her brown eyes actually had a small tinge of green. He froze for a second, then said he was sorry because he didn't have any money. Other students were scattered across the large cafeteria, and Matthew watched Lauren approach several other guys. He couldn't tell if she used the same line on the rest of them, but most of them dug into their pockets for the cash to buy a ticket from her.

Three weeks later, he was returning from a visit to downtown Boston when he spotted Lauren's younger brothers, who were twins, in the North Quincy Red Line train station. It was 9:00 on a Friday night, and Eddie and Silvio DeLuca were being chased down the station platform by three older kids who were sophomores at North Quincy High.

From the twins' faces, Matthew could tell they were not playing a game, but running in fear. The older kids caught them and commenced to give the twins a beating. Their screams didn't seem to affect the few other people standing on the platform, but Matthew ran over to help as soon as he recognized them.

After he broke it up, he was challenged by the biggest of the three sophomores. It was a quick fight with Matthew easily outboxing his opponent, and he enjoyed it so much he wished the other kid hadn't given up so quickly. When the fight was over, Matthew asked the twins to join him for some pizza at a place across the street.

The rest of the DeLuca family heard about it, and Mr. DeLuca, who owned a nightclub and was forever at work, knocked on the Mahoneys' front door to ask Matthew to join his family for dinner that Friday. He wouldn't be there, Mr. DeLuca explained, because he needed to be at the club, but he wanted to thank Matthew on the spot and tell him that the family would show their appreciation with a home-cooked meal.

There were two other, younger DeLuca kids beside the twins, a boy and a girl. When Matthew entered the DeLuca house, he found it filled with the sounds of a family into every aspect of each other's lives, with no problem expressing any opinion or idea that came to their mind, and sharing it enthusiastically in the exact moment that it arrived. But it was all without the acrimony and animosity that Matthew usually associated with such expressiveness in most families he knew in South Boston.

From across the kitchen table, Lauren passed him dish after dish as they were delivered from the stove and the oven. Matthew quickly realized Mrs. DeLuca was an amazing cook. He thanked her for going out of her way to make such a meal. She brushed away the notion with a wave and a laugh, and explained that this was how they always ate, which was the same way every civilized family should eat. As she conversed with Matthew, Lauren's focus was on making sure her siblings' manners were at their best. For most of the meal, she never looked straight at him, but Matthew would catch her shifting her attention his way for brief moments.

He came back the next Friday for another dinner, and another one the following week. He looked for excuses to make his way into the DeLuca kitchen so he could see Lauren, to hear the sounds of the family, and to watch Mrs. DeLuca preparing a meal. She dispensed advice freely, and it was advice that Matthew learned was of hit-or-miss quality at best.

He taught the twins how to box and spent study period sitting across from Lauren at a cafeteria table. They walked to school together in the morning, and that spring they had a running argument over whether *Toys in the Attic* by Aerosmith was better, head to head, than any album by the Rolling Stones. He went to many of her swim meets and track meets, and she showed up at some of his hockey games.

As the weather warmed up, they began spending their nights hanging out at nearby Wollaston Beach with friends. Whenever a joint was lit, Lauren would always pass it without taking a hit, and by the end of summer Matthew was doing the same. One night when they were alone, he told her more about his family back in South Boston, saving his brother Francis for last. Lauren asked a lot of questions about him, and in the end, she said she would agree to keep it a secret from everyone, especially her family.

In fall of their sophomore year, they went to their first school dance together and joked about whether they had really found the person of their dreams. Matthew knew that he had, but it was a question neither one of them wanted to answer seriously until the following year, when college became the topic of discussions at school and at home, at least in the DeLuca home.

Lauren's grades put her near the top of their junior class, and she already knew that she wanted a career in medicine. If she was serious about it, and she was, that meant going to an undergraduate college that would get her into a good medical school. Except for Harvard, the colleges on her list were all far away from Boston.

Matthew was close to a solid B student, and would be looking at a whole different list of colleges than Lauren. When his dream of playing professional hockey faded that year, his future became a blank slate, but he was smart enough to realize that he needed a college education. His father hadn't offered to pay for any of it, which meant Matthew would be looking at state schools, specifically UMass Boston. It was a short subway ride from where he was living in Quincy, and his cousins were willing to let him keep his room there as long as he pitched in a little for food and rent.

In their senior year, Lauren and Matthew spoke about how they would stay together during college despite being apart. There would be holiday breaks when Lauren would return home, and summers. Matthew also promised to visit her at least once a semester no matter what college Lauren chose, which ended up being Northwestern University in Evanston, Illinois.

During spring of senior year, their high school allowed Lauren to spend Fridays working an internship at Boston Children's Hospital, where she was assigned to a hand specialist. After school on Fridays, Matthew would take a Red Line train into the city, then a Green Line trolley out to the hospital on Longwood Ave. The doctor's office, where Matthew would wait for Lauren to finish work, had shelves high up on the walls filled with plaster casts of misshapen hands. On some, fingers were missing. On others, there were too many. Some had two or three fingers merged into something of a single digit, while others were curved and had nails that made them look more like claws. A few were almost indistinguishable from the hooves of animals. Every Friday afternoon, Matthew would scan the grotesque gallery with a mix of repulsion and fascination.

When Lauren got off work, they would walk to Kenmore Square or across the Charles River into Cambridge and grab a bite to eat at one of the many small restaurants that catered to poor college students. They would choose a different place every week and try cuisines that they were mostly or completely unfamiliar with. Then they would walk to one of the small, cheap theaters around Harvard Square to catch an obscure movie or play.

When the weather grew warm, they ended their Friday nights on Wollaston Beach, lying together on the sand until midnight, listening to the sounds coming from the nightclub where biker gangs would mix—and sometimes fight—with locals.

On the second Saturday of June, Matthew showed up at the DeLucas at 9:00 in the morning to walk Lauren down to the beach, where she would take the test to become a lifeguard that summer. It was Lauren's father who opened the front door, though, and he told Matthew they needed to have a talk out back while Lauren walked alone to the beach.

"Is Francis Mahoney your brother?" he asked Matthew as they stood alone on the brick patio in the DeLucas' backyard. The unexpected question stunned Matthew. He couldn't speak, so he simply nodded. For a brief moment, Matthew wondered whether Lauren had shared his secret, but Mr. DeLuca went on to say that a friend of his had told him that Francis Mahoney had a younger brother named Matthew. The friend also told him that the owner of a Boston nightclub had been murdered the week before, and the word was that Francis did it.

Mr. DeLuca said he was very sorry, but he wouldn't allow his daughter to have her life and career ruined by being connected to the brother of Francis Mahoney. They could not see each other again. Not ever. That was an absolute stand from which Mr. DeLuca would not budge one inch, and Matthew would be a fool to ever test him on it.

He and Lauren did see each other, though, during the final week of school. Their talk was limited to Lauren saying that she couldn't disobey her father. He would eventually calm down, she promised, and then they could be together again, but she didn't know how long that would take. Also, she said her summer plans had changed. Instead of lifeguarding at

Wollaston Beach, she would be lifeguarding at a girls' summer camp in New Hampshire. Under no circumstances could he visit her there. They would have to be patient and wait until the end of summer. Her father's mood would change. She was sure of it. Then they would have a little bit of time together, at least a weekend, before she had to leave for freshman orientation at Northwestern.

Matthew spent his whole summer working for the MDC, the Metropolitan District Commission, which maintained local parks and beaches. He was on a three-man truck crew that rode from one public beach to another, emptying metal trash barrels. It was dirty, grueling work that usually left him exhausted at the end of the day, but he got along well with the two older guys on his crew. They'd sometimes get stoned together, which made the rough days a little less so.

As August dwindled down to a week and a half, Matthew grew anxious about whether he'd hear from Lauren at all. One Friday when he got home from work, his cousin was waiting for him on the front porch. A thunderstorm was rolling in and the air suddenly grew cool as Bobby explained that Lauren had called to say she was sorry, but she couldn't see him before leaving for school. Her father had bought tickets for them to fly together to Chicago that night. Orientation started the next day. Lauren was upset, Bobby said, but he didn't see anything that Matthew could do about changing the situation.

Matthew waited until early October before trying to contact her. It took hours on the phone to locate her on campus, and when he finally got the number to the phone on her dorm floor, he hit a dead end. Whoever answered it would go looking for Lauren and return to say that she was not in her room. He wrote her a long letter, but it was never answered.

When Thanksgiving arrived, the DeLuca family disappeared for a week. By early December, Matthew had had enough. He walked down Billings Street and knocked on the DeLucas' front door. It was a weekday afternoon when Mr. DeLuca wasn't likely to be at work. Mrs. DeLuca invited Matthew inside and gave him a warm hug. From there on, everything was cold.

She told Matthew that Lauren had met someone at school. She had a boyfriend now. The family had met him when they visited Northwestern over Thanksgiving break, and he was a very nice young man who was interested, like Lauren, in becoming a doctor. He was smart. They were good together. Mrs. DeLuca said she was sorry, but that's all there was to it. The sooner Matthew could accept the new reality, the better off he would be.

Matthew never finished his first semester at UMass, and never showed up for another class. He spent the next two weeks hanging out in South Boston and getting stoned with his old friend Buzzy. On December 18, he left his old world behind and drove west to start a new life in Seattle.

*   *   *   *   *

The evening air had grown even cooler on the back deck, and a light breeze brought the wind chimes to life.

"Why Seattle?" Jennifer asked.

"My mom and I used to watch this old black-and-white TV show about a pioneer family here. It was something we did together. The show was on for a half hour every week. It was pretty bad, but most shows were back then."

"You came here because of that show?"

"I wanted to be far away, and Seattle was far."

"OK. Here's my opinion. Mrs. DeLuca was way too harsh."

"It gets worse," Matthew said. He paused to go inside the house and make sure Dylan and Nora were asleep. When he returned to the porch, he continued, "Lauren didn't have a new boyfriend. Her mother was lying."

"She made the boyfriend up?"

Matthew nodded.

"That's evil."

"I used to think something like that for a long time," Matthew said. "Now that I have kids, I see it a little different. Sort of. Lauren was their oldest daughter. They were trying to protect her."

"You weren't Francis though."

"What can I say? My brother casts a long shadow."

Sitting on the table beside Matthew was a bottle of water and the bottle of wine. It had about half a glass left.

"So, you never talked to her again?" Jennifer asked.

"We did," Matthew said as he was reaching for the wine. He changed his mind and picked up the bottle of water instead. "About five years ago. She called me out of the blue. Her father had died, so she said the promise didn't matter anymore. I told her what her mother had said. That upset her. Then she told me that her mother had lied to her as well. She told Lauren that I had a new girlfriend and didn't want to see her again."

"Ouch," Jennifer said.

An ambulance drove slowly down an adjacent street. Its siren was off, but its lights sent bright flashes of red and white between the houses as it passed. Matthew followed the movement of the ambulance as he remembered the phone call. "It was a little awkward," he said. "The conversation that we had. And it was sad. Depressing, really. We both knew that we had been robbed. When I think about what we lost…anyway, it's not worth getting angry about anymore. Although every now and then when I really think about it, I do. A little, I guess."

"Is Lauren a doctor now?"

Matthew nodded. "She married a guy she met in med school. They had one kid when we spoke, with another on the way."

"Where do they live?"

"Brookline. It's just outside of Boston." Matthew took the last sip from his water bottle and screwed the lid on tight. "So that's my story." He paused for a moment before adding, "There are no do-overs in this game. I know that. And I'm happy with the life I have. I really am."

*   *   *   *   *

Tuesday, June 6, 2000

The A Crew spent the cool morning ripping two layers of old shingles off a house in the Leschi neighborhood, and at 3:30 they were nailing down the last of the new shingles. Matthew was the first to spot Willard's truck pulling in front of the house. Nobody called out "payday" this time. Matthew climbed down from the roof and walked over to Willard, who stayed in his truck while he handed Matthew a half dozen envelopes, as well as a note with the address of the house they'd be roofing the next day.

"Have everybody there at 7:30," Willard said. "It's a big roof, and it's gonna be a long day." Then he drove off.

When the crew finished cleaning up and loading the trucks, Matthew handed out the envelopes. As he gave Buck his check, he said, "See, sometimes you just have to be patient, and everything works out like it's supposed to."

Buck had driven in that day with the Professor, who said "Let's get these cashed before the bank closes."

The two were walking down the sidewalk toward the Professor's car when Buck suddenly stopped. He had torn open his envelope and was staring at his check when he yelled, "What the fuck?"

As Matthew started his truck, he heard somebody else swearing, so he turned the engine off. He had a bad feeling about what was going on, and he really hoped he was wrong.

The Major came walking over to Matthew waving his envelope. "They shorted me some hours, Matt."

Buck came walking over next. "They stole my fucking money!" he yelled. "I'm like five hours short. Who the fuck do they think they are? It's my fucking money!"

In the glove compartment of the truck was a notebook where Matthew marked everybody's hours at the end of each day. At the end of each week, he totaled the hours and told the crew their numbers, so they knew what to expect for that paycheck. Matthew pulled out the notebook and turned to the week of May 22–26. Total hours ranged from 37.5 to 40, except for the Professor, who had taken that Monday off.

Matthew asked everyone to read out the total hours on their checks, and to a person they were exactly five hours short. He hadn't opened his own paycheck yet, but when Matthew did, he saw that his pay was short by roughly the same amount. So was Sal's. They were both on salary and their pay never changed from week to week.

Buck was seething. "I will kill them both," he said. "I will use a hammer, and I will smash their skulls with it…"

Matthew held up his hands and interrupted Buck. "OK, everybody, before we do anything stupid or rash or whatever, let's take care of the most important thing. And that is to go to the bank right now and cash all your checks. That's what Sal and I are going to do. Get the cash and move on to step two, OK? And step two for me and Sal is to visit the Riegers and find out what is going on. Step two for you guys is to either go home and wait for us to call you, or you can go to Roy's..." Matthew pointed at Buck before continuing, "...where you will relax until Sal and I show up after we visit the Riegers."

Matthew and Sal swung by the bank, where they cashed their checks. Next, they stopped by Sal's apartment in Fremont to drop off his truck and ride together in Matthew's for the 20-minute drive to Wiley Rieger's house in the well-to-do neighborhood of Montlake. Matthew had his radio tuned to KEXP when it started playing "Divine Hammer" by the Breeders.

Sal laughed. "BuckBrain wants to break out his divine hammer for a little justice. I'm surprised he's not in prison already with that temper of his."

"I used to be something like that a long time ago," Matthew said. "You know, if I didn't have kids..." He left the thought unfinished.

As they drove across the Montlake Bridge, which connected the U District to Montlake, Sal said, "You haven't mentioned Anne lately. How are things going with her these days?"

Matthew nodded. "Good. Things are going good with her. We talked about a week ago."

"Have you told her about Francis?"

"I tried a few times." He explained to Sal the challenge he faced in attempting to communicate with her in front of the kids, and how he didn't want to place her in legal jeopardy.

"So you told me instead?" Sal joked.

Matthew didn't hear any resentment in his friend's voice, but he glanced in Sal's direction to be sure. "It was keeping me up at night. I had to tell someone."

"I don't mind. It's not gonna come back on me. But I don't think you should tell Anne. What is she gonna do about it at this point except worry?"

"I suppose you're right."

"She's due home in a couple of weeks, isn't she? Wait till then," Sal said.

"Eleven days, actually." Matthew stared at a tractor trailer they were passing. The back of it was covered in dirt, and someone had drawn a credible rendering of Porky Pig on one of the back doors. Suddenly he realized that he hadn't told Sal, or anyone else for that matter, about what happened between Anne and Bert or about all the fallout. He hadn't wanted to think about it himself. He tugged lightly on his soul patch and wondered if he should share the story, so he glanced at Sal.

"What are you not telling me?" Sal asked.

Matthew glanced at him again. "Anne had a little problem up there a few weeks ago. A guy named Bert." As Matthew began telling Sal the full story, he realized why he hadn't spoken to anybody about it. He was embarrassed. He hadn't been there to protect her from the harassment and the assault. He also hadn't been there to support her after the fact. What kind of a husband lets his wife go through something like that alone? That question had been bothering him for the last few weeks, regardless of what Anne told him about letting her and Andre take care of it.

In a way, he knew that she was right. In another way, he felt that he was also right. There would never be any resolution to the situation that would totally satisfy him. That is, nothing short of flying to the North Slope, tracking down Bert and giving him the beating of a lifetime. And that could never happen, because the fleeting moment of satisfaction would be followed by a mountain of legal troubles and a disappointed reaction from Anne: why couldn't you trust me to take care of this, as I asked you to do?

When he had finished, Sal said, "Well, I know what I'd want to do about it. But you know you can't." He paused before adding, "We can always send Buck after the guy."

Matthew appreciated the fact that Sal got it. There was really nothing more to say about the whole business. He nodded and smiled. "Buck would do it too."

As they approached the Riegers' neighborhood, they turned onto a street that wound its way along Interlaken Park, where houses were hidden behind tall hedges and sprawling gardens.

Matthew slowed as they approached the Riegers' driveway. There were no vehicles parked there, so Matthew backed his truck in. There had been tricky situations over the course of his life when being able to drive away as quickly and easily as possible had twice kept him out of trouble and once kept him out of jail.

After he turned off the engine, he said, "It's funny when you think that he paid for his house mostly with the work we've done."

"You go talk to him," Sal said.

"Are you sure you don't want to go with me?"

"No, I'll wait here."

"OK. I guess it's probably best if only one of us shows up. Otherwise, he might freak out and call the cops."

"Exactly. We don't want the cops showing up, because if they do and something goes wrong and somebody gets shot, we know who that somebody is probably gonna be."

The driveway ended at a three-door garage. It had no windows, so Matthew had no idea if either of the Riegers was at home. Wiley lived there with his wife and two kids, but Matthew knew that Willard spent a lot of time there as well. A brick pathway led Matthew to the front door. He rang the bell and could hear the chimes echoing inside the large house. There were tall windows on either side of the door, but they were covered by curtains so he couldn't see inside.

He didn't know why, but he had a feeling both Wiley and Willard were in the house. Other than trying to knock down the front door, the only way to find out was to walk around the place. Matthew took a second brick pathway, which was shaded by a long pergola overgrown with wisteria in fragrant bloom. It led him to the back of the house and a deck that extended about 20 feet. In the middle of the deck was some patio furniture. Matthew walked up to a table and noticed a drink coaster with a ring of moisture. Somebody was just here, he thought.

He made his way over to the railing at the end of the deck. Almost two stories below was a brick terrace, which extended to a lawn that sloped down to a hedge at the next property. From where he stood, Matthew could see Lake Washington and the Cascade Mountains beyond.

As he was enjoying the sweeping view, a voice called to him from behind.

"Can I help you?" Willard asked.

Matthew recognized the voice and turned around quickly. He was surprised that Willard was able to sneak up on him. "What happened with my crew's paychecks?" Matthew asked. "They're all short five hours."

"That's what it cost us to fix the landscaping damage you guys caused at the house in Magnolia last week."

Matthew remembered the house. It was a remodeled Craftsman on Raye Street. He also remembered doing a walk-around when the job was done. "What exactly needed fixing, Willard? I took a look after we finished, and I didn't see any landscaping damage. I would have noticed."

"It was thousands of dollars' worth, Matt. You're lucky your crew only got docked five hours. My brother wanted to make it ten."

Matthew looked at the sliding glass doors behind Willard. Curtains blocked any view inside. "Speaking of your brother, where is he?"

"He's downtown right now," Willard said.

"Such a beautiful day," Matthew said as he walked over to one of the sliding doors. "And all the doors and windows are covered up. I smell a lie, Willard." Matthew reached for the door handle and waited for Willard to say something. When he didn't, Matthew sensed that something wasn't right, so he turned around. "Here's what I think. You and your brother didn't have quite enough money to pay us on Friday. Then you made up a problem to justify shorting us. I think the real problem is your brother's dot-com business. Your investment funds are drying up, so now you're pulling money out of your roofing business. I bet the next step is a second mortgage on this big house."

He waited for a response, but Willard just stood there in the middle of the deck, saying nothing. Matthew continued, "Your brother's inside the house right now, isn't he? What if I go inside and talk to him about all this?"

"If you don't leave right now, I'll call the cops, Matt. I mean it." To back up his threat, Willard pulled his cellphone from his pocket and flipped it open.

Matthew raised his hands and nodded, suggesting he would leave. Instead, he said nothing and walked in the opposite direction, where the deck continued around the far side of the house.

"Hey!" Willard called out as Matthew disappeared from view.

He checked each window on the far side, and finally found one where the curtains were parted just enough for him to glimpse inside the great room. He saw Wiley crouched down near the sliding glass doors. Wiley had his back against the wall, so he wasn't actually watching the scene on the deck, probably just listening in as best he could. When Matthew looked closely, he saw a pistol in Wiley's right hand. You fucking coward, Matthew thought. You wanted me to step inside the house so you could justify shooting me.

Matthew had seen enough, so he returned to the back deck. He was pissed off now, and as he walked toward Willard, it wasn't so much his boss he was seeing. Instead, it was the faceless Bert he was walking toward, the Bert who would forever escape justice, at least the kind of justice that would give Matthew the satisfaction he craved.

Without saying a word, he grabbed Willard's neck with both hands and began pushing him toward the railing. Matthew's grip was so tight that the only sound Willard could manage was a slight wheeze as he struggled for breath. Willard dropped his cellphone and grabbed onto Matthew's arms, but he couldn't break his grip.

When they reached the end of the deck, Matthew pressed Willard against the railing. Then he extended his arms as far as he could in front of him so that Willard's upper body dangled over the brick terrace far below.

Matthew knew that Wiley might figure out what was happening to his brother and come to his rescue. If so, Matthew could end up with a bullet in his back. At that moment, however, he didn't give a shit. Instead, he glared at Willard and said in a soft voice, "If I drop you just right, you'll break your neck when you land."

Matthew waited for the comment to register. As it did, Willard's stoic façade crumbled. His mouth gaped open and his eyes grew wide in a look of terror. Matthew could feel the blood pulsing through Willard's neck and watched as his face reddened. Willard gasped once, then his moustache began twitching.

That was enough, Matthew decided. He pulled Willard back onto the safety of the deck and let him go. Willard stared bug-eyed as he took the first of many frantic breaths.

When Willard finally managed to compose himself, Matthew pointed a finger at his face and said calmly, "My crew is finished working for you and your brother. You're gonna pay everything you owe us. I'm giving you one week. If you don't pay, we keep all your roofing equipment."

*   *   *   *   *

The drive back to Roy's took almost twice as long as it would have at midday because of rush hour traffic and an accident on the West Seattle Bridge. Matthew gave Sal a rundown of what happened after he rang the front doorbell, including Wiley waiting just inside the door with a pistol.

"What did I tell you?" Sal asked, shaking his head. "Things could have gone wrong in so many ways. But I bet you enjoyed seeing Willard in full panic mode."

Matthew didn't answer for a long time. Finally, he said, "I did. But if I had to do it over again, I would have just walked away."

Sal ignored the comment and asked, "Do you think they'll really pay us in the next week? That's the deadline you gave Willard, isn't it?"

"I'm guessing they won't, which means you can keep their equipment. I'm sure the crew won't mind donating it to you, especially if you become their new employer." Matthew looked at Sal and added, "By the way, let's not mention what I did to Willard. I don't want to give the crew any ideas of doing their own follow-up."

By the time they arrived at the bar, Ferry Hour was over. Dennis, the manager, gave Matthew and Sal their first beer at half price anyway. The A Crew was still there, and Matthew hoped they had taken his advice about using Ferry Hour as a chance to calm down.

"Did everyone cash their checks?" Matthew asked, and they all nodded or said they had. "Good, because…and this is the bad news first…none of us has a job with the Riegers anymore, and I have serious doubts about getting another paycheck from them. That means we'll probably never see our pay for last week or the two days this week."

"Of course not," the Major said. "Why screw us only halfway when they can steal another check?"

"I know where they live," Buck said. "I have their address in Montlake."

Matthew expected to hear as much. "I'm the one who told them that we all quit. I figured if they're stealing from us and lying to us to cover it up, it's not worth putting in another day with them. It's just not worth it."

"But they can't just take our wages like that," Lyka said. "We've already done the work. Can't we call the cops on them, or the Labor Department, or something?"

"All we can do at this point," Buck said, "is cause them pain and suffering by trying to steal business from them. We'll never get the money they owe us. It's gone."

"But it's not right," Lyka said. "We can't just do nothing. We should take them to court, you know. Sue them in a civil case."

"It would end up in small claims court," the Professor said. "We'd have to file separate claims."

Sal waved a hand to get everyone's attention. "Listen up, people. I know you want some justice here, but it'll cost you more time and energy than it's worth to take them to court, and you'll never get what they really owe you."

"He's right," Buck said. "Fuck the legal system. I'll make them suffer. In fact, I'll visit their house tonight and make them feel like they're literally in fucking hell..."

Sal interrupted. "OK, BuckHead, it sounds like somebody is thinking about burning a house down, maybe with people inside. So that's arson and murder one or something like that, and we'll all be forced to testify against you because none of us wants to go to prison for perjury, so let's not get all whacked out about this. At the most, you're out like $800, right? You'll get that back. Don't worry. Matt and I have a plan."

Matthew suddenly felt all eyes on him. "That's right. Sal and his brother are starting up a roofing company. And we have some ideas on how to get it up and running fast."

Sal continued, "We have a couple of jobs lined up and a solid plan to land a whole bunch more. If we can, we'll hire all you guys full-time. It'll be just like working for the Riegers, except there won't be any Riegers."

"No shit," Buck said. "You and your brother are really serious about this? And you'll hire us all full-time?"

"If we can get enough jobs in the pipeline, definitely," Sal said. "I'll even have us working six days a week for anyone who wants extra money. But we have to find the business first."

"How about pay?" Buck asked. "Can you pay us what the Riegers paid?"

"Sure," Sal said, then paused before adding, "but White guys get paid a dollar an hour less on my crew."

Lyka was the only one who realized Sal was joking. She laughed.

Sal enjoyed the moment briefly before saying, "Relax, Buckaroo. I'm kidding. Yes, everyone's gonna get paid what the Riegers paid you all."

"What do we use for equipment?" the Major asked. "You know, ladders, nail guns, staging…"

"That's some more good news," Matthew said. "Sal and his brother have some of it. And right now, we have the rest in the back of our trucks. It's the gear we've been using every day—nail guns, ladders, compressors, generators, staging, the lift that never works—all that shit. Consider it compensation for what they owe us."

Matthew paused and turned to Sal. "That reminds me: we have to unload all of it from our trucks and find a safe place to store it. Once they get over their shock, they might come looking for it."

"Won't they call the cops to get their stuff back?" the Professor asked.

Matthew smiled and shook his head. "I'm betting they won't bring the police into this. I could tell the cops some stories about the Riegers that'll get them in deep shit. And that's besides our stolen wages."

"Is everybody in?" Sal asked. "I need a full crew, and I don't want to be training new people while we're getting off the ground."

"Yeah, nobody pull a Mole and disappear suddenly," Buck said.

Everyone agreed they were in. Then the Professor said, "That reminds me. I got a postcard from Mole. Sounds like he had issues with the camper and had to stop for repairs."

The Professor pulled the postcard out of his back pocket and handed it to the Major. The front of it showed a black-and-white image of a small town on the border between Idaho and Montana, right after the Great Fire of 1910, with blocks leveled and the remains of structures still smoldering. The Major turned it over and read out loud,

"I find myself stranded temporarily in this Pacific Northwest backwater, where the native population (judging from a very limited sample—the two men conducting minor repairs to my camper) has an undue affection for silver mining, filterless cigarettes and the deep-fried organs of small forest creatures. I hope everyone is doing well. Except Buck."

Laughter erupted around the table, with the whole crew looking at a disbelieving Buck. "Very funny, but it doesn't actually say that."

The Major nodded. "Yes, it does. I'm not making it up."

Buck reached out and grabbed the postcard from the Major's hands. "Bullshit it does." But when Buck turned the postcard over, his face dropped and he went silent for a few seconds. Then he said, "What an asshole. What a complete fucking asshole."

Sal laughed. "He's fucking with you, bro. He knows you're gonna read it and get pissed off. That's what he wants."

"I know," Buck said as he flipped the postcard across the table. "But still."

"I'm hoping he'll call soon," the Professor said. "I told him I'd meet up with him if he heads back near the Oregon coast this summer."

Matthew suddenly remembered something and looked at his watch. It was just after 6:30, the time when Anne was scheduled to call. He stood up and threw some money down. "I'm due at the house. I'll see you all soon. Sal, let's get together tomorrow morning, OK?"

"Call me when you're up," Sal said.

Matthew stepped out of Roy's and broke into a jog. It was a short run home, distance-wise, but it was mostly uphill so when he stepped through the front door five minutes later, he had worked up a good sweat. Nora was sitting on the couch with the receiver in her hand and she was fully engaged in a description of the diving lessons she was taking at the Lincoln Park pool. Matthew took the opportunity to catch his breath before sliding onto the couch beside Nora.

He held out a hand in front of his daughter to indicate he was ready to talk, but she curled into a defensive posture with her back to her father and picked up the pace of her chat. Matthew spent the next couple of minutes settling up with Jennifer in the kitchen for her babysitting and shuttling work over the last week.

Dylan joined them in the kitchen and asked his dad, "Can Jennifer stay and have dinner with us tonight? She said she's free."

Matthew turned to Jennifer. "Of course. Please do. We're having... actually I have no idea what we're having or making, but we'll figure it out after I get off the phone with Anne." He returned to the living room couch, where he cleared his throat and tapped Nora on the shoulder. She reluctantly wrapped up her conversation and handed the receiver to her father.

As Matthew began to talk, Dylan walked into the room and held out his hand, indicating that he, too, had yet to speak to his mother. The clock on the bookshelf showed 6:46, so there were only 14 minutes left on the call. Matthew began by telling Anne that there was a lot going on with work, but he could fill her in when she returned in ten…no, eleven short days. The important thing is that the kids were both doing fine, and the school year was winding down.

And how were things going on the Slope, with the temperatures warming and the daylight increasing, Matthew asked. As Anne answered, Matthew leaned back on the couch and closed his eyes.

"What are you doing?" Nora said. "Don't fall asleep on Mom."

Matthew raised a finger to his lips and continued listening. He was loosely following what Anne was actually talking about, but he was more listening to the sound of her voice. He hadn't heard it since the last call the week before, and he was surprised how their intimacy could only express itself through their voices over the phone, and how it was the sound of her voice that made him suddenly miss her all the more. At least that's how it seemed to him, and like a desert plant in a passing shower, he soaked up as much of it as he could before his time on the phone ended.

He opened his eyes and motioned for Dylan to sit on the couch and get ready to take the phone. "Yes, I'm doing alright," Matthew said. "I just needed to hear your voice for a few minutes. We're all good here, Anne, and we're all ready to have you come home."

Dinner that night was takeout from a falafel place in the Junction, followed by three games of ladder ball in the backyard. Jennifer headed home when it was time for the kids to go to sleep. By 10:30, Matthew was in bed staring up at the ceiling and reliving his visit to the Riegers' house. In particular, he was remembering his hesitation at opening the door to the great room and the sight of Wiley crouched inside with a pistol in his hand.

Soon Matthew fell into a deep sleep, but at some point in the middle of the night he woke suddenly. The clock on the nightstand showed the time as 1:46. Maybe it had been a noise that woke him, he thought, like a car door slamming shut. Then he caught a faint sound. It was coming from inside the house. When he sat up, there was light visible at the bottom of his closed bedroom door. His mind immediately went to Willard and Wiley. Had they broken into his home?

His heart began to race, and he felt the muscles in his body tensing up. On hearing the next sound, he sprang out of bed and threw open the door.

In the kitchen he saw the figure of a man, who spun around. It was Francis.

"I know it's late, Matt. I needed to wait until your neighborhood went to sleep. That makes it easier to be invisible." Francis opened and closed a couple of overhead cabinets. "I'm looking for a clean glass. Where do you keep them?"

Matthew was relieved to see that it wasn't the Riegers, but he wasn't happy to see that it was Francis. Nothing but trouble was likely to come of this unexpected visit. He moved to the edge of the kitchen and blinked from the bright overhead light. On the countertop in front of his brother, Matthew saw a plate with a half-made peanut butter sandwich.

"What are you doing here?" Matthew asked.

Francis ignored the question and returned to his own. "A glass to drink from, Matt. A glass that is free of filth. I'm about to enjoy a simple supper as your guest. I've got the sandwich almost finished, and I noticed an unopened can of soda in the fridge. Now all I need is a clean glass to pour it into. If you've gone speechless, I'll say a prayer to St. Anthony. But in the meantime, little brother, could you point to a cabinet in this kitchen where I can find one clean glass?"

He was doing it again, Matthew thought. When they were much younger, Francis had a way of manipulating him, keeping him in a certain place emotionally and psychologically. Matthew could feel it working again, like a gravitational force. What surprised him was how conscious he was of it. When he was a kid, it simply worked. But now he could see through the magic, and he resented his brother for trying to use it on him again.

"I asked you what you're doing here," Matthew said.

Francis tilted his head slightly in a gesture of mock displeasure, which was of course real, Matthew knew. "No handshake, brother? Not even the courtesy of a smile? My, my, what a chilly reception. Speaking of chilly…" Francis opened the fridge and took out a can of ginger ale. He stared at the top, then he used the inside hem of his sweatshirt to wipe the rim of the can before opening it. "Since one clean glass appears to be a bridge too far, I'll dine without it and tell you what I'm doing here. It's about that favor I mentioned at your bar."

Francis took a sip of his ginger ale and spread a final knifeful of peanut butter across a slice of bread. Then he took the other slice and pressed it down neatly and firmly on top of the other. "What I need you to do, Matt, is pretty simple. But it's something that I'd rather not trust anybody else with."

"I'm not doing anything for you." Matthew said it coldly, and he knew his response would irritate his brother. It was the same way a fighter would throw jabs at the beginning of a match to test his opponent's reactions, probe for weaknesses, and possibly provoke him into making a stupid move.

"Your job right now is to listen, Matt, so pay attention."

"You killed Buzzy, didn't you?" Matthew asked, throwing another jab.

The question took Francis by surprise, and for a moment he had no response other than to sweep a hand slowly in front of him in a dismissive gesture. "We are not digging up the past, little brother. I did not travel all the way here for that."

"You need to leave."

Francis calmly took one bite of his sandwich. He was about to take another. Instead, he returned the sandwich to the plate and rubbed small crumbs from his fingertips. "What should we do, Matt? Should we talk about that dear one? Is he a long-lost sheep you've been in search of these many years? Do you think you'll be able to redeem his wasted life? Is that your holy mission?"

Francis' tone told Matthew that he was getting to his brother with the accusation. He knew he needed to keep hitting him with it, so Matthew brought up something that he himself hadn't known about until after his wedding in 1987—that Buzzy, Matthew and Francis all shared the same father. "You murdered your own brother."

Francis stared at his sandwich suddenly, as if he were just noticing it for the first time. Finally, he looked up at Matthew and said, "You want to know what I did to Buzzy, Matt? I gave him a gift. Buzzy Driscoll was the biggest fuckup to ever walk the streets of South Boston. He also framed me for the murder of our dad..."

"It was his dad too."

"Do not interrupt me. He also caused some major problems for my business. He was going to get himself tortured and killed by any number of people, which would have complicated my world immensely. Or he was going to end up in prison, where he wouldn't last a week. Therefore, I intervened, Matt, and I gave him a gift. I gave Buzzy the easy way out. He never saw it coming, and may we all be that lucky when our time comes."

Francis waited for Matthew to reply, but he didn't. Matthew simply stared at his brother.

"What do you want, Matt? An apology? Do you want me to shed tears? I'll be rotting in the ground like Buzzy before you get that from me." Francis paused to pick up his sandwich again, took another bite, then washed it down with a sip of soda. "But I'll tell you what I'll do, Matt. I'll give you a gift too. OK? Then we can move on to the favor."

Francis walked over to the sliding door that opened onto the back deck. Staring out at the night, he said, "It's been almost 13 years since I left South Boston, and people have no idea where I am. They say I'm on the run, like I'm a fox being chased by hounds. The truth is that I'm the one who's in control. I'm still master of my own destiny, and I making plans to build something even bigger than before. My dream has changed, but I've never lost faith in having a dream."

He turned to face his younger brother. "You have no dream, Matt. When I drove through this neighborhood earlier while it was still light, I saw lots of kids. If you ask any of them what they want to do when they grow up, if you ask them what their dream is, they would all have an answer. Because they all have a dream. Some have more than one. But then you look at their parents, and most of them have no dream. I'm gonna say 90 percent don't. They might have a life strategy or a career path or a road map to retirement, but those are not the same as a dream.

"It's a sad thing about growing up. People lose their faith. You can't keep a dream alive without faith, and the world has so many ways to steal it. Life crushes faith like an egg. And when I say faith, I'm not talking about kissing the cross. I'm talking about the big faith. You used to have it when you were a kid. I could see it. But when you came home to get married, I could tell it was long gone. Maybe you lost it when Mom died. In any case, you're part of the 90 percent, Matt. You have no dream

341

because you have no faith. So there it is. Your gift. If you're smart, you'll do something with it."

Matthew listened to everything Francis had said, but he knew he had to dismiss it all, at least for the moment. Letting it sink in was what Francis wanted him to do.

"What?" Francis said. "You're not gonna thank me?"

"What did you do with his body?"

The question accomplished what Matthew wanted it to do. It pushed Francis over the edge.

"Hey, fuck you!" Francis yelled.

The talking was over, Matthew knew, and one of two things was going to happen. His brother would accept defeat and leave, or things would get real ugly.

Suddenly Matthew heard a noise behind him. He turned around and saw Dylan standing in the living room. Matthew wondered how much of the conversation he had heard.

Francis noticed him as well, and in a split second his demeanor shifted. He smiled and said in a friendly voice, "And you must be Dylan. Am I right?"

The boy looked at his father before nodding.

"Well, Dylan, I am your Uncle Francis, and I bet your father never told you about me." He turned to Matthew and said in almost a whisper, "I'll make you a deal, Matt. You want to know where he's buried? Exactly where? You do me a simple favor, and I'll tell you where to find what's left of the dear one."

This was a turn that Matthew hadn't expected. Before considering the offer, he had to handle Dylan. He and Anne had always intended to tell him about his infamous uncle when Dylan was much older. Not only was he discovering the truth far too soon, he was actually meeting Francis, the fugitive, instead of simply hearing about him.

Matthew looked at his son and said, "I need you to go upstairs, Dylan. I'll be up in five minutes, OK?"

Dylan didn't respond at first. He simply stared at the stranger. Finally, he nodded and made his way up the stairs.

Matthew turned his attention back to his brother. "You would really tell me where he's buried?"

Francis raised a hand and showed three fingers. "Scout's honor. After you do the favor."

Matthew hesitated. He had intended to cut his brother off cleanly and send him packing empty-handed. But finally learning where his best friend was buried was very tempting, something Matthew assumed he'd never find out. It had been gnawing at him for almost 13 years. He wanted to do right by his lost brother, and he wanted desperately to come to a place of peace about it for himself. Now that it was suddenly possible, Matthew felt himself being drawn strongly toward the offer.

As he stared at Francis, another thought flashed through his mind, a very odd one. Maybe it would bring him just as much satisfaction to kill his brother right now with his own hands. Matthew knew he was capable of the act, at least in a physical sense. But the moment—and the urge— quickly passed. "What's the favor?"

"Good," Francis said with a look of satisfaction. "I need you to make a phone call. From a payphone that's not anywhere near this neighborhood. In a place where there are no security cameras. You need to figure out who you can still trust right now in South Boston. Who would agree to pass on a message for you, then never whisper a word about it for the rest of his life? That kind of trust. It should be somebody who has a family—a wife and kids. Someone who has a good job with a steady income, owns a house, isn't deeply in debt, doesn't do drugs, doesn't gamble, doesn't have a criminal record, doesn't cheat on his wife and isn't stealing at work. If he coaches a kids' sports team, that's even better."

Matthew did know someone like that. He was an old friend who went back as far as first grade. His name was Jimmy Manning, but as a kid he was known as "Prune" because of the way his skin would wrinkle whenever he went swimming at Carson Beach and stayed in the water too long. When Matthew returned home to get married, he saw him. At the time, Prune bartended at Donnelley's Pub, which was next to the Old Colony housing project. For the last ten years though, Prune had been working at a respected property management company in downtown Boston, and had recently been promoted to director. He fit all the criteria listed by Francis. In addition, he owned a vacation home on Cape Cod.

Matthew told his brother who he had in mind. Francis nodded, then gave Matthew the message he needed to deliver to Prune. He made

Matthew repeat the message twice to make sure he had it right. It was a short, cryptic line that wouldn't make sense to anybody but the man Prune would be delivering it to verbally. That was Chris Farragut. Matthew didn't know Chris personally, but he knew that he ran a bar on West Broadway called Farragut's Four.

When Francis was satisfied Matthew had the message memorized, he said, "Make the call within a week. Don't write anything down. Don't tell anybody else about this."

"When will you do your part?"

"When I know you've done yours, I'll send a message. Be patient. Remember that. You have to be very patient."

"There won't be any more favors from me after this."

Francis smiled. "Don't worry. Using the same intermediary twice is how fools get caught. We won't be seeing each other again. Not in this lifetime." With that, Francis slid open the back door and disappeared into the darkness.

Matthew slid the door shut, locked it and lowered the blinds. Then he walked upstairs. First, he went to Nora's room. She was lying on her stomach, sleeping soundly. After closing the door carefully, he went to see Dylan, who was sitting on his bed, looking more confused than scared. When Matthew placed his hand on Dylan's shoulder, he could feel his son trembling. Then the questions began streaming out, beginning with, "Was that your brother? Why were you guys arguing?"

Matthew held a finger to his mouth. "Let's go downstairs, so we don't wake your sister."

They sat across from each other at the dining room table. Matthew found himself wishing that his son was old enough to drink, because what he had to tell him would go down easier with good bourbon. But there would be no bourbon with the telling, and Matthew wasn't even sure how to start. This was the conversation he and Anne had been planning to have with the kids when they were much older.

"That was my older brother Francis. I didn't tell you about him because he hurt my friend Buzzy."

"Did he kill him?"

Matthew thought hard about how to respond. "I don't know, D-Man. But Francis has done a lot of bad things, and I don't talk to him anymore.

344

We got into an argument because I wanted him to leave. He won't be coming back."

Matthew hoped his response would put his son at ease enough to let up on the questioning. If anything, it only fueled Dylan's curiosity about his fugitive uncle. Matthew considered the fine line he would need to walk with his answers—not lying outright but not revealing any truth that could be kept hidden—and he realized that he was not capable of doing any such thing. Not at such a late hour. So he put a stop to Dylan's questions by saying that they both needed to go to sleep.

"Do you think he'll come back?" Dylan asked.

Matthew shook his head. "He won't."

"How do you know?"

"He would get in big trouble if he came back. So he won't. Not in this lifetime. And you can't tell anybody about him, Dylan, OK? We have to keep this a secret. We'll talk more about him when your mom gets home."

"Are you gonna lock all the doors? And the windows?"

Francis had no problem breaking into their locked house, Matthew knew, but to put Dylan at ease he checked the front and back doors, then locked all the downstairs windows that weren't locked already. Matthew accompanied his son upstairs and sat with him while Dylan slowly surrendered to sleep. As Matthew listened to the steady rhythm of his son's breathing and the occasional tinkling of wind chimes, he wondered whether the deal he had just made with his brother would bring him sweet relief or be something that he would regret forever.

*   *   *   *   *

Saturday, June 10, 2000

Matthew and Sal were eager to start scouting for roofing work, but they waited until the weekend when more people were likely to be home. They used their list of previous customers and knocked on doors from Shorewood up north to Federal Way down south. By mid-afternoon they had drummed up three solid referrals that would provide the crew with about a full week's work. That was what they were hoping for, something

345

to get the ball rolling. Luis was busy setting up digital ads, which they were counting on to bring them even more business.

While they were driving around, Matthew told Sal everything about Francis' visit, even though he wasn't supposed to reveal it to anyone. In Kent, where they stopped at a café and sat down for their third coffee of the day, Matthew got to the part about having a dream and having faith. He had been thinking about it over the last few days, and it seemed Francis might be right.

"So what was your dream?" Sal asked.

"Professional hockey player. But that ended when I was in high school."

"I wanted to be a race car driver. My dad would take me to the state fair track and the Renegade Raceway. I loved the sound of the engines, and how fast those cars moved. It was like a drug. That's probably why I got so many speeding tickets before I was 20. But it wasn't a possibility for me. I knew that when I was about 11 or 12."

"You lost it before me then."

Sal was about to answer when they heard a sudden commotion at the store register. One of the people in line grabbed the tip jar. Carrying it like a football, the thief went running toward the door. He was a young guy with long hair, a beard and a pair of broken sunglasses held together with white medical tape.

The sunglasses reduced his vision to the point where he bumped into two unseen tables and lost his balance. The glass jar flew out of his arm and smashed against the door. A second later, the thief's head slammed into it as well.

There were a dozen customers and employees watching in stunned silence. The thief groaned as he pushed himself off the floor. The jar was now a scattering of broken glass, dollar bills and coins. He sifted his fingers through it all in an attempt to grab hold of as much money as possible. The shards cut his hands, and he began smearing blood across the floor. In response to the pain, he spit out a rapid-fire series of curses.

The store manager emerged from his office and quickly figured out what was going on. He yelled at the thief, who stuffed what he could into the pockets of his jean jacket and stumbled out the front door. As the manager approached, it looked as if he might want to give chase.

Sal caught his attention and said, "Don't do it, brother. Don't get yourself killed by a crackhead. He has nothing to lose."

The manager called for a broom and dustpan. Before they arrived, he crouched down and began carefully plucking coins from the mess. Sal and Matthew watched until a barista arrived to clean what remained.

"I had another one though," Sal said.

"Another what?" Matthew asked.

"Another dream. I had it after I got out of high school. I was living at home and bouncing from farm work to factory jobs to restaurants. All dead ends because I didn't have the right education or training to get one of the good jobs. I hate working for other people. That's something else I realized. Same thing happened to Luis when he got out of high school two years later. We decided we were gonna start our own business."

"Roofing?" Matthew asked.

"We had no idea, but we knew we wanted to be our own bosses. And we wanted to do it in Seattle. When you grow up in Yakima and you want to go big, that means a city like Portland, Spokane or Seattle. When we got here, we both worked landscaping, like you did, and Luis went to school at night to become an electrician. It was a way to make more money while we figured out what kind of company we wanted to start. You know the rest of the story, but we've been working on the dream for years."

They put another dollar in the new tip jar before heading out. On the way back to West Seattle, Matthew considered what Sal had said. It all made sense. For Sal and Luis, that is. For himself, Matthew didn't see it happening. Explaining it to Sal, he said, "For the longest time now, I've been working two jobs and raising two kids. From the minute I wake up, it's just go, go, go, and it's like that almost every day. I just turned 40 years old, and honest to God, I don't know how I got here so fast. But if I was staying in Seattle…"

Matthew stopped mid-sentence when he saw something on the road ahead. They were driving through the Kent Valley, which was one long, flat stretch of office parks, warehouses and the occasional cluster of restaurants and coffee shops. Just beyond a complex of self-storage units was a large empty lot, where an old motel had recently been demolished. On the sidewalk out front, Matthew spotted a lonely payphone sitting next to a light pole.

347

As they drove by, Matthew said, "Pull over here for a second." As Sal slowed down and stopped, Matthew added, "This would be a good place to make that call I told you about. After I get out, drive around the block a couple of times. It won't take me more than five minutes."

"You need quarters?"

Matthew leaned into the back seat of Sal's truck and fished in the pockets of his jacket. "I brought a shitload."

At the phone, he lifted the handset and wiped the earpiece and mouthpiece against his jacket before making the call. It was an old habit when using a payphone. Luckily Prune was home and picked up on the second ring. After a few minutes of small talk, Matthew got to the point. "So here's why I'm calling, Prune. I've got a favor to ask. It's a big favor."

After delivering the message, he asked Prune to repeat it back. Then Matthew told him that he couldn't tell anybody about this call. Not ever.

After the call, Sal asked, "What did it mean?"

"The message? I don't know," Matthew said.

"I know you don't know. But what do you think it means?"

"Are you sure you want to know?"

"Life is short, Mahoney. Of course I want to know."

Matthew began by explaining how Francis had gone into hiding in 1987 when he learned that federal indictments against him had been handed down. Before that, he had controlled a large part of Boston's underworld with the help of a close friend working in the local FBI field office.

Matthew had once seen a chart of Francis' organization in the *Boston Globe*. Right below Francis was someone named Connor McCain, Francis' right-hand man, who ended up serving three years in prison for his work with the infamous Mahoney. He would have served more time, but the FBI couldn't get convictions on some of the serious charges. When Connor was released, Matthew believed, he began communicating with Francis and had helped him elude law enforcement for the last ten years.

"I think Connor has connections with some Boston cops, and they pass on stuff about Francis—like who's reported maybe seeing him and where. Enough information so that Francis can always stay one step ahead of the law. Connor's a really important link for him. But the link also makes Francis vulnerable. If Connor ever flipped…you know, told the FBI where

Francis is hiding in exchange for not being indicted on new charges, Francis would be completely screwed.

"To me, the message sounded like Francis is asking an old friend, someone he trusts, to tell him whether Connor has flipped, or is about to. If that's the case, Francis needs to find a new place to hide. And he needs to change everything about his life that Connor is aware of. That's what I think. But I'm done thinking about everything to do with my brother. All I want now is to end 13 years of worrying about my best friend. I know he's gone, but I want to let him rest in peace. So I can rest in peace."

Chapter 16
Life Begins at 40

(three weeks earlier)
Thursday, May 18, 2000

Anne's return flight to the Slope was different from her first one. There was no Bert to deal with, and she was returning to a place she was now familiar with. This time, however, rather than having a sense of wonder and curiosity about the world up north, she was flying back with a growing sense of dread.

Despite what Andre had told her, she felt that she was in a no-win situation, and that either her supervisor or the director of new drilling operations for Burtonwood would push her out of her relatively powerless contract position. It was their world, after all, and she was the rookie outsider who was upsetting the established order.

Still, she put on a brave face when David picked her up at the airport. He was wearing a big, stupid smile, which helped. "You're not gonna believe this," he said as they were driving back to their camp. He handed her a Polaroid photo. "We finally got the new tripods. Six brand-new ones. Which means we got rid of the old ones. Sent them back to Anchorage, except for number five. Me and Dominic decided to turn it into a sort of trophy. We spray-painted it gold for you! You get to keep it."

Anne looked at the photo of the shiny gold instrument and squinted in disbelief. "Um, I'm not sure how I feel about this, David." She gently placed the Polaroid on the dashboard, where it began to slide back and forth as the truck turned. Anne continued, "Actually, I do know how I feel about it. I don't like it. I know you and Dominic mean well, and I appreciate that, but I don't want to be reminded about the incident. It already jumps into my mind when I don't want it to."

David's look of excitement changed to one of confusion, then disappointment. Anne tried to soften the blow, so she said, "How about if I give the tripod to you for safekeeping? You can hang on to it and…show people if they're really interested."

"Alright. And if you ever change your mind about keeping it yourself, you know, just say so."

"I will, definitely."

"By the way," David said, "I saw him yesterday. The guy. He was getting out of a truck in front of his building, and it looked weird because he had to use his right hand to open the driver's door. His left one is in a cast, and there's a bandage wrapped around his head like he's been in a war or something. A war he lost."

Anne had heard more than enough about an aftermath that David seemed happy to keep talking about. She steered the conversation to her fishing trip out of Seward, which kept David interested for the rest of the drive to their building.

As they pulled into the parking lot, David said, "Sarah flew out this week. She'll be back before you finish up in June. Seth is on his rotational break back in Nebraska."

Anne was relieved to hear that Seth was away. She knew ahead of time that he was scheduled to be off-duty, but schedules sometimes had a way of changing unexpectedly, so she was grateful it didn't happen in this case. With Seth gone, another supervisor named Victor would be overseeing the crew for the next two weeks. Victor was an engineer himself and didn't really do much supervising. He mainly was there to sign unscheduled requisitions and manage any problems that might arise in Seth's absence.

David continued, "And I just got back, so I'll be around until the first week in June because they approved me for a three-week rotation."

Anne smiled. "That's good. You know, I am glad to be back, David, even with everything that happened. It's just like there's this gloomy cloud about it. I'm hoping it won't last." Anne turned to look out at the tundra. "All I want to do is be out there as much as possible."

"Don't worry," David said as he parked and turned the truck off. "I've seen our schedule. Starting tomorrow, there's a long list of project days in the field. We won't be spending much time in camp."

That night, Anne was invited to join a few women from her dorm floor for dinner. She got to the dining hall early and sat down at a table to wait for the rest to arrive. She was reading through some notices and updates that had been issued in her absence when she spotted someone familiar entering the dining hall. It was Gloria, who worked at BG's medical clinic. Anne wondered if Gloria might have been involved in treating Bert's injuries.

When Gloria looked around, Anne found herself avoiding eye contact. She really didn't want to get trapped in an awkward conversation, but Gloria had spotted Anne and came marching toward her table.

Gloria smiled. "Well, look who's back," she said, then shifted to a more serious tone. "It looks like you're doing OK, honey. Is that just for show, or is it real?"

Anne was stunned by the bluntness. It was like cold water in the face, but not necessarily in a bad way. "It truly has been a week, Gloria. But I guess I'm hanging in there OK. Thanks."

Gloria smiled again. "I'm glad to hear that, Anne. You did what you had to do, and everybody I talk to is proud of how you handled yourself."

The words took Anne by surprise, and she felt a swell of emotion. Gloria put a hand on her shoulder and added, "Just remember, he doesn't deserve to be up here. But you do."

*   *   *   *   *

Sunday, June 4, 2000

When Anne had flown out of Deadhorse for her break, the amount of daylight every day had been almost 23 hours. On her return, the sun was officially up all day. It would stay that way until late July, long after she'd be gone from the North Slope. Everyone with a window in their bedroom had been using blackout blinds since early April and would continue to do so until the end of August.

With the increased sunlight came temperatures warming into the mid- to high-30s, which meant more melting snow, so that by the beginning of June little snow remained. Across the exposed tundra were depressions filled with stagnant water, the breeding grounds for what was known as the Alaska state bird: the mosquito. Anne had been familiar with them since her teens living in Alaska, but the only experience she had of the larger variety that feasted on North Slope caribou and ill-equipped oil workers had been on a backpacking trip through the Brooks Range. She and her friends felt their fury for only a couple of days when the temperature rose high enough for them to be active.

"Life begins at 40," David declared as he and Anne drove west across the tundra on the first day when the outside temperature was predicted to rise a few degrees above the 40-degree mark. "It's June. This is when they start to make their appearance."

It was close to noon when the mosquitoes showed up. David and Anne were finishing up some core samples for a proposed drill site when Anne heard the familiar buzzing. By the time they got back inside the truck, they had both been bitten and Anne had swallowed at least one.

Staring through the windshield, she could see them dancing in the air, large dark specks that were more the size of flies than the mosquitoes she had grown used to back in Washington State. "Jesus, I forgot how big they were."

As they drove on to the next location, Anne stared out at the barren tundra. Her mind drifted back to Seattle. For some reason, she was remembering the last time the family went on a camping trip to the Olympic Peninsula. On their drive out to the coast, Matthew sat in the passenger seat and fell into his bad habit of telling Anne how to drive: how fast to go; when to start braking for a traffic light; how to look out for that truck waiting to pull onto the road maybe a hundred yards ahead because the driver might not see them with the sunlight shining from behind their Subaru. He annoyed her enough that she pulled over and let him drive. It was a small matter, but it left her wishing that she had kept driving and told him to shut up.

She came back to the moment and realized she had never driven the truck when she and David worked in the field. She turned to him.

"Do you mind pulling over, David?"

He turned to glance at her, then looked again before saying, "We both peed like a half hour ago. Do you have to go again?"

Anne smiled. "No, I don't have to pee again." When David pulled over, she said, "We need to change seats."

She opened her door and walked around to the driver's side. David stared at her through his window, confused. With a smile and a wave, Anne gestured for him to open his door and get out. Still confused, he complied and stepped out of the truck. Anne patted him on the back. While he walked around to the passenger side, she climbed into the driver's seat.

"I haven't driven once since we've been working together. I figured it was time," Anne said as they drove away.

"Yes, of course," David said, in a voice that betrayed his surprise at Anne's move and how unfamiliar the passenger seat was to him. "In fact, it makes it easier on both of us. It can be draining to be driving all the time, and you know your way around these roads by now. You definitely do."

"Good, I'm glad you're OK with it. It's because of my husband."

David was perplexed by the comment and gave her a look that said as much.

"Whenever we go somewhere together, Matt always wants to be the one driving. He almost insists on it. And if I do drive, he'll start giving me instructions and telling me what to do. He wouldn't dare do that to one of his friends, but for some reason he thinks it's OK to do that to me. It makes me crazy."

David didn't know how to respond, then finally said, "I'm OK with it. Really."

Anne turned to him and asked, "Are you sure?"

David nodded. "I am. Honestly." He was quiet as he stared into space for a few seconds. Then he added, "Oh wow, I just realized something. I think that I might be doing the same thing with my girlfriend. Like, when we go anywhere, I always drive. I wasn't aware that I was doing that until now. It's like a…"

"Revelation?"

"For real."

On their drive back to camp at the end of the day, they spotted a caribou in the distance. Some had been showing up recently, heading down from the Brooks Range for a summer on the tundra. There were just the occasional bulls; cows would show up in larger numbers soon. By late afternoon, the day had cooled down a few degrees, just enough to ground the mosquitoes.

"Those mosquitoes we saw earlier are nothing," David said. "There aren't enough of them around for us to bother with head nets. And they won't be much of a problem until later in June when it's warmer and more caribou show up. That's when there are swarms of them. It's like a pestilence. They attack the caribou mercilessly. I really feel bad for them." David turned to Anne. "And you'll be long gone before the mosquito mayhem really begins."

Anne smiled. "I'm OK with that."

They made one last stop at the commissary so David could pick up some shampoo. As they pulled into the parking lot at the back of the building, David grabbed a bag of trash to toss into a dumpster.

Anne put the truck in park and waited for David to jump out. He had his hand on the door handle, but he wasn't opening it.

"What's wrong?" Anne asked.

"We need to check something," he said.

The dumpster was directly in front of the truck, and David asked Anne to put the truck back in gear and let it roll forward slowly until it bumped into the dumpster. She did as he asked. A second after the bumper made contact, the metal dumpster rocked back and forth, and the massive brown head of a grizzly bear emerged above the open lid. It roared a deep displeasure at having its foraging interrupted.

"Oh shit," Anne said.

David returned the bag of trash to its place behind his seat. "Yeah, we'll just hang onto that trash for a while. By the way, that's something I should have mentioned when you got back. The food-conditioned bears, that is. There aren't many of them around anymore, not since the early '90s when people stopped feeding them. That's one of those unsecured dumpsters. The food-conditioned bears know there's probably a meal in there. Anyway, always bump a dumpster like that to see if anybody is home before you get too close to it."

"I will definitely remember that."

After dropping off their samples at the engineering lab, it was close to 7 p.m. Anne considered a workout at the gym but settled for a quick swim in the pool, then a dash to the dining hall to grab a bite before they stopped serving the evening meal.

At 9:00, she settled in bed with a recent edition of *National Geographic* that examined the Viking culture, most of which Anne knew nothing about. It was a good distraction from what she would face the next morning. Seth was due back from his break, and a meeting of the engineering team was scheduled over the dinner hour. The email invite said, "includes free dinner," which was a joke because pretty much all the meals in camp were free.

Anne wasn't looking forward to Seth possibly confronting her with the fact that she didn't follow his advice and apologize to Bert. If he asked, she'd tell him the truth, plain and simple. She didn't apologize because she didn't do anything wrong, and the incident shouldn't play any part in whether she was offered a staff job with BG or any other company.

On the flip side of things, Sarah was also due back the next day and Anne was looking forward to seeing her again.

The next day passed quickly in the field, and David and Anne were back in camp by 5:00. Before the team meeting, the engineers picked up dinners in the dining hall and carried them on trays to a meeting room next to Seth's office.

"So where is Seth?" Dominic asked after everyone was present and some had begun eating.

"We got back to camp like an hour ago," David said. "I haven't seen him."

Just then, through the door to Seth's office walked a man who nobody in the room seemed to know. Anne definitely didn't. She guessed that he was in his late 50s or early 60s, but the thing that stood out the most about him was that he was way overdressed for a meeting with North Slope engineers. He wore a pressed suit, a dress shirt and shiny black shoes. Victor followed him through the door to Seth's office, and after Victor sat down, the man walked to the only open seat. It was at the head of the table, where Seth normally sat.

Instead of sitting down, he remained standing and rested his hands on the back of Seth's chair. "Hello, everyone," he said and offered the room a warm smile. "I'm sure none of you know me, so let me introduce myself. My name is Jacob Lenz. I work at the BG development office in Anchorage." Jacob paused to take his seat and remove his rimless glasses, then continued, "Please, go ahead and eat your dinners while they're hot. I won't keep you here very long. Let me start by saying that Seth won't be joining us. We met for lunch today in Anchorage, where I informed him that he's been reassigned by BG from his current role as supervisor here."

Jacob smiled again and continued with his explanation. He spent several minutes speaking vaguely on the progress that had been made regarding BG's environmental initiatives and how grateful he was to the North Slope engineering team sitting in front of him for its contribution to those efforts and successes.

Anne scanned the room and realized she wasn't the only one who seemed to be holding their breath and ignoring their meal, despite Jacob's suggestion that they eat. Glancing around also reminded her of something else. She was not quite 40 years old, but she was definitely older than all the other engineers and more experienced with this sort of abrupt management transition.

This was like too many meetings she'd had in her career, when her engineering team had been called into a room and informed that someone they'd worked with was "no longer with the company" or that "the company had decided to let them go." That was an expression that always caused Anne to imagine a person dangling over the edge of a cliff with a human resources manager loosening their grip and letting the person fall into a sort of oblivion. Three times Anne had been the person being let go, and she was all too familiar with the disorienting, and nauseating, sensation of the fall.

Despite how she felt about Seth and his siding against her in the conflict with Bert, Anne felt a moment of sympathy for him. She was pretty certain that his reassignment would not be a career bump but rather a demotion, possibly a reassignment hell specifically designed to force him to retire from BG. If that was the case, Anne knew that her incident with Bert might very well be the cause of Seth's reassignment. Or, more specifically, Seth's reaction to the incident. Had Andre intervened on her behalf to bring about this result?

Jacob wound up his short address by telling the team that BG had full confidence in the work that each and every one of them was doing. The Anchorage office would be appointing a new supervisor in due time, and until then Victor would be acting supervisor. Jacob had discussed it with him before the meeting, and Victor had agreed to take on the temporary position.

As everyone stood up to leave, Jacob turned to Anne and asked if she might have 15 minutes to chat. "We can sit down in the dining hall so you can get yourself a new hot meal. I would have preferred to meet with your team tomorrow morning, but I need to get back to Anchorage tonight."

Anne had only taken two bites of her eggplant parmesan dinner. As they walked down the hall, she said, "I'm actually fine with this meal. I almost prefer it room temperature."

Jacob grabbed a cup of coffee and a slice of chocolate cake before joining Anne at a table.

"You know, your father was the same way," Jacob said. The statement made Anne pause with a forkful of eggplant halfway to her mouth.

"I'm sorry," Jacob said. "I should have mentioned that I worked with your dad up here in the '70s. We were both on the team that developed the VSMs. He and I were roommates for a while. That was a long, long time ago, and the food was not quite what it is now. It was a lot of meatloaf and Salisbury steak. Anyway, Dylan had quite an appetite. He would usually bring a plastic container to dinner and stuff it with a second meal that he would eat in our room right before turning out the lights at bedtime.

"I'd ask him how he could eat meatloaf cold like that, and he'd say that he preferred it cold. Or, as you say, room temperature."

With the anecdote, Anne found herself reconsidering her opinion of Jacob, but not completely. "Well, that's interesting," she said. "I haven't run into anybody up here who knew my dad."

After taking two bites of his cake, Jacob continued, "Back in the office, somebody mentioned that you were working contract on the Slope, or at least that Dylan's daughter was working up here, but I couldn't find anybody on the engineer list with the last name Barry. Then somebody told me that you had your mom's last name, Boushay."

"That was my dad's idea. It's a little complicated."

"He told me a lot, so..." Jacob paused, then shifted the conversation. "Anyway, Anne, it's getting late and I don't want to keep you, but I wanted to throw out an idea for you to consider. First, BG would like to offer you a staff role with our development team." Jacob stopped there to let the news sink in.

Anne lowered her fork and raised her eyebrows. "Really?" she asked, not knowing exactly what the development team did or what her role would involve. "Um, I guess I should mention that I have two young kids...they're back in Seattle with my husband..."

"Yes, I'm familiar with your situation." Jacob gave a reassuring smile. "This role would have you based in the Anchorage office, but you'd have regular visits with the team up here. Occasional short visits, one or two days when it works with your family schedule. I understand that you've enjoyed working up here."

"Very much," Anne said. "I'm fascinated with the environment. And the challenges for the work we do, of course."

"Excellent. This role will keep you connected with what's going on here. More specifically, you'll be part of a team working on a set of new environmental initiatives that will be very important to BG in the coming decade. As you know, there are a lot of changes going on in our field and increasing expectations for how we interact with the environment. In broad strokes, I'll say it'll be a position that you'll find interesting on a team that's doing some groundbreaking work."

The conversation was interrupted by Jacob's phone, which began buzzing. "Oops," he said, looking down and turning off the alarm. "I'm afraid I have to run, Anne. Anyway, that's my brief overview of the role. There's no rush on when you'd start...if you're interested."

"Yes, I'm definitely interested," Anne said as Jacob stood up.

"Good. We'll be able to talk again soon. I know your contract is up here in mid-June. Then I'm sure you'll want to spend some time with your family back in Seattle. I have your phone number and email and all that, so I'll be in touch."

Jacob left his coffee mug and plate in a nearby bus tub, and as he was walking away, Anne called out, "Excuse me, Jacob..."

When he stopped and turned around, Anne continued, "Would you happen to know someone named Andre, who also worked with my dad?"

"Sure, I know Andre."

"Have you talked with him recently?"

"We run into each other from time to time," Jacob said before waving goodbye.

Anne turned and stared out a window and watched an oil rig crawling slowly down a road in the distance. Beyond it were two caribou splashing through a tundra puddle. Wow, she thought. Is it really happening...finally happening? Did I just get offered the job that I'd been hoping to get for so long, one that kept moving just beyond my reach and seemed to almost vanish over the last few weeks?

And it seemed to be happening despite the incident with Bert. Or was it happening because of the incident with Bert, and the fact that she knew Andre? It would have been better to not have so many questions surrounding the opportunity, but it is what it is, Anne decided. As messy as the circumstances might be, this was the job she had been chasing for so long, and tonight it seemed that she had finally caught it. And that was a good thing, for her and her family.

When the oil rig disappeared from view, Anne looked down at her plate. There were two bites left of her eggplant parmesan. After quickly downing them both, she turned to the serving line to see if it wasn't too late to get some more.

Chapter 17

Dies Tenebrosa Sicut Nox

(A Day as Dark as Night)

Friday, June 16, 2000

Matthew's alarm went off at 5:15, a few minutes after the sun had risen. He dressed in light running gear and headed out on his regular route. The clear morning sky was a deep blue, and the air was still and cool, but after the first half mile he had warmed up enough to enjoy the coolness.

He was also feeling a growing sense of excitement, about the big transition the family would be making soon, and about Anne's return. She'd be flying into Sea-Tac in two days, when they could start planning their move to Anchorage. Anne had told him about the job that Jacob Lenz had offered her. There would be interviews in Anchorage, she cautioned, even though Jacob's follow-up email referred to them as "meetings with the development team." As Matthew saw it, the job was a sure thing, and now the only question was what he would do for work once they settled into the cabin. He and Dylan also needed to get their fishing licenses real soon if they were going to squeeze in a little salmon fishing in their remaining time.

Before leaving Seattle, Matthew had to help Sal get his new business going and make sure the old A Crew wasn't forced to split up for lack of work. The last week and a half with Camacho Roofing & Insulation had been a roller-coaster ride. They had three straight days of work for the full crew, followed by two days of nothing.

Sal's brother, Luis, had created a website for the company, and his online ads were appearing on other websites and directing traffic to the Camacho site. They were starting to receive calls from people who wanted to schedule a roofing estimate, so things were definitely looking up.

After tackling the big hill at the end of his run, Matthew walked the final two blocks home while enjoying one of the fresh raspberry scones the opening cook at Roy's had left for him. In Anne's absence the family routine changed slightly, so that while Matthew showered and dressed, the kids got themselves ready and fixed their own breakfasts before going to school.

"My stomach hurts," Dylan announced when Matthew went into his room to wake him.

Matthew sat down on the edge of Dylan's bed and pressed a hand against his forehead, which didn't seem overly warm. Dylan had been asking the occasional question about his infamous uncle since seeing him, but the questions had become less frequent. Matthew wondered if his son's stomach pain could be related to the visit from Francis, so he asked, "What do you mean 'hurts'? Sore because you bumped into something or queasy like you're gonna be sick?"

Dylan didn't respond right away but simply stared up at the luminescent star map on his ceiling. Then he said, "Oh wait, yesterday I tripped in Joshua's backyard and fell into the picnic table." He turned to his father and added, "I think that's it."

"Are you hungry?"

"I guess."

"OK," Matthew said, standing up. "If you feel like a raspberry scone, there's a fresh one in the kitchen with your name on it."

After the kids had breakfast, a quick look at the clock told Matthew that they were running a little early, so he sat with Nora in the dining room and played a game of Go Fish. Within three minutes, she had amassed more than half the cards in a victory deck.

"Got any jacks?" Nora asked.

"Go fish," Matthew said.

After retrieving a card, Nora called out, "Got what I asked for!"

"Again?" Matthew asked. "This is ridiculous. Who shuffled these cards? Hey, you know what, we shouldn't be playing cards. You should be finishing your sign for Mom. You've only got two days left."

Perched on a dining room chair was a large cardboard sign, colored blue with shiny silver letters spelling out WELCOME HOME MOM! Nora's original concept called for a collection of salmon and bears arranged neatly around the border of the sign, but she had only managed to draw three gold salmon and one gold bear across the top. Bears, it turned out, were not as easy to draw as salmon, and Nora had been discouraged at how long it had taken her to draw even one.

The phone in the living room rang. It was Jennifer. In Anne's absence, she had been picking up both kids from school on Fridays. She had also been dropping off Nora at soccer practice, then picking her up when it was over. Jennifer let Matthew know that she wouldn't be able to pick up the kids as planned. Her foot doctor had to cancel her appointment on Monday, and that afternoon at 3:00 was the only time available for her to reschedule. Otherwise, she'd have to wait a week and half.

Matthew said that was fine. He'd call Hadley Epps. It was a short, easy ride for Hadley to take Nora from Arbor Heights Elementary School to the field where her soccer team practiced, then another short ride to pick her up after practice and bring her home. Matthew would be working on a roof in Lynnwood, which was much farther away, but if Hadley wasn't free he could always quit work at 2:00 and pick up both kids.

Matthew called Hadley, and she was in fact free that afternoon and could shuttle the kids. "Thanks, Hadley. Same time. Nora at 3:00. Dylan at…" Matthew covered the phone and called out, "Dylan, what time should Hadley pick you up this afternoon? 3:15?"

"No!" Dylan hollered from the bathroom, where he was applying additional hair gel. He stepped out of the bathroom to explain that all the sixth-graders at Denny Middle School would be going to Lincoln Park after their morning classes. They'd have lunch there, followed by activities. Dylan could walk home when it was all over.

"Oh yeah, that's right," Matthew said. "Just Nora at 3:00."

Hadley added that her husband Neil was taking the minivan to work, so she would be driving their old car."

"OK. Thanks, Hadley."

Matthew looked at the kitchen clock, and once again a morning when they were running early had turned into one when they were running slightly late. They were all out the door in two minutes, and Matthew managed to drop off Dylan first, then Nora, on time. Before Nora stepped out of his truck, Matthew said, "So remember, Hadley will be driving their blue car when she picks you up. And here's our plan for tonight. We're gonna finish the sign. You and me, OK?"

"I don't want to do any more bears. It's really hard to draw bears."

"Alright. Well, I can help you out and draw some of the bears."

"If you don't draw them really good, Mom's not gonna like the sign."

"Then we'll see if I can draw a decent bear. If I can't, then we'll just draw something else instead of bears."

"Like what?"

"I don't know. Let's think about it today. I'll come home with an idea, and you come home with an idea."

"Alright. I gotta go," Nora said. She jumped out of the truck, put on her backpack and dashed down the walkway to the front door of her school. Matthew watched her run and was surprised at how fast she was. Every time he saw her play soccer or simply run around, it seemed like she was moving up another notch with her speed and her skill. Lately he had been thinking that there was little doubt she would one day surpass whatever athletic ability he enjoyed at his peak in high school. As happy as that made him feel, he also felt a twinge of sadness in seeing her leave behind the little girl she had been just yesterday.

*   *   *   *   *

The roofing job in Lynnwood that day was pretty straightforward. The crew would have considered it a boring day if it had still been working with Rieger Roofing, but the job had that special excitement that work had when you weren't sure if you'd still be employed the next day or the next week.

It was a split-level house, and there was a garage out back that Matthew and the Professor were ripping, then shingling. The property sat on the top of a hill with a view of Lynnwood's many shopping malls. Music blared from Buck's cheap, old boom box perched on the chimney of the house. Like most days, there were arguments about which station to listen to. Buck had just changed it to KNDD, or "The End," and refused to honor repeated requests to change it back to KEXP because he was tired of listening to what he called experimental music. He didn't want to hear an experiment, he explained. He let it be known that he would rather hear good, honest rock on stations like KZOK or KISW, but he would settle for KNDD, which was the compromise station that usually put radio arguments to rest for at least a couple of hours.

Matthew stopped work twice during the day to answer calls from people trying to sell him stuff—first a subscription to the *Seattle PI*, then a limited-time offer to switch to a different phone company. He was guessing his number had ended up on some telemarketing list because he was getting more and more spam calls every week.

His phone rang again around 3:45, just as he was nailing down his final course of shingles on his side of the garage. He considered not answering it, but just before the call went to voicemail he stood up and flipped his phone open. A woman introduced herself as Clara Saliman, and said she was calling from the admitting department at Harborview Medical Center in Seattle. Was his name Matthew Mahoney, she asked, and did he have a daughter named Nora Kathleen Mahoney and could he please confirm her birth date.

Matthew sensed immediately that this wasn't good, and he felt the back of his neck tighten. As he listened, he stared out from the top of the garage at a nearby strip mall.

There had been an accident involving the car that Nora was riding in. She had just arrived by ambulance at the Harborview emergency room and was going directly into surgery because of the injuries she had sustained in the accident. The injuries were not considered life-threatening. Clara then asked Matthew where he was and when he could be at Harborview.

Matthew fired off a stream of quick questions: what was his daughter's condition, what exactly were her injuries and, finally, was Hadley Epps injured as well?

There was bruising to Nora's right hip and leg, a possible concussion and an injury to Nora's hand, Clara explained. Nora's right hand. The doctors would provide all the details when Matthew arrived at Harborview. Yes, Hadley had also been injured. She had suffered some bruising as well and was being tested for further issues. That was as far as Clara went into the details. Matthew could learn more once he came to the hospital, she said.

He thanked Clara and closed his phone. When he did, he noticed that the Professor's nail gun had gone silent, and so had the nail guns of the rest of the crew on the main roof. They were all standing up and staring at Matthew.

"What is it, Matt?" Sal yelled across.

"It's Nora...I've gotta go," Matthew said. He made his way to the ladder, where he did a firefighter slide, a move that brought him down quickly but landed him hard.

Sal met him in the driveway and asked, "What happened? Where are you going?"

"Nora was in an accident. A car accident..." Matthew paused when he heard the shaking in his voice. He took a slow, deep breath and continued, "She's at Harborview. They took her into surgery. They won't say exactly what it is...they just said it's her hand, bruises, maybe a concussion..."

"OK, I'll drive you," Sal said.

Matthew saw a set of keys in Sal's hand. It took him a moment to realize they were his truck keys, and Sal had taken them from his own hand without Matthew even realizing it.

"Wait here a second," Sal said, and walked over to the house where Lyka, Buck and the Major were watching the scene silently. He threw the keys to his own truck up to the Major and said, "I'm taking Matt to the hospital. Nora's been in an accident. You guys finish up here and clean up everything good. Then one of you drive my truck to Harborview and call me when you get there."

"What happened?" Lyka asked as Sal was walking away.

Sal turned around and said, "They're gonna take care of her. I'll call you guys and let you know, OK? But don't you all be calling me to ask a bunch of fucking questions. Wait for me to call."

Within a few minutes, Sal was driving south on I-5 in the HOV lane. Matthew noticed that he was speeding. When they first met, Matthew had kidded Sal about how slow he always drove, always careful to go at or below the speed limit. It took a while before Matthew accepted the fact that being White really did mean fewer speeding tickets, fewer hassles with the cops, and being pulled over less often.

Matthew cracked a lame joke about Sal speeding to distract himself from all the thoughts flashing through his mind.

Sal said, "I'm making this one speeding exception today, brother, but don't tell anybody about it."

"Alright," Matthew said, then laughed nervously. When they reached the University District, traffic cut their speed down to ten miles an hour.

As they crept along, Matthew drummed his fingers on the door. "I should call Anne now. I need to let her know what happened."

As Matthew pulled out his phone, Sal said, "You might want to just wait a little bit on that one."

"Why?"

"You're not gonna know everything until you talk to the doctors, right? That's what you said. Anne's gonna ask a lot of questions that you don't have the answers to, and that's only gonna make it worse for her. Let's just get to the hospital. We'll be there in ten minutes. Talk to the doctors, then you call her."

When they reached the Emergency & Trauma Center at Harborview, Sal drove up to the front door. Matthew jumped out and made his way through the lobby to the information desk. It occurred to him that he had been intimately familiar with too many emergency rooms, including Harborview, Highline in Burien, and Boston City Hospital back East, where he went many times to visit friends who had been injured in accidents or fights, or because he had been injured himself.

Dylan's incident with the steak knife had been the first time one of his children needed an emergency room visit, and now Nora had been brought here by ambulance for something far more serious. He could see her face as she was sitting across from him at the dining room table that morning when they were playing Go Fish. Why did this have to happen?

The information desk was busy, and there were a few conversations going on at once. Matthew finally got the attention of a young admitting nurse behind the desk, who had just returned to his station with a latte from a nearby Starbucks kiosk. "You guys called me about my daughter, Nora Mahoney. She was in a car accident…"

The nurse raised a finger as he searched for a safe place to set down his latte. Then he turned back to Matthew. "You say her name is Nora?"

"Yes, Nora Mahoney," Matthew repeated.

"OK, let's see," the nurse said as he sat down and logged onto a terminal. After tapping away at the keys for 20 seconds, he said, "Yes, here she is." He looked up at Matthew. "And your name?"

"Mathew Mahoney."

"Could I please get some insurance information from you, Mr. Mahoney?"

Matthew spent the next few minutes answering questions and watching the nurse enter all the information into the hospital's computer system. Then the nurse handed Matthew's plastic insurance card back to him and said, "OK, very good, Mr. Mahoney. Why don't you sit down while I call the doctor?"

Matthew took a seat that faced a long hallway, and he stared down the smooth, polished floor for a minute before seeing a woman in dark blue scrubs heading in his direction. Something told him this was the doctor, and it was. Dr. Gottlieb was a tall woman around Matthew's age, and she had the ivory complexion of someone who clearly spent almost all of her daylight hours indoors.

She still had a surgical mask tied around her neck as she led Matthew to an examining room down the same hallway from where she came.

"I just checked in on your daughter's surgery," Dr. Gottlieb said. "It's going well."

Matthew noticed a light box on the back wall with three X-rays. Their images were dark because the light box was turned off.

"So exactly what happened? What's the operation for?"

"The car your daughter was in was struck by an SUV. It was T-boned at an intersection, if you know what I mean…"

"Yes…"

"Your daughter…Nora was in the rear passenger seat, and her right arm was outside the vehicle. Her right hand was crushed. It was crushed badly." Dr. Gottlieb paused and stared at Matthew with her unblinking eyes, waiting for her statement to sink in before she continued, "The car she was in was still moving forward, so it was a crushing motion and a twisting motion."

"So exactly how bad?" Matthew asked. "I mean…the operation… you're fixing the damage to her hand, right?"

"Nora's hand was completely crushed, Mr. Mahoney. It was torn apart. Essentially all of it except for two or three bone fragments near the wrist. The rest of the bone structure and everything else: blood vessels, connective tissue, nerves, ligaments, skin…"

"But you can fix it…I mean, rebuild it, right?"

Dr. Gottlieb shook her head slowly. "I'm sorry. There's nothing to rebuild. There's nothing to work with."

Matthew couldn't believe what he was hearing, and he felt the words that the doctor was now speaking bouncing off him. He shook his head. "Don't tell me there's nothing possible here. Don't tell me that." He looked for another answer in her face, and when her expression didn't change, he raised his voice. "I want to talk to somebody else about this. Who else can I talk to here? I want you to get me somebody who can fix this."

Dr. Gottlieb didn't reply right away. Instead, she turned to the light box on the back wall and flipped a switch that illuminated the three X-rays. "This was the condition of your daughter's right arm when she arrived."

Matthew stared at the three images—first the left, then the center and finally the right. Instead of seeing the details of the images at first, his mind saw Nora on a gurney when the X-rays were taken. He imagined her lying there in pain, in tears, maybe unconscious while the X-ray technician manipulated her damaged arm this way, then that, to capture images from all the appropriate angles.

It took great effort to pull himself back to the present moment and see the X-rays and only the X-rays. In them he saw the two arm bones, both of which had been broken. Beyond the wrist bones at the end of the arm, where the palm should be, he saw two or three short, jagged shards displaying nothing like the organized structure of a hand. Beyond that, where the rest of the hand should be, the X-ray showed only a narrow wisp.

Dr. Gottlieb pointed to each image and explained in more detail what Matthew already understood generally. The thin wisp, she explained, was a strip of skin from the top of the hand. About half of it.

"But where did the rest of the hand go...where did it end up?"

"There were some small fragments recovered. Very small. Nothing that can be rebuilt or reassembled, Mr. Mahoney. It really is gone. I'm very sorry. We're doing our best for Nora right now."

Matthew stared again at the three images, moving from the left image to the center, then right, then back again. He did that twice, and he realized he was looking for something to appear in any one of them that could contradict what Dr. Gottlieb had said. Pessimistic, unimaginative Dr. Gottlieb. Then he felt a weight slowly settling on him, the way it would when he played hockey in high school and his team was just about to lose a big game.

It was the sober acceptance that what Dr. Gottlieb had said was accurate and true, and that there was nothing Matthew could do or say or hope that would change that. He wet his dry lips with his tongue, and wiped them dry again with the back of his hand. Without taking his eyes away from the X-rays, he tugged slowly on his soul patch.

"Could I ask what Nora's dominant hand is?" Dr. Gottlieb asked.

"Dominant hand?" Matthew asked, then realized what the doctor was asking. "She's a leftie."

"This," Dr. Gottlieb said, pointing to the strip of skin on the third X-ray, "is what Dr. Sahin is using to form a smooth surface at the end of Nora's right arm. He's created two flaps that will be brought together. He's an excellent doctor, and he's trained in reconstruction and cosmetic surgery. You really couldn't ask for anyone better. The ulna and radius in Nora's forearm were both broken here and here," Dr. Gottlieb said, pointing to specific spots on the X-rays. "The breaks are fairly clean and will heal in a cast. Dr. Sahin is removing some bone in the wrist area and doing light sculpting at the ends of her forearm bones to create a smooth, rounded shape. Technically, it's called a wrist disarticulation."

Matthew's eyes moved back to the X-rays. It was all hitting him so fast and so deeply, and he needed to slow it down.

"I'm a parent myself," Dr. Gottlieb finally said. "I can imagine how difficult this is for you."

Matthew turned to her. "Thank you, but I can't really think about it that way right now. My wife is in Alaska, and I need to tell her. Then I need to tell my son. Dylan is 11. I need to be here when Nora wakes up. So I can't let it sink in like that at this point. Later on, but right now I really have to keep my shit together, if you know what I mean. When will she be out of surgery?"

The doctor nodded. "That depends on how many complications Dr. Sahin runs into. What he's doing tends to be very slow work. It's a lot of microsurgery. The nerves, tendons and blood vessels have to be isolated and dissected, reorganized in a sense, so that Nora has full circulation and full sensation in that area. Or as full as possible. I would guess Dr. Sahin has at least a few hours of work left, likely more. Then Nora will be in recovery. I would say come back around 9:00 or 9:30 tonight."

"I have to pick up my son in West Seattle. We'll be here at 9:00."

"I can have someone call you if her time changes one way or the other."

"OK, thanks. One more thing. The driver of the car...the car my daughter was in...how is she? Her name is Hadley Epps," Matthew said.

"Someone else is treating her, but I was told her injuries are minor. She was having X-rays taken. If they find anything, her doctor may order MRI scans as well."

"I should go see her," Matthew said.

"Check at the desk. They'll know where she is. And from what I understand, Mr. Mahoney, the accident was caused by someone running a red light in his SUV and hitting the car in the middle of an intersection. The other driver was brought here as well, but he was pronounced on the way. Pronounced dead, that is. The autopsy will determine the cause, but my guess is a heart attack. He may not have even been conscious when he ran the light."

Matthew imagined it all happening. He had seen a few car accidents in his time and had heard even more. The sound was like two metal trash cans being slammed together, except much louder, and it was sometimes preceded by the skidding of tires and followed by a secondary collision. Once he heard the cry of a crash victim, whose soft moaning blossomed into a loud, painful wailing within seconds. And in the end, always the sound of approaching sirens.

Matthew thanked Dr. Gottlieb and walked back to the waiting area next to the information desk, where he saw Sal.

"What's the word?" Sal asked.

"It's her right hand. It got crushed."

"Oh shit. Can they fix it?"

Matthew shook his head, then realized that Sal used the same word he had used with Dr. Gottlieb: "fix." Can they fix it? "No, it's gone. It's just gone, Sal." Matthew heard himself speak the words and was surprised at how resolved he already seemed to be to the new reality. Or maybe it wasn't all of him that was responding at the moment. Maybe part of him was detached from the brutal truth of it. And maybe that was for the best.

He continued, "She'll be in surgery for a while. They're working on her arm. Rebuilding the end of it."

"Oh Jesus," Sal said, with a horrified expression that Matthew had never seen from his friend. Sal put his hand on Matthew's shoulder. "She's gonna be alright, Matt. Believe that, OK? Nora is tough as nails. You know that. She'll be alright."

The words meant almost nothing to Matthew, but he knew that they were the best Sal, or anyone else, could offer. And they were better than anything he had. "Yeah, I know," he said.

Sal's cellphone began ringing. As he pulled it from his pocket, Matthew said, "I'm gonna check on Hadley now. I'll be back here in about ten minutes, OK?"

"Take your time," Sal said and waved Matthew toward the information desk before answering his phone.

Hadley had done so much for the kids in the neighborhood, Matthew thought, even though she had no children herself. That included shuttling Nora and Dylan to and from school and soccer practice on so many occasions. And for her generosity, her car got T-boned.

The information desk located the examination room where Hadley was resting. She was wearing a hospital gown and lying flat on her back with her hands folded over her stomach and her eyes closed. When she heard the curtain slide open, she turned and shot up straight. "Matthew! How is she?"

He reached out and hugged Hadley, gently because he wasn't sure where she might be hurt.

"She's in surgery now. It'll be a few hours. There's a really good doctor working on her."

Hadley wore glasses with a bright-red plastic frame, which she liked to describe as rhubarb red. They were sitting on a metal stand next to her. She reached out and put them on. "How will Nora be?"

Matthew shook his head. "She lost her right hand. It's gone." He heard himself say the words in such a blunt way, as he had done with Sal.

Hadley put a hand to her mouth and closed her eyes. "Oh my God, I was afraid of something like that. I saw them put her in the ambulance, and it looked bad. The whole thing was terrible, Matthew. Just terrible. We didn't even see the other car coming. I only noticed something out of the corner of my eye at the last second…I had no time to do anything. I am so sorry, Matthew…"

"No, Hadley, you've done nothing wrong. Really." Matthew paused to turn around because he heard the curtain opening. A nurse appeared, but she immediately realized she was in the wrong examination room and apologized.

"So how are you doing? Have you called Neil?" Matthew asked, referring to Hadley's husband, who worked as a marketing manager at Microsoft.

"He was at a meeting in Redmond, but he's on his way." Hadley reached a hand to the back of her neck and turned her head slowly in both directions. "My neck is a little sore. They took X-rays but didn't see anything wrong. And I've got a little limp. I banged my leg and hip against the door. Nothing broken though. I'm just waiting for the doctor to come back and release me. Anne is coming home on Sunday, isn't she? Have you called her?"

When Hadley asked the question, a look of pain came over her face. Matthew wasn't sure if Hadley was imagining the pain that Anne would feel on hearing the news or the pain that Matthew would feel on delivering it. Perhaps both. Then there was Dylan.

Anne came first. Breaking the news to her wouldn't be easy. Matthew was dreading it. The news hadn't really sunk in with him at anything more than a surface level, and telling Anne would force him to experience it more deeply.

He waited with Hadley until Neil arrived ten minutes later. In the meantime, he made light conversation with her. As he did, he also was trying to compose exactly what he would say to Anne, but he was sure it would fall apart in the enormity of it all. There was no approach other than getting to the point that Nora had been in a car accident. As a result, she had lost her right hand. Just as he had told Sal and Hadley.

He looked for a silver lining and considered the fact that the damage had been limited to the hand—its loss—but then realized how that only took into account the physical aspect, not the emotional and psychological damage done. That would endure long after the bones mended and the skin healed. And how could he begin to assess all of Nora's possible bright futures that may have been taken from her in the accident as well?

In the lobby, Sal gave him the keys to his truck and said that it was parked three blocks north on Ninth Ave. He asked what Matthew was going to do next and if he needed any help doing it.

"I need to find a quiet place outside to call Anne. Then I have to go home and see Dylan. I have no idea how he's gonna react. Then I'll bring him back here with me."

"You should change," Sal said, pulling on the sleeve of Matthew's T-shirt. It was filthy from the day's work. "Take a shower. Have something to eat."

"I want Dylan to come here with me for a while tonight," Matthew said. "I'll be staying overnight with Nora, but he should go home at some point. Someone will need to stay there with him."

Matthew considered his options. He knew Anne wasn't scheduled to arrive home until Sunday afternoon. Even if she could get home sooner, he would have to handle at least this first night alone, and maybe Saturday night. "I'm wondering if Jennifer could stay overnight with Dylan. With all the babysitting, the two have become close. Hopefully that's not too much to ask of her. Lyka would be great too. They'd have to come pick up Dylan here at the hospital."

Sal pulled out his phone and began scrolling through his address book. "I've got their numbers, Matt. I'll call them both. I'll check with Jennifer first. If she's free, what time do you want her to come by?"

"Let's see…if we get back here at 9:00, maybe 10:00 or 10:30."

"Hey, you know, if neither one of them can make it tonight, I can stay with Dylan."

"Thanks. Whatever you can work out, Sal, let me know. I really appreciate it."

Matthew said goodbye and left the emergency room. Outside, it was a busy Friday afternoon with the streets full of rush hour traffic and the sidewalks full of people. It seemed like half of them were in wheelchairs, and Matthew had to move aside quickly a couple of times to avoid a collision. He crossed Jefferson Street and headed toward the west side of the hospital, where there was a small park.

There Matthew found a comfortable place to sit on a low stone wall in the shade of a linden tree. He stared at its leaves and noticed that they were shaped almost like hearts. From his wallet he took out a small scrap of paper that held the emergency number where he could reach Anne on the North Slope. He punched it into his cellphone. After five rings, someone picked up and said, "This is Devin, BG engineering and development, can I help you?"

Matthew said that he needed to speak to Anne Boushay Mahoney. He was her husband, and he needed to speak with her right away. Yes, this was an emergency. Yes, he would hold while Devin went to find Anne. She was in the dining hall at the other end of the building, Devin explained, where her engineering team was throwing a going-away party for her.

*   *   *   *   *

With all the rush hour traffic downtown and on the West Seattle Bridge, it took Matthew almost 40 minutes to get home. He pulled into the driveway and sat there with the engine off to let the tension of the traffic flow out of him. The phone call to Anne had been the absolute worst call he had ever had to make in his entire life. Telling her the bad news opened up the floodgates he had been straining to keep shut. When the call ended, he had to remain sitting on the stone wall for a good five minutes so he could compose himself.

Now he had to go through it all again with his son. First he went to the kitchen for a drink of water. As he was reaching for a glass, he heard Dylan on the back porch. He was talking to Tessa Genot, whose professional popcorn maker had suffered a short circuit at the end of the previous summer, which left the audience for the last two movie nights relying on bagged popcorn from Thriftway. Tessa was explaining to Dylan that her uncle had finally found all the parts needed to repair the machine. It would be back in action for the next movie night scheduled for June 24, the first Saturday after Anne's arrival home.

Matthew watched them chat through the kitchen window. He was hoping Dylan would come into the house alone. He didn't want to be drawn into a conversation with Tessa because he knew it would end quickly and probably awkwardly. While he waited, Matthew pulled out his phone to see if Sal had called. After staring at a dark screen, he realized that the battery had gone dead.

He found his charger and plugged it into an outlet, and after a couple of minutes he got two voicemail alerts. Sal had called and said that Jennifer would be able to stay overnight with Dylan, and she would show up at the hospital around 10:00. The other message was from Jennifer, saying pretty much the same thing. He called her back right away and let her know exactly what had happened.

Just as Matthew was finishing his account, Dylan stepped inside the house, so Matthew told Jennifer he had to go. Dylan looked surprised to see his father and said, "I didn't hear you come in. I thought you'd be home before me." Then when he got a good look at his father's face, he said, "Is something wrong?"

Matthew guided him to the living room, where they both sat down on the couch.

"Is Nora home? Did you pick her up from soccer?"

"Nora was in a car accident, D-Man. Hadley was driving her to soccer practice when they were hit by another car. They're both at Harborview Hospital right now. It's up on First Hill. I just came from there. Hadley looks like she'll be OK. And Nora is having an operation, but she'll be alright. Except that her hand got hit...and she lost her hand. It's her right hand."

Dylan stared silently at his dad, then his eyes slowly grew big. "But they're operating on it, you said."

"They are. The doctors are working on the damage…"

"But you said she would be alright."

"She's going to survive. That's what I mean. But she's lost her hand. For good."

"Why can't they fix it?"

There it was again, Matthew thought. The word "fix." He shook his head. "I'm sorry, Dylan. They can't."

"Dad, you don't understand, they can use technology to fix people when they're hurt really bad…"

"Dylan…"

"No! Listen! I was reading it in a science journal in the school library. And they do it all the time in science fiction, but it's based on real life. They can fix…a lot of things. They have the technology."

376

But not the biology, Matthew thought. He sat silently with Dylan for another five minutes and listened patiently to the power of denial. It's what he had done, but now Dylan was doing it and he was clinging more desperately than his father to a hope beyond hope.

Finally, Dylan signaled his surrender by shifting the topic. "I bet she had her arm hanging outside the window when it happened. You and Mom always let her do it, even though I told you guys she shouldn't be doing it. That's probably how it happened."

It was a stinging comment, but Matthew let it go. He knew that Dylan wasn't trying to assign blame. He was only trying to see the whole event and find the most critical detail to change if he could go back in time and alter the past.

"I didn't think about that, but I bet that's how it happened too," Matthew said.

Dylan held his hands out in front of him and rotated them slowly.

"I have to take a shower," Matthew said as he stood up. "Then we'll go to the hospital. She should be out of surgery around 9:00 or so."

"What about dinner?"

"We'll grab something on the way," Matthew called from the bathroom, where he was undressing.

"We can stop at Dick's Drive-In," Dylan said. "There's one on Capitol Hill. It's not far out of the way."

"OK," Matthew said.

"Maybe we can bring Nora something from there."

"I don't know if they'll let us bring in food," Matthew said. "Or if she'll be hungry, or if she's allowed to eat right after surgery."

"We can get her a Deluxe burger. She likes the Deluxe," Dylan said. Then he continued in a softer voice, "And an order of fries. And a strawberry shake. That's what she usually gets. We could bring her a sundae too, but it would probably melt by the time we got it there."

*   *   *   *   *

After eating dinner in the parking lot at Dick's on Broadway, Matthew and Dylan arrived at Harborview and picked up visitor badges at the Acute Care unit, where Nora had just been transferred from post-op monitoring.

They took an elevator to the third floor and found her room, which faced west with a partial view of Puget Sound. Through the room's lone window, they could see the sun setting behind the Olympic Mountains. It was a room with beds for two children, and Matthew saw that the near one was empty. Then his eyes were drawn to the other bed, where a nurse was adjusting a monitor. There he saw Nora lying on her back asleep. Her face looked peaceful, and her long, braided hair lay in a curl on the pillow next to her head.

When the nurse heard Matthew closing the door, she turned and smiled. "You're Nora's dad?"

Matthew put a hand on Dylan's shoulder, and the two of them walked over. "Yes," he said.

"I'm her brother," Dylan said.

Matthew reached out and took hold of Nora's left hand. Across the bed, he saw the light purple cast that started on Nora's upper right arm and bent 90 degrees at the elbow. It ended before her wrist, which was wrapped in gauze. Matthew guessed it was her wrist, but had to look back and forth between her left and right arms to be certain.

Beyond the place where the gauze wrapped around the wrist, however, there was nothing. If Matthew needed any more certainty about the matter, there it was. A scene from the New Testament came to mind, the one where Christ reproaches the apostle Thomas for needing to see in order to believe. It was an odd thought to have at that moment, and Matthew pushed it out of his mind. Then he leaned over and kissed Nora on the forehead. Dylan hesitated for a moment before doing the same.

"In post-op, she opened her eyes briefly," the nurse said. "But she hasn't really woken yet."

The nurse was in her mid 20s, Matthew guessed, and she had a very friendly way about her, especially for someone working the night shift on a Friday. He heard the door behind him click and turned to see Dr. Gottlieb. The nurse finished her adjustments to the monitors, and before leaving she said, "I'll be on duty until tomorrow morning. If you need me for anything, you can use this call button. I'll be checking in on Nora through the night." Then she pointed out the bathroom in the corner of the room, and said that the vending machines for soda, coffee and snacks were down the hall past the nurses' station.

"You're back just in time," Dr. Gottlieb said with a smile. Turning to Dylan, she added, "And you must be Dylan."

"Yes," Dylan said. "How did you know my name?"

"Nora mentioned you when she was first brought in."

"Oh," Dylan said, and looked at his father with an uncertain expression.

"So here's what's happening now," Dr. Gottlieb said, shifting to a more professional tone. "We've put Nora on a strong intravenous antibiotic. She'll be on that for the next four or five days to prevent infection. We'll be watching for that closely. She may or may not wake up soon, aside from drifting in and out of consciousness. She's still experiencing the effects of anesthesia and the pain medication we put her on. She'll also tend to follow her general sleep pattern, so she may not be waking up, really waking up, until the morning."

Matthew had a few questions for Dr. Gottlieb, but one was far more important than the others and he was struggling with how to word it. Fortunately, Dr. Gottlieb anticipated the question and said, "You may be wondering about the best way to tell Nora about the loss of her hand. If you like, we can have someone from our social support services team talk to her. They're trained to communicate with children about that. They can be really helpful."

"Let's do that," Matthew said. "I'll be staying overnight with her."

There were two chairs against the wall, one of them a recliner. Dr. Gottlieb pointed to it and said, "You'll be comfortable in that when you feel like falling asleep. If you like, you can move it over here to be close to Nora. In the meantime, I'll see if I can get someone from social support to visit in the morning. Also, Dr. Sahin will stop by tomorrow to check in on Nora and talk to you. He'll make himself available to speak with your wife as well when she arrives."

After Dr. Gottlieb left, the nurse came back briefly and helped Matthew move the two chairs to the side of Nora's bed. Before sitting down, Dylan took off a small backpack he was wearing. When he zipped it open, the nurse turned to him and said, "Mmm, something smells good."

"We brought some food for Nora in case she was hungry, but it doesn't sound like she'll be waking up soon."

"Well," the nurse said, "if she does and she's hungry, she could maybe have a little. She might feel a little sick though. If she does, then you should keep the food away from her."

When the nurse left, Dylan turned to his father. "Dad?"

"What?"

"Because she's not waking up until the morning, is it OK if I eat her fries?"

"You just ate."

"I'm still hungry."

"OK, then ask her," Matthew said.

Dylan looked at his sister, then turned back to his father. "She's asleep, Dad."

"I know. But you should ask her anyway. In case she's not completely asleep."

Dylan opened his backpack and sniffed at the burger and fries inside, then asked, "Nora, Dad and I got a Deluxe burger and an order of fries for you at Dick's Drive-In on the way over here. And a strawberry shake. They're for you, but since the nurse said that you probably won't wake up until tomorrow morning, and that if you do wake up you might feel sick and won't want to eat anything, is it OK if I eat your fries?"

Dylan waited only a second before reaching into the bag, but Matthew stopped him. "Give her a minute."

They both stared at Nora's face. To their surprise, they saw her lips part slightly. Then they heard a faint, moaning sound before her lips closed again.

Dylan looked at his father but said nothing. After a moment, he reached slowly into the bag.

"No," Matthew said.

Holding a french fry in his hand, Dylan asked, "Why?"

"She said no."

"I don't think so."

"She said no," Matthew repeated.

Dylan lowered the fry back into the pack, then let out a long sigh.

*　　　*　　　*　　　*　　　*

Over the next couple of hours, the fading light of dusk was replaced by the glow of streetlights. The devices that monitored Nora's blood pressure, pulse rate and body temperature had bright green numbers that fluctuated little. Through the IV dispenser came the steady drip of a clear fluid that ran down a tube and into Nora's left arm.

Matthew and Dylan spent the time talking about many things, including what movies should be selected for the next movie night. It was scheduled for the following Saturday, but Matthew warned Dylan that all bets were off on when it would actually be. In fact, he told Dylan, all bets were off on almost everything for a while, and that family life would be centered around Nora's recovery. One of the exceptions was the move to Alaska. That was happening, Matthew assured him. Once Nora's situation became clearer, they would be able to pick a day on the calendar.

Whenever the next movie night did occur, Dylan said, the adult movie should definitely be *Sleepy Hollow*. It had been released on video less than a month before, and watching it in the backyard with the trees swaying in the breeze and casting spooky shadows everywhere would be the perfect setting. Matthew said that it probably wouldn't be the best movie for Nora because of all the decapitations. *Stuart Little* had also been released on video recently too, and maybe Nora would enjoy watching that again. They would see what Anne thought when she got home.

At the mention of Anne, Matthew pulled out his phone to make sure she hadn't called. They had agreed that she would get back to him when she found out whether or not she could change her flight plans and, if so, what the new flight times would be. Once again, Matthew found himself staring at a dark phone screen. He had brought his charger with him, and he cursed himself for not plugging it in as soon as he got to Nora's hospital room.

After a few minutes of charging his phone, Matthew was able to listen to Anne's message. She had just missed the Friday evening flight out of Deadhorse. Instead, she would be on the first direct flight Saturday morning. For the Anchorage to Seattle leg, she was on standby for a flight that would arrive a little after 9:00 Saturday evening. If she couldn't get on that one, she'd definitely be on a red-eye that would land at 2:30 Sunday morning. She'd pick up her cellphone when she stopped at the cabin on Saturday and give him a call.

As Matthew stared at his sleeping daughter, he thought Anne should be flying back on Sunday to a welcome-home party, and the family should be enjoying a week of vacation together to celebrate the end of a difficult stretch. He and Anne had gotten themselves into a financial bind a few months back, but they had done everything they needed to do to work themselves out of it. And Anne had finally landed a staff job that would let the family move to Alaska and start their new life. There was something fundamentally unfair about this horrible turn of events. And of all things, to have it happen to his beautiful eight-year-old daughter. What he would give to exchange places with her, to lose his own hand and have Nora live on as if the accident had never occurred.

Matthew remembered being in this position before. As a 15-year-old, he had watched his mother die of cancer. Night after night, he sent up desperate prayers that he be allowed to take her place and die of the cancer himself. All the prayers, all the pleading, had been for nothing.

He wouldn't waste his energy this time because he had grown too old and maybe too cynical to think that those kinds of prayers, and perhaps all kinds of prayers, made the slightest difference. Instead, Matthew found himself getting angry at a God who would allow this to happen, at a world in which it could happen. It wasn't a useful emotion to have, but it was there and he knew he had to be careful about it.

As the evening wore on, the Acute Care Unit grew quiet. Occasionally they could hear the distant wailing of a siren coming from somewhere across the city. Around 10:30, Dylan made his second request to turn on the TV that sat on the wall opposite Nora's bed. This time he said that they could keep the sound off. He would be fine just seeing the picture of any cable show that his father wanted to watch. Matthew again said no to the TV being on in any mode.

Just after 11:00, there was a thumping on the door. It was Jennifer hitting it with one of her crutches. When Matthew opened it for her, she came into the room and gave them both a hug. Then she went to the side of the hospital bed and reached down to stroke Nora's cheek. This was so sad, she said. So awful and so unfair.

Matthew thanked her for volunteering to stay with Dylan. Then he put his hand on his son's shoulder. "I'll see you in the morning. Be good with Jennifer, OK?"

Dylan nodded.

"What time should we come back?" Jennifer asked.

"I'm guessing she'll wake up around 6:30. Any time after that is fine, but don't rush. Sleep anywhere you like, downstairs or in Nora's bed. Dylan will show you where the clean sheets and blankets are."

After they left, Matthew positioned the recliner so it was aligned with Nora's bed. He put his hand over hers, closed his eyes and tried to settle his mind. Racing through it were thoughts from the day, sharp moments that flashed over one another so that they almost seemed to be occurring at the same time. He would not get a decent night's sleep, he realized. He'd drift off eventually, but he was pretty sure he'd wake more tired than he was at the moment.

He was still awake the first time the nurse checked in on Nora, but not the second time. At some point in the middle of the night he got up and used the bathroom. Back in the recliner, he closed his eyes and mercifully found that the chaos of his mind had settled down, and now there was only the dullness of exhaustion and a sober acceptance of the tragedy.

The sound of traffic outside had diminished enough for Matthew to hear his daughter's steady breathing. A few times she stirred and he sat up to see if she had awakened, but each time she settled back into sleep.

Sometime later he woke to the sensation of a soft breeze blowing in the room. It wasn't coming from the air vent in the ceiling but from the direction of the window, which was sealed. With his eyes still closed, he put a hand to his cheek, where he had felt the breeze. When he opened his eyes, the sensation ended. He closed them again and fell asleep almost immediately.

Later still, he had a dream where he and his mother were walking from their apartment in the Old Colony housing project to nearby Carson Beach. He was five years old, and it was the peak of summer. Heat radiated up from the sidewalk, and cars passed by with music blaring. He and his mother were heading to the beach to go swimming, to find relief in the cool waves. She held his hand in hers as they crossed an empty baseball field. Then they stood at the edge of a busy street, where they found themselves trapped. On the other side of Day Boulevard was the beach, but they were unable to cross because cars were racing by in an uninterrupted flow.

"Pay attention now," he heard his mother say in her lilting Irish brogue. "You be very careful, Matthew."

The vividness of the dream jarred him awake so suddenly that he sat up straight and caught his breath. He turned to Nora. She was still sleeping soundly. Outside, the darkness of the night sky was surrendering to the soothing pastel colors of dawn. He settled back in the recliner and stared up at the ceiling. There wasn't a prayer of getting back to sleep now, he knew.

*   *   *   *   *

At 6:30, a nurse showed up. It was a different nurse, a middle-aged woman who introduced herself as Helen and gave Matthew a broad smile.

"Good morning, Mr. Mahoney. And how did we sleep last night?"

Matthew eased himself out of the recliner, then pushed it back against the wall so it was out of the way. "Not too bad," he said in a way that barely covered the lie. He glanced at Nora, who was still asleep. "I'm gonna grab a coffee down the hall, Helen. I should be back in two minutes."

Two minutes was all it took for Nora to wake up. Matthew was walking slowly back to the room, being very careful with how he carried his vending machine coffee because the paper cup was filled to the brim. He instantly recognized the sudden screams coming from Nora's room. He picked up his pace, and some of the hot coffee splashed onto his hand. Fortunately, there was trash bin nearby. He threw the cup into it and wiped his hand on his pants.

As soon as he reached her room, he saw Helen trying to comfort Nora. Her eyes were red, and tears were streaming down her cheeks.

When she saw her father, she began yelling, "Dad!…Dad!"

Matthew ran to her side. As he bent over to hold her, Nora reached up for him. Her sobs were interrupted by coughing as she tried to catch her breath.

Helen said something, but Matthew couldn't hear it, so he asked her to repeat it.

"I've given her something in her IV to calm her down. It should help."

It was then that Jennifer and Dylan showed up. They both moved toward Nora, but Dylan remained at the end of her bed, clutching the footboard and staring wide-eyed at his sister. He was seeing the reality of everything for the first time now that Nora was awake and expressing the trauma with so much emotion.

She continued crying, and through her sobs Matthew could hear her asking, "Where's Mom? I want Mom!"

The next moment Matthew felt Nora's grip on his neck loosening. She continued crying but in a less frantic way. Then Matthew heard someone else crying. He turned to the end of Nora's bed, where he saw Dylan suddenly bawling his eyes out. He was staring at his sister and trying to speak through his own tears, but it was all incoherent.

"Come over here," Matthew said, and Dylan stepped to his side. The bed rail had been lowered, so Dylan was able to bend over and lay his head on Nora's stomach. She looked at her brother, then slowly moved her right arm and rested the end of the cast on Dylan's neck. The two continued sobbing, but the level of agitation seemed to diminish in both. With Nora it was because of the medication administered by the nurse, Matthew thought, and with Dylan it was the fact that Nora was calming down.

Matthew turned around to say something to Jennifer. She was sitting on one of the chairs and was sobbing as well. What a mess we all are, he thought. "Thank you for staying with Dylan. I'm really grateful, Jennifer."

When he shifted his gaze back to Nora, he saw her looking at him and moving her lips slowly. Over and over, he watched her mouthing the words, "I want Mom."

*   *   *   *   *

From the moment Anne took the emergency phone call on Friday, her final day on the North Slope turned into a living nightmare. After hanging up, she checked to see if she could get a seat on the last flight leaving Deadhorse Airport that day, but she was 15 minutes late. From the large windows in the dining hall, she could see the Boeing 737 take off to the south and disappear over the sunlit tundra.

Her engineering team was all there with her in the dining hall to throw Anne a going-away party. Instead of unwrapping the two remaining gifts when she returned from the emergency phone call, Anne sat down and explained to everyone what had happened to her daughter. The moment was beyond awkward. Anne was feeling a flood of emotions, but she found herself unable to really express any of them. Everybody on her team did their best to console her. Eventually, one by one, they gave her a hug and said their goodbyes.

Except for Sarah and David. They stayed with Anne and tried their best to distract her for the remaining hours before her 9:30 flight the next morning. They piled into one of their work trucks and took a drive around the different camps, then out toward a remote new drill site. What Anne really wanted to do was walk, just walk for miles on that remote gravel road with David and Sarah. But the temperature was up, and the mosquitoes were out, so they had to stay in the truck while they drove around for two hours and told stories about home.

Back at camp, Anne spent a half hour neatly packing everything in her room. Then she crawled into bed, but sleep wouldn't come. It would not offer the respite she was craving. As bad as Matthew had sounded when he spoke with her, and as terrible as it must be for him to confront the situation head on, Anne was feeling more sorry for herself. She knew exactly what was going on a thousand miles away, but she was powerless to do anything about it. Her daughter had lost a hand. It was gone, and she would live the rest of her life without it. A thousand miles away, Anne thought, and I can't hold her or even talk to her over the phone right now.

By 11:00 Anne felt as if she might be losing her mind, so she knocked on Sarah's door and told her she was going to swim laps in the pool. Sarah offered to join her, but Anne said it wouldn't be necessary. A little after midnight, Anne had swallowed enough chlorinated water and was exhausted enough to return to bed and finally fall asleep.

When she awoke at 5:30, she felt as if she were hungover. But now, at least, she would finally be moving in the direction of home. Her flight had stops in Barrow and Fairbanks before arriving in Anchorage at 2:15. Maddie met her at the gate, and the two waited for Anne's bags to show up before driving south to the cabin. Anne had a half hour to gather up everything she needed to take back to Seattle with her, including her cellphone.

She was booked on a red-eye that night, but she also had standby status on an earlier flight that would leave just before 5:00, so at 3:45 she and Maddie were heading back to Anchorage Airport. On the drive, Anne was able to call Matthew, who detailed everything that had happened since they last spoke.

He and Dylan were in Nora's hospital room. She had a rough morning, he said, a very rough morning. She did a little better after she had something for lunch, and she was sleeping now. The doctor had come by and spoken with Matthew, and a woman from the hospital's social support team had also stopped by to speak with them all. Matthew didn't know if it did any good. Probably, he thought, but it was hard to tell because Nora's mood had been all over the place, and she was on different medications that had the effect of making her sleepy.

At the airport, Anne checked her bags and gave Maddie one last hug before heading toward her gate, where she went directly to the desk to find out about her position on the standby list. She was number six. That didn't sound promising, Anne said to the desk agent, but the agent offered encouraging words. In the next ten minutes, two people were moved off standby, and as the flight began boarding first-class passengers, another person on the list got a seat. That pushed Anne up to number three.

She lingered closer to the gate desk, so she could hear what was happening. The agent was busy updating flight information and answering a phone call. After hanging up, she paged the next person on the standby list. Then she asked passengers in the very back rows to join the boarding line.

Anne waited another five minutes before walking up to the desk again. The flight was full, the agent told her, and all passengers were checked in. Every seat was taken. The agent's tone, which had been so sympathetic earlier, was now businesslike.

Anne felt it like a punch in the gut. She tried to calm down by telling herself that it was only a difference of five or six hours between this flight and the red-eye, where she had a guaranteed seat. There was nothing she could do for Nora at this point that Matthew and Dylan and all the doctors and nurses couldn't do. Still, something inside her refused to accept all that. She didn't want to wait another five or six hours to be with her daughter. She didn't want to wait another second.

As Anne watched the line of passengers slowly moving forward and disappearing into the jet bridge, she calculated that there had to be about 50 or 60 still waiting to board. All she needed to do was connect with one of them and plead her case. But which one? There was a podium at the entrance to the jet bridge where passengers were having their tickets scanned. Against a nearby wall was a row of empty seats.

Anne walked to the wall and stepped up on a seat. A few of the people in line turned to look at her. Oh God, Anne thought, am I really doing this? "Excuse me…" she began. She was surprised at how soft her voice sounded, so she tried again using her outside voice. "Excuse me, please!"

With that, she caught everyone's attention, including that of the desk agent, who didn't seem too pleased with the unfolding scenario. For all the times she had been teased about her height during her life, this was one moment when Anne was appreciating every inch of her six-foot stature and the attention it drew.

With all eyes on her, she continued, "I'm trying to get home to Seattle. I've been working on the North Slope for three months, and I have a seat on a flight that leaves in five hours. I'm trying to get a seat on this flight, though, because my daughter has been in a car accident." Anne paused when she felt her voice quavering. "She's in the hospital right now and I'm trying to get back to see her as soon as possible. If anybody would be willing to give up their seat on this flight, I'd be happy to buy you a ticket on whatever flight you want."

When Anne finished talking, and it seemed there was really nothing left to say, she stared out at a sea of blank faces. Everyone was looking at her, but nobody was moving or saying anything. The moment stretched for another second before one person, then another, then a third raised their hands. One of them left the line and walked toward Anne. It was an elderly woman wearing a bright blue beret and walking with the aid of a cane. She moved slowly in Anne's direction, and as she did a smile broke out on her face.

*   *   *   *   *

The nonstop flight landed ten minutes early, just as the sun was disappearing behind the Olympic Mountains and the pale dusk was stealing the last color from the water of Puget Sound.

Matthew and Sal met Anne at the gate. She and Matthew hugged for a long time, and it was a hug that felt strange to both of them, having spent so many weeks physically separated from the sight and the feel of each other. In different circumstances, it would be cause for a great celebration. Instead, as all three walked to baggage claim, Matthew explained that he and Anne would drive straight to the hospital while Sal would wait to pick up the two bags that Anne had checked. She described the bags and left her boarding pass. Stapled to it were the two baggage claim stubs.

On the short drive to the hospital, Matthew gave Anne another update on Nora, which didn't go much beyond what she had eaten for dinner. He had left for the airport at 8:30, but Dylan and Jennifer were there with her. After finding a spot to park on the street, they walked quickly to the Acute Care Unit.

When the elevator doors opened, Anne stepped out and asked, "So which room is she in?"

Before Matthew could answer, there came a shout from Nora's room. "Mom, I'm in here! I'm in here, Mom!"

Anne moved toward the sound without thinking, without even being aware of crossing the space between where she stood in the hallway and the side of Nora's bed. She felt her daughter's arms wrap tightly around her neck and Nora's tears on her cheek, and she whispered, "I'm so sorry, baby...I'm so sorry. I'll never leave you like that again. Never again."

Book II

Arrival

"Runa found out that there was another mountain on the other side of the world that was even bigger than the mountain in Canada. So she told her friends about it and said they all had to grab their snowboards and go. It took them a whole week to get there. The next day, they went outside and got on a chairlift that went really fast, but it still took a half hour to go to the top. Then they got on their snowboards and started down the mountain, and Runa saw a jump that was bigger than any jump anywhere in the world. Nora's friends were afraid…"

"You mean Runa's friends, right?"

"Oh, right. Runa's friends. Anyway, they were afraid to go off the jump because you couldn't even see the top of it. But Runa wasn't afraid. She went off the jump and flew up in the air so high that she could see all the lights that were on all around the world. But when she started to come down, big dragons came flying after her. They lived on the mountain, and the jump belonged to them. When they saw Runa going off it, the dragons got very mad.

"One of them pushed her into a cloud. Runa lost her balance and started falling and turning upside down. She couldn't see anything because she was in the middle of the cloud, and it was a really giant cloud. Her friends were looking for her and kept yelling her name. They looked all over the mountain until it was almost dark, but they still couldn't find Runa anywhere."

"Did Runa land safely? Was she OK?"

"Nobody knows."

Chapter 1

Hematoma

Immediately after a fracture, blood from ruptured vessels inside the bone forms a hematoma, or clot, that fills the gap between the pieces of bone. In this initial stage of healing, the hematoma aligns itself to the fragments and provides a temporary framework upon which cells carry out a complex sequence of events.

Saturday, June 24, 2000

The alarm clock went off at 5:15. Matthew opened his eyes and stared at the glowing red numbers. Rather than hitting the snooze button, he turned the alarm off. He had been immersed in a waking dream since 5:00, and he didn't want it to end. He was seeing himself and Nora on Friday morning when the two were playing cards at the dining room table. He saw the blue WELCOME HOME! sign resting on a chair and he talked with Nora about painting the remaining salmon and bears, something they were going to do together when they both got home at the end of the day.

They were living in another reality—or in some other plane of existence—where the car accident hadn't occurred. He and Nora would arrive home that night and they would have dinner, then finish painting the sign. All would be well, and this event, this tragedy, would never have happened.

It was an indulgence, Matthew knew, and an empty one at that, but he remained in the dream until sleep overtook him again. He woke two hours later to the sound of his wife's voice.

"I was just thinking," Anne said. "What if Jennifer hadn't changed her doctor's appointment?"

"Huh?" Matthew said as he rubbed his eyes.

"The day of the accident. Instead of Hadley picking up Nora, Jennifer would have picked her up as planned."

Matthew tried to recall the phone conversation on that particular morning. "I think she said her doctor had to cancel the Monday appointment. That's why she moved it to Friday, which is why she couldn't pick up Nora."

"So...the doctor," Anne said. She paused and stared into space. "Who is he? Why couldn't he keep the Monday appointment? Was he sick, or did he want to take the day off?"

"I have no idea. I don't even know his name."

"Maybe he wanted a long weekend in Vegas or something." Anne's voice trailed off at the end of her sentence. She paused again, then turned to Matthew. "In a way, it started with him."

"It sounds like you're blaming Jennifer's doctor for the accident."

"No, I'm saying that her doctor was the first in a sequence. Then came Jennifer, because she decided to change her appointment from Monday to that Friday instead of waiting a week or so. It was a chain of events...like in that proverb—for want of a nail, the shoe was lost."

With that, Anne rolled onto her back and went quiet.

"I wonder who'll end up buying the Pedersen's house," Matthew said, referring to their next-door neighbors, who had recently announced they were moving to Portland.

"I was thinking about that yesterday. Then I realized that we'll probably be moving right after the new owners arrive."

"The neighborhood's starting to change. I hope someone carries on the tradition of movie night."

"Speaking of which, we need to pick a movie for tonight."

"Are you sure she's ready for a bunch of people?" Matthew asked.

"I think so. We need to start bringing her back. It's important."

Nora had come home on Thursday and had spent almost all of the last two days in the house, either in her room or on the living room couch, where she ate her meals and watched lots of TV. A few attempts to take her for a walk succeeded only once, and the six-block excursion lasted a mere ten minutes. She even refused to go to the front door when one of her friends showed up with a get-well card. Instead, she screamed and went charging upstairs.

"How about *The Addams Family?*" Anne asked. They talked about it for a couple of minutes, and it seemed like it could be just the right amount of fantasy and humor. But then Matthew remembered the character called

Thing. It was a hand that emerged from a box. That was the last image Nora needed to see.

"Oh my God," Anne said. "We're gonna have to rethink everything we do from now on. Not just what movies to watch but everything."

"Maybe we should wait on the movie," Matthew said. "Tonight might be too soon. We can have people over for a movie next weekend."

"No," Anne said. "Waiting will make it worse. We need to move her back into the world. She needs to be around the people who know her and care about her. She needs to get used to her new…reality. Showing people, talking about it, learning how to navigate the world with one hand."

"We never watched *Black Beauty,*" Matthew said. "No, wait…*The Nightmare Before Christmas.*"

"It's not exactly the holiday season," Anne said.

"It doesn't matter. She really likes that movie. She almost cried last fall when I returned the video before she could watch it a second time."

"Wait, doesn't the girl puppet character get her arm ripped off?"

"Yes, twice, I think," Matthew said. "But it's different. She sews it back on." He stopped to consider it further. "The way it works in the story is actually a positive thing. Really. Anyway, I'll ask her about it first."

With the movie mostly decided, Matthew reached out and stroked Anne's cheek slowly. Soon they were kissing, then undressing quietly. It had become their ritual some mornings and evenings since Anne's return. Along with sleep, sex was their thirty minutes or twenty minutes or ten minutes of respite from the new reality. In that sense, it was different from any kind of sex in the past. They were grimly referring to it "escape sex."

Fourteen minutes later, the sound of steps echoed throughout the house as Dylan pounded down the stairs in his heavy-footed way. Matthew lingered in bed while Anne pulled on some sweats and headed for the kitchen. He heard a few cabinets open and close, then several more before he heard Anne's exasperated voice calling him.

"What's the matter?" Matthew asked when he got to the kitchen.

Anne stood with her hands on her hips, staring at a bunch of open cabinets. Finally, she said, "Don't get me wrong, Matt. I mean, I'm really grateful that Jennifer could step in and take care of the kids and cook a few meals. But did she have to rearrange half of our kitchen? I can't find anything. I want to make some coffee, but I can't because she moved my coffee filters…somewhere."

Matthew pulled open a drawer and took out a package of coffee filters. "She's not as tall as we are, so she had to move some things from the top cabinets."

Anne ran a hand through her hair and took a deep breath. "OK, sorry."

Coffee was brewed, bread was toasted and buttered, eggs were cracked over a hot pan and one bowl was filled with Rice Krispies Treats cereal and milk. As a rule, Matthew and Anne strictly limited what they called "junk-food cereals" to very rare occasions, but they agreed to allow Nora one box on her return from the hospital.

Matthew walked over to the foot of the stairs and was about to call Nora down, but Dylan stopped him.

"Don't yell for her, Dad. She doesn't like that. I'll go up and get her."

A couple of minutes later, Dylan returned, followed by Nora, who walked down in her pajamas and joined her father on the couch to watch the *Power Rangers*. She crossed her legs, and Matthew placed the bowl in her lap.

As Nora took the spoon in her left hand, Matthew asked, "So did you add anything to your collection last night?"

He was referring to the animals and objects that Nora had drawn on her pale purple cast. The rough woven fiberglass was far from the ideal drawing surface, but Nora had managed to fill most of it with decent renderings of stars, moons, bears and fish of different sizes. However, most of the forearm was taken up by a large elaborate dragon that seemed to be sending the other animals and objects scattering to the fringes, either in fear or confusion.

Nora simply shook her head as Matthew worked free the tangle in her day-old braids. Then he brushed her shiny black hair before rebraiding it.

"Nana B is coming into town today," Anne called from the kitchen. "She's really looking forward to seeing you, Nora. Why don't you come with me to the airport? Her plane lands around noon."

Nora turned to her father and said, "I have enough room to add a plane. And a helicopter. Or maybe a small forest."

"How about up here?" Matthew asked, pointing at the top of the cast where it covered part of her upper arm.

"I'm saving that for another dragon," Nora said. "A girl dragon riding a snowboard."

*　　*　　*　　*　　*

"People are staring at me," Nora said.

She and her mother were standing with a small crowd clustered around the arrival gate for Joan's flight. The plane had just pulled up to the terminal, and the jet bridge was slowly rolling out to connect.

Anne looked around quickly, then said, "Nobody is staring at you, Nora."

Nora's eyes were locked onto a boy who sat with his family a short distance away. He was whispering to his father, who had lowered his head to listen. The boy wore a shiny blue jacket with a Chicago Cubs logo, and when he finished whispering to his father, he pointed in Nora's direction. When the father saw who his son was pointing at, he slapped his hand down and told him to stop being rude. Nora moved to the opposite side of her mother so the boy could no longer see her.

With a loud squeak, the door to the jet bridge opened and people began pouring out. Nana B was as frugal as most New Englanders, but one of the luxuries she granted herself was to always fly first class, so she was among the first passengers to disembark. When she emerged, she spotted Anne and moved in her direction. Then she saw Nora, who pushed between two people and ran to her grandmother.

"Nana B!" she called.

Her grandmother bent down to greet Nora at eye level, and Nora wrapped her arms around her.

"I'll get it," Anne said and grabbed the carry-on bag her mother had let drop to the floor.

With some effort, Nana B picked up Nora and gave her a kiss on the cheek. "My goodness, I can hardly pick you up anymore. And look how tall you're getting. Just like your mother. In fact, I think you'll be even taller than her. And even more beautiful. Look at that wonderful smile of yours. How are you, my sweet thing?"

"I'm alright," Nora said, but as soon as she did the joy quickly drained from her expression. As the tears began to fall, Nora buried her face in her grandmother's shoulder.

Anne signaled to her mother, and the two began making their way from the gate to baggage claim. As they walked, Nana B spoke softly into Nora's ear. "I know about this accident you had, and I don't want you to worry yourself about it. These things happen to us sometimes and they can hurt, and they can make us sad, and they can make life a little more difficult for a while. But we're going to get you back on your feet again, my dear, OK? You'll see. It just takes a little time, that's all. Trust me, your mom and I are going to make sure you get everything you need, alright?"

As they approached baggage claim, Anne could tell that her mother was struggling to hold onto Nora.

"You can put her down, Mom."

"I will do no such thing. Besides, we're almost there," Nana B said, although when they reached their baggage claim carousel and she lowered Nora to the floor, Nana B let out a gasp of exhaustion. "Well, Nora, I'm afraid that will definitely be the last time I'm able to carry you. You're growing too fast, and I'm growing too old. Now let me take a look at your cast."

Nora extended her right arm as much as she could, with the position of her elbow locked by the cast. Nana B ran her hands across the coarse surface and touched the gauze padding at the tip. "I see now. OK. You've got a couple of bones mending, I hear, but you're young, so they'll mend fast. And stitches underneath the dressing here. They'll come out soon, and you won't feel so much tenderness in a couple of weeks or so." Nana B looked up at Anne and continued, "I've been reading up on all this. The procedure is called a wrist disarticulation. She'll have a lot of prosthetic options available when the time comes, but first the wound needs to heal and the swelling needs to diminish."

Nana B had been a math professor at Salem State College, but as she went on about the details of the procedure and follow-up treatment, Anne wondered if she had branched out into medicine. Anne also noticed that people nearby were looking in their direction. It was more like staring, and it quickly became clear that they were staring at Nora. Anne counted three of them. She moved to block their view, then she stared back at each until her glare caught their attention and they looked away.

* * * * *

Kurt, who supplied the impressive audiovisual system that made movie nights possible, reminded them that there was no use trying to show any movies before 9:00 that night because the Seattle sun wouldn't be setting until around 9:10, even with all the shade provided by the maple that towered over the backyard.

That meant Nora's bedtime would once again be suspended so she could watch *The Nightmare Before Christmas*. Neither Matthew nor Anne made note of it because everything to do with family schedules and timetables had been tossed out the window with Nora's accident. The family was supposed to spend the week after Anne's return camping on the Olympic Peninsula with two nights on Shi Shi Beach, three nights at Kalaloch Campground at a site overlooking the surf, and two nights in the Hoh Rain Forest.

All that was canceled. At the same time, neither Matthew nor Anne had worked in over a week. Anne had postponed her interview with BG until the second week of July. She and Matthew agreed that it wouldn't be fair to move the family north until Nora had transitioned out of a cast and had gotten at least somewhat comfortable with her new reality. Along with her physical healing, her head had to be in the right place if she was going to successfully deal with a new life in a new place.

With Joan's arrival, Matthew informed his manager at Roy's that he could work his regular shifts. He even let Sal know that he'd be available to work some days when they needed extra help. Joan, he knew, would be spending a fair amount of time in the house, and he had learned over the years that their small rental was not big enough for him and Joan to spend extended hours together unless there was a party where alcohol was flowing freely.

The guest list for movie night was smaller than it typically would be, so that Nora wouldn't feel overwhelmed. Three of her closest friends and their parents were invited, along with the adults who Nora wanted to see. That included Sal, Lyka and the rest of the A Crew, Jennifer, Kurt, who

401

would run the projector and was the assistant coach on her soccer team, and Tessa, whose revitalized popcorn machine would be making its seasonal debut. Hadley and her husband, Neil, planned to stop by during the movie as well.

While Anne and Nora went to the airport, Matthew and Dylan shopped for groceries and picked up the movie at Blockbuster. Nora had given a thumbs-up to *The Nightmare Before Christmas*. The next stop was Roy's to pick up the quarter keg of Maritime Pacific Pale Ale that Matthew had ordered earlier in the week. At 7:30, he and Dylan were on the back deck working the hot grill. First up were some appetizers: slices of zucchini, yellow squash, garlic spears and eggplant, all brushed with a blend of balsamic vinegar and garlic, rosemary, basil and pepper; chicken skewers served with peanut sauce; and jalapeños stuffed with cream cheese, bacon, lime, garlic and cilantro.

Matthew instructed his son on the proper amount of heat necessary to leave grill marks on the vegetables before turning them, and how soon to remove them so they still retained a degree of crunchiness.

As he was doing that, Matthew heard the doorbell ring, followed by the sound of rapid steps. In the next moment, he found himself falling backwards. Nora had jumped onto his back and somehow was managing to scale her way up to his neck. He stumbled briefly but regained his footing despite Nora wrapping her left arm around his neck in a viselike grip. He pried it away enough to breathe normally.

"Don't choke me, Squids," he said.

Nora's mouth was only an inch from her father's ear, and she whispered loudly, "Someone's at the front door. They rang the bell. I think they want to come in."

"OK, well, that's fine. Is Mom gonna open the door?"

"I think so. She's right there in the living room. And Nana B is there too."

"Alright then. So, are you still OK having people visit us tonight?"

"I don't know…maybe…I guess."

Matthew reached down to the grill and pulled off a chicken skewer. He held it behind him for Nora to take. She switched her hold on his neck to her cast arm and took the skewer in her left hand.

Matthew turned his head to say, "The chicken's really hot, so you need to blow on it first to cool it off."

Matthew heard the sound of Nora blowing on the skewer, then felt wet flecks on the back of his neck from the chicken fat.

"It's all yours, Dylanator," Matthew said. "I'd say another minute or a minute and a half. When they look good, line the veggies up on one platter, and the chicken on another one." Before leaving, he pressed the tongs down on one of the jalapeños, then pointed at them. "These can come off now."

As Matthew stepped into the house, he ducked down so that Nora wouldn't hit her head on the door frame. Nora's friend Naomi and her parents were standing in the living room. As Matthew approached, Naomi called out, "Hi, Nora."

"Hi, Naomi," Nora said softly.

Matthew turned his head and asked, "Do you want to get down, Nora?"

"No," she said.

"I brought you a get-well card," Naomi said. She handed the card to Matthew. He tried handing it back to Nora, who whispered, "I haven't finished my chicken."

In a louder voice, Nora said, "Thank you, Naomi."

An awkward silence followed as everyone listened to the sound of Nora taking her last bites. When she was done, she poked the pointed tip of the stick into her father's neck. "I'm finished now," she said and extended the bare stick forward.

As Matthew took it, Naomi asked, "Do you have your tetherball set up yet in the backyard?"

"No," Nora said.

Matthew and Anne looked at each other with the same question in mind: Is this an acceptable activity? When they both shared an expression in the affirmative, Anne said, "Dad can set it up now if you girls want to play. Nora, you just need to be careful with your cast, OK?"

With that, Nora climbed down, and the two girls made their way to the backyard. Matthew retrieved the tetherball gear from the garage. The base of the pole had been cemented into the back lawn, so it was only a few minutes before the girls were playing. When Nora's other friends showed up, they joined the game. The girls took turns playing against each other, then played in teams. They instituted some new rules: everyone could only use one hand while they played. And they had to decide which hand that would be at the beginning, with no switching of hands allowed.

Matthew, Anne and Nana B all checked periodically to see how Nora was handling the first social situation in her new world. As far as they could tell, she was doing OK. As the evening wore on, they could see, and also hear, more of the girl they knew so well coming back to life. Not so much as her old self, because they all knew there was no going back to the old Nora in a strict sense, but to her new self with most of the core Nora still intact.

As other people arrived and joined the party, they would go to the back deck, where they would wave and call out to Nora, but she was having too much fun with her friends to bother to return the greetings properly. It wasn't until later in the evening when the sun had set, the sky had finally darkened, and the stainless steel cauldron inside Tessa's brightly lit popcorn machine crackled and bubbled over with freshly popped corn that Nora began spending time with the adults who had stopped by to see her.

There was some cheering as Kurt fired up the projector and the movie began playing clearly on the screen against the side of the garage. Rows of chairs had been set up, and at the sight of the movie people began to take their seats. When Nora walked up behind the chair where Jennifer was sitting in the front row, Jennifer turned around and gave her a great big hug.

"Can I sit with you?" Nora asked.

"Of course," Jennifer said, and she patted the seat beside her.

As the opening song played, Nora spoke quietly to Jennifer, and showed her the cast and what she had drawn on it. After a few minutes of talking, Nora leaned over and rested her head on Jennifer's lap. She watched the movie quietly as Jennifer stroked her back.

When Jack Skellington, the Pumpkin King of Halloween Town, was visiting Christmas Town for the first time in the movie, Nora stood up, gave Jennifer another hug, then walked over to Lyka's seat, where she went through the same ritual. She also asked Lyka if she could please redo her braids because her dad had done them earlier, and they were too tight. Lyka asked Anne for a brush, then brushed Nora's hair while she sat on her lap. Then she gently wound it into a French braid.

Next was Sal, who arrived alone. Nora hadn't met Inessa yet, and he didn't want to make her uncomfortable by having to meet a stranger on her first day back in the world. Nora showed Sal her cast, and he told her how he had driven her dad to the hospital that Friday afternoon and how they were all worried about her. Without intending to, Sal ended up talking about the time when he was nine years old and his younger sister Thalia contracted spinal meningitis. Despite two operations, she died just shy of her seventh birthday.

By the time Sal reached the end of his story, he was in tears. Nora got him a napkin from the table on the back deck, then she wrapped her arms as best as she could around him.

Hadley and Neil Epps showed up shortly after that, and Nora went to the back row to take the seat between them. They each gave her a hug. This was the first time Nora and Hadley had seen each other since the accident. Within a matter of seconds, tears were rolling down Hadley's cheeks.

"I'm so sorry," she said as she held Nora tightly. "I'm so sorry I let this happen."

"It's not your fault, Mrs. Epps. My dad told me how it happened. That man had a heart attack, and he's dead now. You didn't do it. It was an accident."

"I know, but still…"

"How is your brain?" Nora asked. "My dad said you had a concussion."

Hadley sat back and smiled at Nora. "It wasn't too bad. I'm feeling better now."

Neil handed Hadley a tissue and she dabbed her cheeks and eyes. Then Hadley reached out to hold Nora. "I'm afraid life is different for both of us now."

"I know," Nora said. "But maybe it will make us friends forever."

Hadley smiled and laughed awkwardly. "That would be one good thing, I suppose."

As *The Nightmare Before Christmas* played on, Nora continued going from one person to the next, spending a little time with each, moving with the care of a young dancer taking her first steps on a new stage.

Chapter 2
Soft Callus

Within several days after the fracture, thick masses appear at the broken ends of the bone as a result of the hematoma. The masses grow until the two ends meet. Revascularization begins to occur, and fibrous tissue and cartilage are created. This tissue is soft and malleable, and can be easily damaged without proper support.

Friday, June 30, 2000

The day after Anne got home, Matthew had told her everything about Francis: his two visits, the exchange of favors, with Matthew still waiting to receive his. It was unexpected news, but in light of the larger crisis Anne accepted it with less surprise than she might have otherwise. Her concern was how the visit might affect Dylan.

They waited until the aftermath of Nora's accident had faded before having a talk with him. That morning, Nana B had taken her granddaughter to the beach at Lincoln Park, where they would spend a few hours enjoying the beautiful weather with Nora's friends. Dylan, however, was spending his Friday indoors, sitting on the opposite side of the dining room table from his parents.

"This is part of being an adult in the Mahoney family, D-Man," Matthew said.

"It's something that you can never tell anybody about, Dylan. Not ever," Anne said. "Do you understand?"

They all spent a moment listening to the sound of the wind chimes on the back deck as Dylan pondered what his parents had said.

"I looked him up on the Internet," Dylan said. "He's pretty scary. He murdered a lot of people. The FBI can't find him, but he was right here in our kitchen."

"That's especially what you can't tell anybody," Anne said. "Do you understand what I'm saying, Dylan?"

As he began nodding his head, the front door suddenly flew open. Nora was there in her bathing suit, with Nana B behind her. Rather than coming into the living room, Nora moved straight to the stairway and up to her room.

"What happened?" Anne asked.

"It'll be alright," Nana B said as she closed the door behind her and put down the bag that carried towels and beach gear. She took a seat at the end of the dining room table. "Her friends were there, and they were playing on the beach. Then they went in the water. I made sure Nora wore a plastic bag over her cast like she does in the shower. I was helping her take off the bag after she came out when someone passing on the walkway called out, 'What happened to your hand?'

Anne shook her head. "God, what is wrong with some people?"

"It was a young man. He likely said it without cruel intent, but you should have seen Nora's friends. They defended her fiercely. I could see that he was shaken up by their yelling. Then the rocks began flying at him. That beach is full of rocks, and most of them are the perfect size. Anyway, I quickly put an end to the rock throwing before someone got hurt. Luckily, no one did."

"Let me go talk to her," Matthew said.

"I'll go up," Anne said. "You're taking her to the doctor this afternoon."

Nana B noticed that Dylan was sitting across from his parents, so she said, "It looks like someone was being lectured to while Nora and I were at the beach."

"Yes," Anne began slowly. "We were talking to Dylan about Matthew's brother."

"You mean the one who's attempting to ruin three centuries of progress in the Commonwealth of Massachusetts with his political corruption?" Sensing that her statement might have been excessive, Nana B turned to Matthew and added, "No offense, Matthew."

"No," Anne said. "The other brother."

Nana B's eyes grew large. "Why in the name of everything holy would you expose him to the knowledge of that relation?"

Matthew could see that Dylan was about to say something, so he raised a finger in his direction and shook his head. Rather than taking a swing at Nana B's question himself, Matthew waited for Anne to respond.

"Mom," Anne said. "It's complicated, OK? Let's leave it at that."

Nana B tsked and shook her head in a disapproving way that Anne knew all too well. "I hope you're not considering exposing Nora to this information as well. She's been scarred enough by her injury, and she hardly needs any additional trauma."

"God no, Mother." Anne said. "Of course not." She turned quickly to Dylan and added in a sharp voice, "That goes for you, too Dylan. Your dad already mentioned this to you, but I'll repeat it: you cannot tell your sister about Francis under any circumstances. Do you understand me?"

Dylan sensed the importance of the demand and he nodded vigorously. "Yes, definitely, Mom."

"Good," Anne said. "Now I need to talk to Nora."

Anne's absence left Matthew, Dylan and Nana B sitting silently after the tense exchange. Matthew knew she would feel somewhat defensive because of her remarks about his brother Jimmy, if not Francis. He also had her alone in front of Dylan, who had always proven to be either a neutral audience when his Mahoney ancestry was discussed in front of his grandmother, or even a loose ally of his father.

Matthew had several choice comments at the tip of his tongue ready to unload in a subtle, measured attack. Not to defend Francis—because there was no defending that brother—but Matthew knew enough political history about his home state to point out not only corruption by the old Protestant establishment, but also centuries of their religious and ethnic oppression. In the end, he decided to keep his powder dry. There would be better opportunities in the future, and he knew he only had to overplay his hand once to become subject to a massive counterattack from the Boushay side.

Instead, he said, "You know, I really enjoy the dry summers out West. It's so much better than the oppressive New England humidity, don't you think?"

*　　*　　*　　*　　*

"Mom said if somebody asks me what happened to my hand, I can say 'What happened to your manners?' Or I can say 'It's none of your business.' Or I can just ignore them. She said ignoring people is usually the best thing to do. But she said I shouldn't throw any rocks at them."

They were on their way to Swedish Medical Center on First Hill for Nora's checkup. Matthew had trouble paying attention to Nora for a number of reasons. It had been almost three weeks since he had made the phone call for Francis, yet he had received no word, in any form, about where Buzzy was buried. Adding to that, he was still annoyed with his mother-in-law. He was also annoyed with Subaru for not making their vehicles more comfortable for people over six feet tall. Plus, he was annoyed at the Mercedes in front of him, which seemed to be moving slower and slower with each passing traffic light. It was something that always happened to him when he was running a few minutes late to an appointment. Slow-moving cars seemed to magically find him, then pull in front.

Finally, Matthew had forgotten to take the turn that would let him bypass the waterfront viaduct, and now he would be forced to drive onto the elevated double-decker roadway that was guaranteed to pancake in the next major earthquake. The road was so old and decrepit that chunks of concrete occasionally fell from the superstructure onto the streets below. It's only a matter of time, Matthew thought, but please, God, give me a pass for the next 40 seconds or so.

When Nora changed the radio station and began finding Matthew's least favorite songs, he was pulled out of his distractions. "Not that station, please. Dad isn't a fan of Britney Spears." Matthew paused to yet again mourn the death of grunge and to resent the music now filling its vacuum. "And yes, your mom is right. Ignoring people who say mean things is usually the best option. But throwing rocks at people is not an option."

"Did you ever throw rocks at people?" Nora asked.

Matthew had a flashback to when he had thrown rocks at people. Then he remembered another time he had done it. He also remembered doing things that were worse. For what seemed like the thousandth time as a parent, he considered how to walk that fine line of respecting the truth without directly acknowledging it. "It's always wrong to throw rocks at people, OK? It doesn't matter who is doing it or why they're doing it."

Nora continued surfing stations until she got bored with them all and turned the radio off. After a minute of silence, she asked, "Do you know what Mom's favorite song is?"

Matthew said nothing at first. Then a smile slowly broke out on his face.

"What's so funny?"

At a red light, Matthew turned to Nora. "I was just thinking about how happy she gets when she hears her favorite song. It's called 'Daybreak' by the singer Barry Manilow." Matthew knew that it was definitely not Anne's favorite song, so he thought he'd have a little fun with it.

"I've never heard of him."

"Well, your mom knows who Barry Manilow is, and she sure loves the song 'Daybreak.' We should play it for her."

They parked in the underground garage at Swedish Medical Center, and as they walked toward Dr. Gottlieb's office, Matthew saw a man at the far end of the hallway who looked familiar. He only saw his back for a second or two before he turned a corner, but there was something about the guy that Matthew couldn't quite put his finger on.

"Well, look at you," Dr. Gottlieb said to Nora with a big smile.

Dr. Gottlieb's assistant had taken Nora's vital signs, which all looked good, then sent her for a set of X-rays to see how her bones were mending. While they waited for the X-rays to arrive, Dr. Gottlieb sat down with Nora and Matthew in the examination room to have a look at the end of Nora's right arm. The stump. Matthew and Anne had been avoiding that term, but in the end they decided it was better than the technical term favored by the medical profession: residual limb.

The stitches on Nora's stump had been removed the week before and the medical tape stretched over the wound as a precaution had fallen off on its own, as designed. Matthew and Anne had been changing the dressing regularly in the days after the accident, but the stump was now exposed and required no dressing other than care against further injury while the soft tissue healed.

"I bump it into things sometimes," Nora said. "And it can really hurt."

"OK, that happens," Dr. Gottlieb said. "Just try to be mindful of it when you're moving around. And are you using sunscreen on it every day?"

"Yes, my Nana B put some on this morning when we went to the beach."

"That's very good, Nora. You keep that up, and you'll minimize any discoloration."

"We're moving to Alaska," Nora said. "It won't be very sunny up there in a few months."

"That may be so," the doctor said, "but until then you should use it. And even next spring and next summer." Turning to Matthew, she added, "A year minimum is a good idea. If you're diligent about it through the end of next summer, it will make a big difference in keeping a more uniform shade to the skin."

When the X-rays arrived, Dr. Gottlieb attached them to a light box and scanned them slowly. Then she turned and said, "So your X-rays look good, Nora. Here, let me show you."

Matthew and Nora came over to the light box, and Dr. Gottlieb pointed out two specific spots. Matthew lifted Nora so she could see better. "You can tell where your body is starting to make new bone material," Dr. Gottlieb said. "Everything is lined up well and the magic is happening, so to speak. But there's still a lot of work left to do, and the connection here is soft and vulnerable. The cast will protect you while the healing continues. All you need to do is be careful with the arm, continue to eat healthy meals and get plenty of rest. And avoid bumping into things as much as possible. Next time I see you, we'll talk about what else we can do."

Looking at Matthew, she said, "We'll start physical therapy and discuss prosthetic options once the bones are healed and the swelling diminishes. That's a ways down the road. You may notice edema, or fluid buildup, at the stump. Once we remove the cast and have Nora exercise the muscles in her right arm, that should clear up. But so far, she's doing great."

After leaving the doctor's office, Matthew told Nora they could stop in the gift shop to buy a package of Life Savers for her and a bag of chips for him. As they walked toward the shop, Matthew noticed that Nora was holding her right arm behind her back. It was awkward for her to do because of the cast, but it was deliberate. He had seen her doing it whenever people were present who might stare at her stump or, even

411

worse, throw out an odd question or comment that strangers often gave themselves permission to do, especially when children were involved.

He understood why she'd want to hide it from people. Anne did too. They had talked about it and agreed that they wouldn't make it worse by saying anything about it to Nora. In a previous visit to Dr. Gottlieb, Anne had discussed the matter. The doctor said it was likely something that would pass in time and that the cast made it impossible for Nora at this point to "find her new natural," or her new way of moving and being herself without her right hand. It was still early, the doctor said, and Nora was vulnerable. If this helped her cope for the time being, then it should be considered acceptable.

They sat on a stone wall in front of the hospital to enjoy their snacks and watch the traffic go by on Broadway. As Matthew ate his chips, he watched Nora holding the package of Life Savers in her left hand and opening it by pulling the little string with her teeth. Then she used her left thumbnail to carefully push each Life Saver to the open end of the roll.

The next thing that caught Matthew's attention was the smell of a burning cigarette. He turned to see someone smoking 30 feet away. It was the same guy he had seen down a hospital corridor earlier. Now Matthew recognized the profile. It was Diego. Matthew's first instinct was to take Nora's hand and head straight to the garage. He didn't want to see Diego, and he didn't want to talk to him. But then Diego turned around slowly and Matthew saw the look of despair on his face. Diego had never been a happy-looking man, but he was now displaying a new level of cheerlessness.

Once he made eye contact with Diego, Matthew felt it was too late to leave without saying something, so he stood up and walked over. As he approached, Diego gave him an up-and-down look that in another context might have meant, "and what do you want from me, you piece of shit?"

"I didn't know you smoked," Matthew said.

"I used to," Diego said.

"Me too. A long time ago."

"That's your girl?" Diego asked, nodding in Nora's direction.

"I brought her here for an appointment. She had an accident last month."

"I heard about that." Diego turned to face the hospital and looked to the upper floors. "My boy is here for dialysis. Something is really wrong with his kidneys. It just happened two weeks ago. They told us it's genetic. I don't think they really know. I think they're guessing. But it's probably a good guess. I don't know."

Diego took a deep draw on his cigarette and was careful to exhale away from Matthew.

"It's good to have insurance," Matthew said. "We're all on my wife's plan, or the COBRA version of it, but what the Riegers offer is decent coverage. It should take care of most of your bills. They can get pretty steep when you're dealing with complicated issues like kidney problems."

Traffic was picking up, and a taxi horn blared on the busy street. Diego and Matthew both turned to see what the problem might be, but it was nothing. When Matthew turned back to Diego, he was met with a blank stare.

"You have insurance." The way Matthew said it was as much a question as a statement.

Diego said, "They canceled everybody's insurance in May, but they didn't tell us. I found out when I filed a claim for Martin. He's the one on dialysis. Our youngest."

"You're shitting me," Matthew said with a rush of anger. "They canceled everybody's insurance, and they didn't tell you? They let you walk around thinking you had health insurance for your family, but you really had none?"

Diego took another puff, then nodded.

"That's incredible," Matthew said. "But I guess I shouldn't be surprised. They cheated my crew out of a lot of pay. Which was alright by me because we kept a bunch of their roofing gear as compensation."

Diego nodded and showed a hint of a smile. "They were not very happy about that."

Matthew smiled and said, "Good." Then he glanced at the hospital and asked, "So what are you gonna do about the bills?"

"My wife and I applied for charity with the hospital. It should work out. At least for most of the bills."

"OK, well," Matthew said and shook Diego's hand. "Maybe I'll see you around here again."

"I'm really sorry what happened to your girl, Matthew."

"Thanks, Diego. You know, you should sue them. All you guys should sue them. Wiley's got a nice big house that's worth a lot of money. That should be paying for all your hospital bills." Matthew then asked, "You're not working for them anymore, are you?"

Diego shook his head.

"Sal and his brother started a roofing company, you know," Matthew said.

"I heard about that."

"They're doing pretty good, but they could use some extra hands. If you want, I can tell them you're interested."

Diego nodded. "Thank you."

Matthew turned and began walking toward Nora.

"It was funny," Diego said.

Matthew stopped and looked back at Diego. He didn't think he had heard him right. "What was funny?"

"My truck. What you put in my truck."

Matthew suddenly realized what Diego was referring to, and he felt a wave of embarrassment at having committed the prank. But then he saw something he had never seen before: a legitimate smile on Diego's face.

*   *   *   *   *

When they got home from the hospital, Matthew grabbed a few things and walked down the hill to Roy's. After finding out the night before that Nana B would be staying late Friday evening and cooking dinner, he called Roger to see if he could steal his bartending shift. He said yes. With so many people heading out of town for the long 4th of July weekend, he was happy to give up a shift that probably wasn't going to be very lucrative. And Matthew got to skip a meal prepared in his own home by his mother-in-law. She hadn't packed any brussels sprouts on this trip, but he was sure she'd find something at the grocery store to make the meal unappealing to him in more ways than one.

Roger had been right. The crowd at the bar was so light on Friday that Dennis decided to close early. When Matthew got home just before 11:00, he learned that he was also right. The front door was ajar, but after opening the screen door and stepping inside, he was hit by an overpowering odor that was bitter, burnt and musky. A fan was blowing in the kitchen.

"Hey," Anne called from the back deck when she heard him.

"Anything?" he called.

"I'm good," Anne said.

Matthew grabbed himself a beer from the fridge and joined Anne on the deck. The cool evening air was such a refreshing break from his quick walk through the foul-smelling house that he wondered how he'd be able to sleep inside later on.

He sat down on the chair beside Anne, opened his beer and took a long pull. "So what did your mother cook?"

"It wasn't that bad."

"Hey, I didn't say anything. The fan is doing all the talking."

"It was a new recipe she wanted to try. Oat porridge with bitter greens, two different kinds of turnip, some Indian spices…um, egg whites, I think. It was going pretty well until things started to burn. She miscalculated the amount of water she was supposed to use. Nora distracted her. For the first time trying the recipe, I guess it went alright."

"Boy, did I make the right call," Matthew said in a low voice before asking, "how did the kids like it?"

"We had some cheese and crackers before dinner, so they didn't eat too much." Anne turned to face the home next to theirs, where the windows were all dark. "I heard the Pedersens accepted an offer. It's so quiet over there these days. I'm used to their kids making noise. Little Jessica was always singing when she was outside. She has such a lovely voice."

"I'm gonna miss Ken's spare propane. He was always there in a pinch when we ran out during movie night." Then Matthew added, "So, anything in the mail today or any phone messages?" It was the question he had been asking almost every day for a week, and it had to do with Francis communicating in some way with Matthew to tell him where Buzzy was buried.

Anne turned to him and shook her head. "I know you don't want to hear this, but you might never get anything, Matt. Maybe your brother used you. He got what he wanted, and that could be the end of it."

"Hmm, I suppose. I would be very surprised though."

"He's killed people, Matt. He killed your brother. You can't trust a person like that for anything."

"He said to be patient. I'll give it a few more weeks or so." Changing the subject, Matthew said, "You know, sometimes I really do miss smoking. When Nora and I were at Swedish, I saw a guy I used to work with. I never knew he smoked. By the way, I don't think I mentioned this, but I made another call to the Anchorage School District yesterday. They got everything from us except the vaccination records, so I faxed them again. The first day of school is August 15. Can you believe that? Two weeks into August and their summer's gonna be over. If I was a kid, I wouldn't be too happy about that."

Matthew turned to Anne and paused when he saw her staring out at the night, not seeming to be paying attention, which was strange because she had been keeping close track of everything related to the move north. "Hey," he said.

The sound pulled Anne out of her distraction, and she looked at Matthew. "Sorry, I was just wondering about something." She turned back to the night sky. "Do you slow down when you get to an intersection? I mean, even when you have the green light, do you slow down and look both ways to make sure that nobody is maybe about to run their red light and hit you?"

Matthew was confused by the question at first. Then he sensed what Anne was getting at. Before he could reply, she added, "I think I do. I think I slow down and look both ways, just to be sure. There's always a one-in-a-million chance that somebody will be distracted because their phone is ringing or because their child is screaming in the back seat..."

"Or because they're having a heart attack?"

"Or that. Yes," Anne said.

Matthew hoped she wasn't serious but saw that she was. "So now are you blaming Hadley Epps?"

"You keep using that word. That's not what I'm talking about at all."

*   *   *   *   *

"How many stars do you think there are in our galaxy? Take a guess." Dylan said. He was lying on the floor beside Nora's bed, using a sleeping bag that was kept in the bedroom storage cabinet and normally only brought out for family camping trips. Since Nora's accident, he had been bringing it out some nights so he could sleep in her room.

Nora's cast dangled down the side of her bed, and her stump was resting on Dylan's shoulder. With her left hand she passed down a tube of Doritos 3D that they were snacking on after their less-than-filling dinner. "About fifty," Nora said before licking the chip dust off her fingers. "No, wait. Two hundred and fifty." They were both speaking in voices just above a whisper to keep their parents from hearing them. A dim glow came from a snowman nightlight plugged into a wall socket.

"One hundred billion," Dylan said. "That's how many stars there are in our galaxy." He pulled the last few Doritos from the plastic tube, ate them, then tipped the tube up to tap the chip remnants into his mouth. "Guess how many galaxies there are in the universe?"

"In the entire universe?" Nora asked.

"Yes."

"Twenty…twenty seven."

"One hundred billion," Dylan said.

"That's the same number as before," Nora said. "They can't be the exact same number."

"It's approximately one hundred billion."

"You didn't say approximately."

"I'm guessing the margin of error is around one percent or less. They have to use estimates."

Nora put her hand to her forehead. "I can't talk about space anymore, Dylan. It makes my head hurt."

They lay in silence for a full minute before Dylan said, "So I'm not supposed to tell you this…" He paused to let the tantalizing thought hang in the air for a moment, and also to give himself one last chance to keep from sharing the unspeakable family secret.

"Tell me what?" Nora asked, suddenly animated by the chance to hear something that promised to be interesting, maybe very interesting.

"You know how Dad has a brother…"

"What about him?"

"Well, he has another brother named Francis, and he's a gangster."

"No way!" Nora said a little too loudly.

417

"Shh," Dylan said. He waited to see if his parents might have heard them. After deciding they hadn't, he continued with his story and shared most of what he had learned from his online research. Then he told Nora about Francis' visit to their house, the visit that Nora had slept through.

"Wow, I can't believe we're actually a Mafia family," Nora said.

"Last night I had a nightmare about him. He was breaking into our house."

After a short silence, Nora said. "I hope we see *Sleepy Hollow* at the next movie night."

"You can't tell anybody about Francis, OK? Especially not Mom and Dad. They'll kill me if they find out I told you."

"Alright."

"Nana B would kill me too. All three of them will kill me. OK? Promise you won't tell."

"I promise."

"Ever," Dylan said.

"Ever," Nora said, then added, "I don't think Nana B likes Dad."

"Me neither," Dylan agreed. "I think it's because of Francis. She doesn't like his family."

"Do you like the name Mahoney better? Or Boushay?" Nora asked. "One thing I don't like about 'Mahoney' is that it rhymes with 'baloney.' What rhymes with Boushay?"

Without hesitation, Dylan said, "Death ray."

They both laughed softly, then were silent.

"Sometimes I can still feel it," Nora finally said. "Like it's there. If I'm not doing anything but just sitting still. Or when I'm waking up. It's like I can feel the skin itching. Or sometimes it feels like my fingers are burning or someone is squeezing them tight."

"I'm gonna build a really cool hand for you. Like the L-hand 980 that Luke Skywalker had, but a real-life one. It'll be a cybernetic hand with as many fingers as you want, and it can be strong enough to crush rocks. Or if you want to play the guitar, it'll be able to do that too. It's pretty amazing what you can make now."

"I want to be able to climb again," Nora said. "I miss climbing."

*   *   *   *   *

418

Joan's morning at the Giffordshire House began at 7:00 when she woke up hungry. The bedroom of her suite had an up-close view of Puget Sound, and she saw a pair of ferries sailing between Vashon Island and the Fauntleroy terminal, as well as a large container ship moving north from the Port of Tacoma on its way to the Strait of Juan de Fuca.

She was the first to show up at the bed and breakfast's cozy dining room, where fresh scones had just been delivered from Roy's. She helped herself to one and spread a generous layer of marionberry jam on each half. She also had a mug of homemade hot chocolate, followed by scrambled eggs, locally made sausage, and a cup of strong coffee with cream.

After breakfast, she stopped at the front desk to see the manager, who had just arrived for work. He was kind enough to allow Joan to take two candles scented with piñon and cedarwood from their supply room at no charge. Then she set out on her walk up the hill to the Mahoney home.

She liked a bracing walk in the morning. It was the same kind of ritual she kept back in Ipswich throughout most of the year. Every morning, with rare exceptions, she walked for an hour along Plum Point Road, by the salt marshes where bitter winds would blow in winter, and past Emerson Orchards, where in fall she would stop twice a week for a bag of fresh fruit or vegetables.

The farm grew several varieties of apples, pears and other fruit. They also grew vegetables, and made jams, jellies, home-baked pies, and hard cider and wine from the harvest of their own fields and orchards. Joan and her immigrant parents had been lifelong friends with two generations of Emersons, and she would often consult with them on matters of growing and pruning.

On the days when she used to teach morning classes at Salem State, she would wrap up her walk by 9:00 to be at school before 10:00. The only occasions when she broke her habit was for foul weather or sickness.

Since arriving in Seattle a week earlier, she had walked the mile and a quarter from her bed and breakfast up the hill to the Mahoney home at a brisk pace. When she arrived that morning at 9:00, the first thing she did was light the two scented candles as amends for her dinner-gone-wrong.

The stench from the night before had already dissipated enough for doors to be closed. On top of that, Anne had just burned two pieces of sourdough toast, so whatever unpleasantness remained was almost completely masked.

Joan was in the middle of apologizing to Anne when she was interrupted by a commotion in the backyard. Despite her cast, Nora had managed to climb halfway up the maple tree. She had dragged a small stepladder from the garage and propped it against the tree trunk to help her reach the lowest limbs. The bigger problem was that she had arrived at an impasse where she couldn't go any higher, but she also was having difficulty reversing course and climbing down. Matthew was standing under the tree and calling up to her, telling her to wait until he climbed up to help her descend.

Soon Anne and Joan were standing on either side of Matthew, offering conflicting directions.

"Get down here right now, Nora!" Anne yelled.

"No," Matthew called. "Stay right there. I'm coming up."

"Nora, you need to climb down," Joan said.

Within a matter of seconds, the situation escalated to where Matthew and Anne were talking past each other. When Joan began peppering Matthew from behind with her unsolicited opinions, he decided to leave the two of them on the ground and make his way up the tree. Once he reached Nora, he got a firm hold of the back of her sweatshirt and guided her slowly down, limb by limb, until he could safely lower her into Anne's arms.

Things seemed to have arrived at a resolution to the problem and a calming to all nerves when Joan let slip one last bit of commentary. Anne was escorting Nora back to the house, so only Matthew heard her.

"If you want your marriage to last," Joan said, "you may want to be a little less vociferous when disagreeing with your wife in public."

Matthew's tolerance for Joan's feedback had exceeded all limits by that point, so he fired back immediately, "I don't think I need any advice from you on how to make a marriage last, Joan."

Even though made in haste, it was a remark designed to cut deep and it did just that. The first indication was Joan's slack mouth, followed by a gasp. As her mouth slowly closed, Matthew saw her lips tighten and he sensed a firm resolve settling in.

He had made a mistake. A big one. He instantly knew it, and now he somehow had to try and walk back his comment. But flashing through his mind were timeless idioms, like Rubicons being crossed and dice being cast.

"Listen, Joan, I'm sorry. Really, I shouldn't have said that." Matthew paused, as it seemed his words were registering with Joan. In her face he saw a shift in her attitude, a loosening of the tension, even a weak smile emerging.

It was a brilliant feint on Joan's part, and she countered with a piercing thrust. "Say what you will about my marriage, Matthew, but my understanding is that your father was no paragon of fidelity."

The not-so-subtle reference was to the fact that Matthew's father had cheated on his mother. He did so more than once, including when she was dying from cancer.

Matthew was stunned, not so much by the comment itself, but by how quickly it shot out of Joan's mouth. It was like a bullet she had kept in the chamber for many years, waiting ever so patiently for the right moment to use it.

He was tempted, very tempted, to take the discussion up a notch by mentioning that when Anne was 11, she had stated her wish to live with her father after the divorce, rather than stay with her mother. He couldn't, however, because Joan was smart enough to seize the moment and declare a silent victory by walking away.

*   *   *   *   *

Monday, July 10, 2000

Anne was the first out of bed on Monday morning. She had a 9:00 flight to Anchorage and she was a notoriously slow packer, even for a short trip that would have her returning home in less than two days. After arriving in Anchorage, she'd be having dinner downtown at the Glacier Brewhouse with members of the BG development team. On Tuesday she'd have a few pro forma interviews and a meeting to set up her onboarding schedule.

Dinner with the team was something that usually followed the interviews, assuming they were successful. However, in Anne's case, she had already gotten approval from Jacob Lenz and others at BG who had seen her job evaluations from her time on the Slope. Some even remembered her father. Dinner would be a chance for Anne's new team to welcome her and introduce themselves.

While Anne packed, Matthew got breakfast ready for everyone. He was moving a little slow after spending Sunday with the Engebretsens in Ballard celebrating Tivoli Days. It was an annual event that featured Scandinavian music, along with a slew of outdoor craft vendors selling everything from beer and food to T-shirts sporting the Icelandic flag. Ballard's Nordic Heritage Museum was also commemorating the Year of the Viking, which increased the number of times Mr. Engebretsen insisted on making toasts.

Dylan was the first one downstairs, and he took a plate of scrambled eggs and toast into the dining room. Two and a half minutes later, he dropped his empty plate in the sink and headed out to his friend Samuel's house, where the two would continue playing a new computer game they had started the day before.

Anne spent a few minutes upstairs in Nora's room before joining Matthew in the kitchen.

"I told Nora that she has to dress herself this morning," Anne said. "She needs to start learning how to do it on her own, and the sooner the better. Which means she'll probably struggle at first, but that's OK. It's a hump she has to get over. My mom was teaching her how to do it, but since she flew home sooner than she was scheduled to because someone made a comment that she didn't appreciate…"

Matthew interrupted, "Which was preceded by a comment that I didn't appreciate and followed by another comment that I didn't appreciate…"

"OK, fine," Anne said, then looked Matthew in the eyes. "My point is that Nora has to learn how to get dressed all by herself."

Matthew nodded. "Sure," he said. "I need to clean out the Subaru before we go to the airport. Give me five minutes."

When Matthew came back inside, Anne passed him on the way out with her bags. As she did, she said, "Tell Nora we need to go now. I don't want to be late for this flight."

Matthew headed up the stairs and ducked his head as he walked into Nora's room. She was sitting on the edge of her bed, crying quietly. Her jeans were not zipped or buttoned, and she had only managed to push her rainbow belt through two belt loops.

Matthew sat down beside her and put a hand on her back. "Hey there, sweetie."

Nora turned to him and tried to speak, but her voice was shaking.

"Come on now, what's with all the tears?"

Nora took a few deep breath before saying, "Mom yelled at me...she yelled at me that I had to dress myself, but I can't..."

"I didn't hear anybody yelling. So, have you tried doing it?"

"I tried, OK? And I can't, and she said that I have to do it myself from now on..."

Matthew said, "Look, we'll work on it this afternoon, alright? When there's no rush. So why don't you stand up and let me fix your belt. Then we'll get Mom to the airport."

With her left hand, Nora gripped her father's shoulder and stood. Then Matthew zipped and buttoned her jeans. He was threading Nora's belt through the final loop in her pants when Anne stepped into the doorway.

"Matt," she said.

When he turned to face her, she continued, "She needs to be doing that on her own."

His first thought was to state the obvious. They could either get to the airport on time, or they could wait for Nora to dress herself. But something told him he should be very careful, so he simply said, "We're gonna work on that later."

Chapter 3
Hard Callus

Ossification takes place during the third phase, with osteoblasts converting the soft callus into a material that forms a solid connection between the bone fragments. Referred to as hard callus, it lacks the full strength of finished bone but is able to stand up to external pressures.

Friday, July 21, 2000

High tide in Puget Sound on Friday morning was a little after 8:00, so Matthew and Dylan showed up at Lincoln Park around 8:30 and walked out to the point. Since it was a weekday, there were only a half dozen people fishing from the beach. Most of them were on the northern side of the point, which Matthew and Dylan knew was the preferred place to stand when the tide was flowing out. As baitfish moved north along the shore with the outgoing tide, the salmon would be waiting just around the point to catch them. It created something of a gauntlet for the baitfish, making it one of the most ideal spots to fish if you didn't own a boat, or have a buddy who owned one.

In the first half hour, they saw two sockeyes caught by people fishing on either side of them. One person had been using a pink Buzz Bomb lure, as Matthew and Dylan were, and the other one used a squid lure. Dylan had one bite with the Buzz Bomb on his second cast but nothing since. He even asked his dad to cast a few times for him to get his lure out farther. After the third time, Matthew told Dylan that he was a big boy and had to cast on his own, even if it meant his lure would splash down 25 yards away, not 40 or 50 yards like his dad's.

"I think I'm gonna try a spoon," Dylan said. He went to their tackle box and found a green-and-silver one.

After Matthew reeled in his line, he told Dylan that he was going to use the bathroom, which was next to the nearby public pool. Three minutes later, as Matthew was walking back to the beach, he heard some excited chatter, the telltale sign that somebody had a fish on. As he neared a line of large boulders that formed a breakwater, he saw that it was his son.

Dylan knew enough to reel in the fish at a steady pace, while keeping a constant tautness in the line. Local fishing regulations required that all hooks be barbless to give salmon a fighting chance. A hook without barbs meant that once you hooked a salmon, it could easily slip off if you slackened the line for even a second.

"Good job, D-Man!" Matthew called after jumping onto the sand. Dylan was standing near the water's edge. His focus was on the fish, and he didn't take his eyes off his line as he continued reeling it in. Other people on the beach shifted their attention from their own lines to enjoy Dylan's drama.

Matthew stepped to his son's side and gauged that the salmon was getting very close to shore. "OK, when you can see it, you need to walk backwards up the beach and hold that line tight."

"I know! I know!" Dylan yelled, without breaking his focus.

Matthew caught a flash of silver 15 yards out in the water as the fish showed its side. It was a salmon, and it was big. "Alright, I see it, Dylan. Time to bring it in. Bring it well up on the beach."

"I know! I know!" Dylan repeated. He stopped reeling and began walking back toward the breakwater, taking slow steps in the soft sand.

Because the tide was still only an hour past being high, the stretch of sand between water and breakwater was short. Matthew could see that Dylan would soon back into one of the boulders. He turned back to the water's edge just as the salmon splashed out of the water and onto the sand. It was a sockeye, and it was at least two feet long, bigger than any salmon he and Dylan had ever caught from shore.

Just as Dylan sensed he might be getting close to the rocks behind him, he shifted his attention away from the fish for the first time since the fight began. The tip of his rod dipped slightly and created a moment of looseness in the line. The salmon continued its instinctive flopping, and with one twist it took advantage of the momentary lack of tension to free itself from the hook. The silver-and-green spoon popped out of its mouth.

As soon as Matthew realized what had happened, he ran toward the fish to try and push it farther up the beach and away from the water. He was only a step from it when the sockeye managed to flop its way back

425

into shallow water, regain its senses and quickly swim away. It showed one last silver flash before disappearing into the Sound.

"Oh hell! What the hell!" Dylan yelled. As he stared out at the water, he began walking toward his father.

Someone nearby called out, "Damn, that was a big fish."

"He was a really nice one," someone else said. "You almost had him, kid."

"It was my fault, D-Man," Matthew said. "I told you to start backing up too soon. I should have waited until it was closer to the beach."

Matthew wasn't sure if Dylan had heard him. He was standing right next to his son, but Dylan had a blankness to his expression as he continued staring out at the water. Then Matthew saw a change in his face, as if he was being overcome by emotion. It surprised Matthew because they had lost plenty of fish before. And Dylan always shrugged it off within a matter of seconds.

Dylan took a couple of quick breaths and looked like he might start sobbing. Matthew put his arm on his son's shoulder and spoke softly. "It's alright, D-Man. We'll be doing plenty of fishing up in Alaska. The salmon are all big up there."

Dylan didn't seem to hear a word of what his father had said. He turned to him and asked. "Why did it have to happen, Dad? The whole thing is so unfair."

*   *   *   *   *

Monday, July 24, 2000

It was 7:00 when Matthew arrived at Maria's Bakery, which was tucked away in a Burien strip mall. Diego was there sitting in a booth, sipping coffee and helping himself to a plate of pastries. Matthew picked up a black coffee at the counter, then joined Diego, who pushed the plate of pastries in front of him.

"I saved you some good ones," Diego said.

Matthew looked down at the plate. He didn't think he recognized any of the pastries, but they all looked delicious.

"Conchas," Diego said, pointing at two pastries in the shape of a shell with cracked sugar on top. There were also pastelitos—soft cakes with strawberry jam and a dusting of coconut—and cheese empanadas.

"I'm game," Matthew said and took one of each.

A few minutes later, Sal arrived and joined them in the booth. "It's gonna be a long day," he said. "A long, hot day. You've both got jobs in Burien." He turned to Matthew and said, "Diego has three guys now from his old crew." He paused and pushed a work order to Diego. "You and I went over some of this yesterday. You've got two small places. A ranch to reshingle and a torch down. Both straightforward and simple, since you and your crew haven't worked together for a while. You've got enough propane, right?"

Diego nodded.

"Matt, your crew has a reshingle on Marine View Drive. A two-story place with a garage and barn. You were with me when I gave them an estimate last week." Sal handed him a work order.

"So, two things," Matthew said, "the Professor's on vacation this week, and I have to leave at 2:30 to take Nora to Swedish."

"That's fine. You guys will need to deal with anything that comes up today. I set up an account at Home Depot under Camacho Roofing & Insulation. Just show them your ID. You're both authorized up to $500. Anything more, you need to call me. I'll be tied up with my brother downtown. We're gonna spend some quality time with a business lawyer, then city hall, then the DMV, the county office, the insurance company and one other place I can't remember."

Diego looked at Matthew and said with a straight face, "All air-conditioned."

Matthew nodded and smiled.

"Hey, fuck you both," Sal said. "I'm the one who's making it rain these days."

*   *   *   *   *

The last place Matthew wanted to be on the hottest day of summer was a roof, where the sun burned from above and dark shingles radiated heat from below. The good news was that the large house they were reshingling was close enough to the water to be a few degrees cooler than if it was just a quarter mile away. The bad news was that Matthew was working the south-facing side of the house. That exposed him to more direct sun and more reflected sunlight off the water because the house was situated where the coastline made a sharp inward turn. No matter how much sunscreen he applied, he knew the chances were good that by the end of the day his skin would have a pink glow to it.

The ever-reliable Buck, who was supposed to be shingling the south side with Matthew, didn't show up at 8:00. At 8:30 Matthew called his cellphone and got no answer, so he left a message. He left another message at 9:00 and a third at 9:30. All morning long, as Matthew sweated and swore, he listened to the nail guns of Lyka and the Major firing away on the other side of the house, the cooler side of the house. With every passing hour, Matthew could tell that they were moving higher on their side than he was on his. And with every passing hour, the sun burned a little stronger, and the dark shingles radiated more heat.

Lyka and the Major offered to swap places with him, but he refused. He had picked the south side when they all showed up to work that day, and he knew he'd never live it down if he waved a white flag because he couldn't take the heat. And if Buck was there, they'd be finishing their side by noon or shortly thereafter. Then, at the hottest part of the day, they could move on to the barn or the garage, both of which were shaded by tall Douglas firs.

As it was, Matthew had only finished a little more than half of the south side as the noon hour approached. He had just lugged two more bundles of shingles up the ladder when he heard Lyka calling.

"He's here, Matt," she yelled. All the guns stopped firing. Lyka walked up to the peak and called down to Matthew. "Buck is here."

"Thanks," Matthew called up to her. He wiped his brow, then pulled a water bottle from his back pocket. It had gotten so warm, that he got zero refreshment value from gulping down the remaining few ounces. After tossing the empty plastic bottle off the roof, he noticed Lyka still watching him.

"It's really getting hot on this side, isn't it?" she asked.

"No," Matthew said. "It's actually a little chilly. Would you bring me a wool coat when you get a chance?"

428

Lyka laughed. "How about a cold water?"

Matthew smiled. "Well, if you can't find the coat, I guess so."

After she disappeared, Matthew heard a rattling on the aluminum ladder leading up to his side of the roof. Eventually Buck appeared, wearing his tool belt and holding a nail gun, which he laid down. He gave Matthew a weak "hey" before reaching into his tool pouch for a nail coil. Matthew walked down the roof, and when he reached Buck he saw how red and puffy his eyes were.

"So, what the fuck happened?" Matthew asked.

"Sorry I'm running late…"

"You lose your phone or something?"

Buck patted his front pocket. "No."

Buck's attitude annoyed Matthew more than the fact that he was late and hadn't called. "Then why the fuck can't you give me a heads-up? I must have called you like five fucking times. And this is the hottest goddamn day of the summer, and I'm stuck shingling solo on the hot fucking side of this house."

Matthew was surprised at how pissed off he sounded, even to himself, and how quickly Buck went from drowsy to alert.

"I'm really sorry, Matt. It's been a bad morning…it was a really bad night."

Lyka called to Matthew from the peak and pushed a chilled water bottle in his direction. It rolled down the roof and into Matthew's lowered hand.

"Why?" Matthew asked Buck with obvious impatience. "A woman?" he added, although as soon as he asked it, he realized how improbable that scenario was.

"My website…something attacked my website…" Buck took a deep breath. When he continued, it sounded like he was on the verge of crying. "I think my website is ruined. I was up all night with technical support trying to fix it, and they said all the galleries…all the photos…they're gone. The files are all corrupted. Or deleted. I had a lot of gigabytes, Matt. It took me so long to find all those images. Like two whole years." Buck paused to take a long, deep breath. "It was one of the best collections of porn anywhere in the world. I know because I've seen them all, and now it's all just gone."

Buck squeezed his eyes tight and put his hands to his head for a second, as if he were trying to stop it from exploding. Matthew was unmoved by the sob story and honestly wanted to punch Buck. But then he caught a flash of something terrifying. It was every roofer's nightmare, and it was about to happen. Buck swayed slightly. Then his eyes shot open, and he threw out his hands in a futile attempt to regain his balance.

Matthew saw the sudden panic in Buck's eyes as he began to pitch backwards ever so slowly. He was standing two feet from the edge of the roof with nothing to stop him except a cement walkway two stories below.

Matthew reacted instinctively by shifting his weight back and shooting his hands in Buck's direction. Just as his water bottle hit the shingles, he got a firm grasp on Buck's shirt and pulled hard. Buck's momentum countered the force, however, and Matthew felt himself stop in his backward movement. Then felt himself being slowly tugged forward.

It was happening very fast, but Matthew knew he was being drawn toward a tipping point where he'd either have to let go of Buck or be pulled over the edge with him. The thought shot through his mind that he had kids, and he needed to be alive and healthy to take care of them. Fortunately, it didn't come to that. Matthew weighed a good 50 pounds more than Buck, and in the next second that was enough to make the difference. Matthew's forward movement stopped, then both of them fell back onto the roof.

They hit with a thud that made the nail guns on the other side of the house go silent. Buck landed on his side and slowly rolled onto all fours. "Oh shit," he said and blinked several times.

Matthew had landed on his back and was staring at Buck. "Are you OK?"

Buck nodded and carefully got to his feet. "Thanks, Matt. I'm OK. Wow, that was close, huh?" He peeked over the edge of the roof, down at the cement walkway, and laughed nervously. "I'm OK," he repeated. "I can work."

Matthew pointed toward the ladder. "Not today. I want you off the roof."

Buck began to protest, but Matthew shut him down. "Get off the roof. Call me later, and we'll talk."

The Major appeared at the peak and called down, "Hey, what happened over here?"

Matthew smiled and called back, "Tell Lyka you guys get to finish the hot side."

*   *   *   *   *

They hit traffic on their way to Swedish Hospital, but Matthew had added 15 minutes to their estimated drive time so that he and Nora reached the waiting room with a few minutes to spare.

"Are you excited to get the cast off?" Matthew asked. An office visit and X-rays on the previous Friday showed that both bones had mended sufficiently to have the cast removed.

Nora seemed distracted as she looked down at the pale purple cast. It had grown paler from the summer sun and was now completely covered in Nora's artistic creations. "I want it off, but I don't want them to cut into any of my drawings. They'll let me keep it, won't they?"

"I think so."

"Hey, when is my godmother coming to visit us? You told me it was gonna be soon." Her godmother was Kathleen Sutliff, who lived back in South Boston. She was like an older sister or aunt to Matthew, and she had been a part of his life since he was a little kid. Having her be Nora's godmother was a way to keep that connection strong.

"A week from today," Matthew said. "I talked to her Saturday. She's really looking forward to seeing you."

Nora's name was called, and they were led into an examination room by a technician. She was a young woman named Kendra, and she gave Nora a big smile before explaining how the cast saw worked. "It doesn't spin like other saws. It moves from side to side, so it won't cut your arm. And it's attached to a vacuum that catches all the dust. It makes a loud noise, but you don't have to worry about that. You let me know if you feel your arm getting too warm, OK, and we'll take a break."

"Can you cut around all the animals and things, so you don't cut any in half?"

"Well..." Kendra said and paused for dramatic effect.

"She really can't avoid it, honey," Matthew said.

"Sorry about that, Nora. I think I'll end up cutting a few in half," Kendra said.

Nora considered Kendra's words, then extended the cast toward her. "OK."

She and Matthew were both mesmerized as they watched Kendra working the saw in a straight line that cut several animals and objects in half, then even more when she moved to the other side. After she finished with the fiberglass shell, she used scissors to cut the padding underneath.

Nora said nothing as Kendra worked, and when everything was removed, she stared unblinkingly at her newly exposed skin, which was fairer than the rest of her arm.

"Ow," Nora said. "I can't move my elbow."

"Don't worry," Kendra said. "It's stiff because it's been in the cast, but it'll be OK soon." She walked Nora over to a sink and carefully washed her arm. "The skin will be tender," Kendra said to Matthew. "Make sure she's gentle when she washes it. When you see Dr. Gottlieb in a few minutes, she'll give you more information about everything."

After drying Nora's arm with a towel, Kendra smiled and said, "There you go. Good as new."

The words struck an odd note with Matthew. When he looked at Nora, he saw her expression change quickly.

"No, it's not," Nora said with sudden irritation. "It's not good as new. My hand is still gone." She flashed an angry look at Kendra.

Matthew knew it was just a slip of the tongue on Kendra's part. They exchanged a glance, and he saw her obvious embarrassment. As she began to apologize, Matthew reached out to Nora. "Honey, she didn't mean it that way."

Nora's anger passed as quickly as it had appeared. She turned around to face the examination table and focused on the two halves of the fiberglass cast that had been an intimate part of her arm and an intimate part of her life for the last five and a half weeks. "I changed my mind," she said in a disinterested voice. "I don't want to keep it."

*   *   *   *   *

Saturday, July 29, 2000

It was most likely the last movie night that the Mahoneys would throw in their backyard before their move north, which meant it would be their last movie night ever. Everyone in the family was running up against different "lasts" in their West Seattle lives.

Nora played in her last summer league soccer game that Friday night. It was the first game where she was allowed to play both periods in her favorite position—forward—because her parents and her coach agreed she was up to the demands as long as she didn't play in a way that was too physical. Regardless, Anne insisted she wrap her right forearm in a protective bandage. On the ride home, Nora began to cry as she listed off the many friends she wouldn't be able to see in the coming school year and the fall soccer season.

Dylan didn't play soccer, and he didn't like watching Nora's games. But since her accident, he had been by her side much of the time and went to her remaining games, so he was there to comfort her on the ride home after the last one.

As for his own "lasts," Dylan had been attending a summer astronomy program at South Seattle Community College with his friend Samuel. The last meeting was in the coming week, and the two were on the phone regularly, conjuring up ways to stay connected. Dylan had done some research and found an online astronomy program and an astronomy club that they could both join. They were also coordinating a visitation schedule that revolved less around school breaks and more around the movement and positioning of celestial bodies in their respective locales.

A few days earlier, Anne had gotten together with girlfriends from her engineering job before her stint on the North Slope. Every month, they would meet up for some kind of activity. That had ended when Anne went up to Alaska. Rejoining the group that Wednesday for one last gathering reminded her how much she missed her old friends. And how much she would miss them when she left Seattle. Anne was surprised to hear that she wasn't the only one saying goodbye to the group. Allison Riordin announced that she, too, was leaving West Seattle in less than three weeks for a new job. To Anne, it reinforced the idea that things and people in the Mahoney world were shifting.

Matthew didn't necessarily mind big changes, but he definitely didn't like thinking too much ahead of time about the life he was leaving behind, so he decided on a strategy of denial. He was picking up as many bartending shifts as he could and roofing most weekdays so that his mind would stay focused on the here and now until the moment came to lock the front door for the last time and head to Alaska. In that way, he hoped the experience would be like a big concert when the final encore ended, the lights came up, and all you were left with was a faint ringing in your ears and the impression that it had been one amazing show.

He had given away his Saturday night bar shift to get everything ready for movie night and to pick up food, a quarter keg of Elysian Pale Ale and two videos. The kids' movie was an easy decision: *Toy Story*. The choice for the adult movie was more elusive. Matthew and Anne knew that Nora would insist on staying up for the second movie, so it had to be appropriate for her. Anne felt that *Sleepy Hollow* would be too much for an eight-year-old. After a lot of back and forth, they landed on *Beetlejuice*.

But when Matthew got to the local video store, both the VHS tape and DVD of *Beetlejuice* had been checked out. He called the only other West Seattle video store close enough to stay on his schedule for prepping dinner. They said their computer showed one copy available, but when he got there the clerk couldn't find it. Matthew made an executive decision and rented *Sleepy Hollow,* hoping Anne might change her mind about it.

* * * * *

Anne wanted to do something special for the final movie night, something she had never done before, so she spent Saturday afternoon in the kitchen. Her friend Miranda had baked small chocolate soufflés for girls' night earlier that week. The soufflés were incredible, and Miranda said they were easy to make. So easy that Anne decided to tackle a recipe that her grandmother had used to make French macarons. She had pulled the recipe out of her grandmother's cookbook several times over the years, but she had always returned it without baking the macarons. Anne hated to admit to anyone outside of the family that she was not a fan of baking. In fact, it was one of the few things in life that intimidated her.

She tried to follow the recipe precisely: Sifting the confectioners' sugar and almond meal together with the salt, then passing them through a sieve twice to remove any lumps; combining the egg whites with superfine castor sugar in a bowl; whisking for two minutes; and adding cream of tartar. Now she had to continue whisking until she saw sharp peaks forming. To confirm the stiffness of the mixture, she was also supposed to turn the bowl upside down without the mixture falling out.

Just when the muscles in her forearm began going numb, she felt a tap on her shoulder. She turned around to see Dylan staring at her.

"I'm in the middle of something, Dylan. What do you want?"

"What are you making? Is it food?"

The question seemed odd, even coming from her son. "I'm in the kitchen. I've got..." She pointed at all the items scattered across the counter. "...all these food ingredients. So yes, I'm making food. I'm going to bake French macarons. It's my Nana B's recipe, but first I have to prepare everything. By the way, where is Nora? Weren't you with her in the backyard?"

"She's in the tree. She climbed up there herself, and it seemed like it wasn't a problem for her."

Anne looked through the window and saw a shape moving among the branches halfway up. "She knows she's not supposed to be climbing yet. Why did she disobey me?"

"Dad said she could."

Anne sighed. "Oh, that is just great." She watched two of Nora's friends come running into the yard and climb up the maple.

"Your father will be home soon. He can deal with it," Anne said before turning back to her macaron batter. Sensation had returned to her forearm, so she began whisking again. She wasn't seeing sharp peaks or anything close to sharp peaks, so she continued. A minute later, she stopped when she caught Dylan out of the corner of her eye. He was standing in the same spot, just staring at her.

"What now?" Anne asked.

"We're not really good at making food, are we?"

Anne stared back at him.

Dylan continued, "I mean, as a family, we're not really good at making our own food. Except for Dad maybe. He knows how to grill pretty good."

"Well, I'm not grilling, Dylan. I'm baking. It's a lot more difficult than grilling. Anybody can grill. You generate the heat, you slap food down, maybe flip it. Then you stare at it until it looks or feels done, at which point you remove it from the heat. That's grilling. I used to do it as a cook at Donovan's in downtown Seattle. And at Roy's, when I was pregnant with you. I understand it the way a professional does. Grilling is simple. Baking, on the other hand, is more challenging because a lot of what has to happen is unseen or, more importantly, variable. As an engineer, I get that."

Anne looked for something to illustrate her point, so she pulled two eggs out of the carton sitting on the counter. She held the two eggs in front of Dylan and asked, "How many egg whites are inside these eggs?"

He hesitated, as if it were a trick question. "Well, two? Because you're holding two eggs."

Anne showed a slight grin and shook her head slowly. "Because these are very large eggs, much larger than average, they could be considered to contain three egg whites. Or perhaps 2.7 egg whites. You see? That's one of the variables. One of many variables that have to be taken into account. Like our elevation, which happens to be about 500 feet above sea level, and the accuracy of the thermostat in our oven." Anne paused to point at the glass window in the oven door. "Every oven thermostat is off by a little or a lot. The temperature shown is either too high or too low. Are you following me? And every oven has different heat zones inside. Another variable, or a whole separate set of variables, ones that are extremely difficult to know and to monitor.

"And there are even more variables. Some we can control; some are beyond our control. Like, whatever the humidity is today. All of the variables affect the outcome of the process. They all conspire against us when we attempt to bake something, like French macarons. My Nana B understood this, and believe me, I saw her frustration more than once when her recipes..."

Dylan interrupted, "Mom, can I go now?"

Anne suddenly realized how much she had been talking and how long she had been away from the whisking. What effect would the pause create? What possible damage had it done? Maybe she'd have to start over. "Go ahead. Just remember what you've learned today. Grilling is simple. Baking is complicated. Know your variables."

She picked up the whisk. After working the batter for a minute, she began to see what might be described not as sharp peaks but more like soft dunes. It was slightly encouraging, so she continued. Once again, just when she felt like she was making progress, she was interrupted.

"What are you doing?" Matthew asked.

Anne turned around and saw him standing there. She hadn't even heard him come through the front door. "Oh, hi. I'm making macarons. French macarons. Nana B's recipe."

Matthew hesitated before saying simply, "Oh."

Anne was about to ask what he really meant by that when she remembered something. "So why did you tell Nora that she could climb the tree? We agreed she should wait a week or so."

"I didn't tell her she could climb the tree."

Anne pointed toward the living room. "Well, your son said you did. Why don't you go find him and see what that's all about?"

As Matthew began to leave the kitchen, Anne noticed two videos sitting on the counter. She walked over and saw that the one on top was *Sleepy Hollow*. "Hey Matt, what's this?"

When he returned to the kitchen, Anne held up the videotape and continued, "We agreed not to show this because of Nora."

"I tried two places. They didn't have *Beetlejuice*. I was running out of time…"

"I really don't think she should see this, Matt."

"Fine," Matthew said. "People love *Star Wars*. We own the original trilogy. We'll show one of those."

As he left the kitchen, Anne said in a low voice, "Great. *Star Wars*. Again."

Dylan wasn't hard to find. He was sitting at the computer in the living room. Matthew walked up behind him and tapped him on the shoulder. "I need to talk to you outside for two minutes," he said.

Dylan turned to his father. "I'm in the middle of something."

Although Dylan had been a really difficult child in his early years, Matthew and Anne were happy with how he had grown out of his bad behavior and was now, generally, an easy child whom they could trust. But there had been a couple of instances lately when Dylan was caught skirting the truth, to put it mildly. Matthew wanted to nip whatever it was in the bud if he could. "Well, you're in the middle of something else with me, so let's go."

When they were standing in the front yard, Matthew asked, "Why did you tell your mom that I said it was OK for Nora to climb the tree?"

Dylan seemed to be trying on different expressions before settling on one and said, "Well, I thought I might have heard you say…"

Matthew interrupted, "Don't do that, Dylan."

"Don't do what?"

"Don't try to cover up a lie with another lie."

Dylan seemed stunned that his attempt could be so transparent. He looked down the street to where Hadley Epps was pushing a reel mower around what was officially the smallest front lawn in the neighborhood. Then he looked back at his father. "She really wants to climb the tree, Dad. I watched her go up, and she's climbing really good. She was hooking her elbow around branches like this." Dylan paused to show his father. "She's not gonna get hurt. I know she's not. She needs to be climbing."

"I'll go talk to her. And you: go inside and apologize to your mother, and tell her why. I'm gonna ask her later, so you better tell her the truth. Tell her I'm talking to Nora and seeing if it's OK for her to be up in the tree."

"OK," Dylan said.

"And you're off the computer for the rest of the weekend."

Dylan protested to the point where his father informed him that the end date to the computer ban remained flexible.

By the time Matthew walked around to the backyard and climbed into the lowest branches of the maple, he saw that there were four other girls with Nora.

"We're having a party," Nora called down. "You're not invited."

"I want you to come down here, Nora."

Nora answered in a raised voice. "I'm not coming down!"

"Come down here for one minute," Matthew said, pointing at where he was standing. He paused to stare at the thickness of the limb and considered the possibility it might have rot. He dismissed the idea. "If you don't, then this whole party is over and everybody has to go home, and you have to go to your room."

Nora said nothing but slowly began to make her way down to Matthew's branch. He watched her moving, and she seemed to have a good handle on the gymnastics involved with climbing two-armed but one-handed. When she reached his branch, he said to her, "You know, your brother's in trouble because he lied for you."

"I didn't tell him to lie for me," she said.

"Well, you better sound a little more grateful the next time you see him. Now let me see your arm."

Nora was wearing a T-shirt, and when she extended her right arm Matthew saw that the crook of it was red, raw and scratched, but not too badly. "OK, I want you to go into the house and grab a sweatshirt. You need to protect this arm when you're climbing."

Nora's reaction was swift and loud. "I can't go down! I'm having a party!"

She stared at him with a fire in her sharp green eyes that reminded him of Anne's intense stare when she was deeply irritated. He felt like smiling but kept a straight face. He knew her audience was split between himself and her friends watching silently, and she had to put up a good front for them. "Then you need to stay right here on this limb until I get back with your sweatshirt. I'll toss it up, and you put it on. If I see you up here and you're not protecting that arm, you're coming down immediately. Understand?"

Nora replied with a single nod.

*   *   *   *   *

The final movie night officially began shortly after 5:30 when Janice showed up. She and her husband lived four doors down and had a woodworking shop in their garage. In her arms, she carried a going-away gift, which Anne unwrapped. It was a sockeye salmon that Janice had crafted from exotic cocobolo wood. Anne was stunned by its beauty. The dense wood was a deep red with lateral bands of orange, yellow and brown. The salmon curved in a way that captured the energy of motion through water, and was finished with oil that gave the cocobolo a subtle sheen. On the back of the salmon were mounting loops, so it could be hung easily.

The carving was just shy of two feet long. When Anne lifted it, she was surprised at its heft. "This is amazing, Janice. Thank you so much. We'll be hanging this above the fireplace in the cabin."

"Send us a picture," Janice said.

"Will do," Anne said. The she remembered something and asked, "Hey, when exactly is Kayla's birthday party? I have it marked down as next weekend, but I don't know the day and time."

"Didn't you hear?" Janice replied. "They're moving to Atlanta. They're flying down next weekend, so the party is cancelled. Or it's being postponed until later in August, but I'm afraid you'll be gone by then."

"Oh no. I'll have to stop by this week with something for her." Then Anne added, "Everybody seems to be moving these days."

"Well, I think you started it," Janice said as she walked to the other end of the kitchen to grab a carrot stick, stopping suddenly when she spotted a large container of hummus sitting on the counter. She spun it around and read the label. It was from a store called Sahani's in Montlake. Janice grabbed a spoon from a drawer and took a taste.

Anne looked over and saw what Janice was doing, but it was too late.

"OK, I think I just figured something out here," Janice said with her back to Anne. She turned around and held up the container. "This is the homemade hummus you've been making for the last, what, five years?"

Anne showed a nervous smile, then laughed. "Ah, yes…that is the hummus that…yes, sorry about that." Anne clutched her hands awkwardly as she considered what to say next. "The thing is…we're really just not that good at making food. You know, as a family."

Janice turned around and reached for a bowl in one of the cabinets. Then she turned back and smiled. "Don't worry," she said. "Your secret's safe with me."

As more people showed up, so did two more going-away gifts: The first was a lamp from their friend Jeremy. It featured a golden cherub holding a torch in its left hand. Jeremy had done a convincing job of mimicking the cherub from the Titanic exhibit. Above the torch, which glowed, but not too brightly, was a lampshade and bulb that cast a warm light. The second gift was a trident maple bonsai tree from Hadley, or more

440

accurately the promise of a Bonsai tree. She had called a nursery in Anchorage and ordered it to be delivered to their new address in a couple of weeks, so they wouldn't have to deal with the hassle of packing it.

Cloud cover moved in after 7:00, and a backyard that was still dappled with the last sunlight of the day shifted in a moment to premature dusk. A half hour later, it was deemed dim enough to begin the kids' movie. With his grilling duties finished for the evening, Matthew sat down with Lyka and the Major. Sal was on his way, and Buck, who was working overtime rebuilding his business, would stop by for a beer later.

Buck had come back to work that Friday when Matthew declared him once again sane, or as sane as Buck could ever be, but he had remained quiet on what exactly had destroyed his database of porn.

The Major, however, had just come from Buck's apartment, where he learned of the cause. "He got infected with the 'I Love You' virus. Or his computers did."

At first Matthew didn't know if the Major was serious, then he was confused. Lyka responded with laughter.

"Technically, it's a worm," the Major said. "Buck opened an attachment that said 'A Love Letter for You' and it multiplied and spread everywhere. It destroyed all of his pictures and replaced them with copies of itself."

"He thought it was a love letter?" Matthew asked.

"I heard about that on the news," Lyka said. "It's going around..." She broke into a laugh again, started to apologize for it, then stopped herself. "OK, it's kind of ironic, don't you think?"

"Kind of?" the Major asked. "How about completely."

Sal showed up at the table with a plateful of food that included two French macarons, one pink and one yellow, neither of which rose to the ideal height but stood tall enough to receive a general thumbs-up from the crowd at movie night.

Anne surprised Sal by sitting down beside him and pointing at the macarons. "I hope you like them," she said. "By the way, Matt tells me you have a new girlfriend who happens to play the violin. And she speaks at least three foreign languages. I was hoping I'd get to meet her tonight. What's her name?"

"Inessa," Sal said. "And she wanted to come, but her group has a recital." Sal went on to explain that Inessa performed with the Cascadia Symphony, a local orchestra. Besides her job as a barista, she also worked at a shop on Capitol Hill that repaired and rented string instruments.

"That's so cool," Anne said. "I hope I get to meet her at some point." Anne stood up and added, "OK, I need to find out what people are thinking about the macarons."

After Anne left, the Major repeated the story about Buck's computers to Sal.

"He's been working pretty hard on it for two years," the Major said. "He figured he'd be rich in five years, then retire in Las Vegas."

"Or some other classy place," Sal said between bites of barbecued baked beans and coleslaw. "Buck likes classy."

"Hey Matt," Lyka asked, "when are you leaving?"

"It's looking like somewhere between the eighth and the twelfth of August."

"What are you gonna do for work up there?"

Matthew shrugged. "Honestly, I have no idea. The kids will be in school a few days after we get there. Then I'll begin my job hunt."

"You should be able to get a roofing job," the Major said. "You have a ton of experience."

The memory of Buck almost falling off the roof earlier that week flashed through Matthew's mind. "Maybe too much experience," he said. "It might be nice to work on the ground for a change. I don't want my luck to run out. Plus, roofing and ice don't mix very well, and that's what you've got in Alaska a lot of the year."

The statement was followed by silence, which was finally broken when Sal said, "Before I forget, I've got some news for you all. I got a phone call today from the Professor."

"When is he coming back?" Lyka asked.

"The middle of next week, I think. But the thing is, he didn't go to Idaho just for a vacation. He went there to interview for a job at some college."

"Whereabouts in Idaho?" The Major asked.

"I don't know anything about Idaho," Sal said. "I always drive around it. Anyway, he got the job. It's in technology and math, or something like that."

"Wow," Lyka said. "He'll finally be teaching again."

"Then I guess they're OK with..." the Major left his statement unfinished.

"His record?" Matthew said.

"Maybe Idaho's a very forgiving place," Sal said. "The Professor said he'll join us for Ferry Hour next Friday. Nobody ever leaves a job without picking up their last check. Also, he told me that he got a postcard from Mole the day he left for Idaho."

"What's Mole up to?" Lyka asked.

"The Professor said he was heading northward to find a more soothing environment and new business opportunities."

*   *   *   *   *

Nora had spent most of the night watching the kids' movie from the tree with her friends. But at 9:15, when Kurt loaded his own personal copy of *Beetlejuice* into the movie player and people were filling the last few seats, Nora descended from the branches and marched toward the brightly lit screen. The opening credits had just begun playing, but when Kurt saw Nora step in front of the screen, he paused the movie.

Nora stood bathed in light and spoke in the direction of her unseeable audience. "I just want to tell everybody two things," she said in her outside voice. "First of all, I'm still not afraid of anything."

When she paused, there was a smattering of claps. One person called out, "We love you, Nora."

Nora replied in an annoyed tone, "That's not what I'm talking about." There was a brief silence before she added, "The second thing is that I used to hate my brother, Dylan, sometimes. But now he's my new best friend. OK, that's all I have to say. You can play the movie."

Most people at movie night had seen *Beetlejuice* before, so as the movie approached its familiar ending, the goodbyes began. Matthew and Anne exchanged hugs with many neighbors and friends, along with slips of paper, on which were written phone numbers and email addresses.

Kurt's audiovisual equipment was unplugged and hauled through two backyards to his house. The light in the popcorn machine went dark, and chairs were folded up and carried off by various neighbors. Those who had brought a dish to share at dinner retrieved their plates, bowls and serving utensils, and a small group remained to help Matthew and Anne clean up.

When the dishwasher was filled with its last load and the final bag of garbage had been tied shut and stuffed into the container at the end of the driveway, they went through the house turning off lights, then headed for bed. The last comment Matthew made before falling asleep was to praise Janice's cocobolo salmon carving for the fourth time.

Anne, however, lay awake thinking about variables. In particular, the variables around the heart attack suffered by the driver who hit Hadley's car. His name was Sheldon Young, Anne had learned. From what she knew, heart attacks occurred when blood vessels accumulated a lot of plaque and a piece of the plaque broke off, caused a clot and stopped the blood flow through a coronary artery. Plaque was caused by cholesterol, if she was right. How much of Sheldon Young's cholesterol was due to a genetic disposition and how much was the result of how he lived, specifically what he ate?

His heart attack occurred at a certain moment on that Friday. If he had experienced it a minute before he actually did, Anne thought, his car never would have hit Hadley because the road approaching the intersection went around a corner and he would have driven off the road before ever reaching the intersection. And if the heart attack had occurred a minute later, he would have been alive and alert enough to hit his brakes as he approached the red light, giving Hadley enough time to safely pass through the intersection.

What if he had eaten one less hamburger in the month before the accident or one less order of spare ribs or whatever fatty foods he might have favored? Or what if he had eaten one more hamburger or one more order of whatever? Would either of those scenarios have shifted the time of the heart attack backward or forward, even by a few seconds? Did Sheldon have an exercise routine, and had he skipped any days at the gym that week? What was his level of stress, and who in his life could have behaved differently to reduce that stress? Or created more of it to move up the time of the heart attack?

444

So many variables, and Anne knew that regarding this person who caused the accident—Sheldon Young—she had only begun to consider them. Her mind ran through the other people involved: Jennifer, Jennifer's doctor and Hadley Epps, and she replayed some of their circumstances, their variables. She hated it when her mind latched onto a situation or scenario like this. It made her think through endless depths and around constantly enlarging circles of possibility. She had been doing it since the accident, and it was exhausting.

Their bedroom window was halfway open to let in some of the cool night air, and through it Anne heard the sound of a car door closing halfway down their street. The car started up and drove away slowly. She looked at the clock on her nightstand. It read 1:47 a.m. Who was leaving at this time of night? Someone visiting a friend? Someone in a relationship? A one-night thing? She heard only one car door close, so it was probably only one person, and they drove away quietly, so it wasn't following an argument or a fight. Unless the person was at the point of exhaustion or a crushing romantic defeat. Anne decided that the visit had likely ended well. Well enough to last this late and end quietly.

OK, that's settled, she thought, and rolled onto her other side. A few more distant sounds drifted in through the window, but they were far away and hard to decipher, and eventually Anne's tired mind settled on the macarons. Her Nana B's French macarons. She had done OK with them, she felt. No, they were not amazing, but they were good enough to put in front of people and say—I finally made these today for the first time, and they're from an old recipe my grandmother gave me, my grandmother from France who would be proud of me, I believe. My grandmother, who was married in an alabaster silk wedding dress that had been tailored in a fashionable Paris salon, and it was the same dress worn by my mother at her wedding and by me at my own wedding. Such beautiful silk, and someday I'll get to see Nora wear it at her wedding too…

* * * * *

Monday, July 31, 2000

"We need to start packing, Matt. Today." Anne was sitting at the dining room table with a pen and notepad full of tasks to be completed, calls to be made, bills to be paid and various other loose ends to be tied up before the move in ten short days. BG would be paying for all the moving expenses, including the truck that would show up on the morning of the 9th and take away everything the Mahoneys owned. All that would be left was gear for camping out in the living room on their last night and the clothes they would need for the first few days in Alaska.

Matthew was sitting at the computer in the living room and called back to Anne, "I'm just reading here that U2 is coming out with a new album in October. I hope it's better than *Pop*."

"I don't care, Matt. Did you hear what I said?"

"I'm going by Home Depot before I pick up Kathleen at the airport. I'll get a shitload of boxes and packing tape."

"Get mostly small boxes. Last time you got all large boxes. When we packed them, they all weighed a hundred pounds." When Dylan walked through the back door, Anne added, "Take Dylan with you. Dylan, where is your sister?"

Dylan opened the fridge door and scanned the almost bare shelves. When he didn't respond, Anne repeated her question and Dylan said, "She's up in the tree."

"Again?" Anne asked.

Still," Dylan said.

"What?"

Dylan saw nothing in the fridge he would be able to eat without some form of preparation, so he let out a long sigh before closing the door and walking into the dining room. "She went up there first thing this morning. She hasn't come down, so she's not up in the tree again. She's up in the tree still."

"It's past lunchtime," Anne said. "Isn't she hungry?"

"I bring snacks and drinks out to the tree and hand them up to her."

"This is getting to be a little too much."

Dylan stared at his mother. "Nana B said you did the same thing. She said sometimes you would climb a tree and you wouldn't come down until it was dark."

"That's an exaggeration," Anne said as she returned to her lists. In a louder voice, she added, "Matt?"

Matthew turned off the computer and stood up. "Let's go, Dylanator. I don't want to be late to the airport."

When they left, Anne placed two phone calls, then made herself a peanut butter and banana sandwich. As she stood looking out the back window and taking her first bite, she felt a tightness in the waist of her jeans, so she decided to only eat half the sandwich. As she was taking her final bite, she saw something in the backyard that caught her eye. It looked like it might be starting to rain.

When Anne realized what it was, she marched onto the back deck and called up the tree. "Nora?"

Nora didn't respond right away but finally said, "What?"

"If you need to pee, you come down here and use the bathroom like the rest of us."

*   *   *   *   *

Matthew and Dylan were running a little late when they reached the airport, but it was alright because Kathleen's flight was also running a little late after a longer-than-expected layover in Denver. They watched her plane pull up to the gate and waited as passengers exited. It had been almost two years since Matthew had seen Kathleen, and his excitement showed when he finally spotted her. He called out, and she walked over to give them both a big hug.

Kathleen Sutliff was ten years older than Matthew and had lived in the same housing project as the Mahoneys. Matthew couldn't remember a time when she wasn't a part of his life growing up. She was close enough to his family to be considered an honorary Mahoney. Kathleen had actually dated his older brother Francis before he became heavily involved in the Boston underworld. Then she broke up with him and married someone in the military. After spending several unhappy years in Texas, she divorced in 1984 and moved back to the Old Colony housing project in South Boston with her daughter, Diana.

They shared an apartment with Kathleen's mother, who still lived in Old Colony. Just as they were settling into their new life in South Boston,

447

things took a tragic turn. One night in early spring, somebody high on angel dust climbed onto a neighboring roof and began firing random rifle shots. One bullet passed through the window of the bedroom Kathleen shared with her daughter. The bullet struck and killed Diana.

Despite her daughter's death and the drug problems overtaking the neighborhood, Kathleen continued living with her mother in Old Colony. She also fell back into a relationship with Francis for a short time. Her life took a turn for the better when they broke up again and she opened a beauty salon on East Broadway called the Hair & Beyond. Her mother and her friends lent the money she needed to get started.

While still running the salon, she started a new career in social work. Matthew thought it was a great fit and told her it was what she had been doing her whole life anyway, so why not start getting paid for it?

She had a great way with kids and was thrilled when Anne and Matthew asked her to be Nora's godmother. Kathleen's mother had been Portuguese, which gave Kathleen a deep olive complexion, and her long hair was a rich black, just like Nora's. When they were in public together, people would often confuse the two for mother and daughter, which Nora got the biggest kick out of.

As they walked to baggage claim, Kathleen asked Dylan, "So what's going on in the sky these days? What have you been keeping your eye on?"

"Well," Dylan began, "we've been looking at meteor showers lately, which is a big thing this time of the year. My dad and I were down at the beach Friday night to spot meteors. We're in the city, so there's light pollution but we can still see a lot. There are a few overlapping showers, and they're all peaking about now. Perseid has the most meteors, although you have to wait until right before dawn to see the best, which my dad and I only did once because it's really hard to get out bed at 3:30 in the morning. Then there's Piscis Austrinids, but that doesn't start until after midnight and you're lucky to see one meteor per hour. The third one is the Southern…" Dylan struggled to remember the full name but couldn't. "Anyway, that one is better because it starts around 10:30, and you can see maybe ten meteors every hour, so that's the one that we mostly watch. You can notice them without a telescope, but I like to use my Sky Surfer 2. It limits my field of vision and meteors go really fast—like 100,000 miles an hour, or faster actually—but I like to get a really close look."

"That sounds like a lot of fun," Kathleen said. "I bet you can't wait to use your telescope in Alaska."

"It's gonna be cool. My friend Samuel and I have been putting together a calendar of what to see up there. Plus, there's the aurora borealis, which is incredible in Alaska, and that's a whole different thing. I don't know how much homework I'll have in school, but I'm hoping it doesn't get in the way too much."

Matthew and Kathleen smiled at Dylan's comment, then she asked Matthew, "So where is my girl right now?"

"She's at home awaiting your arrival," Matthew said. "She's excited to see you."

"She's been spending a lot of time in our tree," Dylan said. "It's a maple in the backyard. Mom and Dad said it was OK for her to climb again. She got her cast off last week."

"She wants me to build her a treehouse so she can live up there," Matthew said. "A treehouse with a bathroom."

He brought Kathleen up to date with more details about Nora's recovery and the imminent move.

As Kathleen told Matthew what was new with her, she noticed a smile breaking out on his face, so she stopped and said, "OK, I can see you're about to laugh. What's so funny?"

Still smiling, Matthew said, "Ah, it's your Boston accent. I haven't heard so much of it in a long time."

Kathleen gave him a playful punch on the arm. "Listen to you, 'Mr. West Coast' trying to pronounce all his R's. I can still hear your accent, Mattie. You're not kidding anybody."

When Matthew stopped laughing, he asked, "So how is Brendan?" Brendan Maguire was Kathleen's boyfriend. They had been in a relationship for the last eight years. They met while he was working as a carpenter on a renovation to the row of townhouses where Kathleen lived. Brendan was a native of Ireland and a member of a folk band. He was also, in Matthew's opinion, the best thing to happen to Kathleen in the longest time. If anybody deserved happiness, Kathleen certainly did.

"He's doing great. As usual, he has more work than he can handle. He sends his hello and promises to join me the next time I visit you guys."

It took them a while to locate the green Subaru wagon in the parking garage because so many other people in the Seattle area drove the same car. When they finally found it, they squeezed Kathleen's luggage into the back, where the boxes Matthew picked up at Home Depot took up a lot of room.

"So how is Anne handling everything?" Kathleen asked.

Matthew was standing with Kathleen behind the car, and he waited until Dylan had jumped into the back seat and closed the door before answering. "It's a little mixed, to be honest. She's a hero for taking that job on the North Slope. She really saved us, and it turned into the staff job we all hoped for. But she's been struggling with the accident. I think it would help if you could talk to her at some point."

They left the airport right before rush hour began, so the drive home was easy. Matthew had borrowed a cot from a neighbor to set up an extra bed in Nora's room. After Kathleen left her bags there, she went out to the back deck and called up the tree. "Where's my special girl? I came all the way from South Boston to see you."

Nora gave a quick squeal before scrambling down the branches in record time. "You're here!" she called as she jumped onto the deck and embraced Kathleen.

"Sit down with me," Kathleen said. "I've been looking forward to seeing you so much."

"Me too," Nora said. The two sat down at the round table on the deck. As Nora's smile slowly faded, she brushed hair away from her eyes with her left hand. Then she held it below the table along with her right arm. "So my dad told you what happened to me, right?"

"He did. You lost your right hand, Nora. I'm so sorry about that." Kathleen looked at Nora's expression, and considered the tone of her voice before deciding what she should say next. "Can you show me?"

Nora hesitated, then said in a soft voice, "Sure." She pulled up the sleeves of her sweatshirt, placed both arms on the table side by side and looked at them as if they might not be her own.

Kathleen reached out and placed one hand on Nora's hand, and the other on her stump. She ran her hand around the stump a couple of times before giving it a gentle squeeze. "Dylan told me you got your cast off last

450

week, and you're already climbing the tree so easily. And your mom said you're playing soccer again."

Nora nodded a few times. Her eyes welled up, but she brushed away the tears before they could fall. In the silence, they could hear Anne complaining to Matthew about the size of the boxes he had picked up at Home Depot.

Eventually Nora took a long, deep breath. She let it out slowly as she continued to stare at her arms. "I can't braid my own hair," she finally said.

"Funny you should mention that because there's a woman who comes into my hair salon. She's my friend. Her name is Heather, and she has one hand like you and nice long hair like yours. And I was asking Heather last week how she braids her hair, and she showed me how she can do certain braids by herself with one hand."

As Kathleen continued, she watched Nora's expression gradually change from resignation to surprise. Kathleen continued, "That's right. She can do some braids by herself. I asked her if she could make a video to show you how she does it, and she's gonna do that next week. I'll be able to send you the video when you're in Alaska, and you can learn how to do some braids on your own."

Kathleen gave Nora's stump another light squeeze. "But, you know, the thing about braiding is that it's fun to have other people braid your hair sometimes too. Right? They can see exactly what they're doing because they're behind you, so it's easier. And it feels good to do someone a favor." Kathleen pushed her chair to the side and gestured for Nora to bring hers closer and turn it around. Nora's braid was a mess after sleeping on it and spending all day in the tree, so Kathleen loosened it. Using a brush from her bag, she brushed Nora's long black hair until it flowed soft and silky down her back.

"How does that feel?" Kathleen asked.

"It feels good," Nora said.

"See, I told you. You know, you're one-quarter French, so how about a French braid?"

Nora laughed and said, "Yes, please. Oh wait, I mean...*Oui, s'il vous plait.* My mom taught me that."

*   *   *   *   *

451

The day had been very warm and with the wind blowing from the north, the evening didn't cool down as quickly as usual, so they had dinner on the deck. Matthew didn't remember Kathleen being very adventurous when it came to cuisine, so they prepared a couple of appetizers, tossed a fresh salad and heated up a pan of lasagna that Anne had grabbed at a gourmet shop in Alaska Junction. Through the first, then second bottle of red wine, the conversation ranged from the past in South Boston, as well as Ipswich for Anne, to how the Mahoneys were imagining their futures in Alaska.

"Once we settle in," Anne said to Kathleen, "you and Brendan have to come visit us. You'll love it up there." Anne paused and remembered that Kathleen, a lifelong city dweller who had made it clear on more than one occasion that only animals should be in the woods, might not actually love visiting Alaska. "Or, at least you'll like it as, you know, a break from the city."

Kathleen tilted her head one way, then the other, to indicate a certain hesitancy to agree fully. "I'll definitely like it. Yes. Although the woods and I aren't really simpatico. But I'll go for walks. Local walks."

"But then you might not get to see any bears," Nora said.

The three adults all enjoyed a good laugh. Then Anne said, "I think that's the idea, sweetie."

It was another hour before the air finally began to cool, so they continued talking on the deck until Kathleen insisted it was time to hit the hay, mentioning that it was actually three hours later for her since she was still on Boston time.

Earlier in the evening, Matthew had placed a fan in the one window of Nora's bedroom, so the room had cooled down enough for Kathleen and Nora to sleep comfortably. Once the lights were out, Nora asked Kathleen if she wanted to hear a story. Kathleen said OK, so Nora crafted a quick tale of mighty Runa surviving a blizzard in the mountains. She sheltered in a cave with her friends, lit a big fire and cooked baked beans, which were stored there by the two giants who got stuck on a nearby mountain by the storm. The story ended with a sudden clearing of the clouds, blue skies, sunshine and an epic ride down the mountain on fresh powder. Kathleen missed most of it because halfway through the tale she was already fast asleep.

*　　*　　*　　*　　*

The next morning, Kathleen and Nora headed downtown in the Subaru. Their first stop was Pike Place Market, where they watched mini donuts being made at the small stand with the donut conveyer. They picked up a fresh dozen in the customary brown paper bag, and a coffee and hot chocolate at the Starbucks next door, then walked down to a waterfront pier to enjoy their breakfast and toss crumbs to the seagulls.

Nora insisted they spend an hour in the strange waterfront shop that displayed tons of curiosities: what a sign described as a shrunken human head, a supposedly authentic baby dinosaur skeleton, whales' teeth, exotic insect shells, a freakish tiny pig in a jar of clear liquid, a lighthouse made of matchsticks, and bizarre specimens of taxidermy, including a two-headed lizard, a three-headed duck, a bird with the head of a rabbit, and so much more.

They walked all over the waterfront, all around downtown and browsed in several stores. Kathleen bought a few things for Nora, including a new sweatshirt because the one she had been wearing was dirty and worn from days of climbing in the maple tree. She also picked up a couple of souvenirs for herself. For lunch, they returned to a fish and chips place at the Market and found two seats together at the crowded counter, which gave them a view of people streaming through the place.

The counter formed a large square around a prep area where two middle-aged women did all the cooking, dispensed soft drinks, prepared the plates, delivered the meals, and scratched out bills on small sheets of lined paper, which they tore off a large pad and placed under a salt shaker when people were done.

As they waited for their food, Nora asked Kathleen about her silver Viana heart earrings and begged Kathleen to let her try them on.

"Not here," Kathleen said. "It's too busy. If I lost one, I'd never forgive myself."

"Oh please," Nora insisted. "Let me just try on one. I promise I won't lose it."

453

Before Kathleen could respond, one of the women running the stand delivered two paper plates full of fish and chips. Then she gave Nora a stern look and said, "Now you listen to what your mother just said, and don't bother her. This is not a place to be trying on earrings, and if you drop them on that dirty floor, believe me, you'll never want to wear them again."

Nora smiled and nodded. When the woman turned away, Nora and Kathleen looked at each other and shared a muffled laugh. "I'm sorry, Mom," Nora said and gave Kathleen a big hug.

When the woman returned with their drinks, Nora played on with the joke. "I promise not to bug my mother about the earrings because she's the best mom ever."

The woman replied in the same serious tone, "You're absolutely right she is. And don't you ever forget that, young lady."

They drove the long way home on Harbor Ave, then past Alki Beach, where the traffic moved slowly because of all the people out on a beautiful summer day. It gave Kathleen a chance to ask Nora about the different adjustments she'd had to make since losing her hand. Nora detailed many, from the mundane task of putting on a Band-Aid to dressing and undressing herself. "Everything takes longer, but my mom and dad helped me learn some tricks when I'm getting dressed. And I got new shoes and sneakers that have Velcro straps or elastic laces. In the shower I have pump shampoo and soap and a sponge on a long stick."

Nora mentioned a few more adjustments. As she began explaining one, she stopped herself. Then she continued in a softer voice, "So I used to hold the toilet paper in my right hand when I wiped myself. I'm not used to holding it in my left hand, and sometimes it gets messy." She wrinkled her nose as she looked at Kathleen. "I know that's kind of gross…"

"It's OK. I'm sure you'll be able to adjust. Just slow down and take your time. You'll get used to using your left hand. And when you do, it won't be messy. The trick with a lot of things is just slowing down a little."

Nora was resting her right arm on the Subaru's open window as they passed Me-Kwa-Mooks Park. A strong breeze from Puget Sound swirled through the car. "I used to hold my hand out the window to feel the breeze," Nora said. "I can still feel it, but it's different. When we get to Alaska, my mom said I can try on different fake hands to see what I like, but I don't think any of them are gonna feel right. Maybe I'll never use a fake hand. Unless Dylan makes one for me."

*   *   *   *   *

Matthew woke up without hearing an alarm. It was set to go off at 5:15, but when he rolled over to look at the time, he saw nothing. The numbers were normally bright red, but there were none showing. His eyes followed the cord to the wall. It was still plugged in, so he hadn't accidentally pulled it from the socket. It was an old clock. Maybe it had hit the end of its road in the dead of the night, he thought.

He stretched for the window and pulled back a curtain. It was somewhat bright, maybe the end of dawn or just after sunrise. He guessed 5:45. Anne was still sound asleep, so he got out of bed and went to make coffee. When he flipped the light switch in the kitchen, nothing happened. After opening the fridge and seeing no light, the problem was suddenly clear: they had no power. He put on some sweats and took a short walk down the street, so he could look into a few windows and find out if other people had lost their power. He saw lights on everywhere. He even heard the sound of a radio or TV coming from Kurt's house. So it wasn't a neighborhood outage, but one limited to the Mahoneys' home.

As everyone else in the house woke up and made their way to the kitchen, Matthew was put in the position of explaining what had happened. Answers didn't seem readily available until Anne woke up and mentioned that it was Matthew who was supposed to call and schedule their last day of service.

"I told them the tenth was the last day we needed electricity. August tenth."

"Are you sure you didn't tell them August first?" Anne asked.

"Yes, I am sure," Matthew said.

"On a different subject," Kathleen said, "I could really use some hot coffee."

It was decided that everybody should get dressed and head down to Roy's for breakfast. Matthew would stay behind and call Seattle City Light to get their power turned back on.

When he finally reached to customer service, he was told that the error probably occurred in data entry, with the zero being accidentally dropped from the number ten. The power would be turned back on in a few hours or so.

With that settled, Matthew joined everybody at Roy's.

The plan for the day was to visit the Space Needle, something that the Mahoneys had never done in all their years living in Seattle. Kathleen compared it to living in Boston without ever visiting Paul Revere's House in the North End, which she admitted she still hadn't done despite living in Boston most of her life.

The only one not going was Anne. She wanted to be home when the electricity came back on, but more importantly she wanted to get on top of some packing with nobody around to distract her. Everyone else was excited to look out upon Seattle and the surrounding area from atop the Space Needle. At least until Dylan began describing the elevator ride to the top.

"The Space Needle is high, like really high," Dylan said. "It's super high. Around 600 feet. And the elevator ride is really cool because it's actually outside, and it has glass doors so you can see the ground getting farther and farther away from you."

"Glass doors?" Kathleen asked. She turned to Matthew and added, "You didn't say anything about glass doors."

"It doesn't even feel like you're on an elevator," Dylan said. "It's like you're flying up in space really fast, then you're just floating up there with the ground incredibly far below you. It freaks a lot of people out. I've heard the stories at school."

"What happens when somebody freaks out?" Kathleen asked.

Her look of concern was evident to everyone, including Dylan. He continued, "I think they just keep going up and up in the elevator until they reach the top. I bet they have someone there, like a doctor, who calms people down when they get out."

"That doesn't sound like a very pleasant experience," Kathleen said.

"Plus, the people who freak out on the way up still have to get back on the elevator to return to the ground, so I'm sure they freak out on the way down too. The only other way down is a giant metal ladder outside. That would be even worse because..."

By that point, Kathleen had heard enough. She turned to Matthew and said, "OK, change in plans here, Matt. I think I'll be skipping the Space Needle today. I'll stay on the ground and help Anne prepare for the move."

*   *   *   *   *

Anne had already finished some of the packing, including all their winter clothes, along with their skiing and snowboarding gear. Her method for the rest was to focus on one room at a time and pack everything except what they might need in the next eight days.

She started in the living room with three small boxes. Down came the photos from the mantel. She wrapped each one in a piece of clothing pulled from one of the bags she had planned to donate—mostly clothing that Nora and Dylan had outgrown. Once they got to Alaska and unpacked, Anne would wash everything and donate it there.

When the first box was filled, she sealed it with packing tape and used a marker to write the room it belonged in and generally what it contained. Now this was how you packed, she thought to herself, not throwing a hundred pounds worth of stuff into a giant box and taping it shut without labeling it.

Anne had just finished sealing the last box in the living room when a light suddenly came on in the living room, an indication that power had been restored. She considered turning on some music when the front door opened, and Kathleen appeared.

"Hey," Anne said. "I thought you were going up the Space Needle."

"I did too," Kathleen said. "Until I learned about the glass doors on the elevator and people freaking out from the height. Dylan really knows how to paint a scary picture."

Anne marked "Living Room & Games" on the side of the last box and stacked it on top of the other two. "He does that because he's afraid of heights himself, but if he can make someone else more afraid than he is, then he thinks he won't be afraid."

"He seems pretty OK with it all," Kathleen said.

Anne smiled. "Wait till he comes home. I bet we'll hear a different story. It's just one of his things."

"Can I give you some help here?"

457

"Sure. First, let's make some coffee."

After Anne brewed a pot, she put a Calexico CD in the player. Then the packing of the kitchen commenced. They had all day, so they took their time. By noon, they had 14 boxes packed, sealed and labeled, and they hadn't even finished the kitchen.

Anne let Kathleen continue to pack what remained there, while she grabbed a pile of extra-large boxes they'd never use and headed off to Home Depot in the truck to exchange them for a bunch of small and medium ones. When she returned, they moved on to the dining room to carefully wrap each piece of china that Matthew and Anne had received at their wedding. The set was missing a few pieces: a bowl that had broken when Matthew hadn't wrapped it during the previous move; a side plate that Dylan had thought he could throw like a Frisbee when he was two years old; and a plate and creamer that Nora had dropped on two occasions of slippery hands.

"She only has one hand now," Anne said. "She's gonna have to be even more careful with everything. For the rest of her life." Anne reached into the bag of clothing to be donated and pulled out the crimson sweater that Nora had outgrown the previous winter. Anne held it to her nose and sniffed. It still smelled faintly of the peppermint hot chocolate that Nora had spilled on it at a friend's birthday party the last time she wore it.

"It seems like she's adjusting well," Kathleen said. "I mean, as well as you can hope for."

Anne took a last sniff of the sweater, wrapped it around a dinner plate and placed it carefully in a box. "She is," Anne said. "She's adjusting better than the rest of us, I think. I envy her." Anne turned to Kathleen. "That probably sounds strange, but it's true. She can't undo what happened, but she's managing somehow to go around it or through it, and come out the other side. Dylan is handling it well too. Matthew seems to be doing the same. But I'm just sort of…stuck about the whole thing."

Anne walked to the near wall and reached for the calendar that Roy's printed for regular customers every year. It was still showing the month of June with a picture of colorful wildflowers blooming in the Tatoosh Range. She removed the push pin holding the calendar to the wall and tucked it into the box.

"I can't get past the accident," Anne said. "I keep thinking about all the ways it could have been prevented." She went on to describe all the variables that had been in play before the event itself, the variables that brought about the moment when the accident occurred. She began with Jennifer's doctor and went on to Jennifer, Hadley and Sheldon Young.

"If you think about it as an equation," Anne said, "it's like a string of variables that led to the accident. If any of the variables change, if any of the people had behaved differently, even in the slightest way, then the outcome would be different, and the accident would never have happened. The other night I was talking to Matthew and I told him that I had missed a variable. He told me at one point that he considered leaving work early that Friday and taking Nora to soccer practice himself, instead of letting Hadley pick her up. If he had done that…"

"So you told Matthew that he was a variable too?"

Anne looked out the window and tried to recall the conversation. "Well, not in so many words."

"What did he think about that?"

Anne shrugged. "I think he got pissed off. A little bit. He said I was pointing a lot of fingers." Anne turned to Kathleen again and spoke as if she were back in the discussion with Matthew. "It's not like I'm blaming anybody for the accident."

Kathleen replied, "He might have felt like you were blaming him. And everyone else."

"No," Anne said. "That's not what I was saying at all. It's not what my whole line of thinking is about. It's about trying to understand what happened, or why it had to happen, and how things could have gone differently if certain people had or hadn't done the things they did, in the exact way that they did them. That's different from blaming."

Kathleen had been holding a plate over one of Dylan's old long-sleeve shirts. She lowered it and carefully folded the sleeves over the top. Then Kathleen said, "So there's Jennifer, her doctor, Hadley, the guy who had the heart attack—Sheldon—and Matthew. Those are all the variables, right? But aren't you leaving somebody out?"

Anne considered the question. She went over all the other people she knew who might have played a part one way or another, but she drew a blank. "There isn't anybody else," she finally said.

"Are you sure?"

Then it came to Anne, and it hit her like an electric shock. "You mean me?"

Kathleen looked at Anne but said nothing.

Anne continued, "I wasn't even here. I was over a thousand miles away in Alaska. How could it be my fault?"

Again, Kathleen didn't reply, and Anne's words simply hung in the air between them. After a moment, however, the words came rushing back to Anne. Her eyes opened wider, and it took another moment before she could reply. "Oh my God," is all she could say at first.

Anne looked down at the fragile china bowl cradled in her hands. "I left Nora. I was the first variable. If I had never gone to Alaska, none of the other variables would matter because I would have left work early on the day of the accident and brought her to soccer practice. That's what I always did on Fridays..."

Anne was standing up, and she felt with her hand for the back of the chair beside her. When she found it, she sat down.

"I have to confess," Kathleen said as she took her own seat, "I knew you were going to say that. I mean, eventually. Although who can say if you would have been busy with something else that Friday?"

Anne hadn't really heard Kathleen's words, but continued working through her revelation. "Matthew must hate me. Nora will too. When she gets older and realizes..."

"I want you to listen to something," Kathleen began. She patted Anne's hand to pull her out of her thoughts. When Anne looked at her, Kathleen continued, "When my daughter died...when Diana died, she was in our bedroom. It was on Easter Sunday, and I let her go back there to put on her butterfly dress again because she loved it so much."

Anne nodded. "I remember you telling me about that."

"I was in the living room with my mom. We were sitting on the couch watching TV after our big dinner. We were watching that show *One Day at a Time*. Anyway, I called out to Diana to hurry up and come back into the living room, and if she didn't hurry up then I would come and get her in the bedroom.

"But I was tired after a busy week and a big dinner and a couple of glasses of wine. I just sat there and watched TV. I didn't get off the couch and go get Diana like I said I would. Then my mom and I heard the rifle shots. And that was that. It all happened in a minute. Diana died because I left her alone in the bedroom. I wasn't there with her. I didn't go get her like I said I would. So, it was my fault that she got killed. I was in therapy every day for almost four weeks before I let go of that story. Diana didn't die because of me. It was an accident. There was no way to see it coming, so there was no way to avoid it.

"I'm gonna save you maybe a month of therapy here, OK? Nora didn't lose her hand because of you. It was an accident. It didn't matter where you were when it happened. Trust me, blaming yourself comes naturally. It's what we do. You can spend energy and lose sleep thinking about your variables for the next 20 years. Nora will be growing into a young woman while you're stuck in the past, reliving the same moment from every possible angle."

The words made sense to Anne. Perfect sense. She looked at Kathleen and nodded gently, but then she looked away. She knew how her mind worked. It was like a castle. As much sense as Kathleen's words made, they would be left standing outside pounding at the front gates because they were in conflict with words already living inside. Anne knew she would eventually accept Kathleen's wisdom, but it would take a little while. At least now she was aware of it, and what Kathleen told her was a great relief to hear. It was a start.

Anne stared into the empty living room, bare of photos and magazines and quirky lamps. Then she heard a familiar sound coming from blocks away. It was a musical tune blaring from cheap metal speakers.

"Wow," Anne said, "I can't remember the last time I heard an ice cream truck in this neighborhood."

"We still have some in South Boston. Mostly at the ballfields when there's a game," Kathleen said. She stood up and added, "Hey, I could use some tea. Did we pack that already?"

Anne closed her eyes, thought for a moment, then pointed toward the kitchen. "It's in the stack of boxes on the far right. Second box down."

After a tea break on the back deck, they finished packing the dining room and declared the day a success. Kathleen offered to buy takeout food for dinner and suggested Thai. Anne gave her directions to the Laughing Monk in Morgan Junction and wrote down a number of menu options that

Nora, Dylan and Matthew liked. Matthew was working a short shift at Roy's, but he would be home by 6:30, which left more than enough time for a run to pick up food.

While Kathleen drove to the restaurant, Anne made another cup of tea and returned to the back deck. She felt a sudden fatigue, and she chalked it up as much to her conversation with Kathleen as to all the packing she'd done that day. The chair she was sitting in had a high back. She rested her head against it and stared up at the one cloud in the sky. Her mind began drifting, and after a while it ended up on Plum Point Road in Ipswich and the Boushay farmhouse.

Anne remembered a conversation with her mother 13 years earlier about the future of the house and the property. Her mother made it quite clear that when her time on this earth was over, she expected Anne to return to Ipswich and manage the property, whether that meant turning it back to more of a farm or simply residing over the place in its current form.

Anne had no intention of doing either, but she never had the heart to tell her mother. To Joan and all the generations of French Boushays, a settled piece of land was your home, your identity, everything. To Anne, it was part of her dead past, a place that it would make no sense at all in returning to. Her future was in Alaska. Nothing could ever change that, not even her mother's death.

Her mind fell again on that day when her father called her from the plum orchard to tell her that he and her mother were getting divorced. Even as a child, Anne had seen it coming. She tried to backtrack from that fateful day to a time when her parents were still happy together, and she wondered if it would have been possible to somehow head off the split that eventually caused the breakup of the family.

She was pulled from her reverie by the piercing shout of a girl. Ten-year-old Jayden Sabella was racing after a crowd of her friends in a game of tag. The group, with Jayden trailing, came charging through the open backyards amid a series of shouts and laughter. When they reached the maple tree, the group of children trying to avoid being tagged paused to catch their collective breath.

Jayden, who had been "it" for a while and was clearly tired, made a feint at one, then another friend. Anne could see that she didn't have enough strength left to get close enough to tag anybody. But then a boy tripped on an exposed tree root and fell to the grass. Jayden leapt at the sudden opportunity, charged toward the boy and tagged him. As Jayden ran away, Anne could see the change in the girl's expression. The burden had been lifted, and there was a big, exhausted smile on her face.

Chapter 4

Remodeling

In this final phase, solid bone is formed, and the healed fracture is able to withstand outside forces and the demands of growth. The external callus, or outer surface, can remain swollen for an extended time while it is slowly sculpted back to a shape resembling its original. Remodeling is the longest phase and may last for several years.

Wednesday, August 2, 2000

The Ferry Hour business at Roy's was brisk for a Wednesday afternoon. Neighborhood regulars mixed with a group of kayakers who had paddled their way over from Vashon Island and were debating how long to linger on the front deck before paddling home.

Matthew had been slammed for the first hour and a half, but by 5:45 things had quieted down enough that he could hear the new Italian music CD playing over the bar's sound system. The music went along with the new special menu: cuisine from the Amalfi Coast of Italy. From the dishes he'd had a chance to sample, Matthew was impressed. His favorites were: squid stuffed with potato, zucchini, garlic, capers, olives and pecorino cheese on a bed of scialatielli—traditional coastal pasta; grilled cuttlefish with celery and lemon; and chunks of lamb and tomato in red wine sauce.

Overall, the new special menu was getting mixed reviews, but during his Ferry Hour shift, there was one Amalfi Coast appetizer that everybody was loving. It was a simple flatbread pizza with basil, spinach, crushed tomatoes and mozzarella di bufala. Since it was a freshly made pizza with a crispy crust, it gave the less adventurous customers at Roy's an escape from special-menu anxiety.

Matthew was delivering his ninth pizza of the shift to one of his customers when he suddenly noticed a Western straw hat sitting on the bar at the far end. After dropping off the pizza, he headed in the direction of the hat. He had a hunch who it might belong to, and it proved correct when he saw Anne sitting at the second to last stool. He placed a cocktail napkin in front of her and poured an ice water.

"Hey," Anne said. "How's the shift going?"

"Pretty good," Matthew said. "A little better now." He smiled. "Dennis just told me that he hired a new bartender. He's giving him all my shifts, so it looks like today's Ferry Hour is the last time I tend bar in this here saloon."

Anne raised her water glass. "We should celebrate," she said and took a sip. "Let me buy you a drink."

Matthew pulled up his sleeve to check his watch. "I will gladly accept that offer in about ten minutes when I'm off duty. For now, you're the customer, so what can I get you?"

Anne scanned the rows of bottles on the backbar. "Oh, I don't know. Maybe I'll stick with water for now."

Matthew topped off her glass and offered her a lemon wedge. "So what brings you down the hill? Taking a break from the packing?"

Anne squeezed the lemon wedge over the glass, then placed it on the napkin. "It's been a busy year, Matt. A lot of things have been happening fast."

"It feels like fast," he said. Someone at the opposite end of the bar caught his attention by raising an empty beer glass. Matthew gave the guy a nod, then continued, "If the accident didn't happen…"

Anne interrupted. "I know, but it did. It happened, and we can't change that. And I'm tired of looking for blame. Really tired."

The ticket machine on the backbar came to life and spit out two drink orders for the dining room. Matthew glanced at the machine, then ignored it.

Anne continued, "Anyway, our anniversary is coming up soon. It could be a chance for us to get back on…I don't know, the right track, if you know what I mean."

"I hear what you're saying. In fact…"

Anne interrupted again. "Here's what I'm thinking: something small. And simple. It needs to be something we know we can do together. And I don't mean a convenience store or a Blockbuster or something stupid like that. I mean something that will challenge us, but won't frustrate us or make us hate each other."

Matthew turned his gaze to the ceiling and nodded in a way that suggested less than full agreement.

"Matt, we need to get our confidence back. That's really important for us right now."

Matthew laid a hand on the bar gently. "I'm not disagreeing with you." Then he walked over to the register and pulled out a magazine that was tucked behind it.

"Check this out," Matthew said and handed the magazine to Anne. She looked at the cover. It was the July issue of *Inside Alaska*.

She gave Matthew a skeptical look and opened to the contents page. "What am I looking at?"

Matthew pointed to one of the feature articles. Anne read out loud, "This summer's can't-miss sizzling seafood festivals."

"No," Matthew said. "The one above that."

Anne looked again and her eyes grew big. "Danish royal yacht *Alexandrine* visits Anchorage in September."

"If we're gonna dream," Matthew said, "we should dream big."

Anne closed the magazine and tapped the cover. "This is what I'm afraid of, Matt."

"Just consider it. We can always choose something else. Take that home, and read the story. The yacht will be in port until early October. That gives us time to get unpacked, get the kids in school. And I'll find a job. Then we do the *Alexandrine*. They'll be hosting public tours every weekend, so we'll get a good look inside. It's almost 300 feet long. And wait till you hear about the artwork they have onboard."

*   *   *   *   *

They enjoyed a late dinner on the deck, with all the Thai dishes that Kathleen had picked up spread out on one table and everyone sitting at another. There was enough food for seconds all around, even thirds for Matthew and Nora. Anne asked how the trip to the Space Needle had gone and was not surprised to hear that Dylan had suffered two small panic attacks, one on the elevator ride up and a second on the ride down.

The talk at the table then turned to the elephant in the room or, more accurately, the elephant in the yard. The Pedersen's house had been sold, and the new neighbors had moved in. One of their first projects was to build a fence that encircled their yard. As long as Matthew and Anne had lived there, none of the six houses on their side of the block had backyards that were fenced. Neighborhood children would use all of the yards as one community park, sometimes staging foot races that would span the entire length.

But a six-foot-tall wooden fence built roughly in the middle of the stretch threatened the shared sense of community and signaled what might me a greater shift in their little corner of Arbor Heights.

"I hate it," Nora said. "I always have to use the sidewalk now to go visit my friends, so I always have to put on shoes first."

"I've met them, and they're very nice people," Anne said. "But they're new here, so I don't think they realize how things work. You know, what the unwritten rules are."

Kathleen nodded. "Except every time a family moves out and a new one moves in, the rules are rewritten a little bit. When that happens enough, there's a change. I've seen it plenty of times in South Boston. Sometimes it's a change for the better, sometimes for the worse. It's like a shoreline. The sand is always shifting because of storms and tides. A beach can be created overnight, and one that's been there for years can suddenly be swept away."

"Maybe it's a good time to be moving," Matthew said. "We were lucky to be here while things were at their peak."

A third bottle of wine was opened, and candles were lit, but the somber mood didn't fully lift until Dylan offered a radical proposal. "We should have a Saint Boushoney Day tomorrow."

"We already had one this year," Anne said.

"So? There's no rule that says we can't have two. We had two Saint Boushoney Days in 1996."

"Yes!" Nora said. She began slapping her left hand on the table, which was her new way of clapping.

"Everyone in favor of a second Saint Boushoney Day tomorrow?" Dylan asked with a raised hand. It was quickly followed by Nora's and Matthew's hands but not Anne's.

"We have a majority," Dylan said. "Mom, you should make it unanimous."

Anne's mind had been focused almost exclusively on preparing for the big move, so she was reluctant at first to lose a day. Then she realized how much they could all use a break from the packing and the cleaning, so she raised her hand.

"OK," Dylan said. "It's unanimous. Tomorrow will officially be a Saint Boushoney Day. We need to agree on a schedule of events tonight. Like, right now."

Kathleen was confused about what was happening. "So was I supposed to be voting? Who is Saint Boushoney?"

"We'll explain," Nora said. "You're gonna like this."

*   *   *   *   *

"I seriously thought about killing him," Matthew said.

He was sitting with Kathleen in a Pike Place Market café, where they had a view of the waterfront. Anne and the kids had descended to the lowest level of the Market to help Dylan search for an English translation of Ptolemy's *Almagest,* a second-century Greek treatise on the stars and planets. Dylan had only a passing interest in actually reading the book. Trying to find it was a competition between himself and Samuel, and he wanted to be the first to locate a copy in a used bookstore.

It gave Matthew a chance to tell Kathleen more about his unexpected visit from Francis. He had shared the gist of it with her earlier, but he had waited to share the part of the story that disturbed him most.

"He was telling me that he'd reveal where Buzzy is buried if I made a phone call for him. You know, trade favors. Then the thought flashed through my mind that maybe I should kill him. Right there in the kitchen."

Kathleen shook her head. "Matt, no, you wouldn't have really…"

Matthew interrupted, "It was a pretty strong urge."

Kathleen gave Matthew an angry look. "You have no business letting your thoughts go there, Matthew. You've got a beautiful family and a pretty nice life. You would have lost it all if you killed your brother. You know why? Because you have no freaking idea what to do with a dead body. Think about it. What would you have done with Francis' body? That alone would screw you. Then think about what it would do to your children. They would only know you through prison visits.

468

"I've known guys who have actually had to figure out how to get rid of a body at a moment's notice because they couldn't resist crossing the line. I shit you not, Mattie, in every single case their lives ended in misery because of their mistake. Real misery. Remember this: every story that starts with a dead body ends badly."

Matthew was sitting up straight in his chair and having a flashback to his childhood in Old Colony when Kathleen would sometimes babysit him and Buzzy. Their greatest fear would be to provoke her fierce side. They even came up with a funny saying about someone getting so angry that they "put the fear of Kathleen into you."

"Will I have to remind you about this again?" Kathleen asked.

"No," Matthew said. "I hear you loud and clear."

"I miss Buzzy, too, if that matters. I have no doubt Francis killed him, and I hope Francis ends up in hell because of it. But I don't want you to join him there." She reached out and patted Matthew's hand. "I hope you find out where he's buried."

"It's been almost two months since I did my part, and I haven't heard anything back. Do you think he just used me to get what he wanted?"

"I don't want to give you false hope, but in the time I knew him, there were certain matters where he could never be trusted and other matters where you could bet your life on his word. He's devil and angel combined, but mostly devil."

Matthew went to use the bathroom, and when he returned Anne and Dylan were sitting there.

"Did you find the book?" Matthew asked.

"No," Dylan said. "But the guy at the store told me about a couple of other used bookstores in the U District that I should check out. I'll call Samuel when I get home, and if he didn't find it today I'll keep looking."

"If we're gonna catch the next ferry, we should probably go soon," Anne said. The plan for the day was to take the ferry over to the peninsula, drive north to Port Townsend and rent kayaks. They could kayak in Seattle, but Dylan and Nora preferred Port Townsend. There was a fish and chips place at the end of a pier where you placed an order by kayaking beneath the pier and pulling on a string. It rang a bell in the restaurant above. They would then lower a basket with an order sheet and a pen. When your order was ready and paid for, they lowered your food and drinks in the basket, and you could enjoy your meal as you floated along the waterfront.

Dylan turned to look out the window at the ferry parking lot. "At this point I estimate the ferry will be about 72 percent full." Something else suddenly occurred to Dylan. He turned around quickly. "Hey, where did Kathleen and Nora go?"

"No idea," Matthew said. "I was in the bathroom."

"Nora wanted to show her something," Anne said.

"You let Nora take Kathleen somewhere?" Dylan asked with an abundance of concern in his voice.

"What's the problem?" Anne said.

"What's the problem?" Dylan repeated. "This is Saint Boushoney Day."

They reached the stairway above Post Alley a few seconds too late. As they rushed down the steps to the gum wall, they heard a woman's shriek, followed by the sound of a girl erupting in giggles.

*   *   *   *   *

Friday, August 4, 2000

The next morning, Matthew woke before the alarm sounded and went on his usual run down to Lincoln Park. The beach was already occupied by a few fishers clustered around the point in the dim light of dawn. There would be no more fishing here for the Mahoneys. All their gear was packed away. As it turned out, their last West Seattle fishing memory would be about the big one that got away, which is how all the best fish stories end, Matthew thought.

After a quick shower, he went upstairs to grab Kathleen's bags. She was already dressed and ready for the airport. Matthew carried her stuff out to the Subaru, then went to wake Nora. At dinner the night before, she said she wanted to go to the airport with Kathleen. He knew she'd be hard to wake, and she was. By the time they arrived at Sea-Tac, a new sunny day had begun. Nora was wide awake and asking when she would see Kathleen again.

"You're still in trouble, girl, for that stupid trick at the gum wall. If I end up getting sick, you're gonna hear about it," Kathleen teased. Nora smiled and stifled a giggle.

Kathleen continued, "Brendan and I will visit you in Alaska as soon as we can. Maybe even for Thanksgiving. But I'm not promising that exactly. And I'll be seeing my friend Heather this weekend, so I'll make sure she sends you that video we talked about. Then I'll call in two or three weeks to find out how the braiding is going, OK?"

They accompanied Kathleen as far as the underground platform, where they said their goodbyes. On the drive home, Nora turned to her father and said, "I'm gonna miss her. She's really good at helping people."

*   *   *   *   *

After dropping off Nora, Matthew headed to work. The day would be bittersweet because it was his last day of roofing with his crew, and probably his last day of roofing ever. Sal tried to get him excited by leaving a message saying that they'd be putting a new roof on Eddie Vedder's West Seattle home that day. Matthew happened to know that the musician's gigantic house was at the end of 44th Ave and only about ten blocks away from Roy's. It was so big and had so many dormers that it would be a real bitch to roof.

He was pretty sure Sal was joking. That was confirmed when he called back for the address. The actual house they were reshingling was so close to where Matthew lived that he would have walked to it if he wasn't the one carrying most of the crew's roofing gear in his truck.

The place was a brick Tudor that might have been just over a half day's work if the roof wasn't so steep. That meant a lot of extra time to set up and take down staging. Although it wasn't Eddie Vedder's home, the Tudor claimed the distinction of sitting on the highest point in Arbor Heights.

When Matthew eventually made it to the peak of the roof, he found the claim to be credible. In every direction, he seemed to be looking downhill. A pretty cool vantage point to scan the neighborhood, except maybe during a storm.

"I hate staging," Lyka said as she nailed in her first metal bracket just above the gutter. She and Matthew were reshingling the west-facing side of the roof and standing on double planks suspended between two ladders. "When I worked on that turret, it seemed like I spent half of my time setting up staging, then removing it."

"It is a pain," Matthew said, "but remember—the more equipment the customer sees you using, the more you can charge for the job." Matthew looked down at the soft bark at the base of the neatly trimmed trees surrounding the house. It would be a relatively soft place to land if anyone fell off the roof today. Still, he didn't feel at all like falling on this, his last day, and he quietly whispered an oath to that effect. Then he suddenly remembered something and turned to Lyka. "Hey, I've been meaning to ask you something for a while, but I keep forgetting."

Lyka gave him a skeptical look and said, "It's about my tattoo, isn't it? You want to know what it means."

Matthew was caught off guard by her response. "No, I don't…I mean, I do, but that's not what I was gonna ask you." He slipped another bracket beneath a shingle and drove a nail through the top hole. "I was wondering what you were going to do when you got tired of roofing. You're smart, and I'm guessing you have some kind of a plan."

Lyka looked below to see if anyone might be within listening distance. In a soft voice, she said, "I'll tell you because it's your last day, but you can't tell anyone else, alright?"

Matthew nodded.

"Especially Sal."

"OK. Go ahead."

"So, here's my plan. I've been saving with what I make on this job and my other side jobs. And I'll be taking enough night classes this fall and next spring to finish my bachelor's degree, then I'll be taking the OAT so I can apply to a doctoral program…"

Matthew interrupted. "Wait, you're losing me here."

"I'm gonna become an optometrist and open a store in West Seattle. It'll take years to make it a reality, but eventually I'll be my own boss."

"I think you'll get there. And you know, Sal wouldn't mind if you told him you were gonna quit in, like, a year. There's usually a lot of turnover in roofing."

When Lyka didn't respond, Matthew raised his hands and added, "OK, don't worry. I'm not gonna say a word. I promise."

With the first line of staging complete, they nailed in eight courses of shingles before setting up the next stage. Unlike most jobs where they could walk up and down the roof easily and somewhat safely, the steep Tudor roof kept them moving slowly and cautiously. Still, by 11:30 they had managed to finish most of their side and were only one stage away from the peak. On the other side, Buck and the Major had only reached their halfway point.

"One thing I like about roofing," Lyka said, "is that you usually have lunch in a different spot every day."

They were about five minutes away from their lunch break on a day that had started very warm and was growing very hot. Everybody was looking forward to cracking open their coolers while sitting on the soft, cool grass in the shade of a big dogwood tree on the back lawn.

As he fired away with his nail gun, Matthew guesstimated that he was about three shingles from the end of his nail coil. When he got there, he'd call it a morning and head down for lunch. Between bursts from his gun, Matthew heard Buck on the other side of the roof say, "No fucking way."

The Major and Lyka had heard him as well, and both of their guns went silent.

"Are you gonna tell me what's going on?" Matthew called out. "Or are you gonna make me find out for myself?" When Buck didn't reply, Matthew put down his nail gun, reached up to the peak with both hands and pulled himself high enough to see over. Buck and the Major were both staring off into the distance.

"I'm not sure," the Major said.

"Oh, I'm pretty sure," Buck said.

"What?" Matthew asked.

"What do you see coming this way?" Buck asked. He pointed toward 106th Street. The road ran straight for many blocks, and in the distance it went up a long, gradual hill that gave a clear view of approaching traffic.

Matthew saw a few vehicles driving slowly in their direction: a small pickup, a sedan and a white van. Then he realized the van was a camper. A white camper with stripes along its side. As the camper came into clearer view, he saw that the faded stripes were pumpkin orange and avocado green. Classic '80s styling.

"You don't see many campers like that around here," Matthew said. "The only person I know who's owned one..."

"It's him," Buck said solemnly. "He has returned."

"Maybe he's taking a break from the road to say hi," the Major said.

As the camper drew near, the three guys went silent. They were waiting to see if it would turn onto their side street.

"How would he know where we're roofing today?" the Major asked.

"He would know," Buck said. "He would know."

Lyka, who had been confused by the conversation, finally asked, "Who are you guys all talking about?"

*   *   *   *   *

He was looking somewhat leaner than the old Mole, who had always maintained a gnome-like stoutness, although he was sporting the same thick brown beard and blue-tinted sunglasses. He joined them all in the shade of the dogwood.

"I'll begin with an answer to the subject you all are no doubt wondering about. Why am I here?"

"I was wondering about that," Buck said.

Mole turned his head like an owl, slowly and deliberately, then stared at Buck through his spectacles. "Which is why I prefaced my statement as such. As impossible as it seems, it would appear you've become even more stupid in my brief absence."

Matthew offered Mole half of his peanut butter and jelly sandwich. Mole declined the offer politely and held up a clear plastic container of blue liquid. "I'm currently drinking a tea made of dried butterfly pea flowers to purge my system of excessive cannabinoids. Solid food would inhibit the process. As to my appearance here today, I am currently in search of employment due to a sudden loss of financial liquidity. To put it succinctly, I was waylaid by a fellow traveler while attempting an unorthodox crossing of the Canadian border. I'd prefer to leave it at that."

"Someone stole your stash of $20,000?" the Major asked.

"The amount was somewhat larger due to a successful spring season on the craft fair circuit. I've been forced to manage the last few days with the small amount of cash in my pocket." Mole paused to glance momentarily at each member of his audience, suggesting a request of confidentiality regarding what he was about to add. "I have also secured a certain amount of agricultural merchandise from British Columbia that I will be offering for sale on the streets of the U District this evening. If any of you are aware of any enhanced law enforcement activities in that area, I would appreciate you sharing that information with me now."

When nobody responded, Mole said, "Very well. If anything changes, you have my cellphone number. It has not changed."

"If you're looking for work," Matthew said, "you should talk to Sal. He's been needing someone to replace the Professor. He landed a teaching job in Idaho."

"Yes, the Professor actually called last week to tell me about his new position. I'm not familiar with his particular institutions of higher learning, but I congratulated him. Then I called Sal. I've arranged to rejoin the crew next week. It'll be safe for me to work on a roof again once my cleansing regimen is complete. I'll also be resuming my living arrangements with the Emerald City shopping complex. They've granted me the same comfortable nesting spot on level seven of their garage in exchange for my former cleaning duties."

A smile broke out on Buck's face, suggesting a certain sense of satisfaction that Mole's fate mirrored his own in a sense. "So you're gonna start over from the beginning? Start saving up until you reach $20,000 again?"

Mole turned to stare at Buck and was considering an appropriate riposte when the Major said, "Buck has been very unhappy lately because his porn business got destroyed. He lost all the pictures he's been stealing for the last two years. There were thousands of them, and they all got infected by a computer virus."

Mole seemed to savor the news and offered a weak smile. "Perhaps not dissimilar from the virus that destroyed his moral compass at birth and has been slowly consuming his gray matter ever since."

*   *   *   *   *

Matthew had one more chance to say goodbye to his crew after work that day when they all went to Roy's for Ferry Hour. It was the first in a final flurry of goodbyes that stretched for six days. As more and more items were packed away in boxes that were bound for Anchorage, the Mahoneys found themselves drifting up and down the street to eat meals at the homes of different friends.

On the morning of Friday, the 10th, two drivers showed up to take Anne's Subaru and Matthew's truck up to Bellingham, where they'd be put on a ship bound for Alaska. Later that afternoon, the moving truck arrived. It was long enough to block almost three driveways on the street, and already had the contents of two other houses on board. It seemed impossible that the moving crew could get all of the Mahoneys' stuff into the space that remained in the back, but they did, and it took them less than two hours.

That evening, their last in West Seattle, the Mahoneys walked down the hill to Roy's for dinner. By 11:00, they were spread out with their sleeping bags on the hardwood floor in the living room. The empty house seemed larger than it ever had before. The cleared rooms, the bare walls that Matthew had patched and painted in places, and the smell of different cleaning solutions gave the house a somewhat anonymous feel that made their memories in the place a little less real, a little less intimate, almost as if they had never lived there at all.

They slept in four sleeping bags clustered together in the darkness. The only sounds were the light tinkling of the wind chimes on the back deck and the occasional snores coming from Matthew and Dylan.

"Mom, are you awake?" Nora asked in a soft voice.

The question was greeted with silence. After a minute, Nora added, "I know you're awake. You can never fall asleep before midnight. You're definitely awake."

Anne sighed. "What is it?"

"What's Dad's favorite song?" Nora waited for an answer but received none. "Mom?"

"I'm not sure, honey."

"I know what your favorite song is. Dad told me," Nora said.

"Oh, really? What did he say it was?"

"He said it was 'Daybreak.'"

"'Daybreak?'"

"Yes, 'Daybreak' by Barry something," Nora said.

"Barry Manilow?"

"I think so."

Anne hated Barry Manilow, so she decided to return the favor. "Hmm, OK. Well then, I think I just remembered your dad's favorite song."

"What is it?" Nora asked.

"I don't know who sings it, but it's called 'Midnight at the Oasis.' We should play it for him on his next birthday. It'll be a surprise."

A moment of silence was broken by the sound of Anne stifling a laugh.

"Mom, you know what?"

"What?"

"I think you guys are messing with me."

"Well, maybe a little bit."

"But if it would be funny, we should still play it on his birthday."

"Oh, we will."

*   *   *   *   *

It was a typical August day in Anchorage, with the temperature just above 60 and partly sunny skies that seemed ready to give way to showers at any minute. Maddie borrowed a van from the resort where she worked to pick up the Mahoneys at the airport.

When they reached the cabin, Nora was the first one to rush through the front door. She was almost knocked over by Luna and Biscuit, who Maddie had left inside as a surprise.

"Oh my God," Nora called out. "They remember me!"

"Of course they do, sweetie pie," Maddie said.

"Can we keep them, Maddie?" Nora asked. "My mom promised we could have two dogs, but I already know Luna and Biscuit, so if you're tired of them, we can just keep them here all the time."

"No, honey," Anne said. "They're like Maddie's kids, and you can't just take somebody's kids away from them."

"I'll tell you what though," Maddie said. "I'll let you guys adopt them part-time until you get settled. And remember the rule." She paused to point at Nora and Dylan. "No wandering in the woods unless the dogs are with you."

"Thanks, Maddie," Matthew said as he brought the last of the bags into the great room. Nora grabbed one of hers and began dragging it toward the stairway until Matthew told her to pick it up and carry it.

"I can't wait to see my room again," Nora said. "Starting today, it's my permanent bedroom."

Maddie turned to Anne. "So you've got two more vehicles on the way up here? You barely have room for one more in the garage."

"We have to wait and see what Matt needs for work," Anne said. "Whatever that ends up being. But we plan on getting rid of one of the trucks. My dad's is pretty beat up, and I wouldn't trust it on a long drive. But Matt's might be more truck than we need."

Dylan had barely spoken since they all boarded their plane in Seattle that morning. As he stood in the middle of the great room, staring at his Game Boy, the batteries on the device finally failed and the screen went dark. He lifted his face and scanned the room with blinking eyes, as if he had just beamed into the cabin by way of a *Star Trek* transporter.

Anne noticed the change in his expression and saw that the device was dead. "Good. You've had enough of that toy for a while."

"I just have to change the batteries."

"No, it's time for you to have a job."

Dylan suddenly grew nervous and said, "I'm still in grade school, Mom. I can't have a job."

"It was the first job my father gave me when I moved up here," Anne said. "I was around your age. Do you see that rack over by the fireplace?" She pointed at the rack, which held about a dozen pieces of firewood but had room for another three dozen or so. "Your job is to make sure that rack is never empty." Then she pointed at the other end of the great room. "And the same thing with the firewood rack over by the wood stove."

Dylan seemed uncertain how to respond at first, then switched to his favorite tactic when tasked with doing something he didn't want to do: he searched for a technicality that would cancel it, at least for the immediate future. "It's still summer, Mom. It's too warm to have a fire. I don't think we're gonna need any firewood in here right now. Maybe in October."

"We live up high, Dylan, and it can get cold here at night. In a few weeks, it's gonna be cold more than it's warm, day and night. You know where the open woodsheds are out behind the garage? This winter we'll be using the wood in the sheds that have a blue circle painted on the side. It's been drying for two years. You'll want to fill both of the racks to the top every time. I never want to see either one of them empty. And be sure you knock pieces of wood together when you take them off the pile. That'll shake the spiders loose. Any spiders you let inside will end up in your bedroom."

With the failure of his first defense, Dylan sought to at least ease what was looking like a monumental burden on his life. "But we don't need...like...a hundred pieces of wood in each rack all the time."

"There will be days when you don't want to go outside because of the weather, and you'll be grateful that the racks hold enough for a few days." Anne walked over to Dylan, smiled and rubbed his shoulder. "Remember, I'm only asking you to do what I had to do every single year I lived here. It's part of your inheritance."

* * * * *

They spent the next day stocking the kitchen and shopping for the last of what the kids needed for school. The following morning, Anne left at 7:30 for her first day of work in Anchorage. Matthew's job was to deal with the moving truck that was scheduled to show up around noon. The moving crew was not too happy when they reached Upper Potter Creek Drive, where the road changed from pavement to crushed gravel.

It had started to rain, and the wheels of the heavy truck sank into the many soft puddles along the road. The first thing the driver wanted to know after knocking on the front door of the cabin was whether there was a place farther down where he could turn his truck around. There was a turnaround for school buses, Matthew told him, but it wouldn't work for their truck. They would have to back up all the way to the paved road before they could turn around. Matthew also advised against pulling the truck up the long driveway, which was more uneven and narrower than the road. The three-man crew left the truck where it was and carried everything up the driveway in the rain.

Three days later, as Anne drove off to work, Matthew walked the kids down the driveway to wait with them until their different buses came. Then he sat down at the long dining room table in the great room with a fresh cup of coffee and the classified section from the previous day's newspaper. With Anchorage being a much smaller community than Seattle, the job listings in the *Anchorage Daily News* were not as extensive or as varied as they were in the *Seattle PI.*

He skipped certain categories, like health care, because he didn't have the required education or experience. He was also on the fence about whether he wanted a job that entailed working outdoors, but if the search went on long enough, he'd have to consider that. After all, he had plenty of experience roofing, and he might have to fall back on it. Bartending was something he could jump into easily too, but he only saw one ad for that. It was at a place in downtown Anchorage that he happened to know was a complete dive bar, rumored to have more fights and stabbings than any other bar in the city.

The retail jobs that he qualified for didn't pay very well but sounded easy, like bartending without the alcohol. Then he pictured himself standing in a department store wearing a cheap tie and a name tag, and that really depressed him. An ad for security guard at the Anchorage Museum gave him a quick laugh. It was followed by more and more dead ends. There was a good reason, he realized, that he hadn't wanted to begin his job search until he moved to Alaska.

To make himself useful, he decided to climb up on the roof and install the new chimney cap. Light rain was supposed to move in by early afternoon and he didn't want to be walking on the smooth metal roof when it got wet. In the garage, he grabbed a ladder, Dylan Sr.'s old tool belt and the new chimney cap. It ended up being an easy task, and the view from the rooftop helped to boost his mood. He enjoyed it for a good ten minutes, then carefully headed down the ladder after feeling the first few drops of rain.

Inside, he listened to a message on the answering machine from Maddie. She had left her restaurant scheduling book at her house and she needed it to assign this week's shifts for her breakfast crew. If Matthew got the message and had the time, could he please pick it up at her house and deliver it to the resort in Girdwood? Anne kept a key to her house in the kitchen. Matthew called her back and said he'd be on his way after he took Luna and Biscuit for a walk.

Girdwood was a 45-minute drive, but Matthew needed to go there at some point anyway to pick up kindling. There was a small hardware store that he knew was selling bundles cheap. Anne made sure they had plenty of firewood for the coming winter—at least five cords—but they only had enough kindling for the next couple of months.

He took his big truck, which had been delivered the day before. After dropping off Maddie's book, he filled the back of the truck with 30 bundles of kindling, then grabbed that day's newspaper at the grocery store. He didn't really like the idea of going back to an empty cabin to scan another set of job ads, most of which would probably be repeats from what he had seen that morning, so he dropped by the Big Wall Bar & Grill to peruse the ads over lunch in a more social setting.

He was ten minutes ahead of the regular lunch crowd, so there were a few stools empty at the bar. He sat down, scanned the menu and ordered the grilled halibut sandwich. When it arrived, Matthew assessed it like a food critic. It was a generous piece of fresh fish served on a firm roll that had a good chew to it. The sandwich came with a light homemade tartar sauce that included capers. That was a nice touch, Matthew thought, but he was even more impressed by the fish, which was as fresh and tasty as any piece of halibut he had ever eaten.

The bartender cleared Matthew's plate when he was done, then quickly refilled his coffee. The bar and restaurant had gotten busy with the lunch crowd, and the bartender, who looked no older than 25, was scrambling to fill orders. As Matthew watched him, he could tell that the guy hadn't done enough prep work before his shift and was now frantically slicing lemons and running to the back of the restaurant for a rack of clean glasses.

Maybe, Matthew thought, he should see about picking up some bar shifts at the Big Wall, assuming there were any available. Andre owned the place, and Matthew knew him pretty well. Anne knew him even better. Just as the thought occurred to him, he heard Andre's distinctive voice coming from the direction of the kitchen. Matthew decided to wait until the end of the lunch rush to try to talk to him.

By 1:30, he had almost finished scanning the last of the job ads when he felt a tap on his shoulder. He turned around and saw Andre smiling at him.

"Matthew!" Andre said, pronouncing the name with a hard "T" sound. "How can you come in here without saying hello?"

Matthew knew he was teasing. He smiled and said, "Just waiting for things to quiet down before I bothered you."

Andre looked down at the newspaper on the bar and said, "Somebody is looking for a job?"

"That would be me. Anne got hers, but I just started my search today. Which brings me to a question..."

Andre interrupted, "You worked in restaurants, true?"

"Yes, in fact..."

"Of course you did. Anne told me. And that made me start to think about something recently because I knew you'd be moving north, and you'd be looking for a job that would fit you very well. Yes, I was hoping to see you soon." Andre turned and pointed to an empty table next to the back window. "Let's go sit down, OK? It's more comfortable over there." Andre paused before adding, "If you have the time, of course."

Matthew couldn't tell whether the look was sincere or mocking. "An unemployed man has lots of time, Andre."

That prompted a quick laugh. "Then let's go sit down." As Matthew stood up, Andre called for the bartender to make two espressos.

The last thing Matthew needed at that point was more coffee because his palms were sweating, a clear sign he was already overcaffeinated, but he wasn't about to refuse an espresso from Andre.

They sat down and talked for a while about Seattle, the move to Anchorage, Nora's accident and her recovery, and Matthew's experience in restaurants. As much as he tried to squeeze in the subject of possible bartending work at the Big Wall, Matthew was instead forced to field the many questions that Andre threw his way.

One of them was Matthew's impression of the halibut sandwich he had for lunch. It was good, Matthew said. Very good, and Matthew explained why. Next, Andre asked Matthew to look at all the Big Wall menus— lunch, dinner, brunch, dessert, beer list, wine list, special drink list—and give his impression of what he would change if he were the owner.

It was a conversation that went on for more than an hour. For the most part, Matthew liked what he saw on the menus, although he said he could give better answers if he also knew what the portion sizes were and how well each item sold. As far as specific changes, he pointed out two items on the dinner menu he might change. One was the salmon dinner.

Andre looked confused. "What's wrong with fresh grilled king salmon? This is Alaska, and it's in season. It's crazy not to serve it."

Matthew nodded. "It's not the salmon I'd change. It's the sauce. If all the ingredients you list here are fresh, then it's probably an expensive sauce that takes a lot of time to make and goes bad fast. I'd start with something simple, like a dill butter, which you can always build on or vary, but keep it light and simple. Or just go without it. King salmon has a lot of fat and you're grilling it over cherrywood. That might be all the flavor you need."

It went the same with the other menus. Matthew mostly liked what he saw and suggested a few changes. On the beer and wine lists, his feedback was a little less Europe, a little more local.

Drawing his hand down the left side of the wine menu, Matthew said, "You'll get no argument from me on the quality of these. I've tasted lots of them and served most of them. And look," Matthew paused for emphasis, "nobody makes better wine than the French."

Andre smirked and waved a hand dismissively. "No bullshitting, OK?"

"What I'm saying is I might list one less French gamay, one less French sémillon and one less...something else from France. Then add a pinot noir from Oregon, maybe one from California. Last year, Roy's started serving this cabernet franc from California, and it's the best cabernet franc I've ever had. Again, no offense, but I'd swap out the French cab franc for that. Same with the beer list. I mean, Heineken? Please, take that green bottle out back and shoot it. People want to see local brews on their menu these days: fresh craft beers that have traveled across town, not around the world on a container ship. That's especially true for young people, and that's what I see when I look around here."

Andre listened carefully to everything Matthew said. As he sat there, his expression shifted slowly from irritation to resignation and finally acceptance.

"Like I said, Andre, I love more than 90 percent of what you have here. And I couldn't pull off a job like yours. There's too much to think about, too much to worry about. Employees who don't show up for their shifts, food that goes bad, ovens that break, books that don't balance, a shitty review in the newspaper...honestly, it would drive me absolutely mad."

Andre nodded. "Yes, Matthew, it will. But I can help you with that."

Matthew stared at Andre and considered what he had just said. It confused him. Andre's English wasn't exactly perfect, so maybe he had made a mistake in his choice of words, but Matthew didn't think so. Which cleared up Matthew's confusion in a way he wasn't quite ready for.

"Andre, I was going to ask if you had any bartending shifts that I could pick up here. That's what I wanted to talk to you about. Just bartending. But that's not what you're talking about, is it?"

Andre stood up. "I've loved running this place, Matthew, but I've been here too long and I'm looking to retire. My problem is that I don't want to sell it to just anyone. But now I think we have the solution to both of our problems." Andre gestured toward the kitchen. "Let's go to my office in the back. I can show you the books, and we can settle on a price."

They spent 45 minutes reviewing the last five years of revenue and profit from the restaurant and bar, so Matthew could see how the numbers fluctuated from season to season, and between a good snow year and a bad snow year. If the crowds didn't show up to ski and snowboard in Girdwood, they didn't show up to eat and drink at the Big Wall.

They also discussed property taxes, liquor license fees, zoning regulations, health inspections, pest control, Andre's relationship with the local government, the condition of the building that housed the Big Wall, and Andre's best estimate of what renovations would likely be required in the next few years.

Finally, Andre threw out a big number. Matthew stared at the amount, which seemed enormous. He had stopped by to ask about a bartending job. Now, it seemed, he was about to buy the place. Or at least commit to buying it. He could always back out later, he told himself. He didn't really know if it was good fit for him, but in his gut it felt like a good fit so he rolled with it.

He countered Andre's offer, and Andre threw out his own counter. Matthew nodded. Then Andre wrote the final figure on a legal pad and drew a circle around it.

"OK," Andre said across his imposing walnut desk, "so we'll break this down into monthly amounts spread over ten years. If you're having trouble, let's say, in one particular month, you let me know and we move that payment to the end of the ten-year term. If it happens two months in a row, then I want to see the books. Unless something drastic changes in the restaurant industry or the town of Girdwood, you'll be making at least a modest profit every month.

"Anyway, my point is that I'm not a bank and I'm not the Mafia, so you don't have to worry about me taking back the business. When a man gets out of prison, he'll fight to the death not to return there."

Matthew was speechless. An old expression came to mind about not knowing whether to shit or go blind. He was more excited than he had ever been about any business venture, including ones that had remained strictly in the talking phase over the years.

At the same time, and despite Andre's reassurance, Matthew was incredibly anxious about being responsible for the entire operation of the place. He could make money with it, sure, but he'd also own every fuck-up that occurred. And he wouldn't be able to leave his work at work the way he had been able to do most of the time with roofing and bartending. It would be a 24/7 commitment. A dream, Matthew realized, was really a two-sided coin, and on the other side was the dream's corresponding nightmare.

Andre opened a drawer and pulled out two glasses and a bottle of pastis, an anise-flavored French aperitif. He poured out two shots and slid one over to Matthew. "We'll do this later with champagne and dinner with your family, OK? And like I told you, I'll be here to help you get started. Do you think Anne's father and I knew what we were doing when we opened this place? No way. You've got more experience right now than the both of us had together back then."

Andre held up his glass. "*Santé, et bonne chance,* Matthew."

They downed their shots. Matthew felt a slight burning in his throat and smelled the sweet scent of licorice.

"OK, one more thing," Andre said. "And it's important. This number," he pointed to the figure he had circled on the legal pad. "When you go home and tell Anne you're buying this place from me, you tell her you're buying it for this amount." Andre wrote out a second number that was exactly half of the agreed amount. "I've always told her that she owns her father's half of the business. When he died, she refused to take a settlement and insisted it was all mine. So when she sees this number, she's going to think I'm giving you a special deal because of her father. She'll say no. Then you come back here for lunch or a drink, whatever. And you return home and tell her—OK, Andre says he'll double the price—so that the final price will actually be this price that you and I already agreed to."

*   *   *   *   *

Anne was as surprised as Matthew that Andre had offered to sell him the place. Her first reaction was excitement that the Big Wall would stay in the family. Later that night, as they were lying in bed, she began bringing up one concern after another. They were pretty much the same ones that Matthew had considered already. It wasn't until the following morning at breakfast that she brought up the price.

"I just realized that Andre is giving you a break because of my dad. I keep trying to tell him that he doesn't owe me anything. You need to let Andre know that it has to be a fair price, Matt. It has to be the same price he'd offer to someone who wasn't related to me."

"I'll go see him at lunch," Matthew said.

The papers were signed a week later, and the family showed up for dinner at the Big Wall to celebrate. Andre hadn't seen either of the kids in more than a year, and he was shocked at how much each of them had grown. He was also shocked at the number of Band-Aids covering Dylan's hands. Anne explained that it was from carrying loads of firewood.

"Yes, I remember the same thing happening to you," Andre said to Anne. "Then you discovered gloves."

The next three weeks were a blur for Matthew. He wanted to learn as much as he could before Andre left for Hawaii on his first vacation in seven years. There were many days Matthew was at the Big Wall from 9:00 in the morning until 11:00 at night. It was sometimes hard to fall asleep with all the thoughts running through his head about being responsible for running a restaurant and bar that had a staff of 18 and countless problems, with new ones arising every day.

One night he awoke with a throbbing headache and a feeling of deep dread. He had gotten in way over his head by buying the Big Wall, and he would come to realize that the decision was the biggest mistake of his life. After a few more hours of sleep and the arrival of dawn, things seemed to be not so awful, and the problems not so unmanageable. He started to believe, for the first time, that he would learn everything he had to learn to master his new job. As with running, he also believed he would find a pace that suited him best, and he would start to anticipate problems rather than being surprised by them.

Still, the learning curve was steep those first few weeks and the days were very long. Matthew missed most dinners at home, along with the family's trip to the dog breeder who had sold Maddie her German shorthaired pointers. He also missed Anne's visit to Nora's school to discuss an incident.

Anne had been surprised to get the phone call from the assistant principal, who said that Nora had started a fight with another student. Nora had been adjusting well to her new school, the assistant principal explained. She was very popular with the other kids in her class and had no trouble participating in lots of activities despite the challenge of having only one hand. In fact, she had a very resilient spirit and was proving to be quite the inspiration for other kids who had their own challenges.

But that morning, Nora had an altercation with a boy. They ended up fighting, and Nora punched him with the end of her arm. "Her stump," the assistant principal said. Anne left work early to pick up Nora and promised that she'd discuss what was and what wasn't acceptable behavior in school.

On their drive home, Nora offered a different version of the story. She said that the boy had been bullying her and that they had gotten into a fight but only after he had shoved her from behind. "So then," Nora explained, "I stumped him."

That was the first time Anne had heard the expression, and she understood right away what it meant. They were only a mile from school when Anne turned the Subaru around and headed back. The assistant principal was still in his office, so Anne led Nora in and closed the door behind them. Nora took a seat, while Anne remained standing.

"My daughter told me that she was being bullied," Anne said. "I believe her. The boy shoved her from behind, so she defended herself. Now, I've told her that she's never to be the one to start a fight." Anne glanced down at Nora, and for emphasis added, "Not ever, not for any reason. But if another student assaults her, she has every right to defend herself and that's exactly what I expect her to do."

Nora looked up at her mother, then across the desk at the assistant principal. "My mom's really tall, isn't she?"

*　　*　　*　　*　　*

It wasn't until late September when Matthew allowed himself to take a whole weekend off from work. On that Friday evening, he brought home two pizzas that a cook at the Big Wall had just prepared. After he slid them in the oven and set the timer, he headed upstairs to change. Anne was sitting on the deck of their bedroom and asked him to join her outside. The air was cool, but the setting sun was still high enough to cast a little warmth.

"Something came in the mail today," she said.

He pulled up a seat beside her and she handed him a postcard. On the front was a picture of Zion National Park in Utah.

"It's from your Uncle Raymond."

Matthew turned to Anne. "I don't have an Uncle Raymond."

"I know," she said.

Then it occurred to Matthew that this might be the long-awaited communication from Francis, and his eyes grew big. "Oh shit. Is this it? Finally?"

"You tell me," Anne said as he flipped the card over.

"Hello Matt. We arrived in Zion over the weekend, and I can't tell you how amazing this place is with its beautiful rock formations. We're loving every minute of it. Our hotel is on the river downtown, and there's a place across the street that serves the best green chili. We hope you're doing well. Please say hi to your parents for us. Love, Uncle Raymond"

488

He looked at Anne and was about to comment. Then he went back and read the postcard again before saying, "OK, I'm gonna say it's probably from him. And he managed to find our new address." Matthew paused and tugged on his soul patch. "Except I don't have an Uncle Raymond, my parents are both dead and this is supposed to be from Utah, but it has a postmark from..." He tilted the card to put more light on it. "From Altus, Oklahoma. Can you figure it out?"

Anne took the postcard and flipped it over. "Did you see what's on the front?"

In the center of the image was a large rock dome. As Matthew stared at it, he noticed a couple of things at the base of the dome. On the left side was a small "1" and on the right a small "1+1". He stared a little longer, then shook his head. "I honestly have no idea. Do you?"

"No."

At the dinner table, they sprinkled the conversation with occasional thoughts about the postcard. None of them provided the breakthrough they were looking for until Anne said, "What's written over the picture has to connect with something that's said on the back."

Matthew shrugged his shoulders. "What does green chili have to do with anything?"

"Nothing," Anne said. "So it's not that."

Nora, who was finishing her last slice of the pepper and onion pizza, asked, "What are you guys talking about?"

"Nothing." Anne looked at Dylan and repeated it because she thought he might have a vague sense of what was being discussed.

After dinner, they returned to the bedroom deck to continue their speculation. Matthew considered each line of the postcard and tried to make some connection with the image. When he reread the final line, he flipped the card over. In the fading light of dusk, the dome was darker and had an almost spooky quality. In fact, it looked like a gravestone.

That's when he unlocked it and said, "Wow."

"What is it?" Anne asked.

He handed her the card and replied, "'Say hi to your parents for us.' My parents are dead, so if I want to say hello to them I have to visit their grave." He pointed to the dome. "That represents their gravestone. If you're looking at it in their cemetery, my mom is buried on the left side and my dad on the right."

"So your mom is one, and your dad is one plus one." Just as Anne finished saying it, she also realized what it meant. "He's buried in your dad's grave."

Matthew nodded.

"You'll need to have the grave opened up, won't you?"

Matthew thought for a long while before replying, "I don't know how it works to have a grave dug up. But the cemetery is in Massachusetts and my brother Jimmy is still president of the State Senate there, so it might help to drag him into this."

"What if he doesn't want to be dragged into it?"

"I won't give him a choice."

*　　　*　　　*　　　*　　　*

Nine days later, Matthew took a red-eye flight to Logan and landed the following afternoon with a sore neck. He stayed the next two nights at Jimmy's house. It had been a few years since Matthew had seen his oldest brother. At five foot nine, Jimmy was the shortest of the Mahoney boys. Matthew noticed that he still had the quintessential altar boy look, with perfectly parted hair and a polite smile. Behind the smile, however, was a politician whose ability to outdebate, outthink and outstrategize his opponents was second to none in the state of Massachusetts.

Jimmy's five teenage kids were all there to greet Matthew at their house on N Street, as well as his wife Peg, who cooked a classic roast beef dinner for the occasion. After bringing everyone up to date on the move to Alaska, Matthew shared more information about Nora's accident. Jimmy's kids were especially interested in hearing about the progress their distant cousin was making in adapting to her new life. Talk around the table then moved on to the upcoming presidential election between Al Gore and George Bush. Sleep came easily that night, with Matthew excusing himself early and heading to the small guest room at the back of the house.

The visit had been agreed to over a phone call, and it didn't take much arm twisting by Matthew. He began by asking his brother what the process would be if someone needed to dig up a grave in Massachusetts. Then he mentioned their parents' graves specifically.

Jimmy sidestepped the obvious question—why dig up their graves?—and told Matthew that he and Peg had recently purchased a family mausoleum with enough space for themselves and their parents. The plan was to have their parents disinterred and their remains moved to vaults within the mausoleum. It was allowed by law, as long as the proper steps were followed. The move was planned for the following spring, and Jimmy had intended to contact Matthew beforehand for his consent.

When Matthew asked whether the move could occur a lot sooner, like within ten days, Jimmy said that the permits and arrangements involved would make such a tight timeline challenging. And more to the point, what was the rush?

Matthew brought the discussion to a close by saying, "We need to dig up Dad's remains now. Don't ask me why."

Growing up, Matthew had never been close to Jimmy, the way he had been with Francis. But on the rare occasions when he would turn to his oldest brother and ask for a favor that couldn't be fully explained, there was an understanding that the situation involved Francis and a full explanation would leave Jimmy culpable, or at least vulnerable. Matthew knew that a request should be made with as few details as possible or, as in this case, none.

The next morning, Matthew woke fully rested. He and Jimmy had a quick breakfast, then headed out to Forest Hills Cemetery on the outskirts of Boston. It was a Tuesday, with the September sky bright blue, and the air cool and crisp. The cemetery was heavily wooded and had gently winding lanes. It always gave Matthew a sense of peace. When they entered, the cemetery appeared empty, but as they approached their parents' graves, Matthew spotted a backhoe.

Nearby was the flatbed truck that had carried it there and a van with the two men responsible for handling the disinterment of their father. Their mother's was scheduled for a later date.

Jimmy stepped out to begin the proceedings while Matthew stayed in the car. He had visited his mother's grave regularly before moving to Seattle, and on his occasional visits home. But following his father's burial next to his mother, Matthew found it difficult to spend time in proximity with the man, even after his death. He and Jimmy had actually been discouraged from attending the disinterment because families often found the process disturbing, but Matthew insisted on being there. If Buzzy was buried in the grave, he wanted to see it for himself.

Lines had been marked on the ground to indicate where the digging should occur. As Jimmy had explained to Matthew on the drive over, the expectation was that the casket would be removed whole from the ground. However, there was a chance that it may have decayed to the point where their father's remains would have to be removed bone by bone, as it were. What Matthew knew, and Jimmy didn't, was that if Francis' information was correct, things might not progress to that point.

The backhoe engine was fired up, and the operator began his methodical task of carefully scooping out bucketloads of dirt and placing them on a tarp spread out on the grass. It was all under the close supervision of William O'Connell, the health official in charge of the operation. He stood alongside the grave to ensure the operator dug no deeper than he was supposed to. Jimmy, who had no interest in watching every step of the process, rejoined Matthew in the car and turned on the radio to catch some morning news.

When the proper depth had been reached, William and his assistant donned gloves and white jumpsuits in order to continue with the careful task by hand. A rectangular structure consisting of four metal walls, like an open box, was lowered into the grave to prevent the earthen sidewalls from collapsing. The assistant, who was the younger of the two, descended alone into the grave and began shoveling dirt into a container attached by chain to the backhoe's bucket. When the container became full, the operator lifted and dumped its contents onto the growing dirt pile.

Matthew was watching from the front seat of Jimmy's car, and through his open window he could hear the assistant calling to William that he had reached human remains. The half-full container was withdrawn and emptied, so that William could join his colleague in the tight space.

The two health officials were now using brushes and trowels to move away dirt, and Matthew could hear snippets of their conversation. It sounded like they were identifying specific bones, namely a radius and an ulna. Then the tone of William's voice suggested that something wasn't quite right. There was talk of uncovering additional bones, and Matthew caught the word "cranium."

Then everything stopped. The two climbed out of the grave, and William called the operator out of his backhoe.

"That's it. We're done," William told his team.

He called for Jimmy and Matthew to join him outside. When they did, Jimmy walked up to the three men and asked why they stopped, while Matthew walked beyond the group to get a look into the grave. He had a clear view of what they had uncovered. There were several bones, including two with round shapes. Matthew had never actually seen a real human skull, but these looked to be exactly that.

"I'm afraid we can't continue," William told Jimmy. "It looks like we have two bodies buried together where there should just be your father's."

Matthew was standing beside the pile of dirt, and as he took a step forward to get a closer look at the bones, something on the pile caught his eye. Sunlight was reflecting off of a small silver object. Matthew glanced at the other men to see if any were looking his way. They weren't, so he reached out, plucked the object from the pile and tucked it into his pocket.

"It also looks like there's been foul play," William continued.

"What kind of foul play?" Jimmy asked.

"That's not for us to determine. I need to get someone from forensics over here. Nothing can be moved any further. As I see it, this is now a crime scene."

*　　　*　　　*　　　*　　　*

The return flight to Alaska departed Boston at 9:00 the next morning, and after a stop in Seattle, it was scheduled to land in Anchorage at 3:45 that afternoon.

Matthew left wondering whether he had done everything he could for his old friend. He told himself that it was time to go home, and Alaska was home now. Although he felt torn, the rest of the work was really up to Jimmy, who said that the investigation would likely drag on for months but that he'd keep Matthew out of the whole process.

There was a chance, maybe a very good chance, that the second body in the grave would be identified by forensics as Buzzy Driscoll. Matthew would wait to see how the investigation played out. If the true identity wasn't established, Matthew would have to reveal to Jimmy the fact that it was Buzzy, so that his remains would be laid to rest properly.

Matthew's plane wasn't even half full, so he had an aisle to himself and plenty of room to stretch out in his window seat. Flying above a thick layer of puffy white clouds created a dream landscape below. Matthew spent much of the first leg with his eyes closed as sunlight warmed his face. With his right thumb, he slowly spun the silver Celtic knot ring on his pinky finger. He had given it to Buzzy as a thank-you for being his best man. The inside was engraved with the date of the wedding and "Coming Home." It was part of a lyric from a U2 song they both loved: "Oh, don't sorrow. No, don't weep. For tonight, at last, I am coming home."

The ring had been sized for Buzzy's middle finger, but it only fit Matthew's smallest, where he knew he would wear it for the rest of his life, then take it to his own grave. Since tucking it into his pocket at the cemetery, he had been treating the ring as an object only, separate and distinct from the memories of his best friend. One was an artifact, the other a deep attachment of heart and soul.

It was Matthew's best attempt to keep all the emotion from crashing through the 13 years and drowning him. He would take his time with that and find the right moment to come to terms with everything once the dust had settled. It was a good plan, but somewhere in the sky above North Dakota the dam began to burst. Matthew made his way to a bathroom at the back of the plane, where he quietly lost it for several minutes.

Back in his seat, he shut his eyes again. He thought about Buzzy and what kind of life he might be living if he hadn't died in that cemetery so long ago, but he found his thoughts being drawn away from his friend and toward his brother Francis. One thought led to another, and in the end they all led Matthew to pose a solemn question: How in this world, how in this lifetime, could he ever forgive Francis for what he had done?

*　　*　　*　　*　　*

Kathleen and Brendan joined the Mahoneys for a week over Thanksgiving, and by that time several storms had dropped enough snow at the cabin's elevation that Dylan had to shovel a path between the back door and the firewood sheds. On Thanksgiving Day, they celebrated dinner with rock ptarmigan that Anne and Maddie had hunted earlier that fall.

Before sitting down to eat at the long table in the great room, Nora insisted on showing Kathleen, Brendan and Maddie how she had trained the two German shorthaired pointer puppies that were now five months old. Maddie had, in fact, schooled Nora on how to train the puppies to obey several commands. One of the pointers was named Runa, and the other Orion. Dylan originally wanted to name Orion after the constellation Corona Borealis, which meant northern crown, but agreed to Orion because it was easier to say. Maddie asked if Nora might consider a name other than Runa because it sounded so much like the name of her dog Luna, but Nora wouldn't budge on that.

The two puppies were full of energy and distracted by new people and the smell of food, so it was difficult for Nora to get their attention. She was persistent, though, and had been for the last three months of training the pups.

"Look at me, Runa," she commanded as she stood with a hand extended toward the dogs. "Look at me, Orion...look at me, both of you...Runa, Runa..." When she had their full attention, Nora said, "OK, go to your room, Runa...go to your room, Orion...listen, go to your room...go to your room..."

The dogs walked across the great room to two large crates sitting against the wall. Then they went into their crates, turned and lay down. Nora went over and gave them each a treat while praising them with the excitement of a mother whose child had just taken their first steps.

Matthew and Anne also hoped to celebrate Christmas in their new home. Kathleen said there was a very small chance that she and Brendan would return to Anchorage for the holiday. Sal and his girlfriend were also willing to fly up and see the place for the first time.

The problem was Anne's mother, who had never visited the home of her ex-husband while he was alive or dead. She let it be known that she had no intention of spending the winter holidays there. Rather than a flat no, Anne interpreted her mother's decision to mean "not quite yet."

Goat Creek Lodge, on the other hand, remained an acceptable option, with Joan being willing to spend Christmas there as she had for several years. She agreed to pay for the family's airfare from Anchorage to Seattle and back. Matthew and Anne contacted the Engebretsens and their other Christmas regulars to say that Joan Boushay and the Mahoneys would join them all at the lodge once again.

They flew into Seattle on the afternoon of the 21st and rented a large SUV at the airport. The first stop was the Giffordshire House. Anne and Nora would be staying that night with Joan. After dropping them off, Matthew and Dylan drove up the hill to stay with their old neighbors Jeremy and Benjamin, who had a very comfortable mother-in-law unit above their garage. Joan had offered to put the whole family up at the Giffordshire House, but Matthew, like Joan, wanted their first meeting since they had exchanged words to occur on ground that was more neutral, perhaps even advantageous to him, like Roy's, for breakfast the next morning.

Anne had agreed to the arrangement, but then called Matthew at 7:00 on the morning of the 22nd and said he and Dylan should join them for breakfast at the Giffordshire House. Matthew wanted to know if Joan was refusing to meet at Roy's or if there was some other reason for the change.

"It's gonna be fine, Matt. Just come on down."

When Matthew and Dylan showed up an hour later in the lobby of the bed-and-breakfast, everyone was there to greet them. Matthew noticed that his mother in-law was wearing a coat. After giving Dylan a big hug, she turned to Matthew and said, "On our walk last night, we saw some amazing holiday decorations at a house just a couple of blocks away. I thought you might like me to show them to you before breakfast."

So they would have a little walk, Matthew thought. He nodded. "That would be nice," he said and stepped aside for Joan to lead the way out.

"Let's have breakfast," Anne said to the kids and pointed the way to the dining room. Dylan's eyes remained on his father, and he didn't move until Matthew said, "Go ahead. I'll be back in a few minutes."

The holiday decorations were indeed amazing, and Matthew got to see them three times because that's how many times they circled the block during their extended discussion. Matthew offered the first awkward attempt at apologizing, followed by Joan's, which was less so.

"I felt hurt by what you said, so I did what comes naturally," Joan said. "I said something that might be hurtful to you. I regret doing that, and I know…Anne and I had a long talk last night…I know you feel bad as well about what you said."

"I was angry in the moment," Matthew said. "And I spoke in haste. I do regret it."

"I see how you are with the kids, my grandchildren, and you're a good father to them. I respect that. And you and Anne have a steady marriage. I'll be brutally honest and tell you that I really didn't believe it would last. I didn't see you two together for more than a few years, at most. But here we are 13 years later, and you seem to have successfully weathered a lot of storms, particularly over this last year."

Matthew was very surprised to hear Joan be so honest and to acknowledge something positive about his relationship with Anne—if not its strength, at least its longevity. He knew it was not an easy thing for her to do, considering that her own marriage lasted fewer than 13 years. He thanked her for that. And he thanked her for all she had done over the years for Nora and Dylan. The conversation moved on to safer topics, but Matthew's guard was still up because he sensed there might be a twist at the end of Joan's kind words. There wasn't.

"We come from very different backgrounds, Matthew, and I suspect we'll always see the world differently because of it. But that's not really the point. We're family, and we should always put the interests of the family first."

*   *   *   *   *

There was one more stop to make before heading to the lodge, and that was Dr. Anderson's office. During the flight to Seattle, a wire on Dylan's braces had broken. They called Dr. Anderson, and he agreed to squeeze Dylan into his busy schedule in order to fix the situation.

Nora went along to Dr. Anderson's office as well and got her parents' permission to make an inquiry. She went to the receptionist and politely asked, "I'd like to see Queen Victoria. Is she at home today?"

The receptionist was in the middle of filling out an insurance form. She smiled at Nora, then began rolling her pen between her fingers as she considered the request.

"Tell her I'm the girl who gets special powers from animal crackers."

"Give me a minute, OK?" the receptionist said.

When she finished with her paperwork, she disappeared for a couple of minutes. On returning, she said to Nora, "The queen can see you now if you're ready."

Nora walked alone down the same hallway as before. This time, no music was playing, but when she reached the royal room, the queen had just donned her tiara and was sitting down on her throne. "Enter please," she called.

Nora advanced to the middle of the room and curtsied. "Good morning, your majesty."

The queen showed a look of surprise, "Ah, someone has been practicing. That's very, very good. You show much respect to my court. And have you brought your magical crackers with you today?"

Nora shook her head. "I wanted to tell you about something else. It's about what happened to me after you saw me before." Nora raised her right arm and pulled back her sleeve, revealing the stump. "I had an accident. I lost my hand."

The queen's jaw went slack. She slipped out of character and simply stared at Nora's stump.

"I have fake hands that I use sometimes, and I go to therapy to help me do things better."

"Oh, my goodness..." The queen said, before finally managing to pull herself back into character. She extended a hand and beckoned Nora toward her. "Approach my throne, please."

Nora took a few steps forward and stopped directly in front of the queen, who reached out her hand.

"May I take a closer look?" the queen asked.

After Nora extended her arm, the queen examined the stump and said, "Ah, such a terrible wound. It appears that that the healing has gone well." The queen let go of Nora's arm and looked into her bright green eyes. "And your spirit, child? Has it been wounded as well? Or do you remain fearless?"

"I'm still not afraid of anything. Every week, I watch *The X-Files* with my brother, even though I'm not supposed to."

The queen smiled warmly and nodded. "That's very good to hear. Now I will tell you something important." She paused to consider her words, then launched into an impromptu speech. "Life is a battle for all of us, whether we be young or old. And there is no avoiding the injuries and wounds that we must suffer. For we are all mere mortals, of simple flesh and blood, and none of us can pass through this life wholly unscathed." She lifted her eyes to the ceiling momentarily and continued, "That life is for the gods only, not for such as you and me.

"Even queens and kings can suffer greatly in their battles. Some have given their very lives, from Edward the Elder to William the Conqueror and Richard the Lionheart. You…you have suffered in battle as well. And for one so young and brave, it breaks the heart to see such a terrible wound. But hear me now, and remember these words. You have been born to a life of greatness, and you are answering your current challenge admirably. This is evidenced by all who share your company, including myself. So, today and all the days that follow until your final rest, you shall carry that greatness with you. And you must always stand straight as you do today, and hold your head high. For as I glimpse the future through unclouded glass, I see that you are one day destined to wear a crown."

*   *   *   *   *

It had been a very rainy December in Seattle, which meant there was no shortage of snow at Goat Creek Lodge and Mount Rainier. More was falling as everyone headed to the lodge that afternoon. Sal was the first to arrive and already had a roaring blaze in the fireplace. He assured Matthew that he had called the owner of the lodge to request that all mousetraps be removed. The owner called back to state that Goat Creek Lodge would be trap-free for the duration of their stay.

Sal and Inessa had brought a load of firewood in Sal's brand-new pickup. Camacho Brothers Roofing & Insulation now had two full-time crews, with plans to add a third in the spring, all thanks to the aggressive online advertising that Sal's brother was coordinating. A new truck was one of Sal's big splurges. He and Inessa had also moved into a townhouse in Queen Anne.

Anne was thrilled to finally meet the woman in Sal's life. She and Inessa made some coffee in the kitchen and sat down in the breakfast nook to get to know each other. Anne was immediately impressed, not only with

Inessa's musical talent but also with her ability to speak a number of foreign languages. The more they chatted, the more Anne realized that Inessa was in many ways her opposite. Inessa had done things that Anne had always wanted to do, and had talents and skills that Anne could only dream of.

"I'll be honest," Anne said. "I'm glad French isn't one of your languages because I'm sure you'd speak it far better than me."

Dusk brought the remainder of the Christmas group: the Lamberts; the Schulers; and the Engebretsens, with a tree tied to the roof of their car. The transmission on their AMC Pacer had started to slip the previous summer, so they traded it in. They were now driving a 1983 AMC Spirit, which only had 40,000 miles on it and had been stored in a garage, so despite its chronological age, Andy Engebretsen insisted, it still had many years of useful life remaining.

After the Engebretsens settled into their cabin, they walked back to the lodge with a box of Christmas ornaments and the ingredients for that evening's glogg. As Mrs. Engebretsen joined others in decorating the tree, Mr. Engebretsen went about preparing his popular Norwegian drink.

Sal joined him in the kitchen, and after they exchanged greetings, Sal got right to the point. "What the heck happened with the whole Y2K thing? I mean, nothing happened, but why? I've been asking people all year, but I haven't gotten any good answers."

Mr. Engebretsen twirled one end of his moustache and nodded vigorously. "I understand, Sal. I, too, was surprised and confused. By the way, take this ginger root and peel it for me, please. So I conducted an investigation. I work for the city, you know, and when you work for the city, you often have time to do other things at work. This is what I discovered, OK?"

Mr. Engebretsen paused to take a deep breath before continuing. "It was the programmers, you see, who rushed into action all across the country…the whole world really. Now, they could have rewritten the code completely to stop Y2K, but there wasn't enough time for that. Instead, they found a short-cut that let them accomplish the same goal in far less time. Also, as I understand it, programmers can be very lazy. The short cut is called 'windowing.' All it does is push Y2K 20 years down the road. It's a delaying tactic."

Sal was more than a little skeptical. "You're saying Y2K is still going to happen but not until 2020?"

"It's a very technical thing to explain, and I'm afraid I've forgotten some details, but trust me on this, Sal. It's going to be bigger than a simple Y2K. Far more chaos because it will be complicated by the windowing. I'm getting old, so I may not be around for it. You and Matthew must prepare, and you must start soon. Y2K 2020 will be here quicker than you think."

Dinner was late that first night, as it took everybody a while to settle in. Seven kids and ten adults eventually gathered at the long table in the great room, where the Schulers prepared a meal that centered around a dish of chicken and pasta with lemon pesto. Three of the children and one adult opted for traditional spaghetti sauce rather than pesto with their main course. Conversations were numerous and loud around the table, with everyone catching up on how their previous year had gone.

The one topic on all their minds was Nora's accident, and the table tactfully waited for the right moment to share their feelings. Anne broached the subject as the first bowl of chicken and pasta was halfway around the table. As she did, everyone else quickly fell silent. Some of them had already spent time with Nora since the accident, but the Schulers and their two children hadn't. Nor had Doug Lambert, so Anne was speaking mainly to them. She talked briefly of the accident and how well Nora had been recovering, and expressed how grateful the family was for all the support they'd received, including that provided by present company.

Nora added a few words, and the discussion ended on a light note. There were statements of encouragement from different people, followed by a toast to Nora's continued recovery. With that, the subject had been addressed and dispatched. A general sense of relief settled over the table, and the conversations moved on to other, more comfortable topics.

When dinner was over and the table had been cleared, hot drinks were served: hot chocolate, tea, as well as alcoholic and nonalcoholic versions of Mr. Engebretsen's Norwegian glogg. With mugs in hand, people headed outside to the fire pit, where Matthew and Dylan had gotten a fire going quickly despite the snow falling at a steady pace. Chairs were brushed free of the powdery flakes and positioned upwind of the flames. Inessa said that she had brought her old backup violin and hoped to play it outside, where the sound would carry beautifully in the still night air. However, the instrument was sensitive to moisture, and being snowed upon was out of the question.

Instead, everyone continued on with their dinner conversations. Those who hadn't seen Nora since the previous Christmas took the chance to speak to her privately and say how sorry they were to hear about the accident. She sat with her snowboard stretched across her legs. The board was plastered with all kinds of stickers, and Nora was wiping dry one of the last open spots and preparing to rub yet another sticker onto it.

As one person, then another spoke to Nora, her reaction was to thank them while staring down at the board and focusing on her sticker task, as if the accident being referred to had happened to someone else. Back in August and September, when students at her school would ask her about it, she would often glance at her stump to confirm the reality. But now, she had moved beyond doing even that.

It wasn't denial. She knew every day exactly what it was that she had lost with the absence of her right hand, and she was starting to learn about a few things she had gained. It was that she had, as Dr. Gottlieb put it, found her new natural, and she had little interest in talking about an accident that was now firmly in her past.

When the new sticker was in place, Nora asked everyone around the fire if they wanted to hear about her prosthetic hands. They all did, so Nora began by saying that she had two. One was a passive functional hand that didn't move at all. She called it her "frozen hand" and wore it when she had tasks that required extra help in lifting, pushing, pulling and similar motions. She also was testing a mechanical version that she referred to as her "robot hand." It had electrodes that picked up electrical impulses generated by the movement of the muscles in Nora's forearm. The hand and the fingers would then flex in specific ways, depending on what kind of muscle movements she made. It would require a lot more training before Nora could make regular use of it.

When Anne had started her job at BG, Nora's limb loss was considered a preexisting condition, so neither of the prosthetic hands was covered by the family's insurance plan. Joan had offered to cover the considerable cost for both, and Anne agreed to accept her mother's generosity.

As Nora was explaining how her robot hand worked, Doug Lambert pulled up a chair to the fire. After dinner, he had to go over to his cabin because the fire in his woodstove had gone out, and he needed to restart it if his family was going to sleep comfortably. He sat down beside Nora and told her he was sorry to hear that she lost her hand.

Nora turned to him and said, "Thanks. My dad told me you might lose your job because your company is part of the big bubble."

Doug smiled and said, "Yes, Kozmo is in a little trouble right now, but if I lose my job I can always get another one." His smile quickly faded when he realized how his statement could be misconstrued. "I'm sorry. I didn't mean..."

"It's alright," Nora said. "I've been telling everyone about my fake hands. I don't really use them all the time." She paused and searched for Dylan, who was sitting three chairs away. "My brother's gonna build me an awesome hand."

When Dylan heard the statement, he nodded in Doug's direction and said, "I'm studying books on cybernetics, and I found some courses I can take on the Internet." He suddenly noticed many eyes staring at him, waiting perhaps for a definitive statement on exactly how he was going to produce a more awesome hand than those already available from the medical world. "So I know I can make a good one, like a really good one. It's just gonna take some time."

Nora smiled in his direction. "It's OK. I can wait."

The snow continued to fall through most of the night, which created great snowboarding conditions for Emily Lambert and Nora up at Paradise the next morning. Nora wore her frozen hand to wield a shovel as she spent 20 minutes building a jump so high that Emily was afraid to go off it.

The Girdwood ski resort had a terrain park where Nora had been practicing her jumps and tricks over the previous month, and she was now in search of challenges that were both more exciting and more risky. Her epic wipeout late in the afternoon ended the snow fun for the day, but the failure of the jump did not diminish Nora's animated retelling of it around the fire that evening.

More snow fell late into Christmas Eve and Christmas morning, which arrived with the sound of a northern saw-whet owl and its soft, peaceful toot-tooting. It sang from its perch on a fir tree just outside the bedroom where Anne and Matthew were sleeping. The owl's song held Matthew in a state of semi-sleep for almost ten minutes. He rose to near-consciousness a few times, only to slip back down into a snowy dream.

The peace was shattered by the sound of a shriek coming from somewhere in the lodge. Matthew sat up and listened carefully to confirm that the sound was indeed real. Then he heard the voice of a woman moaning, "Oh God, no…"

It was Joan. He was certain of it. Beside him, Anne was still sleeping soundly, so Matthew climbed out of bed quietly and got dressed. He crept down the hall, and as he entered the kitchen, he saw Joan with her hands on her hips, swearing softly at something on the kitchen counter.

"Good morning," Matthew said in a voice loud enough for only her to hear.

Joan turned around and said, "Well, there's certainly nothing good about it from where I stand."

Matthew saw a large plastic bag on the counter. The bag was opaque, and through it he could see a pile of small green shapes. Brussels sprouts, he assumed. Also on the counter was a scattering of tiny, dark flecks. His mind began to make rapid assumptions that led to a lightness in his heart, and a faint but growing hope.

"Just look at what they've done," Joan said in disgust.

"Was it…" Matthew began.

"Mice!" Joan said, with a disturbed expression that Matthew didn't think he had ever seen on her before. "They must have eaten through the bag last night. And they've violated my brussels sprouts."

Matthew examined the bag cautiously. It was large and held many sprouts. Pounds of them. On the bottom was a small hole, ragged with chew marks. The top remained tightly secured by a wire twist. He undid it and looked inside. At first, he saw only sprouts, but as he reached inside and spread them around, he noticed a small number of little mouse turds scattered on the bottom of the bag. Yes, this was promising, he thought.

"It looks like they've crapped inside as well, Joan," Matthew said.

Her distress deepened. "Is it bad?"

Matthew spread the bag open, and Joan peered down. "I only see a few," she said cautiously. "Yes, just a half dozen, maybe. And they're all

504

at the bottom of the bag." She looked at Matthew. "I don't see any on the sprouts themselves. I think a quick washing…"

"It might not be that simple," Matthew cautioned. "It's like the old saying—it's not the turds you can see that you have to worry about. It's the turds you can't see…" Joan stared at him, unconvinced, so he added, "…that you have to worry about."

"Nonsense," Joan declared with a fresh resolve. "I'll wash the whole lot by hand right now."

Matthew felt his moment slipping away and said, "Full disclosure, Joan."

"I beg your pardon," she said as she transferred the last of the sprouts from the bag to the large sink, then turned on the water.

"I think it's OK to serve the sprouts as long as people know where they've been," he said. "Or what's been on them. We really should give people the information and let them make up their own minds. I mean, if you ordered sprouts at a restaurant, you'd want the server to tell you if maybe they'd been peed on by the cook's dog, right? It's only fair."

Joan turned off the water, then stared into space as she weighed the argument. Finally, she said, "I suppose so. Although then nobody would eat them if I said they'd been shat upon by mice. It's hardly an appetizing way to describe a dish." She stared down at the sinkful of wet, shiny sprouts.

Then Joan recovered and said, "Wait, we can simply drive to a store and buy new sprouts. They won't be as good as mine, of course, but at least we'll have brussels sprouts for Christmas dinner."

Matthew turned around and looked toward the large windows at the end of the great room. Outside, snow was falling, a dense curtain of snow that swirled slowly in a light breeze. "The snow…" he began, as if staring at his own Christmas miracle. "It's really falling outside. And stores around here don't sell brussels sprouts. We'd have to drive in treacherous conditions. Plus, we don't have time."

"Can't we just give it a go?" Joan asked in a weaker voice. "You have four-wheel drive, don't you?"

With his best poker face, he said, "I love brussels sprouts, Joan. We all do. Especially yours. But no sprouts are worth dying for."

Breakfast that morning included cinnamon French toast with spiced apples and pears, along with three varieties of sausage—one mild, one spicy and one very spicy. The meal stretched to almost 10:30, when it was time to gather at the Christmas tree and open gifts. Nora and Dylan would have to wait until they returned to Alaska to open their larger gifts, which weren't brought to Seattle, but they had plenty of smaller gifts waiting to be opened at the lodge.

Those for Nora included a journal. She had asked for one because, as she said, "she wanted to start writing her stories down." She also received a Furby, a furry electronic toy that was five inches tall, and had big eyes and ears. Furbys spoke an infantile language known as Furbish. Nora had received a Furby two years earlier when they first came out, then quickly lost interest in it. But there was an odd trend at her new school, where kids spoke to each other in Furbish. Nora was beginning to get on her mother's nerves by sometimes speaking it at home. Anne agreed to give Nora another Furby in exchange for banishing the speaking of Furbish forever from the cabin. Nora also promised to keep the talking Furbys in her room unless she was taking them to school or to a friend's house.

Nora responded to the gift by saying, *"Dah-may-may. Dah-kah-oo-nye."* After a look from her mother, Nora added, "Sorry. I mean, it's awesome. Thank you."

Among Dylan's gifts was a set of advanced Rubik's Cubes to train for the upcoming Anchortown Cube Competition, open to all Anchorage-area students under 18.

One of the last gifts to be opened was one that Matthew had wrapped for Anne. It was a long tube, and as Anne slowly tore off the colorful paper, she gave Matthew a look that was both curious and skeptical. Eventually she pulled the plastic stopper from the end of the tube and peeked inside with one eye, then the other.

"You won't know what it is until you take it out," Matthew teased.

Anne figured it was likely a print of some kind, but no particular print came to mind. She pulled it from the tube, and as she carefully unfurled it, a smile spread across her face.

"What is it, Mom?" Nora asked.

"It's a print of a painting by a Danish artist," Anne said without taking her eyes off it. "He was one of the Skagen painters in the late 1800s. They

506

broke away from the traditional style of the day and were influenced by impressionism and realism."

"Somebody's been studying up on her art," Inessa said.

Anne turned to Inessa and smiled, "True, I did a little research. I wanted to know everything I could about this painting. It's called *Mother and Daughter by the Sea*. I'll put it in a frame as soon as we get home. Come take a look."

Everyone got up and walked over to where Anne was kneeling to see for themselves. The print was a simple scene, with a mother and daughter lounging lazily on a porch sofa. The mother was reading to a girl who seemed to have fallen asleep on her mother's lap. In the background was a soft green lawn stretching to a sandy beach and the bright sea beyond.

"I love the light," Inessa said.

"The painter gets it," Anne said. "That's how it is by the Atlantic Ocean on a sunny summer afternoon. Maybe 4:00 or 4:30."

"You're right," Joan said. "That's so much like the view from our house in Ipswich. I used to read to you like that in our gazebo."

Anne turned to her mother. "That's what drew me to it."

"We saw the actual painting," Matthew said. "Right before it was stolen."

"Stolen from where?" Sal asked.

"The *Alexandrine,*" Matthew said. "That's the name of the Danish royal yacht. It was visiting Anchorage last September. They had it open for public tours, and we went on board a couple of times."

"Wait, I didn't go on board anything," Dylan said with a confused look. "When was this?"

"I didn't go on board anything either," Nora said.

"The *Alexandrine* left Anchorage on October 3rd," Matthew said. "The thieves stole it the weekend before."

"Didn't they have a security system on the yacht?" Joan asked.

"Two systems, actually," Anne said.

"And they were not easy to beat," Matthew added.

"Interesting," Sal said.

"It's supposed to be worth about ten million dollars," Matthew said.

Anne took one last look at the print before rolling it up and returning it safely to its tube. "And now it's ours forever," she said.

Christmas dinner was served just after 5:30. It commenced with Joan apologizing to all the guests in the great room. There had been an unfortunate incident earlier that day, she said, and as a result the sprouts of Christmas 2000 were no longer suitable for human consumption. The vegetables for dinner would now be limited to a salad prepared by Renee Lambert and snap peas brought by the Engebretsens. Joan made a promise—which was more like the swearing of an oath—that should she come back for another Christmas at Goat Creek Lodge, her brussels sprouts would make a triumphant return, rodents be damned.

The first items delivered to the table were platters of roasted duck, which had all been neatly quartered in the kitchen. Joan had prepared five of them, and the lodge oven was barely large enough to accommodate them all.

Nora was the first to comment on the main course. When she saw the ducks, she tugged on Inessa's sleeve and said, "I just realized something. On every Thanksgiving and Christmas, we're always eating some kind of bird, but it's always a different kind."

In the kitchen, Matthew was at the sink cleaning the cutting boards and knives while Sal filled the bowls of side dishes, which included coriander-roasted carrots; scalloped potatoes with prosciutto and gruyere; and chestnut, sage and onion stuffing.

Matthew had been telling Sal how the last few months had gone by in something of a blur. Life as the owner of a restaurant and bar was a lot more complicated than bartending or being a foreman on a roofing crew. The job fully owned him, and there were days when the problems piled up so high that Matthew wanted to hand the place back to Andre. But then there were times when the dream really shined through, and Matthew could think of no better life than owning and running the Big Wall.

"In the end, I'm the one who decides on the menu," Matthew said as he finished rinsing the last cutting board. He turned around to make sure he and Sal were alone in the kitchen before continuing, "The menu does not include, nor shall it ever include, brussels sprouts."

Sal laughed. "You really dodged it this year."

"It's a beautiful thing, isn't it?"

"You know, lightning doesn't strike twice, brother. What about next Christmas?"

"I have a whole year to figure that one out," Matthew said. He grabbed a dishtowel to dry his hands, and when he was done he stared at the Celtic knot ring on his pinky. He was still getting used to having it live on his hand all the time. He had shared the whole story with Sal: flying to Boston, visiting the grave and finding the ring.

When Matthew caught his friend looking at him, he held up his right hand and said, "This is it. This is all that's left of him."

Sal shook his head. "You still have the memories. They'll be alive as long as you are."

"I suppose so," Matthew said. He added serving spoons to each of the bowls, and as they were about to deliver them to the table Sal said, "I meant to ask you, did Lyka ever tell you about...you know?"

"About what?" Then Matthew remembered. "Oh, that. No, and I never asked her."

After dinner, people made their way to the fire pit. The evening air was dry and the sky was clear for the first time in days, so Inessa brought out her violin and played a short set from classical composers, starting with Vivaldi and ending with Tchaikovsky. After taking a break to warm her hands, she played a few modern songs, ending with one of the *Metamorphosis* pieces by Philip Glass, which she had recently learned.

At 9:00, Joan announced that it was time for the final event of the holiday. People headed to the lodge and took a moment to grab something from the kitchen or use the bathroom. Eventually they all made their way to the back of the lodge and the illuminated path leading down to Goat Creek for the annual lighting of the floating candles. They would carry away all the problems and worries of the previous 12 months, along with everyone's greatest wish for the coming year.

As Nora was zipping up her jacket in the back hallway, Sal caught up with her.

"There's something I want to ask you," he said with a cautious look on his face. "I hope you don't mind."

"What is it?"

"You remember Lyka, right? I'm wondering if you can tell me…if you wouldn't mind telling me…what that tattoo on her arm means. The one that says 'forgive.'"

Nora considered the question as they walked down the path, then said, "I don't know."

"But didn't she tell you that time when we were all having barbecue in your backyard last summer? You asked her what it meant, and you guys whispered to each other…"

Nora's face lit up and she smiled. "Oh yeah, I remember that now. I asked her what it means."

"So what did she say?"

"She said, 'What do you think it means?' And I said, I think it means that you have to let go…" They were near the end of the path, and Nora looked down to the river, its waters running cold and dark. She seemed to drift off for a moment before finishing her thought. "You have to let things float away." Nora turned to Sal and added, "Or else they can drown you."

Nora spotted Dylan waiting for her by the water's edge. After lighting their candles, they placed their floating lanterns on the water and gave them a gentle nudge. Nora took her brother's hand as they watched their flickering lights join the others and move slowly downstream. Then Nora shattered the silence by announcing, "I hope nobody wished for me to get my hand back because it's not gonna happen."

There were a few gasps, and Nana B told Nora that she should be more respectful during such a solemn moment.

"It's alright. Really," Nora said in a voice full of certainty. "Someday I won't miss it anymore."

Nora's Journal

Monday, January 1, 2001

I was falling through the cloud for a long time and spinning around. I could hear you all calling my name, but I couldn't see you. When I was getting close to the ground, big dragons flew down and saved me. They weren't the bad dragons who pushed me into the cloud. They were good dragons who saw what happened and wanted to help.

I'm living with the good dragons now. They're teaching me things that will give me special powers when I return, like how to fly into the clouds and not lose my balance, and how to make up whole new worlds.

I might be gone for a few years, or maybe a little longer. When my work is done, you can all visit me. I'll be living on a brand-new mountain, and the mountain will belong to me. It will be bigger than anybody has ever imagined before. Wait until you get my message, then join me there. And when you get to the mountain, don't look for me at the bottom. I'll be waiting for you at the top.

From the Author

I hope you enjoyed reading *The Mahoneys of West Seattle*. It's a self-published novel, so I'd like to thank all of the people who were generous enough to read the earlier drafts and give me honest, insightful feedback. I'm also fortunate to have had the manuscript reviewed by the two best copy editors I know. Aside from the Alaska scenes, the story is informed by my 25 years of living in the Seattle area (U District, Capitol Hill, West Seattle and Burien).

If you'd like to read more about the writing of the story, please visit www.MahoneysofWestSeattle.com.

This book is a sequel to *The Chieftains of South Boston,* which takes place in 1987 and begins with the marriage of Matthew and Anne in Ipswich, Massachusetts. Along with providing a fuller look into the couple's early years, the story also takes a deep dive into the worlds of Boston politics and the Irish Mob. I've begun work on a third book in the series, which will be set around the year 2014.

If you liked *The Mahoneys of West Seattle,* please consider leaving a quick review or rating. I'm an unknown writer, so every bit of support helps. You can find out more about me and my work at www.WriterBurke.com.

Made in the USA
Las Vegas, NV
09 February 2022